The

Interstellar

Age

The Complete Trilogy

Valmore Daniels

THE INTERSTELLAR AGE

The Complete Trilogy

Valmore Daniels

THE INTERSTELLAR AGE

Forbidden the Stars

Music of the Spheres

Worlds Away

The Complete Trilogy

For a complete list of available books, visit:

ValmoreDaniels.com

FORBIDDEN THE STARS

THE INTERSTELLAR AGE
BOOK 1

VALMORE DANIELS

THE END

Copán :
Honduras :
Central American Conglomeration :

My ancestors tell us that on a calm, still night, if we listen hard enough, we can hear the planets move. They call it the Music of the Spheres, and its song is a tale of the return of the gods. I have heard this song.

But I am just an old man. What do I know?

My grandson comes up to me to ask permission to play with his friends. I ask him, "Do you want me to tell you the story of the end of the world?"

I know he has already heard me tell this tale, and he does not believe. He would rather play with his friends.

Maybe if I tell him a few more times, he will come to believe.

I can only hope; but what do I know?

I tell him of Hunab Kú, the god of gods, the creator of the Maya. I tell him that Hunab Kú rebuilt the world three times after three deluges, which poured from the mouth of a sky serpent—some say from the mouth of Kukulkan, god of the sun, the oceans, the earth, and the sky.

I tell my young grandson, who grows bored at my tales, that Kukulkan built the first world and the second world. He did this so that the third world would be ready for the People of the Earth, the Maya.

I tell him of the folly of the Maya, of their arrogance, of the decadent ways and human sacrifices, and the foretelling of the white man. I tell him of the end of the third world, of the destruction of our ancestors.

My grandson smiles. He believes I am just a lonely old man who tells grand tales.

I know the truth, and I know the future. I tell him that the fourth world belongs to the white man; but the fourth world is not going to be here for much longer.

The ancient gods decreed this.

The fourth world must suffer under a deluge to make way for the New World. If the white men do not accept the changes, Kukulkan will destroy them.

Above all things, the gods will build the New World.

The gods will return from the stars, and they will need a better world in which to make their homes.

The time is coming soon.

"How soon?" my grandson asks patiently, humoring his old grandfather.

"You will see the end of the fourth world in your lifetime," I tell him. "And you will see the coming of the fifth world. I do not know if I will see it. I am getting too old."

"Not so old, Grandfather," he says to me.

I smile at him, knowing that, at heart, he is a good boy; but he glances out of the corner of his eyes at his friends, and longs to play.

"Now go to your friends," I tell him. "But remember what I have told you."

"Yes, Grandfather. I will remember what you have said."

He runs off, and I know that he will remember. But will he believe? Or does he think I am just a silly old man?

FOR IMMEDIATE RELEASE
NASA Press Release
Re: Orcus Mission

Barring the Oort Cloud and any wandering asteroids or comets orbiting Sol, Pluto is the last celestial body on the outermost perimeter of Sol System's family of planets. Pluto is a signpost signifying the boundary of Sol, and the beginning of interstellar space.

Now, for the first time, NASA is sending a team to explore the farthest planetary body in our system. The flight crew has not yet been announced, but a spokesperson indicated they were close to finalizing the shortlist. Whomever they assign to this enviable mission will need to endure a six-month trip to Pluto, followed by another six months on the return trip. With an additional seven months on Pluto until the planet comes back into optimal orbit for the return launch, the crew of the *Orcus* Mission will be away from home for almost two full years.

Scientists have many questions about Pluto, and hope that this mission will provide them with the knowledge they have sought for over a century.

One senior researcher at NASA indicated the possibility that information about the small planet may provide insight into interstellar travel.

Countless unmanned ships and probes have gone to Pluto on exploration missions in the past fifty years. *The Orcus* represents the first manned mission.

Scientific Addendum:

Pluto orbits Sol at a plodding 17,064 kph, taking 248 years to make the round trip. It is by far the most aberrant of planets, following an eccentric elliptical orbit at 17.148 degrees inclination above and below the ecliptic.

Preliminary readings confirm the makeup of the planet to be methane and nitrogen based, with traces of hydrogen, helium, silicon and a number of other elements.

The Sun itself is no more than a bright star in the distant sky, about four times the apparent brightness of Polaris, the North Star, from Earth. Illumination during Pluto's daytime is less than that of a full moon during Earth's night, and gives the sky a dark purplish hue—quite exotic, and more than a little mysterious.

The stars themselves are visible through the thin layer of nitrous-methane atmosphere during Pluto's 6-day rotation period, but they are easier to see at night, with no icy fog to obscure them.

2,320 kilometers in diameter, Pluto has a gravity of 0.04 Earth standard.

In 1905, the astronomer Percival Lowell predicted the existence of a ninth planet, but died before seeing Pluto—and in fact, the coordinates he had predicted were wrong. Still, in honor of Lowell, the planet is named using the letters of his initials, P.L. — Pluto.

The honor of first sight of Pluto fell to Clyde Tombaugh in 1930. A student of Lowell's, Tombaugh photographed three images of that small planet from the Lowell Observatory. The analysis of their findings, however, did not support Lowell's figures for the mass necessary to affect the orbit of Neptune. That left the possibility that another celestial-body existed near Pluto.

It was not until 1979 when James Christy discovered that Pluto had a smaller twin, Charon…

Macklin's Rock :
SMD Mine Number 568 :
Sol System :
Asteroid Belt :

The sound of the emergency klaxon filled his septaphonic ear-mask.

<Pirates on telemetry-reader; three engine signatures confirmed.> Hucs, the computer personality, spoke to him in succinct tones as images passed through Alex's field of vision via his ocular caps.

In the background, the Ronge Nebula glowed, dark green in large swirls against a magnificent star field. Small pulses of light identified the incoming war-class fighters flown by the pirates infecting this sector of the galaxy. There were three of them.

Captain Alex Manez cursed his backup wingmen who had broken away to chase down a SID—Ship-In-Distress. Obviously a false trail designed to split their forces.

With his first-gen thought-link patch secured to his temple, Alex had no need to relay his commands verbally. It was second nature to do so, however.

"Hucs, key in an emergency call for wingmen Grande and Makato. Tell them to get their butts back here, flank!"

<Message confirmed. Transmitted,> the computer said aloud, as the words scrolled along the bottom of the DMR casement.

"Give me a scan of their defense system, and all possible ordnance arrays," he ordered. There was time for a computer reconnaissance; it would take the pirates three minutes to pass within firing range.

When the assessment came in, Alex pondered it, and made a quick decision.

"I want fore shields at maximum, tap the aft, fifty percent on laterals. Charge two long-distance mantas, and key up maser cannon for close proximity. Confirm!"

<Orders confirmed.>

The clock signaled the pirates would be in range in one minute, forty-one seconds. An indicator light on the DMR casement flashed.

<Mantas are prepped and hot. Enemy trajectories steady.>

"Give me a zero-minus thirty projection of their position," Alex told Hucs. "I want to preempt their attack, see how they react. Target wing men only, leave the leader for maser cannon."

<Orders confirmed,> the computer replied.

A nanosecond later, targeting coordinates appeared on the DMR. Alex knew that the computer never took into account the human reaction to being under fire; the parameters were too great. That was why the ships had to have human pilots.

Once the pirates' scanners detected two deadly manta warheads approaching, they would split and try to separate the mantas; the ship not targeted would then try to disable the mantas with its own ordnance. In the case of the Ronge Pirates, they used standard laser repeaters; not as deadly as maser cannons, but ultimately quicker on the draw. Alex had something in store for them after that, a surprise he had been working over in his mind since his last melee.

"Hucs, alter coordinates for manta 1 to 118.12.335; manta 2 to 136.53.799. Confirm and launch."

<Orders confirmed. Mantas away.>

Before the mantas were halfway to their destination, a message icon flashed in the upper corner of the DMR screen, and Hucs' redundancy told him:

<Incoming directive.>

Expecting it to be his wingmen reporting back and informing him they would be joining the fray, Alex was surprised when the voice that came over the septaphonics was female; he recognized it immediately.

"Alex," his mother said, "We're ready to go *outside.* Come say good-bye."

"Hucs: Pause; Save," Alex told the program, and his game stopped play in mid-attack. He would have to continue later.

He took off his thought-link and ocular caps, as well as the septaphonic ear-mask that his mother made him use when his parents were in the TAHU. He left his personal cubicle in search of his mother and father, and sauntered into the communal area of the Temporary

Asteroidal Habitation Unit.

There was a great show of nonchalance in his demeanor and his stride. He was trying hard not to care that he was once again going to be left alone for hours on end with, by his estimation, nothing to do. He gave a casual flick of his head, whipping his long hair back.

His parents granted him certain privileges on his last birthday. To test the limitations of his new responsibilities, they gave him the choice of how to keep his hair. He decided to grow it long and forestall a hair cut from the programmed valet servochine. Proud of the length of his hair, he took great pains to perfect the toss of his head to the side. The maneuver kept his bangs out of his eyes and elicited a disapproving frown from his parents. He liked to remind them that it had been his decision to boycott the traditional cut.

His mother knew his equanimity was a façade. He knew his mother knew it was a façade. He still acted as if he didn't care that both of his parents had to leave again for the day to go to the site. Inside, he hated it when they left him alone in the small TAHU with only his uplink to the EarthMesh as company.

They had been on Macklin's Rock two months, and his parents worked at least six out of every seven days. That did not leave much time for Alex.

Macklin's Rock, one of the larger natural satellites in Sol System's asteroid belt, resembled a cylinder with tapered ends, an egg stretched out to the extreme. A cross-section of its length would cover an area larger than metropolitan New York, but Macklin's Rock was still just a large, unexciting rock.

Back home on Canada Station Three, the SF holovid rentals showed Sol System's asteroid belt to be a crowded ring of rocks and debris circling the Sun between the orbits of Mars and Jupiter. In the vids, the asteroid belt was usually home to refugees from a Terran global government gone bad, or for expatriates who had to hide from military sweepers trying to weed out the deserters; the ever-present danger of an asteroid collision kept the drama high in these pot-boiler stories.

The truth was a little different. From Macklin's Rock, looking out the view ports of the TAHU, Alex could not see any other asteroid without the aid of a telescope. If there were any danger of collision, Hucs' proximity sensors would alarm the TAHU inhabitants an hour in advance, then fire a deflecting shot with a laser. Rarely did a particle get through the computer defenses. It was all quite boring.

The Sun was nothing more than a tiny glowing marble, giving as little light to the inhabitants of the belt as could be seen on a foggy day in London, but without the romantic atmosphere of that old city.

The other planets in the system were nothing more than tiny specks through a telescope. Earth, at its closest approach to Macklin's Rock, was over a thousand times farther than the Moon from the Earth. It seemed like a greater isolation than all that to a ten-year old without any friends close at hand.

Even Jupiter, more than eleven times the diameter of Earth, was nothing more than a tiny, steady star that could be seen from Macklin's Rock by the naked eye for three-and-a-half months every two years; the rest of the time, it was obscured through normal telescopes by the glare of the omnipresent Sun.

Hucs could filter the image out; enhance it to 200 times magnification to give it the apparent size of Luna as seen from Earth. Alex had seen more than his share of reproductions of all the system's planets through telescopes; it was no different from the belt.

Standing on the surface of Macklin's Rock and looking in all directions, one could get the impression of living on a desolate, dark, deserted island floating through Sol System.

It was all quite boring to Alex; all too mundane.

Not that Alex was lacking in chores. There were lessons to be integrated, and a biosyn analysis he had to make up from the day before when he had played hooky from the lessons given by Hucs, the Home-Unit Computer System; instead, opting to play the latest version of 'Nova Pirates' he had downloaded from the Thai Multimedia Society.

But by and large, Alex was bored.

He sent audio-visual EPS messages to his friends on Canada Station Three, one of the dozens of the various country corporations' inhabited orbitals positioned at the Earth-Moon L4 point.

The EPS communications were more out of duty and obligation than desire; news from home just made him miss it all that much more. The seven minute delay between transmissions made for lengthy but shallow dialog, even on the chat pages.

Alex watched his mother prepping for her excursion.

"Mom, can't you stay home today?" he asked.

Alex's mother turned from pulling on her bio-eco suit-shield and gave her son a gentle smile.

"I'm sorry, Alex, but we've got to verify the new readings. Hucs reported an anomaly in the elemental percentage readout of the Nelson II at site 14. If it is what we are looking for, we can be off this asteroid within the week and leave it to Canada Corp.'s miners. Won't you like going home to CS3 and playing with your friends again?"

"Yeah," Alex said reluctantly. "But that's too long. Hucs is boring. All he wants to do is teach me Fulman algorithms and astral cartography. I want to interface with a real face, you know?"

"I know, Alex," said his father as he stepped into the communal area from the airlock, having finished re-checking the pressure gauges and atmospheric capacitors.

Gabriel Manez was shorter than his wife, his skin permanently tanned in contrast to her pale white flesh; his hair jet black where Margaret's was blonde. Alex had inherited his father's Mayan looks.

His was the voice of authority.

"Just remember that you agreed it would be best to come with us on this dig. You had the choice to remain on CS3; the company would have assigned an *Andy* to chaperone you."

"Yeah. I think maybe next time I will stay home, if it's all right; it's boring up here."

The Manez's went on at least one survey every year. The previous years, Alex had stayed on the station, but this year he had not wanted to be separated from his parents. Considering his current predicament, he regretted his decision.

His father smiled. "Well, you can put in a tight beam to some of your friends after your lessons. I think we can afford the real-time charges. And we just might be home sooner than you think."

Gabriel turned to his wife. "Especially if those readings are accurate, Mags. This could be the find we've been looking for. The bonus the Corp. offers on new strikes will be enough for us to retire on; we can buy a share in the Floating Isle Station like we dreamed."

She playfully batted at him, ignoring his enthusiasm. "You know I hate being called Mags," she scolded her husband, mock annoyance on her face as she initiated the vacuum seal on her suit torso. "Gabe!" she said to him, purposely making a face.

He shot her a dirty look right back. "All right. Margaret."

"Thank you, Gabriel."

"I prefer, 'love of my life.' "

"And I much prefer…" Margaret leaned over before her husband pulled on his artificial atmospheric replicator helmet and kissed him soundly on the lips.

"Yuck!" Alex declared and wandered over to the Digital Mock-Reality hologram screen on the prefab wall opposite the console desk, and set the thought-link patch over his temples.

Using Hucs for the EPS engine, since he did not have a bus generator like the one in their apartment on Canada Station Three, he logged in to the global operating system of the EarthMesh and waited the seven minutes for his personal settings to manifest and his modified cyberscape to be uploaded.

"This thing takes so long!" he said, even as he once again congratulated himself for his inventiveness in design.

His personal cyberscape was based on one of his favorite novels, Homer's *The Odyssey*. He called it Odysscape.

As Odysseus, he had to sail his ship to different lands to access the various programs, utilities and games in his cyberscape. He would change the cyberscape whenever he read a novel that took his fancy, basing his desktop on his latest favorite. Previous desktops included worlds from Lewis Carroll, C.S. Lewis, J.R.R. Tolkien, and Robert E. Howard.

"It takes me forever just to boot the system," he complained, though he had no choice in using the EarthMesh virtual drive. Hucs' LAN did not allocate even a quarter of the memory needed for Alex to run Odysscape. The drives were dedicated to the technical aspects of his parents' work and for the bio systems of the TAHU.

On the Odysscape casement, the tall Greek figure of Odysseus stood on the shore of Calypso's Island, making a raft to try to sail home to Ithaca. The casement showed Hermes, messenger of the gods, floating in the sky off to one corner after just delivering his message to Calypso, telling her that she should let Odysseus go. That signaled the startup of his desktop.

The CGI character was laboriously slow in binding the logs of his raft together, and Alex harrumphed with impatience. Hucs' P-Generator just was not powerful enough.

"Don't forget, it takes a little while for the Electronic Pulse Signal to reach Earth and bounce back. We haven't quite mastered faster-than-light … yet," Gabriel joked, and pulled on his helmet.

Alex's mother pulled on her own helmet, and each checked the other's suit for seal breaches, passing a vacuity loss detector over the seams and bodice of their suits. The contained ecosystem computer signaled that their suits were leak-free and surface-ready.

His mother's voice came over the septaphonic speakers in the TAHU, losing little of its tone in the digital translation.

"We'll see you in ten hours, Alex. You be good, and do your homework. Hucs will report to us if you don't."

The warning came after the lecture of the night before, and Alex dropped his chin to his chest, looking abashed.

"I know, I know!" he replied. The moment they had returned from work and asked for a report on Alex's activities, Hucs informed them he had spent six hours playing Nova Pirates instead of concentrating on his studies. Hucs was nothing if not deadly accurate in his recital.

"Hucs is a tattle-tale," he declared sullenly.

"No," Alex's mother corrected. "A tattle-tale is someone who tells on someone just to get them in trouble. Hucs reports to us for your own good, Alex. It's his program."

"I know, I know." But the timbre of his voice suggested he found the whole idea unfair in any event.

"We'll see you soon, Alex. Be good."

"I will."

Alex's parents stepped through the airlock. With a deep, audible click, the door sealed shut. The vacuum notification light glowed on the control panel to the right of the door at eye level as a chime sounded to indicate pressure equalization was beginning.

There was a low humming sound as the pumps sucked the air out of the lock, and the gravity replicator magnetics slowly dropped its gain, matching the negligible G's on the asteroid's surface.

His parents performed a few light exercises to get their muscles used to the near-zero gravity, and their own relative body weights of less than a gram.

Erected under the surface of the asteroid, the TAHU provided ideal protection for a survey team. The Construction-Engineering team had used pulse charges to create an artificial cavity ten meters into the surface, forming a rectangular box fifteen meters on a side, and four meters in height. AI mechbots constructed the TAHU itself.

With two personnel cubicles, a communal area, lavatory, dining cubicle, computer laboratory, and airlock, it was the perfect size for a two-person survey team. If the surveyors were a couple, a third person, such as an offspring, could be attached to the mission, and not put any real strain on the TAHU resources.

There was enough food for six months, and solar wind particle converters kept the batteries charged to full.

They built a gravity convection magneto into the floor of the TAHU, magnifying the asteroid's natural magnetic field inside the construct by a factor of 85.91, enough to simulate near-Earth gravity. The energy requirements were enormous, but the Sun, four hundred gigs away, provided an unlimited source of power.

Constructed on the surface of the asteroid, the ATV bay held the ATV itself, as well as a small two-person floater in case of emergency. The floater had enough power to escape the gravity of any celestial object smaller than Luna, after which it would emit an alert beacon.

Each personal cubicle inside the TAHU held a security receptacle, which converted to a one-person floater. Safety first.

Alex turned to the DMR.

"Hucs," he said aloud, even though the computer would follow every command he thought at it. "Bring up a VR casement for ATV camera."

For the moment, he ignored his Odysscape, preferring to use Hucs' much faster CPU engine for the local task. He shut down his link with the EarthMesh. After all, he was supposed to be working on his biosyn. Hucs had enough lesson plans uploaded into his Vdrive to last another month.

A connection with EarthMesh was not needed, but Alex felt better knowing that contact with Canada Station Three or Earth was seven minutes away.

Hucs spoke:

<ATV view on-holo, Alex. Please don VR ocular cap.>

Alex picked up the optics but waited before pressing them over his eye cavities.

The interface camera on the dash of the ATV powered up. It would make a visual and audio log of his parents' progress to each of the Nelson II sites, recording their reports and theories, failures and finds, and automatically EPSing it to Canada Corp.'s mainframes in Ottawa on Earth.

The DMR casement in front of Alex showed a 2D image of the camera's current field of vision. Alex slipped on the ocular cap of the thought-link patch. He pressed the cup-shaped caps to his eyes as they form-fitted themselves to the contours of his face.

Abruptly, he saw everything in the ATV bay from the dashboard, as if he were there, sitting on the hood.

Approaching the ATV, his parents were guiding themselves by a system of guy wires attached to the ATV and the bay. With the minimalistic gravity of the asteroid, a strong jump could send a person flying off the asteroid and into space.

The ATV itself used a version of the gravitational magnetos, combined with a reversed polarity magneto to repel itself against the asteroid's surface so that it could float two meters above the ground.

His parents both strapped themselves into their seats inside the vehicle and fired the power cells before his mother saw the green camera light indicating 'image-transmit' as well as 'image-record.'

"Hello, Alex," she said, smiling through the transparent faceplate of the helmet, guessing correctly that it was he who had slaved his VR to the camera. The clear septaphonic voice came over the TAHU speakers.

"Hi, Mom."

"What is it, Son?" Gabriel asked after a moment, fastening his seat restrictors.

"I don't know. I just wanted to let you know that I miss you."

"We miss you, too. Love you, Alex."

"I love you, too." He wasn't yet too old to say that; at least, not in private. If they were back on Canada Station Three, he might feel uncomfortable about telling his parents he loved them in front of his friends.

"All right, then get your lessons completed this morning, pass that biosyn test … and when we get back, maybe you can show me just exactly how that 'Nova Pirates' game works," his father said to him, his grin filling the width of the helmet's face plate.

"All right!" Alex exclaimed, suddenly excited. "See you later, Dad!"

He disconnected the VR link with a thought, and turned his attention to the review of the biosyn material that Hucs had presented in a secondary DMR casement with borders flashing an urgent red.

<Lesson Thirty-Seven Review—Biosyn>

Hucs was as accommodating as ever.

The computer droned on in a childlike voice with the review, but hard as Alex tried to concentrate, he found his attention soon wandering to the suspended 'Nova Pirates' game, and within an hour of his parents leaving, he minimized the lesson casement against the warnings of Hucs.

He maximized the game casement in VR.

Seconds later, he was blasting pirates out of the Ronge Nebula.

Geological Report :
Macklin's Rock :
Filed by Gabriel Manez :

Belt Segment: 14568

SMD Mine Number: 928-3

Name: Macklin's Rock

Age: 237.89 million years (Earth Standard)

Type: Metallic/Carbonaceous Chondrite (C-Type)

Distance from Sun: 425.92 gigameters (mean)

Closest Earth Approach: 276.33 gigameters

Dimensions: 148.11 kms longest diameter / 35.08 kms widest diameter.

Surface Temperature: -103.5 °C average

Mass (estimated): 10,020.5 teratons

Surface Gravity: 0.0000002373 G

Atmospheric Pressure: None

Escape Velocity: 0.009568 km per hour

Mineral Content: aluminum, calcium, carbon, cobalt, copper, helium, iron, magnesium, nickel, silicon, sodium, sulfur, titanium

Potential Value: $14 Trillion (Can) over 50 years.

USA, Inc. Exploration Site :
Mission *Orcus 1*:
Pluto :

Dark, cold, silent, inhospitable.

Wonderful.

Captain Justine Turner stood on the edge of Sol System. As captain of the *Orcus 1*, the historic honor fell to her.

It was another in a series of firsts for her: youngest female astronaut in NASA history; youngest person to get a captaincy of a space vessel; first human to set foot on the icy surface of Pluto.

She tried to think of something notable to say for the benefit of those on Earth who tracked their progress. Overcome with the tide of emotion, Justine could not think properly. The stale recycled air in her suit did not help clear her mind.

"Pluto," she finally declared into her microphone.

Swiveling her head to face the Sun, a tiny glowing pinprick in the low horizon, she imagined she was speaking for the benefit of posterity.

"It's been a two-hundred year journey to get here, since the dark planet's existence was first theorized. Now, that dream is a reality. This occasion is a milestone in human history. From here, all that's left is to conquer the stars."

She took a breath before continuing her speech, but a digitized voice filled her helmet.

"Captain!" called Helen Buchanan over the comlink. On loan from the Canadian Space Exploration Department, Helen had more than proven her administrative competence in her position as second-in-command. Still, she had a tendency for dramatics.

Irritated by the interruption, Justine growled, "What is it, Helen?"

"The science team reports all spectroanalyses are normal. Ekwan again requests permission to venture out on the surface." The first mate lowered her voice to match the captain's tone. "Justine, if he doesn't get his way soon, he's going to drive us all off the end of the planet, you know."

There was always one bad apple in every bushel. Unfortunately, NASA had had no say on who the Japanese included in the mission. They had to accept Ekwan along with the fifteen billion in research money the Japanese Space Administration had invested.

Six months in space with that overblown, opinionated jackass, however, was enough to test the patience of a saint.

I should deny his request, just out of spite. That would be petty, and a blatant misuse of her authority. Besides, it was not a generous attitude to take with any member of the civilian science team.

Looking around, she could barely see twenty meters beyond the landing lights of the *Orcus 1*. Willing to ignore the petty politics of Earth's corporate countries, she had accepted this mission—ecstatic and full of passion—for the chance to touch the heart of Pluto.

Now I am here! She reveled in the fact.

The surface of Pluto was barren and unforgiving. The achievement of reaching it would spur Earth to invest more resources in space exploration. The mantle of that responsibility rested squarely on her slight shoulders, and she dare not let anything untoward happen on this mission. She knew she should make the other members of the eight-person crew wait an hour after her exposure to the surface of the planet, in case there were microbes eating into her suit, or some other fantastical possibility thought up by the NASA scientists. But if letting Ekwan go would shut the seismologist's loud mouth up for just five minutes...

"Permission granted, Helen. But make sure he follows regulations. I'm coming back in. Seen all I need to see for now. I've got enough pics to keep NASA's publicity department busy for a year."

"Very good, Captain."

She could hear the relief in the First Mate's voice.

Justine made her way up the lander's ceramic ladder and entered the belly of the *Orcus 1*. It took a minute to cycle through the airlock.

∞

Inside, she faced an unorganized mob. In an orchestra of confusion, four crewmembers circled about their unbidden conductor, all shouting in a cacophony of anger.

"Ekwan! Slow down," Justine commanded, getting their attention. "We're here for seven months. You'll get all the surface time you need." She stared into his angry eyes. *So much anxiety in such a little man.*

"It's these stupid belts, Captain! There are too many, and they're getting in the way. And she—" He jerked his head at First Mate Helen Buchanan. "—won't let me go out until she has me trussed up like a prisoner."

"Ekwan. Just do it. Would you rather waste time arguing, or get your suit on properly and get out on the surface that much sooner?"

Clearly unhappy, the seismologist allowed Helen to finish strapping his suit together. With comic exaggeration, he stomped into the airlock.

"And wait for the rest of us!" Helen shouted through the intercom. "We'll be ready in a few minutes."

Ekwan's reply was unintelligible, but there was no misunderstanding the frustration on his face.

In a way, Justine could relate to him. Even in modern Japan, the need to excel and surpass everyone else drove their economic and social order. In a small country with such a high population density, it was no wonder people were frantic and short-tempered in their race to get ahead of the pack.

The others in the locker room slowly fumbled their way into their suits.

Justine nodded at Johan Belcher, the European Space Agency's geologist. The handsome Austrian was there to run detailed tests on the makeup of Pluto's icy surface, including depths, densities, and percentages.

If not for her captaincy, Justine would have encouraged his smooth-tongued advances. She had to keep herself set apart from the others, however; to do otherwise would undermine her authority. It was imperative she keep her command and authority for the duration of the twenty-month mission.

Johan returned the nod with a calculated smile as he helped Dale Powers, the NASA astrogator, into his suit.

Two other NASA members struggled to get ready. Henrietta Maria and George Eastmain. Justine suspected the two had become lovers on the long voyage. They giggled at each other like schoolchildren when they thought no one was looking, and whispered in each other's ears frequently.

"Where's Sakami?" she asked the group. The single representative from the People's Republic of China, Sakami Chin was clearly an outsider. He refused to dine with the others, and made no effort at casual conversation. Surly and abrupt, Sakami made no qualms about his aversion to space travel.

Justine turned her head at the sound of boots striking the metal plate that divided the locker room from the rest of the ship.

Sakami pushed his way through the crowd to his suit, and paid no attention to the cries of outrage from the others.

Justine glanced at her First Mate. "I'm heading to the bridge, if you've got everything under control here."

"Sure do, Captain. Take a nap. I'll alert you if Ekwan falls down a crater," she joked.

"Belay that. Only alert me if he kills himself."

She forced a smile, and made her way through the spacecraft.

∞

With the *Orcus 1* empty, Justine made a detour to the galley and helped herself to a squeeze tube of cold tea. She congratulated herself on achieving the most important goal of her life.

Stories of Planet X had filled Justine's young mind and fed her imagination, and as a teenager she studied every book she could download on the subject.

She made it her lifelong passion, reading everything she could find about the planet, scouring two centuries worth of history. With every probe that went past the dark world, she made certain to download all relevant data.

After she graduated from her Arizona State's Astronomy Department with honors, the Lowell Observatory took a shine to her and sponsored her into the NASA training program. Justine had worked hard over her short career. She clawed her way up through the ranks just for the opportunity of fulfilling her dream. Her ultimate goal: the *Orcus 1* mission. It was hers, though it had cost her a marriage along the way.

Brian, her ex-husband, had decided he did not want to play second fiddle to Justine's career. Her single regret was that she never made room in her schedule to have a child. The sense of loss and regret over her decision to put career ahead of family might have sent her into a deep depression, had not the Orcus Mission become a strong possibility.

Duty beckoned. Someone had to staff the bridge. With squeeze tube in hand, she picked her way through the ship.

She reached her command chair just as a klaxon sounded.

Scanning the monitors to no avail, Justine pitched her voice to get the computer to acknowledge her command. "Com: on." The ship's computer beeped, and Justine said, "Turner, here. What is it?"

The replying voice came across filled with a high-pitched whistle of static.

"Captain! We've got something strange out here, you know! Something you just *have* to see!" There was no mistaking Helen's Canadian accent when she was excited, and the woman tended to get overexcited about even the little things. Justine sighed.

"If it's a patch of ice with pink and purple streaks through it, I'm not going to be impressed."

"You want impressed?" Helen's digitized voice asked. "Well, I guarantee you won't be disappointed. Get out here and see for yourself!"

"What is—"

The computer beeped, indicating that Helen had cut off communications.

With a grudging effort, Justine lifted herself out of the chair and made her way to the lockers to suit up and go outside.

She grumbled all the while. "Crazy Canucks. Always with those cliffhangers. She probably loves the weather up here, while I freeze my nethers."

Justine, who weighed 59.8 kilograms on earth, was finding it difficult to maneuver with her Plutonian weight of 2.4 kilograms once outside the *Orcus 1*'s artificial gravity simulator. She weighed about as much as a large bag of salt. A strong leap could send her dozens of meters in any direction. That kind of activity, she admonished herself, was against regulations, and unsafe.

With its surface a slick sheet of methane ice and dunes of frost, any small misstep on Pluto could send her sliding hundreds of meters away. There would be little time to use the ice hooks built into the sleeves of her suit-shields to slow her down. Her boots were equipped with vacuum-suckers to keep them stable on the ice. Even so, a fall into one of the kilometers-deep craters that pocked the surface could mean a chilly death.

NASA publicity department wanted lots of commentary on the trip, and Justine decided to get it out of the way while she could. She spoke into her microphone, and pointed a small mini-cam toward the largest object in Pluto's sky.

"The moon, Charon, whose surface is more water-based without traces of methane, is a dark blue orb filling the sky."

Shifting to get out of the glare from the *Orcus 1*'s landing lights, she skittered across an expanse of ice and caught herself. With a deep breath of relief, she faced upward again.

"Although it is 1,270 kilometers in diameter, a third the diameter of Luna, Charon is more than five times the size of Luna from the Earth because of its proximity to Pluto, 12,640 km away."

Justine got into an ATV and set it to follow Helen's homing beacon.

She babbled while the vehicle rolled over the glacier that made up most of the surface of the planet.

"The primary mission of the *Orcus 1* is to examine the possibilities of methane-based life forms existing on Pluto. Nitrogen is a necessity of life, making up about 78 per cent of Earth's air by volume. It makes up a vital part of protein molecules. As with the Mars microbes a century ago, NASA is hoping to find some evidence of life on Pluto."

The beacon indicated she was within a kilometer of the group.

She struggled to think of something to say that might interest an Earth audience.

"Pluto is named after the Roman god of the dead and the underworld. To continue the allusion to Greek mythology, they named Pluto's smaller twin 'Charon' for the old boatman who ferries souls across the River Styx. In following this tradition, NASA decided to name the first manned mission to Pluto *Orcus 1* after the—"

As Justine came over a rise, she shut her mouth tight with a clack that echoed insider her helmet. Below her, the science team and Helen gathered like acolytes around a divine statue.

Justine's eyes beheld a sight beyond anything she had ever imagined possible.

In a place where no human had ever before set foot, against the cold darkness of Pluto's skyline, there was a monument the size of an aircraft hangar. The bulk of the structure resembled the nucleus of a complex atom.

Orbiting that nucleus, a number of spherical objects formed what looked like an electron cloud, hovering in the space around the monument without any visible tethers or supports.

An alien chill walked icy fingers up Justine's spine.

Humankind was not alone in the universe...

6

St. Lawrence Charity Hall :
Ottawa :
Canada Corp. :

Michael Sanderson, vice-president of Canada Corp.'s Space Mining Division had his best smile on for Stall Henderson, the Mayor of Ottawa, and Ian Pocatello, the National Minister of Finance.

Sharing inane pleasantries over flutes of champagne at the St. Lawrence Charity Hall, Michael groaned inwardly at the need for such a cosmetic façade.

Michael had lost track of how many of these functions he had attended over the past thirty-two years of his career, both in and out of the corporate government. Since his appointment to the VP of SMD five years previous, his attendance to these functions had tripled. They wore thin on him.

His smile, however, never faded.

"I don't usually drink, but after tasting this excellent champagne, I'm considering changing my views." He took a sip to punctuate his opinion.

"My wife spends hundreds of hours finding and sampling new labels, and buys it by the case when she finds one she likes. I'll tell her to send you and Melanie a bottle for Christmas," offered Stall Henderson.

"Wonderful. I'll be looking forward to it."

Mayor Stall Henderson was an open, jovial man, well suited to public office. Short in stature, he had a balding pate and an expanding waistline; a sign of the good times he had brought to the city. Everybody's friend, he had a quick mind, but suffered from a dry sense of humor, which some people found condescending.

Michael genuinely liked him for his personality, and for his integrity and political acumen. He was a politician's politician.

"So, how is the asteroid business?" Stall said. He kept his eyes from glancing at the Minister of Finance.

Stall Henderson was well into his sixties, and had been mayor of the country's capital city for twenty years.

In the past century, Ottawa had grown from merely the legislative capital of Canada to a major international city that attracted investors and researchers from all over the globe. Canada Corp. had resisted the worldwide corporate trend of diversification, and had located all its divisional headquarters in Ottawa and its environs; a major stroke of good fortune for Stall's political reputation.

Michael smiled and set his empty glass on a tray carried by a servochine, exchanging it for a full one.

"Oh, we're doing about as well as can be expected," Michael said. "We have a few more prospects in development, as you've no doubt read in yesterday's press release. If the preliminary surveys are correct, I can see a day in the future when Earth's natural resources will no longer be extirpated. All mining for the globe will be done off-planet. It's quite exciting."

"Fascinating, I would hasten to add," the mayor said. "Anything to do with outer space has my interest piqued. I have a son in post-grad studying the geothermal anomalies of Mars."

"Sted Henderson." Michael searched his mind, and was pleased with his recall. "Yes, I read his graduate thesis on it; published in Sol Weekly's last issue, I believe. Since finding those microbes last century, experts have been arguing about life having once existed on Mars. Sted's thesis points out that the evidence might suggest, instead, that life *will* exist one day in the future on Mars, that the planet is preparing itself for some kind of evolutionary burst. A boon for the naturalist movement. There was talk of degrading orbits or something along those lines. Increased temperatures and so forth."

"Yes! He'll be delighted to hear you've taken an interest."

Ian piped in. "I caught that issue as well, though I bought it more for the cover story about the Orcus mission to Pluto."

Ian Pocatello was the focus of the night, but still an unknown quantity to Michael. Younger than both Stall and Michael by at least twenty years, Ian had won a seat in the House of Ministers in the last round of proxy elections with a resounding majority decision; it had been his first time campaigning, which served to show he was a dangerous political opponent.

Researching Ian's background, Michael learned the man had spent the early part of his life as a successful financial advisor. Upon his election to the legislature, Ian had been appointed to the cabinet as 'Minister of Finance' by Canada Corp.'s long-time CEO, Pierre Dolbeau.

The first two budgets under Pocatello's administration had brought sweeping cuts to every department of the corporate government of Canada. Warning of a trend of global economic collapse—Japan Ltd., Australia Company, India Ltd., and Spain Corporation being the first countries to declare bankruptcy and be taken over by neighboring economic powers—Ian had forewarned of a day when Canada Corp. would be the victim of a hostile takeover from the much more fiscally powerful USA, Inc.

Three years into his Five-Year Plan, he turned around Canada Corp.'s financial outlook, and although the budget was still constricting, Canada Corp.'s debt had dropped by eighty percent and forecasts indicated a possibility of a surplus within the next six quarters.

Ian Pocatello's straight-faced, quiet approach to functions was daunting, however, and it took all Michael had in him to keep the conversation going, trying to find a soft spot in the Minister's defenses.

"I didn't know you were a space buff."

Ian shook his head. "I'm not. Progress in the space industry bears watching, though. If it's profitable, I'm interested."

Around the three men, dignitaries and functionaries in all levels of government—national, provincial, and municipal—as well as lobbyists from differing private corporations and minority groups, swirled in a cacophonic dance of political maneuvers. Behind those smiles and polite nods were feral plans and ambitious agendas.

Ostensibly, they were all there at the dinner to help fund-raise for Child-Find Canada, and it was more than a success at ten-thousand dollars a plate and a full house, but that was an excuse for the participants to lobby other politicians for support with whatever individual goals they had come to the Hall to achieve.

Michael's agenda was straightforward, but he had to play his hand close to the vest or others would dismiss his motives as a smoke screen for some private objective. If he did not portray himself as a political barracuda, he would lose standing and reputation. The mining effort would suffer, and, ultimately, he believed, so would the rest of the sub-corporation.

The SMD needed funds to bolster their research efforts. At present, they had thirteen class 2 nickel mines to show for the $140 billion the Corp. and private stakeholders had invested in the Space Mining Division. Forty-two of their projected asteroidal mines had showed, after additional surveys, to have impure lodes of ore and minerals; in a cost versus product schematic, they were not worth the trouble at present.

Michael Sanderson believed in the SMD as the best hope for Canada Corp.'s financial supremacy in the global economy, and as the best hope for the world. Scientists had estimated that the asteroid belt itself held hundreds of undiscovered new elements with attributes that could improve the quality of life for everyone on Earth.

Already, USA, Inc. and The British Conglomerates of the Commonwealth had aggressive and profitable space mining programs up and running, although most other country corporations were so far as unsuccessful as Canada Corp. A major lode had not yet been discovered on any of the Space Mining Division asteroids, and the race to the proverbial mother lode was getting tense.

Michael knew there were iron ore lodes out there in the Belt that would more than justify the massive investment by Canada Corp. and others. One or two big finds would alleviate the debt the SMD was accumulating.

He needed a few more billion dollars for operating costs and research—there were hundreds of thousands of asteroids to survey— and he was sure the 'Big Find' would occur soon. He had to get the Minister of Finance on his side, and get him to believe in SMD.

Then they could take their case to CEO Dolbeau.

Over the past two months, however, Michael had been unable to arrange a meeting with Ian Pocatello. The minister would not take private meetings with the VP of SMD, and had not returned any of his calls. When Michael discovered that the Minister of Finance was on the attendance list for the night's charity, he had seen to it that he and the Minister would cross paths.

Another man was approaching, and, hearing the last words spoken, commented in a wry voice.

"We have a Canadian on the *Orcus 1*. Did you know that? I'm following the story closely, myself." He laughed. "And I saw a tabloid on the mesh just today promising that landing on Pluto will mean the end of the world. 93% of readers agree."

Which is why they perform extensive mental competency and personality tests before someone can buy a share of the country corp. and can then vote on national matters, thought Michael.

The others curled their lips at the comment as the Minster of Energy, Mines and Resources—Michael's direct co-superior—joined them. He and the Minister of Canadian Space Exploration shared the joint-chairmanship portfolio of the Space Mining Division.

"Michael, how are you?" Alliras Rainier asked. A gray-haired man of seventy-one, Alliras was the foremost champion of the SMD, having made it a personal crusade to pass the bill ten years ago to create the Division, and pushing to have long-time friend Michael Sanderson appointed VP and director of the effort. Michael's meteoric rise through the ranks of EMR could be attributed, to some extent, to his association with Alliras Rainier, a long-time advocate of Michael's philosophies on energy and conservation.

Michael himself had just passed his fifty-third birthday a week before, spending the weekend with his family at his home outside Hull, Quebec. He kept fit by jogging two miles every morning, avoiding animal fats, and eating grains, fish, rice, and plenty of fruits and vegetables. At his last check-up, his doctor said to him, "I have some bad news; you only have about fifty or sixty more years to live."

Family was the most important thing in Michael's life, but a close second was the welfare of his fellow humans, not just Canadians, but everyone in the world. He gave to charity, and did what he could to help the environment, which was why he had gotten into the field of environmental energy at McGill University, where he had met his wife, Melanie, a Humanities Major.

Some small successes early in his career had garnered him the notice of Canada Corp.'s Department of Energy, Mines, and Resources. He had been climbing the ladder of the governmental corporation for the past thirty years and was near the top, where he had gained more influence than he had ever hoped or dreamed.

He was in a position to effect great changes in the way the world found and used energy, and the possibilities excited him. The passion that had sent him into Environmental Studies at University had not dissipated over the years.

His energy level, and tolerance for political maneuvering, however, was fading fast.

When Michael nodded that he was fine, Alliras prompted, "And your lovely wife, Melanie?"

The conversation from this point was choreographed; the two had gotten together at Michael's house the night before to discuss tactics.

"Melanie? She's here, somewhere. I think she's cornered Angela and the two are probably deep in debate over the aesthetics of pre-Columbian art."

"I never should have encouraged her to take that U of Carleton course. I think I've spent over a hundred big ones on ugly statues of pregnant goddesses in the last six months." He laughed, and the other three men joined in obligingly.

Michael could tell that Ian Pocatello was starting to feel more than a little cornered himself, with three pro-mining lobbyists surrounding him. The Minister was tense, as if waiting for the concerted attack.

The whole charade reminded Michael of tigers stalking a polar bear.

They would have to be careful, or enrage the bear.

Turning to Ian, Michael smiled. "I understand congratulations are in order over your last budget?"

"Yes. It was simple, really…"

If there was one thing Ian Pocatello liked, it was listening to the sound of his own voice.

The others settled in to listen, luring the Minister into a false sense of security. They smelled victory.

7

USA, Inc. Exploration Site :
Mission *Orcus I* :
Pluto :

Twelve kilometers from the landing site, Justine, driving the ATV, pulled short.

In front of her was an alien artifact.

Ekwan Nipiwin took a step toward it.

"Stop!" Justine roared.

As one, they turned to her.

She got off the ATV and picked her way down to them. It was a difficult task, considering the treacherous path, and her inability to take her eyes off the artifact for more than a couple of moments at a time.

As she came closer to it, she realized she could see through the semi-transparent surface of the monument. A hectare large at its base, and easily sixteen floors high, it was a massive structure of alien construction.

Justine stared at the behemothic artifact, her imagination running away with her. Thoughts of other life in the galaxy filled her mind. She had no doubt about it. They were not alone in the universe.

What were they like? Where did they come from? How long ago did they visit Sol?

Was this monument a calling card?

Here is where we are ... come visit us.

Or a flag?

We were here.

Or some kind of warning?

Go no further puny humans!

She was sure the thinkers back on Earth would be up twenty-four hours a day trying to answer those same questions, once she transmitted her report. As mission exec., Justine had little in the way of scientific background, compared to the others in the science crew, each of whom had no less than two Ph.D.'s. Her training was more technology based, but even that education did nothing to help her solve the puzzle in front of her.

"It ain't doing nothing, Captain." Helen broke off from the group to join Justine. "Just sitting there. Could have been here for a hundred million years, doing nothing."

"I want to know for certain. If there is even the remotest possibility of danger to the crew, then I'm going to declare this area off limits until we get instructions from Earth."

"Don't be so dense!" Ekwan's lips twisted. "I'll show you." He reached down and grabbed a sizeable chunk of ice and hurled it at the artifact before Justine realized what he was doing.

"Stop!" she commanded, but the ice ball impacted on the artifact and shattered into a million tiny fragments.

The artifact remained a noble, immovable object.

"See, Captain! I already tried that before. It's just there, like Helen said, doing nothing. If you are going to report this to Earth, the least we can do is take some surface measurements, perhaps a mass spectrometer reading; the usual stuff."

The pain-in-the-ass geologist was right, as usual. The immensity of the artifact itself, and the deep-seated awareness that there were others out there, numbed Justine, slowed her reactions. This discovery shook her to her core.

"What do we call it?"

"*Dis Pater*, of course." This from George Eastmain.

The name was apropos. There were many meanings of the word, but the one that came to Justine's mind was "Lord of the Dark Realms." The Romans had called their god of the underworld *Dis Pater*, and later changed it to Pluto. Justine had done her homework on all things Plutonian.

Henrietta mimed blowing George a kiss.

Glad that her helmet obscured the sour look she directed at the two of them, Justine nodded. "Very well. Let's get as much data as we can in one hour. Then we'll have to return for oxygen, and I'll transmit my report."

Like wind-up toys, the team jerked into action and began to set up their instruments.

They spent the rest of the hour taking measurements, readings, still photos, videos, and forming hypotheses. Within minutes, Dale Powers yelled out.

"What is it?" Justine asked, out of breath from running to his side despite the chance of slipping.

The astrogator raised his arm and pointed his finger. Centered on one sloping face of the monument, Justine could see thousands upon thousands of etched glyphs. When she moved to another of the bubbles, she saw it also had strange writing on the surface.

"My God!" Justine turned, looking for the engineer. "Henrietta! Get over here. I need you to get a picture of this. And tell me what you think."

With her camera, Henrietta took a few stills, and then ran the data through her palm puter.

"Forty-nine columns on this bubble," she announced. "One-hundred and seventy-five rows. I can't make anything out. I have to take a closer look." She waited for Justine's nod before turning on her anti-magnetos.

The engineer repelled off the planet's surface and hovered before the engraving, taking photos and video.

"Each column and row represents a unique set of glyphs, maybe like a sentence or something. I can't make out anything here."

"How many sets?" Justine asked the group as they all peered up at their floating colleague.

George, the astrophysics genius, replied, "Eight-thousand, five-hundred and seventy-five lines of glyphs." The figures came to him with little effort. "On each face."

Taking a quick spin around the circumference of the nucleus, George counted, "At least thirty-five neutrons. That's over thirty thousand lines."

"Yeah," confirmed Henrietta. "And I think each line is in a different language; each style is markedly different, and I don't recognize any of them." She measured a few with her palm puter. "Each row is twenty centimeters in height, and each column is seventy-one centimeters in width, separated by forty-two millimeters of blank space. The whole encryption encompasses a square area on the face 35 meters by 35 meters. Here, I'm transmitting the image to your puters."

They all pulled out their palm puters, and reviewed the images. Each line had a varying number of symbols, ideograms, dots, squiggles, or glyphs, from ten to a few hundred characters. Some specimens were simply a thousand or so straight lines inscribed side by side.

At the bottom of the last column, by itself, was a single line of glyphs. Justine thought it might be a signature of sorts.

Justine knew in her heart it was a Rosetta Stone of an interstellar collection of languages.

Imagine! Over thirty thousand other species out there in the vastness of space!

Justine shook her head.

"All right. We have to get back and send a report. Besides, our oxygen is low. In ten hours, we should have a reply to our report, and then we'll go from there."

Justine had to cajole every member of the team to return to the ship.

She, most of all, was the hardest to convince to leave.

[Event Report : Form ER-102] :

Date:
21-08-2090 / 13:23 GMT

Filed by:
Captain Justine C. Turner, Orcus 1
Navigator Helen Buchanan (CSE)

Scientific Team:
Joahanne Belcher (ESA), Ekwan Nipiwin (JAP), Dale Powers
(NASA), Henrietta Maria (NASA), George Eastmain (NASA),
Sakami Chin (PRC)

Nature of Event:
Discovery of unknown artifact. Scientific team named it *'Dis Pater'*
after the Roman god of the underworld, who was later renamed
Pluto.

Origin:
Unknown—not of human manufacture.

Age:
Unknown.

Location:
Pluto. Longitude 120:14:04. Latitude 42:98:31.

Composition:
Unknown. Specific gravity of 100+. Impenetrable by ion

bombardment (laser drill ineffective). Spectroanalysis inconclusive despite repeated test. Uncharted, or unchartable atomic composition.

Dimensions:

35.02 meters NS by 49.38 EW at base of nucleus. 168.27 meters in diameter including electron cloud. 75.91 meters in height.

Remark:

Foundation/base rests on surface of planet; no indentation identified.

Mass:

Estimated 1.44 teratons.

Apparent color:

Translucent. There is a subtle disruption of light flowing through object.

Animation:

None. Object is inert.

Distinguishing Marks:

Every curved surface of the nucleus is covered in glyphs, inscribed by unknown means. Extensive photo catalog included with appendix to report.

Observations:

Obviously of alien origin. We've tried every test we can think of, but none have given us any more than cursory data. Until we can interpret the glyphs we have no idea who the architects are, or for what purpose they erected this monument. Ekwan Nipiwin believes the shape is meant to represent an element, though it is nothing like anything in our current table, or like anything we have ever encountered.

USA, Inc. Exploration Site :
Mission *Orcus I* :
Pluto :

"Captain."

It was Helen.

In her command chair, Justine, lost in thought, blinked and turned her attention to the Canadian.

"Yes?"

All eight of them had been maintaining a silent vigil, waiting for a reply from Earth. Occasionally, someone would point out a reading or an image and make a comment, but in subdued tones. The enormity of their discovery sank in deeper as the day progressed.

To pass the time, Justine had composed a few messages to family and friends, and one or two colleagues. At a time when a single person's existence dwindled to near-insignificance compared with the knowledge of over thirty thousand alien races *out there,* Justine felt she needed to reaffirm the connection to the ones she loved and respected.

It made her feel better knowing she was a part of something that might reveal the awesome secrets of outer space. Never in her wildest imagination had she believed the Orcus Mission would bear such cosmic fruit.

The others perked up as Helen spoke. "We've got a binary EPS from Mission Control. Huh." She glanced up, her eyes wide in disbelief. "And a confirmation of translation of glyphs on *Dis Pater!*"

There was a moment's hesitation. George Eastmain blinked rapidly.

Ekwan's mouth opened in a silent O.

Then Justine spluttered, "A what?"

"I repeat: A translation."

"That can't be!" Dale Powers stood up. "Those glyphs prove there is life out there, and they've visited here." He pointed to the ceiling, and his voice took on a note of incredulity. "But I know for a *fact* that *our* life has never been to Pluto!"

Justine regarded him for moment, contemplating his tirade. "I tend to agree with you, Dale." She scanned the group. "But if Mission Control says they have a translation, we'd best hear it before discounting its validity."

"Helen?"

"I'll put it right through."

They all turned their attention to their workstation monitors.

Luna Station :
Luna :

Chow Yin had spent every one of the last seventy-nine years of his life on Luna. If anyone was aware of that, it would certainly make headline news, and break records. That was the last thing Chow Yin wanted, however.

At the age of three and a half, accompanying his parents on a posting to Luna Station, he had laughingly escaped the grasp of his mother one day and run off. As most accidents happen, he had run through a construction zone and fallen under the tires of a terraloader. His legs had been crushed, his bones splintered into thousands of pieces.

Reconstructive surgery and extensive physiotherapy, combined with the easy Lunar gravity of the time, had given him back the ability to walk, but with a very pronounced shuffle, and only with the aid of crutches; his awkward gait was far beyond a mere limp. Throughout elementary classes on Luna, he had been called troll, troglodyte, Quasimodo, and a host of other unwanted appositives.

He resented his peers—hated them.

Popularity was too far from his grasp to even be considered a dream. Acceptance was unattainable. He was an outcast.

The physicians told him he could never travel to Earth—the bones in his legs would shatter like toothpicks under the hard Gs of a re-entry shuttle, and walking in gravity six times that of the Moon was an impossibility.

For all purposes, he became the only orphan on Luna, since no one besides him was permitted to be stationed there for longer than a year for their own biological safety—his parents included. Yin had fended for himself reasonably well. His parents had visited once a year, but had granted the People's Republic of China legal guardianship of him.

Over the years, as he entered adulthood, his contact with his parents lessened to the point where Chow Yin no longer cared to accept their attempts at contact. To this day, he had no idea of their fate.

When Luna Station installed magnagravs for artificial gravity, only Chow Yin went without the lead-lined outfits. The pressure would be too much for his crippled body.

A lesser man would have let it get the better of him; perhaps even ended it all.

Not Yin.

He had turned his disadvantage to an advantage. The one thing he noticed about everybody who looked at him, especially once he reached his late teens and early twenties, was that their looks of horror and pity and revulsion were their central fixation. If he happened to be lifting their credit flecks from the folds of their coats, they did not notice, for his crippled and pathetic self was their only focus.

At twenty-three, he had been no longer satisfied with the pickings of transients' and tourists' credit flecks; those sums were enough to get him by, but what he really longed for was wealth: enough wealth that people would look at him with reverence instead of revulsion.

As the only permanent resident of Luna, Yin was more familiar with the station than anyone else was. He had converted a low-G storage bay on the bottom-most level of the station to his private quarters. With the help of a young and bored computer whiz whose parents had been stationed on Luna for a year, he erased traces of the storage bay in the main computer, changed security logs, created new access codes to keep out undesirables, and altered the entire computer system of the sector to suit Yin's needs and desires.

From this base, he ventured forth among the teen population of Luna. Most of them were bored and disenchanted with life on the Moon, and Yin recruited them to his cause, especially targeting those with skill in computers and technology.

Set up as a launch site to destinations beyond Earth, Luna Station, by its charter, was a cooperative venture of thirty-two country corporations. As such, no single government had absolute jurisdiction. The main computer was programmed as an administrative governor, and would enforce the policy voted upon by the station's board of directors on Earth.

It was only a matter of time before Yin and his cyber gang cracked the computer's defenses.

Yin's young protégés created a dummy file to accept instructions from Earth, run simulation reports on those initiatives, and send those dummy reports back, keeping the Earth council ignorant and happy.

As far as things went, by the time Yin was twenty-eight he owned the Moon in all but name. The wealth and power he had gathered to him rivaled that of the country corporations themselves. Every pleasure was his; every luxury was his with barely a thought.

Nothing happened on Luna Station without Chow Yin's fingers in the pot, and the only people that knew it were those that worked for him.

Lord of his little empire, Yin watched over the comings and goings of all transients at Luna Station, had his finger on the pulse of the country-corporations who docked their shuttles and temporarily installed their people on Luna.

If Yin wanted, he could have the Luna Computer ground all outgoing flights, or restrict any incoming shuttles from any country or private corporation that displeased him. He could hold all of outer space ransom, if he chose to do so.

He did not do that, however. Discretion, he had learned from experience, was the better part of increasing one's personal wealth.

…And information was the most powerful tool in the pursuit of that goal. He used the information he gleaned in productive ways; revenge and petty tyranny was not his business. Besides, abusing his power would only get him noticed, and he preferred to operate and luxuriate in anonymity.

The only people he let get close to him were the teens, whom he had continued to personally recruit over the past forty-odd years.

As part of his campaign to dominate Luna Station, when the last Chinese station director had rotated back to China, Yin had the computers manufacture an identity for the director's replacement and bounce it into the Hong Kong data base. A non-person had been transferred to the Moon, and the big bureaucratic machine that was the PRC did not even notice, so wrapped up in their petty politics and closed-door communistic efforts. It was a coup d'état, as far as Yin was concerned, though yet an unpublished one.

The entire Chinese Sector was firmly under his control, and the rest of the station was at his mercy.

Classified government documents were his to peruse and use as he wished, and he did so with impunity. He had corrupted the shuttle port governor, diverted tariffs and fees to his own private bank accounts, and appropriated nearly the entire budget allocated to the Chinese Sector from the PRC. So far, he had gathered a net worth that numbered in the trillions. He had invested heavily in many of the Earth nations' private corporations; and with a little manipulation, managed to secure a healthy return on his employed capital, as well as letting him keep his thumb on the pulse of Earth industry.

As part of his daily routine, while slowly consuming breakfast, he enjoyed reading some of the top-secret government communiqués his young techo-wizards intercepted.

When he read one such missive directed from Earth to Pluto, he nearly choked on his orange juice.

Immediately, he rang his secretary and told him, "Call a meeting of all our top snoops. We have a new priority."

11

Macklin's Rock :
SMD Mine Number 568 :
Sol System :
Asteroid Belt :

Taking a break at noon for a bite to eat, Alex slipped off the thought-link patch and ocular caps, blinking his eyes as he focused on the small TAHU. Adults always tried to tell him that too much VR would make him go blind, but if that were true, Alex had never seen any evidence of it.

"Hucs," he addressed the computer. Now that the thought-link patch was off, he had to vocalize his request. "Fries and cola, please."

<Carbonated beverages are on restriction, Alex, as well as fried foods. I am sorry. Would you like a tuna sandwich and a glass of milk instead?>

Alex grumbled to himself. His parents were concerned that he was not eating well enough. He felt all right, but had no choice in the matter; he had not yet figured out how to overwrite the log matrix on Hucs, so that he could override its priority codes with impunity. He decided he would have to work on that problem in the afternoon, or risk severe penalties when his parents found out he had been playing hooky again.

"Yeah, that's fine." When he entered the dining cubicle, his sandwich and milk were waiting for him in the booth, the replicator pre-programmed with the different personal preferences of each of the three inhabitants. Alex liked chopped celery and onion with no extra mayonnaise, but his parents preferred lettuce as their only addition. He sat down and ate quickly, his mind not on the food, but on the problem of the log matrix.

If he wrote a sub-program slaved to the file named "Alex's Daily

Activities and Progress Chart," then whenever his mother or father tapped in an inquiry on him, the dummy file would come up on screen on top of the legitimate file. He could then doctor the dummy file in any manner he so chose.

The problem with that was—

The TAHU alert klaxon sounded, making Alex jump in the booth.

<Proximity warning,> Hucs reported. <Unknown object approaching TAHU. Origin unknown. Velocity near light speed; thirteen seconds to impact. Please proceed to security receptacle, Alex.>

Without delay, Alex tapped the 2D min-monitor in the booth, signaling his parents.

"Mom! Dad!" he yelled, but the monitor showed nothing but white static.

"Look out! I think it's an asteroid!"

<Eight seconds until impact. Energy dampers at one hundred percent. Leak shield secure. Superstructure shields at full. Please proceed to security receptacle, Alex.>

Leaping out of the booth, Alex raced for his cubicle. The emergency drills his parents had forced him to repeat came to him like second nature.

Jumping into the security receptacle, he closed his eyes as the restraints locked around him, securing him from hitting any walls when whatever it was outside hit him.

He had the briefest of moments to speculate what was coming at him. His first thought had been an asteroid, but that would not be traveling so fast. A solar flare? Unlikely, at this distance.

Sweat dripped from his forehead as panic set in.

<One ... >

His parents were outside, unprotected.

< ... second ... >

Unable to control himself, he screamed.

< ... until ... >

12

St. Lawrence Charity Hall :
Ottawa :
Canada Corp.:

As Michael Sanderson and Alliras Rainier began their first round of maneuvering tactics to corner Ian Pocatello into granting them an extra billion dollars in funding, a servochine interposed itself between them.

The AI had been designed in the shape of a humanoid, but instead of legs, it used six rubber wheels to glide across surfaces. The wheels were attached to a rectangular box that could be customized as a refrigeration unit, a file cabinet, a tool chest, or any other kind of container required by the servochine's programmed capacity. As a waiter, the servochine's compartment was used to carry bottles of wine and spirits.

To Michael's slight surprise, the servochine was holding a silver tray on top of which was a white plastic envelope addressed to him.

"How quaint," the Minister of Finance commented. "A couriered message. I don't think I've ever been on the receiving end of one of those."

Alliras said, "Don't know why we ever stopped. Couriers and fax machines were wonderful. Now, we send everything over the EarthMesh. Quite frankly, I'm not comfortable with all the techno hackers in the world having access to the digitally transmitted love letters I send to my wife from work." Both Ian and Stall chuckled appreciatively.

Glancing at the servochine's CPU mount as if the AI would explain its presence, Michael took the envelope, opened it and, muttering a quick "Excuse me" to the three gentlemen looking on with interest, read the lased memo on the plastic slip he found within.

∞

Michael, I'm sorry to have to send this message to you considering your current circumstances, but an emergency has arisen that demands your immediate attention.

There has been a catastrophe that could undermine the entire program. The media is not yet aware of the incident, but it is only a matter of time. We need you, Michael!

—Calbert

∞

Michael looked up at Alliras, blinked, and then forced an equable smile.

"Something has come up."

"Everything all right?" Stall asked, fishing for information.

"Of course. You know SOPs: every time there's a blip on the astrographs, they have to have it signed off."

"A find?" Stall pressed.

Michael smiled. "If it is, I'll make sure to send you an advance press release. And now, if you'll excuse me, gentlemen."

The look on Ian Pocatello's face was a mix of concern over the emergency, and relief that he would not be corralled that night.

The timing was horrible, but Michael had to get back and assess the situation; he trusted Calbert not to exaggerate any catastrophe. If anything, his aide was apt to understate the case; and that scared years off Michael's life. If damage control was needed, he had to get to the SMD event center quickly.

As Michael turned to go, Alliras said, "You don't mind if I tag along?" He read the emotion on Michael's face, and knew that the message was more important than lobbying the finance minister.

"Please do." Michael said it as casually as he could.

Alliras motioned to one of his aides, who hurried over. "Please inform our wives we've been called away, and see that they get home safely."

"Certainly, sir." The man gave a curt nod, and hurried off.

Making apologies as they left, Michael and Alliras headed out of the St. Lawrence Charity Hall, and into the Minister's waiting limo.

"Damn it," Michael cursed once they were inside the vehicle. "Two months trying to get into the same room as Ian Pocatello, and this happens."

He handed the memo to his superior. Before reading it, Alliras commented, "A bit medieval, sending a message on plastic. Quaint, as the Honorable Ian Pocatello put it, but still medieval."

"It's something that Calbert initiated; public thought-comm traffic is mimeocorded by the government. CSIS has legislation allowing them to monitor any thought-comm or AV conversation, even encoded transmissions. Even the CCP can get access to the Corp's messaging system, in a crunch. A hand-delivered message is about the most secure form of communication available to us, as ironic as that is."

"Ironic," the Minister repeated.

"If one of the CSIS agents, or even a worker at the communications network, is of the disgruntled variety, there's always the chance of them selling any vital information over the border. We normally have a code we use over the thought-comm network, but I turned off my system for the charity function."

Alliras read the plastic slip inside the envelope. He whistled. "What does this mean?"

"I'm going to find out soon enough," Michael replied, already tapping in the number for a direct AV comm line to Calbert Loche, powered under SMD's private and secured lines, to allow his superior to listen in. An AV comm, conducted through thought-link patches, could be heard by one person on either end of the transmission.

"What about your internal security?" Alliras prompted.

As the signal beeped that transmission was taking place, Michael answered, "We have our own code for department lines, just like your office, I assume. We use it for emergencies, so no one will have enough examples to decode."

"You take your history lessons to heart, I see."

"I learned from my superior, rather than from textbooks," Michael complimented. Alliras nodded in concession.

To his consternation, Michael's call was bounced to Raymond Magrath, Calbert's capable assistant.

"What's going on?" Michael demanded. "I got the message.

Where's Calbert? Get him on the line."

Raymond looked sheepish. "Sorry, Director; Calbert has his hands full. I know he needs to speak to you, though. Urgently." He struggled to think of what could be said over what passed for a 'secure' line.

"There's a ... a kind of 152, but of indeterminate substance or identification."

Michael chewed on his lip.

"And...?" he pressed after a moment.

"Also, a 489."

"Oh. Damn." He nodded to the assistant. "We're already on our way. Fifteen minutes."

"Thank you, Director." The assistant severed the connection.

Michael hung up the comm line.

"So what's a 152 and 489?" The Minister asked, raising one brow.

"A 152 is a 'Find.' A discovery of a mineral or ore lode."

"That's good, then."

"Indeterminate. We get an average of a dozen 152s a week.

"—A 489," Michael informed him solemnly, "we don't get so often. It means there's been an accident, and there are multiple deaths involved."

The silence in the limo stretched out for a full minute, and then Alliras nodded.

"Then by all means, let's not spare the horses."

USA, Inc. Exploration Site :
Mission *Orcus 1* :
Pluto :

On the bridge DMR casement of the *Orcus 1*, and simulcast on their workstation monitors and palm puters, the NASA insignia appeared along with the emblems from the Canadian Space Exploration division, the European Space Agency, the Japan Conglomeration Space Enterprises, and the People's Republic of China Space Program, all of whom had joined the Pluto mission under NASA authority.

Justine scrutinized every digiface character that appeared on the screen.

The report had been sent in binary code; a video uplink was thought too expensive for routine communications. The power requirements of AV at that distance were astronomical, to say the least.

The computer translated the message:

∞

To:

Orcus 1

From:

Mission Control, NASA, USA, Inc.

Re:

Dis Pater

Message:

The glyph on the last row, last column is confirmed as Mayan Hieroglyph, circa 700 AD

Translation:

'Behold the Mighty Door of Kinich Ahua; Eternity is Now Before You; Beware the Power of Kukulcan.'

Orders:

Discontinue initial mission. *Dis Pater* is primary priority. Local authority granted.

Signed:

CEO Frank Madison, USA, Inc.

Director William Tuttle, NASA

CEO Pierre Dolbeau, Canada Corp.

Thomas Granville, Minister of CSE

Dir. Lassen Kruger, ESA

Dir. Vic Tong, Japan Cong. Space Enterprises

Honorable Tung Jo, PRC Space program

∞

Loud conversation broke out immediately, threatening to escalate into argument.

"What does that mean, 'Behold the Mighty Door of Kinich Ahua; Eternity is Now Before You; Beware the Power of Kukulcan'?"

"And what does 'local authority' mean?"

"What do they expect us to do?"

"Who is going to be in charge? The Mission Chief? Or the Science Chief?"

Johan Belcher asked, "Are there any more details?"

"No."

Henrietta had a concerned look on her face. "Are they keeping us in the dark on purpose?"

"Is there more? Does Captain Turner have a private message?" George Eastmain demanded.

That last question brought silence as all turned to her for an answer. Justine glanced at Helen. "Is there anything for me?"

The First Mate/Navigator of the mission blinked a number of times. It was against regulations to reveal even the existence of coded military messages to the Science Team, but it was obvious the captain wanted to allay suspicion among the others.

Slowly, she nodded—*Yes.*

"Bring it up."

Helen hesitated. "Captain," she began to protest.

"Bring it up," Justine reiterated, her tone forceful and full of command. She brooked no disobedience.

"Very well." The Canadian turned to her comm computer and tapped in a few passages, giving the preliminary codes. She turned to Justine. "Captain?"

Nodding, Justine said out loud, "Voice print confirmation: Captain Justine Churchill Turner, *Orcus 1*. Security Code: Alpha-Alpha-Alpha-Zeta-Alpha-Turkey-Chicken-Rat." There were a few chuckles, despite the tension.

The on-board AI replied, "Confirmation acknowledged, Captain."

Justine added in a mock imperious tone, "Just so everyone knows, I'm changing the code after this." That elicited a few more chuckles.

On the bridge DMR casement, the NASA insignia was replaced by the CEO of USA, Inc.'s official emblem. Unlike the binary EPS, this message was an AV communication, with a length of two minutes, fourteen seconds. The cost for that brief message was in the thousands of dollars.

On screen, the image of CEO Frank Madison and Director William Tuttle appeared, both seated on a couch in Camp David.

The Director spoke first. "I won't waste time, Captain Turner. No doubt you've received the translation of the inscription on that artifact you called *Dis Pater* by now. I know, I know. The words mean nothing without a frame of reference. We've got top Mayanologists and cryptologists working on it along side our best technical and theological experts.

"For now, I want you to inform the Science Team that they should proceed with utmost care, but with utmost urgency in trying to solve the mystery of *Dis Pater*; we need as much information as possible."

The CEO, the most powerful man in America—and some said, the world—interrupted the Director.

"Since the discovery, we've had a number of summit meetings with the involved agencies represented by the Science Team up there, as well as with most of the other countries. There is a widespread movement to make public any and all findings. But the five agencies who are in cooperation on this project are in a position to keep the upper hand with our discovery.

"It's political chaos down here. It is imperative that we have some solid information before making any kind of arrangement with any country outside the five. Therefore, we are depending on you to ride herd on those scientists up there. Bring us something we can use."

The Director of NASA took over again. "Justine, no matter what, I want you to make sure no lives are in danger. Come back to us safely. There's a promotion waiting for you upon arrival." He smiled and gave a quick nod of his head.

The NASA insignia transposed itself over the frozen image, and then the casement went blank.

The argument that threatened to boil over from the collected scientists was cut off as Helen's voice rose above the growing roar of protest.

"Captain! We've got something on the spectrograph sensor at the site of the artifact."

She stared up at Justine, her eyes widened to the size of saucers.

"It's the *Dis Pater*."

Her voice throaty, she spoke in a breathless rush. "It's ... *reacting*."

SMD Catalogue :
Largest Asteroids :
by diameter (km) :

1. Ceres – 952

2. Pallas – 544

3. Vesta – 529

4. Hygiea – 431

5. Intermenia – 326

6. Europa – 301

7. Davida – 289

8. Sylvia – 286

9. Cybele – 273

10. Eunomia – 268

- - -

42. Macklin's Rock – 148

SMD Event Center :
Ottawa :
Canada Corp. :

Michael and Alliras arrived at the SMD Event Center twelve minutes after speaking with Raymond Magrath. Taking the Colonel-By Thoroughfare, they pulled up to the large neo-mod building in the southern section of Ottawa, near Gloucester and the international airport.

Inside the Event Center, the two men made their way to the seventh floor, Operations. Stepping off the conveyor tube, they entered organized chaos.

Technicians and operators were hustling back and forth, hovering over computers and monitors. All along the walls of the enormous room, giant DMR casements showed schematics of Earth, Luna, and the other planets. One showed the entirety of Sol System, with running statistics on each view scrolling up the side bars of the casement screens. Most of the smaller monitors showed various asteroids in the belt.

Rows of desks housing computers and DMR casements divided the floor of the Event Center. Technicians and operators took up every available space.

Filled to capacity, the room held more people than normal. Most of those in attendance were evening shift. A few had not left after their shift ended, and stayed on through the emergency to lend their expertise.

Michael glanced at his watch.

The second night shift would arrive in four hours. It did not matter what the emergency was, tired people made mistakes. Michael would direct them to go home himself, if it came to that. For the time being, he felt secure with the abundance of intellect in the room.

Raymond Magrath spotted them as they entered, and hurried over. With his thought-link patch secured to his temples, he nodded to the two, and directed their attention to the central screen.

Raymond was young, in his early thirties, but competent in his duties, regularly performing beyond his job description as administrative assistant.

Raymond wasted no breath with pleasantries. "It happened just over two hours ago."

"What happened?" Alliras pressed.

Michael glanced over to Calbert, hovering over a technician.

Raymond squinted—a sign he was giving the CPU a command through the thought-link. Everyone had their own way of showing they were thought-linking, even though no physical movement was required. The central DMR casement flicked, and a new image superimposed itself for their scrutiny.

The legend explained that they were looking at Segment 14568 of the charted asteroid belt. The screen showed a number of large bodies, some rotating, others stationary.

The AI filtered out any rock smaller than a kilometer in diameter to avoid creating a cluttered DMR display.

Many of the rocks had a white circle sketched on their surfaces, with a direct legend detailing their physical attributes and statistics, SMD mine number, and name—if they had one.

Michael saw an anomaly in one of the SMD asteroids.

One of the circle designations—Macklin's Rock—showed that the site was in the process of being surveyed, but there was no real-time image of the asteroid itself on the screen.

"What happened?" he asked, repeating his superior's question.

"The whole damned asteroid just vaporized on us. We have the EPS record cued and ready for playback."

Just then, Calbert Loche spied them, and hurried over.

"Two surveyors were on that asteroid when it exploded. Although exploded is not quite the right term," he added. "Disappeared, vaporized, vanished—who knows?"

At the moment, Michael was more concerned with the deaths rather than the technical explanation for the incident. "Who?"

"Margaret and Gabriel Manez, two senior geologists. They were checking a Nelson II at local site 14 when it happened."

Raymond thought-linked to a smaller DMR monitor, and an archived image of Macklin's Rock appeared, magnified, showing the location of the TAHU, and the thirty-seven prospective sites. Site 14 was illuminated in red.

Michael searched his memory. He prided himself on remembering the names of every person in the SMD, all 532 of them. A particular fact came to him, and he had trouble swallowing.

"There was a ten-year-old boy on that rock as well."

"Yes," Calbert answered, his voice low and solemn. "Alex, I believe is—was their son." The hard look on his face told Michael that he felt just as responsible and remorseful as the VP.

"Survivors?"

"Sorry, Michael." Calbert remained silent a moment, then concluded. "We don't know what happened exactly."

"Collision?"

"No. The EPS sent by the TAHU's Hucs indicated something approaching them near light speed."

"Light speed?" he blurted, shocked. "A Sunburst? Electric cloud storm? What was the point of origin?"

"None. We have no indication that it even originated off surface. We think it might be something they found at the site. Their Hucs' long-range sensors picked up nothing, but the short-range picked up the anomaly about thirteen seconds before impact. Again, I'm not sure 'impact' is the right word, either."

"That long? Thirteen seconds at light speed would be well past the boundaries of Macklin's Rock," Alliras pointed out, checking the statistics of the asteroid. "The origin of the pulse could be anywhere between Mars and Jupiter!"

Then Calbert's words registered.

"The *short-range* picked it up? It's geared for a few hundred klicks. That doesn't make sense. Thirteen seconds? Are you sure?"

"That's right, thirteen. The watch probe we have orbiting as sentry to this section EPSed that there was an oscillating pulse of energy— form unknown—at a point *inside* Macklin's Rock.

"Whatever it was, it traveled—or at least originated—under the surface of the asteroid just this side of the speed of light. Maybe it bounced back and forth within the rock a number of times, consuming the asteroid from the inside out. Finally, it impacted or broke through the surface. It was too fast to get a decent measure, to be sure, in any case. Whatever this energy source was, we have no signature on it, no means of identification."

Michael struggled with his chemistry. "Whatever the substance was, it was inert until something triggered it. But what?"

"I agree in theory; there was some kind of fission taking place. Much more powerful than any nuclear reaction. If we only had a sample…"

"What do you mean?"

"All we know is that the energy pulse vaporized the entire rock in a matter of less than fifteen seconds."

"Vaporized? Any traces?" Michael asked. "Resultant gases?"

Raymond shook his head. "None. Mass readings of the quadrant indicate a net loss of 142 teratons and change, exactly that of the Rock."

"That's impossible. Either it moved, or we've got millions of meteorites coming our way."

"As far as we *know*, it didn't move. There's no trace signature of the solar wind tail. And there are no new meteorites in the segment indicating an explosion. None of the sensors picked up anything; but then, again, the energy pulse of that thing was so strong, our sentry probes lost a few seconds of power. Anything could have happened in that time … anything."

Michael sighed heavily. "What do we have to go on?"

"Just the recorded conversation between the surveyors—between Margaret and Gabriel," Calbert corrected himself, his voice somber.

"Bring it up."

"We should go into the conference room to view the log," Raymond suggested, always thinking. "Right now, the techs don't need the distraction."

"Quite right." Michael gestured to a portal leading to the hall, which housed a series of conference rooms on either side.

∞

With Calbert remaining at Ops, the three others seated themselves in leatherback swivel chairs around a large semicircular marble table facing a collection of DMR screens.

Raymond, his thought-link patch still connected, brought up

schematics. The smaller monitors held images of Macklin's Rock recorded two-and-a-half hours before the occurrence.

On the central DMR screen, the casement showed the Space Mining Division symbol for a moment, and then the image flicked to fifteen minutes before the event.

Raymond explained, "It took them a few hours to get to Site 14 after they left the TAHU. They checked the sites in rotation."

A clock on the lower part of the casement showed the time as 12:58 GMT. The image itself was the record from the ATV interface camera, which, as Margaret and Gabriel disembarked from the ATV in their bulky bioshield suits, followed them from about five meters away, hovering over the surface by an antimagneto engine and navigating by micro fuel pulsors.

The septaphonics in the conference room carried the conversation between the two surveyors.

∞

"Here it is, finally," said Gabriel in his unmistakable accent, standing beside the ATV.

Margaret did not hesitate; she approached the site marker.

"Hucs reported the Nelson II had detected traces of a semi-large deposit of something *beyond* the core sampler range, right?"

"Yep. I brought the override code, just in case. We can get an extra twenty meters out of the sampler drill."

He opened the ATV carry compartment, withdrew a telescopic extension for the drill and joined his wife at the Nelson II.

∞

Michael interrupted the playback with a hand gesture. The image froze at Raymond's thought-link command.

"Do we have the readings of the Nelson II?"

"Yes." The assistant brought them up on a secondary screen. "Non-conclusive. The mineral readings were typical as far as a kilometer down, nothing to write home about. No significant lodes. But when the drill reached its maximum depth, it registered a .002 per cent content reading by mass of some unknown substance.

"Obviously, Margaret and Gabriel believed it was a deposit of iron ore, as the record of their dialog shows. This is why the potential value estimate he filed is so high."

"Right." Alliras cleared his throat. "Let's finish the recording."

∞

The playback continued, with the two surveyors speculating on their find, and what they would do with their bonuses once they returned to Canada Station. Michael could not help but smile, even though his throat was tight, and his temples throbbed. It was a grim business.

∞

"The Nelson II indicates the deposit begins fourteen meters below maximum depth," Margaret reported.

Gabriel adjusted the depth cue on the drill, and tapped in the command to engage the Nelson II's engine. The large bit twirled and dug into the asteroid.

"Any indication on size of deposit?" Margaret enquired as she monitored the Nelson II's temp and friction indicators.

Watching the sample analysis display, Gabriel shook his head.

∞

At 13:11:02 GMT, he reported, "Almost there, another minute or two."

∞

At 13:11:47 GMT, the image blanked.

∞

The silence in the conference room drew out for a few minutes.

"Damn," was Alliras's comment.

Michael tried to be analytical. "Obviously, the deposit reacted with something in the drill or sampler, or even with the friction and heat of the operation."

"We've already begun analyses," Raymond told him. "The makeup of the drill is designed to avoid causing a reaction to any known mineral compound, including plutonium and uranium. Whatever happened, it wasn't nuclear."

"So we're left with heat?"

"We can't rule out the possibility of a new element, one that does react to something in the drill?"

"So we are left where? At the beginning?"

"Yes."

"Caught with our pants around our ankles, I would say," Alliras put in. "Damn."

They were interrupted by a message sent from Calbert. The casement appeared over the DMR of the survey playback. "Michael, one of our probe sentries has picked up small mass readings in the event area."

"Be right there," he replied, and the three men hurried back to the Operations Center.

∞

Calbert greeted them with a nod. He pointed his hand to a medium-sized DMR on the east wall.

"Initial readings indicate a number of objects, ranging from 50 kg to 5000 kg mass."

"Meteors?"

"No, ion pulse radar shows the objects as fragments. We should be getting an image in about three minutes."

The technicians and operators in the room all ceased their work and looked up at the DMR as the screen flicked to visual camera.

There was nothing on the screen at the moment, but the radar magnification indicated a range of 932 meters.

At a range of 500 meters, several objects could be discerned. One looked like the remnants of a Nelson II drill. Closer still, and the ATV could be seen, horribly mangled and burned.

One hundred meters in, the probe picked up two objects: the bodies of the two surveyors.

"Alive?" Michael shouted.

A tech punched a command sequence into his keyboard, and reported, "No, sir."

"Damn!" Alliras swore; it was becoming a mantra.

Another technician reported, "All other objects identified as equipment from the survey team. Tools, rations, other accouterments." Specific details at this point was lost on Michael and the others.

"What about the TAHU?"

"No sign, sir."

"Recover everything out there," Michael directed. "I want a detailed report and autopsy on my desk by nine tomorrow."

The probe would magnetize the objects and drag them back to the *Canuck Flyer*, the mining orbiter, a large complex the surveyors used as a way station between Luna and the asteroids. With hundreds of engineers and processing technicians on board at any given time, there was a more than adequate mechanical and chemical laboratory, as well as an experienced medical staff on hand, more than qualified to perform the necessary procedures.

"What happened to Alex Manez?" Alliras said, but no one ventured an answer.

Michael, his body stiff, turned from the operations room and headed for the conveyor.

∞

Alliras accompanied him down the hall. When Michael punched the up button for the conveyor, intending to ride to the seventeenth floor where his office was located, Alliras said, "I think I'll go home to my wife, if that's all right."

"I wish I could do the same," Michael said in a soft voice. "Right now, I have to write a press release for the media, and I have a few unpleasant calls to make to Margaret and Gabriel's families."

"I don't envy you that task. By tomorrow, SMD stock might well be worthless."

When Alliras' conveyor arrived first, he shook Michael's hand. "I'm truly sorry about all this. I hate to sound clinical, but unless we can find out what that element was your surveyors found on Macklin's Rock, there's no upside to this. The media will eat us for breakfast. We'll lose our funding and our charter."

"I know. Take care, Alliras. See you tomorrow."

"I'll stop by mid-morning, if that's all right."

Michael nodded. "Just fine. Convey my apologies to Angela."

"I will. Try to get some sleep tonight yourself," Alliras said.

With a dry smile, Michael said, "Right."

Alliras stepped inside the conveyor tube. He nodded and tried to give Michael a smile as the doors shut.

The second tube arrived, and Michael rode it up to the top floor.

∞

In his office, he placed two comlink calls. One to the Manez Family, and one to the Sheridans, and expressed his condolences as best as he could for the loss of their children and for their missing grandchild.

He then typed a short press release for the media, posted it on the Associated Press Mesh Board, *Highest Priority*, then turned off his computer, opened the liquor cabinet and withdrew a bottle of Scotch. He poured himself a stiff measure in a plastic coffee cup.

After a quarter of an hour, he placed a commlink call to his home.

"Hey, babes," he said when his wife, Melanie, answered.

"You're still at work?" she asked.

"Yeah. I think I might be awhile. All-nighter. Gotta be here in case they find anything."

"What's wrong?"

Michael had to take a deep breath, and then he filled her in. They talked over the link for three hours.

He made sure to tell her he loved her before hanging up.

Michael finally stretched out on the couch in his office to try to catch a few winks.

Unknown :

Disconnected.
Free falling.
Force of pressure.
The depths of space.
Lost in the farthest reaches.
Found by the light of Sol.
All things seen as if one.
Nothing is possible when everything is gone.
Feeling his way through the morass of darkness.
Screaming against the vast vacuum of madness and pain.
Sailing with the solar wind as guide to his destination.
For one instant he feels the power of all.
The next moment the call comes to him.
It is power; it is for him.
The beacon of a million stars.
The shores of all consciousness.
The signal is Home.
It calls him.
Come, Alex.
Come.

USA, Inc. Exploration Site :
Mission *Orcus I*:
Pluto :

Helen's voice of authority cut off the argument that threatened to boil over from the collected scientists.

"We've got something on the spectrograph sensor at the artifact site. It's the *Dis Pater.*" Immediately, Henrietta Maria and Sakami Chin rushed over to the communications desk.

Sakami's eyes flashed all over the communications boards. "What is it?" the planetologist asked.

Helen replied in a voice loud enough for everyone to hear.

"It's glowing—and the sensor reports that it's giving off electromagnetic wave vibrations. Initial wave length at 6662.04 angstroms, a frequency of 450 terahertz increasing in frequency at an accelerating rate of 60 terahertz per hour per hour."

"Can it do that?" George Eastmain, the astrophysicist, shook his head in disbelief.

Helen shrugged; her specialty was navigation and communication. "Maximum wave length of 3997.23 angstroms will be reached in approximately five hours."

The captain speculated, "Some kind of broadcast? Could the *Dis Pater* be some kind of antenna array? If so, where is the broadcast originating?"

"Unknown."

"Between 7000 and 4000 angstroms is the visible spectrum of light. Something's coming at us!" exclaimed Dale Powers, calculating the mathematics in his head: "…At just under the speed of light!"

Justine raced for her bio-eco suit shield, and donned it in record time. With her, the Science Team dressed and entered the air lock, leaving Helen behind to monitor communications and control.

Taking the ATVs, both packed with analytic and survey equipment readers, the group raced for the artifact.

Twenty minutes after the initial reading reported by Helen, the Science Team and the captain gathered around the monolith. For a few moments, they did not move from the ATV, so stunned were they by the change in *Dis Pater*.

The color of the monolith had gone from transparent to a deep cherry red. They heard the cyclic wave emissions as a hum, which resonated in a rising and falling volume.

Justine swallowed. "All right people; let's act like we know what we're doing. I want every kind of reading you can imagine taken on that thing."

When they did not react immediately, she spoke in a loud commanding voice, "And I want it ten minutes ago!"

Quickly, the six scientists spread out to check the existing analytical equipment, and soon reports were filtering in from each area of expertise.

Justine retrieved the AV interface camera and filmed everything as it happened. She gave instructions to Helen to EPS live to Luna station. The power costs would be extraordinary, but if the CEO of the United States of America wanted some tangible information, she was going to give it to him in spades.

Ekwan was the first to call out. "I read temperature change."

"Specify," Justine ordered, assuming temporary command of the Science Team. If Dale Powers had any objections, he did not voice them.

"Surface temperature of artifact rising," the Japanese scientist said. "Minus 210.8°C ... minus 210.1°C ... minus 209.6°C..."

"Projections?"

Ekwan consulted his computer. "At Ground Zero, temperature will read 0.0°C."

"Interesting," Justine said. "Peripheral effects? Climatology of the surrounding area?"

Ekwan shook his head. "It depends on how long *Dis Pater* holds that heat. We could have a few isolated whirlwinds, maybe some nitrogen hail or methane rain. If the artifact cools quickly, there is nothing to worry about. I'm assuming it will begin to cool once ... *whatever* ... reaches us."

George Eastmain reported, "The thing is changing color slowly. It's going through the entire visible spectrum. The color right now equates to about 6,250 angstroms. Over the next few hours, we'll see it get light red, then yellow for a few minutes, changing into the greens, then blues, and finally into the violets at Ground Zero—about 4,000 angstroms or less."

"Wave emissions increasing in pitch." Johan Belcher looked up at Justine. "In about two hours it'll reach a frequency too high for us to hear, but it might wreak some havoc with our communications."

"Noted." Justine played the camera over the artifact, noticing that it had already lightened in color. "Is there any kind of spectral analysis possible? Can we tell what this thing is made of?"

Henrietta and Dale hunched over one of the monitors. Dale glanced up. "It's impossible to tell what *Dis Pater* is composed of. The element is uncharted. Also, we're getting a reading on a second unknown element reacting with the artifact: uncharted as well."

"Suppositions?"

"If I were to make a guess, I would say *Dis Pater* is made of an element that would have an atomic weight of about ten thousand— way off the charts. Carbon has about twelve, nitrogen fourteen, and even plutonium is about two-hundred forty-four. This stuff is way beyond our analytical abilities. As for the reactant, my best guess, based on what this machine is reading, is about half that: 5,000 or so."

"Incomprehensible," muttered Henrietta.

Dale shrugged. "It's naive of us to believe there are only a hundred or so elements in the entire universe, man-made or not."

Justine was growing frustrated. She knew the scientific process was an exercise in patience, but she was a woman of action and it galled her to have to sit on her hands.

"Speculations," she addressed the group. "Solar flare? Electric cloud? Cosmic lightning? Someone must have a theory."

When no one answered immediately, Ekwan, his specialty intergalactic meteorology, shook his head. "I can't tell you what it is, but I can tell you what it's *not.*"

"Well, that's something."

"It's not a solar flare, or solar wind. Solar wind, at best, has a velocity of about 500 kilometers per second, not the 299,792 kilometers per second light travels. A flare would not travel this far out from the Sun.

"An electrical cloud, as we've been calling them, is isolated in one location. They rarely travel more than a few hundred thousand kilometers, certainly less than a gig.

"We've got something that could possibly be coming from as far away as 5,500 gigs. If it is originating inside Sol System, then we are talking about something coming from the general vicinity of Mars or Jupiter. From outside, it's possibly something to do with the Oort Cloud. Cosmic lightning is usually a side-effect of electrical clouds."

"Any other possibilities?"

No one replied for a few moments, and then George shook his head. "It's too early to know."

"Are we in any danger? Should we evacuate?"

Again, there was no reply.

Forced to make an executive decision, Justine said, "We don't have enough time to lift off the planet, so if there's a global effect, we're done for no matter what. But if there is a local effect around the site, I want to be at least a dozen kilometers away at impact. At the very least, I don't want to be here when it begins hailing. Thirty minutes before Ground Zero, we'll return to the lander and monitor our instruments from there. Is everyone in concurrence?"

One by one, the Science Team nodded their heads.

Over the next few hours, Justine left them to their work, occasionally interrupting one person or another to make a statement to the AV camera for the benefit of Mission Control on Earth.

∞

As the final hour approached, for the first time in her life, Justine started feeling claustrophobic. Out in the vastness of space, she felt as if the entire universe was closing in on her, choking her, squeezing the life out of her. The other members of the crew had tasks to occupy them, but all Justine had was her imagination. She never thought something like this might happen to her. Her interests in Pluto had been sentimental and academic; this event was not only an extraordinary anomaly, but it was also a catalyst for Justine's internal priorities. It made her realize that there was more to Sol System, and the universe, than mathematical statistics. The universe was a living organism.

Her bio-eco suitshield was becoming warm, so she turned the

thermo-regulator down a few degrees.

After an eternity, her commlink chimed, the general broadcast light blinked, and Helen's voice filled the silence inside their helmets. "T minus forty-two minutes, Captain."

"Thanks, Helen. All right people," she directed to the Science Team, "get 'em up and move 'em out."

With reluctance, they obeyed. By T minus twenty-six minutes, they were back inside *Orcus 1*, and Justine wasted no time in sounding a Stage One Impact Alert. Stabilizers activated, and magno-repulsors switched on. The occupants kept their bio-eco suitshields sealed tight and belted themselves into their command modules.

Helen continued the countdown. "T minus fifteen minutes. Ground Zero at 18:13:59 GMT."

"There's a continuous EPS to Earth on all monitors, so put your best face on," Justine warned the crew with a light voice; their faces could not be seen through their suit helmets.

On the main DMR casement, Helen filtered in a real-time AV of the *Dis Pater*. Over the past few hours, it had changed as predicted, its color turning yellow, green, and blue. Currently, it was in the deep violet end of the spectrum. The cyclic wave emissions were no longer audible to the human ear, but the computers tracked it unfailingly, despite Johan's supposition.

"T minus ten minutes," Helen told them. A moment later, her voice took on a new timbre. "I have something on the long range radio pulse scopes. I'm getting a bounce-back of a small object about 200 gigs out."

"Identification?"

"Not at this range. Speed approaching 299,792 kmps—very close to light speed."

Justine felt compelled to stand up, despite the restraining belt on her. She had to will her muscles to obey. "Do we know from where, yet?"

George Eastmain called out, "Inside the system. I'm extrapolating origin ... now. It came from the asteroid belt."

Helen nodded. "Confirmed. Inside Sol System."

"Speculation?"

For a change, there was none.

"Keep me posted, Helen. I want to know the instant the computers identify the object."

Time turned to molasses, and the final minutes passed like decades.

"T minus five minutes. Object eighty-nine point nine gigs and closing."

"Identification!" Justine demanded.

"Sorry, Captain."

The crew continued to watch their monitors in silence for the next few minutes.

Justine's apprehension and frustration was getting the better of her. She switched her internal speakers to privacy mode, and made an entry in the captain's log. She directed a short appended entry to Brian, her ex-husband, and ended it with: "…Maybe I could have been more compromising, but … this project is so damned important to me. I hope you understand, and forgive me. If we never meet again, believe me, I cherished the time we had together."

Helen's voice broke through the entry. "T minus two minutes. Object at thirty-five point nine gigs and closing. "Everybody secure?" Justine called out.

One at a time, each responded affirmatively. Justine saw that more than one of them had been logging personal entries as well. That made her feel better.

Helen continued giving periodic reports: "T minus forty-five seconds. Object at thirteen gigs and closing…

"T minus eight seconds. Object two gigs away…

"T minus four seconds. Object at one million kilometers and closing fast.

"Identification confirmed."

Justine barked, "What is it?"

"T minus two seconds to impact…"

"Hold on everyone!" Justine called out.

"One second—"

18

SMD Event Center :
Ottawa :
Canada Corp.:

Early the next morning a commlink call buzzed until Michael woke up. His neck was kinked from sleeping on the leather couch and he tried to stretch it out.

Yawning, he turned on his computer and looked at the DMR monitor. The Coordinator of Administrative Operations' face filled the screen.

"What is it, Calbert?"

"Michael," the coordinator gasped over the link. "Get down here right away! You've got to scan this yourself to believe it! It's the CEO of USA, Inc. on holo—for you!

He blinked twice.

"The Yanks found the TAHU from Macklin's rock, and you'll never guess where!"

∞

Riding the conveyor tube back down to the seventh floor, Michael could not help but tap his fingers against his thigh nervously. The CEO of USA, Inc.! He was quite possibly the most powerful man in the world.

NASA had found Macklin's Rock, but why would the CEO want to speak with Michael when it would be easier to have the Director of NASA contact the Minister of the CSE?

When the conveyor stopped, Michael paused and glanced at his reflection in the full-length mirrors on each side of the tube. He straightened his tie, fixed his jacket, swept fingers through his hair, and felt the stubble on his cheeks and chin. There was no time to shave.

Taking a calming breath, he entered Operations.

Raymond was waiting for him, eyebrows quirked in anticipation and wonder. He quickly told Michael, "I've patched a secure link in Conference Room C. Mr. Alliras, Mr. Granville and Mr. Loche are already inside, waiting."

"Mr. Granville?"

The administrative aide nodded, confirming the presence of the Minister of Canadian Space Exploration.

"Thanks, Raymond. How do I look?"

"Like shit, but I don't get paid to judge any beauty contests."

"Quite right. Anything new out here?"

"Nothing substantial. After we got some of our in-orbit sensor arrays back online, we picked up a slight heat signature from residue in the area, but it had already faded by the time we got an accurate read on it."

"So what happened? Where did NASA find it?"

Raymond just shook his head. "They're keeping us in suspense."

Taking a deep breath to calm himself, he smiled at Raymond, gave a conciliatory nod, and headed to the conference room.

He opened the door to see the Minister of Energy, Mines and Resources deep in conversation with his co-chair of the Space Mining Division, Thomas Granville, who was also the Minister of CSE. Calbert was seated at a command terminal, punching up various displays on the minor DMR casements, checking background information on the situation.

Alliras spotted Michael. He smiled broadly, but Michael could tell it was strained.

"Mr. Rainier," he said in greeting.

"Morning, Michael," Alliras said, motioning him to join them. "I was just giving Thom a situation report. He was out of town until earlier this morning, when he received a communiqué that NASA and the CEO of USA, Inc. wanted a videoconference, top priority. I know it's early in the morning, but from the sounds of it, this is important. I have a source that tells me it has something to do with *Dis Pater*."

Michael cocked an eyebrow. "The artifact they found on Pluto? What does that have to do with Macklin's Rock?"

"I'm not certain, but the director of NASA requested your presence specifically."

Michael glanced at the main DMR casement. Curious.

Sensing his thoughts, Alliras said, "We've already got a line feed, but the conference won't start until our fifth arrives."

Michael started to ask, but Alliras, grinning, answered first. "CEO Dolbeau."

For a moment, Michael was taken aback. The head of the Canada Corp. was not known for attending low level meetings of any kind.

Therefore, he thought to himself, this is now a high-level meeting.

Something important was going down. He could feel the sweat glistening on his forehead. On the other side of the conference table, Calbert looked cool as a cucumber. Typical. Calbert wouldn't let anything as mundane as a meeting between the most powerful men in the world phase him when he had a job to do.

The Minister of CSE was a former military officer, and as such, he turned to Michael, and with a low grumble, handed him a cordless shaver, which he produced from within a briefcase.

Embarrassed, Michael took it. "Thank you." He took a few steps over to the water fountain and applied the shaver to his face.

He finished just in time, as the conference room door opened for CEO Pierre Dolbeau and his personal attaché, Frank Wellman.

"Gentlemen, greetings," the CEO said in his French accent.

"Sorry to bother you so early in the morning, Sir," Thomas Granville said, taking Charge of the proceedings. "I trust you made it here without incident."

"A little ruffled around the edges, I'm afraid. Didn't quite have time to shave," he joked, rubbing the whiskers on his chin, putting them all at ease. Michael's hand went involuntarily to his own freshly shaven face.

Mr. Granville, smiling, made quick introductions all around, and then nodded to Alliras.

Alliras, in turn, gestured at Calbert. "Mr. Loche, you may begin the two-way communications patch connection on the secured line."

Calbert tapped in a few commands into his computer, and the DMR casement lit up with the insignia of the CEO of USA, Inc. above the official emblem of NASA. Michael knew that on the other side, the CEO and the director would be seeing the insignia of each department represented in the room superimposed over a large Canadian Flag.

On the screen, the image of the CEO's living room in Camp David served as a backdrop. Both the CEO and the director were seated on a white cloth couch as aides and assistants bustled about the periphery of their view.

"Good morning, Pierre," the CEO of USA, Inc. offered.

"Et bon jour a toi, Francois!" It was the CEO's way of lightening the tension; he was famous for his Francification of people's names. Michael was sure Pierre Dolbeau was the only one outside of Frank Madison's family who could get away with such bantering behavior.

"How's the family, *Peter?*"

"Ca va tres bien. Et la votre?"

"Good; very good. Please be seated, gentlemen. Make yourselves comfortable." When everyone had found their chairs, the CEO of USA, Inc. got right down to business.

"Let me confirm our intelligence report with you. According to the press release posted by VP Michael Sanderson at 13:12:25 GMT there was an accident involving the asteroid called Macklin's Rock, resulting in the deaths of two surveyors, and also resulting in the apparent loss of their child—no trace of him so far. Against all laws of physics, this asteroid seems to have disappeared, or disintegrated—dematerialized. The actual cause and effect is unknown."

Michael swallowed. "That's right, sir. On all points."

The CEO nodded, and then addressed his Canadian counterpart.

"Let me digress for a moment. We have not made the following information public, and we would appreciate your keeping it under your hat for the time being."

"But of course."

A dark photographic image of an unfamiliar electron model appeared on screen against a backdrop of the stars. Some of the members of the *Orcus 1* mission stood in the foreground to provide perspective on just how large the artifact was.

"Good. As you all might know, the Pluto Mission, *Orcus 1*, has resulted in the discovery of the artifact the lander crew have dubbed *Dis Pater*. On the face of this artifact, we found examples of over thirty thousand forms of writing. Today, our cryptologists have determined that one sample of writing underneath the main text is in an obscure dialect of Mayan."

Michael, Alliras and Calbert shared looks and a few grunts of surprise. "A translation!" For a moment, Michael was completely distracted from his concern over Macklin's Rock and Alex Manez by this revelation.

"In a previous conference, we have discussed this with Mr. Granville and Mr. Dolbeau. The translation is as follows:

"Behold the Mighty Door of Kinich Ahua; Eternity is Now Before You; Beware the Power of Kukulkan."

"What does that mean?" Alliras asked.

William Tuttle, the director of NASA, spoke up: "According to the Mayan Pantheon, Kinich Ahua was the god of the Sun, appearing as a firebird—their version of a phoenix. Kukulkan was the god of the elements. We might have just received a small clue to the deeper meaning in the last few hours."

He shifted position, and lifted a notepad for reference. "At precisely 13:12:25 GMT, the artifact known as *Dis Pater*, originally classified as dormant, began to react."

"React! To what?" Michael was losing his patience, and only calmed himself when Alliras put a calming hand on his forearm.

"First, let me describe what happened. The scientists on Pluto noted that two important changes were taking place. First, the object turned a deep shade of red and began to emit a wave oscillation of 6662 angstroms. Second, the color began to transcend the visible spectrum of light, and the wave emissions began to accelerate at a constant negative sixty nanometers per hour per hour, until, five hours, one minute and thirty four seconds later, at 18:13:59 GMT—about 23:13 Eastern—the object had reached a wave oscillation of 3997.23 angstroms. It settled on a color of deep violet, having gone through the entire spectrum of visible light.

"We began to receive the EPS signal about 23:30 Eastern, and at 04:30 this morning were made aware of a startling discovery from the *Orcus 1*.

"At ground zero," he continued, "the object, *Dis Pater*, stopped glowing and returned to its original transparent. It also ceased to emit any wave pulse. It became, once again, dormant. At that same instant, however, *Orcus 1* detected a foreign object near Pluto, originating from the asteroid belt—"

All six men in the conference room leaned forward, the emotions on their faces a mix of apprehension, surprise, anxiety, and disbelief.

The director concluded, "The foreign object, clocked at a mean speed of 299,792 kph, ceased its incredible velocity, and took up orbit equidistant between Pluto and its moon, Charon. There were no power emissions, or reaction signatures from any engine or other source.

Moreover, there was no electrical or any other kind of activity detected.

"Ion spectrograph indicated the object to be chiefly metallic, with a mass of about one-and-a-half teratons, but indicated small traces of a polymer composite at one location. The *Orcus 1* thereafter used a telescopic magnometer to visually identify the object orbiting eight thousand kilometers above the surface of Pluto.

"The object, gentlemen, was identified as an asteroid of approximately 150 kilometers longest diameter; records identify this asteroid as Macklin's Rock, with a Temporary Asteroidal Habitation Unit erected inside, all property of the Canadian Space Exploration's Space Mining Division. The TAHU had markings on its face matching those of the geological survey conducted by Canada Corp.'s Energy, Mines and Resources Space Mining Division, SMD #568. So far, we have not been able to discover any signs of life inside the TAHU, and there are no power emissions. The TAHU is dormant."

The director of NASA fell silent, letting it all sink in.

CEO Dolbeau broke the silence, his voice thin and uncertain. "Are you trying to tell me that this asteroid traveled over four billion kilometers in five hours?"

"Just shy of the speed of light, yes."

Michael jumped to the same conclusion as the others, that the substance the Manez's had discovered was an element that had the energy and power to propel an object at near light speed. It was the discovery of the millennium. As mind-blowing as that realization was, Michael was more concerned with one other thing. He did not hesitate to ask.

"How soon can you get someone up there to check and see whether Alex Manez is there, and if he's still alive?"

The CEO of USA, Inc. and the director of NASA shared a pointed look.

It was William Tuttle who finally answered.

"Unfortunately, the *Orcus 1* does not have enough power to perform a lift-off and subsequent return to Pluto, and still leave enough power to continue its mission, not to mention making the return trip to Luna Station. The optimal window for their return trip will not occur for another six months. We would lose half a year of scientific discovery if we were to attempt a rescue."

Michael stood. "Are you telling me that you are going to just sit there and allow Alex Manez to die if he's still alive?"

CEO Dolbeau made no comment, but out of the corner of his eye, Michael saw him raise an eyebrow.

The director replied in a level voice, "According to our best projections, there is no sign of life on TAHU."

"You can't tell unless you send someone up. If Alex managed to reach the TAHU's security receptacle, he will have enough oxygen and heat for eighteen hours, even without electricity."

"I'm not disputing the possibility of his survival, only stating that to do as you request will cost a considerable amount of money and an even greater loss of time."

Michael jumped to his feet. "If money is what you want, tell me how much and I'll take it out of my own pocket!"

"Now, now!" Alliras interrupted, pulling Michael's sleeve and gesturing that he should retake his seat.

The director of NASA was about to make comment, but the CEO of USA, Inc. spoke first. "I appreciate your position. Of course, we will abandon the *Orcus 1* mission immediately. We have already transmitted instructions for them to terminate the mission. They will proceed to the TAHU and salvage the entire unit, if possible. Finally, they have orders to return immediately to Luna Station, although the trip back will not be quite as rapid as the TAHU's trip there. Our best projection has them returning in a little over seven months, sometime after the New Year."

"Thank you, Mr. Madison," said CEO Dolbeau. "That is very generous of your government to conduct a rescue mission of this caliber without regard to the astronomical costs of the undertaking."

"It is the least we can do, under the circumstances. We are already drawing up a proposal to initiate a second Orcus mission; we hope to have an exclusive partner in this venture," he offered, leaving the suggestion out in the open. The CEOs smiled at one another, but Michael, his temper cooling, saw that neither man made any indication that the conference was concluded.

He had to wait a few moments before CEO Frank Madison, as if interjecting an afterthought, said, "While I have you all on the line, I would like to informally propose a second joint venture that would be mutually beneficial to us both."

"Of what nature?" CEO Pierre Dolbeau asked casually, though Michael got the sense that he knew exactly the proposal's nature and had been expecting this topic to surface at any moment. If Michael had thought it through, he would have realized that the top man of USA, Inc. would not waste time on a personal interface when a pre-recorded AV press release would have sufficed in this particular instance.

"We are prepared to offer an equal financing contract to you—I would say, ten billion dollars total equity—in a co-development enterprise through a joint corporation, a partnership with equal ownership.

"NASA would loan this new company, a subdivision of NASA and SMD—let's call it Quantum Resources, Inc. for now—a number of research technicians and scientists matching your own contribution. We would stipulate that sub-contracts would be divided equally between NASA and SMD on the *Dis Pater* research, as well as for possible lodes of Element X, shall we call it?, discovered on Macklin's Rock. If this is indeed what was driving the asteroid to achieve light speed, the possibilities for future enterprise are staggering."

He continued: "SMD would retain all mining rights on their individual stake claims, as would USA, Inc. should we stumble on any finds. Exclusive development rights on either side would be given to Quantum Resources. International marketing would be supplied by NASA Space Resources, with a 30% royalty to be disbursed to Quantum Resources."

For brief moment, Michael felt like protesting. What right did USA, Inc. have to come sticking their fingers in SMD's discovery? All SMD had to do was re-analyze the readings of the Nelson II, and collate any other information they received from the recovered TAHU, and they would have a virtual monopoly on the results of light-speed research—if they were able to find another lode of Element X.

Then a few other thoughts occurred to him; thoughts that had probably already occurred to CEO Dolbeau, who would have to be a shrewd businessman to run the third largest corporate government in the world.

The first consideration was that, if a contract was reached, NASA would not release the news of *Dis Pater's* phenomenal reaction, nor the light-speed trip of the Manez's TAHU. This information could be suppressed for the next seven months, and perhaps even well after the return of the *Orcus 1*. That would provide this joint-corporation, Quantum Resources, with an incredible advantage in research time. With NASA Space Resources' large marketing base, any resulting products would reap billions in revenues for Quantum Resources, and the parent companies.

In addition, if SMD closed the information flow and refused the deal, NASA would throw every spare asset into the search for and development of the mysterious Element X. They would start out behind SMD at first, but with their enormous resource base, they would quickly overtake and dominate Canada's world market share.

A joint venture would speed things up for both parties, and the benefits would be mutually reaped.

Politics gave Michael a serious headache.

CEO Dolbeau straightened himself in his chair. "It is apparent to everyone here, I'm sure, that the discovery of *Dis Pater* and its relationship to light speed travel indicates incontrovertibly that we are not alone in the Universe. There are others out there; possibly, many others. I'm sure we would all agree that when—not 'if'—we meet our interstellar counterparts, it would be extremely important to show a unified front, that we present ourselves as a people who freely enter ventures in the spirit of cooperation and beneficial enterprise."

The CEO of USA, Inc. nodded formally. "I see we are of one mind. As we speak, I have lawyers drawing up the initial drafts of Quantum Resources, Inc.'s charter, as well as the joint financing and research contract between SMD and NASA. I'm sure any minor negotiations will be handled diligently and promptly by our respective departments long before the return of *Orcus 1*. In the meantime, I have instructed William to have an open line on the *Orcus 1* mission transmitting non-stop from NASA's Mission Control to the SMD Event Center."

CEO Dolbeau stood. "That is very gracious and kind. I know we will all be watching with baited breath for results of Orcus 1's contact with the TAHU."

CEO Madison, also standing, hastened to add, "If I might propose one more thing."

"Of course."

"In the spirit of cooperation that you expounded upon so eloquently, I would like to propose that the directorship of Quantum Resources, Inc.—or whatever name we eventually agree upon if that one is not satisfactory—should fall to Michael Sanderson. His diligence and concern for the well-being of those under him has been shown so pointedly to us all as of greater concern to him than any fiscal interest; a quality, I'm sure, to which we all aspire. I unofficially forward this motion."

"I can assure you, Mr. CEO, that your proposal is more than adequate as a sign of your good faith. I unofficially second. And, as we are the only two shareholders who count at this early stage, the motion is unofficially passed."

The formal part of the conversation concluded, the two CEO's indicated they wished a closed two-transmission line, through which they offered each other pleasantries and shared a few words on other topics of international concern.

∞

Ushered out behind the two ministers, Michael and Calbert left the conference room to the CEOs and their aides.

"Congratulations," Alliras offered Michael as they neared the door, shaking his subordinate's hand. "You obviously made an impression."

Still dumbstruck by the appointment, Michael shook his head. "I didn't expect…" He took a deep breath.

"None of us are surprised. You deserve this."

"I'm sure I'll have my work cut out for me, but right now, I want to see that tape of the *Dis Pater*. It's the key to understanding Element X, and our interstellar neighbors."

Alliras laughed. "Typical. You're offered the catbird seat, and all you can think of is how to build a better mousetrap."

"I'm sure I'll do a victory dance later, when it all sinks in. Calbert, I want to know exactly when the *Orcus 1* will rendezvous with the TAHU."

Calbert shook his head and chuckled. "All business with you, boss." But he got right down to it as well.

Accessing the data tapes through his thought-link, Calbert informed him, "It won't be until this afternoon. You have a few hours to grab breakfast. The *Dis Pater* files will be in your office waiting for you."

"Thanks, Calbert."

"Boss, we've got six months to analyze the data. Why don't you catch a few more hours sleep; you look like you're dead on your feet."

"I agree," Alliras said, nodding to Calbert. "We all could use a few hours to rest and freshen up."

Thomas suggested, "Why don't we all meet back here at one? While we wait for the rendezvous, and see whether young Mr. Manez has survived his travails, we can discuss a plan of action. There's a hell of a lot of work for us in the next few months, and I want to get a jump start on it, make sure we're all on the same wave length."

Shaking hands, they dispersed.

Michael turned to Calbert. "I'm ordering you to take your own advice. Stand down. You and Ray both. I'll see both of you in seven hours. I'm going to head home and grab a shower."

∞

As Michael exited Operations and took a conveyor tube down to the parking lot where a limo was waiting to take him home, all that had transpired suddenly hit him like a tidal wave.

There were other life forms out there … somewhere. They had left more than a calling card; they had left a possible means of contact, like the recording on the Voyager II probe sent out in the late nineteen-seventies by NASA. Humankind was about to embark on a mission to take them into the Interstellar Age.

And Michael Sanderson was going to be a pioneer of the next stage of the evolution of humankind.

Instead of feeling elated and proud, Michael felt inadequate to the task. Frightened. Small.

He thought of Alex Manez, the first light speed traveler. Had he survived the experience? His parents hadn't; they had become the first victims of Element X.

Was Alex alive?

Michael hoped so.

19

Pluto Orbit :
Orcus 1 :

The tomb was complete; darkness impenetrable, forever. He was a living corpse in a coffin of the unknown; his brain had ceased all higher functions in defense of the impossible data that had bombarded his senses. It was all too much.

Breathing was an effort. It was increasingly more difficult with each passing millennium.

Or was that, each passing minute?

Alex slowly came to realize that he was losing oxygen in the security receptacle. There was no light for him to read the monitors; the devices themselves were not operating.

"Hucs?" he called out. "Hucs?"

Only silence answered him.

Memory was the core of a spider web; Alex was on the outer thread. He followed the silken strands, careful not to fall off into the bottomless depths of insanity.

Something had hit the asteroid. His parents had been outside, on the surface.

"Mom! Dad!" he called out weakly, not expecting them to answer. "Help!"

He tried to move his head, but there was something stopping him; he remembered, the security receptacle encased his head in protective foam, leaving just enough room for him to breathe.

Moving his hand, he drew it up and tried to rip the solidified foam from his head, but it was too hard. He had to activate Hucs; the computer must have gone off-line. Flicking his hand over the control switches brought no results.

Feeling around for the manual override, a panic set in, causing his heart to trip-hammer in his chest. The override, when he found it, produced no effect either. The entire TAHU was dysfunctional.

A scream welled in his throat, his brain rebelling against the claustrophobia that was constricting him. Out in the vastness of empty space, he was trapped, immobile.

Images swarmed through his mind. Voices. He heard voices.

Alex had no idea how much time had passed from when the unknown quantity impacted Macklin's Rock, and when he regained consciousness.

There had been those voices. Calling to him. He had refused the summons, but not because of any conscious decision on his part; he had not been ready.

Ready for what?

He closed his eyes, even though that did not change his view, and thought hard, concentrated. There was the sense of a lightness in his memories. Lightness, or light, or … He didn't know. The universe was laid open for him like an annotated atlas. Time-space had no meaning in that light.

No. That wasn't right. Time had meaning; space had meaning; but past the light—yes!—*past* the light, time-space had no meaning. *Past* the light.

Past.

Future.

There were no such things. He rejected them.

No, something rejected them for him.

Because he was not ready.

Ready for what?

He was beginning to feel dizzy from lack of oxygen. The override did not produce any electricity in the TAHU, although it should under any normal circumstances. Unless whatever hit them had disconnected the solar connectors from the TAHU's battery core.

He had to restore power, or he would die. He recalled the emergency procedures drilled into him before his parents and he undertook the journey to Macklin's Rock. In the event of an accident, the security receptacle was supposed to have enough life support to sustain him for eighteen hours—more than enough time for rescue to arrive from the Mining Orbiter.

He didn't know how long he had been out, but if the oxygen level was any indication, then he didn't have much longer to go. Perhaps eight or ten hours.

There was a sudden thought-flash in his mind. The power of it overwhelmed him.

He remembered:

Sol was laid out in his mind in its entirety, like a map on a table, or the 3D hologram of Sol System in the space museum back home on CS3.

A chorus of voices, like angels, like devils, began to sing. It was a haunting melody, a riveting accompaniment to the images that presented themselves in his mind.

He remembered an image of Jupiter, the massive gas giant with the large red spot, coming toward him at incredible speed. It had been in his field of vision for less than a second, growing larger from a small dot to something that covered his entire view, and then racing past him, out of sight. The intensity of the song diminished—like voices buzzing in the background. The rumble of a crowded hall on Canada Station Three.

The song grew stronger, more insistent.

Empty space for more than a half an hour. As the song crescendoed he saw Saturn, its rings of gas particles forming a perfect halo around its equator. It performed the same second-long appearance as its gaseous brother, Jupiter. The music echoed like the memory of a dream dancing just beyond consciousness.

Another hour or so, and he had the sense that he was crossing the orbit of Uranus, though the smaller gas giant was nowhere to be seen. The song played on.

Ninety minutes later, he was certain he was in the path of the smallest of the gas giants, Neptune, and his course abruptly veered twenty degrees above the ecliptic. A little over an hour later, and more than five hours after Macklin's Rock initially reacted, Pluto and its cousin, Charon, burst into view like a giant net, catching him between their orbits. The song took a change in timbre and tone. It was the denouement of the symphony.

Now, the images and song had disappeared, but he had the lingering impression of two small planets on either side of him.

The entire thought-flash was more like a dream than reality, but now, every time he closed his eyes, he was certain that he could see beyond the bounds of the security receptacle, beyond the TAHU, and beyond the asteroid.

For some unexplainable reason, he was over five billion kilometers away from the Sun.

Panic set in, and he concentrated on keeping his eyes open. The *blink* came on suddenly, and he could sense something approaching Macklin's Rock.

It was a space ship. A different song told him so.

He must be delusional. His mind was playing tricks on him. Pluto was nowhere near where he was—which was the asteroid belt, of course. Wasn't it? And the ship coming toward him was obviously the rescue pod—for what other ship would be out so far from Earth? The only mission Alex had heard of was the *Orcus 1*.

He remembered reading a podcast. There was a mission currently on Pluto.

Mentally shaking his head, since he could not do so physically, he decided he was just imagining things. Most likely, Macklin's Rock had suffered a collision with another asteroid and the resulting impact and subsequent lack of oxygen was making Alex delusional.

A loud, echoing noise filtered through the TAHU, and after a moment, Alex identified it as a fission laser cutting through the top face of the TAHU. It must be the rescue mission from the Orbiter.

Someone was going to save him.

Salivating, trying to moisten his dry throat, Alex called out, "I'm in here!" as soon as he heard the laser cease to cut, and the grinding sounds of polymer ripping as the rescuers opened the TAHU.

It was then that Alex realized that once all the air escaped the TAHU, sounds could not travel in the emptiness of space. The security receptacle itself served as a soundproof encasement. Without a digital septaphonic booster, the rescuers would not know where he was until they stumbled upon him.

Alex closed his eyes...

...and could *see* in his mind's eye the suit-shielded figures of two people drifting down through the opening of the TAHU to the floor of the main room, the soft beams of their palm-lights traveling over the confines of the room, searching for survivors. The song was back in his head, dim, as if he had turned down the volume. His internal vision extended just a few dozen meters outside his security receptacle, rather than millions of kilometers.

Panicked because of the images he should not be able to see, he forced his eyes open. A *blink* brought him a flashing image, quickly fading, of things he should not see. It was like a radar blip. He grunted in surprise at the image. Four more *blinks* produced the same effect.

With repetition, he became more used to the unusual perception, even though his heart raced with the implications. He did not think he could ever get used to the song, however. It was like the babble of a hundred people speaking foreign languages, and there was an imperative message hidden behind the unearthly lyrics.

The next time he *blinked,* he consciously tried to expand the range of his mental perception. He found that he saw not only the figures quickly approaching his personal cubicle, but also the ship which had landed on the surface of Macklin's Rock. In his periphery, he could see the images of Pluto and Charon far off on either side of the asteroid. The song peaked again, urging him, warning him, cajoling him.

Another *blink* and he pushed his range to the limit; he could not see, but he could *sense* all the other planets in Sol System, the Sun, the Earth, and even the larger bodies in the asteroid belt. The song overwhelmed him, made him so dizzy he wanted to vomit, but he somehow controlled himself.

"What's happening to me?" he said. "I must be completely crazy."

At the next *blink,* he tried to see past Sol System, thinking he might as well enjoy the sensational perception while he could. Once he was rescued, and he got some oxygen, he was certain his normal senses would return to him, and he would discover that he had been in the asteroid belt all along.

To his mild surprise, he could not see past the outer orbit of Pluto. There was something blocking his view; some kind of electromagnetic field that imposed a limit on his perception. If he could strain his ears and pick out a few words of that song, the explanation would come to him.

He shook his head. Then, his mind adapting quickly to the new— though obviously delusional—perception, he tried to shrink his field of vision as far as he could. Quickly, he discovered that he could consciously turn it off. A *blink* produced the same blankness of view as with his eyes open inside the protective foam.

No song.

A movement in the security receptacle turned his mind from his experiments. The rescuers opened the receptacle, and, with their much stronger hands, ripped the foam from him.

His first sight as the foam fell away from his eyes was the play of a light, sharp and intense. After so long in the dark, he saw spots dancing in front of him until his vision acclimatized.

Someone pressed a suitshield helmet over his head, and the warm rush of oxygen sent him into a faint. He breathed deeply a few times and felt the dizziness fade.

Sounds filtered into him from the septaphonics.

"Alex? Alex? Are you all right? Can you hear me?" It was a woman's voice.

Alex nodded. "Yes," he replied, though his words came out in a squeak.

His throat was parched. Sticking his tongue out, he touched a plastic nipple inside the helmet, which extended into his mouth. He sucked an ounce of water from it, and opened his mouth to let the nipple retract.

"I'm all right," he said. "Are you the rescue team from the Mining Orbiter?" But he knew they weren't.

The two figures turned to look at one another. Finally, the woman addressed him again.

"I'm sorry, Alex, but no. My name is Captain Justine Turner, from the *Orcus 1*. We were on a mission to Pluto when we discovered your TAHU entering the orbit of the planet."

Alex closed his eyes again.

Blinked out.

Pluto and Charon were still there, ten thousand kilometers away on either side. The familiar theme of the dark planet pounded in his ears, a musical score a million times more intense than Gustav Holst's masterpiece, The Planets. Holst had never written a score for Pluto, since no one had known of the dark planet's existence until years after the original composition. But no one, however ingenious, could ever have produced a symphonic spectacular such as the one in Alex's head when he *blinked out*.

It was real.

And it came to him then, the reality of his situation.

"My parents are dead," he said out loud, but to himself.

The captain of the *Orcus 1*, not hearing him, reached down and helped him to his feet. "Can you come with us? The ship is just outside."

Alex nodded, and, prompted by the second crewmember, donned a suitshield to protect him from the solar radiation that extended out even that far from the Sun.

As they made their way out of the TAHU, the other figure introduced herself. "My name is Helen, Alex. I'm a Canadian, like you."

Alex did not reply, still stunned by his parents' deaths.

A tear slowly trailed down his cheek, hanging a moment on his chin, and then fell from him to land on the base of the helmet. A moisture sensor on the inside surface triggered a tiny vacuum, which sucked up the tear, reclaiming the drop into the water reservoir surrounding the helmet.

Alex suppressed the extrasensory images that came whenever he closed his eyes, and wished he could do the same for the ache in his heart.

20

SMD Event Center :
Ottawa :
Canada Corp.:

After a quick breakfast of sliced fruits and orange juice that he prepared for himself, since the cook had the day off, Michael Sanderson left his house, stepped into the waiting auto passenger transport, and gave the navigation computer the address of the SMD Event Center.

During the twenty-three minute trip, he scanned the Globe & Mail newsvid home page on the EarthMesh, reading the headlines and downloading those stories that caught his interest. The press release he had posted on the Associated Press net did not appear anywhere. The news services splashed the latest celebrity gossip instead. People were not interested in science; they would rather read about who was sleeping with who, or listen to the columnists jaw about what actor was getting a divorce, or plastic surgery.

Michael truly cared about the truth, and he cared about the quality of life in every quarter of society. The best way to bring the standard of living up uniformly was through economics. The natural resources of the earth were taxed to the limit, and expensive to mine.

They had to find alternatives within the asteroid belt. With increased volume of precious materials, there came jobs, wealth, and opportunity for anyone who had the wherewithal to grab it. Handing an average person a couple of dollars did nothing. Like the biblical proverb went, 'Give a man a fish, and he will have food for a day; *teach* a man to fish, and he will have food for the rest of his life.'

Flipping the auto transport's DMR casement back to the Globe & Mail Page, he scanned it for any other articles relating to the mishap.

The deaths of Gabriel and Margaret Manez were reported; but there was no indication that the early morning summit meeting between the CEOs of USA, Inc. and Canada Corp. had been leaked. For that, Michael was thankful. They would have to handle the discovery of Element X and the recovery of Alex Manez with utmost secrecy; outside interference from fringe groups would hamper the CSE and NASA getting to the bottom of the mystery.

Although the translation of the glyphs on *Dis Pater* did not mean anything to Michael at the moment, he was glad there was no mention of the breakthrough. The public had enough wild information on its hands; any more, and there could be panic in the streets. The fewer people who knew humans were not alone in the universe, the better—at least for the short-term until the government corporations could soften the blow.

He turned off the DMR monitor when the auto arrived at the SMD Event Center, and a chime inside the cab sounded. Michael exited the vehicle and entered the Center as his auto transport continued on to the parking garage.

Glancing at a clock inside the conveyor tube, Michael noted that it was nine minutes past one.

He entered the Operations room on the seventh floor to pandemonium.

"What's going on?" he asked, eyes flicking to the monitors. Alliras saw him, and quickly strode over, Calbert following closely behind.

"He's alive, Michael," the Minister of EMR said, his jubilation apparent. "It's Alex. He's alive. They've found him."

"What?" Michael asked incredulously. He had hoped for the young boy's survival, but did not really believe anyone could have endured that kind of trip.

"Yes, and he is perfectly fine. They're just transporting him over to the *Orcus 1* now before they go back to the TAHU to investigate."

Scanning the monitors, Michael quickly found the one slaved to the NASA transmission from Pluto. The astronauts had landed on Macklin's Rock, peeled away the surface of the TAHU like an onion, and at that moment, were emerging from the aperture escorting a small figure Michael immediately identified as Alex Manez.

Michael could barely suppress his joy; his relief was palpable.

Alliras handed him a data fleck. "It's the joint venture contract and a preliminary charter for Quantum Resources, Inc. That's the official name. You had better look the contract over before we sign it. Once your concerns are addressed, I'll pass it up the chain."

"Great." Michael turned to Calbert. "Send up a note to Alex telling him we're happy he's been rescued, and that we're doing everything we can to get him safely home. I'll append a note letting him know that we recovered his parents' bodies, and will broadcast their funeral on closed circuit to the *Orcus 1*.

"Request Captain Turner performs a complete physical and mental analysis of Alex. I want that, and everything concerning *Dis Pater*, *Orcus 1*, and Macklin's Rock piped into my office computer. I'm going to review this contract, and everything we've got from Macklin's Rock and *Orcus 1* so far, and try to figure out a plan of attack. Forward any suggestions to me, will you?"

Calbert nodded. "I've already outlined a number of items."

"Fantastic. And, Calbert, I'd like you to consider whether you want a job in Quantum Resources with me, or if you'd rather have my recommendation for VP of SMD."

"What?" Calbert was flabbergasted at the offer.

Alliras nodded. "If you decide to stay here, you'll have my recommendation as well."

"You have your choice," Michael added. "But I could really use someone like you at the helm in this new venture."

"I'll—I'll have to think on it."

"Of course. Let me know by the end of the day."

He turned to Alliras "Would you like a snifter of brandy?"

"You couldn't drag me from it."

Together, they left Operations, trusting in the competency of those inside to perform their jobs to the best of their ability without supervision.

They took the conveyor tube up to Michael's office, and once inside, sat on the long couch.

Michael produced two tumblers of vintage brandy, and they tapped their glasses together in a silent toast to events gone well.

21

Luna Station :
Luna :
Chinese Sector :

Over two-hundred thousand kilometers from Earth, a teenager named Klaus Vogelsberg watched a pirated link broadcast of the NASA transmission to SMD Ottawa from his computer DMR on Luna Station and knew fear.

Hands shaking, he pressed the auto-dialer on his video communicator to his superior, Chow Yin. A somber round face appeared in the communications casement, dark eyebrows heavy with concern and anger.

Chow Yin had the resources to do just about anything he wished inside Luna Station with impunity. One of those actions, Klaus feared, was to make him disappear. Klaus had no wish to become an anonymous statistic.

He had screwed up, and knew it.

"Have you seen the transmission, Boss?" Klaus asked, his voice cracking. He did not need a reply to know that the other man had watched the same broadcast on a slaved channel.

Clearing his throat, Klaus apologized, "I am terribly sorry, Boss."

It was Klaus's task to monitor all scientific-related broadcasts from Earth, hunting for any hints of discoveries of new products, elements, or any kind of invention that might prove of future value. Klaus would then pass along the information to another, who would quickly fill out worldwide patent forms and have it automatically registered with the World Patent Office under front companies set up by Chow Yin.

Once the real inventors, be they individuals or organizations, got around to processing their paperwork and applying for a patent, they would discover the previous claim. At that point, Chow Yin and his society would sell their bogus patent back to the original research company for an outrageous amount.

It was a lucrative swindle, one of dozens Chow Yin had running.

Currently, Klaus's task was to monitor all transmission to and from Pluto and the *Orcus 1* mission. It was a top priority.

The night before, Klaus had intercepted the distress EPS from Macklin's Rock, but had thought nothing of it and had not passed the information along to his boss. How could he have guessed that an asteroid would spontaneously develop the ability to travel to Pluto in less than five hours? It was an oversight that could possibly cost Chow Yin billions in extortion moneys now that the implications had become clear.

With the discovery of *Dis Pater*, coupled with the seeming light-travel journey taken by Macklin's Rock, Klaus easily put two and two together. Interstellar travel was within Earth's grasp, and he, Klaus, may have let the technology slip right through his organization's fingers.

Before long, USA, Inc. and Canada Corp. would have all possible patents locked up. The fact that Chow Yin would be furious was an understatement, but the eerie calm with which he spoke to Klaus made the young man's stomach clench as if he had an intestinal cramp.

"Of course you are sorry," Chow Yin said, his words coming slowly, methodically. "If you had handled your responsibilities correctly, we would be in a position to capitalize on this now. I am not merely speaking of a payoff. If there is a secret element that is capable of light speed travel, and if we control it, then we could control the entirety of outer space. Instead, there is every possibility that Luna Station will become nothing more than a milestone in the conquest of Sol System with no mention of me or my contribution. Luna Station's global and interplanetary position will be completely undermined, all because of your blatant incompetence."

"Yes, Boss." Klaus averted his eyes.

Chow Yin took a long, deep breath, and regarded his young protégé with the predatory eyes of a shark. "There is a slim chance that we may yet come out of this intact. It is a long journey home from Pluto; am I wrong?"

"Yes, Boss. I mean, no, you are not wrong. It is a long journey, perhaps as long as six months or more … and fraught with dangers."

Chow Yin tightened his lips in what passed for a smile. "I see that we are once again aligned in our thinking. After all, possession is nine-tenths of the law, is it not? Contact some of those 'friends' that you keep bragging about; offer them anything they want to get the job done. I want all the secrets from the *Orcus 1* mission in my hands by New Year's. If luck is on our side, we will come out of this unscathed, and very rich. It would be a sweet victory to dominate the world—in the forefront, this time, instead of hiding behind Luna's dark side."

With that, Chow Yin severed the communication, leaving Klaus's DMR casement blank. A full minute passed without Klaus moving.

At first, the only hint of the coordinator's reacting to the remonstration from his superior was a slight quivering in his cheeks. Then all his emotions spilled out. He punched his open hand and cursed, "Damn it all!"

He closed his eyes and took in a deep breath. Anger would not solve his dilemma.

Opening the bottom drawer of his desk, he removed a small quart bottle of German whiskey he had stolen from his father, and poured a thumb's depth in a plastic tumbler he also kept in the drawer. After throwing it back, his face grimacing from the burn as the hot liquid tore down his throat, Klaus poured himself another, and sat for a long while holding the tumbler in his hand. If Chow Yin caught him with alcohol, he would turn Klaus out.

He stared out the window of his room onto the org-garden and contemplated. Was he doing the right thing? How could NASA be so foolish as to think they could harness the underlying power of the universe in their puny hands? The implications were clear to him. He was a student of technology, and knew that the scientific community regarded faster than light travel as a theoretical impossibility. They had their same old arguments, and would use them at every opportunity to discredit the notion that the stars were within human reach.

Now, Klaus knew, they could stick their theories in their event horizons. That thought made him feel better. Once lauded as great men, those so-called experts would now be scrambling to come up with alternate theories to prove light speed travel was real, and pretend they had never been on the other side of the argument. Hypocrites.

Still, there was a knot in his stomach when he contemplated his task. He had to ensure he could hire someone to hijack the NASA spacecraft. Even as Klaus did this, Chow Yin would see to it that he would never be able to slip out from under his Chinese master's authority. Klaus would be as imprisoned on Luna Station as Chow Yin.

But, if he did not do as Chow Yin directed, Klaus would soon be numbered among the dead.

It would have been better if his father had never been posted to Luna Station, though his job with the European Space Agency dictated it; better still if his father had never touched a drop of alcohol. Klaus shuddered, remembering the drunken beatings he took.

He'd had no choice: either run away from home or suffer the abuse. Klaus had run away, and straight into the waiting snare of Chow Yin's network of teenage thugs.

The anger in him surged. His father, and all those like him, would pay dearly. Chow Yin would make them suffer; and Klaus would make that suffering possible.

With renewed determination, he opened a link to his EarthMesh account and began to make enquiries.

22

NASA *Orcus 1*:
Sol System :
Flight Path Pluto-Luna :

Excerpts from the Official Flight Journal of Captain Justine Churchill Turner—transcribed from voice:

Captain's Journal — August 21, 2090

Confirming the reality of the sudden appearance of Macklin's Rock, we shuttled the *Orcus 1* to the asteroid, abandoning our previous two missions, the first of which was to explore Pluto; the second, to study the alien object we called *Dis Pater*.

Upon arrival at the displaced asteroid, we discovered the sole survivor and rescued him.

Young Alex had enough time to secure himself in the receptacle-floater and, to all outward appearances, arrived quite unharmed. I wanted to perform an exhaustive physical examination on Alex to determine his state of health the moment we brought him on board. There are people on Earth who are anxious to receive that report. Alex understandably pleaded exhaustion and First Mate Helen Buchanan concurred.

"If he feels all right," she said, "then there's nothing that can't wait. Once we brought it back online, the biometrics on his security receptacle indicated all readings within normal range. I'll set up a cot in the medical bay and hook him up to the electroencephalograph AI while he sleeps. It will report any abnormalities to my belt monitor. I know, if I'd been through what he's been through, all I'd want is a quick nutrishake and a dozen hours sleep."

I bowed to the first mate's recommendation on the medical matter. Helen set up a bed for Alex, procured a protein and carbohydrate-intensive drink, and watched him fall fast asleep.

Dale, Henrietta, Sakami, George and I saw to the dismantling of the TAHU. Helen returned to her post and continued to monitor the command consoles. Johan Belcher and Ekwan Nipiwin used the ship's ATV to travel to SMD Site 14 in an attempt to obtain a specimen of Element X, which, according to the NASA-SMD report we received eight hours after liftoff from Pluto. That might have been the catalyst for the asteroid's incredibly swift journey through Sol System. If they do not find evidence of the element, they are to perform a complete spectroanalytic survey of the entire area, and collect a cross-section of specimens for return to NASA.

Addendum:

They did not find a trace of Element X (I wish they would come up with a less mysterious name for it). The spectroanalysis proved completely useless. The specimens they collected revealed no evidence that anything untoward occurred.

Once the TAHU is loaded, we will have to lift off immediately, or miss our window. A lost day at this end could mean an extra two-hundred days of travel before reaching earth.

Nobody would be happy about that.

Captain's Journal — August 22, 2090

An odd thing occurred this morning; something that I'm sure I will ponder at great length during the trip home when we finally lift off.

Our ward, Alex Manez, slept the rest of yesterday afternoon, all evening and night, and woke early this morning. Helen had rigged the electroencephalograph AI to notify her upon Alex's awakening and she quickly dressed and found me in the dining area eating breakfast.

"He should be awake," Helen told me.

"Great." I stood and dumped the remainder of my coffee in the vacuum refuge receptor. "Let's go see how he is. Mission Control on Earth is practically yelling for a report on Alex."

"I'll grab some food and meet you there," Helen said.

I wanted Helen along for two reasons: first, she's Canadian, and I thought that might set Alex at ease having a fellow compatriot there—even though they are of two different ethnic origins; second, as part of Helen's job description, she is skilled in first aid and rudimentary medical techniques. The first mate is a registered nurse, and she is qualified on the bio-analysis equipment. She can make diagnoses and recommendations usually reserved for those with M.D.'s.

Stepping inside the medical bay a few minutes prior to Helen's arrival, I cleared my throat when Alex did not immediately turn around.

He was awake, dressed, and playing with a stethoscope. I said, "Good morning, Alex. Do you remember me? I'm—"

"Yes, of course. Captain Turner." Putting the instrument down, the ten-year old turned and regarded me for the first time that morning. His face was solemn, unreadable. I felt a momentary shudder of apprehension, as if the intelligence behind those eyes were ages old.

"Good morning." He was the epitome of detached politeness.

"That was quite the sleep, Mr. Rip Van Winkle," I commented, trying to sound jovial and friendly. "You've been in here a while."

"Fifteen hours, thirty-two minutes, and seventeen seconds," he replied with easy confidence, his tone one that brooked no disagreement.

"Why, that's about right. How did you know—?" I began, and then realized the answer. "The EEG." I pointed a thumb at it.

The machine would have a running record of statistics on Alex. Heartbeat, respiration, blood pressure, every stage of his sleep and wake periods.

"Where did you learn to read an EEG?" I asked, as I found a chair and sat down, waiting for Helen to arrive with breakfast.

Alex shrugged, but did not reply.

"I guess it's not that hard to figure out." I said. "You must be good with computers and stuff."

Another shrug.

"Well, if you are technically minded, are you going to follow in your parents' footsteps when you're older and join the Canadian Space Exploration department?"

"My parents are dead," was his answer, plain and simple.

Speechless, I stood there in stunned silence as Alex calmly sat down on the cot, folded his hands in his lap, and watched me with the eyes of ancient experience.

I wished fervently for Helen to arrive and alleviate my discomfort;

perhaps Alex would warm to a fellow Canadian. It was ridiculous, but this young boy intimidated me.

Inhaling deeply, I closed my eyes and composed myself, recalled my senior leadership training. I willed myself to keep my wits about me and not be cowed by a child.

"Well, Alex. How did you come to that conclusion?" With tacit agreement from Helen, I had refrained from informing Alex of the demise of his parents.

"It's not a conclusion; it's a fact. They are dead."

I struggled to come up with a response. "How do you feel about that?"

"How do you think I feel?" he returned.

"I'm not certain. You strike me as a very special person. You are correct: your parents did not survive, Alex. I'm sorry to confirm this for you. They were outside of the TAHU, on the asteroid's surface when—"

"When the asteroid, at near the speed of light, traveled here to Pluto."

"How do you know all these things?" I asked.

"I was there. It's a little hard to miss."

I had to take a deep breath and collect my thoughts. "Do you feel sad about your parents, Alex?"

"Of course."

"You seem to be taking this all very well; either that or you're hiding your emotions from me. You don't have to, Alex. I'm your friend."

Alex did not reply to that.

"It's all right to let out your emotions, Alex. If you want to cry, you should."

"Thank you for the offer, Captain Turner, but I'm fine."

He was being irritatingly polite. If I didn't feel so sympathetic for his predicament, I would have felt the urge to slap him across the face, just to get him to show some emotion … even anger.

Whatever else I might have said to him remained unspoken as the hydraulic door unlatched and opened to reveal Helen backing in, holding a large tray of food in her hands. It smelled wonderful.

Helen smiled at Alex. "Breakfast. I hope you like eggs, toast and orange juice."

"Yes. Thank you very much," he replied, looking at the food eagerly. It was the first sign of any emotion in the boy this morning.

Therefore, he was human, I thought wryly. Not an alien changeling or simulacrum.

"Coffee for you, Captain?" Helen offered me a cup. "Aspartame and non-dairy creamer."

"Thank you, Helen."

"You're welcome." She turned to Alex. "How are you feeling this morning? You had quite a rest."

"Fine," he mumbled around the crust of the toast he had consumed in one bite.

Helen said, "I'd like to run some bio-diagnostic tests on you, a little more involved than the electroencephalograph I hooked up to you last night, if that's all right?"

Alex shrugged, intent on his repast.

The first mate's expression turned to one of confusion, and she let out a small harrumph as she inspected the EEG machine.

"What is it?" I asked.

Before answering, Helen initiated the EEG interface and began typing in a sequence of function keys, bringing up differing schematics and charts on the digital screen.

"Nothing," Helen answered finally, her voice tinged with concern. "There's absolutely nothing on the EEG!"

"What do you mean? It was on a few minutes ago! I saw lights!"

"Oh, the machine is on, but it might as well be hooked up to the wall. It recorded nothing all night long." She looked at the cords attaching it to Alex like a collection of umbilicals. "Perhaps I hooked it up wrong."

"Then how did it alert you that Alex had arisen?"

"Well, either there's something wrong with the connections, or— Alex, did you play with this EEG?"

He turned from his eggs and shook his head.

"Never touched it."

"It's not working. If there were data, it's gone now."

Shrugging, as if this came as no surprise, he said, "I could have told you that."

Both Helen and I stopped looking at the EEG interface monitor and stared hard at Alex.

"What do you mean by that?"

"The EEG isn't recording anything. Isn't that obvious?"

I put my hands on my hips. "Then how did you know how long

you were sleeping, down to the last second?"

"I wasn't sleeping," he replied. "I had been in the room for fifteen hours, thirty-two minutes, and seventeen seconds when you arrived."

"What?"

That he knew that information indicated either he was obsessive about time, and kept meticulous track on a clock; or that the marking of time came to him easily, like second nature. I'd heard of people who could tell you the time of day down to the nearest minute, without looking at a clock, or even looking at the position of the Sun. It was like a person who has an internal time clock, and wakes every day at the same time. Perhaps Alex was such a person.

Helen ignored the question of time, and grabbed her stethoscope, dragging a mobile bio-analysis unit from one corner. "What do you mean, you weren't sleeping? Insomnia?"

Alex shrugged. "I guess."

"Didn't you get any sleep at all?"

"No."

Helen brought the bio-analysis unit over and switched it on. The indicator light and the screen showed that the instrument was operational, but when Helen passed the vital receptors over Alex, nothing showed up on the monitor.

"That's odd."

Quickly, she reset the unit, and passed the receptor over me. My heart rate, respiration, body temperature, diastolic and systolic blood pressure measurements appeared alongside a brain wave chart and a micro-display of my major organs and their stats. It was similar to an EEG, but had many advanced functions, and could diagnose virtually every ailment known. All of my readings were at a hundred percent of normal, and my microorganism levels showed satisfactory. I was the picture of health.

Helen reset the unit and tried Alex again, and still got no reading.

"What the hell?" the first mate cursed. She turned and regarded Alex. Bringing the stethoscope to her ears, she indicated to the boy that she wanted to listen to his heart rate.

"Normal," she reported. "For some reason, the machine isn't working; neither is the EEG."

I hovered over them. "Was the EEG working last night when you hooked it up?"

"Yes. That's the funniest part of this whole thing. There isn't even a record of the first few minutes after I hooked it up to Alex. I'm sure I checked it before I left."

Turning to Alex, I spoke in her most authoritative voice. "Now, Alex, are you lying? Did you play with these machines? They are expensive pieces of equipment, not toys."

Alex, having finished his breakfast, eased back on the cot and regarded me with an impassive look that sent a shiver down my spine. "I told you, I never touched them."

"I don't know what kind of game you're playing, but—"

Before I could finish my statement, Alex glanced over at the bio-analysis machine. There was a beep, and the unit suddenly flared to life.

Helen dashed over to the monitor. "His readings are normal. DNA patterns match; there's no sign of foul play. What's the meaning of this?" she asked, her usual patience starting to run thin.

Alex, giving a knowing cock of his head and a twinge of a smile, glanced at the bio-analysis machine again. The readings began to fluctuate past the normal spectrum. His body temperature went up ten degrees; his heart rate increased a hundred beats per minute; his respiration rate dropped to one breath per hour; his blood pressure was all over the place; and the unit began to diagnose Alex with every disease known to humankind.

"What the hell?" I cried.

Again, Alex glanced at the machine, and all the readings disappeared. The unit flatlined.

"What are you doing?" Helen asked, her eyes wide and her face registering pure disbelief.

Again, Alex shrugged. "Nothing much." And he would respond to no more questions on the subject.

Captain's Journal — August 23, 2090

The TAHU and all CSE equipment have been loaded aboard the *Orcus 1*, and we are preparing to lift off the asteroid and begin our journey home. I have scheduled the flight to begin first thing tomorrow morning, at 05:59 EST. It should take us about one-hundred-and-forty days to arrive at Luna Station; the Sun's enormous gravitational pull will boost our velocity by more than thirty kps over our average velocity coming to Pluto.

Our young ward, Alex, displays highly antisocial behavior, though Helen assures me that his reaction to his predicament and the loss of his parents is not uncommon. She refuses to speculate on the events of yesterday morning.

I, for one, will be watching Alex closely.

Once we are in flight, descending toward earth at three-hundred-and-twenty-four kps, I will transmit the first EPS report to Earth; I am not certain whether to include my thoughts on Alex yet, or wait until I have more information.

Captain's Journal — August 30, 2090

It has been nine days since Alex's rescue, and eight since the boy revealed some kind of electropathic kinetic ability with the EEG and the bio-analysis units; since then, he has not shown that the ability remains, or that the events of 22 August had ever occurred. Medical examinations provoke no unusual results, and, as far as the technical readouts are concerned, Alex is perfectly healthy.

Upon questioning, he denies any knowledge that the anomalies with the EEG and bio-analysis unit took place; although his odd behavior from that day persists. He refuses to participate in any discussion or recreation with the science team or command crew, and only comes out of his makeshift compartment in the medical bay for meal times.

Both Helen and I agreed not to include our observations in our report, and to maintain a clandestine vigilance over young Alex, watching should he repeat his feats. Even when alone, he does not experiment with his abilities; all medical bay monitors show steady, normal outputs. There have been no glitches in any other electronic equipment on the ship.

Captain's Journal — September 14, 2090

Although the past two weeks have been spent analyzing the TAHU and its contents, we have found no evidence that proves one way or another what exactly transpired in the asteroid belt.

What caused Macklin's Rock to achieve light travel? Why did it cease its flight when it entered the orbital field of Pluto and Charon. Obviously, the termination of the rock's journey has something to do with the *Dis Pater* artifact.

But what? It remains a mystery.

We received another EPS from NASA informing us that they have created a joint-venture partnership between USA, Inc. and Canada, Corp. to study Element X, *Dis Pater*, and the possibility of repeating light-speed travel.

Quantum Resources, Inc. has confirmed the directorship to the former vice-president of the Space Mining Division of Canada Corp's CSE, the reputed Michael Sanderson, whom I have never met.

With him at the helm, the joint company has aggressively collected, collated, and documented all aspects of the events concerning their charter. All reports we send to NASA (the EPS informed us) will be copied and forwarded to Quantum Resources' headquarters in Toronto, Canada.

We have instructions, upon arrival at Luna Station, to hand over the TAHU, all materials found within the unit, and a full report on all our finds to Quantum Resources, Inc. officials who will meet us at the station. There will also be a representative there who will take charge of young Alex and escort him back to Canada Corp.

So far, Alex has shown no inclination to repeat his remarkable feats of electropathic kinetics, nor has he acknowledged that he ever has, or still retains, that ability. I have decided not to include any observation in our reports to NASA and Quantum Resources, Inc. yet.

Once we have returned to NASA Mission Control, I will hand over this journal to Director William Tuttle, and rely on his discretion and decision whether to make issue of Alex, or report my observations to Quantum Resources, Inc. There is no malice in my decision; I merely do not wish upon Alex any more scientific and psychological scrutiny than necessary. Besides, I am not sure if my observations fall under Quantum Resources' charter.

Captain's Journal — October 29, 2090

In the medical bay, as at every science station on board the *Orcus 1*, there are cameras installed to document all experiments for future study. By no means were these cameras designed for security purposes, so it was with some trepidation that I programmed the computer to turn the cameras in the medical bay on, and leave them to record the room overnight.

This move was prompted by a revelation brought to me by First

Mate Helen Buchanan earlier yesterday. Catching me alone for a few moments, she indicated her concerns.

"I don't think Alex has slept a wink since coming on board the ship," she said.

"What?"

"Do you remember him saying that he didn't sleep that first night?"

"Yes."

"I thought it was just nerves, a mild case of insomnia. What with all he'd been through, it's not that remarkable. After a few days when he didn't complain about it, and since he looked rested enough, it never crossed my mind again."

"And what leads you to believe he's been awake for, what, two months?"

Helen mumbled. "It's not like me, but I left the bioanalysis unit on last night in the medical bay. When I went in this morning, it had stored a twelve-hour record of the only living being inside the room, Alex, in its memory banks. When Alex stepped out for breakfast, I accessed the data, and it proves conclusively that, although he remained inactive for a few hours, he never achieved Alpha sleep, let alone REM sleep. After the few hours, there was an absence of readings, indicating, perhaps, that he had left the room. Shortly before five o'clock this morning, he returned to the room and waited until I arrived.

"I was curious what he'd been up to all night, and so I did a quick investigation."

My mind racing in twelve different directions, wondering what all this meant, I prompted her to continue: "What did you find out?"

Helen bowed her head a moment before continuing. "He accessed our main computer data banks. Although he managed to hide the identity of any data files he used or stored, he may not have known that every time a file or document is opened, the file usage meter is tripped in the log casement. During the past two months, Alex has been accessing the main computer every night. I know it's been him, since I discreetly questioned the science team, and no one has any knowledge of using the machines after hours except on a few rare occasions."

"Thank you, Helen. Don't approach Alex. He'll probably deny it. Let me handle this."

Her relief was palpable. "Just thought you should know. I'll be off to perform my routine sensor cache interactions."

Captain's Journal — October 30, 2090

Helen was correct. Alex does not sleep.

When I replayed the camera recording late this morning, I was shocked to see that at around 20:00 hrs, when everyone had finished their evening meal and sought refuge either in their own quarters or in the recreation cubicle, Alex, as was his custom, repaired to the medical bay.

To my great shock, he lay down on the cot and stared directly at the camera, situated in the corner of the small bay.

For fifteen minutes, I watched as he stared right at me. I had to remember this was just a recording.

I fast-forwarded, but the image on screen did not vary.

Hours went by, right up until 06:00 this morning, Alex did not move from his spot on the cot, nor did his gaze waver from the camera.

At precisely 06:00, when the ship's chime indicated it was time to rise and that breakfast was being prepared by the AI in the dining facility, Alex stood up from his cot, took a step or two toward the camera, and spoke.

"Have a good morning, Captain," he said to the camera, and left the room.

I recall that, over breakfast, Alex had been smiling at me furtively, although at the time I had paid no heed. He knew ahead of time that I was going to access the camera recordings.

There is something not right with young Alex Manez.

I don't think he was this way before the Macklin's Rock incident. He has changed in some fundamental way that I cannot put my finger on. Although he has not shown malice toward the crew, the ship, or me, I am starting to cultivate a fear of the young boy.

Captain's Journal — December 25, 2090

It is Christmas Day, and Helen and I took turns at the helm so we could enjoy the onboard festivities. The entire journey has been long, and we can all imagine ourselves in the comfort of our own homes, for the first time in more than a year. Especially now that we've begun our aggressive braking maneuvers, since we have passed inside the orbit of Jupiter and are fast approaching the asteroid belt.

It is unnerving to think that the outward trip took Alex and his asteroid approximately five hours; it has taken us four months to cover two-thirds of the distance. This boggles the imagination. To think that travel at light speed could be within our grasp! A trip to Centauri System would take a little over four years, instead of five thousand at present technological levels. I wonder what this advancement will mean in terms of the socio-economic impact on our fellow humans.

Every hour, we apply a retrorocket boost, dropping our velocity by a kilometer per second. At current speeds of over three hundred kps, the *Orcus 1* would simply shoot past Luna in the blink of an eye. Over the next two weeks, we will have decreased our velocity to less than a hundred kps.

It bothers me that Alex has not participated even in our Christmas celebration. He has not overcome his antisocial tendencies, and has kept himself in the medical bay during waking hours. At night, he continues to access our main computer files.

Shortly after discovering his nocturnal forays, I enlisted the help of Dale Powers, a whiz at all things technical, and developed a watchdog program to list by name all files accessed on *Orcus 1*. I have determined that Alex has never accessed the same information file twice. At this time, he has read close to eighty-nine percent of the information stored on board *Orcus 1*, including the Science Team's data storage arrays. By the time we land on Luna, he will have accessed every single file contained in the data banks aboard the ship.

I estimate that if he has retained even a fraction of what he has read, then he will already know more about outer space and science than any three members of the Science Team.

I asked him what he was looking for. Expecting him to act shocked that we knew he was reading our files, it was my turn to be surprised when he replied. "It's pretty boring here otherwise."

"You've accessed technical readouts, schematics, hard science files, and encrypted files. Surely, you don't understand them! You're only ten-years old!"

For the first time in any of our discussions, he was forthright: "At first, it was difficult to understand them, yes. But after awhile, I figured it out."

"Figured it out! More than half of that information I couldn't solve with both hands, a flashlight, and a map. Most people take one look at some of NASA's basic manuals and develop a permanent headache. I had to take calculitical telemetronics twice before I could understand just the fundamentals."

"I know; I read your personnel files as well."

"Oh." For a time, I was too stunned to form a coherent response. "Don't tell me you can remember all that scientific and technical jargon."

He smiled, proud. "Every word." Then he proved it, by quoting word for word the calculitical telemetronic manual of the *Orcus 1*. I was flabbergasted, but I had to know.

"And what are you going to do with all this information?"

His reply was as cryptic as I could imagine. I pressed him later, but he would not elucidate for me.

What he had said was, "I have to find out what they are saying."

"What who are saying?"

He turned to me and said, "The planets."

23

NASA *Orcus I*:
Sol System :
Flight Path Pluto-Luna :

EPS Security Monitor : (Command Bridge)

January 10, 2091

3:11:27 PM EST to 3:17:13 PM EST

3:11:27

The EPS view shows the command bridge of *Orcus 1*.

3:11:27

Present are Captain Justine Turner monitoring the command chair, First Mate Helen Buchanan at helm, and Dale Powers (Astrogation) at navigation.

3:11:27

Activity is minimal.

3:11:35

Log indicates routine implementation of braking procedure in anticipation of attaining a solar orbit ahead of Earth's orbit at 58,154 kph.

3:11:58

Proximity klaxon sounds.

3:11:59

Activity increases.

3:12:02

Captain Turner: What the hell is that? Give me a visual right now!

3:12:04

Dale Powers initiates long-range magnification sensor optics from navigation.

3:12:04

Trajectory computations appear on helm computer casement.

3:12:13

Dale Powers: I can't get a fix. Working on it.

3:12:15

Helen Buchanan: It's approaching at 102% present speed; impact in ten minutes, twelve seconds, mark!

3:12:19

Captain Turner: Don't tell me we've got another frigging runaway asteroid!

3:12:20

George Eastmain and Sakami Chin enter.

3:12:21

Alex Manez stands in portal to command bridge, watches.

3:12:23

Sakami Chin: What the hell is going on?

3:12:25

Helen Buchanan: Negative on that, Captain! It's not an asteroid. Magnetic Doppler shift indicates it's a ship. Sensors also read exhaust emissions.

3:12:27

George Eastmain: What did you say? A ship?

3:12:32

Dale Powers: Affirmative on that. We've got a visual; it's not great at this distance, but you can tell it's an artificial coming at us.

3:12:35

George Eastmain and Sakami Chin hurry to their stations.

3:12:58

Helen Buchanan: They're not responding to comm. I've initiated SOS and warning transmissions; they're not responding to either of those!

3:13:30

Captain Turner: Dale, can you verify its trajectory? Is it coming at us on purpose, or is this just a freak coincidence?

3:13:48

Navigation computer runs test simulations with variations entered by Dale Powers.

3:13:49

Helen Buchanan: I've confirmed the computer's emergency instruction set to send live EPS to Earth on continuous feed.

3:13:58

Dale Powers: Confirmation on trajectory. They're definitely coming at us on a collision course.

3:14:01

Captain Turner: Shit! (pause) Helm! I know this ship is not designed for evasive maneuvers, but I highly recommend anything you might suggest. Get us out of this, Helen! Dale, can you get anything on visual that could help? Identify the bugger!

3:14:12

Johan Belcher, Ekwan Nipiwin and Henrietta Maria arrive and, seeing the approaching ship on main monitor casement, quickly take their stations. Captain Turner sees Alex enter, motions for him to stay where he is.

3:15:01

Dale Powers: Negative markings, Captain. The shape of it is unfamiliar. It's not NASA or CSE.

3:15:05

Johan Belcher: ESA doesn't have anything like that either.

3:15:08

Ekwan Nipiwin: It's not Japanese. It looks private.

3:15:10

Captain Turner: What? Are you trying to tell me—?

3:15:12

Ekwan Nipiwin: Pirates did not die out in the Caribbean; they merely evolved. I say we are being attacked by pirates. And if you consider the information we have on board this ship, it's no wonder why.

3:15:34

Alex Manez leaves portal of command bridge unnoticed.

3:15:35

Captain Turner: (shakes her head) How did they know! No one on this ship leaked any information!

3:15:40

Dale Powers: It could be anyone in any of our agencies. There are dozens of people who have access to government information. Not to mention hackers, of course. Or other governments. When you consider everything, I agree with Ekwan; it's not exactly a surprise. We should have anticipated something.

3:15:45

Captain Turner: Anticipated? We're not a military ship! We're scientific! This kind of shit is not supposed to happen!

3:15:48

George Eastmain: Whether it's supposed to happen or not, I just picked up a radar sensor reading on that ship's forward hull. It's a can-opener.

3:15:53

Captain Turner: A what?

3:15:54

Ekwan Nipiwin: The front of the ship is a spike that punctures the hull of the victim's ship, at the same time inserting a reverse claw that will pry open our hull like a can of sardines.

3:16:03

Captain Turner: You mean they're going to ram us?

3:16:05

Ekwan Nipiwin: Yes. Also, if we do not don our suitshields, we will quickly run out of air and pressurization.

3:16:11

Captain Turner: Shit and damn it all! Helen!

3:16:21

Helen Buchanan: Sorry Captain. At current velocity, any drastic alteration in course will tear us apart.

3:16:26

Captain Turner: How long until impact?

3:16:28

Helen Buchanan checks trajectory computer, requests confirmation.

3:16:39

Helen Buchanan: Collision in five minutes, twelve seconds … mark.

3:16:42

Captain Turner: All right. Everyone don suitshields. If they want the frigging ship, they can have it. Dale, can you erase all main computer files?

3:16:47

Dale Powers: Affirmative ... entering command codes now.

3:16:50

Captain Turner: Helen, eject everything from payload bay, let them chase the TAHU and everything else from here to forever. Everybody else, to the security receptacles.

3:16:59

Dale Powers: All non-essential files deleted. Confirmed. All essential files awaiting command code for deletion.

3:17:00

George Eastmain, Ekwan Nipiwin, Henrietta Maria, Johan Belcher leave posts and head for security receptacles.

3:17:03

Captain Turner: Voice print confirmation: Captain Justine Churchill Turner, *Orcus 1*. Security Code: Alpha-Alpha-Alpha-Zeta-Alpha-Turkey-Chicken-Rat. I never got around to changing it.

3:17:09

Helen Buchanan: TAHU and payload ejected, Captain.

3:17:10

Dale Powers: All essential files deleted. Main systems shutting down.

3:17:13

Captain Turner: Good, now both of you to your security receptacles. (Turns around)

3:17:20

—Where's Alex!?

24

NASA *Orcus 1*:
Sol System :
Flight Path Pluto-Luna :

For the first time in months—the first time since he realized his parents had died—Alex was truly scared. Petrified would be a better word, but semantics was beyond him right then.

He had sensed the approaching ship minutes before the *Orcus 1's* sensors alerted the command crew to its presence. At first, he had thought it was merely a rendezvous ship previously arranged by NASA or CSE, but when the klaxons sounded, his curiosity and confusion had brought him to the command bridge where he learned the truth.

Pirates.

And Alex had no illusions that their purpose was anything but to kidnap him. No stranger to the EarthMesh, Alex knew that no information in the world was failsafe. Someone must have hacked the *Orcus 1's* transmissions to NASA and pieced the clues together. They knew Alex was alive, and potentially the key to light-speed travel.

A valuable commodity, to say the least.

It took him three minutes to unfreeze his paralyzed muscles. Once the captain knew of the impending collision between the ships that would destroy the *Orcus 1*, all hands would be ordered to their respective security receptacles. They would jettison the crew's receptacles before impact, and the pirate ship would alter course, hunting down each receptacle in their search for Alex.

But he would not be among them.

There were enough receptacles for the original crew. He was sure no one would have the presence of mind to think of Alex's survival; even if someone did offer him a receptacle in their stead, he would not accept. He had something else in mind.

He raced for his old security receptacle from the TAHU in the payload bay. It was his only chance. Standard procedure dictated that all receptacles be fully charged at all times; and that included the one from the TAHU. Although none of the *Orcus 1* crew had thought to recharge the receptacle, Alex had taken it upon himself to do the job one night a few weeks back. It had been a simple task after accessing the SOP files from the main computer banks.

He congratulated himself on his forethought.

It would take the pirates hours, perhaps even a full day, to hunt down the *Orcus 1* security receptacles, only to discover their quarry not among them. By that time, the emergency alert to Earth would bring military vessels patrolling the asteroid belt to the rescue, and the pirates would have to flee or die. All the while, Alex would be in his old security receptacle in the ship's payload bay, unharmed.

Thirty seconds after dashing from the Command Bridge, Alex reached the payload bay and hurried to the ruins of the TAHU. He crawled through the wreckage to the security receptacle and fastened himself in, initiating a priority code he had programmed. For eighteen hours, he would be safe.

Closing his eyes, he trained his mind outside the *Orcus 1* and tried to locate, with his mental capacity, the oncoming pirate ship.

Just as he was getting a fix on it, and began to magnify his outer vision, there was a deep mechanical rumbling under him, shaking the security receptacle violently.

"What the—?" he called out, steadying himself inside the receptacle.

He interfaced with the status monitor. "Condition?"

The monitor computer could accept voiced queries, but could answer only visually on the screen. In standard computer typeface, the words appeared.

: Unknown interference with SC stabilizers : Sensor findings inconclusive : Waiting :

"Link with *Orcus 1* computer," he ordered.

: Link established : Waiting :

"Computer. What is the cause of recent vibrations in payload bay?"

: Vibrations in payload bay caused by executive order to eject all contents in payload bay by Captain Justine Churchill Turner at 3:16:50 p.m. EST : Waiting :

"Computer!" he shouted. "Abort! Abort! Abort!"

: Unable to comply : Waiting :

Alex did not have long to wait; at 3:17:08, a loud grinding noise filled his ears, blocking out any other sound, blocking out even his thoughts, as the payload bay door opened and the airlock pumps jettisoned the TAHU, the security receptacle, Alex, and a few dozen other objects into space.

Alex ground his teeth together as a sudden motion slammed him face first into the security receptacle's monitor. His elastiplas restraints bit deep into his ribs and thighs.

Within moments, silence replaced the grinding, and Alex's equilibrium returned. He could feel himself rotating at a slow rate. As for his velocity and trajectory, the security receptacle was useless in that regard.

Feeling the panic well up in his throat like hot bile, Alex forced himself to calm down and let his outer vision do for him what the security receptacle sensors could not. Within moments, he found that steady mental rhythm that allowed him to see outside of himself, to see outside of the tiny receptacle into the vastness of the beyond.

Thirty degrees or so from the zenith of his trajectory, he saw the *Orcus 1*. From his viewpoint, it was the NASA craft that was rotating in wide circles around his position, getting farther and farther away by the second.

He saw a smaller ship approaching the *Orcus 1*. Instead of continuing its trajectory, the pirate ship's port thrusters fired, and it changed position, altering course to intercept Alex.

At that point, Alex could have cried at the way things had turned out.

He was completely helpless.

25

Quantum Resources, Inc.:
Toronto :
Canada Corp.:

Michael slammed his fist down on his desk. The windows in his new fourth floor office in the Quantum Resources, Inc. complex north of Toronto rattled from the vibrations. In the hall, his administrative assistant stopped the dicta-shell, glanced up through the semi-transparent fiber wall.

"What? This had better be some kind of sick joke! This is the goddamn twenty-first century! Things like this don't happen!" Michael could barely contain his anger.

"I'm sorry, sir, but we just received the NASA-slaved EPS transmission from the *Orcus 1's* security camera confirming their S.I.D. call."

Calbert Loche was trying hard not to notice his superior's ire, knowing it was not directed at him, and continued with his report.

"At approximately 15:23 EST, an unmarked aggressor bore down on a collision course with the *Orcus 1*. For some reason, the *Orcus 1* ejected its payload moments before impact, and the aggressor altered course for intercept. There are no standard operating procedures for a pirate attack. Captain Turner was just doing what she thought was best. She was making it up as she went along, and only had a few moments to make a decision. NASA has cleared her of any culpability.

"Captain Turner confirms there was a single life form reading in the ejected payload, that of Alex Manez, who is now in the confines of the attacking ship. What he was doing there, I don't know. The payload bay was off limits, but Alex must have thought it a good hiding place.

"The *Orcus 1* had no hope of pursuit, and its sensors were jammed.

They lost the aggressor's signature emissions. The *Orcus 1* is continuing final approach to Luna, and will arrive in fourteen days. NASA has a dreadnought-class protector less than a hundred gigs away, and is sending it to follow the aggressor's last known trajectory, but the chance of picking up its engine emissions signature is minimal. The Space Traffic Commission has been alerted and will investigate, on a random basis, ships entering Earth orbit over the next thirty days."

"For what that's worth!" Michael blurted. "A couple of bottles of whiskey is enough to get those damned commissionaires to look the other way for five minutes. Damn!" he cursed. Turning to Loche, he spoke through gritted teeth. "You know what this means?"

Calbert said, "It means someone out there knows all about Element X, and probably has information we don't. That information, I would assume, indicates that Alex is more involved in this than being a hapless bystander. Captain Turner's reports on Alex are less than forthcoming; Alex has been affected somehow, the kidnappers know more than we do about it, and they took him because of it."

"The possibility occurs to me that either we're not the first ones to encounter Element X, or that someone is reading every file we transmit." Michael paced up and down the office. "We need more information. I want everything we've got on anything to do with Element X, Alex, *Orcus 1*, *Dis Pater*, Macklin's Rock, everything. I want a special team set up to investigate this—take people off the element searcher team if you have to. There's something about all of this that we're missing. Something right in front of our noses. God, I hate being left in the dark; it's infuriating. I want answers!"

"I'll get right on it," Calbert said. "I know just the people to use." He left Michael to brood by himself.

The Director of Quantum Resources did not brood long. There were just too many bits of seemingly unconnected data, and too many pieces of this grand puzzle that did not add up in any way. There was too much that he did not know.

Over the past few months, he had been busy getting Quantum Resources off its feet. Although they did not have any product to show for their efforts yet, their charter provided for a lengthy R&D lapse, considering the scarcity of the element around which their company was based.

Of the forty-seven employees at Quantum Resources, thirty were collating data and trying to determine relationships among asteroidal figures to narrow down the conditions where Element X might be found. It was an astronomical task, but had about as much chance as randomly picking an asteroid and physically surveying it.

Ten employees were engineers determining the properties of Element X based on sketchy data, and attempting to develop theories on possible uses of the mysterious element.

The remaining seven, including Michael, Calbert, and Raymond, were administrative. As it stood, Raymond Magrath was more than capable of handling internal administration by himself. Calbert was effective as a liaison between Quantum Resources and their parent corporations. Michael did not have any concrete task before him except for the odd meeting between NASA and CSE execs.

He decided to roll up his sleeves and get himself immersed hip-deep in this investigation. It was time to get down and dirty.

The first question on his mind, something that had been bothering him for a number of months, was Captain Turner of the *Orcus 1*. Her reports to NASA were inconsistent.

When dealing with the technical aspects of the mission, such as current shipboard conditions, the ongoing investigation of the TAHU, and transmission of theories put forth by the scientists aboard concerning *Dis Pater*, she was exhaustive. Concerning Alex, she was elusive. Although her statements were anything but brief, the content never changed: Alex was fine. Alex was doing well. Alex was normal and healthy.

Obviously, somebody thought Alex was extraordinary enough to stage a pirating and kidnapping of the young boy. Captain Turner had spent the better part of five months with the youngster; she had to have seen something out of the ordinary.

Turning to his desktop, he entered a high-security password in his computer, typed an encoded EPS message. He directed his transmission to intercept the *Orcus 1*.

∞

To: Captain Justine Turner, Orcus 1

From: Director Michael Sanderson, Quantum Resources, Inc.

Security: Level 1 Clearance

I have been apprised of the attack on the Orcus 1, and the subsequent kidnapping of Alex Manez. I appreciate the extremes to which the abductors have gone to complete their task. All measures are being taken by our governments to find Alex.

It has come to my attention that Alex may have been affected by exposure to the element we are temporarily terming 'Element X' in ways that we have not yet fathomed; we suspect the third party involved has obtained information about Alex that may make it imperative we recover him, beyond the obvious reasons to do so. It would be helpful if you could provide me with any observations, however mundane, you have made about Alex that may not have been included in previous reports.

Director Michael Sanderson

Quantum Resources, Inc.

∞

Michael tapped the SEND option on his console. It would take more than twenty minutes for the message to reach the *Orcus 1*; an additional amount of time for the captain to form her response; and another twenty minutes for the reply to reach him. Still, Michael checked his computer a dozen times that hour for messages.

When his secretary informed him she was heading off for lunch, Michael realized he was hungry. To clear his mind, he put on his overcoat and gloves and took a walk down the street to the Webster Family Feed Company for a ham on rye and a tall glass of unsweetened iced tea.

His thoughts were in turmoil. The national and international ramifications of the events of the past few months were staggering, but Michael could not help thinking about Alex.

The poor kid. First, he lost his parents, then was propelled more than four billion kilometers from home; and, as he made the long journey back to Earth, he was accidentally ejected into space, and subsequently kidnapped by forces unknown. How would all that affect a child's mind?

When Michael arrived back in his office, his computer DMR screen was flashing, indicating an urgent incoming message.

Barely suppressing his excitement, he opened the communiqué and read Captain Turner's reply.

∞

To: Director Michael Sanderson, Quantum Resources, Inc.

From: Captain Justine Turner, Orcus 1, NASA

Security: Level 1 Clearance

Against my better judgment, I am forwarding selected excerpts from my private journal—coded with a double-redundant protocol—to you through a trusted colleague; you should receive the uncoded version in a matter of hours. It is painfully obvious no transmission is completely secure; I would have rather waited to present this information to relevant parties in person, but have taken as many steps as possible to keep this information secure. I ask that you keep this to yourself for the time being.

A second copy is being forwarded to Director William Tuttle.

Captain, Justine Turner, Orcus 1, NASA

∞

The wait would drive him crazy. Michael decided to occupy his time answering his other meshmail and browsing the EarthMesh.

Knowing that it could be years before Quantum Resources saw a profit, Michael had diverted a small percentage of the startup capital into a number of secondary investments; hedging his bets, as it were. He logged onto the EarthMesh Global Stock Market and checked the progress of his accounts, selling off a few, buying into a few other companies that looked good to him.

A knock on his door brought him back to the here and now, and he looked up as Calbert Loche entered the room.

"I just wanted to let you know that I've formed a research team of seven for this project. Most of the information available is already in our data banks, but they've decided to start from the beginning and work their way through it all as if for the first time."

"Good. I've made a few inquiries of my own to obtain more data. I'm racking my brains. There's this nagging feeling in the back of my mind that tells me we're missing something crucial. I want to know more. I want Alex found."

"Those are some of the directives I issued them. Also, they are contacting a few other organizations that might have a different angle on the entire *Dis Pater* matter: SETI and some of its independent splinter groups. Crop circle experts are having a field day, saying they've predicted this for over a hundred years. There's a lot of data out there, and a lot of people with even more opinions. There are the Luddites who think progress is the devil's own weapon against the soul, and would do anything to keep this information from being used. If you're looking for someone who's responsible for the kidnapping, we've got ourselves about a billion-and-a-half suspects. And almost as many motives."

"I'd like to narrow that down, just a little," Michael replied acerbically. "And quickly. Within the next week or two."

"You ask the impossible, and we shall provide." Calbert smiled lightly. "Anyway, it's knock-off time. I'll see you in the morning."

Michael looked at the clock in the corner of his DMR. "Already? Where did the time go? I'm going to stick around a while, check a few leads."

"All right."

Michael went back to his computer, but he could not focus on anything. He leaned his chin on the palm of his hand and stared blankly at the monitor, letting his thoughts run away; a free association exercise of sorts.

He imagined traveling to the stars, meeting alien cultures, and charting the entire galaxy. What an adventure!

He was jarred out of his reverie when his communicator chimed. Picking it up, he rubbed the bridge of his nose. "Sanderson here."

The receptionist said, "Hello, sir. Your wife is here to pick you up. She's waiting outside in the car."

"My wife? She's not supposed to be picking me up. I drove here this morning myself. Are you sure it's my wife?"

"Uh, yes, sir. She rang in and said she's been waiting for twenty minutes."

Michael sighed. It probably was time to turn in for the day. He was exhausted and far too frustrated to be effective. He needed a good night's sleep.

"All right. If she rings again, tell her I'm on my way."

"Certainly, sir."

Michael hung up the communicator and put on his jacket, packed his briefcase, and headed down to the lobby. He nodded at Henry as he passed through the front desk security scanners, and stepped outside.

His car was idling in the pickup area. He couldn't see through the tinted windows, but when the horn sounded sharply—a trait his wife had when impatient—he subconsciously relaxed. Walking over to the passenger side, he opened the door and got in.

There was a man dressed in a large winter jacket and with a balaclava pulled down over his face. With a speed that stunned Michael, the man opened the driver side door, slipped his car card in the slot to engage all the locks and close Michael in. Fumbling for his own card, Michael found it and used it to release the doors, and jumped out, but by the time he was on the sidewalk, there was no sign of the stranger.

Looking back inside the vehicle, Michael saw a manila envelope between the driver's and passenger's seats. Sitting back down inside the car, he opened the envelope. Inside was a report.

The front page read:

∞

Decrypted Text
Excerpts From The Official Flight Journal Of
Captain Justine Churchill Turner.

∞

He flipped quickly through the dozen pages of transcribed entries, describing Alex's ability to manipulate electrical devices, and his apparent insomnia. Obvious side-effects of exposure to Element X.

Looking around to see if anyone was watching him, Michael slowly went over the journal excerpts line by line. The insomnia, the computer files, the hidden camera, the electrical telekinesis—all pointed toward something in Alex. A mystery. There was something there.

By the time Michael got to the end of Captain Turner's report, he knew exactly *why* Alex had been kidnapped, and why the pirates had gone to such lengths.

The only question that remained was ... *who* were the pirates?

26

Pirate Ship :
Sol System :

Like a petrified clam within its shell, Alex waited inside the security receptacle and listened for the sounds of the kidnappers coming to pry him out forcibly. He was too panicked to remember to use his special *sight* to watch their approach.

Docking with the pirate ship had been clumsy, and if Alex had not been secure in the receptacle, he would have had numerous bruises and bumps to show for the experience. As it was, he was more scared than if he had been injured; if he had been, at least he would have something to take his overactive mind off what would become of him.

In the DMR game, *Nova Pirates,* a captured fighter would be taken to the pirates' home base where he would be enslaved for the rest of his life, performing menial chores and suffering the abuse of the pirates. That was just a game; this was reality. Over the past six months, Alex had come to know that most of the time reality was much worse.

On the *Orcus 1,* he had felt safe, secure, and could afford to be aloof, reserved, even arrogant in an effort to hide the internalized pains of losing his beloved parents in such a brutal manner. The *Orcus 1* had an accommodating, concerned crew.

On the pirate ship, he would have no such luxury.

He could imagine his future torment. What had he done to deserve such a horrid fate? His parents killed, himself kidnapped. The song in his head threatened to drive him insane. What else was going to befall him?

After a quarter of an hour by himself in the receptacle, Alex thought he was going to go crazy from the isolation and from his imagination. Soon, however, he could hear the sounds of footsteps as the pirates made their way through the defunct TAHU to locate his security receptacle.

Within minutes, they found him, and he finally gathered enough wits to use his *sight* to *see* beyond the receptacle, and to watch his captors. As with every time he closed his eyes to use his *sight,* that haunting song came to him, the lyrical words too soft to define, too far away to catch, too intense to ignore.

There were two of them, he saw. Both were men, dressed in flight suits. One had short dark hair. He looked Asian. The other man was a tall and blond Caucasian.

Though Alex could not quite pin down their ages, he finally decided they were younger than any member of the *Orcus 1* crew. They did not look like pirates; more like astronauts you could find at any space agency in the world.

Taken aback by the kidnappers' unexpected normality, he didn't hear them at first, but they repeated themselves. The tall, blond one had a European accent Alex could not pin down.

"We are not going to hurt you, Alex. I'm going to open the receptacle, and I would like it very much if you cooperated with us, and didn't try to run," one of them said. "There is no place to run, anyway; but if you are a good boy, things will go better for you. Can you hear me?"

Alex's tongue did not want to work for him.

"Can you hear me?" the man repeated as he withdrew a pair of handcuffs from a pouch tied around his waist. "Tell me you'll cooperate, and I won't have to tie you up."

"I won't fight," Alex finally replied loud enough for them to hear on the other side of the receptacle. He waited as the men punched the release button, allowing the door to swing open easily.

Alex stepped out cautiously, and looked up at the men, making no effort to run from them. They had spoken the truth: he had no place to go, except open space. He was in their power.

"Good," the man said. "I see we have no need of these."

He raised the handcuffs before Alex a moment before putting them away in his pouch. "Now, my name is Captain Gruber, and this is First Mate Chung."

"Who are you?" Alex had to ask. "Pirates?"

"We work for a private organization that has taken a great deal of interest in you, Alex. They have followed your progress quite closely since your unfortunate accident last August, and would like to meet you. I assure you, no harm will come to you if you cooperate, but make no mistake, we have taken you prisoner and you will do as we say, or there will be repercussions. Do you know what that word means?"

Alex nodded. "In *Nova Pirates,* prisoners are tortured and made slaves."

Captain Gruber gave him a sour look. "Very funny. No, we are not pirates … exactly. Nevertheless, if you do not cooperate, you will be dealt with severely. Certain privileges that I am in a position to grant you will be withdrawn. It will be a few weeks before we return. How you spend those few weeks—either in comfort, or locked in your room with no entertainment—will be your choice. My orders are to keep you incommunicado. Do you know what that means?"

Alex shook his head, even though he knew the answer.

"It means no contact with anyone, locked in a room for the rest of the trip; but if you are a good boy for us, I will let you have certain freedoms. What do you say to that?"

"I won't try anything," Alex promised.

"Good. Now, if you will follow First Mate Chung, he will show you to your accommodations and then bring you to the mess to get some food. We have recreation facilities for the crew that you may use to occupy your time until we attain orbit. The only requirement we have of you until our landing is a daily physical examination. I understand that you have some small ability with the manipulation of electricity." He gave the boy a stern, uncompromising glare.

So, they had somehow hacked into the *Orcus 1's* secure data bases, as had Alex. How they had done it from space was beyond him.

"I don't know the extent of this power, but I have no interest in a demonstration, Alex. Do I make myself clear?"

"Yes, sir."

"Good. Off you go, now. I'm looking forward to a comfortable, uneventful return. I trust you share my optimism, and that you will make every effort to be a good little boy."

"Yes, sir."

"Good. We understand each other perfectly." He turned on his heel, and strode away.

∞

After being shown his room by the First Mate—a small, cramped space marginally larger than a coffin, with a military bunk and a glowlamp—Alex was familiarized with the latrines and the mess hall. Chung brought him to the common room that was empty right then. There was a DMR television with an extensive library of foreign language videos; a video entertainment console with a number of games also in other languages, but Alex thought he could get around that with the games. There was also a refreshment kiosk that, Chung explained, contained files on every beverage Alex could want.

"Now, remember, Alex: this common room is for the crew members, a place to relax. They have been given orders not to talk to you, so when they are off duty, you may not come in here. You can play the videos when the room is free, and you can read any of the books in here if you can find one in English. However, under no circumstances are you to contact any of the crew for any reason. If I hear one complaint, you will be locked in your room for the duration of the trip. If you have any questions, you may approach me. Do you understand?"

"Yes, sir."

"Good. Now, we must go to the medical bay for some tests."

∞

The physician at the medical examination room was a pleasant looking older man with a disarming manner.

When Alex arrived, the doctor smiled and beckoned the young man to come in. True to form, the doctor was dressed in a lab coat, and wore spectacles over bright blue eyes. His hair was balding, and what hair he had left he swept over the bare skin of his pate. Chubby hands held a stethoscope he had just been donning when Alex arrived.

When he spoke, it was with an accent from one of the southern states of America.

"Have a seat young man. I promise this will be much easier than you think. I'd just like to take a few readings—heart beat, respiration, all on the EEG bio-reader; and if I could, a small sampling of blood, if you don't mind. Then you can be on your way."

"That's all right," Alex told him. Taking off his shirt, he lay down on the examination bed.

"My name is Doctor Hyndman, but you can call me 'Doc.'"

Doc began his examination by attaching a few electrodes to Alex's torso and temples. "I understand there is some kind of electrical disruption field you are able to produce."

There was no use denying it. "If I want."

"Remarkable. Could you show me now? I already have readings for normal state of rest."

"Captain Gruber said—"

"It's all right, Alex. The captain is not here right now, and I don't take orders from him. But, if you don't wish to..."

Alex, despite himself, liked the doctor. "All right. But you have to tell me how you knew about it."

The Doc smiled. "Our organization has many resources, both financial as well as human. A little bribery is all it takes to obtain remote codes. A laser EPS to the *Orcus 1* when we know no one is monitoring the computers, and 'boom', everything is laid out for us. Now, I have shared a secret with you; it is your turn to show me what I would like to see."

Alex, with as little effort as it took to breathe, caused the EEG bio-reader to flatline.

"Remarkable. How do you do it?"

Alex shrugged. "It just happens. I think it, and I can just ... I don't know ... take away the power. Or, I can add to it." Again, he flexed his ability, and the EEG bio-reader began to beep and quip, the readings fluctuating wildly. "Like breathing. You don't think every breath, but if you concentrate, you can hold it for a while."

"All right! All right, Alex! The machine will explode."

"Sorry, Doc."

He smiled. "No worries. You say you just *think* it? Do you get tired when you do it?"

"No."

"Not even a bit?"

Alex shook his head.

"Dizzy, like when you hold your breath?" he asked.

"Nah-uh."

"I understand you have not slept in months. Do you feel tired at all?"

"Well, no."

The doctor raised an eyebrow.

Alex explained, "Not sleepy tired, but sometimes I feel a little slow."

"Slow?"

"Like when you haven't eaten in a while. Low energy or something."

"Interesting. Any other side effects you can think of?"

Alex shook his head, while the doctor rubbed his chin thoughtfully.

"I wonder ... but then, it is not my place to delve. They have facilities for this at the station; my colleagues will be eager to begin their studies of you."

Alex sat up as the doctor produced a syringe for taking blood. "Doc," he said hesitantly, and for a moment, the doctor assumed Alex was nervous about the needle.

"It will only feel like a small pin prick for a moment," he assured Alex.

"I'm not afraid of the needle. I just wanted to know... What are they going to do to me?"

The doctor paused a moment, gave Alex a quizzical look. Then his expression changed to one of amused assurance. "Well, I haven't been told everything, you understand. But I can promise that no harm will come to you. Our organization is powerful, but we are not frivolous. There are many things we do that might threaten others. They want to stop us. But everything we do is for the betterment of humankind, ultimately."

"They didn't have to kidnap me—"

"But I'm afraid we did, Alex. You have a power, beyond the manipulation of electricity, which is of vital importance to the world. Your home country, and others, is ill-equipped to deal with your potential. There would be disasters, possibly war. Even now, some countries are drawing lines, taking sides.

"We have the facilities to explore and observe, and want no part in Earth's wars; I assure you, no one will come to any harm, especially you. In this, you must trust me. It is for your own good that we have taken you. In the wrong hands, you could do great harm without wanting to. You don't want to hurt people, do you?"

"No."

"There, you see? Already I have proven that what we are doing is for the greater good."

Alex furrowed his brow, unable to understand the doctor's logic. "But this ship was going to ram the *Orcus 1!*"

"I assure you, Alex, we would not have done that. You see, none of us wishes for death. The captain would have turned at the last moment."

The doctor leaned forward, his face drawn in concern.

"No, Alex, all we wished to happen was the evacuation of the ship, so that there would be no confrontation. We had expected you to be ejected along with the rest of the crew, but, as it happens, you came out alone, before the others. That made our job easier, and we have avoided hostilities with the NASA ship."

"But..." Alex struggled with the dichotomy of the doctor's argument.

When the needle was jabbed in his arm, and blood taken, Alex barely registered the pain; his mind was awhirl.

"Done. Moreover, as I promised, it did not hurt so very much. You see I keep to my word. So you must trust me now."

Alex nodded solemnly.

"Well, Alex. You may go now, but my door is always open. If you are confused, or you have questions, you may approach me whenever you feel the need. All right?"

"All right."

First Mate Chung entered the MER and shot a questioning glance at the doctor.

"All done, First Mate."

"The Captain wishes to receive a full report on your readings, Doctor."

The Doc cocked his head to one side. "And he shall have access to all medical findings taken aboard this ship, as is his right; but you know under our contract that information about Alex is top secret. You and your captain are not privy to our business."

"I don't like this skullduggery, Doctor! And neither does Captain Gruber. Frankly, the money does not seem all that much now, not enough by far for pissing off the entire USA, Inc."

"Ah, but how will they ever know? We would never reveal your participation in this endeavor, for it would reflect badly upon us. And I'm sure you would keep your own counsel as well. A double indemnity clause, if you will. Now, I'm sure our young ward will be hungry, and it is almost dinner time."

∞

Alex followed the grumbling First Mate to the mess and ate his meal in silence, not even bothering to identify the food he shoveled into his mouth.

Everyone was being more than nice and convivial to him, and this disturbed him in a rudimentary way. Not only did he expect to be handled with brutality and callousness, but also he had fully anticipated being summarily locked away. Was the doctor telling the truth, in that this mysterious organization had kidnapped him because they saw no other way to keep him from using his powers against others? For the betterment of humankind?

And what about the powers that so concerned the doctor? Besides being able to freeze or bolster existing electrical pulses, something which Alex could find no great use for except being able to use a computer without a thoughtlink patch, or fool EEG machines, the other ability he had was seeing beyond his range of vision. How could either possibly harm anybody?

As nice as everybody was, Alex was determined not to let them win his trust. They were kidnappers, right or wrong, and he did not like that.

He planned carefully what he was going to do.

27

Pirate Ship :
Sol System :

Alex spent the next two weeks in a state of futility. The crew's apparent apathy toward him provided him with no opportunities to question them, or innocently overhear conversations—the ones in English—that could have given him a clue as to who these people really were and what their purpose was in kidnapping him.

The rules stated that he was not to enter the recreation room when the crew was off duty. Alex kept to his quarters, and only wandered the small area of the ship where he was allowed to be.

He was able to raid the ship's computer files, but besides technical jargon and schematics, routine logs and reports, he found no information about the organization that had taken such an acute interest in him. If Alex had not known better, he would have sworn they knew about his ability to go into computer files from a distance, and had taken steps to erase any record of themselves.

The only break in Alex's monotony was his daily physical examination. Doctor Hyndman was a jovial man, and Alex enjoyed his company, although the Doc was the enemy. Alex quickly realized that the Doc was himself digging for information about Alex, dropping casual questions that seemed innocent enough.

How far away can you control an electronic device? What do you do all night while you are awake? Do you never get sleepy? What do you think about? Can you tell me if you have dreams? Not even waking dreams? Do you still feel fatigued? Any other symptoms?

Two thoughts occurred to Alex: first, this organization, whilst it knew more about him than anyone else on Earth knew, still had many gaps in its database.

For instance, they had information about his ability to manipulate electricity, and to cause computer files and programs to activate without physically touching the keyboard. For some reason, they thought this power to be singularly dangerous.

However, they had no idea about his ability to *see* beyond himself, to *see* outside the ship, and into the vast reaches of local space. He decided to keep this a secret; how it was going to help him, he had no idea, but if he had something they did not know about, it meant that he retained a certain amount of power over them.

The second thing that Alex spent many a night pondering was the ambiguous nature of the enemy. The captain and crew, although they had kidnapped him—and broken several laws in doing so—beheld Alex with very little regard. He had expected them to be mean, callous, and to go out of their way to cause him grief. As long as he did not get underfoot, and obeyed the rules set out by the captain the first day of his capture, the crew completely ignored him. They didn't extend him any courtesies if they didn't have to; but neither did they seek to harm him. He was a passenger, little more.

Then there was the Doc, who genuinely seemed to like Alex, although he was Alex's captor, and obviously had an agenda.

It made thinking of them as the enemy that much more difficult; but to think of them of such, he was determined.

Perhaps they thought they could fool him; but Alex was no ordinary boy concerned with play. His parents had been assiduous in ensuring Alex's education, and awareness of the world outside his family. There was always time for play, but only after the lessons—although Alex often cheated and played first.

Now was not a time for amusement.

He decided he was not going to learn anything significant until they reached their destination; so every night when he was alone in his small room, laying back on the lumpy mattress with his eyes closed, he floated outside himself, outside the ship, to check their progress.

Alex wondered how they were going to circumvent the radar monitoring orbitals every country corporation used to control and check the flow of Earth-bound and space-bound flights. Anything larger than a two-meter meteorite was logged and traced. Surely, Alex's kidnapping had been reported to all countries concerned with the Orcus project; and knowing the EarthMesh grapevine, word would have leaked out. NASA would approach the United Earth Corporate and demand a strict traffic watch for any ship approaching Earth in the time window they calculated the kidnappers would return there.

It was a few days before final approach, as Alex learned from the Doc. He would have to wait and see until then. The Doc, when questioned, only smiled.

Two days out from Earth, Alex used his extrasensory *sight*. He wanted to watch the Earth become larger and larger against the backdrop of the immense starfield of space, but when he did so, he was taken by a strange feeling. It was more of a certainty, an intuition.

Suddenly, he knew deep within himself—as assuredly as he knew his own name—that the ship was on a course that would not take them to Earth.

He thought back and recalled that not once had anyone said that their destination was Earth. Even when he had assumed it was so, and mentioned it, the doctor had not corrected him.

In his field of extraspacial vision, he saw the Moon appearing from behind the horizon of the Earth.

Luna Station.

An independent port, owned by all, but accountable to none.

The perfect hiding place.

28

Quantum Resources, Inc. :
Toronto :
Canada Corp.:

Calbert Loche knocked tentatively on the Director's office door.

When Michael looked up, Calbert raised his eyebrows, silently asking permission to enter. The Director nodded, waving his loyal assistant in, and leaned back into his leather chair, rubbing the glare of the DMR casement from his eyes.

It had been a long morning. So far, there had been no developments in the hunt for Alex Manez, and no clues to the mysteries of *Dis Pater* or Element X.

However, there had been a deluge of meshmail requests from various news agencies and mesh newsletter groups requesting information. As part of Quantum Resources public relations campaign, Michael had decided to offer full disclosure on anything the governments of Canada Corp. and USA, Inc. had de-classified; as well as any 'non-sensitive' research Quantum Resources itself developed, releasing this information only after it had been confirmed.

The info-pirates and leftist groups that monitored NASA (as if that agency were run by malevolent forces) attacked Quantum Resources' computers with a passion that frankly shocked Michael. He thanked his lucky stars for Calbert Loche, who implemented his philosophy of clean computers. The research machines had no possible access to any mesh account, and no company secrets could be saved on any computer that had an EarthMesh connection. Outside correspondence was done on separate computers—dumb terminals only.

Michael could imagine what would happen if any information on Element X was leaked. The mesh tabloids had had a field day on the subject of *Dis Pater*, that find being declassified by NASA within hours of discovery, but the farcical stories those rags generated had no end.

It never ceased to amaze him how some groups obtained their information, and how much of it they managed to acquire. Their accuracy was as alarming as their theories were ludicrous. They spread enough misinformation to keep the masses on the edge of doubt.

Since Michael had little function outside of administration matters until there were any developments, he took it upon himself to deal with the news agencies and mesh groups. If nothing else, it reminded him how important it was not to let himself be swayed by the tabloid stories and opinion columns.

As the one with the facts, he could check them against the accounts generated by sub-news groups. The tabloids fell short every time. Opinion columns sometimes had a few informed participants, but most entries came from lonely, bored, or deranged people who had nothing better to do.

He looked up at his aide.

"Tough day?" Calbert enquired politely.

"Yeah. It never ends."

"Uphill battle?"

"Something like that." Michael nodded.

Calbert smiled. "Is there any other kind?"

That elicited a chuckle from Michael. He saw Calbert was holding a folder. "What have you got for me?"

Calbert lifted the folder, glanced at the cover. "Preliminary Budget for the Fiscal Year 2091—Quantum Resources, Inc." He made a sour face. "It reads like award-winning fiction; only the writer can understand what the hell it says."

They shared a small laugh.

Lifting his eyebrows, Calbert said, "No, I came by to tell you we've downloaded the preliminary investigation report from NASA on the *Orcus 1* incident."

"Incident?"

"That's what they're calling it until they can find a responsible party and lay charges. Also, the weekly *Dis Pater*/Element X update has been downloaded as well. I didn't know if you caught it on your meshmail."

"No. Too busy with the media subculture." He gestured to his computer.

Calbert grimaced. "Tabloids. Never touch them. I stick to the *Globe and Mail,* and the *Washington Post.* Everything else is trash. Too bad the rags have ten times the circulation of any legitimate paper. Crackpots and unrateds."

"On that, we agree."

There was a short silence where Michael decided Calbert was gathering himself to ask something of personal importance. He gave his assistant all the time he needed.

"Uh," Calbert began, "My wife asked me to invite you and Melanie, if you're available, for dinner this Friday. We're having a few couples over for cards. If you don't have any other plans."

"No, our schedule is clear. Mel would be delighted. We haven't really socialized since moving to Toronto. How is Joan?"

"She's adjusting, but preferred Ottawa. The generous raise you approved for us helps keep her mollified, though. She's got her eye on an Alaskan cruise this spring."

"Sounds wonderful."

"Yeah. If you like boats."

"I think they're called ships," Michael joked.

"Change the 'p' to a 't' and that's what I get when I board them. Anyway, I've got to bring this budget down to Ray and see if we can figure it out together."

Michael laughed. "The mysteries of physics are laid to waste by your brilliant minds, and you can't figure out a simple budget."

Calbert mimed offering the report to Michael. "Then you won't mind going over it yourself."

Raising his hands in a forestalling gesture, Michael shook his head. "Not on your life."

Offering a conciliatory laugh, Calbert got up and said, "Talk to you later."

"Later."

When Calbert had left, Michael sighed, took a sip from his now-cold coffee and grimaced. Clearing his throat, he went back to his computer and pulled up the files from NASA.

The incident report told him nothing new, and he closed the casement screen. The weekly update on NASA's efforts in the *Dis Pater* investigation did not offer Michael any new insights, and he skimmed the long-winded paragraphs, scanning for anything of interest.

He brushed over one paragraph, and the meaning of it did not register in his mind until he reached the end of the report. The author had alluded to an interview, but the report did not have any attachment that indicated where the interview was. He read the phrase again:

∞

[Ref: n:\982563\\nvstgtn.dispater.ntrvw325.nasa.gov]

'The translation of the sacred scroll the old man revealed to me leads me to believe a further investigation is fully warranted. There is a possible link between the fall of the Mayan civilization around 800 AD, and the discovery of Dis Pater…*'*

∞

Michael checked the file location on the NASA LAN, to which he had been given access, but it was not there. He went back to the report and checked the file details. The author's name was George Markowitz, and it gave his meshmail and vidcomm addresses.

Dialing George Markowitz's vidcomm through the DMR casement, Michael waited patiently as the ringer sounded four times. He was expecting a voicemail message, but was surprised when the screen blinked on to show a live person. George was man in his forties with a receding hairline and a sour expression on his chubby face. He wore a simple blue shirt with no tie.

"Hello—" George checked the display bar on the bottom of the screen that flashed the caller's identity. "—Director Sanderson." The irritated look on his face did not alter with the knowledge or recognition of his caller's identity. "What can I do for you?"

"Hello, Mr. Markowitz. I'm sorry to disturb you, but I was wondering if you could help me."

Markowitz nodded impatiently.

"I've just finished reading the weekly NASA update on *Dis Pater*— Element X, and I saw your report. In it you make reference to an interview with a an old man from Honduras."

"Yes." There was a decidedly bitter tone to his confirmation.

"I tried to find the attachment, but couldn't. I was wondering if you could direct me to where it is posted."

George Markowitz looked around him at the other end, as if ensuring no one was listening in. "Look, Director, I could get into a lot of trouble for this."

"My interest is strictly official," Michael assured him, momentarily confused.

"That's almost worse. If you must know, I presented the interview to my Investigation Supervisor, and he dismissed it as irrelevant and ordered me to remove it from my report. He also directed me not to bother any of my superiors with this again. I haven't shown the interview to anyone else, and erased it from the NASA LAN as I was instructed. The editing department must have forgotten to delete my header info in their daily update. It has been posted for a couple of days, but no one is all that interested in the oversight; you're the first to say anything about it to me."

"So the interview was deleted?" Michael pressed.

There was a moment's hesitation as George considered his reply. "Officially, it never existed. But—" He sighed ponderously. "I have a copy on digital."

"Would it be too much trouble to ask you to transfer it to my LAN at Quantum Resources here in Toronto? I wouldn't ask otherwise, but I have a bit of a vested interest in all aspects of this investigation."

"Yeah, I know." George took a few breaths. "All right, but I'll send it through a proxy mesh service, so there's no official log, and no immediate link to me, even though, officially, the interview is no longer considered NASA property, but declassified and Public Domain; my Supervisor might not see it that way. It's a lengthy video, so the upload might take a few minutes."

"That's perfectly fine. Here's my mesh address." Michael typed it onto the video transfer so that it appeared at the bottom of Markowitz's DMR casement. The NASA investigator copied it to his mailer.

"Maybe you can do me a favor in return," Markowitz suggested. "If it's not too much trouble."

"Of course."

Markowitz's demeanor had transformed over the course of the conversation. He became more relaxed and eager, finding someone interested in his work.

"I would like to meshmail you my resume. I've been keeping up with your press releases, and reading your meshpage. I think you could use someone with a knack for gathering information. It's not that I'm dissatisfied with NASA. I'll be honest; there is a personality conflict between me and my supervisor. I ... married his sister when we were all in university, and he's never forgiven me for that.

"Circumstances threw us into the same department a few months back, and he won't authorize a transfer for me. I don't mean to burden you with personal problems, sir, but just wanted you to appreciate my motivations."

Michael cocked his head. "I can't promise you anything right now. If we don't find any more samples of Element X, it might be me peddling my resume around town. But I will take a look at it and give it due consideration."

"That's all I can ask. Thank you. I'll transfer the interview file shortly, after I log on to my mesh service."

"Thank you."

They disconnected the transmission, and Michael decided to go get a fresh coffee while he waited for the download. By the time he got back, his inbox had a new item.

There were two messages from George Markowitz. The first was his resume. Michael quickly perused it, and found himself growing increasingly impressed with the man's qualifications and career history. They were wasting him as a junior investigator at NASA's R&D department.

He was thinking, *Raymond could use a catch-all information analyst like this,* and forwarded the resume to his assistant.

Then Michael opened the second message.

It was straightforward.

'Here is the file you requested.'

Michael loaded the file into his DMR AVOT Viewer, donned his equipment—ear-mask for audio, and ocular cap for visual. There were also the options of a nose filter for olfactory input, and even a full electronic suit for the complete tactile experience, both of which he opted out of. Michael was more interested in the content of the interview than smelling anyone's perspiration.

He ran the file.

29

Orcus 1 :
Sol System :
Luna Approach :

Justine had been in space four times before. Whenever she returned home, she had watched in rapt fascination as the Earth began as a tiny speck against the black backdrop of space, and slowly grew to the size of a walnut on the monitor screens. As the days progressed, the blue orb gradually encompassed her entire range of vision. She loved this part of it, and looked forward to it every time.

There was little else for Justine to do on final Earth approach. The ship's navigation computer handled most everything. A human observer was only needed in case the NASA guidance computer lost contact with the ship. When not in the observation lounge, Justine whiled away the days in her cabin, going over her notes on Alex, and on the coup that had taken both him and the CSE TAHU. She wondered whether she should have been able to predict any of it, or could have prevented it from happening.

Standard procedure did not include the event of space piracy. Justine had used her judgment; and that had resulted in disaster. She knew she should not blame herself, but there were those in the Administration who would blame her, especially those who would use this incident as their own personal stepping stool for promotion.

Her chances of redeeming herself were practically non-existent.

She was on the verge of handing in her resignation, with plans to rejoin the Lowell Observatory, when her communicator chime captured her attention.

Depressing the receive button, she mumbled a desultory, "Mmm-hmmn?"

Helen's voice came over the non-video communication transfer. "Priority message to you from Director Tuttle, ma'am."

"I'll take it in here."

"Very good."

Justine's computer beeped a few seconds later, indicating that it had accepted the data dump and was ready for her perusal. She entered the appropriate commands, and on her small DMR screen, the NASA Director's face appeared.

Justine listened carefully to all Director Tuttle had to say; then, her heart pounding with barely suppressed excitement, saved the message on the public drive and immediately called a meeting of all crew and science team members.

∞

In the Command Bridge, she waited until everyone was assembled before addressing them.

"I have just received a priority message from Director William Tuttle. I won't waste time on any lengthy preamble trying to explain the content of the message. Instead, I will play it back for you, and let you come to your own choices."

At the use of the word 'choices' everyone began to talk at once. Justine waved her hand at them for silence, then she motioned for Helen to begin replay of the message on the large DMR in the Command Bridge.

Director Tuttle's face appeared when the NASA insignia faded into the background.

"Justine," the image said. "Conferencing with both the heads of the Canadian Space Exploration, and with the CEO of USA, Inc., we have come to a unanimous agreement to launch a return mission to Pluto, exclusive to both our country corporations. This has been achieved in compliance with a new contract between Canada Corp., its subsidiary, CSE, and with USA, Inc. and its subsidiary NASA. Part of this contract is the creation of a new joint-partnership corporation, Quantum Resources, Inc., which has been set up to exclusively study the phenomenon of the asteroid, Macklin's Rock, its sole surviving occupant, Alex Manez, and all aspects of the mysterious Element X.

"However, since the bulk of our scientific evidence has been pirated from the *Orcus 1,* including Alex Manez, the information concerning our plans, and our future agenda, has been brought into the public spotlight. Under amendment of our initial exclusive contract with Quantum Resources and its parent companies, we have agreed to offer limited partnerships on this new mission to Pluto, to be called the *Orcus 2* mission, to all original participants of *Orcus 1*. No doubt the space agencies concerned will be EPSing messages to your crew and scientific team presently; so I have taken the initiative to warn you and inform you of these developments.

"It is our consensus that any members of the crew or scientific team who wish to extend their tour to the *Orcus 2*, and return to Pluto, may do so. For those who are ordered back by their respective space agencies, or do not wish to participate in the *Orcus 2* mission, we have made arrangements for the *Orcus 1* to rendezvous with Luna Station, instead of returning home. Flight trajectories will be uploaded into your ship's navigation computer within a few hours.

"There, at Luna Station, a crew transfer will be initiated, as well as a refit and restock of supplies. There will be a two-week shore leave on Luna Station following a debriefing.

"Both myself and the CEO of USA, Inc. extend our most hopeful request that you should head up this subsequent mission, Captain, if it is your wish. In return, we will be extending your tenure, and offering you a substantial flight and mission bonus. We leave it to you whether you wish to present this news to your crew, or wait until they are contacted by their respective space agencies. Your replies will be required no less than twelve hours from the time of this transmission.

"Director Tuttle, out."

Justine turned in her command chair and watched as members of the *Orcus 1* began the process of realizing that their initial mission, although it had technically failed, still brought reward. Most of them would be given the opportunity to try a second time.

The pall that had settled over the members of the ship over the past six months, and more especially, after the pirate attack, had suddenly lifted with the news that they would be going back to Pluto.

"We all have some thinking to do—" Justine began, but was interrupted by Helen Buchanan.

"Sorry, Captain, but I don't require any time. The minute the CSE sends me the offer, I'm going to EPS back that I'm staying for the duration. I know I don't have much to do with the scientific aspects of this mission, but I've always been one to see it through to the end. I wouldn't miss this for the world."

One by one, the members of the science team agreed with the First Mate's sentiments, in their own words. Not only were their careers going to be saved by this opportunity, and their professional sense of duty appeased, but their personal ambitions to unlock the secrets of Pluto and *Dis Pater* were being granted in a way none of them had even entertained.

In the end, Sakami Chin bowed out when the order from the People's Republic of China Space Agency ordered him to return to their country, to be replaced by Chin's esteemed colleague, Dr. Soon Tek.

Justine, however, was going back to Pluto, and nothing was going to stop her.

30

Quantum Resources, Inc. :
Toronto :
Canada Corp.:

George Markowitz had personally traveled to Honduras to get the interview.

Being one of the Senate's favorite hobbies, NASA benefited from generous government corporate transfers, and was able to buy the latest in high-tech equipment. Quantum Resources did not have an AVOT, or Virtual Tourist Camera (the name by which they were marketed in the private sector), in their inventory, but luckily, the output could easily be played on any DMR casement with a specialized adapter.

Michael had the option of viewing the flat screen output (slightly distorted), or taking in the full 270° visual 3D audio and full factory and tactile experience of the Virtual Tourist operator.

The VT Camera took samples of the air around the helmet the operator donned, and recorded the scents as part of its database of over sixteen thousand smells. When played back, the DMR could, if the option were desired, give off a small spray of one of its twenty-three basic scents, and send electronic pulses to the brain that tricked it into thinking the viewer was experiencing the actual smells from the field.

Normally, those wanting to go on a virtual vacation without leaving their homes or offices on lunch break used the full experience tapes.

Michael's interest was purely business. He turned off the extra features and just used the VR helmet to watch the A/V interview.

∞

[Copán :
Honduras :
Central American Conglomeration :]

Once a great city of the ancient Mayan people, Copán was now nothing more than a tiny village of less than five thousand residents forty miles outside of the much larger Departmental Capital, Santa Rosa de Copán. It was in a smaller village between the two that Mr. Markowitz first donned his Virtual Tourist and turned it on.

A map of the area appeared superimposed for half a minute over the picture.

"We are here in the mountainous region of Honduras, very near the site of the ancient Mayan City of Copán. This village is the home of the Mayan who originally translated the hieroglyphs we found on the artifact, *Dis Pater*.

"The man, Yaxche, named after the tree of heaven, is said by the locals to be the only one in Copán Departmental who can still accurately translate the earliest forms of pictograms from the ruins of ancient Copán City."

The image on the DMR, taken from the perspective of George Markowitz, showed a dirt road defined by a number of ramshackle houses running down its length, the houses themselves on the verge of ruins.

Sitting on a handcrafted rocking chair at the nearest house was an old man, short, stocky, deeply tanned with black hair and a remarkably round head. He grinned as George approached. Not all of his teeth had survived the many decades of the old Mayan's life.

"This is Yaxche," George said.

Yaxche rocked once, twice, and grinned deeper as George arrived at the front of the house. He clicked his tongue against the roof of his mouth, and said, "Ahyah. Heloo."

"Good day, sir. I'm George Markowitz from NASA in the United States. I was wondering if I could ask you a few questions."

Still grinning like a fool, the old man blinked and replied, "Ahyah."

"You are the man who translated some hieroglyphs for us last summer?"

"Ahyah." He clicked his tongue. "I read some of the old writing. Goozal Kinich Ahua; Inti ba Rahn; Goozal Kukulcan."

George translated from memory. "Beware the Mighty Door of Kinich Ahua; Eternity is now Before You; Beware the Power of Kukulcan."

"Ahyah. You remember. Very good."

"Thanks. Now, we have heard from some of the scholars in Santa Rosa de Copán that you have in your possession a document that dates back over a thousand years, but they have not been able to appropriate it from you or this village."

"It is legacy," Yaxche said, still grinning. "Belongs to Copán. One day I will pass on to Mitnal, maybe go with Hunab Kú—I don't know where I will go, who will take me. That day, when I pass, it will go to my grandson."

∞

Michael wondered why Yaxche grinned so, and then he realized that, to this villager, George must look like some kind of idiot with the Virtual Tourist helmet recorder on his head.

∞

George asked, "Could I see the document, sir?"

"Ahyah." Yaxche turned to face someone off-image, said something in his language, and a boy ran off toward a building down the street.

George turned back to the Mayan. "How did this document come into your possession, if you don't mind my asking?"

"Ahyah. I was given this gift of legacy by my grandfather, Chictzi, who was given it by his grandfather, who was—"

"I see."

"Ahyah. Maybe you do."

Waiting for the young boy to return, George asked, "And how old are you now, Yaxche, if you don't mind my asking?"

"Ahyah. Don't know. Many seasons. Too many for this old man to count. Not to worry. Not many more to count. No. Not many more."

Presently, the boy returned with a polished wooden box, handed it reverently to Yaxche, and disappeared with the alacrity of any pre-teen, no matter their culture.

George paid him little attention, and focused on the parchment

151

scroll the Mayan began to unravel.

"Amazing!" was all George could say.

Then: "It's made from what looks like a kind of bark-cloth. Whatever its source, it has lasted for over ten centuries!"

Yaxche regarded George as a teacher might a pupil. "Ahyah. Made from bark of pine tree; chew until soft and thin, then dry under sun."

"Wonderful. What does it say?"

For a long while, the old man did not reply, turning his gaze to the scroll. It was as if he were lost in the past. Finally, he began his tale.

"It is a story of the downfall of the Mayan Peoples. Ahyah. For hundreds of seasons, the People were wealthy and prosperous. But we grew complacent. Hun Ahua, ruler of Mitnal, the realm of the dead, became angry with the People because of their arrogance, and made a plan to gather them to his realm.

"Hun Ahua whispered in the ear of Ah Hulneb, god of war, and suggested it was time for the People of the South to go to war with the People of the North.

"So the People gathered their women and children, and put them on an island to keep them safe; then they went to war.

"Hanub Kú was creator of the Maya; he had rebuilt the world three times after the three deluges which poured from the mouth of a sky serpent. The first world was for dwarves, who built the cities; the second world was for the Dzolob, the offenders; and the third world was for the Maya. But Hanub Kú was displeased with this war of the Maya, and decreed the world would be rebuilt again a fourth time for the White Man.

"He sent Kinich Ahua, the firebird god of the Sun to come down and burn the Mayan cities while the People were off at war. He sent Kukulcan, the feathered serpent god of all elements, to rise from the oceans and swallow up the island on which all the Mayan women and children were hiding. He took them back into the depths of the sea with him so that the Maya could not breed any more disobedient children.

"When the People came back from their war, they saw their cities destroyed, and their families gone, and they hung their heads in shame and allowed the enemy warriors to come and defeat them, to use them as sacrifices to the gods, and slaves for their kings.

"Kukulcan was so disappointed in the People's behavior, that he later became Quetzalcoatl and ruled the Aztecs.

"It is said that Hunab Kú went back to his home in the stars to make plans for the fifth world, after the deluge that would destroy the White Man."

His tale finished, Yaxche looked up at George expectantly.

"Incredible," the NASA researcher said, the DMR image shaking with his head. "If this is to be believed, then the Mayan gods predicted the coming of the Europeans some five centuries before it happened!"

"Ahyah. It is said to be. And the fifth world is soon to come. But what do I know? I'm just an old man."

"The fifth world…"

George spoke in an aside to the VR. "Could this be a prediction of the discovery of the light speed element on Macklin's Rock? Could it be that this 'Fifth World' is what lies beyond Sol System? Is it possible, as so many theologians and philosophers have toyed with, that the ancient gods were space travelers who visited Earth and bestowed great gifts upon our ancestors? How else do we explain the hieroglyphs found on *Dis Pater* if they were not put there by travelers from the stars a thousand years ago who visited the Mayan people?"

∞

The interview went on for a few more minutes, but Michael cut the sound and did not watch the DMR anymore. True, George's speculations were wild … but no more ludicrous than the other explanations the so-called respected scientific community had brought forward.

Could it be…?

31

Luna Station :
Luna :

"Luna port control, this is *Orcus 1*, NASA BJN-1145 requesting final approach clearance to Luna Station, over."

: *Orcus 1*, this is Luna port control. Please confirm approach vector trajectories, velocity and current payload, over. :

"Luna port control, approach vector at 92 degrees, 14 minutes, 42 point 556 seconds at separation of 92 point 348 thousand kilometers, mark. Payload at 14 thousand kilograms, over."

: *Orcus 1*, vector confirmed. Your position is marked on approach radar, submitted to docking governor for calculation. Hold for calculations, over. :

"Luna port control, waiting, over."

: *Orcus 1*, authorization granted, logged. Please turn over navcom control to docking governor computer on mark, three, two, one, now, over. :

"Luna port control, navcom control slaved to docking governor, check, over."

: *Orcus 1*, slave confirmed. You will be docking at nub 43, station 12, one hour, twelve minutes, fourteen seconds, mark. Authorization number for refit and restock requested, over. :

"Luna port control, authorization number is as follows: NASA BJN-1145 AD-324-19-44-4, please confirm, over."

: *Orcus 1*, authorization confirmed. Stopover of 15 days authorized. Departure time scheduled for 01-30-92 at 0923 hours, over. :

"Luna port control, departure time confirmed, over."

: *Orcus 1*, please transmit manifest of any goods to be transferred from *Orcus 1* through Luna port, over. :

"Luna port control, manifest is being transmitted. Also note an exchange of crew member Sakami Chin, PRC, for Soon Tek, PRC, over."

: *Orcus 1*, crew roster change noted, over. Soon Tek confirmed presence on Luna Station, check. —Protocol completed, over. :

"Luna port control... Thank you, Luna port control, over."

: *Orcus 1*, enjoy your stay, over. :

32

Quantum Resources, Inc. :
Toronto :
Canada Corp.:

The memo on his computer concerning the confirmation of the *Orcus 2* mission was of cursory importance to the Director of Quantum Resources, Inc.

Privately, Michael was glad Captain Turner was commissioned to lead the next mission to Pluto; she had been there before, and was more than competent enough to handle an extended duty in space. It would be good for her career. She had stuck her neck out to give him the information on Alex before it was completely safe for her to do so, and that had put her in Michael's good books.

He had EPSed a message to Justine through her office at NASA, thanking her for the effort, and offering his future help whenever she felt the need to call on him.

He was far more occupied, however, with the news Calbert Loche had brought to him a few minutes after he stepped into his office that morning. Although Michael had ordered the bulk of his staff to look into the Alex Manez kidnapping, the small detail that had remained on the search for Element X had worked steadily towards a resolution of the problem. Calbert divided his time between the two teams.

"Michael, I think we're on to something," Calbert had said to him.

"What?" Michael asked, standing. "Alex?"

"No. Element X. There is an anomaly in the preliminary survey report. Our new man, George Markowitz, thinks he can extrapolate something that might give us a clue how to find Element X."

"George! He just started a couple days ago!"

"Yeah!"

Michael was pleased that his recommendation to Calbert had led to the hiring of George. He had hoped he would not be sorry for hiring the man. Retaining the master researcher might have just paid off.

"Let's hear it."

Calbert Loche held up a forestalling hand. "His presentation isn't completely finished yet. He has some back-reports coming in from NASA that he has to verify and compare, and he's also sent feelers to the Europeans and is hoping for a few replies this morning. I just wanted to know if you could set aside an hour this afternoon to hear the team out."

"Absolutely!"

"Great, say, about 13:30?"

"Perfect."

∞

In the conference room, Michael sat at the head of the table facing a large DMR screen set into the back wall. On the left, Calbert Loche leaned back in his chair with a confidence that served to increase Michael's anticipation.

On the other side of the table, Walter Johnson, Peter Cloud, and Gary McNally sat with folders arranged on the table, pens at the ready, making notes as George Markowitz made his presentation to the Director.

George brought up a display Michael recognized as the preliminary geological survey of Macklin's Rock performed by the Manez's.

To begin, George came right to the point, "I'm not really scientifically literate, but I can check and compare facts. At first glance, this survey in and of itself says nothing. Until now, we had been staring at it for months before we realized that, instead of looking at it, we had to look *through* it."

Michael silently applauded the man's use of 'we,' even though George had just come on board. It showed he was willing to be a team player. His personal problems with his previous supervisor obviously did not interfere with his professionalism or his passion for his work.

George and his wife, Elizabeth, had joined Michael at the Calbert's for cards over the weekend. Michael was instantly taken by the couple, who were open and fun loving. George was not at all shy about explaining to Michael that Elizabeth had been pursuing a teaching career in university before they got married, and gave up her schooling in favor of having children. She showed no regrets, though Michael could imagine Elizabeth's brother being upset at the situation.

George brought up a display on the DMR.

∞

Mineral Content: Aluminum, Calcium, Carbon, Cobalt, Copper, Helium, Iron, Magnesium, Nickel, Silicon, Sodium, Sulfur, Titanium

— Percentages Unknown

∞

"What's important is the Mineral Content. At a casual glance, there is nothing out of the ordinary. All of these elements have been discovered on other asteroids; some rocks have additional elements, and some are not as inclusive as this one. We decided to go element by element, and compare it with other asteroids in the SMD mine catalog, checking against anomalies, but although we were on the right track, we were on the wrong train, if you take my meaning."

He brought up another display.

∞

Site 1: Aluminum, Carbon, Cobalt, Copper, Iron, Magnesium, Nickel, Silicon, Titanium

— Percentages Unknown

Site 6: Aluminum, Calcium, Copper, Helium, Iron, Magnesium, Nickel, Silicon, Sodium, Sulfur, Titanium

— Percentages Unknown

Site 14: Aluminum, Calcium, Carbon, Cobalt, Copper, Helium, Iron, Magnesium, Nickel, Silicon, Titanium

— Percentages Unknown

∞

"This is representative of all thirty-eight sites conducted by the Manez's on Macklin's Rock. The differences between the sites showed us nothing. There was nothing at site 14 that was not found at every other site.

"We were left with nothing, until Paul noticed an anomaly in site 14 itself. Not a variance between it and another site, but between its own reports. I want to show you the following three time-sensitive reports."

∞

Site 14: 13:12:23 GMT

Aluminum, Calcium, Carbon, Cobalt, Copper, Iron, Magnesium, Nickel, Silicon, Titanium

— Percentages Unknown

Site 14: 13:12:24 GMT

Aluminum, Calcium, Carbon, Cobalt, Copper, Helium, Iron, Magnesium, Nickel, Silicon, Titanium

— Percentages Unknown

Site 14: 13:12:25 GMT

Aluminum, Calcium, Carbon, Cobalt, Copper, Iron, Magnesium, Nickel, Silicon, Titanium

— Percentages Unknown

∞

"Each of these reports was generated one second after the other. The final report was generated an instant before detonation. Do you notice a difference between the three?"

Michael blinked. "Helium, of course. But—"

"Helium is not an uncommon element in all celestial bodies, although not as readily found in asteroidal forms. The Sun itself is composed of 25% helium. The thermonuclear reactions in the Sun that provide us with light and energy turn the 75% hydrogen content into helium. Now, helium has the atomic number of 2, and a weight of about 4. That means there are four protons and/or neutrons in the nucleus—in this case, two of each—and two electrons in the K-shell. Specific gravity of 0.00018—"

"Yes, yes," Michael said impatiently. "I know it's been a few years since high school chemistry, but I do recall my periodic table."

"Actually, this is all new to me. Peter was kind enough to give me a crash course late last night." He nodded to his colleague. "But you'll soon realize that the second report was, in fact, in error in determining helium as one of the elements found in the drill site."

"What?"

"Even I know that elements are usually identified by mass spectrometer—the instruments are so common that every geologist and physicist here has a small pocket spectrometer alongside their calculators. Going back over the reports, the large spectrometer at the Nelson II site initially identified the substance as helium not because it detected a color that indicated helium, but because it identified two electrons in a questionable element, and temporarily assumed it to be helium rather than an isotope of hydrogen or lithium. The spectrometers we employ on surveys use a free electron count to bolster our identification process to help determine isotopes as well as basic elements.

"Then, in the third sampling, the spectrometer did not find a color to match helium, or any isotope of hydrogen or lithium, discounted the electron count, and dismissed the element as unidentifiable."

"Unidentifiable? Hydrogen is usually found in pairs—" Michael suggested.

"No, the spectrometer showed nothing even remotely in that spectrum."

"What about two lithium atoms sharing an L-shell electron?"

"No." George smiled knowingly. "The spectrometer reading is completely out of that range."

"Then what good is this information?" Michael demanded.

"First of all, we know that whatever this element is, it has two electrons, so obviously we thought it is an isotope of helium, say, a heavy helium to some degree. At first, we dismissed these findings because of the impossibilities of it. First, with a mass of .002 per cent of 10,000 teratons, give or take, would mean about 200 billion tons of helium. At a specific gravity of .000018, that would mean a volume of about 360,000 cubic meters. Initial drill samples indicate the pocket to be no more than 10 cubic meters."

"What does all that mean?"

"Well, a rough estimate would be an isotope of helium with a nucleus, or atomic weight, of about 271, and a specific gravity of about 210 grams per cubic centimeter."

There was a stunned silence in the room, until Michael said, "Impossible!"

"Certainly … but then, so are luminous or super-luminous speeds."

Michael rubbed the palm of his hand across his mouth and chin. "All right, for the sake of argument, say this is possible. Either this is a super-heavy helium—"

"Which is beyond the laws of physics," added Paul, "even more than the impossibilities that we're discussing now."

"This, in turn, would mean that we had a super-radioactive helium isotope on our hands. About a thousand times more radioactive than uranium."

"—Or," the director prompted.

George nodded. "Or, we have an element that is supposed to have upwards of 271 electrons floating around it. Something with anywhere from 110 to 271 protons in the nucleus, missing its electrons. A super-positively-charged ion."

"That would be…"

"Anti-radioactive. Although not so far-fetched. It could be compared to solid-state technology that currently exists; like semiconductors and superconductors; though this would be the most pure form found naturally; a supraconductor, if you will. The core temperature of the asteroid is probably what keeps this super-superconducting material so pure. The elemental atoms would want to absorb as many electrons as they could from any source."

"Or neutrinos, or even photons from gamma rays," Paul added. "Any available particle. We won't know until we have a sample."

"Right, and Newton's Law of Physics states, 'Every action has an equal and opposite reaction'."

"Absolutely. So if this new element absorbs the photon, the energy of that traveling photon is translated as…"

Michael finished for him. "Electricity, heat, light … or … motion."

"In those amounts, translated at just under the speed of light. There would be a time delay, such as the thirteen seconds between detonation and launch of Macklin's Rock, while the atoms fill to capacity. Once that has been achieved, the only thing left is, as in any radioactive reaction, for the massive energy to be released. Perhaps through the natural valve created by the Nelson II site drill, or, we think more likely instead of the propellant theory, these photon-charged atoms travel on an anti-magnetic propulsion basis, perhaps even in relation to the Sun. A kind of super-quantum reaction. We won't know for certain until we have some of this element for tests."

"But that kind of sudden acceleration— Wouldn't that have crushed Alex?" Michael asked.

Paul spoke up. "Normally, yes. The most-pressure a person could sustain for any length of time is about 8 Gs of force. At 8 Gs, it would take a thousand hours—five weeks or so—to achieve luminous speeds. There is an old theory about light: that it, in and of itself, has no weight. We've played with the physics of the Macklin's Rock phenomenon, and all we can surmise is that, in some way, Element X operates in such a way that everything that piggybacks on it assumes a kind of superluminosity. It would, therefore, feel no effects of the acceleration, even at the supposed five million Gs of force the asteroid would have had to sustain over the course of the first minute. That would have pulverized even diamonds into fine dust.

"The Rock, the TAHU, even Alex, would have taken on an accelerated molecular condition, which could have left the cells of his body in a semi-charged state. This would prove the unofficial theory you presented last week that he is somehow able to manipulate electrical pulses in his immediate area—this phenomenon is not uncommon to people who have been struck by lightning. They, themselves, have become living ions."

"This all sounds impossible."

"Rationally, it seems so, but we've half a dozen theories that prove it on paper."

Rocking back and forth in his chair, Michael thought about it. "For the time being, forget about the theories. How do we go about finding more samples, and if we find any, how do we keep it from reacting? What you're saying is that this thing was in a pocket of minerals, surrounded by…" He looked to Gary, who held up a sheet of paper.

"It was a titanium pocket, if the Nelson II depth indicators were accurate. Our present Nelson II's allow a small gap of open space between the core of the drill hole and the surface of the asteroid …

more than enough room for photons to breach."

"Then, when the drill pierced through, photons from the Sun entered, and—"

"Reaction—or, should I say, anti-reaction."

"Like the hypothetical tachyon, on this side of the speed of light."

Michael raised an eyebrow at the possibilities.

"Right. We've discussed this with the engineers at CSE, and they think they could easily rig a Nelson II with a vacuum drill. We use a similar drill in the clean rooms when we don't want samples contaminated."

Michael knew that, but his mind was buzzing with the new information and theories. "How do we go about determining the location of this … what shall we call it besides Element X? That sounds so mysterious, and we're already on the road to solving this particular mystery."

George Markowitz cleared his throat, already prepared for the question.

"Well, unofficially, we've been calling it the light-heavy element, as a kind of joke, but I've discussed this with a few of the others on the team, and when the time was right, we were going to put forward either the name, Manezum—" He waited for Michael's reaction. "—or 'Kinemet'."

"Kinemet?"

"Kinetic metal."

"Appropriate." For a few moments, Michael considered. "Well, traditionally, the discoverer of an element has the honor of naming it. Since those discoverers are not with us, then I think the task would have to fall to the theorists who first identified and classified the element. In honor of the Manez's, we could call the anti-reaction 'the Manez Effect.' For the element itself, 'Kinemet' it is, and I will make a memo of it."

"Thank you, sir."

Michael waved his hand at him. "How do we find more of this Kinemet?"

"Well, the most obvious, though hardly the most reliable, method is to look for anomalies in the masses of charted asteroids when compared to their volumes. Anything that throws the specific gravity of an asteroid to above, say, ten or fifteen—depending on how stringent we want to get—then we give it a closer look. A specific gravity of seven is what we have found as the median of the asteroids in our catalog, with fluctuations between about four and twelve with those rich in heavy metals. But with Macklin's Rock, we've calculated, based on composition and size, and preliminary mass readings without the space tugs, that it had an overall specific gravity of forty-eight."

"Forty-eight?" Michael could not believe that.

"Yeah. That throws the estimated mass of Macklin's Rock up to over sixty-eight thousand teratons. Based on that, there must be a number of pockets extant. Only problem with Macklin's Rock is that it's about six billion kilometers away."

"Have you told anybody about this? About the theory?"

"No. When we contacted NASA and went through the SMD mine catalog, we found a number of asteroids with similar anomalies, summarily dismissed as faulty data. We'd like you to propose a follow-up survey to these asteroids."

"Of course. As soon as you give me the mine numbers and the vacuum drill, I'll have a survey team there ready to dig. We'll postpone informing NASA until we have some evidence; then they can go through their catalog and try mining their asteroids."

The director took in a deep breath.

"So, then, if this is all true, we have to ask ourselves one question … and while we're discussing impossible theories and new rules of the Laws of Physics, I think I know the answer to my own question."

"What's the question?" Calbert urged.

"Why did Macklin's Rock *stop?* What acted as a damping rod to stop the luminous reactions?"

The men gathered in the room were, by nature, the best physics theorists Quantum Resources could hire. They did not waste time in stunned silence pondering a question that had not yet occurred to them.

Immediately, Peter suggested, *"Dis Pater?"*

Michael shook his head. "I don't think so. I think *Dis Pater* is nothing more than an indicator, a gauge to measure estimated times of arrival, put there by another space-faring race—whether for our benefit or theirs, that is yet to be determined…

"No, something else stopped the Rock from hurtling out into interstellar space, and I want you to include this possibility in your report."

The scientists in the room pondered for a few moments before

Michael supplied his supposition.

"I think, somehow, Alex stopped it."

33

Luna Station :

Luna :

Once the pirate ship reached the docking port at Luna Station, Alex was summoned to the bridge, escorted by First Mate Chung.

He had been keeping his mental eye on the ship's approach, reveling in the sights that seemed so much more exhilarating than pictures on a holovid; there were not many people who could claim first-hand eyewitness to the docking of a space ship.

At first, he wondered how they had managed to negotiate their landing without the docking governor informing the authorities of the nature of the ship, but then, Alex realized the governor was just a computer that carried out instructions. Whoever programmed the governor was probably in the pay of the pirates, or the pirates' masters.

On the bridge, Alex faced Captain Gruber for the first time since being brought on board. The bridge, although Alex had surveyed it with his *sight,* seemed more ominous and foreboding in person, mostly because the command crew were consciously ignoring him, and the captain was glaring at him as if deciding whether to chew him up, or skin him alive.

Trying to avoid making eye contact under the captain's glare, Alex flicked his gaze over the DMRs and stat monitors.

As far as he could tell, most of the controls and stations were identical in function and presence as those onboard the *Orcus 1.*

On the *Orcus 1,* Alex had studied each station and its purpose, and was confident that he could identify them on the pirate ship's bridge— or any other space vessel, for that matter.

"Alex," Captain Gruber's voice grated in dire warning.

Alex snapped his attention back to the command chair, though did not lift his eyes to the occupant.

"Yes, sir?"

"We are going to depart the ship now, you and I. I'm going to be taking you through the port where there will undoubtedly be other people. You might think about running, or shouting for help, or something equally stupid."

"Yes, sir."

Gruber shook his head. "I advise you against it. I could threaten to kill you, but our client has expressly forbidden that kind of action. However, he said nothing about killing civilians." He pulled out a lasrod; it looked lethal. "If you run from me, I will shoot one person at random until you return. If you shout at someone to help you, I will shoot that someone. Do I make myself perfectly clear?"

Alex's eyes narrowed. He knew now that these were true pirates, callous and mean. The Doc might be something of an anomaly, but that might have something to do with the fact that he was a doctor, trained to save lives; nevertheless he had still thrown in with these brigands. Alex suddenly hated every one of them.

He would go along complacently, and not try to escape. He would not, however, fully cooperate if he could help it. He had been on the verge of spilling his secrets to the Doc, explaining about the *sight,* and about the other thing.

A few days before, in his weekly allocated shower, Alex noticed a clump of hair clogging the drain. When he pulled the hair out of the gap, he was shocked to realize it was his own. Since then, he had found strands of his hair everywhere. He was a ten-year-old who was slowly going bald.

As alarmed as he was by this revelation, he knew he had been wise to keep his mouth shut. The less information the doctor had, the better.

"Do I make myself clear?" Gruber repeated in a tone that brooked no disobedience.

"Yes, sir."

Going along with the captain would not only provide for the safety of innocent bystanders, but would allow Alex to see for himself who had contracted their services; if he ever got away, he could report the man behind the kidnapping, with a full description.

"I won't try anything," Alex assured the captain.

"Good." Gruber holstered the rod. "First Mate Chung and the Doc will accompany us. I don't want to hear a word from you for any reason from now on, got that?"

"Yes, sir."

Gruber's eyes turned hard. "What was that?" he demanded in a growl, his teeth grinding together.

"Y—" Alex stopped himself from speaking another word, held himself still.

"That's better," Gruber said. "Let's go."

34

Luna Station :

Luna :

The bartender gave her patron a confused glance when she ordered an iced tea with no ice. Justine was more than accustomed to people blinking at her request in restaurants. Iced tea went down better when it was warm.

The lounge was full, and every chair was taken, so Justine nursed her drink as she slowly neared the observational domed windows. She was wearing a Lunar vest, the fabric lined with metal shavings that increased her apparent gravity by a factor of six; large magnagravs had been installed in the foundation of Lunar station to help counteract the effects of long-term exposure to light gravity on the Moon. Weightlessness and near-weightlessness over time caused bone deterioration, calcium deficiency, and muscular atrophy, among other things, in many people.

Free-fall had many benefits that balanced the dangers, but with Luna established as a base of commerce, every precaution was taken to provide an Earth-like environment to minimize any dangers.

The antigravs on a ship could not be used on the Moon; the expense was far too great.

Justine passed by a few people she knew, nodded or exchanged pleasantries, but quickly moved on. Hoping to catch a glimpse of Earth from the radiation-shield window, she was disappointed. A small digital counter on a support beam indicated it was three hours to Earth's dawn.

Because of the Moon's synchronous rotation, the Near Side always faced Earth, and the Far Side always faced away; however, there was a slight variation in its orbit of five degrees. These variations, called librations, allowed the Earth-view terminator—the line that separated the near and far sides of the Moon—to fluctuate.

It was in the median of that fluctuation that Luna Station had been erected.

The reason for this was as a compromise between astronomers, who wished an unadulterated view of the sky, and the United Earth Corporate Council merchant traders, who, it was found, were psychologically ill-at-ease conducting business out of sight of the Earth.

A Lunar 'day' was about two weeks in length. Currently, the Sun was in the northern Lunar hemisphere, shining brightly as it did for fourteen days straight out of every twenty-seven-and-a-third days, though this did not affect the apparent color of the sky from Luna Station. The Moon had no atmosphere, no molecules of nitrogen, oxygen, carbon dioxide, water vapor and other trace elements and particles for the Sun's light to catch and scatter in the many shades of orange, purple, and blue that bespectacled the Terran firmament.

Justine sighed, and took a sip of her iced tea. She had spent the last two days since landing on the Moon doing nothing but going over and filing paperwork and reports. The liaison from NASA demanded much of her time; each of the crew had been segregated with their respective agencies and departments. They had had no contact with one another.

The little spare time Justine found, she used to avoid all the bureaucrats and functionaries who descended upon her relentlessly; as well as the media who pursued her like sharks to blood.

The news of Alex's kidnapping, and of Macklin's Rock, still hadn't reached any public channels, although the NASA attaché had informed her that the country corp. governments who had participated in the Orcus project were well apprised of the situation.

The media wanted a quip on *Dis Pater*. What did she think it was? they asked her relentlessly. Did aliens put it there? For what purpose? Did she think aliens would be arriving soon? Did she think they looked like the popular representations in the holovids? Did she think the aliens would want to have sex with her? And on and on, each question more ludicrous than the last.

She hated the media, and what they stood for. Vultures, all of them. They made her want to scramble back to the refuge of the humorless bureaucratic monotony.

In a way, though, she was glad she had things to occupy her mind. Otherwise, she might sink into a morass of guilt over having failed to bring Alex home safely. The kid had gone through more than most adults, and had borne up considerably well, even though he had not been offered any comfort from Justine or any of the other crew: their lives were based on science, not sociology.

She glanced at a clock, remembering that she had another meeting in a few minutes. She set down her empty glass for the servobots to fetch, and made her way out of the lounge.

Traversing the warren of halls and corridors, her keen sense of location kept her from losing her way. Her mind tended to wander in an attempt to try to forestall thoughts of the upcoming meeting, but her alertness sharpened when, out of the corner of her eye, she thought she spotted a familiar form.

She turned her head to see the backs of three men and a boy rounding a corner. They were gone too quickly for her to be certain. What made her think it had been Alex? The thought was ludicrous. Alex could be halfway across Sol System for all she knew. Stopping, she debated with herself for a few precious seconds. The attaché would be uncompromisingly furious.

"Ah, they can start without me." Her curiosity had to be satisfied.

She quickly backtracked to the public corridor where the four had entered, and squinted her eyes to scan down its length.

The four must have gone off on a side corridor. Justine stepped up her pace to try to catch up.

At every intersection, she looked one way and then the other. At the third cusp, she thought she spotted a recognizable jacket, and hurried, jogging.

By the time she reached the elbow of the corridor, the forms were disappearing again around yet another corner. At the last second, one of the men glanced behind him, and Justine got a brief look at an Asian man. He did not see her.

Throwing caution to the wind, she broke into a run, but when she rounded the corner, the four had disappeared from sight down a long passage decorated with red trim near the ceiling junction. There were two guards barring her way. She glanced at the map on the wall.

She was at the People's Republic of China section of Luna Station. Whereas most country corporations allowed free passage to anyone, practically inviting them to visit their PR information booths and facilities, it was still each country corporation's right to privacy. It was a long-standing tradition that PRC did not encourage uninvited guests.

Justine pulled out her identification badge.

"Captain Justine Turner, NASA," she barked at the two guards holding flechette rifles and giving her stony looks. "I wish to enter; a friend of mine just passed through here, and it's urgent I speak to him."

The one guard shook his head. "Sorry. No."

She thought about trying once more, then realized that if the Chinese were behind Alex's kidnapping, there was no way she could wheedle or bluff her way into the PRC hall.

"Very well. Good day." Turning on her heel, she stalked off.

∞

She was still worked up, and when she backtracked and found her meeting room, the NASA liaison immediately asked her what was wrong, detecting the flush in her cheeks and the quickening of her breath.

"Are you all right?" There was a trace of an East Sussex accent in his voice.

He was tall, English-born, with a thin mustache and a receding hairline. In England, they called him Duke Wexhall, but since his mother had been American, he held dual citizenship, and had used his American status to gain employment with the National Aeronautical Space Administration, a boyhood dream, he'd told her when they'd first met.

With his natural charm and approachable demeanor, Clive Wexhall waited patiently for Justine to explain why she was so upset.

The internal debate whether to tell the liaison took a few moments. "Either I'm going crazy and seeing things or Alex Manez is being held here at Luna Station. I think the Chinese have him." Succinctly, she gave him an account of the morning's chase.

Before she was through, Clive was EPSing a message to NASA. "It may be nothing, but I think we can't be too thorough in our search. Holding him here would explain why Earth Space Traffic Commission has no trace of them yet. I also find it odd that you mention the Chinese."

"Why is that?"

"Well, I didn't want you to be alarmed, but ever since you landed, I haven't been able to contact Sakami Chin for debriefing. The Chinese consulate refused to answer my calls as well. Washington will have to become involved if we don't get any cooperation from the Chinese. If both sides start getting their backs up on this…"

He shrugged, leaving the obvious conclusion unspoken.

"Shit," Justine said after a moment.

"Yeah," he agreed.

35

Quantum Resources, Inc. :
Toronto :
Canada Corp.:

Determining the specific gravity—or density—of a sample element on Earth is a relatively easy task; not so for an asteroid floating free in space, even a smaller one that has an estimated radius of 4.3 kilometers, such as the spherical one on the top of Calbert Loche's list for the Quantum Resources team to re-evaluate.

On Director Sanderson's orders, the complete survey on SMD #1596 was to be repeated from scratch, no mistakes. It took sixteen hours for the astronautics team to arrive at the asteroid from the Canuck Flyer orbital.

Work began immediately.

The specific gravity, or density, of an object is the ratio of the mass of a given volume compared to the mass of an equal volume of water at a temperature of either 4°C or 20°C, measured usually in x grams per cubic centimeter. The survey team first had to determine the volume of SMD #1596, using a laser topographer to calculate surface area.

With area defined, the mean radius could be inferred with the formula of $4\pi r2$; in this case, the asteroid had a surface area of 231.2727 km^3, and a mean radius of 4.29 km. The volume of a perfect sphere would have a formula of $(\pi D^3)/6$, but with the imperfections of the surface, the craters formed through impacts with other asteroids and meteors, and any oblongs jutting from the surface, the scientists could determine the volume of SMD #1596 with an error factor of plus/minus one percent. SMD #1596 had a volume of 330.72002 km3 ±1%.

Once volume was determined, they had to calculate mass. As there are no scales in outer space, another method had to be used.

Given that one Newton of force acting on one kilogram of mass can change its velocity by one meter per second every second, as specified in Newton's second law of motion, this was where the pilots with the space tugs came in. Using telemetry to study rotation and eccentricity of orbit, they also determined the asteroid's velocity in orbit, which was 31,215 meters per second, similar to Earth's, though it had a much longer distance to traverse around the Sun to complete one orbit.

The tug placed itself behind the asteroid and, using its propellant engines, pushed on the asteroid until the acceleration gauge registered a constant of one meter per second per second, and how many Newtons of force were expelled to do so. With acceleration predetermined at one meter per second, and the Newtons measured at 6,945,120,423,298.4 N, that translated as 6,945,120,423,298.4 kg, or 6,945.12 teratons, compared to Luna's 74 million teratons, or Earth's 6 billion teratons.

Adjusting for the temperature difference, the asteroid's 6.945.12 teratons in a volume of 330.72002 km^3 calculated down to approximately 21 grams per cubic centimeter, or a specific gravity of 21 ± 5%.

Gold has a specific gravity of 19.3, and since the top layer of asteroid SMD #1596 was made primarily of iron (Sgrav=7.89) and nickel (Sgrav=8.9), there was a large discrepancy which could be accounted for by the presence of a heavy element, such as the asteroid's entire interior being pure gold ... or a portion of it being Kinemet.

∞

Watching on the DMR screens at Quantum Resources, Michael was about to nod approval to proceed with the massive vacuum core drilling campaign. Everyone had agreed that location was the most likely to contain a pocket of Kinemet. But then the fire klaxons sounded, and a voice came over the intercoms.

"Please do not panic. This is Major Bernard Nally of the Canadian Armed Forces, CFS Petawawa, on authority from CEO Dolbeau of Canada Corp. to secure this building. Please remain calm, stay where you are, and do not transmit any EPS or fiber-op messages from this building until you receive further orders.

"Thank you. More information will be forthcoming."

36

Luna Station :
Luna :

He had a plan, and had been prepared to wait decades to see it through. Chow Yin was nothing if not a patient planner. However, recent developments could accelerate his strategy by several years, even decades.

The first phase of that master plan was being effected before Yin even woke that morning.

Six months ago, Yin's people, having access to all incoming and outgoing EPS messages received or sent out through the LS antenna array, had intercepted perhaps the most important byte of intelligence that could have ever been forwarded to him. One of those EPS's they routinely had monitored concerned the disappearance of Macklin's Rock.

It had been a message from USA, Inc.'s NASA headquarters to the attaché posted to the American sector. Without leaving any ghost traces, Yin's prodigious computer hackers had copied that message and transferred it to Yin's attention. Almost, it had been overlooked, but with careful planning, Yin had shifted events in his favor.

After the Macklin's Rock incident, he slowly gathered more and more information about the occurrence, and how it was related to *Dis Pater*. Yin had sent out an interception satellite to record the EPS echoes sent from *Orcus 1* to NASA Houston. He had thoroughly researched the remarkable ten-year-old survivor of the first luminous flight.

Yin, as had key personnel on Earth, quickly and effectively put together the pieces of the puzzle.

He grasped the import of this intelligence as keenly as he realized that the outcome of this adventure bore directly on his continued survival, and his future control of Sol System.

If interplanetary space was opened up with light-speed travel, then the country corporations of Earth would fly direct, and bypass the Moon. Those tariffs and fees that kept Yin in luxurious comfort would be diverted to other stations on the nine planets, and to outposts that would quickly be erected on the other thirty-three official moons of Sol System. Luna Station might still retain some influence through its proximity to Earth, but the resources that Yin had enjoyed would henceforth be severely restricted.

Unless … Yin himself held the technology of light speed travel, and licensed it out under front corporations. There could be quadrillions of dollars involved, power enough to control the Country Corporations of Earth (behind the scenes, of course).

Or … enough capital to launch his own interplanetary real estate development project, build those stations on the planets and moons under his own banner. Earth would belong to the Terrans, but the rest of outer space would be his. And those who wished to leave the safety of their little blue planet would have to pay dearly for the privilege.

He knew that acquisition of more of the new element was paramount to control of the interplanetary industry, and he had two teams of researchers working on it; and one team of spies well-placed in various space organizations: ESA, PRC, CSE, and NASA.

Another team was using the information gained through subterfuge, and attempting to apply it in finding their own deposit of 'Kinemet', the term the researchers were adopting for the element.

But the key to unlocking that element's power days or months before anyone on Earth—something that had evaded the scientists on Earth to date, as far as Yin's intelligence could discover—was crucial. The key was in young Alex Manez. Yin knew this as certainly as he knew that his leg would ache when he rolled out of bed and put pressure on it.

Whoever could study Alex first would have a head start on opening up the secret of Kinemet.

Yin was determined to have Alex; and his plan to capture the youth, if the memorandum on his personal computer console was accurate, had come to fruition. The pirate ship he had hired had successfully kidnapped the young boy.

Yin had given orders to have Alex brought to him immediately. He wanted to see for himself that the child was undamaged.

Then, the research would begin, and his domination of Sol System would be assured.

Fate had denied him Earth; he would turn his back on that ancient Nemesis, turn the tables on destiny, and take the universe for his own.

37

Quantum Resources, Inc. :
Toronto :
Canada Corp.:

What the hell is going on?" Michael roared.

Calbert Loche stared at him dumbly, as at a loss for an explanation as everyone else in the room.

One of the techs turned in his seat. "Sector cam shows five men in the lift. They'll be here any minute."

In anticipation, everyone turned to the doors, awaiting the new arrivals much like barracudas in their lair ready to spring on anything that came within view.

When the doors opened, three men dressed in army fatigues and holding submachine guns entered the room in standard military fashion, deploying themselves one on either side of the door, the third entering halfway into the room. All stood at the ready, their SMG's held vertically across their chests.

The fourth military man entered, his narrowed eyes assessing the room strategically, expertly. He wore the dress uniform of a Major-General, his branch cap and collar badges showing him to be attached to the infantry corp. His cool assessment of the room seemed to pass right by Michael and the others.

He turned around and said to someone beyond the doors, "Secure, sir."

"As if I expected otherwise, General," said Alliras Rainier sardonically. He strode into the room, and despite the tone in his voice, gave the military man a nod of concession.

Ignoring the look of cool detachment with which he was being regarded by Michael, Alliras stepped up to the CEO of Quantum

Resources, Inc., and held out his hand.

Michael took it, but kept his silence, forcing his old friend to explain himself and the presence of armed men on private property.

"Michael," Alliras addressed him. "For the time being, I would ask that you suspend all communications to and from this site until I can debrief you."

"What is going on? We've got a team stranded and cut off from all communication almost five hundred million kilometers from here—"

"We should talk in private." Turning, the Minister's eyes found Calbert Loche. "You might want to hear this, too."

Making up his mind immediately, Michael nodded approval for Calbert's participation, and then said to Raymond Magrath, "I'd like you to join us as well, if you don't mind."

"Not at all."

A concerned look came over Alliras, but he did not protest as he followed Michael and the two other men into one of the conference rooms.

Inside, they quickly took their seats, though Michael had the urge to stand and pace. He waited for Alliras to begin.

Because of Alliras's position, and their long-standing relationship, he gave the Minister the benefit of the doubt, and granted him a certain degree of respect. With any other person, Michael would have not been able to check his impulse to shout and badger.

As CEO of Quantum Resources, Michael was technically a part of the private sector, and although his company was accountable to the Canadian Space Exploration department as well as NASA, that did not preclude his deferment to them, or allow for any surprise inspections or unexpected takeovers. Alliras's explanation would have to be very good.

"The USA, Inc. has gone to Defense Condition Two," was the first thing the Minister said, and that was sufficient to grab Michael's full attention. "Canada Corp. followed a few minutes later."

"What?"

"Unofficially, of course. It's the Chinese."

"The Chinese?" Calbert protested. "Again?"

"I thought we had treaties in place. There hasn't been any serious trouble with the Chinese in over a year!" Raymond furrowed his brow. Michael recalled that Raymond's wife's grandmother had been born in Hong Kong before the reversion to mainland China a century earlier, and had immigrated to Vancouver shortly thereafter. China was the only bastion of communism left in the world, after the death of Castro in the Cuban Papal Revolution that had led to that country's pledge to democracy and joining the United Earth Corporate many decades before.

Alliras sighed. "Two days ago, the *Orcus 1* landed on the Moon. The captain, one Justine Turner, was touring the station this morning, and because of her close involvement with the Alex Manez affair, came under the impression that the young boy was on the Moon with her. She thought she spotted him under escort of three men, one of them decidedly Chinese. She saw them enter the Chinese Sector of Luna Station, and was refused admittance to the area. She reported this back to NASA."

Before anyone could pose any questions, Alliras continued, "Also, this morning, Dr. Sakami Chin was scheduled to report for debriefing under arrangement with the Chinese Government. Standard procedure. Both he and his governmental representative failed to show up. Now, in the political spectrum of things, such an occurrence would not necessarily precipitate any kind of military response—it is a minor infraction of our treaty with the Chinese Republic.

"When the USA, Inc.'s Foreign Secretary approached the PRC for comment, he was stonewalled for most of this morning, then, the Chinese Consulate in Washington issued a statement to the effect that NASA was responsible not only for the kidnapping of the valuable world resource of Alex Manez in an attempt to monopolize the technology he represented, but went so far as to thereafter kidnap two Chinese nationals, Dr. Chin and his governmental representative."

"What?" Michael cried out. "That's preposterous. They think we kidnapped our own citizen as well as two of theirs?"

Alliras shook his head. "Not as preposterous as the fact that the Chinese have also declared that the United Earth Corporate has conspired and effected the takeover of their allotted sector of Luna Station."

"Their—? You mean—?"

"Yes," said Alliras. "The Chinese seem to have lost communication with their people on the Moon."

Michael rubbed his chin. "You know what this suggests to me?"

"Of course." Alliras pursed his lips. "A third party interest. The politicians are negotiating with the Chinese as we speak to form a joint investigative committee. The Chinese know well that it wasn't NASA or any of the other country corp.'s, but their foreign policy requires they cover their own ass first. We'll get to the bottom of this soon enough; but for now, we have a rogue element that is obviously tapping into secure links with our space operations."

"Speaking of which," Michael reminded the Minister, "our team in the asteroid belt have probably starting to feel like they've been abandoned."

"Not to worry. I've already commissioned a skimmer from the Canuck Flyer to rendezvous with your team and explain that we need a blanket on communications until we resolve the lunar crisis. They should arrive in a matter of about twelve hours or so. I'm sorry, but your operation will have to be temporarily suspended."

Michael shared a conspiratorial look with Calbert, and then said to the Minister, "What if I can promise you an absolutely secure communication with our team? Could we continue then? Every moment we delay costs us a lot of money and resources. Our team will have to be replaced if this goes on for a few days or more, and knowing politicians, it just could. If I can clear security with you, may we proceed?"

Alliras was on the verge of summarily rejecting the proposal, and then he caught himself.

"How?" he asked.

"You remember the charity last summer, when I got the message about the Macklin's Rock incident?"

"The code you and Calbert worked out. Messages on plastic and such."

"Yes. Public thoughtcomm is mimocorded as standard procedure. This is the same kind of situation, only at a longer distance."

"You can't send a plastic memo five hundred gigs in any reasonable amount of time," the Minister protested.

"Right. But the regular EPS is being monitored, just like thoughtcomm here on Earth. Even if we used just our code, there is always the possibility that it would be cracked. It's not the message that has to change, it's the medium."

"What? The only other method we know of sending messages is radio. Electronic Pulse Signal can be intercepted at any frequency, if the hackers know where to send out their nets."

"This time you are wrong. There are infinite means of sending messages. Radio broadcast is only one of them. How do you think we keep up-to-the-minute account of our craft in the asteroid belt? Radio or EPS is too broad a frequency, too cumbersome. We track our ships with optical radar. Lasers. It's just a matter of programming to piggyback a message on the beam in either direction. As far as security is concerned, any attempt to intercept the laser beam will register on our monitors; we can then change our code.

"Although the ships used by us are charted from CSE and NASA, Quantum Resources members all know our codes and rotations. I can guarantee a secure up- and down-link to the asteroid mission. Any attempt to intercept the beam would be known to us immediately. I would think that, given the current political climate, any positive discovery of Kinemet would be in our mutual best interest."

Michael let the Minister ponder this for a few moments. He was fairly certain Alliras would agree, and he was not disappointed when his old friend finally nodded.

"All right. I'll trust your techs. But I have to leave the guards here and downstairs as a matter of SOPs."

"Of course."

They stood, and Michael accepted Alliras's offered hand. They shook, and exchanged slight smiles.

"And I hope you keep me updated on Luna Station. I have a vested interest in Alex Manez, and more than just because of his connection to Kinemet. His parents were under my sphere of responsibility."

"I understand," the Minister told him. "I'll keep in touch."

The four men exited the conference room and, with little more than a nod to Alliras, Michael got right down to business.

"Calbert, initiate laser 1 protocol. I'm sure there are more than a few of our fellows up there eager to hear our voices."

"Yes, sir. Initiating protocol," was the reply as the control room burst into activity.

38

Luna Station :
Luna :

Alex was marched through a maze of corridors. Finding his way out would be impossible: the halls all looked the same and the only markings on various doors were written in Chinese characters. The pirate captain on his left was grim-faced. It was as if he knew he was selling Alex's life over to whoever had hired him, and though it left a sour taste in his mouth, was determined to see the contract through to the end.

Alex suddenly realized that the games he played on sim were nothing but fantasy. Nova Pirates was much easier to play when the lines between good and evil were easily defined.

The captain was on the side of evil, but so was the doctor who had tried to be nice to Alex, and make him feel comfortable. But were they any different from Justine and the people back on Earth? They all wanted Alex for his powers, for his relationship with *Dis Pater*. Did anyone, good or evil, truly care for Alex himself?

The long walk finally came to an end at a nondescript freight elevator. They entered the elevator and the pirate punched the lowest button; since the buttons were inscribed with Chinese characters, Alex could only assume they were heading for the basement.

Not a word was spoken on the short trip down, but Alex looked up at both of his escorts; neither would return his glance.

The elevator door opened to opulence. The sight before him was so grand that it was a good minute before Alex became aware of the absence of artificial gravity in the room; the magnetos were not operating this deep below the surface of the Moon.

It was as if this were a whole new world within Luna.

Alex had never seen such luxury displayed before him except in elaborately produced DMR vid-flicks.

The room was large enough to dock a mid-sized space freighter. There were extravagant furnishings and draperies covering the floor and walls.

Settees, couches, antique chairs, vases that must have dated back centuries filled the room. Several fine works of art Alex recognized adorned the walls. Four thick pillars had been erected at geometric points within, though only for decoration; the polysteel used to construct the station was strong enough to support itself without the use of any kind of structural supports.

Red, gold, green, and purple dragons were embroidered on long banners of silk and satin, and were hung from the ceiling.

Any kind of wood was almost as expensive as gold on Luna, when including the cost of transport, but in the middle of the far wall of the room there stood an enormous oak desk, waxed to a brilliant shine, its legs carved with images from Chinese mythology.

From behind the desk, a figure dressed in a robe of richly woven red and gold silk stood. There was a satisfied smile on his round face as he shuffled around the desk toward Alex and his two captors.

"Greetings, gentlemen! Greetings. Welcome to my humble little slice of the universe." He spread his arms in a welcoming gesture.

As if he hadn't spotted Alex the moment the boy stepped out of the elevator, and had not moved his penetrating gaze from the object of his obsession, he said, "Ah, I see you have brought me my prize, for which—I believe this is how they say it in those pirate vids—you will be handsomely paid."

As if struck by an out-of-place sense of conscience, the captain said, "You're not going to hurt him—"

The Chinese man looked deeply offended. "Hurt? Why, I would sooner cut out my own heart. Young Alex here represents the world to me. Nay, shall I even say it? He represents the entire Universe. Hurt him? On that account, my dear swashbuckler, I can assure you, your fears are completely unfounded.

"I have received the data report sent by the doctor, and the results are everything I expected. You have honored your end of our pact to the letter. Now, if you would be so kind as to leave Alex and me to get acquainted, my personal assistant will see to your generous reward."

From nowhere, it seemed, a teenager with bad acne appeared and gestured for the pirates to re-enter the freight elevator.

Yin said, "I thank you, gentlemen, for your service to me. You have no idea how you have benefited me, and yourselves, for I shall remember the alacrity with which you have completed your objective.

"Good day."

The pirates were immediately dismissed from his awareness, all his attention focusing uncomfortably upon Alex.

Feeling his heart beat faster, Alex had no choice but to wait. He had briefly contemplated making a break for it, but to where? The pirates would not offer him sanctuary. And he would very quickly lose himself if he ever managed to find his way out of this room of splendor.

He blinked when he realized there was an open hand thrust out before him. "Good day, Alex. My name is Chow Yin. I'm sorry that we had to put you through that terrible, terrible ordeal, but I assure you, it is for your own good."

Alex debated whether to shake Chow Yin's hand, or bite it and try to run. Demurely, he extended his own hand to his new captor.

"Good. It seems you are not only a fortuitous youth, but one who has intelligence as well. That is good. Come, Alex, and make yourself comfortable."

Chow Yin led Alex to a voluminous couch placed in front of a short table covered with fruits and pastries and glass carafes of juice—one-hundred percent pure, if Alex had to guess.

"Help yourself, if you are hungry."

"Thank you," Alex managed to say as he chewed on a macaroon.

Any normal ten-year old would either be completely terrified in Alex's situation, or completely oblivious. Alex was neither. Although he felt some trepidation when contemplating his future, the knowledge of his own powers helped comfort him. If the circumstances turned malevolent, he knew he could plunge the entire room into darkness. With his vision, he did not need light to see. He doubted Chow Yin could match that skill, even with all his money.

And he did not doubt that Chow Yin had paid for his capture precisely so that he could plunder that ability from Alex. He had to form a plan of escape. He saw no way out, and for the moment, he could only bide his time.

Chow Yin sat upon the couch very close to Alex—too close for comfort, really, but Alex had no room to move farther away. He paused in mid chew as Yin put a thin hand upon the boy's shoulder.

"Now, Alex. I brought you here for reasons you might at first suspect, but rest assured, I have your best interests in mind. My best interest as well. I will not hide that fact from you. Yes, you have some special abilities that could benefit me in ways that would change the very face of Sol System. Oh, how I've longed for those changes.

"You see," he said, "I am exiled from Earth. I cannot return. Not for any reasons political or criminal, I can tell you. It's because of a twist of fate."

He pulled up the silk pant of his pajamas to show Alex the wreck life had made of his leg. Alex couldn't swallow the half-masticated piece of chocolate and coconut sweet in his mouth, and nearly vomited it out, but somehow managed to keep it right where it was.

Yin dropped the pant leg, and mercifully covered the mass of scar tissue.

"My bones are brittle. They could not hold up my body weight in Earth's gravity. Even the artificial gravity on the Moon here that they have installed in the last ten years is too much for me; that is why I have had to retreat to my little haven here under the surface. Even Luna Station is forbidden to me. I am trapped.

"But space ... ah space ... now that is wide open.

"Up until now, there have been so many physical limitations on exploring space. What, a trip to the asteroid belt takes upwards of a month? Insane! And costly. Too costly. Why should it be that only the ultra-rich country corporations can go and plunder the incredible wealth in the belt? The rest of us grow relatively poorer as they grow so much richer. It is a story that has been repeating itself for centuries on Earth.

"It is time to change that. If quick, cheap space travel is provided, then anyone with a little entrepreneurial spirit could start up their own asteroid prospecting business. How many people grew wealthy in the Alaskan Gold Rush? Entire families pulled themselves from the muck of poverty and became powers unto themselves, able to determine their own futures, instead of being the puppets of their governments.

"You, Alex, have the ability to cause greatness to come once again to our universe. We need to determine the extent of your ability. I am certain in you is the key to light speed travel. You can unlock the mysteries of Kinemet. Yes. Once we have explored your powers, all you need do is to share your secrets, and everyone will benefit."

Chow Yin smiled benignly upon Alex, but the boy was not looking at his captor. His determination to say nothing was breached with a thought. He had to be sure, be certain that Chow Yin was truly malevolent, and wanted the information inside Alex's head all to himself.

"Why can't I just share it from Earth?" he asked the man. "It would be easy enough to go on the newsvids and tell my story."

Chow Yin shook his head disapprovingly. "But then you would be mobbed by a thousand different organizations, all demanding that you submit yourself to their tests. You would spend the rest of your life like an animal in a zoo. Is that how you envision your future?"

Without waiting for a reply, Yin stood and waved his hand to encompass the room. "Why not share your secret from here, and live in luxury? You would have my protection; I will keep away all the crackpots and unreasonable organizations that would only want to tear you apart to see how you work.

"Stay here with me, and you can choose when and where you share your information. I will be your agent," he suggested. "Your guide, your mentor. Your friend."

"Agent?" Alex had to ask, "Why would I need an agent if I share the information freely?"

"Oh Alex, you have so much to learn about people. If you give someone an ounce freely, they will demand a pound of your flesh, if they take you seriously at all. But if you require that they pay a nominal fee for the license of your information, and a small royalty, then they will be more inclined to deal with you on a professional, serious basis. You will cut through ninety percent of the riffraff.

"I will guide you through this confusing process. You won't have to worry about anything. I will take care of all that needs to be done, present a proposal to the world, and deal with those who are serious enough to line up in wait for your wonderful gift."

Alex could barely believe his ears. It sounded like a speech rehearsed from some bad vid. Did Chow Yin really think Alex only had the mind of a ten-year old? The body, perhaps, but Alex was far more intellectually advanced than that. And he had more insight into people than most pre-adolescents could be credited with.

He had to be careful in dealing with Chow Yin. The man had achieved his incredible wealth somehow, and there was no indication that the means were legitimate. He had hired pirates to kidnap him, attacking a NASA vessel. The man was unscrupulous, and very dangerous.

Best to play along.

"I guess," he said in that offhand agreeable way that most young, naive, children had. "Could I have my own room?"

Chow Yin broke out in a big smile. "Of course." He rubbed his hands together.

39

Quantum Resources, Inc.:
Toronto :
Canada Corp.:

"Michael!"

It was Calbert.

Michael straightened from the desk over which he was leaning, trying to figure out coordinates for a secondary Kinemet survey mission. His assistant's eyes were wild, exhilarated.

"What is it?"

"We did it!" Calbert replied. "We struck Kinemet. They have positive spectrometer readings, identical to the ones George discovered on the Macklin's Rock data. The MS can't define the element, but the characteristics are exactly the same."

Michael never thought this moment would happen. Macklin's Rock was a fluke, he had said to himself half a dozen times a day. An astronomical anomaly. An isolated phenomenon.

But it was true. It was real. It was here.

Kinemet.

"Are you sure?"

Calbert waved a digiscreen report. "Read it for yourself."

Michael had to, in order to completely believe. He was so excited, it was difficult to keep his concentration, and he had to start again three times before he read the entire finding report.

"If the number of asteroids on our list of candidates is only partially valid, there will be more Kinemet out there than we know what to do with!"

It was the time for decisiveness. "All right, begin the excavation procedure as we discussed. I'll talk to the colonel, and get Ottawa on the comm. If this is it, we're going to need maximum security on this. From now on, everything is top shelf. Need to know. I don't want any screw-ups, especially if our communications are being monitored."

"Gotcha, boss." Calbert turned on his heel, and was off at a run, a big grin on his face.

Michael undertook the task of finding the colonel, who was in charge of Quantum Resources, Inc.'s security. He was in the coffee room talking with a couple of his lieutenants, discussing what seemed to be the security of the perimeter of the Quantum Resources outbuildings. He looked up from his conversation when he noticed Michael approach.

"Aces," Michael said, his face caught between a professional stoicism, and a juvenile grin. "We have confirmation of the existence of Kinemet, and I've just ordered the team up on the asteroid to begin excavation. It's time to put your security contingency plan into effect."

The colonel glanced at the digiscreen, raised an eyebrow, and wasted no more time. His implanted comm speaker turned on with a movement of his tongue, and he began issuing orders to his men.

Michael practically vibrated, waiting for the colonel to complete his directive so that they could contact CSE and EMR in Ottawa, and plan a conference to coordinate their security with NASA and the USA, Inc. military.

Before the colonel finished his briefing to his men, he blinked twice, his face taking on a surprised look for an instant. Then his eyes became distant. It was obvious he was getting a private comm on his ear implant receiver.

Trying to contain his anxiety, Michael waited patiently until the colonel's eyes focused on him, his communication terminated.

"Michael, I'm sorry to have to tell you this, but we've been ordered a complete cease and desist of all operations until further notice."

"What? You can't be serious. Not right now! We're on the brink of the most important confirmed discovery in the entire history of the world. We—"

The colonel cut off his growing tirade with a sharp chopping motion.

"There's been an incident on Luna. And," he added with a twist of his mouth, "some politician put a comma in the wrong place in a memo, and pissed off a communist.

"Michael, we're now officially at war with China."

40

Klaus Vogelsberg was deep in concentration.

His DMR screen was aglow with explosions as he tried to maneuver his Starspear through the mass of enemy warships and battle cruisers. If he couldn't get past the globule defenders this time, he swore he was going to kick in the damned computer's casement.

It was a long game, and he hadn't beaten it in eight tries. Each attempt, he had spent hours every night for a week to get to the globule level, only to be defeated. He had never taken so long to beat a computer game. When he mastered this one, he was going to celebrate with a huge toke he'd been saving for just the right occasion.

He was approaching the final vectors of the globule cluster when the door to his room swung open and Marty Middlefield flicked on the overhead lights. Klaus's eyes, unaccustomed to the brightness, were momentarily blinded.

"Hey, jerk-off. Enough time for play." Marty cackled in pleasure.

Klaus leaped out of his seat, the thought-link patch falling to the floor as he bunched his fists.

"You little pain! That's the last time—"

"Stuff it. The big cheese wants you; probably to take a bite out of your bitter ass. And on the double, slacker!"

Klaus hurled a half-full glass of cola at him. The glass, which had no metal content—and thus contained no attractors to Luna Station's magnagravs—sailed out into the hall straighter than any arrow, flying at its target. Marty ducked out of the doorway an instant before the projectile would have impacted with his head. The glass shattered spectacularly against the door of the room opposite Klaus's, the shards falling impossibly slowly to the ground.

"Asshat!" Marty shouted as he ran down the hall.

"I'm gonna make you cry for your mama!" Klaus yelled after the kid, who was three years younger than he was, and had been a constant sore point the past few weeks. To himself, Klaus swore, "If I get my hands around his neck, he won't be dishing out too many more of his little comments, I promise you."

But the message Marty had delivered was more important at that moment than the messenger, however much Klaus wanted to throttle the newcomer.

Yin wanted Klaus. There was no delaying.

Pushing his rage to the back of his mind for future use, Klaus turned off his game, careful to save it, and headed out to Yin's offices, making sure to lock the door to his little room behind him. He didn't want any of the others crawling around his personal space. His room was the only thing he could call his own.

All the while he made his way through the underground complex of Yin's secret empire, Klaus swore to himself. Things had been getting worse and worse over the past few months. Once it was public knowledge about his near-screw-up with the Alex Manez - Macklin's Rock affair, the others who worked for Yin had treated him with disdain.

Trying to distance themselves from him if the figurative meteorite ever hit the dome, the others had treated Klaus as an outcast. Wherever he went, the contemptual glances and mocking comments followed like vultures to carrion.

Klaus had tried to broach the problem with Yin himself, but the old despot had laughed and told him that if he couldn't handle his own problems, he would have to take away Klaus's position and seniority.

A week later, a fistfight with one of the other guys over the incident resulted in a severe reprimand from Yin, and a revoking of certain privileges and Klaus's status as senior monitor. No longer would Klaus be able to create the shift schedule, which had given him the opportunity to dole out to himself the best times; now, he had to take orders from Rick Janzen, a hacker a year younger than him. That grated on Klaus like a sandpaper enema.

In the last month, Marty Middlefield had been recruited to Yin's team of adolescent outlaws, and quickly learned that he could tease

Klaus Vogelsberg with impunity. Nobody would defend Klaus, or allow the older boy to exact his revenge on the newcomer.

Klaus had had enough. He had, in fact, even gone to the lengths of carefully planning every stage of Marty's murder, right down to the celebration he would throw after the little brat was no more than a red stain on the carpet.

A few days before, Klaus had been wandering the main floor of the station, and followed a security officer on his way to dinner. Placing himself at a table nearby, Klaus watched the man withdraw his flechette holster and put the weapon on the table while he dined.

With the patience of dire purpose, Klaus waited, praying mantis-like for any opportunity, and was rewarded when the officer dropped a utensil, and got up to get another one.

Adroitly, Klaus palmed the flechette and holster, and casually found his way out of the diner, and back to his room.

The flechette was the only projectile weapon officially allowed on the station. A bullet, even from a .22, packed enough power to damage any of the protective shells that domed the station and kept out the vacuum and radiation of space. Even Yin proscribed illegal firearms; Luna Station was the only home he would ever have.

The flechette was loaded with a clip of fifty small needle-like projectiles, each containing a small amount of tranquilizer, enough to immobilize a fugitive for up to fifteen minutes.

If Klaus decorated Marty's body with all fifty flechettes, that would be a definite end to the little brat's continuous harassment. That was a fact.

Putting his thoughts of murder on hold, Klaus entered Yin's main office, stood at the doorway until he was noticed and acknowledged.

"Ah!" Chow Yin said when he looked up. The old coot actually looked pleased to see him. "You have arrived."

The potentate stood from his couch, and it was only then that Klaus saw a young boy present and sitting beside Yin patiently.

At first, Klaus did not recognize the youth, but after a moment, realized who he was looking at before Chow Yin introduced him.

"Come on over here for a moment, Klaus. I have someone I would like you to meet. I am sure you have already heard of our guest, by name as well as reputation. You have intimate knowledge of our most honored visitor, since it is by your own devices that he has joined us today.

"Klaus, I would like to present to you, for the first time in the flesh, young Alex Manez. Alex, this is Klaus Vogelsberg, my young protégé, who so aptly discovered you, as it were. Even though you have never met, your destinies have been intertwined for the better part of this last half a year. I do so hope you will enjoy each other's company."

Klaus took a few steps into the room, because it was expected of him, as well as to get a better look at this kid who had sent the entire world—the entirety of Sol System, to wit—into turmoil.

Unimpressed by the kid, Klaus pursed his lips. He glanced up at Yin and blinked.

"Company?"

"Yes." Chow Yin smiled in his patrician manner, and folded his hands in front of himself expectantly. "You see, I am making you directly responsible for our young charge. He has agreed to enter into a joint venture with us to our mutual benefit, and until his potential can be realized, I would like you to see to it that Alex wants for nothing.

"Treat him as a prince; treat him as you would … me, for instance. Cater to his every whim. I want you to be his personal guardian, Klaus."

Without waiting to see Klaus's reaction, Yin turned immediately to Alex Manez, and began reassuring him that he was in the best hands with Klaus Vogelsberg, but Klaus could hear nothing above the roar in his ears.

Guardian! Baby-sitter was more like it. To a freaking ten-year old! Take orders from a little brat!

It was too much. The abuses that had been piling up on Klaus were reaching critical mass. This was no mere straw to break the proverbial camel's back!

The outrage that Klaus felt at that moment threatened to send him into a psychopathic fit, but somehow, he managed to get a rein on it.

Yin was speaking to him once more. "All right, Klaus, see to Alex's accommodations, will you? And bring him for dinner around seven-thirty. He and I have much to discuss. Much to discuss, indeed!"

At least Klaus's father had been direct with his intentions of brutality. Klaus had almost trusted Yin, almost come to respect him as fellow soul, a fellow victim. But now, it turned out Yin was no better than Klaus's own father. Worse, even, for he employed trickery.

It was everything Klaus could do to keep his mouth shut; he had to bite down on his tongue to stifle the cry of indignation that longed to well out of him. The acrid, metallic taste of his own blood served to calm him. A cool wind of icy purpose settled over his thoughts.

Like an automaton, Klaus nodded acknowledgment of Yin's decree. "All right."

Without a word to Alex Manez, Klaus turned on his heel and headed out of Yin's master chambers, leaving the kid to follow as he would.

"Oh," Yin called after Klaus, simultaneously giving his newest prize a gentle nudge forward, "ensure that the other boys do not mistreat young Alex. Should he come to harm of any sort, you can be certain you will receive a severe punishment of the sort only found in your darkest nightmares." He grinned sublimely. "I trust you will take every care with your little ward."

Klaus paused only long enough to reply, "I will treat him like he is my little brother."

"Good. Now, off with you two youngsters." Yin waved paternally to them.

Klaus smiled, but it was motivated by a private thought. *Yeah, I will treat him like you've treated me...*

Outraged at Yin, Klaus turned to Alex as he led the boy silently down the hallway. *You,* he thought, *will regret the day you were born.*

∞

When Klaus got to his room, it was in chaos. The door he had locked was busted wide open, his bed was disheveled, the mattress turned over, and all of his personal belongings were strewn over the floor.

It took Klaus a moment to realize that his computer had also been the object of the vandalism. The screen was on, even though Klaus had turned off his DMR before he left.

His personal cyberscape, which he had spent months designing, was not on the DMR casement. Instead, the default factory desktop was shown. With a feeling of dread, Klaus approached his console, and opened his data manager.

He prompted it to show a list of his files, and saw right away that all the data in his personal folders had been erased. His games, his letters, his notes, his journal—everything.

For a half a minute, he stared at the screen, as if willing this all to have not happened. The earlier rage he felt in Yin's apartment was nothing compared to the anger in him now. At first, he did not even notice the hand that tapped his shoulder.

"Are you all right? What happened?" Alex Manez asked him.

Klaus turned around, and looked at the little kid with eyes that could have been dead.

"Fine. Just fine." He stared at Alex for ten full seconds, not seeing the boy for all the thoughts and plans that went through his mind.

It had to have been Marty Middlefield. Trying to get even, or pulling one of his great jokes at my expense. That's all right. I'll play a little joke on him.

And Yin, threatening ME! Telling me that my ass is grass unless I sit up and play nice like a good little doggie. Well, I'll show him that this dog has more to it than a sharp bark.

I'll fix this little upstart brat, too. He's the root of my problem; but I'll deal with him last.

The plans began forming in his mind, like crystals in a jar of sugar water. How to deal with Yin, Marty, and the little kid behind him.

An evil smile pulled at the corners of his lips as he donned his thought-link patch and opened his meshmail account. All his saved messages, both the ones he had received and the ones he had written, were erased, but Klaus didn't care at that moment.

He wrote a quick memo, and posted it on the Luna Station's Public Bulletin Page, marking it:

!!! URGENT !!! OFFICIAL !!!

Not bothering to turn off his computer, Klaus stood up from his desk, and fell to one knee beside his bed, where he reached underneath and behind a pornographic magazine he had tossed there. When he pulled his hand back out, the flechette pistol he had stolen was in his firm grasp.

Alex backed away, eyes widening. "What are you going to do with that?"

"I'm just going to set a few ground rules."

With that, he strode out of the room, his determined eyes probing the compartment complex. The anger fired deep within him translated easily to his facial features, and some of the other hackers who encountered him on his way stepped back, eyes wide and fearful.

Some followed, but Klaus didn't care. He was past any point of caring about the rest of them. They were all losers, anyway.

As stragglers gathered courage in numbers, and slowly gathered in Klaus's wake, the noise level of the group grew to a jumbled murmur as they speculated what was on Klaus's mind. A few knew about the room being trashed and giggled nervously.

"Marty's gonna get it. Just watch," one said. It only confirmed Klaus's suspicions, and hardened his mind.

Someone asked who the new kid was, but the group was more excited about the fight they saw coming; no one had yet noticed the flechette in Klaus's palm.

When the entourage reached Marty's room, Klaus, ignoring them, kicked in the door, already ajar, and nearly knocked it off its hinges.

"Marty," Klaus growled. "I really enjoyed your *last* practical joke."

Marty, who had been sitting on his bed reading a cybercomic on his digipad, was at first startled, and seemed on the verge of trying to make a break for it, even though his only exit was blocked.

At Klaus's words, Marty's fear was quickly masked by his cockiness. He grinned like a hyena. "I thought you might."

Klaus struggled to remain calm for a few moments more.

"I don't think you understood exactly what I said," he told the younger boy. "I said: I really enjoyed your *last* practical joke. Because, you know, it really will be your *last.*"

"Oh, don't threaten me, you—"

"The time for threats is over. The time for promises is here."

Before Marty could wrap his small mind around Klaus's meaning, Klaus raised his arm straight out, as if to point an accusing finger at the younger boy.

It was then that Marty, and some of the others, saw the flechette.

Marty's shouts of "No!" were matched by some of the other boys, but no one thought to try to stop Klaus before he shot half a dozen needle-like projectiles into Marty's writhing, screaming body.

Somebody tried to jump Klaus, knocking Alex fully into the room, but Klaus, powered by his rage, threw the assailant off, and turned on the group.

"Anyone else tired? Want to sleep for a while? I hear they can revive you from toxic shock if they get to you in time, but you'll be holding conversations with vegetables for the rest of your life."

Everyone backed away.

Reaching out to grab Alex Manez by the collar, he pulled the ten-year old roughly to his feet.

"And you! You're coming with me!"

He dragged Alex behind him as he made his way through the unresisting crowd.

With his thoughts dwelling on the brutal act he had just committed, Klaus did not think about why Alex Manez, who should have been weeping with fright or struggling to get away, simply followed along without a word of complaint or resistance.

Instead, Alex had a contemplative smile on his face.

41

Luna Station :
Chinese Sector :
Luna :

Justine paced.

Occasionally, she snarled as she contemplated the Chinese Sector's stalling. Loud expletives shot out of her whenever she mentioned the Chinese Republic, and their adamant refusal of cooperation, even though they, too, had lost all contact with the Chinese Sector on Luna Station.

"Calm down, Justine," Clive said to her, an attempt at placating the wild beast in his office.

"I can't, dammit! There has to be something we can do! Something!"

"I'm sorry." The diplomat shrugged eloquently. "I'm afraid that our hands are tied at the moment. All that can be done, has."

Justine gestured at him. "We have all our soldiers watching their soldiers, their soldiers watching ours, and neither side actually looking in the right direction. What makes you think that's going to do any good?"

"Do you have another suggestion?"

"Yeah! Let's go in there, get Alex out, and worry about diplomatic relations later."

Clive pressed his lips together disapprovingly. "That might end up worse for everyone," he interposed.

Justine scowled. "I'm not just going to sit on my hands here."

Clive offered Justine a smile of reason. "Our countries on Earth are working on it as quickly as possible. China has long been under the gun from the United Earth Corporate for their centuries-old track record in poor humanitarian relations. Of course, they're reluctant to treat with us. Sakami Chin was something of an olive branch; now, he's gone missing. If, say, Dale Powers had been on assignment in China, and suddenly disappeared, wouldn't your defenses be up as well?"

Justine's scowl turned into a grimace. "Yeah, you're right again, but that doesn't mean I have to like it."

"That's diplomacy. Give it time, Justine. We'll get their cooperation. We're entering the interstellar age; I'm certain China is just jockeying for a better position. Alex is a valuable asset right now, not just because he's a kid, or a representative of 'our' side, but in the potential for space exploration. Everybody believes that boy is the key to interstellar travel. Right now, there isn't anything else to pin our hopes on. That's why the poor child is being fought over like dogs over a bone."

"I know. It stinks."

Clive Wexhall wisely made no rebuff. He wasn't in the business of opinions, anyway. Smoothing things over, calling for cool heads and objective thinking was his strong suit.

"Here, I'll ring down for a few sandwiches. Do you still only drink iced tea, or would you like something with a bit more bite?"

Blinking, Justine was forced to think, however momentarily, about something other than the Chinese Sector and Alex. Clive smiled up at her, pleased to have distracted her turbulent thoughts.

"Uh, no, I'll stick to the iced tea, thank you."

"Certainly." Clive flipped his commlink on, pressed the autodial to the cafeteria and put in the order. Before he could turn off the commlink, an urgent flag began blinking on his meshmail account.

Opening the mail, he read the first few lines, and exhaled.

"What is it?" Justine pressed.

"You've got to read this for yourself." He made room at his desk for Justine to read the correspondence over his shoulder.

∞

To: All Luna Station Account Members

From: A Hostage!

Help! I am being held against my will in the Chinese Sector of Luna Station, along with about two dozen others from different Country Corporations. We are being forced to commit larceny, forgery, theft, and various other international crimes through the

EarthMesh by Chow Yin, an expatriate who has taken over the Chinese Sector and falsified political attachment to the People's Republic of China.

Please, help!

∞

Underneath, there were links to various documents that, when opened, showed the extent of Chow Yin's criminal activities. One document also showed that Chow Yin had forged the identity of the Chinese Consulate, the actual personage not existing anywhere except in computer records.

"Holy Damn!" Clive swore in exhilaration, a wide grin spreading over his face. "We've got it!"

"What? That doesn't do us any good, except as evidence for a trial later on ... or does it?"

Clive, barely able to suppress himself, said, "Do us any good! Of course it does! It proves that there is no official Chinese Government representative present on Luna Station."

"So?"

"Part of the Luna Station Charter specifically states that, in order to maintain claim to the individual sectors of the station—since it is a combinative station, accessible to all—there must be, at all times, a valid representative of each respective government. If there is no Chinese Consulate, and has not been for the past few years, that means that the Chinese no longer have a legitimate claim on that sector until they actually place someone on the property.

"In the meantime, we have a legal ground for going in; backed up by reasonable suspicion of international felonies."

A brief instant passed as Justine absorbed all this. Then, she blinked once. "What are you waiting for? Call in the army!"

The Captain of the *Orcus 1* did not linger while Clive Wexhall made the call to the military adjutant on the station. She turned on her heel, and ran out of the room full bore, heading for the Chinese Sector.

She was determined to be on hand when Alex was rescued, and protect him from further harm.

∞

By the time the army arrived in the Chinese Consulate, and invaded the Sector (backed up by warrants as well as weapons) they discovered from some of the 'hostages' that two of the boys in Chow Yin's adolescent harem of outlaws were missing. One of them, Justine knew by the description, was Alex.

The boy said, "I think they were heading for the airlocks."

Leaving the army to clean up the mess of the Chinese Sector, Justine took off at a run.

She was damned if she was going to let Alex get away now, when he was so close.

42

Lunar Surface :
Luna :

The surface of the Moon had a calming effect on Alex. He couldn't quite pinpoint what brought on his reaction, but the gentle rumbling of the electric motor in the ATV, combined with the rocking motions as the vehicle headed overland called to mind a certain serenity that Alex found ultimately appealing.

Beside him, driving the vehicle, was a lunatic; only seventeen years old, but a maniac nevertheless. Alex should have been trying to escape this young psychopath's influence, railed against his captivity, fought against the inevitable conclusion of this misadventure—that Klaus wanted him dead. Instead, Alex found himself willingly accompanying the older boy.

There was something beyond his mind's grasp, urging him on.

The Moon seemed almost like home, to Alex. It was barren, desolate, and uninhabitable by anyone unless they were safely wrapped in the cocoon of technology. And yet, Alex was at peace with it. The vastness of space, horrible to most, was a black blanket of comfort to him. And the Moon was the signatory of that unimaginable expanse.

The Earth represented suppression, claustrophobia—everything inherently opposite of outer space. Alex never wished to return there. Even though they had spent most of their life on Canada Station Three, Alex's parents still called Earth home sweet home. Alex's only memories were visiting Earth irregularly on yearly vacations, holidays and such. It was as much an alien planet to him as was Jupiter.

…And it would be nothing more than a prison if Alex ever returned there.

Suddenly, Alex realized why the Moon inspired such tranquility in him, beyond the murderous intents of his companion.

The voices in his head no longer made demands of him, no longer stalked his thoughts. Instead, the melody of their words was that of a comforting lullaby.

Soon, they promised, you will be made aware of all that is. We have no need of haunting you into action; you are already firmly set on your course of destiny.

Be calm. Soon, you will return to where you belong.

Alex turned his head slowly toward Klaus and smiled benignly.

∞

Klaus nearly veered into a small crater when he glanced to the side and saw his captive grinning back at him like some kind of retarded baboon.

"What the hell are you smiling at?" Klaus hissed after he regained control of the ATV and put the vehicle back on course.

They were going way too slowly. Klaus didn't want to take any chances. If the damned yahoo Americans hadn't used his message as a political loophole to invade the Chinese Sector and take down Yin's empire, then Chow Yin was going to be on the warpath for Klaus. When Yin wanted revenge, he didn't waste time about it. There would be a dozen ATVs after him and Alex, each carrying men with real guns that fired bullets, not poison-dipped flechettes.

And even if the Americans had gone through with their task the way Klaus hoped, they would soon learn about him, and that he had kidnapped Alex. Their prize would be too great to ignore for long. Any way he looked at it, Klaus was going to be a very wanted person.

Because of Alex.

He looked the kid square in the face for a moment. Alex hadn't replied to his question, nor had he ceased his smiling, although he had turned his attention to the Lunarscape ahead.

"Quit that grinning, you fool. What do you have to be so happy about. You know that I'm going to kill you, don't you?"

Alex slowly rotated his head. "No, you're not."

Klaus's nerves caused him to jerk the steering bar of the ATV a bit, not enough to put them in jeopardy, though. Damn the kid. How had he known that Klaus had changed his mind about offing the little kid?

Over the past fifteen minutes, Klaus had also been taken with the tranquility of the lunar surface, and had done some thinking.

Revenge was good and all, but if he continued his spree of violence and mayhem, there was only one possible end to the whole affair: his own death. People would not put up with that sort of behavior for long, and would quickly organize to stop Klaus's rampage.

Alex was a valuable commodity, perhaps even the most valuable commodity in Sol System.

And at the moment, Klaus had complete control of him. Yin had schemed to use Alex to gain personal wealth, and that would have been due solely to Klaus's efforts. What would Klaus have gotten for his troubles? Nothing.

But now, Klaus could use Alex to his own gain. No partners, no bosses, no fathers; nobody but him.

He had no aspirations of mining the depth of Alex's reported abilities. He didn't have the time or the inclination. Instead, he would settle for a modest ransom. The Americans or the Canadians would surely pay up. Klaus was not greedy; a few million dollars would keep him happy for the rest of his life.

Klaus knew exactly who he could turn to for help: the very same smuggler who had pirated Alex from the *Orcus 1,* his uncle, Trent Gruber. Captain Gruber would *have* to help Klaus. He was willing to offer his uncle a healthy percentage. If that didn't work, and the smuggler was unwilling to participate, Klaus had enough blackmail material on him to send him to United Earth Corporate prison for the rest of his natural life, relative or not.

Gruber, brother to Klaus's long-deceased mother, had a small base on Luna, a few hundred kilometers away from Luna Station. That was where Klaus was heading.

But how had Alex known that Klaus's intentions had changed?

"What do you mean, I'm not going to kill you?"

"I won't let you," Alex replied simply. "I have far too great a purpose to allow that to happen. I need you to help me, though."

"Help you? What for?"

"That is my business. I can tell you no longer want to murder me. You have something else in mind. Extortion, ransom, something like that. I've read enough space opera to guess that you've got a plan for squirreling me away. All I want is for you to bring me to your hiding place, and keep me there for a while. Help me, and I guarantee you will be rich."

"And what if I don't happen to want to go along with your stupid little plan, pipsqueak?"

The answer came in a form that was a thousand times more effective than any verbal threat. The ATV's electric motor ceased to fire, and the vehicle slowly came to a standstill. "What the—?"

Klaus's breathing apparatus slowly stopped pumping air into his helmet. Klaus was soon inhaling the same air he was exhaling, and the oxygen content was dropping as fast as the carbon monoxide level was rising. He would quickly poison himself if he didn't get any air.

Panicking, Klaus began flailing about, desperate for a lungful of clean, life-giving air.

He had the presence of mind enough to realize he could get air from only one source. "All right! All right! You win! I'll do whatever you say, only give me some—"

The influx of oxygen was like cool water washing over a feverish forehead, a warm fire in the arctic cold.

Klaus took several deep breaths, remembered that he shouldn't inhale so deeply, or the oxygen itself would adversely affect him, and slowly, slowly, evened his breathing.

The ATV's motor flared to life, and Alex said, "Come on, Klaus. Let's get going."

"You know," Klaus said once he had his breath back and his nausea firmly under control, "you really are a little shit."

43

SELECTED ARTICLES :
FROM WORLD ASSOCIATED PRESS :

JUNE 2091

In an historic move, United Earth Corporate Council has abolished the long-standing Luna Charter in favor of a direct administration. Spurred by recent events involving a Chinese expatriate who managed to usurp most of Luna Station's resources and property, an act which nearly brought the UEC to the brink of an international incident with China, the UEC has penned a new charter nullifying all land claims on Luna Station by country corporation and individual corporations. An official explained that the Station will be independent of any country corporation's political influence, and in the future, the UEC will lease space on Luna Station on a yearly renewal basis.

JULY 2091

The Chinese Ambassador is in New York today, for the first of six scheduled meetings attempting to bridge the gap between Western Corporate philosophy, and the long-standing Republic philosophy that has been a cornerstone of Chinese politics for centuries. In a statement issued prior to the first meeting, the ambassador reasserted that his government would not hold NASA or any other agency responsible for the kidnapping of Sakami Chin on Luna Station seven months ago. He also expressed an interest in continuing to build a dialog between the two great nations in order to further the newest science of Kinemetics. The Chinese, who own more than a hundred asteroid mines, have revealed suspicions that one or more of their asteroids may have the faster-than-light supraconductor element called

Kinemet.

AUGUST 2091

The second Pluto mission has successfully launched this morning at 6:23 a.m. local time at Kennedy Space Port. The *Orcus 2* is a joint mission between NASA and CSE with a mandate to further investigate the artifact known as *Dis Pater*, and study its relationship to the Kinemetic influence known as the Manez Effect. With pressure from the European Space Agency as well as the Japanese and South American Organizations, NASA has begun to organize a third Pluto mission, *Orcus 3,* and has invited representatives from every nation to accompany the flight to our farthest planet. Captain Justine Churchill Turner, Captain of both the *Orcus 1* and *Orcus 2,* is scheduled to helm the third mission as well.

NOVEMBER 2091

A NASA spokeperson has announced in a press release today that surveyors have discovered a small cache of the element Kinemet on the small asteroid, Nimow. According to preliminary tests, Dr. Caven Oahe estimates that the 102kg find contains enough potential energy to send a ship to Centauri and back. Although the Jet Propulsion Lab, in conjunction with Quantum Resources of Canada Corp., has not yet released a timetable, sources indicate that designs for such an interstellar craft are in the works. Physicists and Engineers at the University of South Carolina estimate the first light speed ship could be ready within four years.

MARCH 2092

In today's technological society, organized religion has long been relegated to history books and small gatherings in basements. But in Central America, there is a growing religious movement that some say is a doomsday cult. The Mayan Spiritualists, who have been gaining in number over the past year and a half, foresee the end of the world's civilizations as they stand. When asked, a high-standing member of the organization indicated that, as the Mayan Culture was once the most advanced society in the world, it will again inherit mastery of the Earth.

MARCH 2092

Scientists from the *Orcus 2* have not been able to discover the origin or intent of the Plutonian artifact, *Dis Pater*. After weeks of investigation, members of the *Orcus 2* mission are no closer to solving the puzzle of the huge monolith on the Dark Planet. A NASA spokeswoman says this is not unexpected. The last time the artifact showed any kind of activity was during the first Orcus mission, when it responded to the triggering of the element, Kinemet. The *Orcus 2* mission is not mandated to conduct any Kinematic experiments; instead, that will be reserved for the *Orcus 3* mission, an undertaking which will be shared by all active space agencies of the Earth. The *Orcus 2* will takeoff from Pluto tomorrow morning, and is scheduled to arrive on Luna in an estimated six months.

AUGUST 2092

Quantum Resources Inc. of Toronto, Canada Corp. has released the latest results of its joint research project with the JPL of NASA. The mystery of Kinemet, once referred to as Element X, has been solved. With recent discoveries of Kinemet deposits on more than twenty asteroids in the past year, research has been shifted into high gear, and has yielded fantastic results, says a Quantum Resources spokesman. "It is only a matter of time before we can outfit an interstellar ship with a Kinemet-powered engine." The complete report on Kinemet can be found on the Quantum Resources Meshsite, mirrored at NASA.

NOVEMBER 2092

The *Orcus 2* has returned to Earth, and its seven-member crew is in debriefing in Houston. NASA and CSE declare the mission a success, even though very little new information has been accumulated on the artifact, *Dis Pater*. A complete sensor array was left behind on Pluto to document any future reaction from the artifact.

JANUARY 2093

NASA and CSE have announced the upcoming schedule for the test launch of the first interstellar spacecraft. The *Quanta,* as the ship has been dubbed, is a one-man ship designed without a payload. Its primary mission will be to achieve the first recorded light speed flight. The ship will travel from Luna Station to Pluto, where it will rendezvous with the *Orcus 3* mission for the jet-propelled return trip. A date for the launch has not been announced, but analysts from the Canadian Astronomy Association say the next window for a flight to Pluto will be October 2094, landing on the farthest planet seven months later, approximately May 2095. The most probable date for the light speed test flight will be then.

OCTOBER 2094

Major Justine Churchill Turner is on her way to Pluto for the third time. The *Orcus 3* successfully blasted off Luna Station early this afternoon. Three and a half years ago, Major Turner played a key part in the capture of international criminal Chow Yin on Luna Station; she is something of a celebrity there, with a planetarium named after her.

Of historical note, Major Turner is a descendant of Percival Lowell, the astronomer who first theorized the existence and possible location of Pluto.

MARCH 2095

NASA has announced the name of the pilot who will take the helm of the first light speed flight. Captain Mitchel Kincardine of Canadian Space Exploration has been selected from nearly three hundred qualified applicants to undertake this historic mission. Capt. Kincardine, father of two, has long been a pilot for CSE.

APRIL 2095

The *Quanta,* NASA/CSE's interstellar spacecraft, which is scheduled to make the first light speed flight next month, is en route to Luna Station where it will be outfitted with a Kinemet engine and tested in zero gravity a few thousand kilometers above the Moon's surface. Captain Kincardine is accompanying the ship, and has been quoted as saying that he is looking forward to seeing his name written alongside those of Christopher Columbus, Yuri Gagarin, and Neil Armstrong.

44

The unrelenting chorus repeated itself in his mind, and had done so for four long years.

The sounds of the planets were slowly driving him insane with their message of urgency.

Come to us, Alex. Come to us.

He was working towards that as fast as he could, but he had to wait for others.

Wait.

Always wait.

Watching every move, reading every word published, communicating with others who could provide him with any scraps that would help him complete his task.

They had announced a date, and he had to shift his preparations into high gear.

The Music of the Spheres told him so.

Come to us, Alex. Come.

45

The *Quanta* :
Luna Station :
Luna :

May 2095

Alex Manez took a deep, agonizing breath and ran his fingers through the thin wisps of his hair, once long and luxurious.

The fourteen-year old then strapped himself into the leather-back pilot seat of the spacecraft and began systematically flipping switches, turning dials, and pressing specific buttons on the panoramic console surrounding him in the cockpit. Every so often, he took readings from the diagnostics readouts and consulted the computer monitor, rechecking this figure or that.

He had to be sure that everything was running smoothly at this stage of the game. A project of this magnitude would ordinarily require the input and coordination of hundreds of personnel, and Alex was completely on his own. Alex was also undertaking this task of his without the permission of those hundreds.

Alex was stealing the light speed ship they had dubbed, the *Quanta*.

The highly experimental vessel was owned by the United Earth Corporate. Each member country had invested heavily in the project with the hopes of reaching the outer planets of Sol System in a matter of hours, rather than the months that it took at present.

Because of the unusual mission assigned to the *Quanta,* the only means of piloting and navigating the craft was via the onboard computer—the mission control's part was only an observe-and-assist position.

Because Alex could manipulate electrical machines, it was child's play to create enough distractions in the lunar hangar for him to pass unnoticed.

Once Alex had snuck onto the ship where it had been temporarily docked in Luna Station's port—all the while ensuring no one else was yet on board—it had taken him only a few minutes to orient himself and take command of the vessel.

The first thing he did was to disconnect all online communications with the mission control centers on the Station and on Earth. The only link he kept alive was to the docking computer, which, in turn, he had already fixed with a virus that would recognize launch requests from him, but disregard any commands from other sources.

Then he secured the hull, locked the ship electronically, and, finally, after obtaining the proper launch permission from the station's docking computer, he fired the ship's main engines. He had to do this before setting the trajectory and acceleration controls—the ignited jet fuel of the mundane engines would keep the security force that had just arrived at the port well away from the *Quanta* while Alex went through the rest of the preliminary launch procedures. Oxygen control, cabin pressure, launch stats—all checked. He reset diagnostics one more time, and aligned the launch trajectory to put him in a gosling orbit following Mother Moon once he lifted off. He could not rely on the mission control computer. Access to that resource was denied him.

As Alex programmed the ship, and prepared for takeoff, he smiled. It was the first time he had smiled in years, ever since returning to translunar space from Pluto.

Getting aboard the *Quanta* and pirating it had been easy; it would have put the Nova Pirates to shame. Nobody paid attention to a fourteen-year old wandering about.

He was certain no one would recognize him.

Four years ago, once the search for him had been exhausted, the world had turned their attention to developing Kinemet and their precious *Quanta* spacecraft. He had been left by the wayside to sink or swim on his own.

It was a simple bargain he had made with Captain Gruber and Klaus. They sheltered him in their station for the duration, and he loaned them his services. Alex did not participate in their illegal activities, but he was the perfect early warning system for when security patrols gave surprise inspections. And with his ability to scan more than a hundred kilometers away, he often accompanied them on salvage hunts and could detect wrecked vessels to which Captain

Gruber could lay claim. It was a profitable arrangement for both parties.

It was only after a few months of his stay that Alex had started to develop the debilitating sickness in his bone marrow. Lunar gravity had helped prolong complete dysfunction, so long as he avoided any area powered by gravitons, but it was only a matter of time before a single step would shatter his bones.

Like Chow Yin.

It was the exposure to Kinemet that had done this to him. He knew it as well as he knew that to drink a liter of strychnine was to ensure you did not see tomorrow.

He also knew that, in order to save his own life, he needed once again to come in contact with Kinemet. Over the past years, his powers had faded somewhat, but even being within a hundred meters of the fantastic super-metal now onboard the *Quanta,* he was already feeling rejuvenated.

The launch countdown began, the numbers displaying on his DMR Casement.

10 – 9 – 8 – 7 – 6 – 5 – 4 – 3 – 2 – 1 … Launch.

Alex tried to imagine the looks on the faces of those few hundred people at Mission Control, as well as those observing from the station lounges as they watched the eighteen-billion-dollar *Quanta* being hijacked on its maiden voyage. Alex wasn't mischievous by nature, but just to see the surprise on their faces…

The *Quanta*, all thirty meters and 29.82 metric tons of it shuddered as the mundane jet-powered rockets started pushing the vehicle up and out of the launch port, giving off enough thrust to accelerate the ship above the 2.4 kps required to escape the Moon's gravitational influence.

The ship picked up speed at an alarming rate.

Below, he knew, people would be scurrying about in a panic. They would try to figure out how he had overridden their security redundancies and cracked the internal security codes.

Alex had managed to interface with both the *Quanta*'s computer and the Luna Station port computer without alerting the electronic alarm reticulums from Mission Control, or from Luna Station itself.

Most of all, they would try to figure out how he had gotten onboard the craft, waiting until the ship had been vacated for a mere five minutes while the ground crew offloaded, and the pilot had been preparing to come onboard.

Yes, the electropathic power had faded, but it was still there, to use as he wished. And little Alex had used that power.

The *Quanta* required 737,765 kilopascals of thrust just to escape the Moon's gravity. Ordinarily, a ship of comparable size would need less than half that output. The extra thrust was needed because of the Kinemet store in the Kinemetic engine attachment, which increased the ship's overall mass by nearly 175%.

All of the requisite information of the mission and operation of the *Quanta* was ingrained in Alex's photographic mind—another side-effect from his exposure to the Kinemet on Macklin's Rock; the exposure that had cost his parents their lives.

It was almost second nature, even though he had physically never performed the operations himself, to guide the ship out beyond the gravity well of the Moon. He drifted out and away, and slowly decreased the engine thrust until he fell behind the Moon's trajectory around the Earth. Once he had attained an orbit around the Earth mimicking Luna's, he increased thrust to match the Moon's 3,700 kilometers-per-hour velocity.

When the onboard computer confirmed a stable orbit, Alex cut the engines, took a deep breath and reveled in his accomplishment.

Even if it ended here, he would be satisfied. How many fourteen-year-olds had successfully flown a spacecraft by themselves, and achieved a stable orbit around the Earth?

But there was so much more to do.

Alex leaned back into his seat and wiped his forehead with his sleeve. Already the null-gravity was taking much of the pressure off his laboring lungs, and his bones seemed to be getting stronger every minute. He was in his environment; he could never leave the Kinemet for any extended amount of time; that was a fact of his life, now.

Glancing at the digital clock on the console, he noted that the entire procedure had taken less than six hours. To Alex, every second he was free of the Earth and the Moon was an eternity to be cherished forever. The familiar comfort of the Kinemetic influence so close to him was enough to make him cry with joy. He could already feel his bones knitting, his health restored to him. If he wanted to make it all count for something, he couldn't quit now.

Running his fingers expertly over the keyboard, he brought up the current flight stats and requested a quick diagnostic scan of internal systems. Everything was up and functional.

For the next part of Alex's plan, however, he had to contact Mission Control on Luna Station. Even though he had cracked into their computer and downloaded every byte of information stored within, the fact that so many countries had worked together on this project—countries that were by nature untrusting—had precluded the omission of many of the more sensitive mission objectives and data.

He needed those to continue with the mission; more specifically, the cooperation of the Director of NASA, William Tuttle, who had temporarily traveled to Earth's Moon for the occasion, along with many other top-shelf space executives from differing agencies. Michael Sanderson, Lassen Kruger, Vic Tong, Tung Jo, Henry Franks, to name a few.

It would be nearly impossible to persuade them, but there was no other option. Alex had to convince them of that.

Alex reached over to the console and flipped the AV switch. Indicator lights came to life, and abruptly, two-way communication was established with the Mission Control center on Luna Station.

His DMR casement revealed a frantic Ops room. Dozens of administrative clerks, techies, computer operators and even a few Canadian, American, and Japanese soldiers were rushing around in a heated frenzy of activity.

It took a few moments for one of the technicians to notice that his monitor was active and showing the smiling face of a fourteen-year-old boy seated in the command chair of the *Quanta*.

The man hastily thrust his ear-mask on and started flipping switches and pressing buttons. He leaned in to his microphone.

"This is Luna Station Mission Control for Operation *Quanta* chartered under the authority of the United Earth Corporate Council. I hereby order you to cease and desist all activity and prepare to be boarded by a tug which we will shortly be sending to rendezvous at your position. Young man, you are in deep shit!" His face was bunched up with rage.

Alex cocked his head, deciding not to take offense at the man's inflammatory remark. "Please get someone with authority on the line," he requested politely. "Preferably Director—"

A new face popped into view. Michael Sanderson, the Director of Quantum Resources, was aging by the minute. His shirt was bereft of a tie, and the top two buttons were undone. Sweat glistened off his forehead, and the look on his face was a mix of desperation and outrage. He was getting up there in years. The trip to the Moon had cost him.

∞

Michael recognized Alex as the hijacker, rather than some industrial spy or foreign agent they had obviously all suspected. Since Alex's kidnapping four years before by Chow Yin, when the Chinese felon had pirated the *Orcus 1,* relations between the People's Republic of China and the rest of the world had been more than strained.

Michael quickly recovered from his surprise, and donned an ear-mask as he struggled to find his voice. "Alex Manez. You remember me?"

"Yes, Director. Quite well, as a matter of fact. I have nothing but respect for you; I know you tried to do right by me. It is not your fault. I don't blame you for my parents. I just wanted to let you know that. What I'm doing now is motivated by none of those things directly."

"—Well, if I had never come in contact with Kinemet in the first place, none of us would be in this position today."

"So are you taking the ship hostage for some reason? I assume this is not just a joy ride." The edge to Michael's voice betrayed his conflicting emotions. It was as plain as the nose on his face that he was having a difficult time trying to come to grips with the fact that an adolescent had just stolen a multi-billion dollar space craft right out from under his watchful gaze.

"No," Alex confirmed. "This is no joy ride, I assure you. It's a matter of survival."

"I see." The Director put his hand over the microphone and started dispensing orders to the dozen people that had congregated around the DMR casement. Finally, he turned back to Alex.

"You seem to know a lot about computer security, space travel, and this mission in particular."

"You'd be surprised what you can find on the mesh."

Cocking his head in a conciliatory gesture, Michael replied, "No, I wouldn't be. But that still doesn't explain how you obtained access to sensitive mission parameters. There are no hard copies, and the only electronic copy is stored on my portable."

"Do you remember the big splash about my clairvoyant ability, sir?"

219

"Yes."

"Well, I never revealed the extent. It has waned somewhat, but—"

"Somewhat?"

"I don't have my full capability, but the ability still exists. It is difficult, but from a room away, I can easily psychically peer over someone's shoulder and see what they are reading on their portables."

"Oh." Michael seemed to be trying to place exactly when and where Alex might have been in close enough proximity to perform the task he had just described, but the fact of the matter was that on Luna Station, the opportunities were abundant.

"I apologize for putting you all in this position, but there are facts that I have that you don't," Alex said.

"All right, then why don't you fly that spacecraft back here and land it. I will ensure a team of specialists, including myself, gives you ample opportunity to present your facts to us."

"It's not as simple as that, sir. You see, I'm dying. My bones cannot stand any more gravitational pressure. The very Earth has rejected me. It is the Kinemet, sir. None of your test pilots has ever been exposed to it when it is active in space. Only three people have that dubious distinction, and two of them, my parents, are dead as a result.

"The Kinemet offers wonderful things to whoever accepts its embrace. A kind of far sight similar to clairvoyance, electrokinesis, eidetic imagery with no retroactive inhibition; all the skills necessary for light-speed flight. You've tried to compensate with redundant computer profiles and even put an untested pilot onboard to physically return power to the ship once the flight has terminated.

"I assure you, Director, all these precautions will end in disaster. You do not yet comprehend the power of Kinemet. Compared with simple atomics, Kinemet is like trying to describe color to a blind man. My eyes have been opened by Kinemet, and I can't tell you what I've seen.

"I can guide others to the light of this power, but there is a cost, which I am paying every day and with every codeine pill I swallow. I am exiled forever from Earth, and from every planet that has any significant gravity well.

"You should know this already, but in your ignorance, you've overlooked the facts."

"I'm sorry, Alex. If you would just come in, perhaps we could try to—"

"You still don't get it, do you!" Alex shouted at the Director. Taking a moment to compose himself, and get his emotions under control, Alex breathed deeply. "I don't blame you, sir. You can't understand. You have nothing to relate this to. That's why I have to take matters into my own hands."

"What do you plan on doing, Alex?"

"Isn't it obvious?" the young man replied.

Michael shook his head. "No. I'm sorry, but it isn't."

"I plan on fulfilling your mission. I know everything about it, even the classified aspects. I know that there is more involved here than you have released to the public—I know where you are sending this space ship.

"Of course, both of us realize that the *Quanta* is perfectly capable of withstanding light speed flight, capable of harnessing the small amount of Kinemetic energy it will release, that your precautions to safeguard the small payload will bear fruit, and that this mission has a better-than-ninety-nine percent chance of succeeding."

Alex lowered his voice as he continued.

"However, I also know that under your mission parameters, the ship will never return to Earth, and neither will the pilot."

He paused for effect, his face growing serious. "Your pilot has a family, Mr. Sanderson. I know he does not have a wife or children, but he has a mother and a father, grandparents, a sister in Tacoma with a husband and three kids of her own; two nephews and a niece who will never see him again.

"I have nothing to lose, no family, no ties; and everything to gain—my life, my future, my own personal survival. Secondly, if this mission fails, you know as well as I that the political situation on Earth will preempt any subsequent missions by at least a decade, or perhaps forestall them forever if war breaks out. Everyone is trying to claim the discovery for themselves, vying for position out among the stars when they have not even left the comfort of their armchairs. If there is going to be light speed space travel, the piloting can only be undertaken by those like me. Those directly exposed to the radiation of Kinemet without the protection of an ion-nullified protection receptacle.

"So you see, I am your best option."

"You can't be serious!" blurted the Director. "You can't understand the ramifications, the—"

"I understand completely, Mr. Sanderson. You should know that as well as anyone.

"—As I have told you, Kinemet offers wonderful advantages. But the cost is much higher than you can understand. Given a choice, I would take my parents back. But I'm up against the wall. I don't have the resources to live in null-gravity for the rest of my life; and this mission will be a disaster without me—unless you wished to postpone until you can expose one of your test pilots to the effects of unshielded Kinemetic radiation. And that would permanently damn him, exile him from ever living on Earth."

Michael averted his eyes from Alex's balding head, his pigmentless face, and the atrophy his muscles showed. "No, we cannot postpone the flight."

"It seems to me that it is in your best interest to cooperate with me on this." Alex waited for their decision.

"What if we do decide to abort?"

Alex shook his head. "As I have said, without this, I have nothing. It would be better for me to point this ship at the Sun, see how much of a tan I can get.

"However, if you let me undertake this mission in place of Captain Kincardine, I will cooperate with you one-hundred percent, and you will get everything out of this experiment that you had hoped for. You may think I don't know what I am doing, but let me assure you that I have read and memorized—and understood—every byte of information I could find."

The Director just stared at him for a long time. Finally, he spoke. "Alex, I think we need a few minutes here to confer."

"Of course. The flight window will stay open for another fourteen hours. Take all the time you need."

∞

Alex turned off his casement, terminating communication.

He took a deep breath to calm himself.

They would be racing through his file trying to find some foothold on him, some way to rationalize all of this, find some way to convince him not to go through with his madness. Everything about Alex, his parents, his life, was in that file, he knew. But no matter how many different ways they tried to sort the information, they would have no choice but to accept that Alex's offer was the only option they would have. His back was to the wall, and so was theirs.

Nevertheless, Director Sanderson would try to talk him out of it. Alex was ready for the argument.

He reached over and took a heavy three-ring binder labeled 'TOP SECRET' off a hook on the edge of the console. The manual contained the specific instructions and procedures for the safe operation of the *Quanta*. It also contained mission directives for the pilot once his destination had been achieved.

Alex had not had access to this manual before, since it was never kept on computer file, and the only two copies had been kept on board the ship for security reasons. He decided to take advantage of the time and read it.

First, he checked the monitors to ensure the ship was still on course in stable orbit following the Moon. Satisfied, he leaned back into the pilot's chair and opened the manual to the first page, memorizing the book word for word, as he read.

∞

Halfway through the book he noticed a light flashing on his console indicating an incoming call from the launch control center. He flipped on his monitor to reveal Mike Sanderson once more.

"I assume you've considered my proposal," Alex said, tossing the manual on to a shelf—it began floating away, and he hastily snatched it out of the air and hooked it on the wall again before the Director noticed.

Sanderson ran his fingers through his mussed hair before answering, "Yes. We've discussed this at length."

"Then you see why you have no choice, why you can't talk me down?"

"Yeah," the Director sighed. "But I still can't allow you to go on with this."

"Why?" Alex demanded.

"I have superiors—there are the authorities—a dozen reasons: like you're unqualified, underage, and possibly insane—oh, Alex, why don't you just come down from there? Nobody here in their right mind will let you go through with this!"

"No!" shouted Alex. "If you don't have the authority to approve this, then get someone who does! Get the damned CEOs of USA, Inc.

and Canada Corp. if you have to!" he demanded.

Michael looked at him with a sympathetic look that Alex did not want.

Grasping for straws, Alex added: "Don't you realize that at the very least I am saving the pilot's life by taking his place?"

"Alex, that pilot is fully aware of the risks he is taking and fully cognizant of all of the factors involved."

"So am I!"

"No, you're not!" the Director yelled in frustration. A hand on his shoulder stopped him from saying anything more. Somebody whispered in his ear and he turned back to Alex with a haggard sigh.

"Director William Tuttle is coming up to Ops; he wants talk to you as soon as he gets here."

Michael leaned closer, as if everyone in the center could not already hear every word that had passed between the two. "Alex, I'm sure you won't get in very much trouble if you just come down right now. You'll save all of us so much hassle."

"No. If it's all the same to you, Mr. Sanderson, I think I will wait and talk with the Director."

"Fine," answered Michael, and in frustration he turned off the monitor.

Alex had time recheck the flight stats, as well as go back into the cargo bay to make sure he had enough food and water, and also had time to finish off the manual before he got a call from the Director of NASA.

While he was reading the manual, he looked over at the pull-ring set in the wall many times—it was the final test in this mission, the final test that would bring Alex to the apex of his life—but first he would have to win past the Director of NASA.

He turned on the monitor when it blinked to notify him of an incoming link.

"Hello, Alex," said an older man. He was sitting next to Michael with another headset on and smiling disarmingly at Alex.

Alex immediately grew wary. "Hello, sir," he answered, a bright smile on his face.

"Oh, you just call me Bill, son," the Director offered in a sprawling Georgian accent. "Now, you've got an awful bunch of folks here up in arms about you, uh, appropriating that vehicle. Now, why don't you just bring it back down here and give these nice folks a break?"

"I'm afraid I can't do that, Bill," Alex replied in a condescending tone to match the Director's. Tuttle kept his unwavering smile as Michael started whispering in his ear. The microphones couldn't pick up what was said, but Alex knew just the same—they were talking about him.

When Sanderson finished his monologue, the Director focused his smiling attention back on Alex.

"Hmmn. It seems here that we have what my folks back home would call a dilemma. But I'm gonna make an administrative decision here and, considering your case and the situation at hand, I'm gonna instruct Mission Control here to go on with the operation as if you were the regular pilot. However," he added in an aside to Michael, also meant for Alex's ears, "since nobody but ourselves in this here room knows what's just transpired, we're gonna keep it hush-hush. No one is to know about our li'l switcheroo."

"What?" Alex demanded, nearly jumping from his seat. His head fogged a little as he saw his name being wiped from all future textbooks. No one would know him, no one would know what he had done—and that was half the reason why he had undertaken this project of his in the first place! But now it would be all for naught!

"Oh, sorry, son," the Director said quickly. "But we are just like a little mouse forced into a corner by a cat. We have to let you do this, else we stand to lose an awful bunch of the taxpayer's money. But if the public ever got wind that we let a fourteen-year-old go on such a mission, why we'd never hear the end of it."

"But—" Alex began, eyes wide, brimming with tears.

The Director raised a hand to quell the protest. "However, we have to come up with some name to satisfy the history books—especially since our other pilot will be about and alive. I'm sure the Director here can quickly make up a pilot file under the name 'Alex Manez'. And I'm sure that Michael's people at the Government in Ottawa will be more than obliged to change your birth date officially to make it seem as if you were old enough to go on this here mission. I'm sure I can get NASA and the Pentagon to come around. Now, will that satisfy you, son?"

Alex sank back into the pilot's chair in relief. The main reason he was doing this was for his parents' benefit. They had lost their lives for Kinemet. If Alex could make use of the new element, make it a success, then his parents' deaths would have meaning to him. But that hadn't been the only driving force behind his decision, that hadn't been what had forced him across the final length of the Lunar tarmac and into the *Quanta*.

The past few years he had been nothing but a freaky little kid who limped like an old man—a spectacle, a sideshow attraction to be goggled at for a few minutes, then discarded. No one paid attention to him. He wanted the world to know his name as a person, to know he had changed the course of history.

But even if posterity remembered him as a slightly different, slightly older Alex Manez, then all was well. He would be known, and his parents' deaths would have meaning.

"Yes, Sir," Alex answered finally, "that's all right by me." Alex knew the Director did not give a damn about him, and only acted with the propensity of an administrator trying to meet an end. That suited Alex just fine.

The Director smiled even wider. "All right, then." He turned to Michael in an aside that Alex could hear. "I trust you can take matters from here?"

"Yes, sir," came the muted reply. The Director removed the head set and, with a nod and smile to Alex, moved out of the way of the technicians and controllers to let them get on with the experiment.

∞

Because of the nature of the new element, the Kinemetic reaction would disable all electronic systems on the ship. As with Macklin's Rock, there had been no energy left to even power the security receptacles. This phenomenon had been studied at length, and, the techs thought, solved.

Alex stared at the pull-ring placed a few inches below the manual.

The techs had surmised that a kick-start could return power to all systems. Once he reached his destination, the pilot would have about ten seconds to grab that ring and pull it...

Or so they thought.

Alex knew better. The kick-start would not be enough to overcome the Kinemetic influence. The pilot would die out in space from lack of oxygen, or lack of heat, whichever got to him first. Although he would be exposed to the Kinemetic power, and become clairvoyant and electropathic as Alex was, the pilot would not have enough time to orient himself, and develop that ability. It had taken Alex a few days to be able to grasp the power and wield it effectively.

Only someone with the electropathic ability could restart the power generator. Someone like Alex. He would explain this to Mission Control later, when he had proved his theory.

He got a signal from ground control: they were beginning the secondary countdown.

10 ... 9 ... 8 ... 7 ... 6 ... 5 ... 4 ... 3 ... 2...

Alex took a deep breath and closed his eyes as they reached the number 1...

... and then he was struggling for reality.

His vision doubled, faded, tripled, doubled, refocused; his hearing echoed, muted, expanded; his sense of touch was beyond description.

Time was nothing.

Four hours to Pluto?

It was merely four instants for Alex.

46

USA, Inc. Exploration Site :
Mission *Orcus 3* :
Pluto :

Justine stood on the edge of Sol System with bated breath. For the first time in four years, *Dis Pater* was reacting once again.

With the exception of Sakami Chin, who had been recalled to the People's Republic of China after his capture and subsequent rescue from Luna, the entire crew of the *Orcus 1* had returned for the *Orcus 3* mission to witness the first planned light speed flight from Luna to Pluto.

Helen, George, Henrietta, Ekwan, Dale and Johan were joined by Allan Yost, a South African whose credentials surpassed their previous planetologist's qualifications.

The eight of them were dressed in their suitshields and standing in a protective outbuilding they had erected as close to *Dis Pater* as Justine would allow. Once again, as with the first time, Ekwan called out the changes.

"Surface temperature rising. The monument is changing color as well."

It was as if they had gone back in time and were replaying the events of five years previous again, reciting lines in a play.

Nevertheless, it was just as exciting as the first time, and Justine could barely contain herself.

Ekwan's voice rose with excitement. "It should be here in less than thirty seconds."

Helen looked up. "Captain?"

Justine had wandered near the door of the outbuilding. She laid her hand on the latch release.

"I'm just going to get a look from out there," she replied.

George Eastmain cocked his head. "You'll actually get a better view of the *Quanta* from the monitors here."

"It's all right. I want to see if I can spot it myself. Besides, you don't need me until it's time to send in the reports." She smiled.

Dismissing her from his attention, George focused his eyes on the monitors.

Justine cycled the lock and stepped out onto the icy surface of the Dark Planet.

It was just her and *Dis Pater* who would truly witness the culmination of the last decade of her life's work, as far as she was concerned. Everything she had done, everything she had sacrificed was for this moment, and she was not about to watch it second-hand from a monitor.

In her ear-mask, she heard Ekwan's voice over the static. "Ten seconds."

Despite herself, Justine felt butterflies in her stomach. She was as nervous as on the night of her high school prom.

She looked up into the sky in the direction she estimated the *Quanta* would arrive. Of course, she wouldn't be able to see the vessel itself; it would be too far away to spot with the naked eye. However, Justine hoped she would see some kind of trail, a distortion of light and space that would mark the ship's progress.

Beside her, *Dis Pater*, the monument that represented almost exactly the atomic model of Kinemet, had turned its final color.

Justine scanned the skies.

"Three," called out Ekwan.

Almost, Justine thought she saw a smear in the firmament of the heavens.

"Two."

There was a faint streak of multicolored light that appeared in the distance, as if some giant invisible artist had painted a swath through the dark blanket of outer space.

"One!" Ekwan called out.

The heavens exploded.

Justine screamed and collapsed on the ice.

∞

"Are you all right?"

Justine regained consciousness slowly. "What happened?" she asked. As she stood, she quickly steadied herself. A preternatural calmness settled over her.

Dale Powers' voice filled her ear-mask. "It didn't stop. It kept on going. The *Quanta* is, by now, racing for the Oort cloud at light speed."

Helen, concern visible in the expression on her face, spoke next.

"You screamed and fell down. When we got to you, you were out like a light. What happened to you?"

Justine reached for the clasp on her helmet and undid it. She slowly pulled it off her head.

"I was looking right at it when it passed," she told them, her voice quiet and even.

Helen, who stood right in front of Justine, waved her hand in front of Justine—she didn't react. "Captain, what's wrong with you. You seem to be looking past me?"

"Sorry, Helen. But you know how they tell you not to look directly at an eclipse?"

"Yeah."

"I looked directly at the *Quanta* as it passed. I should have stayed and watched it from the monitor like Dale suggested.

"Helen," she explained to her second-in-command, "I'm afraid I can't look at you because I'm blind."

The *Quanta*:
Pluto :

Once he reached Pluto, Alex did not stop.

He knew, instinctively, that Pluto was not his destination; it was merely the jumping off point.

All he knew was that the artifact, *Dis Pater,* was there, a beacon in the starry blankness of space, and then it was gone.

He was past it.

Past the limits of Sol System.

Out there in that vastness between the stars.

From one point of view, the years ticked by.

From Alex's point of view, it was merely another instant.

And then...

Then he could detect another beacon, a twin to *Dis Pater.*

Come to us, Alex.

Over here.

This is where you are heading.

We are waiting for you.

The *Quanta* :
Centauri System :

Four Years Later

Somehow, Alex knew that there was no such thing as time, but he also knew that he was over four years older chronologically—though his body had not changed. He was an eighteen-year-old in the body of a fourteen-year-old.

It was as if he had taken a detour through another dimension, a dimension without distance, depth or time. A second *Dis Pater*, this one on the outer planet of another solar system, registered his arrival.

(One second)

But now his ship had re-entered reality in another sector of space— the Centauri System a little over four lightyears away…

…the problem was that he wasn't following! His physical body remained in that alternate reality.

(Two seconds)

He tried to reach for the pull-ring with a hand that was not part of reality.

(Three seconds)

He was a ghost.

(Five Seconds)

No, he wasn't a ghost. He was something—somewhere? somewhere?—else.

(Eight Seconds)

He kept trying to grab the pull-ring, but his hand only went through it. He started panicking—he was going to die!

(ELEVEN SECONDS)

He had forgotten! The pull-ring did nothing. It was he who had to…

(!!!TWELVE SECONDS!!!)

Alex screamed as…

(!!!!TWELVE POINT FOUR SEVEN THREE SECONDS!!!!)

…the ship…

49

Quantum Resources, Inc. :
Canada Corp.:
Toronto :

August 2103

A little more than eight years had passed since Alex Manez had stolen the world's first interstellar spacecraft. Michael Sanderson was celebrating his sixty-fifth birthday, and his upcoming retirement, at home when there came a knock on his door.

After receiving the message from the young army private, Michael hurriedly pulled on his jacket, retrieved his briefcase and followed the man into a waiting car without a word to his family or guests.

As he was being driven to the Center, Michael Sanderson opened his briefcase and read over the file on Alex Manez and the *Quanta* for perhaps the thousandth time in the last two years.

Everyone at the Center involved with the project had all but forgotten about Alex and the *Quanta*, and had dismissed the possibility of success.

The original mission plan was a light-speed trip to Pluto. When the *Quanta* shot past the outermost planet, every astronomer and astrogator on Earth raced to plot its course. Centauri System was the confirmed destination.

Assuming there was a twin to *Dis Pater* there, and also assuming the *Quanta* would stop once it reached Alpha Centauri, and also assuming Alex Manez was able to stop the *Quanta* from exploding, Michael had every available space telescope aimed at Sol's closest neighbor, hoping against hope for any sign of Alex's ultimate fate.

They should have had some result several months earlier—even a signal that the ship had exploded in Centauri space—but after weeks and months of waiting with no signs, they had finally given up. It seemed that their news release of the failure of the *Quanta* and the death of Alex Manez had been correct after all. Or perhaps they would never know what had happened.

But now this.

What was this?

The unmanned outpost on Pluto detected an anomaly and would be relaying a full report to Earth.

Was it a bona-fide message from Alex, or a pick-up of an explosion that had happened over four light-years away, nearly six years ago? All the young private had known, indeed all that anyone knew was that the station had received some kind of signal from the nearest solar system to them.

Michael did not want to become optimistic, but his mind kept going over the details of the project, and Alex's part in it.

Kinemet was the key to interstellar travel, but no one had expected it to happen for decades. There was too much research to be completed first.

The secret of Kinemet was that, when it was ignited, it randomly converted mass to energy and energy to mass, making anything it came in contact with into quanta of light.

The science teams from the ten space agencies around the world had worked on containing that energy and harnessing it. The result was the *Quanta* project. The Kinemet would convert the ship into a light wave and send it out to be received by *Dis Pater* on Pluto. Once the alien artifact had snared the *Quanta* into an orbit, the Kinemet would reverse its electronic polarities and convert its energy back into its original mass. The only loss of energy would be in the Kinemet itself, thus theoretically leaving the spaceship intact.

They had tried to perform this experiment with unmanned spacecraft but there was a difficulty—once the craft was reconverted to mass, any residual Kinemet left in the fuel tanks would re-ignite and destroy the vessel. They could not rig up an electronic trap to discharge the Kinemet before it reacted since electricity could not work while the reacting Kinemet was present—it was a Catch-22.

From the data they had received, they found there was an average twelve-second delay from the time of mass reconversion to the time the Kinemet re-reacted. Just enough time for an astronaut to discharge the Kinemet fuel bays manually.

But this was not what Michael Sanderson had been worried about. He was confident that Alex Manez, if the matter–energy conversion had not killed him—which was a possibility, but then they would have had word, wouldn't they?—would be able to flick that switch and keep the *Quanta* from exploding. What he was worried about was something he had read in Alex Manez's file three years after the young man had begun his journey. And that something might be an even more significant factor in the success or failure of this project—but Michael would only know for certain once he found out if the signal coming in was an explosion, or a message from Alex.

Michael sighed and looked out the window of the car. He watched the landscape whip by him for a time before flicking his eyes heavenward.

"Hurry driver!" he ordered the private. The driver nodded sympathetically and pushed his foot down on the accelerator, getting the Director to the Space Center in record time.

∞

White knuckles was the contagion as Center officials, video-paper reporters, and Michael Sanderson all waited for the message to be relayed from Pluto and be decoded.

He didn't even notice as a rather slight figure sidled up to him. "Sure is a whole whack of people here waiting for word from our young Mr. Manez."

Michael turned his head to see Major Justine Turner give him a big smile. She wore sunglasses, even though they were indoors, and in her slender hands she held a white cane.

He replied, "I didn't know if you would make it."

Justine let out a throaty laugh. "I *need* to be here. Nothing could have kept me away."

Michael nodded his head, and then, because she wouldn't be able to see the action, said, "I know how you feel."

The two of them had kept in contact over the past eight years, as colleagues, and as the surrogate parents of Alex Manez. They both had a vested interest in today's outcome.

After returning to Earth, Justine had had to hang up her pilot's wings, but instead of retiring from NASA, she had taken up an instructor's position.

"Once I got the message, I hopped a hypersonic with a student. I think we broke Mach 10." She laughed. "We'll have to call Guinness on that one."

"What's with the cane?" he asked. With the advent of the second-generation thought-link technology, Justine had a very limited ability to *see*. Sensors in her glasses measured space between her and objects around her, and translated the information directly to her brain as impulses. It was primitive, but Justine was able to navigate a crowded corridor without assistance.

"I don't know. I got so used to it those first few years; it's like a safety blanket now."

Michael was about to reply, when a klaxon sounded.

"Message incoming. We are decoding it now," the female voice of the communications officer sounded over the intercom.

"I never thought—" Michael could barely form a sentence, the anticipation was so high.

All the voices hushed as the result of eighteen-billion dollars and almost fifteen years of work and waiting came to a head.

The communications officer's voice was recalcitrant, and everyone's eyes and ears were unwilling to believe the words she spoke.

"Confirmed: the *Quanta* exploded twelve and a half seconds after reestablishing mass and orbit in the Centauri System."

Statistics began scrolling up the screen detailing, in numerical figures, what had happened.

A thousand voices rose in astonishment and dismay, but one lifted above the multitude: "Then why did it take so long for us to get word? We should have received this information months ago!" Michael called out in a demanding voice. A dozen people began pouring over the computer data trying to find the answer to that question.

His grief and sense of loss was not for the *Quanta* but for Alex, who had died over four years ago. The realization just came home to him. It was as if Alex had died the moment the words were spoken over that impersonal intercom.

"I'll be in my office!" he informed them. Without waiting for a reply, he turned about and stormed away. He did not notice Justine following until he was already in his office with the door closed.

"What are you doing?" he shot, losing all sense of civility.

The former astronaut shrugged and gave Michael a wide smile, as if she were completely unaffected by the tragedy.

"A lot of time has passed," she began, inviting herself into a chair on the other side of the Director's desk. "I had plenty to think about over the past few years. The world is different from when I stood out there on the end of Sol System, looking across the miles of space to watch Alex Manez and the *Quanta* pass me. I never had a child of my own, and I probably never will. Alex is the closest thing I will ever have to a son," she said, then fell silent for a time.

Michael strode over to a water cooler and poured two cups. He gave her one which she took automatically and sipped.

She said, "At one point in my life all I cared about was being a pilot, or an astronaut, or the first person on Pluto, or a dozen other milestones that people would kill to list on their resume. But since that day when Alex became Earth's first interstellar traveler, my entire perspective on life shifted. My world shifted polarities."

"I'm sorry about what happened to you," Michael said.

"I'm not. I may be blind, but for the first time in my life, I can finally see. Achievements are not what's important. What is important are the people in our lives, and how we are remembered by those we love. Alex may be dead, but I will always remember him as that unique individual who stole a spaceship, and as the brave little boy who so completely changed my life."

Sanderson opened his mouth to speak, to console her, to say he finally understood, but the phone on his desk rang. Annoyed, he picked it up, leaving Justine to her own thoughts.

After a few seconds, Sanderson burst out: *"What?"*

Finding himself standing, the Director fell back to his seat as he hung up. He stared at Justine for a few seconds before saying: "I think you should hear this also."

With that he pressed a button on his office intercom.

A hauntingly familiar voice crackled through...

Copán :
Honduras :
Central American Conglomeration :

My grandson stands by me, tall and proud. It is his eighteenth birthday, and he is trying to act like a man, stoic and wise and focused.

But his eyes betray him. I can see how he glances over to Artek's granddaughter and tries to hide his blush. Romance blossoms. Thus the world works, thus my line will be continued. It is the same everywhere. And it is good, so I say nothing.

I am getting old. Too old, some say. I know sometimes my grandson thinks so, but I also know that sometimes, like now, he is rethinking his opinions, especially when the big white men in blue and gray suits fly from their important cities in America just to visit an old man like me.

I am too old to go to them, so they come to me; this, my grandson respects. He is finding his wisdom slowly, but it is there, and I am happy to see that he will make a fine leader of our people when I am gone.

The entire village has come out to the council courtyard to see the white men and their special visitor arrive in our humble community. I see a few faces as old and familiar as mine; most are new, some I do not even recognize. They must have traveled from other villages to see also. That is good. Perhaps Copán will one day return to its splendor of a millennium ago.

Perhaps that is just the wishful thinking of an old man.

My grandson hears the roar of the white men's cars long before my old ears pick up the rattle of engines and pings of rocks from our gravel roads.

Turning my head, I see their rented vehicles. Ten of them, all filled with white men in suits.

All but one.

I disregard the white men. They think they are important, but in the greater scheme of life, they are no more important than anyone else.

The only important one slowly exits the middle car.

He is short compared to the men from NASA, with jet black hair, and a deeply tanned, round face. He appears young, even younger than my grandson, though he bears himself like a council elder.

To honor the village, he is wearing the ceremonial dress of a Mayan priest, which is right and good.

As he approaches, I reach out for my grandson to help me out of my chair and to the ground, where I kneel before the visitor.

The white men gathered around shuffle uncomfortably. They think I am just an old man who knows nothing.

It is they who do not know anything, and their confusion only increases when I pay my respects to the visitor.

I speak in both Mayan and Spanish, so that the villagers can also understand me. One of the white men translates for his fellows.

"He said: Greetings Colop U Uichkin, welcome to our humble village. Your mercy is our salvation.'

"—I think this Colop," the man whispers, though loud enough for me to hear, "is their god of the sky."

I laugh deep in my throat at their poor translation. Colop means Sky Traveler in our language.

Colop ignores them. Their purpose was only in bringing him back to us, and that has been served.

Smiling, Colop beckons me back to my chair.

"Please, Grandfather," the Sky Traveler says respectfully as the white man translates, "rest your old bones. Do not kneel on my account." It is so with the kindest of men.

Colop and my grandson help me back to my seat. My knees crack and pop, but I manage to find the chair and fall into it.

"Everything will be all right now," Colop tells me. "I am here, and your job is complete, Grandfather. Our people on this world are well prepared for the return of the People of the Stars. Your Cousins will have many stories to tell you when they arrive. They look forward to meeting you."

It is then that my grandson speaks out of turn. Alas, I have not taught him as well as I should have. It is obvious that he now believes in my stories; but he is still young, and has doubts.

My grandson looks down on this visitor from the stars who looks like a boy, and says: "Colop. You must answer me a question. When our people were taken to the stars, why were us few left behind? Did our ancestors displease them?"

"No, cousin. The People who were left here were chosen because of their loyalty and intelligence. The ones who were taken needed to be shown the mysteries of the universe so that they could understand their role in the great scheme.

"One day, they would have to return to the world, and their coming would require guides to bridge the gap between the fourth world—the white man's world—and the People's culture. That will be your role in the new, fifth, world of this earth, cousin. You will serve as an ambassador between the People of the Earth and the People of the Sky."

"I am sorry for my impertinence, great Colop. Forgive me." Thus my grandson makes me proud.

"And now," I say, "we must feast and celebrate your coming, Colop."

The Sky Traveler turns to the white men who brought him here, and dismisses them, telling them to return tomorrow when he will discuss the future.

The white men grumble and argue, and they glance at me with suspicion, all the while reassessing my worth and value in their political minds. It will serve me to keep the peace between our cultures, but for now, it is time for them to go.

"NASA men," I say to them. "A great change will come upon us in our future. There will be hundredfold benefits for all the peoples of the world. You need time to think about how you would like that future to be shaped. Perhaps if you went back to your hotels and talked with each other, you could develop a plan and bring it to us, so that both our peoples can talk this over together."

The white men are fond of talking, and making plans. Almost eagerly, they bustle into their cars and drive away.

Colop, the man in a boy's body who the white men call Alex Manez, remains with us. He must tell us about his time with the People of the Sky, what he has learned from them, and what they expect from us.

"For a millennium, you and your ancestors have protected the ancient scroll," he says to me. "It is in that scroll where we will find what we need in order for the People of the Stars to accept us into their cosmic tribe. You are the only one who can read the scroll, grandfather. It is you who must lead us into the next age."

My grandson looks at me with newfound respect.

I may be an old man, but now, with renewed purpose, I feel young once more.

THE BEGINNING

to be continued in *Music of the Spheres*...

MUSIC OF THE SPHERES

THE INTERSTELLAR AGE
BOOK 2

VALMORE
DANIELS

INCEPTION

Copán :
Honduras :
Central American Conglomeration :

My shame is unimaginable.

For years my grandson believed I was just a silly old man. I had hoped he would change his mind and grow to respect me and my knowledge when Colop—the Sky Traveler; the one they call Alex Manez—returned from the stars to thank me for helping the scientists.

I know my grandson never truly respected me, and he has proved to me that I am unworthy. I can no longer bear to face the people in my village.

Perhaps I was too prideful after Colop told me that they needed my help to discover the key to the fifth world so that we may become one with the People of the Stars. He told me the path to the stars was still clouded, and only I could unlock the secrets of the ancient scroll. I had to help him complete his journey.

He is the only one who can hear the Music of the Spheres, but it is not enough. He must also be able to hear the Song of the Stars.

It has been two summers since I spoke with Colop last, but I have worked very hard to translate the scroll for him.

They sent translators to help me when I refused to let them take the scroll away, but since they came to our village, they have been more than useless. They try to find English words to match the ancient Mayan symbols, and they do not listen when I tell them they are traveling down the wrong path.

I told them Colop should be here to learn the story, but they say it is impossible; they will send him images and recordings instead. They do not understand that their machine will only strip the meaning from my story, and so I declined their offer.

Frustrated with me, they took images of the scroll and sent them back to their labs; they used microscopes and chemicals to tell them if the secret was in the paper; they entered the Mayan symbols and pictograms into their computers.

Afraid of damage to the sacred scroll, the translators encased it in a plastic cover for me; for this contribution I am pleased, and I have hung it on the wall in my home.

All their efforts produced nothing more than gibberish, however. After a time, their irritation led them to threats, and then bribes, and then to more threats.

When they demanded to know if I am keeping the secret from them, I told them I have nothing to hide. I can only tell them what my grandfather said to me: true understanding lay not with the story, but in the telling of the story. I offer to tell them the story again, but I don't think they are capable of listening.

One week ago, my grandson, who has also been frustrated with me for a long time, asked me to tell him the story one more time. I had hoped that my telling would give him understanding, but he ran from my house before I finished the Song.

Yesterday, he brought a friend he said he had met on his city adventure. The stranger asked me plainly why I would not help the scientists learn the secret. If I made them happy, he said to me, perhaps the knowledge could help raise the status of the Mayan people in the eyes of the world. At the very least, they would send us wealth.

I told my grandson's friend we did not need any more computers or machines. Such conveniences are secondary and unimportant in the great plan. Our status is not necessary, either. Our purpose should be to help Colop complete his journey and become one with the stars; that is all that truly matters.

My grandson said that his friend would like to listen to me tell the story once more. I hoped, perhaps, that their young ears would hear more than the old ears of the scientists from the north.

We sat on the long couch in front of the scroll and I told the story to my grandson and his friend one last time. I was very careful to tell it in the manner it was told to me by my own grandfather.

When I finished, I looked at them expectantly. At first, the other man's face was clouded over, but my grandson was excited.

"Do you not hear it?" he said to his friend.

After a moment, the stranger nodded. "Yes. I think so. I think you are right."

My heart swelled with pride. Finally, my grandson understood something in the tale. It was his destiny to hear the story. My grandfather had passed the legacy to me, as his grandfather had passed it to him. And now my grandson will become ambassador to the People of the Stars.

"You know the secret?" I asked him. I was hopeful.

My grandson nodded. "Yes, Grandfather, I believe I do. Thank you."

"Good." I closed my eyes with satisfaction. When I opened them again, I said, "Then you must find Colop and reveal the secret to him so that he also may hear the Song of the Stars."

He smiled at me in a way I had never before seen. "Oh, Grandfather. No, I will not find Alex Manez. And no, I will not give him the secret."

"I do not understand," I said.

He stood, and I saw that he clenched his fist at his side. "It is now *my* secret. It is *my* destiny to conquer the stars, not his."

My grandson tore the plastic-sealed scroll from the wall. When I stood to protest, his friend pulled out a gun and pointed it at me.

"What is this? What are you doing?" I demanded of my grandson.

"Sorry, grandfather. You have to come with us."

Two more men entered my house, then. They had rifles. I had no choice but to go with them.

How could I have been so blind? How could I not have seen all these years how my grandson despised our humble life in the village, and envied the power of Colop?

There is no use left for me. I have failed the gods, and must surrender myself to their mercy.

Selected EarthMesh Forum Excerpts
keyword search: *Quanta*

September 2103

"…think the mission was a total fail. Now they're touting him around on the newsfeeds as if he's a conquering hero. He didn't even see any aliens or anything. The *Quanta:* ship of fools. What a waste of money and time…"

October 2103

"…was on a liner to Luna Base last week. Someone said Captain Alex Manez was on board. I tried to get a look at him, but the security was too tight. NASA's meshsite said they're gearing up to launch another one of those *Quanta* ships…"

November 2103

"…you hear about the *Quanta 5* test flight yesterday? The quantum drive lasted about two seconds before it blew the ship right into the cosmos. This is—what?—the eighth astronaut they've either killed or maimed trying to get this right. Not to mention how many billions each of those ships cost. When are they going to give up? There are more important things to think about…"

January 2104

"…I guess it was my own fault. I sank our life savings into USA, Inc. stock before the *Quanta* flight, and I kept it there even when they missed the scheduled return date and the value started to sink. Now they've put Quantum Resources on the auction block because their stock is at an all time low and they don't have any more money to spend. I just hope that stops the devaluation. It's going to be a tight Christmas…"

February 2104

"…saw a report that NASA and CSE officially released Captain Alex Manez from their active roster. He was the pilot for the *Quanta*. Now that they've scrubbed the interstellar program, I guess they don't need him anymore. I can't seem to find any pictures of him…"

March 2104

"…and after fifteen years, now I'm out of a job. USA, Inc. needs a new CEO. First he spent trillions on *Quanta* ships, all of which either blew up or just didn't work, or the pilots died in training exercises. Now he's sold all Quantum Resources stock to Canada Corp. for pennies on the dollar. Didn't he think about all the people who worked in the Houston office? I'm fifty-two; with the economy in a shambles, who's going to hire me now…?"

August 2104

"…finally getting their heads out of the sand. I just read a press release from Canada Corp.'s SMD stating that they're no longer actively searching for that Kinemet element. I mean, without a working *Quanta* ship, the stuff is far too costly to mine. We can use iron ore; that'll get people building again, jumpstart the economy and create some jobs…"

August 2105

"…you guys remember that position I was applying for with Quantum Resources? They were the ones spearheading the first *Quanta* missions ten years ago, but they're more of an applied astrophysics think-tank operation now. Heavy into theoretical research—right up my alley. Well, I got the job! I start orientation in four weeks…"

3

Canada Station Three :
Lagrange Point 4 :
Earth Orbit :

December 2105

Alex Manez sat in the cockpit of the *Quanta*. All on-board electronics were dead, the heads-up displays were blank, and the only sound he could hear was the soft beating of his heart in his chest.

To the side of the pilot's chair, a pull ring hung from a short length of wire. All he had to do was to reach for that ring and give it a sharp tug. The reaction would switch on the generator and charge the battery, which would in turn power the computers and other electrical systems, including the Kinemetic dampers.

Alex reached out for the pull ring, and his fingers—the slender fingers of a teenager—touched the cool thin metal. The last time he had done this, his hand passed through the ring, as if he were a ghost caught between the living and spirit worlds.

The last time, the ship had exploded.

Now, there was no urgency in his actions. With minimal effort, he drew the ring back until it clicked, and watched as the holoslate in front of him flickered to life.

A green light indicated that all systems were operational and ready for normal navigation.

Disinterested, he brushed a thin strand of hair out of his eyes and longed for the time when he had a full head of hair. It seemed like a lifetime ago.

He looked up when a short, high-pitched binging sound came out of the holoslate.

Superimposed on the screen over a schematic display, a sour-looking face appeared, and narrowed eyes stared directly at Alex as if looking straight through him.

"And then what happened?" asked Kenny Harriman, the newest physicist to join the Quantum Resources research team on CS3. He was considered something of a whiz at the University of British Columbia, from where he had been recruited.

Biologically only a few years older than Alex, Kenny acted like a tenured professor. It was as if he had something to prove. From the moment he arrived in the lab, he had insisted on reading every report concerning the *Quanta* missions, reviewing every diagnostic ever run on Alex, and making sure he was supervising every simulation exercise.

He also had an annoying habit of making every question or statement a challenge. Kenny was a very excitable young man who obviously loved the pursuit of knowledge. At the same time, he was on a personal mission to drag Quantum Resources back into the spotlight of the world's scientific community.

In contrast to the physicist, Alex was the epitome of calm. "I told you. Nothing happened."

"Nothing!" Kenny tapped something on his haptic console, and the canopy of the life-sized flight simulator snapped open.

The hydraulics lifted the top up and away from Alex. He blinked to adjust his eyes to the brighter light of the simulation room. Through a large pane of glass, two analysts hunched over computer schematics in the adjacent room.

The light continued to sting Alex's eyes, but he watched as Ellen Yarrow adjusted the rim of her glasses over her pert nose.

Once, when Alex had first arrived on CS3 after his interstellar flight, he had tried to strike up a conversation with Ellen. She'd acted like she was uncomfortable, and excused herself. Since then, she had gone out of her way to avoid him.

Alex had no idea why he tortured himself over her, or over the possibility of any relationship. Even if he looked as old as his birth certificate stated, he was still a freak of nature, a science experiment gone awry.

He was doomed to solitude.

"What do you mean, 'nothing'?" Kenny demanded.

Alex fixed the physicist with a smile of innocence. "I don't mean anything by it. Nothing happened when I pulled the ring on the flight."

Kenny seemed completely unaffected. "Tell me why I don't believe you."

"It wasn't enough of a kick to turn the *Quanta* back on." Alex explained. "I had to provide the charge to initiate the systems."

"Right. This 'electropathic' ability, which you've failed to demonstrate to us time and again." The physicist pulled a disbelieving face. "All we have is your say-so you have the ability to manipulate electrical systems ... oh and the questionable reports from the crew of the *Orcus 1.*" He waved his holoslate in front of Alex.

Alex had had the same argument for the past two years with every scientist, technician and administrator Quantum Resources and Canada Corp. had sent up to Canada Station Three.

Before the real *Quanta's* first interstellar voyage, Alex had judged that the Kinemetic influence on the electrical systems of the ship would far surpass initial estimates. The shielded battery would not hold nearly enough power to start all the shipboard computers. And he had been correct. The pull ring had done absolutely nothing.

The longer Alex had been in proximity to the kinetic metal, the more of a charge he had built up. Once the *Quanta* had reached Centauri space, there was enough electrical current at Alex's disposal for him to start the computers and bring the life-support systems back online. That effort—among other things—had completely depleted him for a very long time.

Alex said, "I will be more than happy to show you how it works. I just need an adequate amount of Kinemet to replenish me."

Kenny gave him a cool gaze filled with disbelief.

Alex repeated himself, and there was a tone of quiet desperation that slipped into his voice. "I need it."

Without Kinemet, Alex was not only powerless to control electrical currents around him, but the longer he spent away from it, the faster his physical body deteriorated.

As with all living things, there were certain vitamins, minerals and amino acids an organism needed in order to maintain and sustain life; with Alex, it was as if exposure to the kinetic metal had added one more required element to his biological makeup when he had been irradiated on Macklin's Rock.

The physicist shook his head. "Even if I could authorize a small quantity—which I can't because we don't have any—I'm not convinced that mere exposure to the element will suddenly infuse you with some kind of supernatural power."

"It's not a sudden effect."

"Besides," Kenny said, narrowing his eyes, "according to these reports, when they were still building *Quanta* ships, they allocated half a milligram of Kinemet here for testing purposes. You were in contact with it."

"It wasn't enough," Alex said. "A drop of water for a man dying of thirst." Without the influence of Kinemet, his health had deteriorated drastically. The doctors couldn't prove that lack of exposure to Kinemet was causing his issues, and without a substantial quantity of the metal, he couldn't prove that it would help.

Kenny waved his hand in the air frantically. "We can go around in circles forever on this. It wasn't the question I was asking, anyway."

"I know," Alex said.

"I know you know!" Kenny was not as capable of hiding his frustration as his predecessor. He took a long, deep breath. "You say you were able to start the generator."

Nodding, Alex said, "I was."

Kenny sighed. "Then why did it explode, and why didn't you die in the explosion?"

"It's in my report," Alex said, his voice weary. "I got the systems up, but it was too late to engage the dampers. The secondary Kinemetic reaction had started; there was no way to stop it from exploding. I barely had enough time to eject the escape pod."

Kenny blinked. "It's too bad the flight recorder can't corroborate your story."

"I told you, when I used the electropathy to start the generator, I pushed too hard and it wiped the storage drive."

"Convenient," Kenny said.

Alex frowned. "You should have shielded it better."

Kenny flicked his hand dismissively. "Never mind about that. You had rations for one week—two if you pushed it. So how did you survive *after that?* What happened in the almost two-and-a-half months between when you arrived in the Centauri system and when you made the return trip. You just—what—floated in space all that time in the pod?"

"It's a little foggy," Alex said. "I think I was suffering some aftereffects from being quantized. Time didn't really flow in an ordinary way." He wasn't a very good liar. From the look Kenny gave him, the physicist didn't believe him on that point.

In his debriefing to Quantum Resources—when it was still a joint venture between USA, Inc. and Canada Corp.—Alex had reported that his escape pod had detected a star beacon, an identical cousin to Sol System's *Dis Pater,* on the outer rim of the Centauri System. Another huge monument that resembled an electron cloud, the alien structure rested on the surface of a minor planet a fraction of the size of Charon.

Alex repeated himself for the hundredth time in the past two years. "I used the pod's jets to head for the alien star beacon. When I got there, it just ... sent me home."

Fixing Alex with a look of frustration, Kenny said, "And if all of the Kinemet blew up with the *Quanta,* how did 'it' send you back to Sol System?"

That was one of the many questions the Quantum Resources scientists kept asking, but they continued to disbelieve any answer Alex gave them; and they were right. It was unfortunate that he was unable to tell them the truth.

He hated that there were things about his story he couldn't share. But if he shared his secret before the world was ready, it would lead to...

He didn't even dare think of it.

The frustration he felt had only sharpened over the past few years. The world needed to develop the Kinemet technology as fast as it could, but they had encountered a brick wall. Coupled with the worsening economy, it seemed no one was that interested in investing in Kinemet.

At times, Alex wanted to scream to get the world motivated, but he knew he had to bite his tongue.

Time was running out; at the rate of things, it might take decades for the science of Kinemet to get where it needed to be.

Because of his health, Alex didn't have decades; he most likely didn't even have years.

But whenever Calbert Loche or Raymond McGrath sent up a new physicist to Quantum Resources, Alex did his best to help them, hoping they were the ones who could unlock the secret of Kinemet.

Inevitably, due to his reluctance to tell the complete truth, and also because those details he did share were difficult to believe, those newcomers eventually discounted the rest of Alex's story.

Kenny was a little more stubborn than his predecessors, but he was on the wrong track. Alex knew where today's conversation was heading, and the day's events had taken a toll on him. He didn't have the strength to endure an argument, and at this point, he didn't care if Kenny Harriman pitched a fit over it.

Alex said, "I'm tired. I need to rest."

Vibrating with barely suppressed anger, Kenny stormed off and tapped his report into the haptic console. One of the lab assistants approached and assisted Alex out of the simulator's cockpit.

∞

It had been over two years since Alex's return from the first interstellar voyage. The world financial crisis had intensified in Alex's absence. USA, Inc. and Canada Corp. had banked heavily on a successful mission for the *Quanta*. Contact with an alien race would have made the country corporations' stocks soar. New technologies, medicines, and even the possibility of interstellar trade would have boosted shareholder and consumer confidence.

With Alex's report that he had seen nothing out there except the distant flare of the Centauri system's red dwarf star, Proxima, the media had descended on the two country corporations, hungry for blood. They accused the United Earth Corporate Council of wasting trillions of dollars on an empty space fantasy when they should have concentrated their efforts on the realities of increasing population, famine and energy depletion. The UECC had backed out of the *Quanta* trials, and after NASA and Quantum Resources' repeated failures, USA, Inc. decided to follow suit.

Quantum Resources barely survived USA, Inc.'s downsizing efforts by selling all shares to Canada Corp. and relocating its quantum research facility to Canada Station Three.

Without a steady supply of Kinemet for practical trials, Quantum Resources had turned into more of a theoretical analysis laboratory. At the moment, their only solid asset was Alex Manez. Despite his agreement to be their guinea pig—and as his body continued to fail him—he found himself becoming more and more obstinate.

As had happened during his self-imposed exile on the pirate base on Luna, without the direct influence of Kinemet, Alex had begun to physically deteriorate once more. It was as if the radiation emitted from that element, while basically harmless to those who had not been exposed during a transfer reaction, had become a requisite substance for Alex. He fed off it; it replenished him and kept him alive.

He had no idea how long he would live without it.

The harshest side effect of his condition was that he could not tolerate Earth's high gravity anymore. While the main labs, administration areas, and the common and recreation centers on Canada Station Three were all fitted with the latest in artificial gravity technology, the levels in the living quarters were completely adjustable by the occupants. Alex, when home, kept gravity to a bare minimum.

Unable to stand on his own for more than a few short minutes at a time, Alex had purchased a set of hydraulic leg braces which would support his weight. He purchased them with the proceeds from the severance package given to him by NASA.

When not in his quarters, Alex wore his hydraulic braces. Using fluid dynamics, biomechatronics and environmental pressure sensors, the braces were able to compensate for any external factors, such as walking on an incline or stairs, or—if he were back on Earth—snow or rain. They provided him with a more natural gait. From a distance, most people would not be able to tell he wore orthotics. Not that it made any difference: Alex looked pale and sickly; his hair was thin and stringy, and his bones continued to atrophy no matter how many vitamin shots the medical staff administered.

All the researchers and corporate administrators treated Alex like a child. Even Ellen Yarrow looked at him as if he were something she discovered in a Petri dish. Although his body appeared to be that of a sixteen-year-old boy, according to his birth record, he was twenty-five; legally an adult. During the eight or so years when his body had been in a quantized state, he had not aged physically.

Once the assistants secured him in the leg supports, Alex pulled on his loose-fitting trousers and fastened them at his waist.

Out of the corner of his eye, he saw Kenny returning, and steeled himself for a confrontation.

Kenny watched as Alex finished dressing.

The physicist finally said, "Look, I don't want us to be enemies. I want you to trust me. I just want what's best for everyone."

Alex scoffed.

Kenny threw up a hand. "Fine. I want what's best for me, but that can only lead to helping you. So please, can't we start the dialogue over again?"

"If you truly want to help yourself," Alex said, "then you'll listen when I tell you that what you are doing right now is irrelevant—and quite possibly counterproductive."

Shaking his head, Kenny asked, "How can the study of the most advanced technology in the universe be irrelevant?"

Kenny often spoke as if he were in a lecture hall.

Alex sighed. "That's not what I'm saying. It is the most important thing in the world. We need to master it before—"

"Before what?"

Alex shook his head. "First, you need to understand the basics of Kinemet. And we don't even know how to stabilize it. We need to focus on how Kinemet affects people, not how to build a better quantum drive. Everyone keeps looking at the power of Kinemet as if it's just the key to light-speed travel."

"But it is!"

Alex shook his head. "Yes, it can be a trigger for quantizing matter into light and powering a properly equipped vehicle at near light speeds. But that's only the most rudimentary of its properties."

"What are you talking about?" Kenny scanned his notes, but Alex knew none of his predecessors had written anything about this.

Normally, he wouldn't try to explain himself. However, of all the researchers sent up to CS3, Alex had a feeling that Kenny's mind might be open to new possibilities.

Alex said, "It can do so much more than just be a fuel for light-speed travel."

Voice low, ears alert, Kenny asked, "Such as…?"

Alex pointed to himself. "Human chrysalis, for one. Though we've failed miserably in that regard. And then there's the Grace."

Kenny stared at Alex as if he were speaking another language.

He blinked. "The grace of what?"

Alex cursed himself and said, "Nothing. Sorry, I'm just too tired to think straight. I have to go to my quarters."

4

Interim Report :
Health Status :
Alex Manez :

From:
Dr. Naryan Amma, Ph.D., CS3 Medical Chief of Staff

To:
Canada Corp. Health Services, Dept. of Nutritional and Metabolic Diseases.

Diagnosis:
The subject, Alex Manez, displays symptoms indicative of massive vitamin deficiency, particularly D and C, though all levels of those vitamins are with normal ranges.

Despite bombardment of multivitamins and a diet of citrus and dairy products, Alex Manez suffers from continued hair loss, chronic insomnia, pale skin and osteoporosis.

There is indication of onset muscle degeneration, and I expect other symptoms to become prevalent as his condition worsens.

While his mental acuity remains in the top percentile, his emotional state has become volatile, and he is prone to depression and anxiety.

Treatment:
All attempts to correct the subject's condition have failed to reverse or even stall his deterioration. Physical exercise exacerbates his pain, multivitamin injections and supplements show no effect, and growth

hormones only serve to cause gastrointestinal distress and may lead to kidney and liver failure.

Prognosis:
Alex Manez has no more than six months to live.

5

Houston Interplanetary Spaceport :
Texas :
USA, Inc. :

It had been over ten years since Justine Turner had seen a sunrise or sunset, since she'd looked upon the face of another person with her own eyes, and since she had even been able to look at herself in a mirror.

She'd gone blind at the edge of Sol System. While she did not regret the events that brought her to that point—and would not trade those experiences for her sight—she found some days more difficult than others, especially in the beginning.

One of the toughest transitions was the loss of her command status. She wanted nothing more than to captain a ship again; to breathe the stale cabin air of a control center; read digital displays and make decisions that would take her vessel out into the vast reaches of space.

The months she had spent on the journey back from Pluto had been the hardest, when she was completely cut off from all sight.

When she got home, she underwent optilink surgery to allow her brain to interpret electrical pulses from an optical-neural translation sensor, which she clipped to the bridge of her nose.

Still, she had struggled with the most basic of daily chores: cooking, dressing and personal grooming to name a few. She had hired an assistant to help her the first year home, but that only reminded her how helpless she was.

Holoslate interfaces were based off haptic technology. It was a perfect match for those who used Braille. After learning the system, Justine was able to read any eBook, manual, or meshmail with the built-in Braille application as easily as a sighted person.

But adjusting to a world where she was blind wasn't the worst part; it was the boredom. She'd had nothing to do.

So once she'd mastered the optical sensor technology, she had pleaded with the officials at NASA to reassign her to the active duty roster.

When they offered her an instructor's position, she jumped at the chance, knowing it was most likely the closest she would ever come again to being in command, or tasting the exhilaration of space flight.

There was a second reason she had so eagerly accepted an instructor's position. The feeling of satisfaction and accomplishment in passing her knowledge on to the young trainees was something she had come to love.

She would never have a child of her own. Biologically, it was still a possibility—there were women much older than her who had children—but at this stage in her life, and with her own personal challenges, she just couldn't see herself making that decision. By the time he or she was a teenager, Justine would be in her late sixties, and she couldn't imagine that she would have enough energy to keep up.

The closest she had ever come to having a child was during those short few months aboard the *Quanta* with Alex Manez. It had given her a fleeting taste of motherhood, and for the first time in her life, she had understood the power of that instinct. To care for and impart her experiences to those who would follow in her footsteps gave her as much of a sense of completeness as she could ever have wanted.

The years she spent as a flight instructor were some of the best in the last decade.

Now, however, that was all behind her.

In the past two years, NASA and USA, Inc. had suffered a great many setbacks—not to mention the loss of many lives on the *Quanta* experiments. That had resulted in the sale of Quantum Resources to Canada Corp. and the shoe-boxing of the entire Kinemet program. There were far too many problems here on Earth to spend any more money on interstellar exploration; or at least, that was the reason the directors at USA, Inc. had given for their decision to sell.

Many of NASA's independent contractors had been released from their contracts, and even many regular staff members had been offered severance packages and early retirement.

They had offered Justine a very generous sum, enough that she could easily have weathered the troubled financial times in relative comfort for many years to come. She had taken the settlement, and wondered what to do with the rest of her life. For a time, she thought about returning to the Lowell Observatory and completing her studies there, but the call of space was too great for her to simply retire.

With her background, she managed to secure a position with Lunar Lines Ltd., who ran their space liners between Houston Spaceport and Luna Base, as a public relations hostess.

It was a one-week round trip, and Justine worked two flights on, one flight off. The position was much more than being an attendant or a tour guide; she was also responsible for the comfort and general safety of the passengers, as well as their peace of mind. While travel to Luna Station and the various space stations orbiting Earth was becoming more frequent, only a fraction of the population had ever undertaken the trip, and for many of those who took a liner it was the first time. They were understandably nervous flying into the void of space.

That morning was the beginning of another of Justine's rotations, and she always looked forward to this leg of the trip for more than just the chance to be in space.

At the Earth-Moon Lagrange 4 point was Canada Station Three, among the Kordylewski clouds. Lunar Lines always had a one-day stopover there before heading to their ultimate destination, and it was Justine's only chance to see Alex Manez.

She worried about him; he seemed to become more pale and sickly every time she visited him. The last time she had stopped there, over two weeks before, he had been significantly more tired than usual and had cut their visit short.

This time around, she hoped to get a word in with someone in charge of the Quantum Resources labs, and find out what they were doing to help him. And if she didn't get satisfaction from them, she would just have to call in a few more favors.

The apartment's home-unit computer system sounded a chime on the main holoslate, indicating there was a vehicle in her driveway.

"Identify," she said out loud.

<Ace Taxi Service,> Hucs informed her. *<Cab Number 3419; the driver's name is Tomas Salenko, four-year taxi license holder.>*

"Oh, he's early. Thank you. I'll be a just another minute."

<Relaying message.>

Justine hurried back to her bedroom and approached the bed.

Resting on the sheets were her two travel bags and a specially developed harness.

The optical recognition scanner on her optilink fed her brain rudimentary spatial data. It allowed her to navigate between one room and the next, and even gave her the ability to discern the difference between a fork and a spoon. It didn't have the capability to show her color, texture or patterns. She could detect the frame of a painting hung on a wall, but she had no way of telling whether it was a blank canvas or a Van Gogh.

Meeting people was just as challenging. It was as if she were face blind. Until someone spoke, Justine had extreme difficulty telling one moving biped from another, unless they had very distinct physical traits.

Optimedia Labs, the company she had originally purchased her optilink through, was also the company who had invented the Virtual Tourist.

A few months back, they had released the next generation in recognition software. Intended for the digital mock-reality entertainment industry, the Personal Environmental Recording Suit—PERSuit, as it was trademarked—was a step up from their Virtual Tourist Camera.

It recorded and interpreted over ten million coded shapes, sounds, smells, colors and textures. Thousands of micro-sensors in the fabric of the harness constantly scanned all audio, video and olfactory data within range.

Contestants on game shows or adventure shows would wear the PERSuit while participating, and then viewers could download those episodes into their septaphonic masks and experience those events for themselves, as if they were there in the contestant's place.

While the downloads were relatively inexpensive, the harness itself was pricey, and getting the techs to integrate the PERSuit sensors with her optilink required signed affidavits that she would not sue in the event of a sensory overload. Combining her body's natural senses with the artificial sensors was not recommended by any of the company's medical staff.

The result was more than she had hoped for, and while she wore the specifically tailored harness, it was as if she had her sight back. There was a major drawback to the garment.

Within a few days of wearing it, Justine began to feel the effect that the company had feared: extended exposure caused her to develop severe migraines. She couldn't wear the harness for more than twelve hours in a day before the pain became unbearable—her mind just couldn't process the enormous amounts of data.

Through experimentation, Justine had also found that if she wore the harness four days in a row, the headaches would start as well.

As a compromise, she never wore the harness at home—she had memorized every nook and cranny in her apartment and didn't need it anyway—and she rarely wore it in public.

For the most part, she wore it when she was working. In her newest vocation as a liner hostess, being able to identify passengers by sight was a valuable ability—especially since the majority of those passengers were country-corporate decision makers, department heads for various science and tech companies, and influential members of the media.

Folding the harness carefully, she packed it in one of her travel bags and headed out to catch her taxi to the spaceport.

∞

Houston Spaceport was bustling with activity. As the taxi pulled up the long stretch of road to the main entry gates, Justine could sense many human forms gathered on the grassy hills in front of the twenty-foot-high fence. While her optilink sensor picked up that the protestors held signs, she could not read any of the slogans written on them; she could, however, hear their angry shouts when she opened the window a crack.

"Feed the people—not your greed!"

"Space is a waste!"

"We need jobs on Earth, too!"

"God gave us Eden; only those who are unworthy seek to leave the garden!"

It was nearly impossible to explain to such protestors that space exploration had opened avenues to new technologies and conveniences which they themselves used on a daily basis. Mining the asteroid belts did provide jobs as the raw materials were shipped back to Earth for processing; it also saved the Earth's natural resources.

There were protestors at nearly every facility in the country that promoted science and technology. If someone suffered a job loss for whatever reason, they often didn't care to look closely at the actual cause; it was easier to point the finger at the nearest target. In the past few years, it was the space industry. Nearly gutting the NASA program was not enough; they wanted to ground all space exploration.

There were also outcries from many of the world's religions, which had started from the day Justine and her crew had discovered the *Dis Pater* on Pluto. Many thought it blasphemous to consider that humans weren't a unique and divine species. To entertain the notion that there were thousands of alien races among the stars was sacrilege.

Some pundits theorized the only reason there hadn't been a full-out religious revolution was because of the failure of Alex's mission. He had come back without any evidence of alien contact; that, to the religious extremists, was proof that the entire affair had been a hoax, and humankind's status as the sole intelligence in the universe was secure.

Over the past year, the crowds of protesters had gradually dwindled, and their rants had not held the vehemence they once carried.

Security, however, remained tight. Once the taxi arrived at the main entrance, it was scanned before any of its occupants were allowed to exit the vehicle. The taxi was quickly cleared of any harmful substances, such as explosives, weapons, or contraband. Justine got out, gathered her bags, and headed for the main building.

The automatic doors parted for her as she entered the spaceport, but when she stepped in, her way was blocked by a tall, thin figure whose back was to her.

Many first time visitors to the port were intimidated by the size and scope of the main terminal, which also doubled as a kind of museum of space flight. Large reproductions—most life-sized—of NASA's various rockets, shuttles and other craft from its long history were displayed throughout the interior of the large building. Crowds of tourists came just to look at the scale models, even if they didn't have tickets for an outbound flight.

Justine assumed the man in her way was simply taken aback by the scope of the space terminal.

"Excuse me," she said politely.

The visitor turned, and though Justine could not make out his features, what struck her as odd was that he wore glasses. With current technological levels, they could correct nearly everything short of blindness. It was rare to see someone still wearing spectacles. When he spoke, there was a hint of a foreign accent that Justine couldn't quite place.

"My apologies, ma'am. I am not sure where I need to go."

Justine, who had been in the port a hundred times, said, "Are you here for a tour or a flight?"

"Flight."

"Check-in is right over there." She pointed to a bank of kiosks to their left. "Then you'll have to go through security."

"Thank you," the man said with a slight nod, and then he headed off.

Justine had no need to check in. She went straight to the security gates and said good morning to the ever-watchful guard. She had to remove her optilink so that he could perform a retinal scan. There was a gentle chime as the computer confirmed her identity, and then a second chime indicating she had a personal message.

Justine put her optilink back on and turned in the direction of the holoslate. While any words written in analog format on a sign were nothing more than a blur, the optilink sensor had the ability to receive digital data and feed it directly into her optic nerve—the original purpose of the technology. Her name, position, and other vital information popped up on the floating slate beside the scanner, and the blinking message icon hovered below her name.

She touched the icon, and it transformed into a terse sentence: *Please report to Director Mathers.*

The guard, trying to be helpful, pointed down an adjacent corridor with his neuro-baton and said, "Administration is that way, ma'am." He sat back down on his chair, looking bored. "Director Mathers' office is there."

"Thank you," Justine replied with a smile, though she knew exactly where his office was, and headed off in that direction.

∞

"Sir?" she spoke softly at the entrance of Director Mathers' office.

Behind the large oak desk, a high-backed leather chair swiveled around towards Justine. Director Allan Mathers held up one finger for her to wait. His other hand was touching the comlink on his ear.

"—Yes, she's here now," he said to whoever was on the other side of the call. "—Yes. Consider it handled... All right. I'll brief her and send her right down."

He pulled the comlink off his ear and dropped it on the desk.

"Justine," he said. "Close the door and come in. Sit."

Usually, the director greeted his employees with a smile, but today his face was grave and drawn. He looked out the window into the distance while Justine closed the door and approached the desk.

"What's up, sir?" Justine asked as she eased herself into the small guest chair.

Director Mathers turned back and leaned his elbows on his desk. He touched the tips of his fingers together and leveled his gaze at Justine.

"Did you scan the news this morning?" he asked.

Justine shook her head. "Sorry, sir, I was in a bit of a rush." Then, when the director didn't follow up his question, she asked, "What's happened?"

"Justine, you are aware that with all the cutbacks, quite a few of USA, Inc.'s subdivisions, like NASA, have been outsourcing a number of their flights to commercial lines like ours. We even sometimes provide transport for armed forces troops and military cargo to Luna and the outlying space stations."

Nodding, Justine said, "Yes, of course. Why are you telling me this?"

"I'm not comfortable about it, but the directive came from corporate." He glanced up at her, then looked back at his hands.

"What directive, sir?" Justine wrinkled her eyebrows. "I'm not sure I follow."

The director took a deep breath. "Well, apparently a report just came in that the original Mayan scroll—the one they say was transcribed from alien visitors a thousand years ago…"

"Yes," Justine said, gulping. "I know which one you're talking about."

"Well," he continued, "it's been stolen, and the old man who had it has gone missing. They think he might have been kidnapped."

"Oh?" Justine hadn't heard any news about this. She wondered what the kidnappers thought to accomplish. At last report, translating the document was a bust. That was one of the reasons for mothballing the *Quanta* experiments.

Director Mathers nodded. "That's not all. The Honduran Cooperative passed some intelligence on to the CIA. There's a growing movement within the Departmentals in that country. Many of them consider that, because the aliens"—he made air-quotes—"picked the Mayan people to visit half a millennia ago, they are the 'chosen ones' and should be in the forefront of any interstellar commerce. They've been grumbling for years about being sidelined. The governments, though, now think this group might be behind the kidnappings and theft."

Justine pursed her lips. "I've heard something about them. What do they call themselves?"

"Cruzados," the director said. "But now NASA feels keeping their supply of Kinemet here in Houston is a security risk. They've suffered enough bad press, and don't want to see themselves in any more headlines. They're not doing anything with the Kinemet currently, and so they want to transport it to Luna Station. They feel the rebels don't have the resources to attempt any extra-planetary action."

"How much Kinemet are we talking about?" Justine asked.

"About a thousand kilos."

She whistled. "That's a lot!" They had used about a hundred kilograms of the kinetic metal on Alex's flight, and they'd overestimated how much they would need.

"We've got the room," he said with a shrug.

Then Justine cocked her head. "So, what does this have to do with me?"

"Understandably, NASA wants to keep this shipment hush-hush until it has arrived safely on the Moon. An army squad is providing protection." He pointed at Justine. "But NASA wants a liaison to go with them. Someone who has security clearance, and apparently yours has never been revoked, right?"

"That's right."

"You were attached to NASA from the Air Force," he said. "Best of both worlds. So they've requested you accompany the security detail."

Justine didn't want to get her hopes up. She swallowed, then said, "Accompany? What does that mean? What do they want me to do?"

"Same thing you always do. Only this time you'll be attending the soldiers they've assigned to the cargo."

"Oh," Justine said, trying valiantly to keep the sharp disappointment out of her voice.

"You're to report to hangar twelve for a briefing with Colonel Niles

Gagne before the other flight crew or passengers embark."

Justine got to her feet and sighed.

The director said, "This is not a crap assignment."

"Yes it is," she told him.

"It came from up top, Justine," he said by way of apology. The expression on his face showed his sincerity. "Look, just do this one boring flight—"

"A week in a cargo hold babysitting a squad of soldiers is more than just a little boring," Justine said and headed for the door. She would never be recalled to active duty. No one needed a blind pilot. "It's demeaning. If you recall, my actual position with Lunar Lines is in public relations. Now you want me to serve coffee to soldiers?"

"I'll make it up to you," Director Mathers said.

Justine opened the door, but paused before leaving. "Well, I can think of one thing that would make this worth it for me."

"What?" he asked.

"I have a friend on CS3," she said.

"You mean Alex Manez, don't you?"

Justine nodded. "Yeah."

"What about him?"

"He's not doing so well." Justine pulled at her lower lip. "On the return trip, I'd like to take some shore leave up there; spend a little time with him and see what I can do."

"That can be arranged." The director smiled. "Consider it a bonus. We'll arrange some rooms in the Starwatch Resort. I'll even write it up as a training expense."

Justine smiled. "Thanks, Allan."

She closed the door behind her. Feeling much better about her newly assigned duty, she strode off to find hangar twelve and the colonel.

6

Canada Station Three :
Lagrange Point 4 :
Earth Orbit :

Within moments of entering his apartment, a sudden bursting pain literally knocked Alex off his feet.

That haunting song that he heard whenever he used his *sight* filled his mind, pushing out every rational thought.

How is this happening? he screamed to himself. The Kinemetic radiation had long since left him.

The song was there nevertheless. It urged him—no, *compelled* him—to finish what he'd started over a decade before.

Alex was not whole, and unless he could complete his journey and transform into a full Kinemat, he would die in agony; and very soon. Time was his enemy.

For the rest of the day, hiding in his apartment, Alex floated in and out of consciousness.

Since the first time he had been exposed to Kinemet, Alex had not been able to sleep or to dream. He could do neither, and did not seem to have suffered any of the physiological or psychological effects of sleep deprivation. Apparently, his mind could still shut down.

As if drugged, his thoughts soared and wandered. Images appeared before him, and flittered away before they could fully form.

Always, though, there was the Song, calling to him. No matter what he did—taking painkillers, turning off the lights, lying down—it was always there.

It was difficult for him to think clearly. Like a gas-powered automobile running on empty, he needed an infusion of Kinemetic radiation before he succumbed.

His exposure to Kinemet a dozen years before had begun to transform him, but the change was far from complete. Alex was a hollow shell, a ghost, trapped between two dimensions. The key, he knew, was in translating that ancient scroll. No one had been able to solve the riddle, and they'd given up trying. Alex knew the answer was in the scroll. It had always been right there.

As he thought about it, fighting off the pain of Kinemet withdrawal, the certainty grew.

With great difficulty—and struggling to maintain his wits—Alex commanded the communications system to make contact with Michael Sanderson. If there was anyone who could figure out his puzzle, it was Michael.

But the pain! He couldn't remember if he had connected with Earth and spoken with Michael, but before he could try again, the song filled his head … and then something happened to him that tore him away from reality.

His body, ill-equipped to deal with the pain, betrayed him.

He began to shut down.

The last thing he heard was the ancient voice calling to him: *Alex, come home.*

7

Sanderson Family Barbeque :
Hull, Quebec :
Canada Corp. :

A cloud of smoke billowed out of the barbeque when Michael's brother, David, opened the lid to reveal half a dozen charred steaks.

"You think maybe they're cooked enough?" Michael asked, standing off to the side.

With his fingers wrapped around the neck of a beer bottle, he lifted it to his lips and tipped the drink up enough to let a stream of golden liquid pour into his mouth. Several drops spilled over his beard, and he wiped them away with the back of his hand.

"Wise-ass remarks will not get you invited back," David said, waving a spatula in a fan-like motion over the burning steaks to dissipate the rising smoke.

"Probably better for my health, anyway." Michael winked at his brother.

"If you're worried about your health, you'd best watch what you say." David lifted one of the barbeque utensils and pointed it at Michael. "I have tongs, and I'm not afraid to use them."

Michael laughed. "I'll go get some plates," he said and headed toward one of the picnic tables scattered around the yard.

Halfway there, he stopped and turned around. David was poking at the blackened meat with a long knife.

"And a fire extinguisher," Michael added in an attempt to keep the banter going.

"Bah!" David made a shooing motion, but he was grinning when he went back to his attempts to resuscitate their dinner.

Laughing, Michael closed the distance between the barbeque and the tables. By the time he got there, though, his smile faded.

His humor never lasted long these days.

After Alex Manez made his miraculous return from Centauri, Michael had returned to Quantum Resources as a consultant to help coordinate the *Quanta* trials. For reasons the technicians could never adequately explain, none of the test pilots who were exposed to the Kinemetic radiation had fully developed the electropathic ability that Alex had. Without that control, they were unable to return the ships to normal space once they were quantized as light. Several of those who volunteered died during the initial Kinemetic irradiation.

Failure after failure caught up to the corporations, both financially—each ship cost in excess of seventeen billion dollars—and from a public relations perspective. Coupled with the continued economic instabilities as more country corporations went into bankruptcy on a global basis, USA, Inc. had decided to mothball most of their experimental sub-companies, including Quantum Resources, which they sold to Canada Corp. at a bargain basement price.

Rather than relocate to Canada Station Three and administer a team of theorists, Michael decided to let them release him from his contract. Although Alliras Rainier had offered him his old position with the Space Mining Division, Michael and his wife opted for retirement. He had enough savings for him and Melanie to live comfortably for the rest of their lives.

But what Michael hadn't expected was that the rest of Melanie's life was cut short a year ago when a city autobus's brake line failed and slammed into her one-seater automobile while she was out on a shopping excursion. She had died instantly. A day did not go by that Michael didn't miss her fiercely.

Over the following months, Michael fell into a deep depression, let his beard grow out, and spent most of his days wandering from room to room in his empty apartment. The only times he ever emerged was for the monthly family dinners his brother held.

No wife, no job, no purpose.

The only thing that held Michael together was the weekly call he placed to Alex Manez; but it was getting harder and harder for Michael to maintain his hope that something would be done to help the boy and his deteriorating health. Without his political contacts, Michael was helpless to prod the medical staff on Canada Station Three to figure out a cure for Alex's condition.

During their conversations, Alex invariably told Michael not to worry; that it would all work out in the end.

"Are you all right?" a voice said, breaking Michael out of his reverie.

He looked up to see Andrea, David's wife, fixing him with two very concerned blue eyes. She was a slender woman with smile lines at the corner of her mouth and eyes. Streaks of silver had begun to flow through her raven-black hair.

Andrea and Melanie had been very close friends, and once in a while she would drop over to Michael's apartment and look in on him, do his laundry and try to clean up the place.

Michael realized he had just been standing in front of the picnic table with a stack of disposable plates in his hand.

He gave her a smile. "Yeah," he said. "Just lost in thought."

Turning around, he brought the plates over to the barbeque.

In addition to David and Andrea, Michael's two nephews, and their wives and kids, were also in attendance. Andrea's sister and her family were also there. David's son was out of town, but his daughter-in-law Debbie and her two children were spending the weekend. All told, David Sanderson's backyard held over twenty people.

Michael was grateful for the crowd. Not just for the company, but because, with so much hustle and bustle, he could blend into the background and not have to interact. He loved his family, but lately he had found himself detaching from human contact. It was good to be around people—it reminded him of his humanity—but he just didn't have the energy to cultivate any kind of relationship with anyone.

David looked up when Michael approached. "Good timing; the steaks are ready."

"They were ready fifteen minutes ago," Michael said, lifting the corner of his mouth in a half-smile.

"Just..." David mimed scraping the burned parts off with a knife. "And smear it with sauce."

Michael laughed. While David put steaks on the plates, Michael carted them over to the tables. While he trucked back and forth, he noticed he had picked up a little shadow.

He looked down to see his six-year-old grand-nephew staring up at him with a grin. "Hello, Carl," he said.

"Hello, Great-Uncle Michael." Carl waved his hand in a sweeping motion.

"Just call me Uncle Mike—I haven't felt great in a long while. Did you want to be my helper?"

"Sure, Great-Unc—sure, Uncle Mike."

Michael handed him a plate with a thick steak hanging over the lip, and watched while Carl balanced it and carried it over to the tables. All the while, he stuck his tongue out of the corner of his mouth in concentration.

Michael and David smiled while they watched him go.

"Grandkids," David said. "They'll keep you young."

Then his smile faded. "Sorry, Michael. I know you and Melanie tried hard."

"I guess it's for the better," Michael said after a while. "I was always working fourteen-hour shifts. Barely had enough time for Melanie. If I had kids they'd probably have grown up strangers, full of resentment."

When Carl came back for his second load, Michael said, "You okay, sport?"

"Yeah. Aunt Ginny says she only wants a half. And one that isn't a burnt offering."

With a laugh, David quickly sliced a steak in two and put the slightly smaller portion on a plate, which Michael handed to Carl.

"There you go. Steady now," he added when Carl overbalanced the plate.

"You know," David said, and there was an uncomfortable quaver in his voice, "if you're not doing anything, why don't you swing by next weekend? Andrea and I are going to a bridge tournament. There's a lot of single people our age there."

"I'm not ready."

Dave held up his hands. "Hey, don't mean to push."

Michael shook his head. "I'm just not sure what to do with myself is all. I always thought this would be my chance to travel the world with Melanie."

"You can still travel." David prepared another steak for Carl when the young boy returned. "There are chartered tours for practically every destination."

"Wouldn't really be the same."

"You've got to get out of this funk," David said. "I'm saying this as your brother and your friend."

"I know. I appreciate it, really. I guess I just need to figure things out. I can't explain it."

David put his hand on Michael's shoulder. "You don't need to explain a thing. Just know we're here for you."

"Thanks, bro." Michael didn't need to force the smile he gave David.

When Carl came back for the last time, he said, "It's just you and Grandpa left, Uncle Mike. —And me."

"Well," Michael said. "Looks like your grandfather saved the juiciest steak for you, a reward for all your hard work."

Carl beamed as he took his prize back to the picnic tables, shouting at his mom, "Look what I got."

David served the last two steaks, and he and Michael headed to the table to fill their plates with potato salad, pickles and buns.

While everyone ate, they shared jokes, gossiped, and just basked in the familiarity of family.

Michael's appetite wasn't what it used to be, and when he had only finished half of his supper, he excused himself from the table to use the washroom.

"Don't fall in!" someone joked, and Michael waved a hand in the air as he went into his brother's house.

On the way to the facilities, he passed by David's front room. A large DMR casement was playing the highlight reel of the last Roughriders football game. At the bottom of the flat screen was a scrolling newsfeed, and it was one of the sentences there that caught his attention.

He quickly moved in for a closer look, but only caught the last part of the announcement:

"...NASA spokesman discounts the impact of the missing Mayan scroll." Then the newsfeed went on to other political matters.

Michael sat on the couch next to the control pad and typed in a command to flip the screen to his favorite bulletin board. He cursed when he had to physically toggle back and forth between pages.

Within a few minutes, however, he had the entire story—the kidnapping of Yaxche and the theft of the ancient scroll—and his face grew dark.

"What's wrong?" asked his brother from the doorway.

"Who uses a damned DMR casement anymore? Why don't you upgrade to a holoslate with an organic user interface?" Michael asked. "You know, haptic consoles have been around for five years now."

"I really don't need to multitask while watching the Jays get beat by the Cubs," David said matter-of-factly. "I'm fine with one screen at a time."

Taking a deep breath, Michael said, "Sorry."

"Hey, no problem. You okay?"

Michael looked up. "Looks like the Cruzados kidnapped that Mayan translator, Yaxche. He was the one who helped us interpret the Mayan text from Pluto." He flipped a page on the casement. "And they also stole the scroll that was supposed to help us figure out how to use the Kinemet."

"Oh?" David blinked. "I thought they had given up on that."

"Yeah. They had." Michael glanced back at the casement. "And it looks like they won't be doing anything about this either." He sighed.

"Well, if NASA and everyone else thinks the document is a dead end, why would the Cruzados go to all this trouble?"

"I don't know."

David spoke again, and Michael could tell his brother was trying to make it sound casual. "Why don't you call up that Calbert Loche fellow? Get your info straight from the horse's mouth."

For a moment, while Michael had read the boards, there had been a spark there, a hint of the passion that had fired him throughout his forty-year career. David was obviously trying to fan those flames.

Michael had to admit that his natural curiosity had gotten the better of him for a moment.

He said to his brother, "You know, I think I might do that."

∞

Most nights Michael couldn't sleep. His thoughts troubled him: how much he missed Melanie; his lack of purpose; his growing disconnection with everyone who had been a part of life.

That night, however, he couldn't sleep for another reason. His mind kept working over and over again about why, after so many years and after NASA and Quantum Resources had devalued the worth of the Mayan scroll, that anyone would go through the trouble to steal it. Or kidnap Yaxche. Did they want to hold him for ransom? Who was going to pay?

Unable to sleep, Michael threw on a thin robe and went to his computer. Although many of his files were classified and confiscated when he 'retired' from Quantum Resources—both as director and as a consultant—he maintained a folder of his own collected data and musings. Shorthand notes that held no meaning to anyone but himself were added to various documents he had downloaded off the mesh. He also kept a copy of all the declassified material that had been on his computer when he left the company.

Michael began the long and arduous task of sorting and filtering through every file on his computer. He hoped, somewhere in the morass of information, there might be something they had missed. Maybe someone else had stumbled on a vital piece of datum that would reopen the doors to interstellar travel.

It was three in the morning when Michael finally noticed the time. He yawned and rubbed his eyes. He needed a couple of hours sleep to process all the documents he had read, and he had only gone through a small percentage of the notes.

Michael laughed to himself about how much his brother would applaud the change in him, the sudden purpose. He went to the refrigerator and poured himself a tall glass of milk. There was no way he was going to get to sleep with a full mind and an empty stomach. At least if there was something in his gut he had half a chance of getting a few precious hours before morning rolled around. He wanted to be alert when he contacted Calbert Loche.

No—he thought suddenly to himself—when he *met* with Calbert. Michael decided right then and there that he needed to speak to his former colleague in person.

He went to his computer and logged onto his travel account and purchased a ticket for Toronto, where Quantum Resources maintained their earthbound administrative offices.

Calbert would see him; Michael's strong endorsement had launched him into the director's chair. And if anyone in the industry had an inside track on what was really happening, it would be Calbert, who always had both Raymond Magrath and George Markowitz nearby. The trio were an intellectual powerhouse when they put their respective heads together. Since the restructuring of Quantum Resources, the three had been delegated to more of a public relations and administrative role.

Satisfied in his plans, Michael headed for his bed. His empty bed…

He had an unexpected pang of loneliness and loss when he approached the bed he had shared with his wife for more than forty years, and he had to choke back the tear that welled in his eye.

Melanie…

He lay down and was on the cusp of sleep when the comchime sounded and gave him a start.

Looking at the clock again, he willed his lungs to pump air in and out once more. Every time someone called unexpectedly, Michael had a flashback to when he answered the phone to a somber but officious voice asking him if he was the husband of Melanie Sanderson.

Regaining his composure, he said, "Who is it, Hucs?" to his apartment's home-unit computer system.

<Voice chat from Alex Manez,> was the answer.

"Oh?"

That was odd. Usually it was Michael who initiated contact with Alex. Michael hoped there was nothing wrong.

"Put him on."

The call came through, and at first Michael thought the link had been disconnected because all he got was static.

"Hucs, can you amplify?"

But there was no need because Michael heard Alex speak then, and the boy's tone sent a chill through him.

"Michael." Alex's voice was hollow and haunted.

Michael asked, "Alex, are you all right?"

"It's getting harder," Alex said. "The Song is in my head but I can't hear it because it's too loud. They want me."

"Alex? What are you talking about?"

"I don't know how much longer I can hold out," Alex said, and Michael wished he could look at the young man. Over a year ago, Alex had disabled the video feed on his communicator. He had said he didn't want anyone to see him looking the way he did.

"Alex, do you need me to come up there?" Michael hadn't been up to CS3 since before Melanie passed away.

"No," Alex said. "But I do need you to do something for me."

"Anything. What do you need?" Michael asked.

A silence stretched out for an impossible length of time and for a moment Michael thought they had been disconnected. But then Alex said, "Find him."

"Find him? Find who?"

"He has the answer. He's always had the key; he just never knew it." Alex's voice was becoming thin, and Michael could sense that the conversation would not last very long, and neither would Alex.

He said, "Tell me who you mean, Alex. You need to help me if I'm to help you."

When there was no immediate answer, Michael barked out a command. "Hucs, get the communications officer of Canada Station Three—"

"Yaxche," Alex said, interrupting Michael. "You have to hear him tell you the story."

And then the link went dead.

Michael repeated his command to Hucs to reestablish communication. After several minutes, he managed to connect with a CS3 operator.

"This is Michael Sanderson," he stated. "Former Director of Quantum Resources. I need to get in contact with Alex Manez. It's an emergency."

"Right away, sir," the woman said.

While he waited, Michael pondered the emotions running around inside him.

In the space of a day, he had gone from a lost soul to someone with purpose. Was it the thrill of a scientific mystery, was it the promise of untold wonders, or was it the concern he held for this young man who was at the heart of the matter? Or a combination of all three?

The operator came back on. "I'm sorry, sir, but Alex Manez has been admitted to our care facility. He's had some kind of episode. I'm afraid he will be unable to take your call."

"Of course," Michael said. "Who is attending him?"

"Dr. Amma. She's the top neurologist in her field."

"I'm sure she is. Listen, I know it's not really your job, but if you could do me a favor and transmit updates to me at this link, I would appreciate it."

"Yes, sir. I understand your concern."

Michael hung up. He sat on the bed.

Find Yaxche?

How odd that earlier in the day Michael had learned about the old man's kidnapping, and now he'd received a message from Alex—almost four-hundred-thousand kilometers away in space—telling him to get to the bottom of this mystery.

One option Michael had was to chart a flight with Lunar Lines and go see Alex. The rational side of him knew that there was nothing he could do except stand vigil beside his young friend, and in the end that might be the only course of action that would do either of them any good.

But Michael had to hold on to the hope that there was, indeed, something that could be done. If finding Yaxche and figuring out why the Cruzados had kidnapped him—and what key he unwittingly possessed—gave Alex any chance of surviving his disability, then Michael really had no choice when it came down to it.

Resolved in his sense of purpose, he slipped inside the bed sheets and forced himself to fall asleep.

He had a very busy day ahead.

8

Canada Station Three :
Lagrange Point 4 :
Earth Orbit :

When Alex came out of his trance, a nurse hurried over to him, looking concerned.

"What happened?" he asked her in a groggy voice. He couldn't focus. The lights hurt his eyes.

"It's going to be all right, Alex," the nurse said. Her voice was muffled, as if she were speaking to him from a great distance.

"Where am I?" he asked.

The nurse put a cold pack on his forehead. "You had a minor cerebrovascular attack—probably just a side effect of your condition coupled with stress. You've developed a fever, but Dr. Amma told me you would be fine in a day or so. Just rest."

He lay back and closed his eyes, not to sleep, but in an attempt to get back to that superconscious state and figure out what it all meant.

Exhaustion, however, prevented him from reaching that transcendent plateau. He opened his eyes once more, but the nurse was gone.

Alex lifted an arm to press the call button, but his muscles were far too weak to respond.

Despondently, he remained in the hospital bed the rest of the night, struggling to recapture his thoughts, but finding them as elusive as his long-gone dreams.

∞

Dr. Amma visited Alex early the next morning.

"How are you feeling, Alex?" she said. "You gave us all quite a scare last night."

She was middle-aged, very thin and short. With her hair pulled back in a tight bun, she took on a vague ferret-like semblance. Of all the people on Canada Station Three, and all the Quantum Resources staff, Dr. Amma was the only one Alex thought truly wanted to help him. Everyone else treated him as a lab rat or an untapped gold mine.

"I'm fine," Alex said.

"Did you get any sleep?"

"I don't sleep." Alex smiled when he said it. Dr. Amma often asked him questions like that, as if trying to trip him up. There was a touch of the psychologist in her, he thought.

"Ah, yes. One can always hope." Dr. Amma looked down at her holoslate and read from her notes. "Well, it looks like your electrolyte count is back to normal. Vitals are stable."

"I'm fine," he said. "It wasn't a coma and it wasn't a stroke."

Dr. Amma leveled her gaze at him. "All the readings indicated you were presenting symptoms of a hemorrhagic event. We couldn't take a tomography scan because of your pre-existing condition, but it resembled a stroke."

Although Alex's electropathic ability had been reduced to a shadow of its former power, there was a minute amount of residual radiation in him, enough to skew the results of any X-ray or electroencephalograph. Lack of proper testing reduced any medical diagnosis to nothing more than an educated guess.

"I was aware through the entire incident," Alex told her. "Though it was clouded."

Dr. Amma narrowed her eyes. "And how would you describe the incident?"

Leaning back into his pillow, Alex stared at the ceiling. "I was separated from myself, but at the same time I went deeper into myself than I ever had before."

"A dissociative fugue?" Dr. Amma guessed.

"No. It was more of a trance. I think … I belong in a different place, or a different state, and my consciousness wanted to go there."

"Do you know where that is?" she asked.

"No," he said. "I lost the connection."

"I hope you won't be sending the medical teams into a panic again."

Alex smiled. "No. And I'm sorry if that frightened everyone. It was unintentional."

Dr. Amma pulled the holoslate to her chest and folded her arms over it.

"Alex, I want to help you. I need to know everything. If you have any idea how to make you better—"

He said, "Get me next to a supply of Kinemet."

"You know I can't," she said. "They stopped mining it, and whatever they have left over they're hoarding like it was the key to the gate of heaven."

Proposed Holocommercial :
Lunar Lines PR Transcript :

The sun slowly settles over the crescent of Earth's horizon. As the sun meets the Earth, it's corona explodes in a flash of light.

ANNOUNCER

From the Earth...

The sun disappears to darkness, and a full moon, bright and silver, rises in its place in the night sky.

ANNOUNCER

...to the Moon

Cut to:

Several passengers lounge on large seats and at a bar in the luxurious interior of a Lunar Lines vessel. They are laughing and smiling.

ANNOUNCER

Why not travel in style?

Cut to:

A female passenger lays her head on a pillow on a contoured bed and pulls a comforter blanket around her.

ANNOUNCER

Lunar Lines – We'll get you there.

Lunar Lines Vessel, *Diana*:
Earth—CS3 Transit :

Normally, Justine would be circulating around the cabin of the *Diana* once the space liner reached escape velocity and the passengers were free to roam about.

Like a minor celebrity hired to mingle with customers at a restaurant or political event, Justine's primary job description was to socialize, tell stories of her days as a pilot, and offer technical explanations for every aspect of their voyage; anything to put the travelers at ease.

Her position as flight guide didn't give her the rush of actually captaining a ship, but at least she was in space and talking about the things which held her passion.

This particular trip, however, was going to be excruciatingly boring for her.

The cargo bay itself encompassed nearly the entire length of the liner and the lower half of its height. From a fiscal standpoint, Justine knew, most of the company's profits came from freight rather than fares. Taking on passengers was more for the public relations exposure than anything else.

Since a good deal of the cargo was perishables intended for either Canada Station Three or Luna Station, they kept the heat in the bay at minimum. Justine needed to wear a thick sweater over her PERSuit harness to keep from freezing, and this severely hampered the sensors. Unfortunately, the harness was tailored to fit snugly, and wouldn't fit on top of a sweater or jacket.

Not having the harness on made her job navigating through the maze of containers something of a nightmare, especially when she had to cart drinks and snacks from the kitchenette one floor above to the soldiers guarding the insulated crate of Kinemet at the back of the cargo hold.

It was ridiculous to think only someone with security clearance was permitted to serve the guards, but she was determined to make the best of it.

The eight uniformed men took their jobs extremely seriously. They were a very tight-lipped crew, and when they were on duty, they held their post in complete silence. At all times, two of them stood guard on either side of the container holding the Kinemet. They had M72 ion pulse rifles at the ready. A third and fourth soldier walked the perimeter of the cargo bay. Every three hours, they would relieve each other in rotating shifts.

When she first arrived in the cargo bay and was introduced to the squad members, they were very formal and would only address her as Major Turner, even after she repeated to them, "Just call me Justine."

Once they were in space, Justine asked them for their orders, and they stared at her in frozen terror. Here was a retired NASA major fetching drinks for them.

"Guys," she had said, "if you don't tell me what you want, it's going to be a very thirsty trip."

Having grown accustomed to putting people at ease with her former celebrity, Justine cracked a few jokes and made sure to ask them questions about their family back home in order to get to know them. After a few hours they relaxed around her, though they all remained very respectful and polite.

They would respond to direct questions from Justine, but the only one who went out of his way to engage in conversation with her was the squad leader, Lieutenant John Jeffries. He was quite young—all the soldiers were—and Justine could tell he was trying to set an example for the men under his command. Soon, however, he truly warmed to Justine and there were moments she was certain he forgot her former status as a major.

When the soldiers were off shift they snoozed, read books or watched vids on their holoslates. Lieutenant Jeffries had brought an old-fashioned crib board and challenged Justine to a game when he wasn't on duty. It killed the time.

Ordinarily, with her optilink sensor, she was unable to discern standard print on paper or cardboard. When the optilink was hooked to the PERSuit harness, however, she could interpret changes in color and translate the two-dimensional images to her mind.

The only problem was, while she played the game, she had to take off her sweater, so she usually had to stop after a few games before she got too cold.

During Lieutenant Jeffries' second stint off-duty, they played for about an hour. Justine was up six games to five over the lieutenant, who had won most of their previous matches. She was on a winning streak, and didn't want to quit, despite the fact that she was shivering.

Lieutenant Jeffries was five points behind the skunk line, and Justine needed six points to win. She kept her pegging cards, since it was his first count.

He played his first card. "Three," he said. "Try to 'fifteen' that."

Justine laid down a 'three' of her own. "Six for two." She took her points while Lieutenant Jeffries pondered his next play. It was obvious he had kept his small cards as well in an attempt to avoid being skunked. He played what Justine assumed was his highest card: a seven.

"Thirteen," he said.

She dropped her deuce and smiled. "Fifteen for two. Two to go."

He hesitated and took a second look at her harness. "You sure that thing doesn't have X-ray vision or something?"

Justine laughed. "No excuses. Get ready to be humiliated."

"Okay," he said. "Here's my other 'three'. Eighteen."

With an exaggerated motion, Justine placed her own 'three' down. "Twenty-one for two. And game."

Clicking his tongue, the lieutenant flipped over his last card. "I had a 'five'."

"I had you either way." Justine showed him her 'four'.

Throwing down his card in mock outrage, the lieutenant said, "I can't let you get away with that. One more?"

"I wish I could, but you won't have much competition against an icicle." Justine chuckled and slipped her thick sweater over her head, reducing her vision to the regular optilink level. "It's time for me to make a round anyway. Did you need anything?"

"No thanks," he said. "Hey, I know this must be the worst assignment you've ever had."

"Not the worst," Justine said with an equivocal smile.

"Compared to flying to Pluto?" he asked while packing up the crib board. "Working as a hostess must be difficult."

Rubbing her hands together to get the circulation flowing, Justine gave a half-shrug. "It may not be as exciting," she said, "but at least at

I get to tell tall tales, and they pay me for it."

She got up and, after polling the other soldiers for their orders, made her way to the elevator and up to the kitchenette.

Besides the flight crew and the hospitality staff, no one else knew Justine was on board. She was recognizable, and if any of the passengers saw her, it might lead to questions NASA and the military didn't want to answer.

While she was loading a cart with snacks and drinks, one of the stewardesses, Brandi, popped into the cramped room and walked directly toward her. Justine couldn't see the look on her colleague's face, but the woman's voice was a mix of concern and puzzlement.

"There's a call for you," Brandi said.

Justine shook her head. "No one knows I'm here. Are you sure it's for me?"

Brandi nodded.

"Who is it?" Justine asked.

"Don't know. It's encoded."

Thinking it might be Director Mathers checking in with her, Justine nodded to Brandi. "Thanks."

After securing the food cart in the walk-in cooler, Justine made her way toward the cabin, outside of which there was a tiny communications cubical.

It was a video chat, so there was no need for Justine to take her sweater off. The regular optilink sensor could translate the digital images on the screen as if she had normal vision.

She stepped inside the cubicle, closed the door and turned on the holoslate.

A familiar but unexpected face appeared, and Justine was momentarily taken aback.

"Clive?"

When Alex had returned from Centauri, Justine had wanted to be there on the Moon when Alex got back, and had spent a few hours catching up with him. After Alex was whisked off by NASA officials back to Earth, Justine had remained for a few days for a debriefing with Clive Wexhall, who was still NASA's liaison on the Moon.

The first evening, he had invited her out for dinner. Justine didn't know whether it was her euphoria at having Alex back safe and sound, or her own sense of isolation because of her blindness and demotion from flight status, or if it was just too many glasses of wine, but she had ended up spending that night—and every subsequent night during her visit—with Clive.

Once she had returned to Earth, she had chalked it up to nothing more than a brief fling, but Clive wanted to see her again.

Despite his regular calls to her afterwards, she had tried to keep her emotions in check, and keep their relationship on a casual level.

When she had secured her job with Lunar Lines six months ago, Clive had somehow found out and had been waiting for her the first time she docked at Luna Station.

They had spent every moment of the two-day layover together as if they had never been apart. Justine had told herself not to let her feelings get the better of her. She had explained to Clive that she wasn't ready for anything more serious in her life. He said he was perfectly fine with that.

Whenever Justine was away, they remained friendly and platonic; but whenever she was on Luna Station, she would stay with him at his apartment. They had fallen into a routine, and Justine didn't want to change their arrangement.

She had not had time to contact Clive before the space liner took off, and normally he wouldn't call her while she was on duty, so she was surprised that he managed to track her down. No one was supposed to know about her presence on the ship.

"Nice to see you, too," he replied with a playful smile and a hint of sarcasm.

When Justine didn't respond right away, Clive pretended to look hurt.

"Sorry," she said. "Of course, I'm happy to see you. You know that. I just wasn't expecting you to call me here."

"You don't like surprises?" he asked with a smile. "I would have called before you left, but I've been up to my neck in paperwork, arranging for the transfer and storage of your, ahem, precious cargo."

"You know about the shipment?" she asked.

"Who do you think suggested you for the assignment?"

Justine's eyes flared. "You! You're responsible for me spending the last ten hours in a freezing cargo bay? And you didn't give me a heads-up?"

His smile grew wider. "Sorry about that," he said, not sounding apologetic at all. "But I figured it would be a great opportunity for you."

"What?" Justine couldn't believe her ears. "And how is this a great opportunity for me? It's so secret I didn't know about it until a few moments before I came on board. And it's so tedious, I'm about to go crazy from the boredom. And did I mention," she added, "that I'm freezing my extremities down there?"

Clive laughed. "I have some news that might warm you up."

She pointed a warning finger at him. "It had better be good."

"I've arranged to escort you—and the shipment—from CS3 to Luna Station."

"You have?" Justine felt herself flush. Then she blinked. "Where are you calling from?"

"I just arrived on CS3 about a half hour ago. I've also made reservations for a private booth at the Terra Vista Restaurant, and I have balcony tickets to *La Danse Des Étoiles.*"

"I've always wanted to see that," Justine said, her voice softening.

"There's no sense in spending the eight-hour layover—as you say— freezing our extremities on the liner's cargo bay. There are plenty of things to do on CS3."

"Clive, if I didn't know any better, I would think you were trying to butter me up for something."

He laughed. "It's all for purely selfish reasons, I assure you. I just want you to start thinking of me as more than a bi-monthly boyfriend." Clive's tone turned serious at that last part.

Justine balked at his declaration. She was comfortable the way things were. There had been far too many changes in her life over the past few years, and she was just starting to get her feet under her and adjust to her circumstances.

She truly looked forward to spending a couple of days every other week with Clive on the moon. With his busy political schedule and her traveling, Justine didn't know if there was any way they could bring their relationship to the next level. Or that she wanted to.

The thought of anything more than what they had already scared her. Justine's long-ago marriage to Brian had been a disaster, and it hadn't been his fault. She had always been a career-minded woman, and had her eyes—and heart—set on the stars.

Even now that she could no longer captain a ship, deep down she held the desire to return to space as something more than a tour guide. She did not want to be bound to Earth or the Moon. It was a ridiculous notion, but she hoped technology would advance to the point where it could either completely restore her sight, or provide her with a less cumbersome prosthetic device than the PERSuit.

"Hey," Clive said. "I didn't mean to bring you down."

"No, not at all." Justine smiled to show she wasn't upset. "But while you're in a generous mood, maybe I can get you to do me a very special favor."

He raised an eyebrow.

Justine said, "Maybe you can help me with Alex Manez."

Clive made a gruff sound in his throat. "Not this again. Since Quantum Resources is under full Canadian ownership, I don't even have clearance to *ask* if they have any Kinemet, let alone get them to allocate any for—"

Then he suddenly figured out what Justine was getting at.

"No way." Clive's face turned red and he dropped his voice. "I seriously hope you're not suggesting we smuggle any of our Kinemet off that liner."

Justine shook her head and clicked her tongue. "Clive, you know I would never ask you to do anything like that."

"Then ... what?"

"How about the exact opposite?"

Clive stared at her for more than a few seconds, confused.

"But—" Then he sighed. "Oh, I see." He sounded reluctant, but said, "Yes, I think that can be arranged."

11

Quantum Resources :
Toronto :
Canada Corp. :

Toronto was vastly different from Ottawa, both in architecture and culture. While the city planners in the nation's capital tried to keep the city's expansion spread out over a large area, Toronto was home to some of the most impressive skyscrapers in the country. Where Ottawa was a hub for politics, Toronto's focus was commerce.

When Quantum Resources was first chartered, its mandate had been to develop Kinemet into a usable fuel source for interstellar flight. Since the *Quanta* missions had consistently failed, and Alex's mission had turned into a public relations disaster, Quantum Resources' ability to capitalize on the new technology had been severely hampered. After Canada Corp. bought all outstanding shares and put Quantum Resources under the umbrella of the Space Mining Division, the Director of SMD had changed QR's mandate in order to put the company back on a profitable basis.

In their early years, Quantum Resources had attracted some of the best thinkers in the field of astronomy and physics, and it would be a shame to put their collective brain-power to waste. While some of the company's resources were reserved for analyzing what they knew about Kinemet in the hopes of one day turning it into a viable fuel, the main thrust of their efforts was to improve existing technologies and increase their efficiency.

As a former employee, Michael was still subscribed to their quarterly meshmail reports. In the last two quarters, and for the first time since its incorporation, Quantum Resources was in the black.

When the autotaxi dropped Michael off at a high-rise office

complex he didn't recognize, he rechecked the destination he had entered into the navigation screen. The directory confirmed this was the location for Quantum Resources.

It had been several months since Michael had spoken to Calbert, but at that time his former colleague had not mentioned any upcoming relocation.

Michael authorized the debit charge, and with his overnight bag in hand he stepped out of the vehicle and entered the building.

In the foyer, he approached the reception kiosk and skimmed the list of companies. Quantum Resources offices were on the thirtieth floor.

When Michael got out of the elevator, he stepped out into a scene of chaos. Construction engineers and electricians were putting up walls, stringing power lines, and setting up computer workstations.

Stepping up to a foreman, Michael said, "Hello, I'm not sure if I have the right place. Is Calbert Loche here?"

The foreman pointed down a half-built hallway. "Yeah. His office is back there."

"Thank you." Michael smiled and let him get back to work as he picked his way through the piles of ceiling tiles, steel frames and scattered tools.

When he reached the end of the hall, he heard the unmistakable voice of his former second-in-command.

"I don't care how you do it," Calbert Loche said as he stared out the window, his back to the door and to Michael. "We need that meshlink up and running by tonight."

Calbert turned as Michael stepped inside the incomplete office, and the clouded look on his face disappeared as he recognized his old boss. He motioned for Michael to take a seat while he finished his conversation.

"Yes, there'll be people here all night. I don't care about overtime, just get your guys to have the link hot by morning." He paused while listening to the response, then nodded. "Good. That's what I want to hear."

Calbert gently touched the comlink sensor at his temple to disconnect it. His smile widened as he reached across his desk to shake Michael's hand.

"Long time no see," Calbert said, and pointed at Michael's chin. "Looks like the weeds are taking over the lawn."

Michael chuckled, and rubbed his fingers through his graying beard. "It's from the stress of dealing with all my sassy employees over the years," he said with a grin.

Gesturing to a guest chair on the other side of his desk, Calbert eased himself into his seat and leaned back.

He regarded Michael with a convivial smile. "How've you been keeping?"

Michael nodded. "Good. Good."

"Staying busy?"

"Doing a lot of reading." Michael motioned his hand around the office. "I didn't know you guys had relocated."

"Expanded."

"What?"

Calbert's eyes widened. "We're keeping the main labs where they are and just moving administration here."

"Oh? Breakthrough?"

"Ha," Calbert said. "I wish. No, without any Kinemet, we're just spinning our wheels. About six months ago, our grant money ran out, and we all thought that was it. But then the Chilean Corp. found out about our experiments with 'steam cracking'. As it turns out, it's totally useless for quantum purposes, but there are other possibilities. They approached us about using the technology to increase the efficiency of their hydrogen plants. We applied some of our theories on their systems and nearly doubled their production with only a marginal increase in expenditure. Since then, we've secured contracts with a dozen other power plants around the world. It ain't glorious work, but it does pay the bills."

"That's fantastic," Michael said.

"And the extra profit keeps Ottawa off our backs, and allows us to maintain our labs on CS3, which," he said, his voice measured and careful, "is why you're here. Right?"

Nodding, Michael said, "Yes. I got a strange call last night from Alex."

"I know. I received the report this morning." Calbert stood up and looked out the window. "You know my hands are tied. SMD holds our charter and they call the shots. I'm just a pencil pusher, as far as they are concerned. I wish I could help."

Michael cleared his throat. "Maybe you still can."

"How?" Calbert asked. "I know you've tried to go through Alliras, but since USA, Inc. stopped funding us, SMD isn't willing to spend resources actively looking for more Kinemet. We don't have any in our possession, and if NASA has any left over, they're not fessing up."

"I know."

Calbert, sounding defensive and frustrated at the same time, said, "I've got some contacts on the SMD survey teams. If anyone uncovers even a hint of Kinemet, you can be sure I'll know about it in two shakes."

"I know," Michael repeated.

"I'm sure things will turn around in a few years and we can begin mining Kinemet again."

Michael shook his head. "Alex doesn't have that long. But that's not what I want to talk to you about."

"It isn't?"

"Do you have a transcript of the call I received from Alex?" Michael knew Calbert did. Alex was a very well guarded and unique secret, and anything and everything he said was catalogued, charted and analyzed.

"Yeah…?"

Michael cocked his head. "He asked me to find Yaxche."

"I heard about the kidnapping and the theft. I feel bad for the old man, but as far as that scroll is concerned, it's a lost cause. I'm not sure why anyone would go to all the trouble."

"But someone did." Michael leaned back in the chair. "Alex obviously thinks there's more there than what we've uncovered, and the thieves also think so as well. And, I'm not sure if you noticed, but Alex asked me to find the man, not the scroll."

Calbert slowly sat down again. "I did notice that. What do you think it means? Do you think Alex knows something we don't?"

"If he does, he's not conscious of it. But it feels like there is some validity to this, even if there's no concrete evidence. Maybe there's something that's been lost in translation."

"All right," said Calbert. "Let's say there's some merit in finding Yaxche—outside of the humanitarian reasons. What makes you think the Honduran Conglomerate isn't already doing its best?"

"Maybe they don't think he's as high a priority as I do," Michael answered. "Or as important as Alex does."

Rubbing his upper lip, Calbert said, "Not saying I agree or disagree, but even if I did, what can I do?"

"Is George Markowitz doing anything important for the next

couple of weeks?"

"George?" Calbert sat forward, looking genuinely surprised. "What does he have to do with this?"

"I'm going to Honduras to look for Yaxche. I'd like George to come with me. More specifically, I'd like you to *assign* him to come with me."

"Why?"

Michael lifted his hand and ticked off a finger. "First of all, he's the only person I know who's met Yaxche. George has been down there a few times. He knows the area. Besides, he's extremely good at research and these kinds of practical puzzles."

Touching his next finger, Michael said, "Secondly, if you give him this assignment and put it on paper, it will give us a certain amount of legitimacy with the Copán Departmental. We can say we're on official business. Otherwise I'm just a nosy tourist."

Calbert took a breath. "This is all a bit much before I've had my second coffee, Michael. Have you even given any consideration to the Cruzados? If they are indeed the ones who kidnapped him, do you think they'll just hand him over to a retired desk jockey?"

"I'm not planning a guerilla incursion," Michael said. "Once we track down where he is, we'll call in the Honduran authorities to take over. I know they consider the document a national treasure. They'll take action. Besides, I'm getting arthritis in my knees; I'm no hero."

Calbert leaned back in his chair. "I'm still not convinced."

"Tell you what, give us a couple of weeks. If we end up with nothing but dysentery, then we'll come home. Unless, of course, you need George for anything…?"

"No, we've got him analyzing hydro fluctuations; any intern can do it."

"Well, then?"

Calbert shrugged. "All right. Fine. Let's go talk to George and see how he feels about it."

∞

Calbert fought traffic all the way across the city as he drove Michael to the Quantum Resources labs.

As one of the few country corporations that still operated on a profitable basis, Canada Corp. attracted immigrants from all over the world. The national policy had always been to welcome the influx of people, but in the major cities the infrastructure was strained to the limit. In the past two years, the government had issued a moratorium on new visas.

Population and overcrowding had always been a concern. Space stations and moon colonies were far too expensive to provide a feasible solution to overcrowding. In the back of Michael's mind—as with others, he was sure—the possibility of life-sustaining worlds in other solar systems would become a primary consideration once they made contact with the alien culture that had built the star beacons.

When the first *Quanta* mission was announced, there had been a swell of hope for the future, and as a result there had also been something of a population explosion as people anticipated interstellar trade, commerce, and migration.

That hope had been dashed when Alex returned with the news that he had not made contact, and that there were no signs of life in Centauri. The failed attempts to develop the electropathic ability in other pilots, and the subsequent mothballing of the *Quanta* projects only served to decrease worldwide confidence. As markets plunged and country corporations fell, there was an increase in civil unrest and crime rates around the world.

In his mind, Michael felt as if he had a responsibility for the direction in which humankind was going, since he had been involved from the start. Perhaps some of his discontentment in the past few years was because he considered the entire affair unfinished business.

He wanted to help Alex, there was no doubt of that; but at the same time he felt reinvigorated now that he had renewed his purpose.

"I've been thinking," Calbert said as he swerved to avoid hitting a courier drone. "With our current expansion, we're going to be recruiting more technicians and researchers. They're going to need someone grounded in science in an administrative capacity."

"Oh?" Michael's interest was piqued.

"Maybe when you get back you might consider taking a position with the company. I was going to ask you a few months ago, but..."

A few months ago Michael would have said 'no'; he had been too torn with grief over his wife. Melanie had always been supportive of his career, and he knew she would not have wanted to see him wallow in a directionless existence. Now, things were different.

"That sounds perfect," he said immediately, unable to keep from grinning like a boy.

"We'll work out the details later. Of course, there are a couple of conditions."

Michael nodded. "Shoot."

"First, you would have to be able to take orders from me. It's a bit of a role-reversal from the last time we worked together."

"I have no problem with that," Michael said, and he meant it. He had always had complete faith in Calbert, otherwise he would never have recommended him for his current position as CEO of Quantum Resources, Inc. "Anything else?"

"Just one more thing," Calbert said in a drawl.

"Yeah?"

Calbert pointed. "Get rid of the beard."

∞

They arrived at the Quantum Resources labs without incident, and went in search of George Markowitz. When they found him, he was sitting inside a sealed glass tank filled with water. He wore a wetsuit and a complex mask that looked like something out of a science fiction novel. Inside the green-tinted lenses, lights flashed as sensors picked up data and transmitted it to a computer off to the side.

When he spotted Michael and Calbert, George surfaced and pulled the mask off.

"Michael!" he said. "Long time."

"It is. I hope we're not interrupting."

"Nah. Just testing a new compound sealant against stress. Some of the tropical countries are a lot hotter and more humid than others and sometimes the standard sealant breaks down." He had a wide smile on his face. "I'd shake your hand but I don't want to get you wet."

Calbert said, "Actually, if you don't mind taking a break, we'd like to talk to you about another project."

"Yeah, sure." George lifted himself out of the tank and climbed down the step ladder in lively fashion. For a man in his fifties, he remained in very decent shape. Laugh lines at his temples counterbalanced the shock of silver running through his dark hair.

Michael missed George's boyish enthusiasm for all things scientific. The man had completely changed from his bitter days at NASA working under his vindictive brother-in-law. Even with his current mundane task, he flourished at Quantum Resources. It was nice to see people in their element.

George stood there looking back and forth between the two new arrivals expectantly.

"Maybe you should change," Calbert suggested. "This might take more than a few minutes."

Michael said, "Or we could all go to an early lunch."

∞

They went to a pub down on the corner to eat. While George decimated a Reuben sandwich, washing it down with a frosted glass of beer, Michael related what happened with Alex, and the request to find Yaxche.

"I heard about the kidnapping," George said. "He was a very nice old man. I hope he's all right."

Michael grimaced. "I'm sure he is. The Cruzados must believe he knows something more about the scroll than what he told us."

Shaking his head, George said, "You don't think he misled us all this time? I only spoke with him a few times, but deception isn't in his nature. I don't believe he'd lie."

"Neither do I, but maybe something just kept getting lost in the translation. I believe we've reached a pivotal point in all this," Michael said. "Alex—and the rebels, obviously—think the scroll will provide the breakthrough we've been looking for. I think so, too."

George wiped his fingers on a napkin. "All right. Sign me up."

"You sure?" Michael asked.

Glancing at Calbert, who nodded, George grinned like a kid with a new robocycle. "You know, in a way, I always felt like I was one of the pioneers, discovering the scroll in Yaxche's possession. It pained me that no one could figure it out. I've spent hours looking over the reports and studying the simulations and recordings, but I would love to take a crack at this in person."

Calbert finished tapping a few commands into his portable holoslate and said, "All right. I've sent in the orders to head office, reinstating Michael to active duty and informing them of your field assignment. You're both booked on a flight to Tegucigalpa." He nodded at them and winked. "You'd better get packed!"

12

Canada Station Three :
Lagrange Point 4 :
Earth Orbit :

Alex sat at a table by himself in the mess hall. He was alone in a crowd of adults. A few familiar faces would nod and smile when he looked up, but no one invited him to eat his meal with them.

In a way, he couldn't blame them. He was an anomaly. History's first and only interstellar traveler, Alex looked nothing like a pioneer or a hero. He looked like a sickly boy, and most people shied away at the sight of him.

Picking at his plate of fries, Alex sighed and turned his mind back to his memories. Since the night of his collapse, he hadn't been able to achieve that transcendent state again. It had been exhausting, and Alex had felt extremely weak for several days afterward.

But there was something out there that he needed to understand. Some metaphysical connection had been made when he was quantized. Was it that haunting voice? What did it want?

Earlier that morning he had tried to message Michael to let his friend know he was all right, but he only got the answering service saying Michael was out of town, but would check his messages periodically.

"Mind if I join you?" someone said, interrupting his thoughts.

Alex, surprised, looked up to see Kenny smiling at him.

"Uh, yeah. Sure."

Kenny sat down and arranged his lunch on the table. It was some kind of vegetable soup and a toasted sandwich.

"Are you feeling any better?" Kenny asked as he broke some salted crackers into bits and sprinkled them in his soup.

"I guess." Not knowing what motivated Kenny to sit with him, Alex was reluctant to say much.

"You gave everyone a pretty good scare."

"Did I?" Alex spoke in a dramatic voice. "That's good."

Kenny stared at Alex for a moment and started to say something, but Alex smiled to show he was being facetious.

Using his spoon to dunk the more stubborn cracker pieces under the soup, Kenny said, "I guess everyone tends to walk on eggshells around you. No one really knows what you can and can't do. I'm sure it makes you feel less than human sometimes."

"Or more than human."

Kenny took a deep breath. "I'll say it again. I think we got off on the wrong foot, and that's my fault. I'm new and I just wanted to impress the hell out of everyone. I'm sorry if it felt like I was using you as a stepping stool. I'm really a nice guy when you get to know me."

"Thank you."

Motioning to Alex's lunch, Kenny asked, "You not hungry?"

"I'm starving," Alex said. "But not for food."

"Look, if I could do anything about that…"

Alex offered him a conciliatory smile. "I know."

Twirling his spoon in his soup absently, Kenny drew his face into a look of concern.

He said, "I wanted to talk to you more about what you mentioned in the lab."

"Chrysalis." Alex picked up a fry and bit it in half.

"For starters, yeah." He stared into Alex's eyes. "I went through all the reports. I only found one where it's mentioned, and Dr. Hoit, who was head of the *Quanta* experiments at that time, basically dismissed the notion. I'm reluctant to repeat his exact words."

"You don't have to. I read the report."

Kenny looked startled.

Alex said, "Back then I still had my abilities. I could *see* beyond my normal range of vision."

"Uhm." Kenny looked uncomfortable. Not everyone could accept that Alex had once had those powers, unless they saw it with their own eyes. "Okay. So, let's pretend I have a more open mind than some of the others. Do you want to tell me about this chrysalis?"

"There's not really much to tell," Alex said. "Both NASA—when it was in charge of the project—and Quantum Resources have been going about this the wrong way from the start. What they don't realize is that I should not have survived my first exposure to Kinemet. I tried to warn them, but they classified everything I said. Sometimes people get a notion stuck in their head and they're unwilling to believe anything that goes against that."

"I have to admit, it comes with the territory," Kenny added. "Scientists can be the most close-minded people you've ever met."

Alex laughed without humor. Then he said, "The entire *Quanta* project was doomed to failure from the start. One of the reasons I involved myself early on—"

"By hijacking the *Quanta*," Kenny added, twisting his lips in a half smile.

"—was because they assumed that the pilot, once exposed to Kinemet, would automatically return to a material state and turn on the electrical systems when they arrived at their destination, and in turn be able to dampen the reacting Kinemet."

"And you knew there would be a greater delay than what was required? The report said it was several seconds—too long, as it turned out—before you rematerialized."

"I didn't know there would be a delay in my returning to normal space, but I knew there wasn't enough time to start the generators, charge the battery and engage the dampers. The first time I was exposed to Kinemet I was far too disoriented to be of any use. Any pilot in that situation would take too long remembering what they had to do before being able to do it. It was also foolish of the physicists at NASA to think they needed to irradiate a pilot *during* a quantized flight to transform him."

Alex took a deep breath. "But that's not the only thing they were wrong about."

"The only thing?" Kenny was obviously struggling to understand what Alex meant.

"Light-speed travel is important," Alex said. "But the way they're going about it is all wrong. You have to learn to crawl before you can walk, and you need to learn to walk before you can run. From the moment Kinemet was discovered, everyone wanted to go straight from the crib to flying through interstellar space. They've skipped a number of necessary steps before they can understand Kinemet, let alone master it."

"Steps?" Kenny asked.

"To begin with, like with any radiation, radical exposure will result in death. That's why they scrubbed the *Quanta* projects—nearly every pilot who they exposed to the element died, and those that didn't die are in comas."

"But you were exposed," Kenny said. "Twice."

"The second time I was already partially transformed. Additional exposure had no effect. The first time I was exposed I was partially shielded by the TAHU, and I was also far enough away from the point of origin that the effects were somewhat lessened. It was a fluke; I should have died ... like my parents. But I believe there was some kind of catalyst that changed the nature of Kinemet before it irradiated me."

Kenny chewed on his lower lip. "You mean how we charge it with hydrogen particles to initiate the quantum reaction?"

"Yes," Alex said. "And I tried to tell them when I got back to Earth, but either I didn't explain it correctly or they were so focused on other things they weren't prepared to listen."

"So ... what's your theory?" Kenny asked.

"I think there is a connection between anyone irradiated by Kinemet and those alien monuments. Because I'm only partially changed, the connection is not clear, but nevertheless, I feel it. It's like a voice in my head calling me. It was very strong when I was in Centauri, and I have to believe if I had been fully transformed I would now know the answer. There would have been no need to cool the Kinemet because it wasn't supposed to be used like it was, and the *Quanta* would not have exploded as a result."

"Do you think..." Kenny struggled for the words. "...that voice was a broadcast from any aliens in that system?"

"There were no aliens in Centauri," Alex said, his voice tight. He carefully avoided looking at Kenny. "Just me."

Taking in a deep breath, as if absorbing all the new ideas that way, Kenny slowly let it out again. "So that brings us back to the original conundrum. What is the proper procedure to become ... whatever it is that you would become?"

"Kinemat," Alex said.

Kenny raised his eyebrow. "Kinemat?"

"Someone who has been fully transformed by Kinemet. They started to call it 'the Manez Effect' but I hate that."

"I'm still not clear on what becoming a Kinemat means."

"Part of the problem," Alex said, "is that I don't know either. I don't know the correct method to become transformed by Kinemet, and I don't know for certain what the result is supposed to be. It's difficult to convince someone they're wrong, when you can't prove that you're right."

"Forget what you can prove," Kenny said. "What do you think?"

"I think I'm in a transitional state that should only have lasted a very short time. Days, maybe, or hours. My transformation is incomplete. That's why my health is deteriorating. I need to finish changing."

"I'll say it again: changing into what?" Kenny asked. "And how?"

"I don't know the answer to either of those questions," Alex told him, starting to grow frustrated.

"Do you have a theory?"

Alex took a deep breath to calm himself. "I'm not completely sure, but I believe there are instructions on how."

Kenny made the connection. "The stolen Mayan scroll."

"Yes."

Pulling a disbelieving face, Kenny said, "We had every cryptographer, programmer, and analyst in NASA picking it apart for years. Their conclusion was it's a nice story, but there's nothing there that gives us any more information about Kinemet or the ancient races who built the monuments on the edge of the solar systems."

Alex shrugged. "Just because we don't know how to read the scroll properly at this time doesn't mean it doesn't hold the information we need." Alex absently popped a fry in his mouth and chewed without tasting.

"So," Kenny said, his voice measured, "what you are saying is, we can't truly begin to understand how to use Kinemet for superluminal travel—at least the way the aliens do—until we are able to complete your transformation?"

"Right."

Kenny picked up his spoon and stirred his rapidly cooling soup. "And our only manual is missing."

"Yes."

∞

Although Justine had not sent Alex a message, he knew she usually worked on the *Diana,* and wanted to come and see her when the ship docked. He'd tried to call her from his apartment, but the Lunar Lines receptionist said they couldn't connect him for some reason. But he wanted to take the chance she would arrive today.

Promising Dr. Amma that he was feeling much better, he got her permission to go. It was an excruciating trip to the main terminal of the space port, but he made it with time to spare. Exhausted from the effort, he sat down on one of the benches.

He didn't have to wait long before he spotted a familiar face.

Clive Wexhall approached with a warm smile. "Alex, how are you?"

"Hello, sir." Alex stood up. "I'm good. It's been awhile."

"Yes it has." He shook Alex's hand. "They don't let me off the Moon very often."

Alex found that he developed an ache in his knees if he stood too long. His braces, designed more for walking, didn't take any of his weight off his joints when he was standing still. If he shuffled his feet or subtly walked on the spot, the biomechatronics would kick in. When he made the motion, though, people looked at him strangely or asked if he was all right.

Alex sat back down on the bench. "Are you waiting for Justine?" he asked.

There was a slight flush to Clive's skin. He said, "In a way, yes; but I also wanted to see you."

"Me?"

"Yes. Unfortunately, Justine won't be disembarking today. She has to stay on the liner."

Alex scrunched up his face. "Oh?"

"But," Clive said, "she asked me to get you clearance to go aboard for a visit while the *Diana* is in dock."

It didn't take any mystical powers to see there was more going on here than the liaison was letting on. Although Alex hadn't had a lot of dealings with Clive, he knew Justine trusted him, and that was good enough for him.

"All right. That sounds fine." He stood up and followed Clive to the security office.

∞

The cabin of the liner was completely empty of passengers when Alex and Clive entered. There were a few members of the cleaning crew there. Bypassing the workers, Clive led Alex to the kitchen area and to the elevator.

Clive motioned for Alex to go into the one-person lift first.

"Where are we—" Alex began to ask, but Clive winked at him and put a finger to his lips.

"I'll be right behind you," the liaison said.

Without another word, Alex entered the elevator. The door shut and it descended to the storage area. When it stopped, Alex stepped out and looked around. He didn't see anyone, and for a brief moment he wondered if he'd been tricked, but then he heard muffled voices.

Without waiting for Clive, he walked down the aisle of containers and spotted a group of soldiers at the opposite end of the storage bay. One of them looked up and grabbed his ion rifle, but then someone said, "It's all right. He's with me."

Alex recognized the voice. Justine beckoned him down, and he waved as he made his way to her.

The soldiers looked at him with a mixture of wariness and curiosity, but Justine didn't offer any explanations to them or to Alex.

She was wearing her PERSuit harness and looked like she was cold. She gave Alex a wide smile, and he quickened his pace as fast as his braces would let him.

Alex was always surrounded by people, but he usually felt alone except when Justine stopped in on her visits. He always looked forward to his voice chats with Michael, but it wasn't the same as seeing someone in person.

As he neared, he felt a change come over him. At first, he thought it was a feeling of happiness at seeing his friend, but by the time he was halfway to her, Alex knew what he was experiencing was something different. He could sense it.

Kinemet.

It was like a ray of sunshine to someone who had spent months in the dark. He could feel it radiating through him, replenishing him. Like a homing beacon, it called to him.

Everything else became peripheral to Alex, and with a renewed energy, he made directly for the large container in the middle of the group. He was barely aware of Justine or the others, and only peripherally registered their presence.

"This is Alex, my friend," Justine said to the group with a lightness in her voice. "I hope you guys don't mind, but he's going to spend a couple of hours here with us during our layover. Don't worry, I've cleared it with the higher ups. Ah," she continued after a moment, "here's the NASA liaison now."

Clive appeared from behind the containers and waved as he spied Justine. As if completely understanding Alex not greeting her in the traditional manner, Justine waved back at Clive and met him halfway down the hall.

Alex couldn't hear what Justine and Clive said to each other. He knew he should at least make the effort to pull himself away from the container of Kinemet and say something sociable to Justine. She had obviously gone out of her way to arrange this for him. But the kinetic metal was a siren's song for him.

When it was not in the midst of a reaction, Kinemet was only mildly radioactive—less than a percent of ultraviolet radiation from the sun. A person who had not been altered by exposure to reacting Kinemet would need to be exposed to the dormant form in close proximity for several months before starting to feel any effects, and then it would most likely only be about as harmful as a sunburn.

Dormant Kinemet did, however, give off enough radio waves to play havoc with some electronics in close proximity. As a precaution against causing any shipboard disasters, the Kinemet on board the liner was encased in a thick container lined with titanium—the same material used in Kinemetic dampers.

Even through the sealed container, Alex could feel the waves penetrating through to his core.

A few hours? If that was the limit to his time, he would need to get closer. He turned around and said, "Can we open it up?"

With Clive in tow, Justine returned to the circle of guards and nodded. "Go ahead, Lieutenant."

As the lieutenant unlocked the main opening by tapping a code into the magnetic lock, Justine grabbed one of the cots and dragged it closer to the aperture.

When the door opened a fraction, a wave of Kinemetic energy poured over and through Alex, and he basked in it. Justine gently guided him to lie down on the cot, and at that moment, she made an odd face.

"Well, there goes my optilink," Justine said with a laugh. "Might as well put my sweater back on."

"It is safe for us?" asked the lieutenant.

Justine turned toward the sound of his voice, but she appeared to be looking past him. "If you have a digital watch, it probably won't tell the time correctly. And forget watching any vids unless you go to the other end of the cargo bay," Justine said. "But, yeah, the rays are mostly harmless."

The lieutenant called out a few orders to his men to patrol the area, and told the ones off-duty they could go up to the main floor kitchens.

"I'll pop back down to check on you in an hour or so," Lieutenant Jeffries said. With that, the soldiers made themselves scarce.

Whatever Justine and Clive talked about over the next few hours, Alex was completely oblivious to it.

As his body re-energized from the proximity to Kinemet, he found himself once again entering something very similar to that fugue state…

The ancient voice called to him: *Alex, come home.*

13

Lunar Lines Vessel, *Diana* :
Dock Seven :
Canada Station Three :

Leaving Alex next to the Kinemet, Justine and Clive moved as far down the cargo bay as they could while still being able to maintain line of sight.

The Kinemetic radiation continued to interfere with both Justine's PERSuit harness and the optilink; the sensors gave her such static feedback she thought her head would overload with the influx of scrambled data. Even though it meant she was once more plunged into complete darkness, she disabled her optilink and put her sweater back on. At the very least it helped keep away the chill of the cargo bay.

She was fine with her loss of electronically enhanced sight, because she had Clive there; he held her tightly in his arms as they sat on a turned over crate and spoke in soft tones.

"I meant it, you know," he said.

She didn't have to ask what he was referring to, and she was never one to play coy; she would not pretend ignorance and make him repeat himself.

Over the past few hours she'd had some time to think about what he'd said, but she was still torn. On the one hand, she was acutely aware that she wasn't getting any younger, and she wasn't looking forward to spending the rest of her life alone. On the other, her twilight years were still far away, and there was so much more she wanted to do with her life.

Justine couldn't have asked for a nicer man than Clive. He was understanding, compassionate and kind. Although he could be a bureaucrat both at work and off duty, and could be a stickler for doing things the 'proper' way, he also had a singular wit and could make her laugh. The thought of giving her future over to him and making a life on the Moon together was not unappealing. At the same time, she had this fire in her belly that told her she wasn't ready to settle down just yet.

"I know you meant it," she said to him. "But it's been a very complicated couple of years."

"So that's a 'no'?" he asked, but he said it with a half smile, as if he'd been expecting the answer all along.

"It's not a 'no'," she said. "It's not a 'yes'; but it's not a 'no'." She squeezed him a little tighter and buried her head in his shoulder. "I just need to get a little more comfortable with who I am now before I can make that kind of decision."

After a moment, he spoke in a quiet voice. "You won't mind if I ask again at a later date?"

Justine laughed and gave him a playful slap. "I'd be upset if you didn't."

They held each other in silence for long minutes.

"This is nice," he said after a time. "Not quite *La Danse Des Étoiles,* but it's still cozy."

She playfully slapped his arm. "You're such a liar!"

"Ha." He laughed. "So, what's this supposed to do anyway? To Alex?"

"I don't really know how this works for sure," Justine said, "but I think it has something to do with how he was exposed to Kinemet the first time. It imbued him with its inherent radiation which changed his physiology. Now he needs it like we need Vitamin C."

Clive said, "I'm not sure I completely understand."

"No one does. That's why he's gone so long without it; why he's deteriorating physically. No one believes he needs Kinemet to survive."

"He seems content now."

Justine couldn't see anything. "Does he?"

"Yes. He looks like he's sleeping, but there's a serenity about him."

Justine could feel herself smiling. "That's good."

"How much longer do you think he'll need?" Clive asked. "The liner is set to reload passengers in a couple hours. We'll have to get him off before anyone sees him."

They sat together for two more hours, enjoying one another's company and talking about nothing and everything.

Though she just wanted to rest in Clive's arms forever, Justine finally squeezed his hand, indicating it was time to go. They had things to do.

She stood up and headed back to Alex, and could hear Clive following.

Alex sat up on the cot. "Thank you so much, Justine."

"You're welcome, but really, Clive arranged it all." She felt around for the door of the container and pushed it shut. It locked automatically, and Justine quickly removed her sweater.

As the Kinemetic radiation was cut off once more, Justine's main optilink connection came back online, and she immediately turned on her harness. At last she could look on Alex and Clive's faces with those electronic eyes, courtesy of Optimedia.

Putting his hand out for Clive to shake, Alex said, "Thank you, Clive."

The two shook, and Clive stepped back and put an arm around Justine. "Not a problem, young man. I just wish there was a more permanent solution for you."

"This was good enough," Alex said. "I feel much better."

"How long will it last?" Justine asked.

Alex shrugged. "I don't know. But one thing I do know: I won't be needing these braces for the time being."

Justine watched as he undid the biomechatronic device from his legs.

Alex stood to give Justine a hug, and she blinked away tears. "If I could find a better way," she said.

"I know."

Justine heard footsteps approaching.

"Are we about wrapped up here?" asked Lieutenant Jeffries.

Nodding, Justine said, "Yes. We need to escort Alex out before the passengers embark. Thank you, Lieutenant. You have no idea how much I appreciate this."

"Uh, I really didn't do anything," he said to her in a modest voice, and checked the lock on the container.

"Sometimes," she said, "that's more than enough."

Justine put her hands on Alex's shoulders, and then pulled him close for a hug. It was difficult to explain to people why she cared so much for this boy. Although she never had any children of her own, that maternal instinct was still there.

Alex was like a foster child to her in some ways, and she didn't realize how much his deteriorating health had affected her until this very moment. Seeing him looking hale and happy brought a sudden torrent of tears to her eyes, and she hugged him even tighter.

"I feel much better," he said to her in a low voice. "Thank you."

Justine gave him one more squeeze, then stepped back, but still kept one hand on his shoulder.

"We need to figure out a way to make it permanent."

Alex smiled. "Working on it. Now I have a little more time. And," he added, "now I have something that might help Kenny."

"Kenny?" she asked.

With a subtle glance at Lieutenant Jeffries, Alex spoke in a low voice. "Kenny Harriman. He's the new physicist they sent up from Vancouver. He's trying to figure me out. Since I haven't been able to use any of my gifts, I don't think he fully believed my story. Maybe now if I demonstrate, it might give him some ideas."

Justine was one of the few people who had witnessed firsthand Alex's ability to manipulate electricity and his uncanny capability to see far beyond the normal range of human vision.

It had not occurred to her until that moment that those gifts would once again be restored to Alex once he was recharged with the Kinemetic radiation. He was connected to that element in a fundamental way. As Alex said often, he needed it.

For the past few years, as Alex's capabilities diminished along with his health, it had been harder and harder to convince the corporate governments to take an interest in Alex. Justine hoped that this new physicist, Kenny, would be able to help in time; she had no idea how or when Alex would have access to more of the superluminal metal.

Wiping away her tears, she said, "I'll be interested in hearing about it all when I come back. Speaking of which, I have one more surprise."

"Oh?"

"I've arranged to take a few weeks' vacation time, and on the return trip, I'll start them here on CS3."

Alex's smile stretched wide. "That's great!"

His delight in the news touched a chord in her, and she realized that she had just as strong a connection to Alex as he had to the Kinemet. It was a good reason to reconsider Clive's offer. If she took a position on Luna, she would be much closer to Alex on CS3. There were daily flights between the Moon and the space station.

"Maybe we'll go on a tour of the Kordylewski clouds or something," Justine suggested.

"I would love that."

Clive tapped Justine on the arm and repeated, "We should get Alex off before the passengers embark."

Justine nodded, and the three of them started back toward the elevator. She mouthed a silent thank you to Lieutenant Jeffries, who gave her a salute in return.

Justine noticed that Alex was no longer walking like an old man. Once again, he seemed to be an energetic youth.

When they all got to the upper level and reached the gangway, Alex stopped and turned around.

"Thank you both again. I don't know how much longer I would have been able to last if not for today."

"No need to thank us," Justine said. "I just wish we could do more."

They hugged and, as Alex left the liner, Justine felt an acute pang of guilt. She had spent the past few years clinging to the hope that she could once again recapture the glory of her days in NASA. She had nothing to prove to anyone in that regard, and it was time for her to make some realistic choices.

She followed Clive back to the elevator, and as he gestured for her to go first, Justine hesitated.

"What's wrong?" Clive asked.

Shaking her head, Justine smiled at him. "Nothing. I think I've made up my mind."

∞

Justine and Clive returned to the kitchen area and she enlisted his help to restock the refreshment cart with cold beverages and snacks. She brewed an urn of coffee and liberated a couple plates of fresh pastries for the soldiers.

When she and Clive had descended to the cargo area and distributed the snacks, the men expressed their gratitude as they helped themselves to the donuts, Danishes, and crullers. Their morale seemed high.

Lieutenant Jeffries, flicking icing residue off his uniform as he finished a bear claw, approached Justine.

"Thank you for this."

"No problem," she said. "I'm just sorry none of you got a chance to visit the station."

"Goes with the territory." He held his smile for a moment, then turned serious. "Do you mind if I ask what that was all about, with the boy?"

Justine hesitated to answer. Any explanation she offered would only raise more questions, and she wasn't certain how much she should reveal.

The lieutenant added, "I will have to make a report. I just want to be sure to get my story straight."

She glanced at Clive, who nodded his assent. Clive had cleared the visit with administration, but Alex's status was still classified.

To Lieutenant Jeffries, she said, "Do you remember the news a few years back about the pilot who returned from Centauri System?"

The lieutenant blinked in surprise. "From the *Quanta* flight?"

"Yes. You just met him."

He looked back and forth between Justine and Clive, disbelieving. "But he's only a kid."

"It would appear so," Clive said in a low voice, "and that information is strictly on a need-to-know basis. When you make your debrief, you can report that Captain Alex Manez, retired, performed an unscheduled inspection of the cargo. Make no mention of his apparent age."

"Yes, sir," the lieutenant said, and if he was uncomfortable with that, he kept it to himself.

A soft chime sounded, indicating the liner was beginning launch procedures. A pre-recorded voice came on the loudspeaker and encouraged everyone to find their seats.

Justine and Clive found their way to the temporary webbed seating that had been installed for the troops, and buckled themselves in opposite Lieutenant Jeffries.

Justine knew she owed the lieutenant more of an explanation, if for no other reason than plain courtesy.

As the liner fired its engines and eased out of the docking bay, Justine told Jeffries how exposure to the Kinemet had affected Alex on a cellular level, and now he required a certain proximity to the element to maintain his health.

She also explained that, because of the shortage of Kinemet, obtaining it for Alex had been near impossible. Justine and Clive had understandably taken advantage of the situation just to help out a friend.

"Most of your superiors are aware of Alex and his condition," Justine said. "However, I would suggest you keep this information in confidence. I don't think it's something you want to be drawn into."

" 'Unscheduled military inspection' sounds good to me," Lieutenant Jeffries said, one side of his mouth turned up in a half smile.

The voice that suddenly spoke through the cargo hold's holoslate was not pre-recorded, and was not recognizable by Justine as one of the crew; it had a thick Spanish accent.

"Attention American soldiers. Remain calm. Because of the corruption of the corporate countries who have kept humankind in ignorance for far too long, the Cruzados have liberated this vessel and its cargo.

"Cooperate, and you will not be harmed. Resist us and you will be ejected into space."

Tegucigalpa :
Honduras :
Central American Conglomeration :

His Mayan name was Te'irjiil, but only his grandfather ever addressed him as such. Most Hondurans spoke only Spanish and had difficulty pronouncing his given name, so he went by the name Terry Fernandez. That was the name he gave to the desk clerk of the hostel in Tegucigalpa, the capital of Honduras, after he ran away from home in Copán Departmental.

That first night away was the most frightening experience in his life. He had to share a room with three others, one of whom looked pale and sickly and coughed throughout night. The second resident of the room snored heavily, and the third occupant wouldn't stop talking about how he was going to plunge a knife into the next person who crossed him.

It was the first time Terry had ever been alone, and the strangeness of the city was overwhelming. The pungent stink of the streets, the hard faces of the citizens, and the screams of police sirens and honking of horns all together nearly sent him running home with his tail between his legs.

He had never seen a group of more than a hundred people in one place at one time before. Now in a city of millions, Terry felt incredibly small and insignificant. He told himself to be strong, and was proud that he survived the night.

The next morning, as he stood on the sidewalk outside the hostel, he counted the few lempira he had saved over the past six months. He calculated the cost of the hostel and meals; he knew his money would not last him more than a week, even in the poverty-stricken barrios of the city.

At twenty years of age, Terry's only viable trade skill was as a laborer in the coffee plantations that employed more than half the population in his home departmental. He had no idea what he would do in the city, but when he spotted a truck with the name of Ruiz Coffee, the company he had worked for back home, he followed it to their warehouse and asked to speak with the foreman.

"I'm young, strong and healthy," Terry said after the foreman—an extremely grumpy-looking man with grizzled grey hair—initially told him they weren't looking for help.

"We already have too many workers," the foreman said and flicked his hand at Terry. "Every day we turn good men away."

"I will work for free today," Terry offered. "Just to prove myself."

The foreman sized him up and pressed his lips together as if tasting something sour. Finally, he said, "All right. We have a truck that needs to be loaded on dock three. Start there. See if you can keep up with the others. We'll see how you do."

With a grin, Terry headed down to the loading docks and pitched right in.

While waiting between trucks, one of the other laborers struck up a conversation with Terry.

"I'm Humberto," the man said. He was middle-aged and stocky, with short-cropped hair and a thick moustache. He sized Terry up a moment before extending his hand. They shook.

"My name is Terry."

Humberto asked, "First time in the city?"

Terry wasn't sure whether he should reveal too much about himself, but he didn't think he could come up with a believable fiction. "How can you tell?"

Humberto pointed at his clothing. "I used to wear homespun outfits when I lived in the country, too."

Looking down at his rural-style clothing, Terry felt suddenly conspicuous. The other workers wore denim pants and factory-made shirts with logos and slogans on them.

At first he suspected Humberto was making fun of him, but the other man did not have a smirk on his face. Instead, Humberto looked concerned and maybe a little sad.

"Yes," Terry admitted. "I don't have enough money to buy new clothes. Yet."

"I know a place you can get jeans cheap, some sneakers and a shirt that doesn't scream 'country'. After the shift, I'll take you there, if you like."

"I don't know…" For a brief moment, Terry wondered if he should trust someone he'd just met. He'd heard stories about criminals in the city who preyed on unsuspecting victims.

Humberto shrugged. "Offer's open if you want."

A new truck arrived, and then they were too busy loading to talk.

At noon break, Terry went and sat by himself to eat some fries he purchased from a lunch truck. He listened to the other workers joke and laugh, and though he wanted to join in, he kept to himself.

Deep down he knew running away from home the way he had was childish. Though he wasn't sure if he could make a life in the city, he knew there was nothing for him back in his village.

For the longest time he had courted Itzel, whose grandfather, Artec, was friends with his own grandfather, Yaxche. Both of the old men had conspired to arrange the union, and Terry had been smitten from the start.

His parents—who both worked long hours—had delegated Terry's upbringing to his grandfather, and usually deferred to his authority. They approved the marriage, but that was the extent of their involvement.

Terry and Itzel had spent many evenings sitting on the porch making plans for their future. Then Itzel became feverish with typhoid seven months ago.

Honduras continued to be one of the most impoverished country corporations, and Copán Departmental was severely lacking in medical facilities and supplies. Within two days of the first symptoms, Itzel had succumbed to the disease. With her death, all hope Terry had for a future died as well.

His anger, at first, was without direction. As the lonely days piled up, he realized that there had been a chance of Itzel's survival had the village had proper sewage, treated water, or a qualified doctor— amenities that many other countries in the world enjoyed.

Their village had had its chance. With so much interest from USA, Inc. and NASA in that ancient document, the leaders of the community could have negotiated access to it for better medical care, infrastructure and a better way of life. They also could have sold it outright, as the NASA officials had first wanted.

Instead, his grandfather had chosen to keep the old scroll with him as a cultural and religious artifact, and he basked in the self-importance he received from his new status. It would be blasphemy to charge admission to view the relic, his grandfather had told Terry one time. The ancients had intended for all humankind to benefit from the knowledge contained within.

But no one had figured out the meaning of the inscrutable words, and so no benefit had come from it, only a continued lack of medicine and technology that could have saved Itzel.

Terry's traditional upbringing would not let him direct his rage at his grandfather or the leaders of the community for not bargaining with the scientists. And so, the only option he could think of was to abandon the people who had failed him and make his own way through life. He had spent the past half a year planning and saving.

But now he was alone, friendless and more than a little frightened. The rudimentary education he had received in the village was enough for him to read and write, but Terry did not even have basic computer skills. The village only had one computer and it didn't have an EarthMesh connection. When the scientists from USA, Inc. left, they took all their machines with them.

At one end of the spectrum, humankind had traveled to another solar system, and at the other end, there were millions of people who lived in squalor. This was the inequality that kept Terry going. He had no idea how he would do it, but he vowed to set things right and bring balance to the world so that no one would have to suffer and die needlessly, like his darling Itzel.

With renewed passion, Terry threw himself into his work that afternoon, enough so that at the end of the day the foreman invited him back.

"You're not union so you'll work on a day-by-day basis." With that, he gave Terry his first day's pay.

"I said I would work today for free," Terry protested, holding the lempira in his hand uncertainly.

The foreman shook his head. "You need proper clothing. That outfit you have on makes you look like a beggar. If any of the supervisors came around, they would write me up for it." He made it sound as if Terry were doing him a favor by accepting the money.

The foreman shooed Terry off and he immediately went in search of Humberto, who was walking toward the main gate.

"Is it too late to go to the store with the cheap clothes?" he asked the larger man.

"Change your mind?" Humberto didn't break his stride, and Terry matched his pace.

"Yes, you were right. I need to look like I belong."

"So old sourpuss is keeping you on?" Humberto jerked his thumb back in the direction of the foreman's office.

"Just as a day worker," Terry said. "For now."

"All right. Let's go."

As he led Terry off the factory grounds towards the city centre, Humberto surprised him by saying, "I know who you are."

"You do?"

"Yes." Humberto glanced at Terry out of the corner of his eye. "I saw you on the news a few years back."

Terry answered in a sullen voice. "Oh, that."

"The way the reporter told the story, your village was host for all those rich NASA men. Good fortune for you."

"It could have been," Terry said. "But it wasn't."

As if measuring Terry up, Humberto took a long while before prompting him to tell his story.

"It's all right if you want to keep yourself to yourself," Humberto said finally. "But I left a village very much like yours because I was angry at how poor our conditions were. I didn't want to live like that anymore. No one should have to live like that."

Sensing he finally had someone who would understand him, Terry started at the beginning and told Humberto about his grandfather and the ancient scroll, about NASA and Alex Manez, and when he ended his story with the account of how Itzel had died unnecessarily, there was a catch in his throat and a tear in his eye.

Humberto clapped his hand on Terry's back. "After we get you some clothes, there are some people I want you to meet. They all have a story like yours," he said. "They also have a plan to put things right. I think you'll like hearing what they have to say."

∞

Terry was nervous about going to a secret meeting. He had heard the stories of criminal organizations operating in the city, recruiting ignorant farmers and villagers into their operation and either corrupting them into their way of life, or using them up and discarding them in the most unpleasant ways.

The only thing that kept him steadfast was Humberto. He seemed perfectly at ease as the two of them wound their way through the narrow barrio alleyways to a ramshackle building. It looked like an abandoned storage warehouse.

"Don't worry," Humberto said. "I called ahead to let them know we are coming."

Upon entering the building, Terry was surprised to see only two people waiting for them. He had imagined a gang of cold-eyed men brandishing weapons. Instead, the first man was scrawny and wore glasses. His pock-marked face was split in a wide grin as he stepped forward to shake hands.

"Hello, I'm Jose Arroyo."

Uncertainly, Terry shook the man's hand as Humberto introduced him.

"His first day in the city," Humberto said to Jose, "but I feel he is the very person we have been waiting for."

Jose nodded. "You're from the village with the alien scroll?"

"Yes," Terry answered. There was no use trying to hide it. If he had been on a newsvid, he would be recognizable to many. "But the scroll is not alien. It's ancient Mayan. My grandfather is its caretaker. He believes it is the story of the end of our gods; the NASA people thought it was the story of an alien visit."

"Ah, yes." Jose gestured to a table with four chairs. "Please sit. Would you like something to drink?" He nodded to the other man who dug into a picnic cooler and withdrew four bottles of beer.

When the man popped the cap and offered the drink to Terry, he said, "Pleased to meet you. My name is Alberto." Though his voice was deep and rich, there was a hardness in his eyes. Terry noticed a scar that ran from Alberto's left ear to the corner of his mouth.

Being polite, Terry tipped the beer to his lips and drank deeply. They all sat down.

"First off, I want you to know that Humberto, Alberto and I all have Mayan blood running through our veins to some extent. In that, you are like our brother. That is one reason we have arranged this meeting."

That was unexpected information, but Terry immediately felt a little more comfortable and trusting of these men.

"I believe in being honest with my friends and family, and I believe in coming straight to the point," Jose said. "Do you mind if I am blunt with you?"

Terry shook his head. "No. Not at all."

Jose leaned forward and smiled. "We want you to go back home."

∞

At one point in pre-Columbian history, before the colonial invasion, the Mayan civilization had been more advanced than any other culture in the Americas.

Along with art, music, and architecture, the Mayans had also been the first in that part of the world to develop a written language. They studied mathematics and astronomy, and in some ways their development rivaled those who lived on the other side of the world.

"It is no wonder," Jose told Terry, "that the alien visitors chose the Mayan people as the custodians of their technology. If history had progressed as it should have, the Mayan culture would today be the dominant force on Earth."

Unfortunately, the wars with the northern tribes, the arrival of the conquistadors and the flood of aggressive Europeans over the last thousand years had drowned out the Mayan culture and reduced their civilization to small pockets of communities.

Jose's mother, he told Terry, was a half-blood Mayan, and had married into a reasonably wealthy Honduran family. Growing up, Jose's mother had told him stories of his culture. "My legal name is Jose, but my Mayan name is Huehuetlotl."

It was while Jose was in university studying law that the story of the discovery of Kinemet had broken. For years, he followed the story with interest. After the first interstellar mission, NASA had tried to acquire the ancient scroll for themselves.

A legal aid by that time, Jose and a few sympathizers had organized themselves into an activist group. At the time, they had called themselves the Mayan Spiritualists, and they tried to put pressure on the Honduran government to restrict, or at least regulate access to the scroll.

"NASA was spending a lot of money in the area and in the capital region," Jose said. "Too many government officials were lining their pockets with bribe money from businesses and contractors who wanted to work for the wealthy Americans. Our movement was denounced, and those same politicians instead pressured my law firm to have me fired and blacklisted. The only work I've been able to find in the past year has been as a tutor to university students."

Jose gave Terry a very intense, impassioned look. "For centuries our people have been taken advantage of, when all along we were meant to lead the way to the stars."

His words stirred similar emotions in Terry. The Mayans had been stepped over by those with money and power, and kept poor and ignorant. If the Mayan people had continued to be a power in the Americas, tragedies like the death of his darling Itzel would never have happened.

Jose continued. "It was then that my friends and I began our work in earnest. There are more than a hundred of us now, and our numbers are growing. We even have a rich benefactor—unfortunately not Mayan, but he believes in our cause."

Terry asked, "And what is your cause?"

"We now call ourselves the Cruzados, and our mission is to restore the Mayan people to their rightful place as ambassadors to the people of the stars."

"How will you do that?" Despite his initial misgivings, Terry was becoming intrigued. If he joined a group who shared his beliefs, the possibilities were limitless.

"The world will not simply grant us the status we deserve. They have already shown their disdain for us. Therefore we must make them give it to us." There was a hard edge to his voice and fire in his eyes.

Terry balked momentarily. "Make them? You mean, by force?"

"If necessary," Jose said, his hand balled into a fist. Then he relaxed his hand and opened it; the smile returned to his face. "But it will be better if we secure our position with a different kind of power: knowledge. If we have something no one else has, then they have no choice but to deal with us."

"The secret of the scroll," Terry guessed.

"That's right."

"But their scientists have been working on that for years. They've given up. No one knows how to decipher it, not even my grandfather. What can we do?"

Jose put his hand on Terry's arm. "We can have faith in our destiny. The secret will be revealed when the time is right. And when that time comes, we must be prepared."

∞

Over the following weeks, Terry met with the Cruzados a dozen more times, often talking or arguing late into the night. They formulated a number of plans, and by the end of Terry's first month in the capital, he had thrown his full support into the cause.

∞

Terry returned to Copán Departmental in a rented pickup truck four weeks after leaving. The bed of the truck was filled with food, clothing, and medical supplies. In his pocket, he had more lempira than he could make in a year working the coffee fields.

When he arrived in his village, he recounted to his grandfather and parents how he had made his small fortune at a casino one night, and his first thought was the welfare of the village. He told them he had contracted with an engineering company to rebuild the village's water processing and sewage system, and had arranged for a doctor to visit the village once a month. Regaled as a hero, Terry spent the better part of the year working to improve conditions in their community.

Terry also brought a pocket-sized holoslate with a mesh connection. Jose had supplied it to him, and instructed him to keep this device secret from his fellow villagers.

Every night, when he was by himself, Terry used the computer to learn to read and write English. He also took courses in math, history and science. Jose believed firmly that knowledge was power, and insisted that all Cruzados had the benefits of an education. As a side benefit, Terry also discovered world music, and spent hours listening to everything from classical to rock to the latest progbeat rage.

Jose had insisted that Terry also spend as much time as he could learning the customs and culture of USA, Inc. and Canada Corp. and the history of the NASA space program—the *Quanta* missions in particular and every scrap of information they could find out about Kinemet.

During the day, his task was to find out as much as he could about the ancient scroll. Though he still found himself with unresolved feelings of anger towards his grandfather's stubborn and backwards ways, Terry forced himself to ask after the history of the document and pressed his grandfather to speculate about the secrets it held.

Once a week, Terry would check in with Jose or Humberto to exchange updates, and once every two months Terry would leave the village for a weekend. He told his grandfather he was going to visit the friends he made in Tegucigalpa. In reality, he went into the countryside at a secluded camp where he would train with the Cruzados in combat techniques.

Initially, Terry resisted the idea of military action.

"Sometimes, in order for your voice to be heard," Jose told him the first time Terry picked up a weapon, "you may need to raise it."

∞

The months rolled by without any new developments until the day when, in frustration, Terry demanded that his grandfather repeat the story of the ancient scroll over and over again.

Listening to the words his grandfather spoke, the key to unlocking the secret of the document came to Terry as if it were preordained.

Running back to his own house, Terry contacted Jose on his holoslate.

That call set in motion a whirlwind of events that ultimately brought Terry to where he was today: standing on the bridge of a Lunar Lines ship with an ion pulse rifle in his hand while Jose announced their takeover to the passengers.

To Terry, the past year seemed more like a dream or a nightmare, and it was then that he realized he had lost control of his own destiny.

15

Tegucigalpa :
Honduras :
Central American Conglomeration :

The virtual tourist flicks on to show a city bathed in heat and humidity. The sky is a clear blue with barely a trace of clouds behind the skyline of the airport.

A cacophony of noise from the loading trucks, taxis and passenger vehicles outside the terminal is loud enough that Michael—who is framed in the two-dimensional image—has to raise his voice to be heard.

He looks cranky and tired.

"What are you doing?" he asks after tapping a request for an autotaxi into a kiosk.

George's voice comes from off-screen. "Documenting our trip."

"We're still at the airport," Michael says. "I'm not sure they care whether we can get an autotaxi or how much we paid."

"Well, you never know. Don't worry, I'll edit out the boring parts before I submit the recording. But I think our arrival in Tegucigalpa is a good bookend."

Michael presses his lips together. "You look conspicuous. We need people to trust us before they'll talk to us."

The image bounces. "The only fieldwork we do is looking at reactors. Calbert never saw any reason to upgrade us to the new PERSuit system. Now that's a toy I'd like to get my hands on."

Shaking his head, Michael says, "We'll just have to make do with what we have. Let me do the talking when we get to the consulate."

"You got it, boss."

Michael grimaces as he waves down a cab. "Sorry I barked at you.

It was a long flight."

"No worries."

An autotaxi pulls up and they throw their bags in the storage compartment. The image jostles dizzyingly as they enter the vehicle.

The computer personality prompts, *<Destination?>*

The image pans to Michael, and George says, "Why don't we go to the hotel first, check in and get cleaned up?"

"That sounds good." Michael scratches his beard. "Maybe I'll shave, after all. I didn't think it would be so hot down here."

"The Ambassador Arms," George says to the computer, and the autotaxi pulls out into the street.

∞

The virtual tourist image turns back on outside the glass doors of an office on the third floor of the Centro Financiero Banexpo building. The frame zooms in on the sign of the Canadian Embassy.

Michael, who looks energetic and confident, stands at the door and pauses. With a clean-shaven face, he is dressed in a loose-fitting white shirt and brown pants.

He removes a wide-brimmed hat and faces George and the camera eye.

"All right. I guess if we're documenting everything, I'll narrate." Michael clears his throat. "We're here at the embassy office to get our travel papers, maps, and to meet with John Markham, who is the consul's aide. We hope he can give us some additional information on the theft of the Mayan scroll and the kidnapping of Yaxche, the translator."

Michael enters into the reception area where a smartly-dressed woman smiles a greeting.

"Hello, I'm Michael Sanderson and this is George Markowitz. We have an appointment."

"Mr. Markham is expecting you. Go right in." She points down a carpeted hallway. "It's the office at the end."

Michael nods and then proceeds to the consul's office.

Inside, John Markham stands up from his desk and comes around to shake Michael's hand. Deeply tanned skin stretches around his mouth as he greets them. His eyes glance at the VT camera.

"We're recording our progress for our report," Michael says.

"Oh, that's fine. Come in. Have a seat." He returns to his side of the desk.

The image briefly flashes on George's hiking boots as he awkwardly finds his chair and sits down. As he points the camera back up, John is handing Michael a thin memory card.

John says, "After your supervisor called to let me know you were coming down here, I took the liberty of compiling some local newsvids that reported the incident."

"Thank you." Michael takes the card and inserts it in his holoslate to transfer the files. "Every little bit will help."

"I'm afraid there isn't much there. Whoever these Cruzados are, they've kept a very low profile up until now. They've never taken part in anything more serious than a protest at the Office of the Interior when NASA first tried to purchase the document. For the past year, they've been so quiet we assumed they'd disbanded."

"Do we know the names of any of their members?"

"Just one. Jose Arroyo, who we believe is their leader. I talked to my counterpart at the US embassy and he forwarded a copy of all the data they've gathered on the Cruzados, and a timeline of their activities. Like I said, it's not much."

"Do you have any contacts with the *policia?* Someone we can talk to about this?"

John frowns. "Yes, but I'm not certain they will tell you anything useful."

Michael looks up from the holoslate. "Oh?"

"Well, for one thing, the government of Honduras doesn't think the theft and kidnapping are much of a priority."

With a glance at George, Michael says, "They don't?"

"The only reason the National Department of Investigations even opened a case file is because of pressure from USA, Inc. and the Honduras Office of Tourism."

"They don't think kidnapping is important?"

John shakes his head. "It's very important, but it happens so often in this part of the world that unless there is a ransom demand or an imminent threat to a VIP, the authorities simply don't have the manpower or resources to investigate. And so far, the Cruzados are only *suspected* of this crime. They haven't taken responsibility or communicated any demands yet. As a matter of fact, according to the consul in the U.S. Embassy, the only reason we know the Cruzados are involved is because of an unsecured EPS to a contact in Houston."

Michael and George share a grim look between them.

John shrugs apologetically. "I want to help you as much as I can, but I have to tell you I think you're wasting your time. Until the Cruzados surface on their own with a list of demands, you're just spinning your wheels."

Michael has a thoughtful look on his face. "I appreciate where you're coming from, but we have to follow through on this."

"Of course."

With a quick look to George, Michael says, "We thought we would begin our investigation in Copán, where it happened. Interview some of the local residents."

"I can certainly help you with travel arrangements. There's a bus that runs daily between Tegucigalpa and Santa Rosa de Copán. From there, perhaps you can hire an autotaxi. I believe Yaxche's village is less than an hour away."

George shakes his head, causing the image to move side to side. "When I was there last, I rented a truck from the owner of the hotel where I stayed. The autotaxis won't run rurally."

John smiles and stands up. "Excellent. I'll call down for some bus tickets while you get your travel documents from my receptionist." He walks around the desk again and shakes both George's and Michael's hands. "And if you have a few extra days while in Honduras, you should visit Copán Ruinas. It's quite astonishing. If you're a history buff, it's a must-see."

∞

There are a series of images of the landscape looking out from inside a bus. The noise of the vehicle's engine is too loud for anything to be heard other than garbled audio.

∞

A short nighttime shot of a hotel in Santa Rosa de Copán slowly pans to a busy sidewalk filled with pedestrians. On the street corner opposite the hotel an old beggar holds his hand out while gumming his teeth and staring into the distance.

∞

The morning sun casts shadows on the dirt road of a small village. A couple of barefoot kids kick a partially deflated soccer ball back and forth near a well which serves as their central plaza.

Michael steps into the frame. "We're here in the village where Yaxche and the document were taken. What's the village's name again?"

George says, "Pueblo de Santa Brio, but most everyone here just calls it the *pueblo.*"

Michael makes a motion with his hand for George to follow him. "We're going to try to find one of Yaxche's relatives and see if they can give us any more information than what we already have."

"If I remember correctly," George says off-screen, "his house is the last one on the end. Maybe his daughter or his grandson is there."

Michael heads towards the far side of the small village. As he walks, a few of the residents stop and look up at him and George in passing curiosity.

There are no more than two dozen ramshackle houses in the village, all looking in dire need of repair. The front of one of the homes has a few tables set out. On one of the tables are baskets of fruit, bread and two dead chickens. On one of the other tables a number of handcrafted trinkets are arrayed. A plump woman smiles at them and says, *"Comprar?"*

Michael glances at George with a helpless smile. "I forgot to pack my translator."

"She wants to know if we want to buy something."

Michael shakes his head. "Maybe later."

To the woman, George says, *"Más tarde. Gracias."*

She smiles and waves at them as the two make for Yaxche's house.

The home itself is of typical construction: the walls are made of adobe, and the roof is constructed with clay tiles. Unlike many of the other houses, this one has a small porch and the floor is made of wood rather than packed earth. The front door is partially open.

George calls out into the house. *"¿Hola?"*

There is no answer, but one of the soccer-playing children trots over.

"La casa está vacía," he says.

"Do you know what happened?" George asks in Spanish,

immediately translating the conversation for Michael's benefit.

The boy shakes his head. "They were taken by men with guns."

"They?"

"The soldiers came and put Terry and his grandfather in a truck. They drove off. This was many days ago."

"Have you ever seen those soldiers before?"

"No. I know nothing of them." The boy pointed to a house two doors down made of thatch and clay. "Terry's mother is there. She waits for them to return."

"Thank you," Michael says and passes the boy a twenty lempira bill.

Yipping with joy, the boy runs off to show his friends the money.

Michael turns to the camera. "This is news. We had no idea Yaxche's grandson was abducted as well."

The two of them cross the packed dirt street to the house the boy had indicated and knock on the flimsy door made of wood planks bound together with a weaved rope.

A middle-aged woman opens the door. Worry lines stretch across her face; her eyes flick back and forth fearfully between Michael and George. Recognition blossoms when her gaze settles on George, who had been to the village over a decade earlier wearing similar headgear.

Behind her are two pre-teen girls who look on with curiosity.

The woman speaks in Spanish, and George translates between them.

She says, "Please come in." She turns to her children and tells them to go play outside.

Michael smiles politely and nods as he follows the woman into her sparsely furnished house. Handmade chairs surround a carved table. A shelving unit holds plates and glasses, and on the mantle over a rudimentary fireplace is a photographic portrait of a young man.

Michael points to it. "Is that your son?"

"Yes," the woman says, wringing her hands. "He and my father have been missing these past days. Taken by the bandits, for what reason I do not know. We have nothing of value." She glances at Michael and George out of the corner of her eye. "You are not the police. Why have you come?"

"We want to help find them," Michael answers. "Though we only found out today that your son was also kidnapped. Can you tell us about him?"

"Yes." She sits down on a chair at the table. "He is my only son and

I love him, though this past year he has grown apart from me and his father. Terry was engaged to be married, you see. Itzel was beautiful and brought joy to him and our family, but she was struck down by sickness and died. Terry ran away from us in grief and did not return for a month. He left a boy but came back a man. He brought a great many supplies and ideas to our village."

When she spoke, she did not look proud, and Michael shot a quick look at George before saying to her, "You don't look happy about that."

"Something happened to Terry when he was away. My husband does not hear me when I say that he is not the same; he and the other villagers only see the improvements to the village and the wealth he brought back with him. But where did he come by this money? He says he won it gambling, but I think he may have done something shameful. I think—"

She falls silent and stares at her hands. "It is not my place to say."

Michael puts a hand on her shoulder. "You can tell us. It might help us in our search for him and your father."

There is a tear in her eye as she looks back up at Michael. "My husband tells me I am being foolish, but I think my son may have … stolen the money from the banditos. That is why they have taken him and my father. They will either ransom them to the village, or they will take their anger out on them."

She grabs Michael's arm. "Please. I beg you. Find my son and my father before something terrible happens to them."

With a grim face, Michael says, "We will do everything we can. Is there anything you can tell us about these bandits?"

"No one saw them closely. They drove a black truck and had hunting rifles. That is all I know."

Michael turns to George and says, "Maybe we can track the Cruzados by their truck? It might be a long shot, but if there was a satellite in the area the night of the kidnapping we might be able to see which direction it went."

George taps his holoslate. "On it."

Michael pats the woman's hand. "Thank you," he says. "We will do our best to bring your family back to you."

∞

Inside the rented truck, George punches several commands into his hololslate while Michael drives.

"Anything yet?" Michael asks.

George nods. "Talk about a needle in a haystack. There was a geological satellite in this section of the departmental looking for mineral deposits. They pick up all kinds of heat signatures. It looks like there were three hundred vehicles traveling on the main road between Santa Rosa de Copán and the Copán Ruinas that night—maybe even double that."

"Double? What do you mean?"

George shakes his head. "The satellite tracked in a zigzag pattern, so there are dozens of gaps in the record. The three times it passed over the village, there was no thermal activity."

"Damn."

George taps a few more commands. "Maybe I can run a filter. Eliminate any commercial vehicles or transports. Autotaxis. That kind of thing. Maybe we'll get luck—"

"You don't have to search any further, George," Michael says. "I think they found us."

George looks up. In the camera view is a large black van traveling towards them at high speed, kicking up a cloud of dust behind it.

Michael edges to the side of the road. The truck veers to cut them off, so Michael slows the vehicle to a stop.

"What are you doing?" George asks, his voice rising.

"Well," Michael says. "It's not like we can outrun them. After all, this is what we want, isn't it? If these guys are Cruzados, maybe they'll tell us where Yaxche and his grandson are. And the scroll."

The black van skids to a stop a dozen meters away and four men with rifles jump out, pointing the weapons at Michael and George. The men have kerchiefs covering their mouths.

They yell in Spanish, and George translates: "Get out of the truck with your hands in the air. Do not try to run."

Michael says, "We'd better do as they say."

The two of them open the doors and step out. They put their hands up as Michael calls out, "We mean you no harm. My name is Michael Sanderson from Quantum Resources in Canada."

"We know who you are," one of the men says in English. "Keep your mouth shut."

Another Cruzado walks purposefully toward George. He

commands, "Turn it off."

George says, "Turn what off?"

The armed man reaches out and grabs the Virtual Tourist. He pulls it from George's head.

"The camera," he says, as the image bounces around showing the dirt road, a pair of booted feet, the sky, and then complete darkness.

16

Lunar Lines Vessel, *Diana*:
Unknown Transit:

Justine could feel the *Diana* pulling out of the Canada Station Three dock. The massive ion pulse engines gave off severe vibrations when initially engaged, and the first jarring motion of the ship as it uncoupled from the dock was enough to knock someone off their feet if they weren't safely fastened in their seats.

Both Justine and Clive clung to each other for balance as they quickly made their way to the canopy seats and strapped themselves in.

Lieutenant Jeffries' men had taken up defensive positions around the cargo, in case the hijackers decided to come down to the cargo bay. When the engines shuddered, two of them grabbed on to the container's handles to stabilize themselves while the other two, who had dropped to one knee, lost their balance and fell over.

Two of the men who had raced toward the elevators after the announcement—ion rifles up at the ready as if expecting the hijackers to burst into the cargo bay with guns blazing—were thrown from their feet into heavy metal boxes when the liner jerked into motion. One of them got right back up, but the other took a very long time to recover.

Once the liner stabilized, Lieutenant Jeffries and his corporal hurried over to the man to check his condition. He looked back and gave Justine a nod that told her, although battered and bruised, he was otherwise fine.

Justine had been through an attempted hijacking before, though the assailants had been successful in their main purpose: kidnapping Alex Manez. But Alex wasn't on the *Diana*. He had disembarked safely.

Fighting back the panic welling inside her, Justine clung to Clive's arm. His face was set in a stoic mask, but his eyes betrayed his fear.

"It's the Kinemet." Clive stated the obvious. "They want it."

"Why are they letting them take the ship?" Justine asked through clenched teeth.

"CS3 isn't really designed to stop a ship from *leaving,*" he said.

Justine shook her head. "I mean the flight crew. All liners have protocols against this. The cabin is self-contained and sealed—in which case they would never initiate takeoff procedures. And even if someone were to manage to get in and hold the pilot at gunpoint, the system is designed to disengage electrical if there are any other biometric readings in the cabin besides the captain and navigator."

Clive glanced at Justine. "Unless they are a part of it."

A dark look settled on his face and he called out, "Lieutenant Jeffries?"

"Yes, sir?"

"I don't think you need to worry about them attacking us."

The soldier turned his head to look back at Clive and Justine. "Why not?"

"Check the elevator," Clive said. "I'm sure it's been disabled. As are, I'm certain, all our communications. They have no intention of fighting with us. Why would they? We are exactly where they want us, safely tucked away in this little prison of our own making."

Clive laughed, but it was a hollow, bitter sound. "You may as well stand down until we arrive wherever it is they are taking us, or until they initiate contact."

∞

The forward velocity increased, and the liner's vibrations lessened to normal levels as the ship finished its launch from Canada Station Three and started in on its trajectory.

What destination? Justine asked herself. "They can't be heading for any of the other space stations. Everyone will be alerted to them by then. They can't be going to Luna Station or anywhere on the Moon for that matter," she said out loud to Clive.

After the abduction of Alex Manez had revealed the extent of Chow Yin's infiltration into the station, security measures had tripled not only on every settlement on the Moon, but for all space traffic coming to and from the planetoid. Non-commercial or non-military vessels were under the highest scrutiny.

Whoever they were, the hijackers were obviously well organized and funded. Another thought came to her: were they hostages? Or were they incidental cargo? If all the hijackers wanted was the Kinemet, they didn't need her and the soldiers. It would be an easy enough task for them to shut down the life support system in the cargo bay and just wait until any threat was neutralized.

She clung tighter to Clive's arm.

Justine still had her PERSuit harness on—she would be completely lost without it—and watched as Lieutenant Jeffries and his men did a full recon of the cargo area, checking the elevators to confirm Clive's supposition. It wasn't that they didn't believe him, but Justine knew from her days in the military that redundant confirmation had proved itself time and again.

Corporal Marks, the second-in-command, tested his communications equipment, and tried to tap into the onboard computer. The result was as Clive predicted. Dead air.

After stationing his soldiers at strategic locations around the cargo area anyway, the lieutenant returned to report. "We're completely shut in and shut off. Grounded."

As if reading Justine's thoughts, he added, "Life support is still fully functional."

"So they want us alive," Justine said in conclusion.

Ever pragmatic, the lieutenant said, "Maybe."

"What do you mean?"

The officer shook his head. "There are a lot of scenarios that could be played out. Holding us as hostages is only one of them."

Justine let her thoughts follow some of the possibilities. They could hold them for ransom. They could release them at a later time as a gesture of goodwill. They could kill them later to serve as a warning, or a distraction. They could sell them into slavery—human trafficking was uncommon, but still an issue in the world.

Before her imagination took her down paths even more frightening, she said, "What now?"

"Now," Clive said in a drawl and glanced at Justine. "Now we need to figure out where we're going. Maybe that will give us a clue to the hijackers' intent."

Lieutenant Jeffries turned as Corporal Marks reported. "I tried to tap into the onboard computer, but it looks like they set up their own firewall."

"It's too bad we didn't have Alex here," Justine said, and then when Clive gave her a curious look, she quickly added, "Because of his ability to see extraspacially. We're all blind in here without instrumentation."

Clive put his arm around her and growled. "There has to be something we can do other than just wait for them to initiate contact."

Corporal Marks had an odd look on his face as he fixed his eyes on Justine's harness. "Even if I had something more powerful than my holoslate, it could take weeks to break the firewall. But…"

"What is it, Corporal?" the lieutenant prompted.

A hint of a smile played at the young man's lips. "That's a PERSuit, isn't it?" he asked Justine.

"Yes."

He said, "I believe it has built-in gyroscopic sensors and an inertial reference platform."

For a moment, Justine had no idea what the corporal was getting at, but then she clued in. "As well as an attitude indicator, vertical and horizontal positioning. Along with visual and olfactory sensations, the suit can also provide inertial sensations to viewers. If I were at sea, or on a roller coaster, viewers who are susceptible would experience motion sickness, it's that real." She sounded like a brochure.

The lieutenant, excited, asked the corporal, "Can you access the suit and the data?"

Corporal Marks nodded. "I think so. With any luck, I should be able to track our course from the moment we launched. I have astrogation charts in my holoslate—maybe I can figure out where we're going."

He cocked his head to one side and said to Justine, "You'll have to remove the suit, though."

∞

Though she had been blind for years, there was always a part of Justine that hadn't completely accepted the fact. There was that glimmer of hope that one day she would wake up and be able to see. The universe had played a cosmic joke on her, and at any moment, it would deliver the punch line, everyone would have a good laugh, and then she would be normal again.

Sitting back in the webbed cargo seat without her PERSuit sensors or her optilink, which the corporal needed to interface with his holoslate, her world had completely plunged into darkness.

She experienced a few moments of all-too familiar despair. It wasn't a joke, it was a cruel prank and she was only fooling herself into thinking it wasn't permanent.

Then she felt a warm hand slip into hers. Clive. He gave her hand a quick squeeze of reassurance.

She leaned into him. "Thanks."

"For what?"

"Just being here."

He laughed hollowly. "All things being equal…"

"Same here." She smiled at him, though she had no idea if he was looking at her or watching as Corporal Marks rigged a connection from the PERSuit to his portable holoslate.

"Listen," he said, "we'll get through this. The hijackers haven't turned off our life support so they obviously need us alive. That gives us an opportunity."

"I know," she said. "I just wish I could do more. I feel so helpless."

In answer, Clive put an arm around her shoulders while they waited.

It was only a few minutes later that the corporal called out that he'd made the connection.

Clive stood up from the seats to approach, and Justine went with him.

"What have you got?" Lieutenant Jeffries said.

"It's compiling the data at the moment. We should have a readout in less than a minute."

There was a hushed silence as everyone circled around the corporal and his computer. Justine felt a deep frustration that she couldn't see the screen and had to wait for someone to feed her the information secondhand.

"Here comes the trajectory now," the corporal said.

A moment later, Lieutenant Jeffries spoke, and his voice took on a caustic tone. "That can't be right."

"What?" Justine asked.

Jeffries said, "Are you sure you have the correct information? Maybe the computer reversed the coordinates or something."

"What coordinates?" Justine asked again.

Corporal Marks tapped repeatedly on his computer again. "No, it's right."

Justine grew frustrated. "What's right?"

She heard Lieutenant Jeffries take a deep breath and let it out in a hiss. "Well, according to our current trajectory, the hijackers are pointing the *Diana* directly at the Sun."

17

Lunar Lines Vessel, *Diana* :
Solar Trajectory :

It had been a frightening and crazy week for Terry. At first, when he and Jose had confiscated the alien scroll—along with Terry's grandfather—he had felt empowered.

He was finally taking control of things and able shape future events. With like-minded people on his side, Terry had taken the first steps toward returning the Mayan people to their rightful place in the world. If he had anything to say about it, his people would not suffer and die needlessly like Itzel.

As with any revolution, there were bound to be casualties. Deep down, Terry knew this; he wasn't so naïve as to think all they had to do was brandish their weapons and people would simply give in. Though he steeled himself for the possibility, he still wanted to avoid violence as much as possible. Jose assured him he felt the same way. He assigned Terry and another Cruzados, Carlos, to guard the shuttle's cabin, in the unlikely event one of the American soldiers managed to get out of the cargo hold and infiltrate the upper decks.

Since joining the Cruzados, Terry had been surprised at the size of their network of sympathizers in the USA, Inc. government and NASA. There was an even larger number of people who they could bribe or blackmail into doing what was needed for their principal mission.

One of those they had bribed was the ship's navigator, Lieutenant John Franks. Terry didn't know the details, but from what he had overheard, he guessed the navigator may have had a gambling problem and rising debts.

Within an hour of successfully breaking away from the station, Franks stepped out of the cabin and demanded to speak with Jose.

Pointing a meaty finger at the man, Carlos said, "He's busy. What do you want?"

Franks growled. "I want more money."

"You'll get what you agreed on."

Franks shook his head. He looked very frazzled. His hair was in disarray, his skin flushed and his pupils were dilated. Terry thought he might be on drugs.

Franks growled. "I need more. And I want to settle this now."

Carlos kept his voice even, but the lids of his eyes dropped, and his irises unfocused. "It's too late. The deed is done. When we get to our destination, you'll get paid. Now go back to the cabin and do your job."

Either Lieutenant Franks didn't recognize that he couldn't bully or cajole Carlos, or he was too far gone in his panic that he didn't care. The navigator held up his holoslate and showed them the screen.

Even from a bad angle, Terry was able to make out the message someone had sent to Franks. He had obviously received it just before the hijacking, but by then it was too late for him to do anything until they were well under way.

The message was from Lunar Lines head office. Franks had been suspended pending a criminal investigation for smuggling.

"See this?" he said. "It was just a couple lousy cases of rum. People do it all the time. Why'd they have to pick on me?"

"Sorry to hear that," Carlos said. "But it's not my problem."

"Don't you see? They're already on to me. I need to completely disappear, get a new identity. I need more money for that."

Carlos was losing his patience. "You're getting enough from us to do that."

"I need more!" Franks said.

His eyes flicking wildly back and forth, the lieutenant made a motion as if to race past Carlos and Terry. Holding out one hefty arm, Carlos clothes-lined the navigator, and the man fell back into the wall.

Carlos produced an ion pistol and pointed it at the navigator. "I said: get back to the cabin."

"You son of a bitch!" Franks screamed and rushed Carlos.

A crimson flower blossomed out of the middle of the navigator's forehead. Terry barely registered the whir of the ion pulse.

Franks' eyes widened in sudden shock for a brief moment before the life went out of him, and he sank to his knees and toppled over on his side.

"What the hell did you do?" Terry yelled at Carlos.

"He was crazed. High or something. We couldn't have him creating a panic right now. Or sabotaging the flight computer. There's no telling what people like that will do." Carlos was once again completely calm. He showed no more concern than if he had slapped a bug with a flyswatter.

"But you killed him!"

Carlos turned his full attention to Terry. "Are *we* going to have a problem now?"

Terry stammered. "N-no. It's just—"

"What?"

"I don't know. Couldn't we have just knocked him out? Tied him up or something?"

Carlos scratched his hair behind his ear. "I thought you were on board with this mission."

"Yeah. I am." Terry stared down at the blood pooling under the navigator's head. He could feel Carlos's eyes watching him. "It just caught me off guard, you know. Sorry."

Anything else they might have said to each other went unspoken as two men approached at a jog. It was Jose and one of the other Cruzados, Alberto.

Jose surveyed the scene and asked, "What happened?"

With a shrug, Carlos said, "He got out of hand."

Jose glanced at Terry for confirmation. Reluctantly, Terry gave a quick nod.

The leader of the Cruzados took a breath. "All right. Clean up the mess. We'll have to find someone to take his place and help our pilot fly the liner." He pointed at Terry. "You up to it?"

Terry, still trying to come to terms with the killing, blinked dimly at Jose. All three men were looking at him expectantly.

"Uh. Yeah," he said finally.

The Cruzados leader nodded and left with Alberto. Carlos tapped Terry on the shoulder.

"Take his legs. Help me get him into one of those freezers."

∞

Terry remained somewhat withdrawn over the next two days as he assisted the pilot—the first non-Mayan Terry had met in the Cruzado movement.

Captain Gruber was an older man who spoke English with a heavy German accent. Terry's English was not very good, so it made communication difficult at first, until Gruber ran a translator program from the ship's haptic console.

At first, Terry had been overwhelmed with the myriad controls and banks of computers, but that quickly settled into tedium.

Captain Gruber told him that, for the most part, he could pilot the liner himself; all flight crew were trained to fly solo should the need arise.

"Basically," he said to Terry, "I just need you to babysit the console when I sleep. Someone needs to be here at all times or the sensors will shut the ship down. Don't worry, it's on autopilot, and if anything happens, the alarm will sound. Your main duty is to call me or come and get me if that happens."

They rotated in twelve-hour shifts. It gave Terry a lot of time to think about his role in hijacking the liner and whether he had made the right decision.

He had spent most of his life believing everyone in his family had made bad decisions. His parents lived in squalor, never trying to better themselves or providing a higher standard of living for their family. His grandfather had a precious artifact which he could have traded for great wealth for his community. And now, he had to admit, Terry had followed in their footsteps. In an attempt to make a difference, to better his family and community, he had fallen in with a group whose ideals were aligned with his own, but whose methods were extreme.

And Carlos! He had killed the navigator without batting an eyelid. There was no remorse or doubt afterwards. With no more thought than stepping on a bug, Carlos had ended a man's life.

Terry was certain they could have restrained the man and resolved the situation without resorting to murder.

There was a line Terry had vowed not to cross. Now, upon reflection, he realized that the line had been breached the moment he agreed to kidnap his grandfather and steal the ancient scroll.

How far was too far? It was all too far, Terry knew. But the problem was that he was in too deep to back out now. They would certainly eliminate him if he made too much trouble. The Cruzados had Terry's grandfather and they had the document. They did not need Terry any more.

If he was to survive this thing, he would have to continue to play along and wait for an opportunity to escape.

Where they were going, however, there was no place to run.

∞

It was three days later that Captain Gruber, looking ruffled from a broken sleep, came in while Terry was on shift. He offered up a token smile of greeting, then motioned for Terry to move aside.

"What's happening?" Terry asked.

In a gruff tone, the captain said, "We're stopping."

"Stopping? We won't have enough fuel to build velocity again."

Glancing up at Terry in annoyance, the captain said, "We don't have more than a day's worth of fuel left anyway. What did you think, that we were just going to coast the rest of the way?"

Terry hated to admit it, but that was exactly what he had assumed.

The captain pressed his lips together. "We're going to rendezvous with another ship and unload the cargo."

"And the hostages?"

Frowning, Captain Gruber did not reply.

A dark look settled over Terry's face. "We can't just abandon them and let them drift in space. They'll run out of food and water before any rescue ship finds them."

The captain either didn't have a reply, or chose not to say anything. Instead, he concentrated on bringing the liner to a dead stop.

Within an hour, a bright speck appeared in the distance, and Terry pointed at it. "Is that the new ship?"

"Looks like," the captain said and called up a display. "Yup. It's the *Ultio.*" He pressed the intercom button and announced the new arrival.

Moments later, Jose and Carlos entered the cabin.

"He's here?" the leader of the Cruzados asked. His face was lit up with anticipation.

Terry wondered who, but didn't ask out loud. He had the realization that he had been kept in the dark about many things. Though he hadn't spent a lot of time thinking about it earlier, he knew now that he wasn't as trusted as he had originally thought back in Honduras when the Cruzados had first brought him into their revolution.

When he looked up at Jose, he saw that the other man was watching him ponderingly, and Terry flashed a smile to show that he was still on board with the operation.

They all watched as the other ship grew larger until it completely filled the display. The *Ultio* pulled alongside the liner and an umbilical tube extended out and attached to the main door.

All four men exited the cabin and made their way back to greet the new arrival.

It was with growing anticipation that Terry waited as the cabin door unlocked with a hiss of escaping air, then slowly opened. Only one man stepped out.

"Jose, I'm glad everything went well." Tall and blond, with piercing blue eyes, the man was in his late twenties or early thirties, though he carried himself as if he were years older. He wore a black suit in a modern cut without a tie. His white shirt did not have a fold at the collar, but instead circled the man's throat in a restrictive circle. His smile held no humor.

It was at that moment that Terry detected a faint resemblance between him and Captain Gruber. His notion was confirmed when the two of them stood together and shook hands.

"Uncle," the younger man said in English. "How was the trip?"

"Uneventful."

Jose, a wide grin on his face, stepped up and shook the blond man's hand as well.

"Your plan worked perfectly," he said.

"I'm glad to hear it." The man turned his steely gaze on Terry. "And is this who we must thank for providing the opportunity?"

"Yes," Jose said. "This is Te'irjiil, who goes by the name Terry Fernandez. Terry, I would like you to meet our benefactor, Mr. Klaus Vogelsberg. His uncle is Captain Gruber. Without their support, we would still be meeting in deserted buildings and just *talking* about the movement."

A corner of Klaus's lip went up in a humorless smile, and he extended his hand to Terry. "Very pleased to finally meet you. We've been waiting years for the so-called geniuses at NASA to figure out the ancient scroll, and in the end, the secret is unlocked by a simple villager. How perfect is that?"

Terry felt very uncomfortable under the other man's penetrative gaze. He didn't know if he was being complimented or insulted, but didn't want to say the wrong thing, so he nodded and offered up a smile of his own.

Turning his attention back to Jose, Klaus asked, "I trust we didn't have any trouble with our guests down below?"

"No. They are completely secure. All entrances are magnetically sealed. They already had enough food and water for the journey down there, and aside from one of them attempting to blow open the elevator door with some small explosive—which failed of course—we haven't heard a peep."

"That's good."

Terry found his voice. "They aren't going to be harmed, are they?"

Letting out a sudden barking laugh, Klaus said, "Going to be harmed?" He shared an amused look with his uncle, then continued: "If we wanted them harmed, we wouldn't have taken them hostage."

The relief Terry felt was quickly replaced by a measure of embarrassment. These people must think him some kind of country rube. He vowed not to open his mouth again until he had something intelligent to say.

Klaus turned to Jose. "Speaking of which, you may transfer them and the cargo to my ship. Use knockout gas; filter it through their air system." He glanced at Terry and gave a wink. "No conflict, no fighting, no harm. You see, we've thought of everything."

Terry flushed red.

Jose, a pleased smile on his lips, motioned to Carlos and the other men. "Let's go secure the prisoners." As he left with them, he called back over his shoulder to Terry. "You can stay with Captain Gruber and help him."

Gruber gave Terry a level look. It was obvious what the pilot was thinking: Terry's status in the movement was on a downward slide.

When Jose and the other Cruzados were gone, Klaus took a step closer to Captain Gruber.

"Once we have everything aboard, I need you to set the autopilot to point the liner back at the Sun. With any luck, the authorities will waste time trying to save a ghost ship. By then, we'll be very far away. We have a lot of work to do, and we don't want to be interrupted."

Terry started to say, "But, I thought…" And once again, he felt the heat rise in his neck and cheeks as Klaus looked at him with an amused smile.

"What," Klaus said, "did you think the governments of Earth were just going to give in to our demands if we turned over the cargo and hostages? Restore you to your rightful place as ambassadors to the stars? Ha!" This time, his laughter had the sound of a threat in it. He was obviously growing tired of entertaining Terry's ignorance.

Terry knew he was pushing the limit of Klaus's tolerance, but he had to ask one last question:

"If we aren't holding the Kinemet for ransom, what are we going to do with it?"

There was a chill moment when Terry thought Klaus was going to order his uncle to shoot him where he stood, but then the younger man's face broke into a wide grin.

"I'm glad you asked," he said to Terry. "Because I need you to work with me to complete the translation of the scroll, and uncover its secret. For that, we need the Kinemet, and a few test subjects."

With that, Klaus gave his uncle a nod, and then headed in the same direction as Jose and the others.

Captain Gruber gave Terry a tap on the arm with the back of his fingers. "Let's get moving."

∞

Trying not to be too obvious about it, Terry took a careful look at the unconscious hostages as they were loaded on gurneys and transported one by one from the liner to the *Ultio*. Aside from a few bruises here and there, and an overall pallor of gauntness from lack of nutrition, they all seemed to be healthy.

He did notice the one woman among them, a civilian, and recognized her from the news. It was the captain from the missions to Pluto. Terry was quite surprised to see her, but made sure to keep his expression neutral around the other Cruzados.

Within an hour, the hostages and the Kinemet were transferred to a safe hold on the *Ultio*, and Captain Gruber asked Terry to help him fire up the *Diana's* engines and set its course for oblivion.

For the most part, Terry had no idea what he was doing, but whenever the captain said to press this button or that, he did. Soon, the liner was fully prepped and ready for its final voyage into the Sun.

"If we aren't going to return to Earth or Luna," Terry asked after screwing up his courage, "where are we going?"

"You know, you ask a lot of questions," Captain Gruber said in German. Though the translation came across in a pleasant programmed voice, the captain's original tone had been acerbic. He switched to English. "Curiosity could get you in trouble. If Jose wanted you to know, he would have told you."

Terry forced himself to keep his voice light and casual. "Maybe it slipped his mind. He's quite busy." When the captain didn't immediately reply, Terry asked, "What's the big secret, anyway? I'm going to find out soon enough. So what's the surprise?"

Eyeing the young Mayan, Captain Gruber took a minute out from his final preparations and flicked on a backup navigation holoscreen. He tapped in a few commands on the haptic console and the image of a familiar planet came into view.

Terry's lips fell open as if to make an exclamation, but no sound came out. He finally found his voice. "I would never have guessed."

"Precisely why Klaus chose it," Captain Gruber said. "Not only is it right there in plain view, but who would think to look for us in a ball of poisonous gas and sulfuric acid?"

The captain finished programming the computer and got up to leave. "My boy, if there is such a thing as hell, where we're going is the closest thing to it in this universe."

NASA NewsFlash :
May 2102 :

Nearly one hundred and forty years after Venus became the object of the first successful interplanetary mission, the Lucis Observatory orbiting Earth's sister planet is now vacant and abandoned.

Citing budgetary constraints and lack of public support for the research station, NASA's board of directors voted early last year to cease manned operations to Venus. The final crew disembarked this morning after finalizing the automation of the remaining sensor equipment. They should be arriving home by the end of the month.

For more details, please follow our MeshSite...

Canada Station Three :
Lagrange Point 4 :
Earth Orbit :

The one thing Kenny insisted on was to record the experiments on holo.

Since they wanted to keep the administration of Quantum Resources out of the procedures until they could come up with some solid conclusions, both Alex and the physicist decided to conduct their tests in Alex's apartment after official hours.

For the most part, Alex's involvement in the core research at the lab had become minimal—there were only so many experiments they could do without any Kinemet. It had only been on Kenny's original insistence that Alex had been there on a more regular basis the past few weeks. Now that Kenny's official reports did not show any progress, Alex was allowed to spend his time as he saw fit, so long as he remained on call should the need arise.

Since recharging himself with the Kinemetic radiation on the liner before it was hijacked, Alex was completely restored. He had not, however, reported his recovery to the administration, and wouldn't until he and Kenny had a chance to do some of their own research.

His complexion was hale, his legs were strong, and he had more energy than he'd had for years.

He had not gone to see Doctor Amma for his regularly scheduled checkup, but sent her a message that everything was going well for him. Although the doctor had the best of intentions, Alex knew any diagnosis she reached would not provide him with any great insight into his condition. It would, however, raise some serious flags back on Earth if they reported he had gone into complete remission. For the time being, he could not afford that kind of attention.

Alex wanted time to investigate other aspects of the Kinemetic ability without the hindrance of the scientists who had spent most of the last ten years getting him to perform the same useless tasks and scratching their heads when they couldn't figure out what it all meant.

In Kenny, Alex saw the spark of someone who wanted to know the answers without using the knowledge for their own political or professional gain. Although Kenny had come on strong—trying to prove himself—once he had a glimpse of what Alex was, and what he could become, Kenny's primary instincts kicked in.

Most scientists initially entered their fields in the pursuit of knowledge, to be the first one to solve the puzzle. After years of the politics and squabbling inherent in the scientific community, many lost sight of their purpose. Right under the surface, Kenny was still motivated by his original passion, and Alex recognized it.

But while NASA and Quantum Resources *wanted* to know the extent of Alex's condition, Alex *needed* to know. And if it meant going behind the backs of the administration to find those answers, so be it.

At first, when he no longer needed the hydraulic braces, Alex was certain someone would notice him walking around Canada Station Three under his own power, but after years of dismissing his presence, no one seemed to be able to tell the difference. Still, Alex kept mostly to himself in his rooms, except to go to the mess hall, or to the labs when he was called.

He didn't need to go to any physical location; once again his clairvoyant ability allowed him to visit any area on the station without leaving his room. All he had to do was close his eyes and concentrate. It was a simple matter of will for him to push his senses outward. Like a ghost or an astral walker, he could frequent every corner of Canada Station Three.

Alex was able to see Kenny with his ability long before the physicist arrived at the apartment for their nightly experiments.

A moment before Kenny pressed the buzzer, Alex extended his thoughts to the door panel. While it was just as easy to walk over and press the release, or even use voice control to allow the door to open, Alex preferred to exercise his electropathic ability to trip the switch. It was good practice.

"Hello, Alex," Kenny said as he stepped inside.

Without any additional preamble, Kenny pushed a cart filled with equipment toward Alex's computer station and began to connect the sensor leads to the bus ports.

"You had an idea, Kenny?"

The physicist nodded. "Yesterday I noticed that there was a fluctuation in the ambient temperature when you used your *sight*." He glanced over at Alex. "I hate using the word 'clairvoyance.' Sounds like something a fortune-teller would say."

Alex shrugged.

Kenny continued explaining: "I'd like to run a series of tests to measure the temperature change around you in relation to the distance that you extend your *sight*. It could be important; if you require more energy to see farther, it could make a difference to how much Kinemet someone would need to pilot a ship to different locations."

"I keep telling you, piloting a ship in that manner is not what was intended. That's just incidental."

Kenny looked up from the computer and nodded. "Yeah, I know. But if we're going to get the government corporations on board with this—and get you more of the Kinemet—we need to give them some tangible purpose. They want to see black on their profit and loss statements, not red. They need results. Things they can get behind; like cheap space travel."

"All right. But tonight I'm going to try to push my *sight* farther than I ever have before," he said, adopting Kenny's word for the ability.

"What do you mean?"

Alex lay back on the sofa while Kenny trucked the cart over and placed the sensors around and on Alex.

"The very first time I experienced the *sight*, I saw the entire solar system laid out for me. It happened over a four-hour period, but in my memory, it was more like an afterimage from a bright flash. There was no controlling it. It was almost like something in my mind was calibrating my senses, getting my location.

"After that, my range was considerably less. I could only see about a hundred and fifty kilometers away. Before I went to Centauri, I used that ability to help the group who was sheltering me, by warning them of incoming ships. When they went on salvage missions, I would scout for them. I had plenty of time to practice and push my ability."

Kenny asked, "You worked for the pirates who kidnapped you, right?"

"We came to an understanding." Alex closed his eyes and tried to relax. "I've never been able to go farther than about a hundred and fifty kilometres, and when I try, it's been an enormous strain." He looked at Kenny. "I can sense there's something out there, beyond the limit of my clairvoyance—my *sight*. Maybe there's something out there I can only see if I'm quantized."

"You mean, when you shift out of our reality?" Kenny paused to look at Alex.

"Yeah. But when I enter a quantized state, I don't have any senses at all. It's like I'm in some kind of stasis. I know that's not the way it's supposed to be, but… It's like I'm a baby bird that has ventured out of its nest for the first time and sees the limitless sky. It can tell it's supposed to be able to fly, but hasn't figured out how to use its wings yet. Until I can complete my transformation, I won't know what I'm capable of when I become quantized."

"So what is it that you are proposing tonight?"

Alex breathed deeply, and paused to collect his thoughts. "When I spent those few hours on the *Diana* recharging myself with the Kinemet, there were others there who were also exposed to the Kinemetic radiation."

"Yes?" Kenny's interest was piqued.

"Perhaps if I focus on them, since they've been marginally irradiated, I'll be able to bridge the gap between us."

"And," Kenny added, a knowing smile on his lips, "perhaps get a location on your kidnapped friends?"

Alex nodded. "That's the plan."

"I'm on board with that. Let me just finish hooking you up."

It only took Kenny a few more minutes to complete the set up. As he tested the sensors and got an initial reading before they started their experiment, Kenny looked as if there was something he wanted to say.

"What's wrong?" Alex asked.

"It's only been three days since you were restored," Kenny said. "I know you've used your abilities far more than what I've seen."

Alex admitted, "Yeah. So?"

"So, the Kinemetic radiation in you is not unlimited. You're going to run out of juice at some point, and we have no idea when we'll get more for you."

Alex leaned back into the sofa and smiled dismissively. "I know, but I'm good for a while longer. Let's get on with this, Dr. Frankenstein."

Once Kenny finished attaching the sensors to Alex, measuring his vital stats as well as brain waves and electromagnetic emanations, he flipped on the spectrograph and gave Alex a thumbs up gesture.

Shutting his eyes, Alex willed himself back into that transcendent state. Over the past few days he had become quite adept at the technique.

This time, instead of visualizing the station and allowing his senses to float through the corridors and rooms, he pushed his senses outward. Trying to ignore anything tangible within the scope of his *sight,* he focused on any Kinemetic energy signatures in the area. There was a link between him and that element, and if he could simply train his extra-spatial senses to detect it, he was certain he could send his incorporeal form out to find Justine and the others.

As he scouted in a sweeping pattern outside the station, he felt an extrasensory tug, accompanied by a note or two of the haunting melody that always seemed to be in the periphery of his senses when he was using his Kinemetic abilities. Without being conscious of what he was doing, he gathered all his will and pushed himself in that direction.

At first, his spectral senses soared at an alarming speed, but it was as if he were on the end of a giant elastic. Once Alex reached approximately a hundred and fifty kilometres distance from the station, the effort to move himself even a meter more became exponentially more difficult. Like a marathon runner who reaches their glycogen limit, Alex felt a sudden burning fatigue and lost focus.

Disoriented, he suddenly could not determine which way to return to his body. He was lost, adrift in space, and he didn't have enough energy to sever the link and snap back to reality.

Alex panicked, and he felt his consciousness fade away into a nothingness as dark as the farthest regions of space.

20

For what seemed like an eternity, Michael and George lay on the floor of the van as the Cruzados transported them to an unknown location.

Trussed up like a hog around his ankles and wrists, Michael was unable to find a position where every pothole they hit in the road didn't send him bouncing and jostling against the steel floor. Twice he banged his head against a metal tool box; the second time he nearly blacked out and almost vomited from the sudden nausea. He wasn't sure his kidneys would survive the ride.

Like George, Michael was gagged, and could only glare back at the rebel soldier who watched over him with callous eyes. Unlike George, Michael was still conscious.

The first time George had tried to protest his capture, struggling against his bonds, the solider guarding them kicked him in the side and barked, *"Silencio!"*

After a particularly jarring bump, George once again growled through his makeshift muzzle. The soldier struck him in the side of the head with his rifle butt, and then gave Michael a challenging look when he tried to wriggle over to check on his friend.

A small trickle of blood ran down George's face. He was knocked out, but breathing. Still alive, though he didn't regain consciousness during the remainder of the journey.

It was hard to judge how much time had elapsed, but it seemed like hours before the van slowed, turned a sharp corner, and then rolled up to its final destination.

Michael heard shouts in Spanish as orders were given,

acknowledged and carried out. He estimated from the voices that there were more than a dozen men in the vicinity.

When the back doors of the van opened, and he and George were pulled out into a moonlit compound, Michael saw that his assumption was correct.

A number of armed men approached to assist in unloading the prisoners. While two of the soldiers grabbed Michael by the arms, a third cut the rope around his ankles. They escorted him from the van to a large storage shed. Four other men lifted the prone figure of George out and carried him.

In addition to the shed where they were heading, there were three other outbuildings—barns converted to barracks, Michael guessed as he spied more men milling around in front of them. The buildings had been erected on either side of a packed dirt road which led up to a main house. It was dark except for one room on the second floor. A silhouetted figure stood in the window, as if overseeing the activity below.

One of the soldiers yanked on Michael's arm, getting his attention and dragging him roughly to the storage shed.

Stepping inside first, the soldier pulled a thin string attached to a bare light bulb hanging from a rafter, and harsh yellow light bathed the inside of the shed. Wooden barrels were stacked in one corner. Against the other wall was a dilapidated gas generator that looked as if it hadn't worked for a decade. The floor was of packed earth, but there was a dirty straw mattress near the back of the shed. The soldiers carrying George dropped him on it without exercising any amount of care.

In heavily accented English, one soldier said, "Sleep now. No trouble."

Turning off the light, the Cruzado exited the building. Michael heard the snap of a padlock and the soldier ordering a man to stay posted out front.

There was one small dirt-stained window beside the door, but it was large enough to let in some light from the moon, and Michael's eyes soon became accustomed to the night.

With his hands still bound behind his back, he moved over to check on his friend again. He got down on his knees and leaned in for a closer look. George was still unconscious, but his breathing was evening out.

Michael spoke in low tones, "It'll be all right George. We'll get through this."

He looked around the shed again, his mind racing. First things first, Michael wasn't going to be able to do much with his hands tied together.

Awkwardly struggling to his feet, he approached the generator and turned his back to it. Reaching out with his fingers, he felt a sharp length of broken metal jutting out just far enough that he might be able to cut the rope at his wrists. He worked the rope over the edge repeatedly.

Soon enough, the rope fell free from him, and Michael brought his hands out front to examine them in the dim moonlight for damage. Several tiny cuts marred his skin and a few trickles of blood ran down his arm, but he was otherwise unscathed.

He set to work untying George's bonds and trying to arrange the man into a more comfortable position until he regained consciousness. That accomplished, Michael sat on the foot of the mattress and leaned back against the wall.

With the shed locked and guarded, and Michael unarmed, there wasn't much else he could do. They had been sending updates to John Markham every morning. When they failed to check in tomorrow, Michael hoped that John would send out an alert to the authorities and contact Calbert at Quantum Resources. However, even if they were made aware that Michael and George were missing, they would have no idea where the two were.

Michael had no idea what had become of their equipment. George's video mask had a GPS tracker in it. If the Cruzados had taken it with them, then all Michael had to do was turn the camera back on and wait for someone back home to notice. If the machine were destroyed, then Michael would have to find some other way to let their location— wherever that was—be known.

In the back of the van, Michael had been disoriented and distracted. He'd had no bearings. Had they gone north, west, east, south? And for how long? Hours for certain. But that could mean they were anywhere, even in one of Honduras's bordering countries, like El Salvador or Guatemala.

Michael sat up for another hour, worrying over their situation and speculating on what would happen the next day. After a time, exhaustion crept in and sleep took him.

∞

It was one of the most uncomfortable nights Michael had ever spent, and he woke with a sharp pain in his neck from sleeping upright against the wall.

George was already awake, and sitting on the edge of the mattress, elbows propped on his knees, one hand gingerly touching the swelling bump on his head.

"You look like I feel," he said to Michael in a grave voice.

"Thanks." Michael tried to work the kink out of his neck. "How's the head?"

"Feels like a watermelon in a microwave. But no permanent damage, I think."

"That's good."

With exaggerated care, George pushed himself to his feet and tested his balance. He looked around the shed and then stepped closer to the small window. "Where are we?"

"Not sure of the exact location, but it's obviously some kind of base camp for the Cruzados."

George glanced sharply at Michael. "Our equipment? The camera?"

"I'm not sure. They may have destroyed it."

"We can only hope!"

Michael stood up. "What?"

With a knowing smile, George winked. "I installed a backup circuit running off a lithium battery. It was in constant contact with one of the geo satellites we were using. If the link is severed, it trips an immediate alert back home. The GPS uplink would give them our last coordinates. At least that would give them a starting point from which to track us."

"What if they didn't destroy the camera?" Michael asked.

Shrugging, George said, "Well, the longer it takes Calbert to notice we're missing, the harder it will be for him to find us."

"That's what I thought," Michael said, pressing his lips together in a grimace.

They both turned when they heard the clanking of metal. Someone unlocked the shed's padlock, and the door swung open. Two Cruzados with rifles at the ready stood just outside, looking in. One of them glanced down, saw their hands unbound, and narrowed his eyes. He made a gesture with his weapon and said, *"Siga con nosotros."*

With one soldier in front, and one behind, the two prisoners were led up the packed road to the main house.

Inside, they were greeted at the door by a dark haired, middle-aged man with a thin black moustache which drooped around the corners of his smiling mouth.

"Please come in," he said with a sweeping gesture of his hand. "My name is Oscar Ruiz, and this is my plantation. I apologize for the unpleasantness of your quarters last night, but we were unprepared for your arrival. We have had many guests of late, and we are not always able to accommodate everyone."

Michael blinked, unsure how to respond. He shared a look with George.

A burly man with a thick moustache appeared from another room. He was dressed in a dark grey shirt and denim overalls. At the end of a leather strap slung over his shoulder was a submachine gun. It rested between the back of his arm and his side.

Noticing the new arrival, Oscar nodded in his direction while keeping his eyes on Michael and George. "This is Humberto, who is part of my new protective detachment, and is assigned to household security. If you will follow him upstairs, he will show you where you can clean up. Breakfast will be served shortly. I cannot wait for you to try our own home-grown coffee—it's world famous, you know."

Oscar gave them a quick nod, took one step back and spun on his heel. As he disappeared into the same room Humberto had come out of, he called out some instructions in Spanish to the house staff.

In a thick accent, Humberto said, "Upstairs." When Michael didn't move right away, the soldier put his hand on the back of his arm and pushed him gently but firmly toward the staircase. "Now."

George needed no prompting, and led the way to the second floor. Humberto followed them up, and called out directions which brought them to a sparse bedroom furnished with a single mattress flat on the floor, a wooden chair in one corner, and a ratty looking sofa.

There was a four-pane window looking out over the plantation, and a quick glance showed dozens of *campesinos* tending the rows of plants. Thick iron bars covered the window, providing no means of escape. Not that it was an option at this point. Even if Michael and George were able to get away from their captors, they were both unequipped to survive in the open on their own for any length of time; at least for however long it would take them to make their way to a populated area where they could call someone for help.

Humberto took a few steps to the wall opposite the sofa and pushed back a slatted door.

"Wash here," he instructed them.

Without another word, he left the bedroom, closing the door behind him and locking it.

Michael looked at George. "What the hell is going on? Are we prisoners or guests?"

"Yes," was George's answer. He smiled. "If I were to make a guess, I would say Mr. Ruiz is a supporter of the Cruzados movement, but he might not be a willing supporter. I wouldn't count on him knowing much more than whatever rhetoric they feed him."

"How's that?"

"Look at it from his perspective," George said. "He's a wealthy landowner with a profitable business, at least by local standards. Central America has been rife with civil war of some sort for centuries, and someone who wants to maintain their status needs to work within that reality. I'd say he's just hedging his bets. Obviously the Cruzados are a larger organization than we suspected. If they manage to attain their objectives, then he'll be remembered for his contribution. If their revolution gets put down, he can always point to his 'guests' to prove how hospitable he was; he could maybe even go so far as to claim the Cruzados forced his cooperation."

George was the first to enter the water closet and he grunted in disapproval. "Well, at least it's indoor plumbing," he said when he turned on the tap and watched rusty water pour into the cracked porcelain sink. He did his best to wash the sweat and dirt from his face and neck while Michael sat on the chair and waited his turn.

"So how do we play this?" Michael asked.

George stepped out of the washing room, dabbing at his face with a towel. "We don't have a lot of options. We don't know where we are; the authorities don't know where we are and we don't have any means of contacting them. They're not going to kill us, and I don't think they'll hold us for ransom—at the most we'll be used as hostages. In the meantime, we should act as guests, ingratiate ourselves with Oscar, and pump him for as much information as we can get. Even if he's not directly involved in the Cruzados' politics, I'm sure he knows more than we've been able to guess so far. Your turn."

Michael barely had enough time to wash up before there was a knock on the door for them to head back downstairs.

∞

Michael smelled the fresh-brewed coffee well before Humberto led them into a large dining area. The table in the center of the room was filled with breads, fruits, sausages and fried potatoes. Eyeing the breakfast hungrily, Michael almost didn't notice there were two people sitting at the table.

As Michael and George entered the room, Oscar stood up and motioned to two empty chairs. "Please, sit. Join us. I implore you to tell me what you think of my coffee; the beans were freshly roasted and ground only a few minutes ago."

But Michael didn't reply. Both he and George stopped short when the second man turned and directed his toothy smile at them.

In Spanish, Yaxche said, "George. Hello. Where is your funny hat?"

21

Lucis Observatory :
Venus Orbit :

Justine was the first to regain consciousness, and a knife of panic sliced through her awareness when she couldn't hear or sense anyone else in her vicinity. She began to hyperventilate.

Without her PERSuit harness or optilink, she had no idea where she was or who was with her, if anyone. The after-effects of the sleep agent made her feel like her head was filled with cotton, and there was a persistent ringing in her ears.

She thrust her hands out to try to grasp something—anything— familiar and orient herself. Her fingers brushed against fabric, and then with both hands she tentatively felt along its length. It was the sleeve of someone's jacket. Only one person in their group wore a suit.

Gently shaking his arm, she whispered, "Clive? Are you all right?"

A moan escaped his lips as he came to. "Oh, my head," he growled. "Did a planet land on me or something? How are you?"

"I'm all right." Now that she wasn't alone in the darkness. "Can you see?" Justine asked. "Where are we?" Absently, she scratched at the inside of her elbow.

She heard him groan as he sat up. "We're in a large room of some sort," he told her. "Maybe a conference room or a lab. All the furniture has been removed. There's one door; it's barred, but it has a small window. There's light coming in from it."

Clive made some rustling sounds as he struggled to his feet. "The others are here, too, but they're still unconscious."

Justine experienced a moment of unreasoning panic when Clive stepped away from her, and her fingers reached out for him of their own accord. If Clive was aware of her momentary desperation, he did not acknowledge it. She took a deep breath to center herself. She was stronger than this; succumbing to her fears wouldn't help the situation.

Justine heard Clive rouse Lieutenant Jeffries, and after a moment, the squad leader groaned and coughed as he awoke.

"That was one hell of a Mickey Finn," he said, his voice rough as sandpaper. A moment later, he asked, "You two all right?"

"Aside from the mother of all hangovers, yeah," Justine said. "Do either of you have any idea where we are?"

"Obviously we didn't crash into the Sun," the lieutenant said, his voice sardonic. "Though it feels like it. My skin is on fire." A moment later he said, "It looks as if they've taken all of our weapons and equipment. They even took my boots and belt."

Before they had been rendered unconscious, when they were in the hold of the liner, the soldiers had their ion rifles and supplies. Of course, they were completely ineffectual, but it had provided Justine with a psychological cushion. Now, it sunk home that they were completely at the mercy of their captors.

Justine heard the lieutenant go from man to man and shake them awake. Most of them woke in a symphony of moans and complaints, and Corporal Marks made a remark that he felt a tingling sensation in his legs, as if they were still asleep. When one soldier woke, Justine heard him roll over and vomit.

"Do you see anything out there?" Lieutenant Jeffries asked, his question directed to Corporal Marks, who answered from a distance away.

"An empty hall. I see a few other doors. We're in some kind of lab complex, I would say. None of the other windows are lit."

"Any markings?" the lieutenant asked.

"Just room numbers. Wait—" There was a moment of silence, and then Corporal Marks said, "Huh."

"What?" Justine asked.

"I know where we are," he said, his voice rising in surprise.

"Well?" she prompted.

Clearing his throat, Marks said, "At the end of the hall is a little trolley. There's a symbol etched into the front of it. A circle with a small cross hanging from the bottom."

Lieutenant Jeffries asked, "The symbol for a female?"

"No," said Corporal Marks. "Venus."

"Venus?" the lieutenant asked. "I thought Venus was a ball of hot acid."

The answer popped into Justine's head. "Lucis Observatory."

"Right," said Clive, back beside her. "In Venus's shadow. It's the perfect hiding place. The orbital has been abandoned for years, but the computer still collects data and transmits it home on a regular basis. As long as the computers keep spitting out periodic data to Earth, no one would ever suspect anyone was here."

Using a wall to stabilize herself, Justine stood up. "We're missing something."

"What?" Clive asked.

"Right before we were knocked out, the liner slowed."

Corporal Marks said, "Docking here?"

"No, I think we were docking with another ship, and we were transferred over."

Clive took a step closer to her. "What makes you say that?"

Justine reached out and took his hand, and lifted it up. "Two reasons. First, the liner wouldn't have had enough fuel to make the trip here." She pushed up his sleeve and ran her fingers along the skin at his elbow. There was a tiny bump there. She pressed it.

"Hey, that hurts," he said.

"Second, we weren't merely unconscious, we were given a dose of thiopental or some other barbiturate. If you check, we all have a puncture where they had us on intravenous."

Clive whistled. "Induced coma? How long were we out?"

Corporal Marks spoke up. "Rough calculation, based on how far the liner had traveled, and the remaining distance to Venus, I would say at least two or three days in transit. There's no way to know how long we've been here, but judging by the scab on my arm, we've been off the IV for the better part of a day."

Justine nodded, not knowing if anyone saw the movement, and said, "So if you add those two facts together, that would mean they want to keep us alive, but they want to keep our—and their—existence a secret."

She had continued to keep her grip on Clive's arm, but now she squeezed it hard. "I don't think we're being kept here as hostages."

Lieutenant Jeffries asked, "Then what do they need us for?"

His question was interrupted when the soldier who had vomited earlier cried out, "What the hell?"

"What is it, Private Jackson?" asked the lieutenant.

"Sir, my apologies, sir. I couldn't help it. I—I voided myself. But, sir, it hurts."

Justine heard some of the others hurry over to investigate, and she let Clive lead her towards the group.

Clive said, "Oh my."

"What?" asked Justine.

"That's not shite," Clive said.

Corporal Marks' voice was tight. "It's blood."

And that's when the pieces of the puzzle fell into place for Justine.

22

Ruiz Plantation :
Honduras :
Central American Conglomeration :

It took Michael a moment to regain his thoughts. The last person he had expected to be there was Yaxche. The old man looked healthy and hale.

George was the first to speak. *"¡Hola! Ha sido un largo tiempo."* He stepped around the table to shake Yaxche's hand, and continued speaking in Spanish: "Unfortunately, I don't know where my funny hat is, but I wish I had it right now."

Without the benefit of a translation program in his portable computer, Michael struggled to keep up with the conversation. His Spanish was very rusty, but he knew Yaxche didn't speak English, so he let George do most of the talking. Whenever he could, he translated for Michael.

"We came down to Honduras to find you," George said to Yaxche. He took a seat at the table when Oscar, with a gracious smile, motioned to two chairs and then snapped his finger for a servant to pour two cups of coffee.

"I am right here," Yaxche said, as if that had been an obvious fact all along. There was a slight crack in his smiling façade that Michael noticed. The old man was just as much a prisoner as they were.

"Are you all right?" Michael asked. One thing he realized quickly was that Yaxche's grandson was not present. Was he someplace else? Was he ill? Dead?

"Yes." Yaxche nodded. "Oscar has been very kind."

"The only thing that separates us from the beasts is manners," Oscar said. "Please, fill your plates. Eat."

They didn't need any more prompting. Michael's stomach rumbled as he loaded his dish with half a dozen strips of bacon, two hardboiled eggs, and spread jam on a hot piece of toast. He dug into his breakfast with gusto. It was a feast fit for a king, as far as Michael was concerned, especially after having had nothing to eat since the previous morning.

He wanted to grill Yaxche, but without knowing more about the situation and getting all the facts, Michael decided to hold off on his questions for the time being.

Between mouthfuls of food, George nodded to Señor Ruiz. "Perhaps we can impose on your generosity with a question?"

"Of course," Oscar said, with a flourish of his hand.

"What is to become of us?"

"For now, the three of you will remain here as guests, so long as I have your word that you will not abuse my hospitality." He looked into Michael's eyes for a moment, and then George's to ensure both men understood and agreed to the condition. "As for the future, I cannot say; though it is my understanding that you will not be ransomed."

So they were to be held as hostages, Michael concluded. A second thought occurred to him. If they didn't need to ransom them, then the Cruzados already had enough money to fund their operation. It was a little scary to think this organization had grown so quickly without the notice of the international security agencies.

There was still the question about where Oscar's loyalties lay, but Michael had to assume their host would report every word of their conversation to whoever gave him orders. The entire *hacienda* could be bugged, for all he knew.

Although his mind screamed for answers about the events surrounding Yaxche's kidnapping—and their own—Michael instead took a long drink of his coffee. "You are right. This is the best cup of coffee I've ever tasted."

Oscar beamed with pride. "Thank you. It is from my personal stock. Only the best for my guests."

George, picking up on Michael's lead, asked, "Perhaps you could give us a tour of your operation sometime."

"Of course," their host said. He looked up as a younger man dressed in a light grey suit appeared in a doorway and nodded to him. Absently, Oscar said to George, "It would be my pleasure, but we will have to do this at some other time. Right now, I have some business matters to attend." He stood up and bowed to his guests. "Please, finish your breakfast. Help yourselves to as much as you want. You may, if you wish, stretch your legs with a walk around our grounds. I'm sure Humberto, as always, will escort you."

With that, Oscar took one last sip of his coffee and left the room.

Michael was chomping at the bit to grill Yaxche, but he wanted to find a place where they could have at least some semblance of privacy. Waiting until George had cleared his second helping of breakfast, he looked back and forth between his friend and Yaxche, and said, "Perhaps we could take our coffee outside, and sit for a while?"

One of the servants, picking up on Michael's suggestion, immediately loaded a serving cart with the coffee urn, a dish of sugar and a small pitcher of cream, and led them outside to a veranda.

Half a dozen palm tree saplings had been planted in large ceramic pots and placed strategically around the veranda to provide as much shade as possible. It was still early morning, but the tropical sun was already beating down. A few dribbles of sweat began to form on Michael's forehead and neck.

They sat in wicker chairs around a patio table, the base of which was made of carved wood, and the round top was a mosaic of various pieces of hand-cut stone.

Humberto took up a position at the edge of a set of stairs, putting himself between the hostages and the field—and possible escape. He was far enough away that, if the three of them talked in low voices, they wouldn't be overheard. There was no way to guarantee there wasn't a hidden microphone in their vicinity, but Michael had to assume they had enough privacy to discuss the events that had led the three of them to their present circumstances.

As they conversed in Spanish, Michael interrupted only occasionally when he didn't understand a word or phrase. Again, he let George do most of the talking.

George started off by telling Yaxche what they knew; which wasn't very much.

"When we arrived at your village, we were told your grandson was also abducted. Did they take him someplace else? Is he all right?"

Yaxche's face fell at the mention of his grandson. "He was not taken," he said. "It is my great shame to say he was the one who took me."

Michael and George shared a surprised look. "What do you mean by that?"

"He is not the boy he used to be. He has changed. His heart, I believe, has seen too much pain."

Concern in his voice, Michael said, "We spoke to your daughter. She told us about his fiancée."

"Itzel," Yaxche said in a whisper. "She was an angel, but her time was short. Te'irjiil could not forgive himself, or us."

"You?"

"He blamed all of us—me, the village council, even our country—for not saving her. He always thought we should have sold the ancient scroll to NASA for medicine and machines."

"But," George said slowly, casting his eyes back and forth between Michael and Yaxche, "your daughter said he came back from a long trip with medicine and technology. If he blamed the people from your village, why would he help them?"

Yaxche stared out into the field. "It may be darkened, but I believe it is still a good heart that beats in his chest."

Michael asked in broken Spanish, "I understand he told everyone he made the money gambling. Do you think he may have sold the scroll instead?"

"Not the scroll," Yaxche said. "Its secret."

Michael immediately glanced up to see if Humberto was listening in. The Cruzado was busy looking bored and chewing a dirty fingernail.

"We've had hundreds of cryptologists, translators and decoding computers working on that document for over a dozen years," Michael said. "NASA has all but given up on it providing them with any significant meaning, and I believe Quantum Resources has mothballed the project." Michael gave George a glance for confirmation of that last point. "And all this time, Alex was right; you had the secret?"

Yaxche looked down at his hands, folded on his lap. "No. I do not know the secret. I have failed my ancestors. I was entrusted with the story, but I now realize I have never understood its true meaning. I had hoped to pass the scroll on to my grandson, that he might protect it through the next generation, but his eagerness to learn the story was a trick. I saw in his eye that he discovered the truth that been hidden from me all along." The old man fell silent while Michael's mind raced.

What was the secret that had eluded so many scientists and educated minds? How had a simple villager figured it out? Was it something so obvious and plain that seasoned professionals had dismissed it? Or was it a genetic puzzle that only a descendant of the first transcribers could comprehend?

George lightly touched Yaxche's wrist with his fingers. "No one blames you. But perhaps if you could tell us exactly what happened, what sparked the Cruzados to kidnap you, we might be able to help you understand."

Yaxche said, "For a year, Te'irjiil had sat with me every evening, reading the story with me. Talking about its meaning. He would hold up a small box—one of your computer machines—and tell me it agreed with some of the story, but not with other parts. At times he would get angry and say the scroll told nothing more than a bedtime story, and there was no meaning. That we wasted our time.

"I thought, the last night I saw him, he would once again leave our village and not return. But he asked me to tell him the story again. I do not know how he came to understand the secret of the scroll, but I saw it in his eyes. And then came his betrayal."

Once again, Yaxche fell silent, and Michael could tell it was difficult for him to tell the tale. It was obviously very personal and very painful.

Over the past decade, Michael had read and re-read the translation of the scroll, telling the story of how the Mayan people—one of the most advanced civilizations of the pre-Columbian world—had come to the brink of extinction over a thousand years before, after a failed civil war caused their gods to abandon them. Like Yaxche's grandson, Michael had always thought it more of a parable than fact.

Yaxche had always claimed that the story had been transcribed from the words of their ancient gods before they left Earth to return to the stars. The scrolls themselves were of human manufacture, and of biological origin, as was the ink with which the story was written. The only fact that lent credence to the scroll's ancient link was the Mayan inscription on *Dis Pater*.

Goozal Kinich Ahua; Inti ba Rahn; Goozal Kukulcan.

"Beware the Mighty Door of Kinich Ahua; Eternity is now Before You; Beware the Power of Kukulcan."

Both the scroll and the inscription on the monument on Pluto mentioned Kinich Ahua—the Mayan god of the sun—and Kukulcan—the feathered god of war who could affect the elements and cause earthquakes.

Historians had struggled to comprehend the symbology behind these ancient deities and what the scroll was trying to tell the descendants of the Mayan people. At one point, a group of physicists from Arizona had assigned each of the gods mentioned to various elements from the periodic table. They tried combining these elements with Kinemet in various formulations to no discernible results. For years, the 'secret' of how to effectively use Kinemet for effective interstellar travel had eluded the best minds on the planet.

But for some unknown reason, Te'irjiil—the son of a plantation worker without the benefit of a formal education—had solved the puzzle.

"Yaxche," George said, "I hope you know that we are here to help you. Do you remember Alex Manez?"

"Yes, Colop is always in my thoughts, though I have not spoken with him in many years."

Uncertain that what he had to say would come across correctly in Spanish, Michael asked George to translate: "Alex sent us a message from one of our space stations to find you. He said that you have the secret, even if you don't know it. He couldn't tell me anything more, because he fell into a fugue state."

"Ahyah. He has had a vision, then."

Michael understood the reply, but continued speaking in English: "I don't know that. I haven't had the opportunity to talk to him since then, though I received word that he had recovered. But before he went unconscious, he said I needed to hear the story. Wait—"

Eyes widening, Michael glanced up at George and said, "You know, after all this time, I just realized: I've read the translations and interpretations, and I listened to the recording you made when you first interviewed Yaxche, but I've never actually *heard* the story itself."

"What do you mean? You heard Yaxche telling us the story on my recording."

"In Spanish. And then translated into English. I haven't actually heard it in Mayan."

George blinked at Michael. "I'm sure we have the Mayan version on record somewhere. We had a few linguists on retainer who could interpret the Mayan glyphs, and I recall several of them reading the scroll out loud. Are you sure you didn't access one of those recordings?"

"I don't think so, but I also don't think it matters. Alex said, specifically, 'You have to hear *him* tell you the story.' Not one of our linguists, but Yaxche himself."

Shaking his head, George said, "What good will that do? Without a computer to translate, it will all just sound like jumbled words to us."

Michael opened his hands. "At this point, what harm can it do?"

George shrugged and turned to Yaxche. "Are you able to tell us the story on the ancient scroll from memory?"

"Ahyah," the old man said, as if the question had stung his pride. And then he closed his eyes and began to recount the tale of the end of the Fourth World in his native language.

At first, Michael strained to listen to the words and phrases, trying to find anything familiar in the lyrical sound of the story. He hoped his brain could make any kind of connection, that some kind of revelation was forthcoming.

Soon, however, he realized George was correct. It was just a big jumble of incomprehensible sounds. Out of politeness, he waited until Yaxche finished reciting the complete tale, and then turned to George to acknowledge the researcher had been right all along.

But when he looked at George, he saw in his eyes what Yaxche must have seen in his grandson's eyes. A quick glance at Yaxche confirmed it.

Somehow, George had figured it out, too.

"What?" Michael demanded. His voice was a little too loud, and Humberto jerked his head and took a step toward them.

Raising his hands in a pacifying gesture, Michael said to the Cruzado, "Sorry. Everything is all right. We're just debating something. A scientific point."

With a grunt, Humberto eased himself back into his post, but he kept suspicious eyes fixed on the three of them.

Yaxche took a deep breath in anticipation of what George would say next. There was a pained look in the old man's expression, and Michael guessed that having not one, but two people understand something he did not, something that he was entrusted with, was difficult to accept.

"What is it?" Michael pressed.

"I wish I had a computer right now," George replied in a growl. He licked his lips. "I can't be a hundred percent, but I think I know the key to the secret, at least."

His eyes moved back and forth, as if scanning his own memory. "You know how, in grade school, when you wanted to remember something for a test, there were a number of mnemonic techniques you could use?"

"You mean like acronyms or acrostics?"

"Or rhymes or songs," George said. "In this case, I think the tale itself is a way to get the teller to remember the song itself."

Michael made a connection. "When Yaxche was telling us the tale, it did have a lyrical quality to it." He tried to quell his excitement, in case it drew Humberto to investigate. "You think we need to analyse the story as if it were a song?"

"Not for the lyrics, but for the melody. I think the story is just that: a story. It could probably be of any subject. It's simply there to help the keepers of the scroll remember the *melody*. There were certain parts of the tale where Yaxche's voice hit a certain note and used a particular inflection. I think that's important."

George turned to Yaxche and spoke very quickly in Spanish, summarizing his theory.

"Yes," Yaxche said in Spanish. "That is how I was taught the Song of the Stars. It is very important to sing those parts in the correct manner; to honor the gods."

"The Song of the Stars?" Michael asked. "That's the title of the story? I've never heard mention of this in any of the translations. It's not written on the scroll. Is it?"

"No," George said, "but then again, no one ever asked what the name of the story was." He let out a breathless laugh. "It's more than a lack of translation, it's about a lack of a common frame of reference."

"What do you mean?" Michael felt his face flush as he couldn't put the pieces together in his own mind.

"From Yaxche's cultural point of view, he must have assumed we would already know that the tale was in the form of a song. After all, that's how stories have been passed down from generation to generation. We have ballads that date back centuries.

"On the flip side, from our scientific point of view, we were so busy looking for measureable evidence in this document that we didn't take into account the one fact that was obvious from the start."

Michael still didn't make the connection. "And that is?"

"The song itself is a translation from another language. Not in the literal sense of the words on a page, but as a means of passing down the melody itself."

"Sonics," Michael said in a gasp. "When Macklin's Rock first reacted, the *Dis Pater* gave off cyclic wave emissions which corresponded with the changes in its light spectrum."

"Different notes on the musical scale can be charted by their compression waves," George said. "And although the difference between the wave-particles of light and the frequency in sound would be in the factor of, I don't know, a billion hertz or so, I think there is a solid correlation, and I think this is something a suitably advanced civilization—one that used computers—could program and calculate."

"We need to get you to a computer," Michael said in conclusion.

"And we need to record Yaxche's song in a sound room."

All the while the two of them talked, Yaxche looked back and forth between them. The look on his face was a mix of consternation and panic. He had no idea what they were talking about.

George, flicking his eyes up to make sure Humberto wasn't listening, said to the old Mayan, "We need to get you out of here and to safety."

"I am not concerned for my well-being," Yaxche said, making no effort to lower his voice. "But if you wish, I can show you a way out."

Michael cocked his head. "You know a way to escape this place?"

"Ahyah," Yaxche said. "My friend Humberto told me of it."

23

Lucis Observatory :
Venus Orbit :

The Mayan culture had always placed great significance in Venus, which they referred to as both the morning star and the evening star because it could be seen at either time.

As some of the most sophisticated astronomers of the time—and being a calendar-conscious and mathematical civilization—the Mayans had charted Venus's yearly cycles and discovered that five of Venus's years correlate almost exactly with eight Earth years. To them, this was an obvious sign of its link with Earth and proof that Venus itself was a deity. The Mayan people would time any of their great events, such as a war or the coronation of their leader, with the cycles of *Noh ek'*, their name for the sky god.

And so, when Terry first realized Klaus had set up his main base of operations on Venus, a part of him felt it was more than coincidence; it had to be some kind of divine influence.

From the moment Terry had joined the Cruzados, he had imagined that he had been chosen to spearhead a holy revolution, that he would singlehandedly restore the Mayan culture to the frontlines in the quest for interstellar progress. In his naive fantasy, the world would honour him as an ambassador for Earth once mankind had overcome the limitations of travel between the stars, and made first contact with the thousands of alien races who were waiting out there.

Terry had been taken in by the romantic notion of a holy crusade, with an army of Cruzados at his back.

Terry, however, had no idea how he was going to accomplish that, and after two days on the orbiting observatory, he began to give in to despair. Gradually, he realized that once he had handed the Song of the Stars to Jose and Klaus, his dream had begun to unravel bit by bit, and it looked more like a nightmare with each passing hour.

The Cruzados were not an honorable group. They did not have the ancient Mayan spirit in them. He was coming to understand that they were just another gang of disgruntled peasants and greedy opportunists who, in turn, had thrown in their lot with someone Terry could only describe as a madman—granted, one who certainly knew more about computers, Kinemet and astrophysics than most.

In one of the Lucis Observatory's workshops, Klaus Vogelsberg sat hunched over a haptic console. There were seven holoslates set up in a half-circle around him. Periodically, he would adjust an input or type in a series of commands.

Terry stood half a dozen steps to the side and waited. He had been relegated to the role of Klaus's personal servant, and though it grated on his pride, he knew he only had himself to blame.

There was one other person in the workshop. Jose watched as his partner in crime tended his programs. There was a look of dark concern on his face as he stared at the monitors, clearly unable to decipher what he saw.

"You've been at this for days. Are we any closer to the solution," Jose asked.

"Every minute that passes brings us closer," Klaus said sardonically.

"You know what I mean." Jose pointed across the room. "He's the third, so far. At this pace, we will soon run out of lab rats. And every day we spend here increases our risk of being discovered."

Terry grimaced at the words, and couldn't help but look past the two men where Jose had pointed. Adjacent to the workshop was a lab, shielded with titanium and electromagnetically sealed. A wide pane of tinted glass—created with particles of titanium—allowed them to see inside the experiment area.

Strapped on a medical gurney, one of the captured American soldiers lay unconscious and naked. Dozens of sensors and leads were attached to his arms, chest and head.

Beside him was a tray on which rested one milligram of unshielded Kinemet—which Klaus had shaved with what had looked like an invisible saw. He had told Terry the beam was simply a non-reactive laser coupled with a chemical coolant, and that he required complete concentration to get the cut just right, "so kindly keep your mouth shut from now on, unless I ask you a question," he had said through gritted teeth at one point.

When Klaus didn't reply to his last statement, Jose said, "You promised us you could unlock the secret and give me complete control of space travel. That was the only reason we agreed to your terms. I wonder if you maybe overestimated your capabilities."

"There is always a measure of trial and error when conducting scientific experiments," Klaus replied evenly, speaking with much more patience to Jose than he had to Terry. "I assure you, I will have the proper sequence locked down very soon."

A moment later, however, he matched Jose's harsh tone. "And don't forget, the power will be ours together. You may have contributed men and the ancient scroll itself, but without my money and knowledge, you would still be sitting in a darkened warehouse making empty plans. We are *partners* in this."

A ripple of irritation passed over Jose's features, but he quickly reined in his emotions. "Very well, *partner*. If we are equals, then we should both know exactly what you are doing now."

"I'm not sure you would understand the scientific terminology."

Jose narrowed his eyes. "I have taken a few physics courses at university. I'm certain I can follow."

Klaus shrugged and turned back to his computer. He took a deep breath and seemed to debate his next words. "All right," he said finally. "We have a little time before we can measure our subject's reaction, anyway."

He called up a file and played one of the many animated presentations of the Kinemetic reaction which had peppered the EarthMesh newsfeeds over the past decade.

"Back when Quantum Resources was in its heyday, they used a bombardment of hydrogen photons to create a reaction in Kinemet; it caused the metal to convert into a quantum kinetic force. As a raw fuel, this works, but there's no control once it quantizes. Whatever is in proximity to its sphere of influence at the time of reaction gets quantized—turned into light. Any electrical impulse is neutralized. When the Kinemet stops reacting with the photons, and returns to solid state, all the electrical systems are disabled. Someone, or something, needs to kick start them, or you're adrift in space without light, heat … air."

"Yes," said Jose. "I know this much."

"Just making sure."

Klaus called up another animation. This one was watermarked with the NASA logo on the bottom right, the Quantum Resources stamp on the bottom left, and the word 'Confidential' along the top. It was a conceptual recreation of Alex Manez's voyage to Centauri.

"Now," Klaus continued, "that problem is compounded. After rematerialization, there is a secondary reaction in the Kinemet, a nuclear fission, which causes the Kinemet to release its photons in an exothermic reaction—something like an atomic bomb. Why? Well, when you drop a rock in water, and it causes a temporary void, when the surrounding water rushes back in to fill that void, there's a splash. Energy is released. The splash is enough to cause the Kinemet to start reacting to itself. Instead of quantizing, it fissions, and this happens quite quickly.

"The 'pilot' is there to give the electrical generators a kick start, so the dampers can prevent the fission from occurring. In the case of the *Quanta,* the pilot was too slow to rematerialize, and that is why the ship exploded, and that's the problem they've been struggling with for the past few years. How to stop the bomb from exploding once the fuse is lit." He chuckled at the concept.

Jose asked, "So how does the ancient scroll fix that?"

"The problem is not with the Kinemet. The problem is with the pilot, or more specifically, the irradiation process to create a Kinemetic pilot. It's something far beyond the quantizing process, which in and of itself is biologically harmless.

"Alex Manez was exposed to the reacting Kinemet under unknown and uncontrolled circumstances, and was irradiated during that process. Among other things, he became electropathic—and gained the ability to manipulate those electronic dampers needed to stop the 'splash'—but there is something in him that failed to complete the change. He was unable to materialize in time, and the Kinemet exploded. The incomplete Kinemetic process also resulted in his deteriorating health and will be the cause of his inevitable demise.

"Unfortunately, no one has been able to reproduce the exact conditions that created Alex's new physiology. They tried photons from other elements like helium and the other noble gases, but that had no effect. The closest they came was to try to prime the Kinemet with a burst of ultraviolet rays. They were on the right path working in the electromagnetic spectrum, but their methodology was wrong— they didn't have the proper sequence to prime the Kinemet, and so the *Quanta* experiments continued to fail.

"Some pilots died moments after initial exposure in the lab environment. Two lived for a month before radiation poisoning killed them. Those were the earliest experiments. Five survived the process, but in the field they—like Alex—were unable to rematerialize quickly enough to engage the Kinemet dampers. Boom. Even though Alex somehow managed to survive the explosion on the *Quanta*, he is also considered a failed conversion.

"So now, the question remains: what is the correct process to create a Kinemetic pilot?"

Klaus pointed to the ancient scroll, which was resting at an angle on a nearby worktable. "You see, the Mayan document contains a key code, a sequence of sound waves which the computer can map to their particle-wave counterparts. We then bombard the Kinemet with that frequency before the quantizing process. Different frequencies—and combinations of frequencies—elicit disparate reactions in the element, conditioning it to give off a subtly different form of radiation." He shook his head. "It's an amazing element, and I'm certain it will take decades to chart every aspect."

Klaus turned in his chair to face Jose and drew in a deep breath. "So you see, I'm reproducing some of Quantum Resources failed experiments, but using the correct frequencies I recorded from Terry's vocal rendition of the story to prime the Kinemet first. Of course, this is all assuming Terry recited the story exactly as his grandfather taught him—" Klaus glanced over at Terry, who stiffened at the implication that he had made any mistakes.

Klaus continued, "I've mapped the notes where he used particular inflections, and I'm hoping they provide the proper combination to unlock the puzzle."

"Hoping?"

"Well, it's been a millennium since the scroll was first written. Even if Terry recited the song exactly as he'd been taught, how can we know that every generation passed down the sequence without a single mistake? There are a few other dynamics to consider."

Jose took a few measured paces towards the window, as if he could see the internal changes in the soldier in the other room. "What are you telling me? How many uncontrolled factors are there?"

"I don't have complete records from Quantum Resources, so I have had to repeat some of their failures."

Jose ground his teeth. "How many more failures?"

There was a hint of a smile playing across Klaus's lips; it seemed he enjoyed tormenting Jose. "Quantum Resources underwent more than a dozen full trials, and established a number of constants. For the purposes of my trial, I've been using those confirmed results. There are still some variables in their tests, however, and once we get past candidate number three, here, I only have two more factors to account for, and then we will know whether Terry's rendition of the Song survived unchanged over the centuries."

Jose inhaled, then let his breath out in a slow hiss, as if to release the tension that had built up inside him. "Good. Then by all means, proceed." He turned back to the window to watch.

Klaus wrinkled his forehead in annoyance, but Terry was the only one to see the movement. There was obvious friction between the two partners, but Terry didn't know if he had the wit to use that against them.

He knew any action he took that made him look more disloyal at this point would most likely earn him a bullet. Now that he had given them what they wanted, the scroll and the song, they had no use for him outside of being Klaus's personal attendant. After Terry's behavior on the liner, Jose didn't trust him anymore and wouldn't allow him to even carry a gun.

For now, Terry would bite his lip, endure the heartache brought on by witnessing the inhuman experiments, and bide his time until he saw an opportunity to repair the wrongs for which he was responsible.

∞

They did not have to wait long until one of Klaus's monitoring programs let out a short alarm.

"Ah," Klaus said. "The sequence is now programmed into the computer. We can proceed with trial number three."

"How long will this take?" Jose asked. "When will we know if it worked?"

Without answering the question, Klaus punched in a command to his console. "Here we go. Now I'm bombarding the Kinemet with the thirty-two ultraviolet frequencies of photons in the prescribed order, and the sensors indicate the Kinemet is undergoing the transformation. All right, now for the main attraction: hitting it with hydrogen to start the quantization."

All three men looked up into the shielded room to see the Kinemet suddenly light up in a fashion similar to a magnesium flare. A moment later everything in the room turned into the same light. If not for the Kinemetic dampers in the other room, the Kinemetic radiation from a milligram of the element could conceivably quantize most of the Observatory, as Klaus had informed Terry earlier.

The entire lab room was filled with a brightness so sharp Terry had to put his hand up to protect his eyes. The sensors that had been attached to the soldier stopped transmitting data to Klaus's computers, since they were also affected.

"They've quantized," Klaus said by way of commentary. "During the Macklin's Rock incident, Alex Manez was exposed for approximately four hours. The actual length of time required could very well be four seconds, for all we know. Quantum Resources used the four hour marker as a constant, so I've been doing the same."

Jose, who also had his hand up between his eyes and the lab, asked, "So that's when we'll know?"

"We'll know if he is altered or not. Once the Kinemet has completed its process, everything in the room will return to a solid state, and then we can go in and take some readings on the subject. After that we'll perform a simple quantization procedure and see how quickly he rematerializes. Anything more than nine seconds is a failure; the pilot wouldn't have enough time to get his bearings and initiate the dampers."

Giving a nervous cough, Jose asked, "What about the 'splash' effect you mentioned?"

"There won't be any Kinemet left for a secondary reaction," Klaus said. "If they had only packed enough Kinemet for a one-way trip to Centauri, there would never have been any fission and the *Quanta* would never have exploded."

"So we're safe?"

"Yeah." Klaus typed a few more commands into the computer, and then spun around on his chair. "The lab is electromagnetically sealed. No one can get in or out. Meanwhile, I'm hungry. Time for something to eat."

∞

Before leaving, Klaus punched a key on one computer, and the window between the main workshop and the lab room grew darker, enough so that it was no longer physically uncomfortable to look directly at it. Of course, there was nothing to see beyond the glass other than a bright blur.

Following Klaus out the door, Jose ordered Terry, "You stay here. Make sure no one enters except us. Anyone else tries to get in here, send me an alert on the comlink." Almost as an afterthought, he added, "I'll bring you back a sandwich or something."

∞

Terry, who had remained stoic while the co-leaders were in his presence, let out a curse and punched his open hand with his fist in frustration once he was alone.

His anger was directed not only at Klaus, Jose and the Cruzados, but at himself for being such a sucker.

Everything he had done had been to honour Itzel, and to ensure what happened to her never happened to his people again.

And he was right at the center of it; he was the catalyst. If he hadn't run away from home like a petulant child; if he hadn't naively taken up with the Cruzados; and if he hadn't betrayed his grandfather by stealing the ancient scroll, none of this would have happened. How many people—innocent or not—had died because of Terry's actions? How many more would die?

In the past two days, Terry had been helpless to do anything but stand by as Klaus experimented on the American soldiers. Once he had determined the first subject had failed to change completely, Klaus ordered the victim taken out of his sight, and never followed up on his progress. Terry had never seen anyone with such a lack of remorse or conscience. Klaus was completely absorbed in his task, and didn't exhibit any signs that he cared who lived and who died in the pursuit of his goal.

One day, while eating lunch by himself, Terry had overheard some of the other Cruzados a table over talk about Klaus, and how he and his uncle had been the ones who had kidnapped Alex Manez a decade ago, and had been somehow betrayed by him.

Terry hadn't seen much of Captain Gruber. The man spent most of his time teaching the Cruzados combat techniques for ship-to-ship battles and how to fight inside space stations.

That last bit of information drove home the reality that Terry was part of an insurrection, rather than the liberation and rebirth of the Mayan culture he had dreamed of.

And it had only been possible because of him.

There had to be something he could do to stop them. But he knew he wasn't clever enough by far. He didn't know how to fight, and he was too transparent to become a politician and sway the Cruzados to his views.

He took a few measured paces towards the window of the lab, and he felt a pang of guilt knowing that the soldier inside would most likely endure hours, days, or weeks of agony before dying of Kinemetic exposure. He hadn't even found out what the soldier's name was.

His grandfather was most likely completely ashamed of Terry. He hoped the old man was all right. Jose had promised to keep him safe and secluded in case anyone from Quantum Resources or NASA tried to use him to figure out where the Cruzados were and what they were doing. Terry realized now that they were, in effect, holding Yaxche hostage against Terry's continued cooperation.

It was a complete disaster. He probably couldn't have screwed things up any worse if he had planned it that way.

He pulled up a chair near the window and sat down to wait out the rest of his vigil. Although he wasn't the kind of person to give in to despair, he half-hoped the Kinemetic radiation might leak through the window somehow and permanently turn him into a being of light.

∞

A few hours later, Terry looked up when he heard footsteps out in the hall.

The workshop door opened and Jose entered the room.

"How is it going," Jose asked, and Terry shrugged.

"All right, I guess." Terry looked, but he didn't see a plate of food or even a bottle of water in Jose's hands. The Cruzados leader must have forgotten. Stomach rumbling, he said, "You mind if I take a break?"

Jose, stepping toward the window as if he could see what transpired within, waved his hand dismissively to Terry. "Sure. Be back in an hour, would you? That's when the experiment should be over. We'll find out if the price we paid is worth it."

∞

Before heading down to the mess hall, Terry stopped at the lavatory. Inside, he entered one of the stalls and sat down on a chrome toilet lid. He had no need to relieve himself, but just needed a few moments to pull himself together before facing any of the Cruzados.

They were all very rough men, raised in some of the most poverty-stricken regions of Mexico, Guatemala, El Salvador and Honduras. If Terry didn't act as tough as them, they would see it as an act of weakness. He had already lowered himself in their eyes by his protests on the liner. If he had any chance of getting out of his situation alive, at the very least he had to maintain whatever status he had left in the eyes of the Cruzados.

While gathering up his courage, Terry heard the washroom door open and two men entered. He recognized them by their voices. It was Klaus and his uncle, Captain Gruber. Making himself as still as could be, Terry waited for them to go about their business and leave.

The two men spoke in German, so Terry had no idea what they said, but their tones were full of menace.

Klaus said, *"Achten Sie darauf, Ihre Männer sind bereit. Ich werde Signal, wenn der Vorgang abgeschlossen ist. Sie wirst sie töten Jose und Terry."*

When Terry heard his name, the hairs on the back of his neck stood straight up, and he cursed himself for not being able to understand what was said.

In English, Captain Gruber asked, "What about the rest of the Cruzados?"

"I have enough evidence to convince them Jose was just using them for his own benefit; he was never a true believer. Don't worry about them; without a leader, those sheep will soon flock to my banner. — Oh, and if you can, make sure it looks as if it was Jose who killed Terry. Fuel for the fire."

After a moment, Gruber said, "Shouldn't be too hard."

"Soon, Uncle, we will finally take what Alex Manez promised but failed to deliver. I won't rest until that little brat is dead, too."

∞

"You're late," Jose said in a reprimanding voice when Terry returned to the workshop. "The Kinemet has almost burnt out."

Klaus didn't look up from his computer. Captain Gruber stood off to the side, but the older man didn't look directly at Terry. His eyes, however, took everything in, and a chill ran down Terry's spine.

"Uh, sorry," Terry said and shrugged as Jose shot him a scathing look.

He tried to make sure none of the three other men in the room saw how his hands shook, how his breathing was ragged, or how hard his heart thumped in his chest. Almost, he had decided to run and find a hiding place somewhere in the observatory. He knew, however, that if he had, it would have only been a matter of time before they discovered him.

He was a dead man anyway. He knew it deep in his heart. Even if he returned to the lab, once the experiment was proved a success, Captain Gruber would murder him. After all that Terry had done, he felt he deserved it, and decided to face his destiny. If he was to die, at least he would die brave, instead of running like a coward.

"Not a moment to spare," Klaus said and motioned toward the other room.

The light inside the lab flared and suddenly extinguished, and Klaus retracted the window tinting.

Soon, everyone could see the soldier slowly rematerialize as thousands of tiny flashes of light coalesced and went out.

The entire transformation took less than six seconds, according to a timer display on one of the monitors, and Klaus stood up, obviously excited.

"Did it work?" Jose asked.

"I don't know," Klaus said, never taking his eyes off the soldier. "I need to revive him and run some tests. If he shows all the signs of a successful metamorphosis, then we can run him through a simulation and measure his reactions." He tapped a command, and an intravenous tube in the lab turned blue as some kind of stimulant was introduced into the subject's system.

Within moments, the solider stirred. His legs jerked as sensation and consciousness returned to him.

Through a microphone, Klaus called out, "Private Teegs, can you hear me?"

"Whass," the soldier said, his speech clearly not at full capacity. He licked his lips, forced his eyes opened and tried again. "What's going on? What happened?"

"How do you feel?" Klaus asked. "Can you describe the sensation?"

"I heard it," the young man said, voice filled with wonder. "It was a song. Haunting. It filled my head. It—"

Just then, his entire body shook with a convulsion. A look of panic spread across his face and his eyes bulged out. Veins popped up on his forehead and neck.

"What's happening to me?" he cried out.

Klaus spoke in a hard voice into the microphone. "Calm down. It's just an after-effect of the procedure. I assure you, you'll be fine."

But the man was anything but. Both Terry and Jose ran forward to look as another spasm took the soldier and he fell off the gurney to the floor.

Like a fish out of water, he writhed and twitched, all the while howling in agony. The imaging machine and medical monitors sparked as they were overloaded with electricity. Most fizzled and went dead, but one caught fire and popped with a couple of tiny explosions until the overhead sprinklers shot CO_2 into the room to smother the flames.

"You have to help him!" Terry shouted, looking over his shoulder.

There was no concern or empathy evident in Klaus's eyes; merely a look of disgust and frustration. "It's over."

"But he's dying."

Without replying to Terry, Klaus turned to his uncle and shook his head. Captain Gruber, who had looked as tense as a tiger ready to spring, relaxed visibly.

Jose, watching the soldier's final death throes, asked, "What now?"

"We'll have to clean up the lab, reset everything and try again tomorrow. Only one variable left; at least we'll have a fifty-fifty shot." With that, Klaus walked out of the workshop, his uncle following a few steps behind.

Terry turned to Jose. "We can't just stand here and do nothing. He's dying."

"He's already dead," the leader of the Cruzados said, his voice hard and steady. "Nothing we can do at this point."

Trying not to let Jose see the tears streaking down his face, Terry turned away from the window. His hands continued to shake.

If the soldier had lived, Terry would now be dead at the hands of Captain Gruber. Which was the more just outcome?

Terry remained alive, but now he had more death on his conscience.

"Sometimes," Jose said quietly, "I wonder if you are fully

committed to our cause."

24

Edgar: "Good morning, Alex. My name is Edgar Janz. I'm the assistant to the science advisor for USA, Inc.'s Board of Directors' oversight committee for Quantum Resources."

Alex: "Morning."

Edgar: "Did you have any questions before we begin? I've cleared the entire day, so there's no rush."

Alex: "I had hoped to be debriefed by Michael Sanderson."

Edgar: "I'm sorry, he's retired from Quantum Resources. I'm afraid his security clearance has been downgraded since then. Anything you speak to him about must be of a personal nature only."

Alex: "What about Captain Turner?"

Edgar: "*Major* Justine Turner is attached to the training facility at Kennedy Space Center. I'm sure you can arrange to speak to her after your debriefing. Are there any other questions I can answer for you?"

Alex: "I guess not."

Edgar: "Well rested after your trip to Honduras?"

Alex: "Yes, thank you. I'm sorry if that delayed your report."

Edgar: "I won't lie. There are a lot of people waiting to hear your story. It wasn't easy putting them off. But that isn't a big problem. I have a preliminary report I already submitted, but we need to verify some facts. Are you ready?"

Alex: "Yes."

Edgar: "Excellent. All right, let's do this. *Ahem.* This is the official debriefing of Captain Alex Manez, first human to travel to another solar system. It has been five days since his return to Earth. All medical and psychological tests have come back, and aside from the difference in his biological and chronological ages, Alex Manez has been given a clean bill of health. —Yes, Alex?"

Alex: "I've been a little achy since yesterday."

Edgar: "Uh. I'm sure that's just an after-effect of all the traveling. The doctors cleared you."

Alex: "All right."

Edgar: "Good. Now, can we start at the beginning? Can you describe your experience traveling in a quantized state?"

Alex: "For me it was instantaneous. I didn't experience anything. One moment I was here; the next moment I was there."

Edgar: "I'm going to ask you a series of questions. They might seem repetitive or obvious, but this is for the benefit of the oversight committee. I would like to start with the events leading up to the explosion of the *Quanta*."

Alex: "Of course."

Edgar: "Was there power in the ship when you first materialized in Centauri System?"

Alex: "No there wasn't."

Edgar: "According to pre-flight experiments this was expected. Just for the record, can you explain why?"

Alex: "Of course. There were two separate quantities of Kinemet on the ship. One for each leg of the trip. As I understand it, the Kinemet that had been primed with photons would burn out just as I arrived in Centauri. The second load, which had not been primed, was merely quantized as was every other substance on the ship. The astrophysicists determined that once the non-charged Kinemet rematerialized, it would re-react with its own photons and cause a secondary reaction. Without applying a coolant, it would reach critical mass and undergo a nuclear fission."

Edgar: "And this is why there is a need for a human pilot at this point, correct?"

Alex: "Yes. Assuming I would be rematerialized as well, my only task was to restart the onboard electrical systems. I merely had to turn on a generator, which would return electrical power to the ship. The onboard computer would then initiate the Kinemetic dampers and interrupt the second load of Kinemet before it reacted."

Edgar: "And was there a problem preventing you from sparking the generator?"

Alex: "Yes. The ship had turned solid, but I remained in a semi-quantized state and was unable to physically grab the pull ring to charge the generator."

Edgar: "Do we know why you didn't fully return to a physical form?"

Alex: "One of the analysts surmised the longer a biological entity was in a quantized state, the longer the transition to a normal corporeal form."

Edgar: "Do you agree with this theory?"

Alex: "No."

Edgar: "Uh … Alex. I don't have anything in my notes about your disagreeing with that assumption."

Alex: "I know."

Edgar: "Well, what do you think is the reason?"

Alex: "I believe I have not been fully transformed into a Kinemat. I am an aberration. I didn't know this before the trip, but I do now. We need to stop thinking about using Kinemet for light-speed travel and start examining its other properties before more people end up like me."

Edgar: "Will you excuse me a moment, Alex?"

Alex: "Of course."

Edgar: "I just need to make a call."

∞

Edgar: "Hello, Alex. Sorry that took so long. I hope you're comfortable."

Alex: "They served me an early lunch."

Edgar: "Good. I've been instructed to strike your last comment from the official record and concentrate on the actual verifiable events only. Please restrict your answers to facts rather than conjecture."

Alex: "All right."

Edgar: "Where were we? Right. There was a delay between when the *Quanta* rematerialized and when you returned to physical form."

Alex: "Yes. But during that short time, I was conscious and aware of where I was. I was halfway between light and matter."

Edgar: "And how long, exactly, were you in this transitional phase?"

Alex: "It was about eight or ten seconds before I brought myself back to material form. It's hard to judge."

Edgar: " 'Brought yourself?' Alex. I have nothing in my records stating that you brought yourself back."

Alex: "I know."

Edgar: "Did you tell anyone this before?"

Alex: "Of course, but they think it was just my imagination, or my memory playing tricks. Did you need to leave the room again?"

Edgar: "No. Let's just skip that last part for now."

Alex: "All right."

Edgar: "So you rematerialized. How long did you have before the ship exploded?"

Alex: "Just a few seconds. I wasn't thinking straight, and tried to pull the kick starter ring."

Edgar: "But ... I thought that's what you were supposed to do."

Alex: "It didn't have any effect. I tried to tell them before we left. The generator needed more of a boost to get started than a simple pull cord—being quantized for that amount of time, the electrical system was weakened. I had to use my electropathic ability to start the generator."

Edgar: "Electropathic ability? What is that? Alex, I'm not sure I can report any of this. My record and your story doesn't match up. I have nothing here that says anything about this."

Alex: "I'm sure they'll edit the parts they don't want to hear."

Edgar: (coughing sound)

Alex: "Okay ... the generator started, but it was too late to start the dampers."

Edgar: "It was too late?"

Alex: "There was only about a second or so left before the Kinemet reached critical mass, and the coolant required at least four seconds."

Edgar: "How did you survive the blast?"

Alex: "Well, the automatic capsule ejector launched the cockpit just as the *Quanta* silently burst into fragments of light."

Edgar: "All right. That's what I have in my report as well. What happened next?"

Alex: "I was a little stunned by the escape, and I was dazed. After a few minutes, I realized I was stranded more than forty-trillion kilometers from home with no way back, and I started to panic."

Edgar: "That's understandable."

Alex: "All traces of the *Quanta* were gone. The capsule only had about a week's supply of oxygen and food. I ... felt completely alone."

Edgar: "What happened next?"

Alex: "I instructed the shipboard sensors to scan the vicinity for trace electromagnetic vibrations. The ship's spectrographic analyzer picked up a signal."

Edgar: "The signals were similar to those emitted by the artifact in our solar system, the *Dis Pater?*"

Alex: "Yes. The computer calculated it was a little over twenty-thousand kilometers away."

Edgar: "Then what?"

Alex: "I programmed the navigation system to fly to it."

Edgar: "Based on the calculations you provided, at the capsule's top speed, it would take a little over a month to get there."

Alex: "Correct."

Edgar: "You only had a week's worth of oxygen and food. So how did you survive the trip?"

Alex: "I put myself back into a quantized state."

Edgar: "You put—? Alex, there are significant discrepancies between my reports and what you are telling me. I'm not sure we can continue until I get this straightened out."

Alex: "I tried to tell the analysts, but no one believed me."

Edgar: "We'll continue this debriefing tomorrow. Right now I need to get to the bottom of this."

25

Lucis Observatory :
Venus Orbit :

Justine had never been more frightened in all her life. She had never fully experienced the acute isolation and helplessness of being blind like she did now.

When she had first lost her sight on Pluto, she had run the full gamut of emotions on the six-month voyage home: anger and frustration, denial and false hope, depression and finally acceptance.

During the trip home, however, she had never once feared for her life. The entire ship's crew had been as supportive and accommodating as anyone could be. NASA had kept in constant communication with her and made arrangements for her optilink surgery upon her arrival back on Earth.

For those first six months, she had begun to compensate for her blindness in a natural way, relying more on her other senses: hearing, touch and smell. After the surgery, even though she had adjusted to life as a blind person, her visual prosthetics had been a huge crutch for her. The only time she was without technological aid was in the comfort and safety of her apartment. The sensory skills she had begun to cultivate over that first half a year had never fully developed.

Now, she had no time to expand her natural abilities and compensate for her loss of sight. Her current situation was indeed dire, and her life was in very real danger.

The Cruzados had shown their complete disregard for life by experimenting on the captured members of the security squadron, and Justine was more than helpless; she was an added burden on the remaining soldiers, and on Clive.

She was relieved and more than grateful to have him with her. As if she were a toddler, he hovered over her day and night. From helping her navigate to the lavatory, to ensuring she was able to eat the tray dinners their captors brought in, to holding her hand whenever there was a sharp unexpected sound; Clive never left her side. Justine knew he had to be going through his own emotional journey, and the shame of putting the burden of her wellbeing on him filled her with guilt and despair.

…And anger.

She had been a commissioned officer of the United States Air Force, the decorated captain of a NASA space vessel. She had traveled to Pluto and been on the team that discovered evidence of alien cultures in the galaxy. And here she was, hiding in a darkened room, barely able to care for herself, and fearing for her life.

There were others in her group who were far worse off.

When she had realized Private Jackson was the Cruzados' first attempt at creating a Kinemetic pilot, she was outraged.

That outrage quickly turned to horror when the young man went into spasms and cried out in agony as his body began to die from radiation poisoning.

Over the next three hours, he developed an angry rash that turned first red, then black, as Clive described to her in a very low and somber tone. The private's skin bubbled with melanomas, and he continuously secreted bloody pus from all of his orifices. At the end, he could barely summon the strength to moan before he finally died. Justine could still recall the wretched sounds the poor man made; they haunted her.

Dormant Kinemet carried extremely little risk to humans. The minimal radioactivity it gave off was considerably less than getting a medical X-ray.

Kinemet reacted differently to other forms of radiation. Once it was bombarded with hydrogen photons, it quantized and became an extremely powerful fuel source.

Justine knew, from reading some of the briefing reports, that Quantum Resources had experimented with ultraviolet radiation and Kinemet. When exposed to this combination, humans exhibited symptoms similar to Alex Manez's: a few of the subjects who had volunteered for the experiment reported a heightened sensitivity to any electronic field in their area; they seemed to experience a kind of heightened perception, as if they were dislocated from their corporeal bodies; and they described a high-pitched sound that permeated their hearing. It was like a ringing in the ears, if the ringing changed pitch on a random basis.

They also exhibited classical symptoms of radiation poisoning, and died of rapid mutagenic melanoma. The same melanoma that the private exhibited.

The remaining members of the security detail kept a silent vigil while Private Jackson died a painful death. Over the next thirty-six hours, two more soldiers were taken.

Private Anderson was the next subject; he was gone for ten hours, and when they brought him back, he seemed physically unaltered, except that he was completely catatonic, and had to be force-fed by one of his fellow servicemen. His condition worsened, and though he displayed no physical symptoms, he was dead for an hour before they realized it.

Private Teegs was missing from the room before Justine had woken up that morning.

The soldiers had largely grown silent with despair.

Lieutenant Jeffries made his best effort to boost their morale, but no one laughed when he cracked jokes, no one responded when he tried to make idle conversation, and he had no takers when he attempted to start a few parlor and word games. He gave up trying after a few hours, and the entire group settled into a general atmosphere of malaise.

The injustice of it all made Justine simultaneously want to rage against her circumstances, and curl into a little ball in the corner and cry until she ran out of tears.

Justine did neither, however. She was determined to put on a brave face, despite her handicap, and try to think her way out of this situation. A kernel of thought had gestated in her mind over the past few days, and if she could only concentrate hard enough, she might come up with a solution.

The only comfort Justine found, as they passed the anxious hours, was being as close as possible to Clive. The two of them found a spot a little way off from the others to get some semblance of privacy. Backs against a wall, they both sat with their legs touching. Justine folded her hands in Clive's and leaned her head against his shoulder.

"I'm so sorry to get you involved in all this," he said to her quietly.

"Nonsense." She clucked her tongue. "It's not your fault."

"Maybe, but I feel responsible just the same." Clive reached an arm around her and pulled her close, tucking her safely to his side. "We all feel like there should be something we could have done differently. Second-guessing is part of being human."

"And so is speculation," Justine said.

"How's that?"

"I've been so scared over the past few days my brain feels like it's been dipped in molasses."

"Not to mention lack of proper sleep," Clive said. "I would kill for a mattress or even a blanket. I think my hip bone is going to come right through my skin."

Justine patted his hand. "Do you get the sense that there's something we're missing in all this?"

"Like what?"

She thought about it for a moment. "Well, up until a week ago, I had never heard of the Cruzados movement. No one was forewarned about this uprising until they stole the old Mayan scroll. Since then, somehow, they've managed to infiltrate Canada Station Three, hijack the *Diana* and bring us to Venus. I mean, they've obviously been here at the observatory for some time, setting things up. From the briefing I received in Houston, the authorities didn't really think the Cruzados were a serious threat."

"And what do you make of that?" he asked.

"First of all, if they didn't think the Kinemet was at risk, why move it to Luna? Why not just put it on a military base?"

She felt Clive shift. He said, "Perhaps they thought moving the Kinemet was a preemptive measure. Remove temptation and all that. Like you said, no one thought the Cruzados had spread beyond Central America."

"Then why on a commercial liner? Why not on a military transport?"

"That was the first plan," he said. "However, a few hours before take-off, the rocket developed some kind of computer glitch. It would have been days before it was repaired."

"Still," Justine said with an edge to her voice, "there's something more going on here than we've seen."

"How so?" he asked.

"I don't think the Cruzados are the only threat here."

"Uhm—" Clive started to interject.

"No, listen," she said, holding up a finger to illustrate her point. "Honduras doesn't have a space program at all. Even the nearest spaceport is Mexico City. There has to be someone else behind the Cruzados. It can't just be a grassroots historical preservation movement. Someone has supplied them with arms and training. Someone got them to Canada Station Three. Someone set things up here on Venus. This whole thing had to have been planned for months, or even years. And—"

Justine fell silent as the missing piece of information came to her. A hundred thoughts bombarded her, and she struggled to make sense of it. She stood up suddenly, as if the motion would clear her head.

A moment later, Clive got to his feet. "What?"

"They had to have inside information and help." Justine tapped a finger against her lower lip.

Clive scoffed. "How would that be possible?"

"Someone has to be using the Cruzados as a cat's paw," Justine said. "They can't have the resources or information to pull this off."

She had spoken loud enough that Lieutenant Jeffries and the others heard.

Corporal Marks, sitting across the room, asked, "Then who would have the resources?"

With a quick tilt of her head, Justine said, "At this point, it could be any of the major country corporations. USA, Inc. and Canada Corp. haven't been keen on sharing the tech, hedging against the future. World resources are strained; one of the country corporations might be getting desperate enough to make a play. They might think they can do a better job, or they might have been doing their own research all along and thought they'd made a breakthrough which we overlooked."

Lieutenant Jeffries said, "If that's the case, they've been playing it pretty close to the vest. I haven't heard anything through military channels."

"I'm on the mesh all the time," Corporal Marks added. "If an entire country corp. were making this kind of move, no one's made a peep about it."

"Then who?" Justine wondered out loud. "They had to have someone who could pilot the liner. Someone who knew the Kinemet would be on the flight, and according to Clive that was a last-minute decision."

With one hand lightly touching a wall, she stood up and began to pace. "Maybe if we work backwards," she said. "I know it's a wild shot, but if we can figure out who might have pulled the strings, maybe we can make the connection."

Corporal Marks asked, "Do you think it might be someone in Lunar Lines?"

Shaking her head, Justine said, "I found out about the shipment the morning of the flight from Director Mathers. He's been with the company for almost twenty years. He's a family man, a decent guy. I can't believe he had any part in this. What about you?" she asked the soldiers. "When did you find out about the mission?"

Lieutenant Jeffries said, "I was called in for a briefing by Colonel Gagne the day before. He told us he'd received the request for a security squad from NASA that morning. The decision to move the Kinemet had been made only moments after we found out about the theft of the Mayan scroll. The way everyone was scrambling, it was all news to the military. I wasn't even aware there had been another ship involved."

"Well," said Justine, "none of this explains anything. It's obvious someone higher up is involved. Someone with access to both the military and NASA."

"I have a question," said Corporal Marks. "And I really hope this isn't out of line, ma'am."

"Go ahead, Corporal."

"Why you?"

For a moment, the question caught Justine off guard. "What do you mean, why me?"

"Well, pardon me for saying so, but the only factor that doesn't make sense is why they chose you to accompany us. I've been on two missions in conjunction with Lunar Lines in the past year; we've never had an attendant assigned to us before. We've always sent a private up to get food. And, no offense, ma'am, but why would the military request someone with a handicap as part of an important operation like this?"

Lieutenant Jeffries cleared his throat. "That'll be enough, Corporal."

Justine fought to control the flush of heat that rose to her cheeks. "I certainly hope you don't think I had any part in this? I'll have you know I have dedicated my life to NASA. I've—"

"That's not what I'm saying." Corporal Marks sounded clearly uncomfortable. "But if you remember, Lieutenant, even Colonel Gagne sounded bewildered that we were assigned an attendant at all.

The request must have come from NASA itself."

Justine barked out a hollow laugh. "It's nothing so nefarious as that. Clive is the NASA liaison. He just thought it was an opportunity for us to spend some time together. Right?" she asked Clive, turning her head in the direction she thought he would be.

But he didn't reply to her question. Justine, unable to see, felt a sharp needle of panic at his lack of response.

"Clive?"

"That'll be quite enough of this," he said finally, but his voice came from the far side of the room. "Everyone stay where you are."

Justine shook her head. "What's going on?" she demanded.

It was in a low, steady voice that Lieutenant Jeffries said, "He has an ion pistol."

"A gun? —Clive, what's going on?"

But then, the pieces of the puzzle fell into place. Her mind screamed that she was wrong; that she'd leapt to the wrong conclusion. She didn't want it to be true. How could it?

"You arranged everything?" she said in a gasp. "No, you can't be part of this. It's a mistake. It has to be."

She took a step in the direction of his voice, but Lieutenant Jeffries' firm hand held her back.

"Clive, tell them they're wrong."

She heard a vigorous knock from the inside of the lab door. "You weren't supposed to know until it was all over, and we had the power," Clive said, his voice harsh and angry.

"The hijacking … the experiments!" Justine could not fathom any reason why Clive would be involved in such a heinous conspiracy. A man she had begun to love. She had opened her heart to him. "No, I can't believe you had a hand in this. It's treason. It's murder!"

"It was necessary," he said, and Justine heard him knock on the door again, this time harder. "NASA is filled with bureaucrats and politicians, more worried about their funding than about progress."

Lieutenant Jeffries growled. "How long have you been working against us?"

"Since the beginning," he said. "Every time the news announces massive layoffs, or higher taxes, or government corruption, it makes it easier to see what needs to be done. People are tired of having their lives run by faceless corporations who don't care about them."

"Clive!" Justine still couldn't wrap her mind around it. "You've been lying to me all this time?"

"Not about us," he said. "It's not too late, Justine. You can come with me. You were there at the beginning. The world needs to unite under one banner, one power. You can be part of that."

"You're insane!" Justine screamed, and Lieutenant Jeffries could not hold her back as she lunged towards Clive's voice.

She heard Clive yell, "Get back, all of you!" and then the electric whir of the ion pistol.

Someone beside her screamed, and she barely registered it as she collided with Clive. Not thinking about what she was doing, she lashed out at him in an attempt to knock the gun out of his hand. He was stronger than she was, and he was not blind. It was all too easy for him to disable her, grabbing her arms and pushing her to the ground.

Another heavy body crashed into the two of them, and they all fell in a tangle, Justine pinned beneath them. She heard someone grunt as a punch connected.

With her feet, she tried to push herself out from under them, all the while flailing about with her hand, trying to locate the ion pistol.

Just as she felt the metal of the nozzle, and tried to grab for the handle, the gun was pulled from her grip.

There was another whirring sound, and then the two fighters were no longer in motion.

Justine heard the sounds of the three other soldiers rushing over to help their lieutenant.

Justine, her head ringing from the fight, reached out and, in a ragged voice, demanded of anyone, "What's happening?"

A voice, thick and deliberate, answered, "Justine."

"Clive?" Her fingers touched the fabric of his jacket, and she squeezed her hands around his arms.

"It was supposed to be you and me until the end. I made a place for us in the new regime. I'm so sorry," he said, and let out a wet cough. And then he spoke no more.

She moved her hands up to his chest and felt the warm spread of blood running from a gaping wound. A sob came out of her, and her eyes stung from the sudden tears that flowed down her cheeks.

Corporal Marks spoke from just off to the side. "Someone help me get Lieutenant Jeffries up. He'll be fine. Just knocked out."

Her mind threatened to close in on itself. There was too much happening in too little time. It was as if she could hear the sound of her heart breaking.

"Clive," she gasped out, calling to the memory of the man she thought he was; not the man he turned out to be.

"You," Corporal Marks ordered to one of the soldiers, "see if Miss Turner's all right."

The soldier—Justine couldn't tell who—gently drew her away from Clive's dead body and pulled her to her feet.

"It's over now," he said in a soft, consoling voice.

Grief, fresh and raw, swelled inside her, and Justine let out another cry, and buried her head in the unknown soldier's shoulder.

Before anyone had time to catch their breath, though, a new voice permeated the room.

"That will be quite enough of that. Put the gun down, Corporal, or my men will open fire."

Justine heard the sound of boots on the floor as a number of men entered the room.

"Thank you. Now if you would all be so kind as to move back to the other wall, we can sort this out."

The newcomer had a slight, somewhat familiar accent. Justine's mind, hit by too many revelations and too much emotional pain at once, was muddy and slow to respond. She didn't move from where she stood.

"What's going on? Who are you?" she asked meekly.

"Major Justine Turner," the man said. A moment later, she could smell his hot breath as he stepped in close to her. "Do you not remember me?" he asked. "We never met, but I'm sure if you think about it, you'll figure it out."

"Klaus Vogelsberg!" she gasped. "You? You were behind this? Why?"

"Your golden boy promised me something, and I mean to collect it. Now that we no longer need you to keep Clive happy, you can help us next."

"What do you mean by that?"

To the Cruzados, he said, "Bring her."

She heard the American soldiers protest, but the sound of rebel guns raised into position stopped them.

Rough hands grabbed her shoulders and pulled her out of room.

26

Ruiz Plantation :
Copan Departmental, Honduras :
Central American Conglomeration :

It was all Michael could do not to choke on his coffee. "Humberto?"

George swatted him on the arm. "Not so loud."

But it was loud enough for the large Cruzado to hear. Shooting the three guests a dark frown, Humberto quickly shortened the distance between them.

He kept his voice low and spoke in English, but it was edged with warning. "It is important you continue to act the gracious guests of Señor Ruiz. Do nothing suspicious. I will tell you when it is safe to move. Perhaps tomorrow; perhaps not." It was the most Humberto had ever spoken to them at once.

Michael opened his mouth to ask a question, but Humberto silenced him with another look of warning. He then moved back to his post at the patio steps, narrowed eyes scanning the fields of the plantation dutifully.

Clearing his throat in an obvious way, George lifted his coffee cup. "I think I'll have one more, and then maybe we can have a look around the house. I thought I spotted an art gallery of sorts at the other end of the main hall."

When he got Michael's attention, George pulled on one ear lobe and flicked his eyes at the manservant who was hovering just inside the house—the servant glanced over at them, and then quickly looked away. Michael got the message.

He nodded and moved his own coffee cup closer. George poured for both of them. He then motioned to Yaxche's cup.

Giving a small shake of his head, Yaxche stood and excused

himself. "It is almost time for my morning game of checkers with Alondo, the cook," he said in Spanish. "He can only play one game before he must go back to the kitchen. Either of you are more than welcome to come and play a game after, if you have nothing better to do today."

Michael answered Yaxche. "Thank you. That sounds good. I look forward to it."

With a pleasant smile and an unconcerned gait, the old man ambled off to find the cook.

Michael watched him go, his thoughts racing in every direction, but he schooled himself to remain outwardly calm. Pouring a small amount of cream into his coffee and adding a teaspoon of sugar, he sipped his drink slowly.

Trying to be as casual as possible, he scanned the area around them. There were three patrols of two Cruzados roaming the grounds outside the house. Inside the big windows, he saw several servants cleaning up the breakfast dishes. Everywhere he looked, there was someone who could overhear anything he said. Most likely, their conversation with Yaxche had already been reported.

"We need somewhere to talk."

George grimaced. "Yeah. Harder to do than to say, though. As gracious as our host has been, I don't think giving his hostages any level of privacy is high on his list of priorities."

Michael continued to look around, but he couldn't think of anything they could do that wouldn't raise suspicion. Humberto, while maintaining his proximity, pointedly looked away from them. Obviously, he was one of those people who would not say anything until he was good and ready to do so.

George leaned in slightly. "Let's just bide our time. We can't do anything about it without more data anyway. And I don't think Señor Ruiz would be so accommodating as to give me access to a computer with an uplink to Quantum Resources." He barked out a dry laugh at the thought. "Meanwhile, it might make it easier if we pretended we were on vacation."

Raising one eyebrow, Michael said, "Vacation? This is the weirdest vacation I've ever been on. I don't think I'm going to recommend it to any of my friends."

∞

405

Michael almost went crazy from the waiting.

As a man who had spent the majority of his life in a position of authority, he was used to getting constant updates and progress reports from those who worked under him. He was also accustomed to having people answer him when he asked questions.

The few times Michael tried to extract information from Humberto, the most he could get out of the Cruzado was a monosyllabic response and a dark look of warning.

Michael was not used to subterfuge. A straightforward man, biding his time wore on his nerves. He had trouble sleeping, and the next morning he was slow to wake, and was very groggy.

There was only so much they could do to pass the time. They wandered around the house and admired Oscar Ruiz' collection of art and handcrafted furniture. Careful of the hot sun, they sat out on the patio and lost innumerable games of checkers to Yaxche.

They didn't see Oscar the rest of the day. When questioned, one of the servants said he had several plantations and could be at any one of them.

All the while, they were under the watchful eyes of half a dozen Cruzados who were posted in and around the household. Though Humberto was one of them, he rarely spoke to any of the rebels.

The day took forever to pass, and that night, despite being overwhelmingly tired, it took Michael hours to finally nod off to sleep.

His mind was whirling in a hundred different directions. How would the discovery of the Song of the Stars change Kinemet? Of course, he would ensure Quantum Resources was involved at every stage of development; but with the world economy so tight, and public interest in space programs at an all time low, would NASA and the CSA re-open their *Quanta* programs? Would this discovery help to heal Alex?

∞

"Wake up!" a voice whispered very close to his ear. At first, Michael flicked his hand at the disturbance, as if one of the many flies buzzing around the room had found a way under the mosquito netting hanging over his bed.

There was a gentle nudge on his shoulder, and Michael snapped awake. It was the black of night, and only a vague light from the crescent moon outside illuminated the room to any degree. A shape loomed near him, and he quickly identified George as the person who had roused him.

"What?" he asked, his mouth still dry from sleep.

"It's Humberto. He said we need to move now."

Swinging his legs over the side of the bed, Michael untangled himself from the netting and slipped on his shirt. "I'm ready. Let's go."

In the hall, Humberto and Yaxche were waiting. The old man rubbed one eye and smiled a greeting.

Humberto spoke in English, and George translated for Yaxche.

"Make no sound," the Cruzado said. "Señor Ruiz is still away, and half the guards are sleeping, as are the household servants. The entire perimeter of the plantation is wired with an electric fence. I have arranged for my cousin to 'accidentally' drive his jeep into one section. Several of the guards have gone to investigate. You will make your way through the rows of coffee plants to the other side of the property—I showed Yaxche the trail. I left an unregistered truck behind a large group of trees off the road, hidden from view. It has a full tank of gas, enough to get you to Santa Rosa de Copán; it is a little over one hundred kilometers from here. I left a map."

"Wait," Michael said. "You're not coming with us?"

"No. They will find me downstairs in the main hall. I will be unconscious from a blow to the head by one of Señor Ruiz's very heavy and priceless vases."

"How will that happen?" George asked.

"You will have to do it," Humberto said, and turned to lead them toward the stairs.

Michael grabbed him by the shirt. "Why are you helping us?"

Clenching his jaw, he answered, "Because I believe in our cause; I just do not think our leaders believe in our cause. They believe in money and power. Once they are removed, the Cruzados will once more stand for what is right and just."

George whispered. "Come with us. With your inside knowledge, you could assist the authorities directly."

Humberto leaned closer to them. "I will not betray the movement; only correct it. Taking hostages was wrong. There are many of us who feel the same, and soon we will act."

Michael said, "Our liaison in the capital is John Markham; he's with the Canadian Embassy. You can trust him. If you can get information to him, he may be able to help you overthrow your leaders."

Humberto paused, as if considering. He nodded, finally, and then turned to Yaxche. Putting his hand on the old man's shoulder, he said, "Do not be too disappointed in your grandson. His heart was blinded by memory of a loved one. He, too, can be saved."

∞

George was reluctant to hit Humberto over the head with the vase, and when he passed the artifact to Yaxche, the old man scrunched up his shoulders and shook his head.

Sighing with resignation, Michael took the vase from George and eyed Humberto. "Are you sure about this?"

"Yes. You only need to swing hard enough to break the vase, not my skull. When I hear them approach, I will pretend to regain consciousness."

Lining up his shot, Michael swung the ceramic at Humberto, who braced for the impact. As it turned out, he didn't hit hard enough, and the vase remained intact. Humberto, however, stumbled forward a step and rubbed at the back of his head, wincing. He shot a perturbed look at Michael, but instead of bracing for a second blow, he yanked the vase out of Michael's hands and threw it on the tile floor.

It smashed spectacularly.

Still touching the tender part of his head, Humberto said, "At least I'll have a nice bump there to show them. Good enough." Looking back and forth between Michael and George, he slowly got down on his knees. "They'll be back soon. You had better be off. I've cleared the path, so you shouldn't need to use any more light than what the moon gives off."

With a final look at the three of them, Humberto sank to his belly and lay down.

"Good luck," Michael said to him, and the three men hurried out the back way and into the coffee fields.

∞

As if he had walked the path a thousand times, Yaxche marched at an even pace down through the rows of flowering coffee shrubs in Oscar's plantation.

Although Michael wanted to hurry the old man, he appreciated the surefootedness of their guide, and made his best effort to follow Yaxche's footsteps exactly.

They were most of the way to the tree line when they heard a distant shout coming from the main house.

Michael's first reaction was to run, but he caught himself when he almost ran over Yaxche, who had come to a complete stop.

"What is it?" he asked. "They've figured out we're gone. They'll be after us."

Yaxche turned around slowly. After listening to George repeat Michael's words in Spanish, he replied in a very quiet voice. "Ahyah. We must wait here."

Michael opened his mouth to ask what for, but Yaxche raised his arm and pointed to one of the trees near him. At first, he couldn't see what Yaxche was pointing at, but then he saw a brief silhouette of some kind of small animal jumping from one branch to another directly over their path.

As if it spotted something amiss, it paused and scanned the surrounding forest for signs of danger.

"Monkey," George said in a breathless whisper. "If we spook him, he'll howl like a banshee."

Michael couldn't make out what kind of monkey it was, and he didn't want to get any closer to find out. Silently, he prayed the little primate would go on its merry way.

More lights flicked on from the main house, and the shouts grew louder. The monkey stood up straighter, hearing the sounds, alert for danger.

Holding his breath, Michael waited an eternity before the monkey decided to get as far away from the disturbance as possible. Letting out a short chittering sound, it leapt into the branches of the next tree and scooted off.

George, who was also holding his breath, let it out with a whoosh. "That was close," he said.

His words startled a second monkey they had not spotted.

It screeched in alarm, shook a tree branch, and then raced after the first monkey.

Several flashlights from the main house turned in their direction, and before Michael could duck, the beam passed over him. One of the Cruzados hollered a command in Spanish, and the entire group broke towards them.

"Go!" Michael barked out. "Run!"

Yaxche looked to be a man in his late seventies or early eighties, Michael was in his late sixties, and George was well into his fifties. The men who chased them were much younger, and would soon catch up.

Even though they had a head start, the road where Humberto had stowed the truck was at least a kilometer away. By the time the three men stumbled through the copse of trees, the Cruzados were almost on top of them.

Making painful sounds as he tried to catch his breath, George took a quick look over his shoulder to check the distance between them and their pursuers. He promptly lost his balance and tumbled to the ground, crying out in pain as he twisted his knee.

The lead Cruzado yelled, "¡Alto!"

Michael reached down to help pull his friend back up. Gasping for air, George shook his head. "I'm done!"

"Bullshit!" Michael said. "Get up!"

With a grimace that showed he was in excruciating pain, George tried to get to his feet.

There was a loud snapping sound, and George abruptly looked up at Michael in surprise. At first, Michael thought he might have broken his leg, but then he saw a shadow spreading out from George's white shirt. It looked black in the darkness of the woods, but the metallic smell of blood wafted up.

"My wife…" was all George managed to say before he fell back to the forest floor.

"George!" Michael said, and tried in vain to pull his dead body back up.

A firm hand grabbed his arm. "¡Vamos!" Yaxche said.

Michael couldn't think. He was frozen by the shockingly sudden killing. George had been his friend for over a decade, both when they had worked together, and when Michael had retired.

There had been no reluctance or second thoughts when he'd agreed to join Michael's expedition to Honduras. George, ever-curious, ever-helpful, was dead.

When the two of them had been captured by the Cruzados, it had been a frightening few days, but at the back of his mind, Michael never really thought their lives were in imminent peril.

It was Michael's fault. He had dragged George halfway around the world only for him to be murdered in a jungle.

Before his grief could consume him, Michael heard a sharp whistling sound as a bullet sped past his head and splintered a tree branch.

Yaxche grabbed his arm with both hands and shook him. *"Prisa,"* he said, and Michael's paralysis broke.

They were only a few dozen meters from the road. Though he hated himself for leaving George's body behind, Michael knew he and Yaxche would most likely join him in death if they tarried.

Trying to block out thoughts of his friend, Michael hurried down the makeshift trail after Yaxche. Another shot rang out, and Michael ducked. He felt a tug at his shirtsleeve as the bullet narrowly missed him.

There were angry shouts behind him, but Michael couldn't make out any of what they were yelling.

Quelling the blinding panic that tried to seize him, Michael scrambled up the embankment at the main road and quickly scanned for the copse of trees Humberto had mentioned.

He pointed. "There!" Pulling Yaxche alongside him, he raced across the dirt road.

By the time they got to the patch of trees, the Cruzados had crested the road. There was another brace of shouts as the men spotted them.

One of the men chasing them dropped to his knee and raised his rifle to take careful aim. Michael pushed Yaxche out of the way as the man fired.

Letting out a curse in Spanish that Michael couldn't identify, the Cruzado started shooting wildly in their direction.

For a brief moment, as Michael and Yaxche reached the other side of the copse of trees, he thought either they had run to the wrong area, Humberto had set them up, or someone had stolen the truck before they got there.

Michael let out an expletive of his own and threw his hands up in frustration; but then Yaxche tapped him on the arm and pointed. In the shadow of a jicaro tree, under a hasty covering of leafy branches, was a beat up gasoline-powered truck similar to the one he and George had rented, though this one was a light blue color and had a canopy over the short bed.

They both sprinted toward the vehicle and jumped in. The keys were in the ignition, and when Michael pumped the gas and turned the switch, the engine fired up immediately.

Slamming it into gear, Michael drove the pickup as fast as he could through the field, directly away from the Cruzados.

The rear windshield suddenly spider-webbed as a shot ricocheted off it, but by the time Michael got the truck back up on the main road, they had left the Cruzados too far behind for them to have any hope of hitting their fleeing quarry with another bullet.

Michael hit the steering wheel with the heel of his hand in anger.

Yaxche spoke in an assured voice. *"Tu amigo vela por nosotros desde el cielo."*

'Your friend watches over us from heaven now,' Michael figured out after a moment.

Setting his jaw, Michael fixed his eyes on the road ahead and concentrated on finding his way to Santa Rosa de Copán.

27

Lucis Observatory :
Venus Orbit :

Terry saw himself as a young boy at the height of the Mayan civilization. Dressed in traditional costume, he stood on a raised platform with four others his age.

In the field, throngs of Mayans were gathered together as the astrological advisor to the king spoke about the coming of the fourth world, and that it would be signified by a great omen: the sky would turn to fire and the heavens would burn. Lightning would strike the earth and destroy their temples, and the gods themselves would fall from the sky and smash into the world. Conquerors from a distant shore would arrive in the aftermath and rebuild the world according to their own design.

In order to save themselves from the wrath of Hanub Kú and survive in the fourth world, they must build a monument in his honor; a staircase to the heavens where they could rise above the coming disasters and ride out the chaos.

The king, his priests and his most trusted astronomers had chosen that spot where Terry and the other four boys stood to begin construction.

To commemorate the undertaking, they had chosen the five boys as a special sacrifice to gain Hanub Kú's favor.

Two large men grabbed Terry by his arms and bent him backwards over a sacrificial altar.

The priest approached him with a long knife—

∞

Terry shot straight up from his cot and gasped in panic. His eyes scanned the darkness of the small room he'd been sleeping in, and he clutched one hand to his chest where his heart thumped like a hammer. Slowly, his breathing returned to normal when he realized he'd been having a nightmare.

Swinging his legs over the side of the cot, he found his shoes and slid his feet into them. He closed his eyes, held his head in his hands, and thought about what he had just dreamed.

Terry's grandfather always stressed the importance of dreams, and the need for remembering nightmares. The Mayans of old believed dreams were a way of communicating with the gods, and with other people both living and dead, revealing knowledge that could not be shared during their waking hours.

Always regarding this as mysticism, Terry had never paid too much attention to his grandfather's interpretations. Now, however, with the realization that there was far more substance to the legends his grandfather had recounted, Terry had become a believer.

Calming himself by sitting up straight and regulating his breathing, he tried to remember his nightmare before the threads of his memory evaporated like smoke in the wind.

He had no idea what it meant, or why he had dreamed it. Although he'd had more frequent dreams of the ancient Mayans since Itzel's death, none of them had ever dealt with human sacrifice or portents of the remaking of the world before; nor had any seemed so much like a vision.

Before he could sort out the reasons for his nightmare, and whether it had been one of the special dreams his grandfather had talked about, the chime on his nightstand sounded and a familiar voice issued out of it.

Jose said, "Terry, we're heading up to the lab to begin with the next subject. Klaus wants you there standing by in case he needs something during the experiment."

Like coffee or a sandwich, Terry thought to himself. Out loud, he said, "All right. I'll be there in a few minutes." And then he clicked the communicator to shut it off.

He rubbed his head as if the action would clear his thoughts from the nightmare. Padding over to the washroom, he splashed cold water on his face to wake himself up. Finally, he went out to fulfil his role as servant to a madman.

∞

Terry arrived at the lab just moments before Klaus and Jose. Both men bore determined looks. Behind them, several large Cruzados escorted the fourth subject for the Kinemet radiation trials.

It was the woman. Major Turner.

Terry had completely forgotten about her. He had been preoccupied with the recitation of the Song of the Stars for Klaus and performing menial tasks for him. At no time had he gone to check on her or any of the prisoners, but even if he had wanted to look in on them, he couldn't have. The section of the observatory where they kept the prisoners was under heavy guard, and no one was permitted entry without express orders from Klaus, Jose, or Captain Gruber.

As they dragged the woman past him, he got his first good look at her. Her eyes did not focus, and he recalled that she was blind.

Her long hair was disheveled and her cheeks were streaked with tears. Major Turner looked like she had been through a tough few days, but she held her head high and set her jaw defiantly as her escorts steered her past Terry and toward the lab.

"Jose," Terry said, finding his voice. "She is a woman, and she is disabled. We can't do this."

Jose glanced up at Terry, but it was Klaus who raised his hand sharply to cut him off. "On the contrary, boy, we can and we will. If it makes you feel any better, I really have only one more variable to test for. She's got a fifty-fifty shot of becoming the first fully transformed Kinemetic human. Of course," he added with a wry smile, "she still might die from radiation poisoning. We're really just stumbling around in the dark hoping for the best here."

It was too much for Terry. He knew there wasn't anything he could do against six men who were much larger and more prone to violence than him. He could feel himself shaking from frustration and anger.

Although he had undertaken combat training at the monthly camps the Cruzados held, Terry had never really taken it as seriously as the others, and never committed himself to the instruction. He had believed from the beginning that his destined part in the movement was geared more towards a leadership role than as a fighter. But he wasn't even a figurehead in the Cruzados revolution; once he had unlocked the door to the Song of the Stars, they had relegated him to being nothing more than Klaus's servant.

All he could do was stand there while the brutish Cruzados herded the woman into the lab.

Inside, one of the men reached over to unbutton Major Turner's shirt at the collar. She swore at him, and Terry couldn't make out her exact words. Her meaning, however, was very clear. She punctuated her words with a slap to the Cruzado's face.

The man immediately belted her across the cheek with the back of his hand, knocking her into the examination bed.

Terry instinctively stepped forward to help, but a strong hand grabbed his shoulder. Klaus's fingers dug into his skin.

Reaching up, Terry ripped the hand away from him with as much strength as he could summon, and glared at Klaus, who was smirking back.

Terry pointed toward the other room. "Is that really necessary?"

"We can't risk the possibility of contamination from her outfit," Klaus answered, mistaking the cause of Terry's protest. He weighed Terry with a critical eye, and his voice carried a heavy undercurrent of disdain when he spoke again.

"You really aren't cut out for this, are you? You're a dreamer, and dreamers never survive in the real world."

There was a scream from the lab, and Terry turned to see the four Cruzados forcibly strip the clothes from Major Turner. Naked, she fought wildly, but another slap disoriented her long enough for them to haul her up on top of the table and strap her down. One of them inserted a needle in her arm from an intravenous drip. When Justine tried to pull her arm away, the man punched her in the face.

Blinded by outrage, Terry pushed Klaus out of the way and raced over to the door of the lab.

One of the Cruzados, a big man named Esteban, saw the movement and hurried over to block the entrance. He was far too large for Terry to handle, and by the time Terry could figure out how to get past the big man, both Jose and Klaus grabbed him.

Klaus spat out his words. "I thought you said you could control him, Jose."

Instead of answering Klaus, Jose barked an order out to his man. "Esteban, take him to his quarters and seal the door."

To Terry, he said, "I'm very disappointed in you, *niño.*"

As he was dragged out of the lab, Terry saw behind him that Major Turner was already unconscious, and Klaus had returned to his computer station to begin the Kinemetic transformation trial.

Once again, Terry had completely failed in his efforts, and the cost would be another life.

∞

Terry only had three meters of floor on which to pace, and he made the round-trip at least a hundred times. All the while, he fumed at Klaus and Jose, damning himself for his role in the entire affair.

When history wrote his story, they would not hail him as a hero, or visionary, or savior of the Mayan culture. No, he would go down in the books as a traitor to humanity. A thief, kidnapper, and accomplice to murder.

There had to be a way to redeem himself.

But what could he do? He was just one small man against dozens of Cruzados.

By now, Major Turner would be well into the experiment. She would be nothing more than a series of photons swirling around the room. In less than three hours, the speck of Kinemet Klaus used to kick-start the reaction would expend itself, and then she would either be transformed into a quantum navigator, or she would die a horrible and painful death, as had the previous subjects.

Terry had to do something.

As he paced, the seed of an idea formed in his head. Maybe he could play Jose and Klaus off against each other?

He held his breath, as if the plan might escape with his next exhalation.

Could he do it? Was he capable of following through? Or was his mind leading him into yet another foolish act?

Forcing himself to calm down, he closed his eyes and tried to even out his breathing. When his heart returned to a normal rhythm, he slowly opened his eyes once more, and then began to work out a plan of action.

He returned to the door and checked the peephole once more, but didn't see anyone in his limited range of vision.

The doors of the residential quarters only had locks on the inside. Carefully, Terry slid the latch open and gently pulled the door back a crack, and then peeked out.

Esteban was half a dozen meters down the hall, sitting in a chair and leaning back.

Keeping the door as close to the jamb as he could while still giving him enough of a gap to see through, Terry watched him. The man had to be bored out of his mind with the mundane guard duty. He already looked as if he were ready to doze off. Terry just had to be patient. With slow movement, Terry removed his boots and then approached the door once again, this time in his stocking feet.

Like a jaguar stalking its prey before an ambush, Terry peered through the gap and watched and waited. He kept his eyes fixed on Esteban and stood still.

When the big man's head dropped a notch fifteen minutes later, Terry still did not move.

Even when he heard the first light snore come from the Cruzado, Terry remained motionless.

He waited an additional five minutes after he thought Esteban was asleep, and then delicately opened the door wide enough to slide out into the hall.

The layout of the observatory's residential area was such that there were two ways Terry could have gone. The first was out toward the cafeteria and common area, but there would assuredly be any number of Jose's men loitering there. The only other way was in the direction of the laboratories. That was where Terry wanted to go anyway, but in order to do so, he would have to creep by Esteban without waking him.

He raised one foot and put it softly down in front of the other as he picked his way past his guard.

He was directly in front of Esteban when a loud clanging sound echoed down from the opposite end of the hall in the direction of the kitchen. Terry heard someone curse lightly, as if they had dropped a pan, and he froze, staring intently at Esteban.

For a brief moment, he thought the guard had woken with the sound and was staring back at him. But it was a trick of the shadow and light in the hall; Esteban continued to snore.

Terry resumed his deliberate pace until he rounded a corner two sections down, and then he quickened his steps.

At the lab area, he turned toward a flight of stairs and followed them down to the lowest level.

He would need help if his plan were to have any chance of succeeding; and there was a distinct lack of friendly faces in the observatory.

∞

The hallway to the empty lab where they kept the American soldiers was unguarded. The lock on the main door to the room had been reconfigured to lock from the outside, and there was no way the prisoners could get through the electromagnetic latches. No one expected any of the Cruzados or any of Klaus's men to open the door and let the soldiers out.

The locks were keyed with an infrared scanner. When Terry had first come aboard the Lucis Observatory, Captain Gruber had sprayed the back of his wrist with a laser. It left no visible mark, but the old smuggler had assured him it was a kind of sub-dermal tattoo that would last for at least a few weeks. It would give him access to all the labs and common rooms with a mere wave of his hand.

There was a moment of doubt when Terry reached the door. If Klaus had updated the security databanks and removed Terry's clearances, this trip—and his plan—would be cut short. But the door opened into a darkened room. The smell of unwashed humans wafted up and he had to force himself not to gag.

He had some expectation that once he opened the door, the Americans would rush him and knock him down before he could talk to them, but when he flicked the overhead lights on, he saw that the soldiers looked weak and defeated.

One of them looked up as Terry stepped into the room, and said, "Who are you?" in English.

The others spotted Terry. Their eyes narrowed and their jaws clenched.

Terry had spent the better part of the past year learning their language, and though he still had trouble with aspects—especially slang—he felt confident enough to relay his idea to them.

"My name is Terry Fernandez. My grandfather is the guardian of the Song of the Stars scroll. I am as much a prisoner here as you. Our captors are experimenting on your *compañera*, Major Turner, and if you don't help me, they will most assuredly kill her."

∞

Klaus was hunched over a computer monitor, tapping one long finger against his lips as he scanned the diagnostics.

A few meters to the side, Jose was looking at the brightened window between the lab and the workshop, as if mesmerized by the display. He had his hands folded over one another behind his back, and every few seconds he would make a rocking motion, lifting himself up on the balls of his feet, and then settling himself back down.

Sitting on a tall stool at a lab table, Captain Gruber held half a deck of cards in one hand. The rest of the cards were arrayed on the surface of the table in a game of solitaire. At his hip was an ion pistol in its holster.

On the other side of the room, two of Jose's Cruzados were looking bored. One of them leaned against a computer server rack and rested his elbow on the top. The other was chewing his fingernails with his teeth. Both of them had ion pulse rifles, but they were propped barrel-up in the corner a few paces away.

"How much longer, do you think?" Jose asked. His voice sounded casual, but there was a note of anticipation in it.

Klaus popped his head up from the display. "Any minute now, I—"

Then he blinked, noticing that Terry had entered the lab without anyone knowing.

A moment later, everyone else turned their heads, sensing something wrong in Klaus's voice.

Terry willed his breathing to remain steady, and his heart to beat normally and not jump right out of his chest as every person in the room glared at him, first in surprise, then with alarm.

The two Cruzados stumbled into each other as they both went for their pulse rifles, but Captain Gruber already had his ion pistol out and pointed at Terry.

"What the hell are you doing here?" Jose demanded. "Where's Esteban? That idiot!"

Terry kept his eyes fixed on Jose. He didn't want to rush anything at this point. Unless he kept his voice level, the leader of the Cruzados would not take him seriously.

"I have something to tell you, Jose," Terry said after he was sure he had everyone's attention. He was impressed with how calm he sounded.

"Oh?" Jose blinked and shot a quick glance at his two men, making sure they had found their pulse rifles and were ready to handle any kind of trouble.

"Your life is in danger." Terry didn't make any threatening gestures, but he could immediately see the fear and uncertainty in Jose's eyes as he looked up and down to see if Terry had a weapon.

"Really?" The sarcasm in his voice was tinged with doubt. "I understand if you are upset," Jose said, stalling for time, "but I'm sure we can talk it out."

With a slight shake of his head, Terry said, "The danger is not from me."

Jose narrowed his eyes.

"When I was in the washroom earlier, I overheard Klaus and his uncle say they were going to kill both of us and take over your men once the experiment was successful."

Whipping his head first to the left at his men, who looked as confused as him, then back to the right at Klaus, Jose said, "Is this some kind of joke—?"

But he went silent when Captain Gruber swung his ion pistol away from Terry and pointed it at Jose.

Klaus, who had been watching the exchange with a half grin, said, "No joke, Jose. The little man has it right. You see, I thought it over, and even though the entire galaxy is really big, I've decided I really don't need a co-commander. But I'd like to thank you for your contribution to the cause—my cause, that is."

Jose, wild-eyed, threw a look at the two Cruzados. "Don't just stand there! Shoot him."

The men raised their pulse rifles, but they didn't point them at Klaus or Captain Gruber.

"Oh," Klaus said in a smug tone, "and I'd like to thank you for your men. As it turns out, most of them really weren't interested in your silly crusade, or in following your incompetent leadership."

Jose opened and closed his mouth in shock.

No one was paying attention to Terry all the while, and he slowly backed away from the conflict, heading toward the lab door. He unlocked it with a swipe of his wrist, and a moment before he opened it wide, he shouted:

"Jose! Run for your life!"

Seeing the open door, Jose took one step toward safety.

Captain Gruber fired the first shot, and that pulled everyone's attention back to the center of the room.

The ion stream hit Jose high in the arm, and he spun around, but did not fall. Screaming from the pain, he dove behind a table.

Just then, five American soldiers burst into the room and rushed Gruber and the two Cruzados, who fired blindly at the men without hitting anyone. Trent Gruber, however, did not panic under fire, and shot an ion stream directly into the head of the first man to reach him.

In the confusion, Terry lost track of Klaus, who must have dived for cover. He quickly skipped to the side, looking for the man, and saw two sets of legs kicking wildly from behind a metal table.

Dashing around, Terry saw Jose, bleeding from his arm, sitting on top of Klaus, his hands around the other man's throat, trying to choke the life out of him.

An ion stream from one of the rifles hit the tiled drop ceiling, and a small section broke free and crashed down on Terry. He threw a hand up to protect his head and glanced over to see two of the Americans tackle the two Cruzados on the other side of the room. Malnourished and weak, they were barely able to pull the pulse rifles out of their opponents hands. In hand-to-hand combat, the Cruzados were getting the better of them.

Captain Gruber wasn't able to get off another shot before the two other Americans, Lieutenant Jeffries and Corporal Marks, collided with him. They fought for control of the gun.

In front of Terry, Klaus and Jose rolled around on the floor, each trying to squeeze the life out of the other. Terry was all for letting them finish each other off, but he knew he couldn't chance either of them getting away.

He threw himself at the two men who had been the engineers of his downward moral spiral. The sudden anger he had for them surprised him, and he found himself punching them indiscriminately.

They had lied to him, tricked him, led him to betray himself and the people he loved, and then planned to kill him. The injustice of it all filled him with such a rage, he didn't even notice that one of them had stabbed him in the stomach with a screwdriver. It was only when Klaus, with a curse in German, kicked him off and onto his back, that Terry felt the shooting pain in his abdomen.

He couldn't breathe, and it took everything in him to get to his feet.

Klaus was bleeding from his nose and a few other cuts on his face. He spat blood as he used the metal table to haul himself up.

Jose remained on the ground, still and glassy eyed.

With his vision tunnelling, Terry saw that the Americans had managed to subdue the two Cruzados and were keeping them pressed to the ground.

On the other side of the room, Lieutenant Jeffries was on his knees, holding his hand over his face. Corporal Marks and Captain Gruber had both hands on the captain's gun.

With a vicious kick, Captain Gruber knocked the wind out of Corporal Marks, and the American released his grip on the ion gun. Captain Gruber shot him in the chest, point blank.

Klaus, seeing this, ran to help his uncle.

Like a predator, Terry let out a war cry and charged after Klaus. He had to prevent the two from escaping. If they got out of the room and sounded the alarm, the rest of the Cruzados would easily overcome Terry and the surviving Americans.

Captain Gruber swivelled at Terry's cry, and fired a charge at him without a moment's hesitation.

Two things happened at the same time.

First, there was the feeling of a sledgehammer pounding Terry square in the chest. His forward momentum kept him from falling back to the ground, but he couldn't breathe, no matter how much he tried to force his lungs to inhale.

Secondly, a fraction of a moment later, an ear-shattering explosion sounded from behind him and the entire room filled with light as the ion stream passed clean through him and into the window of the lab.

With the window blown out, the particles of light that Major Turner had become were now free from any barrier, and spilled out into the lab.

Above the ringing in his ears, Terry heard Klaus scream, "No!" as the photons swirled and escaped out into the hall.

Terry saw Lieutenant Jeffries spring up, face bleeding, to collide with Captain Gruber, and he sensed the other soldiers race past him to help bring Klaus and his uncle down.

But the last thought that went through Terry's mind was not that he had managed to defeat Jose and Klaus, but that he finally figured out what his dream meant.

The gods of old had spoken to him. In order to save his people, Terry had to be sacrificed.

And as he sank to his knees, and the final darkness enveloped his

consciousness, Terry decided he was all right with that.
His grandfather would be proud.

28

Frank: "Good morning, Alex. My name is Frank Galloway; I'm the senior advisor for USA, Inc.'s Board of Directors' oversight committee for Quantum Resources. I'll be taking over the debriefing from my assistant."

Alex: "Where's Edgar?"

Frank: "I wouldn't worry about him. He's been reassigned."

Alex: "I'm not worried. But I still want to know why he isn't here."

Frank: "If you must know, this conversation is outside the scope of his security clearance."

Alex: "And you have enough clearance?"

Frank: "To be honest, I don't think anyone has enough clearance. But at the very least I'll be able to determine whether the information you provide can be disseminated, and if so, through which channels."

Alex: "But your scientists need to know what I know, or we'll never be able to use Kinemet the way it was intended."

Frank: "I've spoken with the department heads at Quantum Resources. They've all assured me that they can make Kinemet a viable fuel for space travel."

Alex: "Maybe, but the way they are using it is dangerous and very inefficient."

Frank: "And how does it need to be used?"

Alex: "I don't know, exactly. But you need to stop them from repeating the *Quanta* mission. People will die. They need to start over from scratch."

Frank: "Alex, you strike me as a highly intelligent young man, but this is the real world. There are other factors that need to be taken into consideration."

Alex: "Such as?"

Frank: "...All right... For one thing, the space program is extremely unpopular at the moment: we are spending billions every year, and so far we haven't been able to recoup those expenses. Alex, we were hoping for a different result from your mission; something we could use in our PR campaign to bolster support, something that would fire the imaginations of the population. Heck, we'd have settled for a little green man in a flying saucer.

"In the eyes of the media and the public, the *Quanta* mission was a failure. The ship was destroyed, there was no contact with an alien race, and the viability of Kinemet as a fuel is still years—if not decades—from refinement. We need a success, and soon. The USA, Inc. Board of Directors are generally not scientifically inclined; they're motivated by opinions and polls, and if they enact policies and expenditures that go against the shareholder majority, they may lose their seats in the administration."

Alex: "Politics, you mean."

Frank: "Yes. Exactly. And so, you must also understand that any information you reveal today that goes against the *Quanta* missions may never go beyond this room."

Alex: "So you would let Quantum Resources continue down a path doomed to failure rather than set them straight? All for politics?"

Frank: "I'm afraid that's not my call, but if that's the final decision, it will come from the CEO's offices."

Alex: "It will cost lives."

Frank: "That's why I'm here. I want to know everything you know so that we can prevent future accidents."

Alex: "Nothing I say at this point will help you."

Frank: "Now, Alex, please be reasonable."

Alex: "...Do you believe that I was able to put myself into a quantized state when I was in the Centauri system?"

Frank: "The consensus with the department heads indicated that what you think happened may be a result of disorientation or fatigue."

Alex: "But what do *you* think?"

Frank: "I'm not certain there is any way to verify your story. I mean, it would go a long way if you could quantize yourself again and allow our scientists to observe the effects."

Alex: "I used up all the Kinemetic radiation in my system in Centauri. And it's also not something I can do here on Earth—there's too much geomagnetism on a planetary body. If I was recharged, and back in space, I think I might be able to do it again."

Frank: "That might be a difficult request to fulfill, Alex. There are many people in key roles who cautioned against letting you go on the first mission. They are using the failure as leverage to forward their own agendas and to ensure your removal from the program."

Alex: "What you are saying is everyone has already made up their minds."

Frank: "Not everybody, but enough of them to make your request difficult to grant."

Alex: "So what does this mean for me?"

Frank: "I'm sorry, Alex. I've been instructed to tell you that if you cooperate, and reconfirm your non-disclosure agreement, we can offer you a generous compensation package. You'll never have to worry about money again for the rest of your life."

Alex: "What if I refuse?"

Frank: "Well, as far as the world knows, Alex Manez is a seasoned pilot for the Canadian Space Force on loan to NASA, and who is of a considerably more mature age. We even have a digital composite image of a few actors made up for the press release and any future interviews. There's no possible way we can reveal to the world that we let a teenager lead the *Quanta* mission. That would be a public relations nightmare."

Alex: "I don't like to be threatened."

Frank: "I don't like to make threats. So what will it be?"

Alex: "I want the agreement all in writing, then I'll tell you the rest of what happened out there."

29

Unknown :

The Music of the Spheres fills her mind and soul.
Raw and exposed, all Sol System lies before her.
The energy of the Sun floods her senses.
Like children, the planets dance in orbit.
Come and play, they call out.
Each have their own laugh.
Their voices are songs.
They are alive.
Another song…
Alex?
So small.
He is lost.
There, but not there.
She pushes her thoughts out.
His song is faint and distant.
He needs her help to come home.
A new being of light, she lacks control.
Her essence explodes outward; the galaxy is wide open.
The Song of the Stars fills her mind and soul.

30

Quantum Resources :
Toronto :
Canada Corp. :

It was as if he had been an entire world away.

When the skybus circled the Toronto Pearson International Airport to line up with the runway for final approach, Michael looked out the window at the buildings and streets whipping past in a blur; and for the first time in over a week, he breathed a sigh of relief. It was like seeing an old friend after a long separation.

In a way, arriving back in Canada was very surreal. Michael had been through so much in Honduras it almost seemed as if he had lived two different lives.

Yaxche sat in the aisle seat, his fingers wrapped around the armrest in a stranglehold, his eyelids pressed closed tightly. He had never been on an aircraft before. At first, he'd been excited by the experience, but his enthusiasm had dimmed at the sudden pressure put on the passengers upon takeoff, and turned completely to fear with the first bout of turbulence that shook the skybus like a baby's rattle.

The old man wouldn't listen to Michael's explanations about aerodynamics or the safety of modern air travel. The only thing he spoke in reply was a prayer to the sky gods.

Even when the plane had stopped, Yaxche still would not relax his grip on the armrests. It was only once they disembarked the plane that he regained some of his normal color.

In the terminal, Michael spied Raymond McGrath in the large hallway, waving to get his attention.

"Over here," Michael said to Yaxche in English—he had purchased a clip-on translator for him at the Tegucigalpa airport—and crossed the distance to Raymond. "I'd like you to meet an old friend of mine."

After Michael introduced the two of them, Raymond said, "It's a pleasure to finally meet you, sir. We're all very excited to have you join us in the labs. Calbert and I have been speculating like a couple of old gossips."

Raymond turned to Michael. "We'll grab your luggage and head over to the hotel. We booked you two a suite. You can get cleaned up, rest."

Michael shook his head. "I'd rather head straight over to QR—if that's all right with you," he said to Yaxche, who nodded. To Raymond, he said, "Maybe we can get some fast food on the way." They started down the hall to the baggage area.

"I miss fast food."

∞

They all slid into an autotaxi after loading their bags in the trunk, and the vehicle engaged its forward drive the moment the doors sealed.

With his thought-link implant, Raymond was connected with the EarthMesh, and was able to instantly communicate with any linked computer. While the autotaxi had a manual interface for the majority of people—like Michael—who didn't have one of the implants, Raymond was able to send the vehicle their destination with a simple thought.

While Michael always considered himself an adopter of new technology, thought-link was one advance that did not appeal to him, though he understood why a certain segment of the population jumped at the chance to be connected to the mesh twenty-four-seven.

In his life as an administrator, Michael had spent most of his workday being constantly interrupted. It took extreme organization to juggle the hundreds of daily requests from staff, review info bulletins from the scientific community, process directives from his governmental superiors, and find time in his day to tend to personal needs. To have access to the millions of meshposts, blogs, forums, and newsvids around the clock would only be another distraction.

The downside was that, unless Michael was physically in front of a computer, he had to get his news secondhand.

So when Raymond's eyes widened as he received an alert that was obviously important, and he said, "You'll want to see this," Michael had to flick on the holoslate built into the autotaxi's dash to find out what was going on.

He quickly logged into this favorite news channel and selected the headline.

∞

Honduran Rebel Movement Crushed.

In a concerted effort, the Honduran Military and the Honduran Public Police Force raided several holdouts across the Central American country corp. at dawn this morning following reports of rebel activity.

A spokesman for the Honduran Minister of the Interior reported that the armed force sustained zero casualties, though a number of rebels were killed in the process. Over two hundred arrests have been made, including several prominent land owners and government officials who are suspected of involvement.

Calling themselves the Cruzados, the movement's political mandate was to assume leadership over Earth through a monopoly of space travel. According to one source, the rebels believe their actions are destined by ancient Mayan doctrine. The Cruzados are also suspected in the hijacking of the Lunar Lines ship, the *Diana,* out of Canada Station Three. The whereabouts of the vessel and its passengers are still unknown.

In a joint statement, representatives of the Honduran and Guatemalan Heritage Societies condemned the Cruzado movement.

∞

Accompanying the story, there was video showing helicopters descending on a plantation—Michael couldn't tell if it was Oscar Ruiz's or not—and Honduran soldiers pouring out and taking up positions against Cruzados, whose faces were obscured by long kerchiefs. After a quick exchange of gunfire, the Cruzados, obviously overmatched, surrendered. In handcuffs, they were marched into armored vans.

Raymond said, "I just linked with Calbert. He received word from John Markham that Humberto was integral in the raid, feeding them all the information they needed on the other Cruzado encampments."

Yaxche said, "Of course; he's a friend of mine," as if that explained everything.

Raymond paused a moment and spoke in a somber tone. "And they've recovered George's body. It'll be flown back here within the next few days."

Michael's face was rigid, and his jaw clicked, but his reaction was not because of Raymond's last statement. The raid and the recovery of George's body was good news, but he'd been expecting it after Markham had let him know Humberto had made contact.

"What?" Raymond asked. "What's wrong?"

"Why didn't anyone tell me?" Michael growled his words.

"Tell you what?"

"About the *Diana* hijacking." Michael could feel his face flush in anger. He punched in a dozen search queries and brought up all the information he needed to get up to speed. He was particularly alarmed to read that they suspected the liner itself may have been pointed toward the Sun.

"Justine works for them," he said in a flat voice. "Was she on that flight?"

"I'm sorry," Raymond said, nodding in confirmation. "I know you two are friends. I thought you knew. It's been all over the news for a—" He shut his mouth with a snap, as if only just then realizing that Michael had been out of contact for all that time, and grimaced in apology.

Michael dismissed the apology with a slight headshake. "I've seen what the Cruzados are capable of. They couldn't have engineered that hijacking without some serious help. Tell Calbert to clear his day; we need to make some enquiries."

∞

When they arrived at the Quantum Resources administration offices, Calbert was in the lobby waiting for them.

"Glad to have you back," he said to Michael, clasping his hand in greeting.

Michael gave him a single firm nod. "Glad to be back. This is Yaxche."

Shaking hands with the Mayan, Calbert said, "We've been looking forward to this since Michael contacted us about George's theory." He glanced at Michael quickly. "It's odd that we don't have a single audio recording of the Song of the Stars, just the translations and the attempts by our own linguists, who were obviously incorrect in their recitation."

Turning back to Yaxche, he said, "We have an entire team of technicians standing by to hear your story… Unless, of course, you're too tired from the trip."

His mouth splitting wide in grin, Yaxche said, "Old men never pass up an opportunity to tell a story." He barked out a laugh.

Raymond, smiling, said, "I can take him over there if you two need to debrief."

Calbert said, "Thanks, Raymond."

The two headed off to the recording lab. Raymond wasn't a very tall man, but he towered over Yaxche, and seemed to enjoy not being the shortest person in the room for a change.

Raymond started relating some of the theories floating around about the Song to Yaxche, his voice fading out the farther they got.

Michael turned to Calbert. "Can you fill me in on what happened with the *Diana?*"

Motioning toward the elevator, Calbert headed off first. "What you read in the news is pretty much it. Since Canada Corp. bought out USA, Inc.'s shares of Quantum Resources, we really haven't had any kind of pipeline into their governmental channels for years. Even most of the scientific information we get from NASA has already been screened and cleaned."

They reached the elevator, and Calbert let Michael get in first. He punched the button for his floor.

Michael said, "You have to have a few contacts who might give you some unofficial information."

"Yeah, I do. But no one I've talked to has any more idea what's going on that we do. Apparently, it's been a military operation from the get-go, and you know how hush-hush they are."

Michael jerked his head. "Military?"

"Someone got some information that the Cruzados were launching an operation to raid NASA's store of Kinemet, and they decided to move it all off planet. Since the Chow Yin incident, the American sector on Luna is the most fortified location in Sol System."

"If they moved the Kinemet off-planet, they assumed the Cruzados didn't have space capabilities," Michael said. "As it turns out, they did, and the information was obviously a plant to get the Kinemet in transit, where it was most vulnerable." Michael punched his fist into his hand. "You know damn well the Cruzados aren't working alone."

"The Canadian Space Force has offered its assistance to the Americans, but so far, no one is any closer to figuring it out."

When they reached Calbert's floor, they quickly exited the elevator and made their way to his offices. They entered a small conference room set up with several holoslates and a long work table. One of Calbert's assistants was there, dropping off a large food platter and an urn of coffee.

"I ordered up a few sandwiches for us. I figured we'd be working most of the day."

Taking off his jacket and draping it over the back of a wheeled chair, Michael sat down and reached for a coffee cup. "Thank you."

After practically guzzling down his first cup, Michael poured another and grabbed a sandwich. He bit off a piece and while he chewed, he launched a timeline app on the main haptic console. He began to fill in all the major events that had taken place over the past few weeks. Then he linked in as many mesh searches as he thought relevant to the situation.

Calbert got on his comlink and contacted John Markham to see if they had a complete list of the Cruzados arrested in Honduras.

It took them a few hours to collect and collate the data, but at the end of it all, they still couldn't figure it out.

Calbert moved over to his desk and opened a drawer. "Drink?" he asked.

"I'd kill for a Scotch, if you have it."

"Of course I do," Calbert said, and produced two tumblers. He poured a measure into one of them and handed it to Michael who nodded his thanks and took a sip.

"It's all connected," Michael said, turning around to look at the board. "And everything was sparked by the original theft. Nothing else would have even been initiated unless they knew they had the key to solving Kinemet. Everything hinged on that, and everything was set up way ahead of time: the rumors of an attempted theft on American soil; getting their people in position on CS3 to intercept the shuttle. They had to have people high up in administration, and—" He whistled at the thought. "—they had to have a lot of resources and money at their disposal."

"What do you think?" Calbert mused. "A rival government? There was a lot of drum-pounding back during the first *Quanta* mission. Quite a few country corporations were upset that we weren't sharing the Kinemet technology."

"The Chinese?" Michael raised a speculative eyebrow. Their voice of opposition to Western control had been the loudest after the failure of the first *Quanta* mission.

"I don't think so. They have their own space mining program. If they really wanted Kinemet, they could just go get it." He waved his hand spaceward. "It's out there; the only problem is getting it. No one's been officially looking for it for the past several years, and there hasn't been any scuttlebutt on unofficial operations."

Calbert stood up and paced over to his desk. "And then what do you do with it? As far as most everyone is concerned, we're decades away from being able to convert it into a stable fuel. Without the conversion technology, the expense is not worth it. Not when the world economy is in a shambles. People are more worried about putting food on the table than whether we can travel to other stars—especially when we don't have anything more than a hint on a floating ball of ice over four billion kilometers away that there's anyone out there besides us."

Michael set his drink down and sat back in his chair. He rubbed his tired eyes.

The entire world had gone through an emotional upheaval over the past couple of decades. With the failure of the first *Quanta* mission to make first contact, the initial euphoria of interstellar travel had deflated quickly. Once subsequent efforts to reproduce a Kinemetic navigator had failed, public opinion had turned to a level of cynicism he hadn't seen since he was a boy during the wheat crisis and the fall of public governments. Back then, the reorganization of governments into country corporations had sparked economic recovery.

Though now, he thought to himself, the health of country corporations rested solely on consumer confidence. And since confidence was low, the corporations were taking fiscal losses left and right. Budgets were cut. There was an increase in unemployment and a rise in civil unrest in most of the harder hit countries.

There was no better time for a revolution. Someone saw it coming and had gambled big. Whoever could offer a bright light for the future could write his own ticket. Michael could not believe any of the Cruzados he had met, even the gracious Oscar Ruiz, had that kind of foresight or access to enough resources to have prepared for this eventuality years ahead.

"So someone was coming at the problem from a different angle," he said out loud. "Figure out how to use Kinemet first, and then source the metal—only they decided to steal the stuff instead of doing any of the heavy lifting."

"Right. So what did they know that we didn't?" Calbert asked. "We must have spent thousands of man-hours on the translation of the Mayan scroll. Of course," he added with a dry laugh, "with all our brilliant minds we never figured out that the medium *was* the message."

Rubbing his eyes with his knuckles, Michael yawned.

"Why don't we take a break for the day?" Calbert said. "I know a nice steakhouse around the corner. We can take Yaxche there to try some Canadian cuisine."

"Yeah," Michael said. "My brain is tired from over thinking everything. I'm probably missing the obvious."

On his comlink, Calbert connected with Raymond. "How's everything going down there?"

"Oh, we've been done for hours. The team is busy crunching numbers and looking for patterns. It could take them a while to come up with any possibilities. I've been showing Yaxche around the building. He seems to like the roof garden the best."

"We're going to break for the day, go out to the 'Beef and Brew'. Can you ask Yaxche if he's hungry? And you're welcome to join us, if you can."

There wasn't more than a moment's hesitation before Raymond said, "If I can? We're already halfway to the elevator." He laughed. "We'll stop at your floor and meet you."

Michael stood and stretched. He reached for his jacket. "Have you had a chance to talk to Elizabeth?" he asked. "I've tried to reach her a couple of times, but all I get is her answering service."

There was a sudden pained look in Calbert's eyes.

Michael knew he and George had become more than just colleagues since Michael's retirement. Before Michael's wife had passed away, the three couples had vacationed together every other year. It was Michael's own fault that he had fallen out of touch since her death. At the time, he didn't want the sympathy his friends had offered, instead preferring to wallow in his anger and loss. He hoped Elizabeth knew she could lean on him for support.

"Yes," Calbert said. "Once she found out about what happened, she flew down to Florida to be with family. I contacted her this morning as soon as I learned they'd recovered his body. She said she was making arrangements to bring George's parents and sister here for the funeral."

At that point, Michael was uncertain what to say. There were so many emotions roiling around inside him that he thought any words he spoke would get caught in his throat.

He was saved when Yaxche and Raymond appeared in the doorway of the conference room, both with bright smiles.

Calbert asked, "Everyone ready?"

"Uh," Yaxche said into his translator, "I would like to talk to Sky Traveler now."

"Alex?" Michael asked. "He's not here, Yaxche. He's on Canada Station Three. In space."

Yaxche gave him the same look one would give a small child. "I am aware of this. Perhaps we could use your EPS. That is how I spoke with him two years ago, when I was in Santa Rosa de Copán."

"Of course," Michael said, looking sheepish as Calbert smiled at his discomfiture.

Raymond blinked in the way only people with a thought-link blink. He was sending a command into the building's systems.

"I can patch the uplink right in here, if you like," he said. "We should probably update Kenny on the scroll anyway—he's our lead physicist on Kinemet development up there," he told Michael. "Only been with us for a few months, but he's come up with some very promising theories."

All four of them turned to the holoslate as it flashed the corporate logo along with an animation of a radio wave.

After a few seconds, the screen flicked to show a young woman with short blonde hair and a pretty smile. A small inset square in the top corner showed Raymond reflected in the frame.

"Quantum Resources, Canada Station Three," the blonde woman said. "How may I help you? Oh, hello, Raymond."

"Terra," he answered, "how are you? Is Kenny there?"

"Kenny?" There was a quick flash of uncertainty in her eyes. "Well…"

Calbert took a step forward into her view. "What's wrong? Where is he?"

Chewing her lip, Terra said, "I'm sorry, I thought you all knew."

"Knew what?" Calbert pressed.

"He's been arrested."

Raymond's voice went up in alarm. "Arrested? For what?"

Terra looked decidedly uncomfortable relating the information. "Someone should have told you this," she said, and shook her head. "They discovered Alex Manez in Kenny's apartment early this morning. He's unconscious—in a coma or something. The station police think Kenny did some kind of experiment on Alex. He claims he didn't do anything, but they're holding him anyway."

"Where's Alex?" Michael demanded, too distracted to follow EPS courtesy protocols and step into Terra's line of sight.

"He's in the medical wing under observation. They said they have no idea what's wrong with him. Dr. Amma said this was the second time he's gone into a coma, a deeper one this time, and she's worried he won't come back out of it."

Calbert and Michael shared a concerned look.

Raymond spoke to Terra. "Thank you for filling us in. I'll call back in an hour." He cut the uplink.

Before anyone could say anything, Yaxche, who was following the conversation on his translator, grabbed Michael by the arm.

"We must go to him right away," he said, his tone brooking no argument. "Alex is in a spirit walk, a dream state. I think he has lost his way. I might be able to guide him home."

Calbert said to Raymond, "You book them on the next flight to the Nova Scotia Space Port and get them on a shuttle to CS3; I'll find out what's going on up there."

31

Unofficial Transcript :
Alex Manez Interview Part Three :
Dated August 2103 :

Frank: "Is the agreement to your satisfaction, Alex?"

Alex: "Yes. Thank you."

Frank: "All right. We are recording this. Please tell me, in your own words, what happened after you set the escape pod on course for the source of the electromagnetic signals. —And leave nothing out."

Alex: "May I have a glass of water?"

Frank: "Of course. Evan, please bring in a pitcher and a glass."

Alex: "I have one more request."

Frank: "Alex, our patience is running thin."

Alex: "It's a little thing."

Frank: "All right. What is it?"

Alex: "Is there any way you can get me a small sample of Kinemet?"

Frank: "I'm sorry, I can't authorize that. It's extremely expensive to mine, and there's a limited supply on Earth. Seems like a very extravagant souvenir, Alex."

Alex: "Well, can I just see some for a little while?"

Frank: "Why?"

Alex: "I think I need to be around it."

Frank: "I'll see what I can do, Alex, but I can't make any promises. Are you ready to tell us the story now?"

Alex: "Yes."

∞

Alex: "I think I already told you that the trip to Centauri felt instantaneous to me, but I didn't mention that it left a kind of residual memory in me. It's hard to describe the feeling. It's like someone tells you about how they went skydiving, and described it so well that you can imagine it was you who jumped out of the airplane. Now, pretend that no one ever described that feeling, but you still have the sensations of the dive. It's an echo of a memory.

"The moment the ship was quantized, there was a link between me and the *Dis Pater* on Pluto. The only way to describe it is as a kind of compulsion. It drew me to it. That the *Quanta* itself was pointed directly at it is beside the point; even if it hadn't been, I would have felt drawn to the monument.

"When the ship reached Pluto, for a moment it felt to me as if the entire galaxy was laid out in a spider web of connected monuments, and all I had to do was *connect* myself to one of those strands and fly along its path. I believe, if NASA had not put the *Quanta* on a direct trajectory to Alpha Centauri, I would still have been able to course correct and travel along that thread. I couldn't, of course, because this thought didn't enter my consciousness until after the ship had arrived in the next solar system.

"When the ship arrived, I was able to sense the Centauri version of the *Dis Pater*, as if it were a homing beacon.

"This is why I believe we are not using Kinemet the way it was intended. I was only partially altered by exposure to the reacting Kinemet, and was never able to fully transform into what I should have become. Yaxche called me 'Colop u Uichkin', which we've translated as a god of the sun, or stars. A closer interpretation is 'Master of the Stars' or, as the term I've been using for myself, 'Star Traveler'.

"I did some reading on the way here from Pluto. The ancient Mayans were a very cosmic-minded and spiritual people. One of their beliefs was that a person was made of pure energy. Every object in the universe is made of that same kind of energy. Energy can be interpreted as frequencies. The Mayans believed that all things had the ability to transfer that energy—if they found a compatible frequency—to any point in the universe.

"Where do you think they developed that philosophy?

"I believe if I had been transformed the way it was intended, I would not have been unconscious during that trip to Centauri. With the powers I have developed since I was irradiated, I believe I should have been able to pilot the ship. My 'clairvoyance' would be for navigation, and my 'electropathy' would be able to control the amount of power put out by the quantized Kinemet.

"Of course, I was exposed to Kinemet by accident, so I am incomplete. If you conduct tests on others without fully understanding how the Kinemetic radiation will affect them, they could quite possibly exhibit worse symptoms than I have, even death."

∞

Frank: "When I said leave nothing out, I meant about the events you experienced. We need to leave the conjecture for the scientists."

Alex: "But this is something they need to hear."

Frank: "Again, that is yet to be determined. I'm sorry, but that's the way it has to be."

Alex: "Fine."

Frank: "Alex ... you also understand that in order for us to fully honor our end of the agreement, we must have full disclosure from you ... we need the truth. If all the Kinemet on board the *Quanta* exploded in the secondary reaction, how did you manage to return to our solar system?"

Alex: "While you may or may not believe what I just told you, I promise you that what I'm about to say is the complete truth..."

∞

Alex: "I could do the math. I had less than a week of oxygen and water, but the escape pod would take more than a month to reach the source of the signal. It was a pure survival instinct that I attempted to put myself back into a quantized state. I had enough Kinemetic radiation in my system to maintain my state for the duration.

"What I didn't take into account was that, without a catalyst, I had no way of reversing the process. I could float for months or years before I burned off whatever radiation I had in me. In my theory, a properly conditioned star traveler should be aware while quantized; I was not.

"If I hadn't been pulled into dock in the alien space port, I most likely would have drifted until I died."

∞

Frank: "Stop right there! Alien space port! Alex, are you saying you made contact with aliens? If so, this is a serious breach!"

Alex: "No. No aliens. I didn't lie to anyone about that."

Frank: "Okay. Continue."

∞

Alex: "I assure you, the spaceport—the source of the signal—was completely deserted. Everything on board was fully automated. I can only assume their sensors detected me and retrieved the escape pod. I was pulled inside a large hangar. There was a series of platforms that looked as if they were docks for ships of all sizes, but besides my pod, there were no other vessels. The hangar itself was very sparse. I couldn't see any windows or bay doors anywhere. The walls looked like they were made from some kind of polished stone, rather than metal.

"My first thought was to open the escape pod to step out, take a look around, but my pod's canopy was jammed. Besides, I didn't have an EVA suit, and I didn't know what kind of atmosphere the port had, so I had to remain where I was. There must have been a quantity of Kinemet there, because I began to feel rejuvenated, almost immediately.

"Automated arms extended from along the platform and attached themselves to the pod. At first this scared me, because I thought they were going to open the canopy, but the gauges on the pod indicated that they were merely refuelling me with oxygen and electricity."

"Once the pod was recharged, another set of arms affixed a large object to the underside of the pod. I couldn't tell what it was, but I have to assume it was attached with some kind of magnetic clamp. The moment the mechanical arms retracted, the pod began to move away from the dock. I had no control over the navigation systems as the pod moved towards a tube. Inside, I built up speed and was shot out from the port at what I would imagine would be the escape pod's maximum speed."

"The entire process from the moment I regained consciousness was less than five minutes.

"As my pod left the space port, I was once again quantized. I have to assume the object they attached was some kind of temporary portable Quantum engine. The next thing I knew, I was in orbit around

Pluto, and the ground crew were trying to contact me on the radio. The portable quantum drive had been completely consumed during the flight.

"The rest you know."

∞

Frank: "Alex, I'm not sure what to say. That's an incredible story. Are you leaving anything out?"

Alex: "You don't believe me?"

Frank: "Well … that's not for me to say, but, I have to warn you that, well, pretty much everyone who reads this transcript is going to dismiss your report as wild speculation at best, and juvenile fantasy at worst. The problem, unfortunately, is that we can't corroborate any of this."

Alex: "I know."

Frank: "You understand that it would be extremely difficult for people to reconcile your story with established scientific fact."

Alex: "Yes. Sometimes the most closed-minded people are scientists."

Frank: "Be that as it may, I don't think the board of directors are ready for this information. As a matter of fact, I think they will dismiss it out of hand."

Alex: "I'm sorry I don't have any evidence for you, but I'm sure it's there if someone wants to look, they just have to return to Alpha Centauri. The space dock is sitting there, empty and waiting."

Frank: "That, my boy, is easier said than done. To be honest, your account raises more questions than it answers."

Alex: "I'm sorry if I've upset you."

Frank: "I'm just not sure how to present this information to the board … or if I should."

Alex: "The world needs to take a closer look at Kinemet, and understand its relationship with human beings."

Frank: "If your story is true, then I agree, but we need verification … All right, well, at this point, all I can do is to submit the report and get it on record. I'll leave it to the board to decide."

Alex: "So what happens now? I mean, to me?"

Frank: "For all intents and purposes, 'Captain Alex Manez' is a commissioned member of the Canadian Space Force, and will be honorably discharged. You, on the other hand, share nothing with him other than a name. Once we release you, you will be free to do as you will. I believe the current CEO of Quantum Resources, Calbert Loche, has spoken with you about a position in the R&D department on Canada Station Three?"

Alex: "Yes."

Frank: "That sounds like a very good deal. But I want to remind you: to speak about your experiences in Centauri to anyone outside of this room will be considered a breach of contract and could be actionable in court. That would be very unpleasant for you."

Alex: "I'm not a child. I understand."

Frank: "I hope you do. Now, is there anything you would like to add before I submit the report and end the debriefing? Alex...? Alex...?"

Alex: "No. That's everything."

32

Lucis Observatory :
Venus Orbit :

It was the most unique and wonderful sensation Justine had ever experienced.

Although she was no more than a collection of photons held together by her electropathic ability, she was aware of herself and her surroundings. Alex had remarked to her that he had no recollection during the quantized state, as if he were in the midst of a deep sleep.

In her corporeal form, Justine was blind, and could only use her senses of touch, smell and sound to interact with the world; now, she had a sense of sight that was far more powerful than human vision. When she concentrated, she could zoom her consciousness in to any object—as if through a powerful microscope—and see the very particles of matter in their continuous ballet.

She could also sense the planets in their inexorable orbit around the Sun. It was as if she could feel their presence in Sol System, hear the sounds of their heavenly song.

In a more subtle manner, she could sense the alien monument on Pluto, the *Dis Pater,* like a dim beacon in the dark of space. Beyond that, if she strained to the limits of her ability, she could also sense an entire network of those monuments—thousands of them—spread throughout the galaxy.

Justine had a moment of consternation when she sensed another presence within Sol System. It was like a very faint flash in the distance, and it took her a minute to realize that it was another Kinemetic being: Alex!

She wondered if Alex would be able to sense her, now that she was irradiated with Kinemet.

When she focused on him, it came to her that he was incomplete.

His physical form was in one location, but his consciousness was someplace else.

Alex's essence was adrift, lost in the depths of this ghost world they inhabited. Justine pushed her senses out to search for it, but could not detect his consciousness.

It took her a moment to work through it. Alex wasn't in a quantized state. He had spoken before about the clairvoyant ability he had, and was able to utilize when not in a quantized state. Justine assumed it was the same as what she was currently experiencing—only, when she was in the quantized state, it was an extremely powerful ability, far more than anything Alex had described. In the back of her mind, she hoped that when she returned to normal, she would retain the *sight* as Alex had. That would more than compensate for her blindness. But she would worry about that later.

Right now, there were three issues she needed to address. One was trying to figure out where Alex's consciousness was.

The more immediate problem was that, as she moved her photonic essence out of the lab, she saw that the main room had turned into a war zone. People were dying.

There were two casualties already, though she did not recognize their faces. She spotted Lieutenant Jeffries on his knees holding his hand to his bloodied face while Corporal Marks wrestled with Klaus's uncle.

Four other soldiers were busy restraining two Cruzados, while Klaus seemed to be aware of Justine and was staring at her with a startled look on his face.

The third thing Justine realized was that she was burning through the Kinemetic radiation in her system at an alarming rate and would very quickly run out of fuel. Like someone suddenly experiencing a pang of hunger, she knew she would require more exposure to Kinemet if she was going to continue existing in a quantized state. And she guessed that she wouldn't be able to help Alex if she was corporeal, nor would she be much use in the fight.

So, last thing first, she needed to refuel.

It only took a moment for her to sense where the cache of Kinemet was kept in the observatory, and though it was difficult for her to cause her photonic particles to move in tandem through physical space, she put all her concentration into the task and exited the lab in a flash.

Klaus screamed after her as she left.

∞

She tried to devise a plan while she pushed her photonic form down the hallway. In her quantized state, she had the ability to affect electrical impulses—a quick test on a nearby light proved it—and she figured that would carry over when she returned to normal, but only if she was irradiated by enough Kinemet. When Alex had been depleted, he lost both the clairvoyant and electropathic abilities, though he had retained his eidetic memory (which, she surmised, might have been a more permanent physiological aspect of the Kinemetic transformation).

Although she had only seen a dozen or so Cruzados on her journey through the hall, she knew there had to be many more of them. Even if Lieutenant Jeffries and his men were able to overcome Klaus and his uncle, they were still outmatched by the rest of the observatory's complement of rebels.

Justine was not a trained fighter or tactician, though she had taken the basic mandatory courses in boot camp. They were outnumbered, under-equipped, and malnourished. Brute force was not the answer, but she had a thought that she might still be able to user her newfound abilities to their advantage.

She sent her vision out, tracking ethereally to where the Kinemet had been stored on the observatory's lowest level, near the docking bay.

Though she was reduced to a mass of protons, she was still unable to pass through solid matter, and she had to take the long way. In her photonic-quantized state, it was actually more difficult for her to move her essence through normal space than if she were solid matter. All of her photons, held together either by some kind of mental force or physical attraction, were in constant motion inside that intangible bubble.

When she finally reached the end of the hall, she began to wind her way down the flights of stairs near the elevator.

Two floors down, she ran out of Kinemetic radiation, and abruptly rematerialized into her human self. She was, however, a meter and a half in the air and was still in motion.

In solid form, she arched and fell sharply to the landing in a tangle of barked shins and banged elbows. The breath knocked out of her, head ringing from impacting it on the wall, Justine lay in a stunned heap for almost a full minute, naked and vulnerable until her breathing returned to normal.

Very slowly, and with great care, she gingerly gathered her arms and legs under her and pushed herself up off the floor. Resisting the urge to vomit from the combined effect of the de-quantizing and nausea from hitting her head during the fall, Justine took a moment to steady herself by leaning against the wall.

Once the feeling returned to her hands and feet, she took a deep breath and oriented herself. There was a thin dribble of blood coming from just under her hairline. She touched the wound experimentally, and winced at the sharp resulting pain.

Now that she was corporeal, she had hoped that she would retain the ability to see beyond herself, but couldn't because she didn't have any of the Kinemetic radiation left in her system. She felt a sharp pain of ethereal hunger. She *needed* Kinemet. If this is what Alex had gone through for the past few years, no wonder he had deteriorated physiologically.

Justine would have to find her way to the stash of Kinemet from memory, and she found that, as Alex's memory had improved, she now possessed a perfect image in her mind of the layout of Lucis Observatory.

Conscious of her nakedness, she drew one arm over her breasts and resumed her descent of the stairs barefoot, hoping against hope that none of the Cruzados had heard her crash and come to investigate.

∞

When she reached the bottom of the stairwell, she stopped at the door and leaned her head against it, trying to hear any sign of the rebels on the other side.

The resounding silence prompted her to pry the door open a crack. She paused, listening, then opened the door all the way and tiptoed down the hallway.

When she got near to the docking bay, she started to feel an electrical buzz. The hairs on her arms stood up and she felt a warm tingle go through her. The Kinemet was close.

As she moved farther down the hall, the sensation intensified, and once she arrived at what she assumed was a storage lockup, she knew the Kinemet was secured inside.

She tried the door, but it was locked. A sudden bout of panic hit her. She had come all this way only to be stopped by a door lock.

Mentally, she kicked herself. Although the Kinemet was in a different room, and most likely inside the titanium container, there was a trickle of radiation leaking out. That was how she was sensing it. All she had to do was stand there long enough to build up enough of a radiation level to regain her electropathic ability, and then she could easily pop the lock and gain entrance.

Pressing the entire length of her body up against the cold door, she stood there, allowing the Kinemetic radiation into her system. She was painfully aware of how vulnerable she was, and prayed that her luck would hold out a little while longer.

She worried that by the time she was in a position to help Lieutenant Jeffries and his men, it would be too late, but there was nothing more she could do until she had recharged.

After what seemed like hours, but was probably only a few minutes, she felt the flow of energy course through her veins as if she had just taken a vitamin shot. The energy level in her was akin to a drop in a bucket, but it was enough for her purpose.

A mere flicker of thought was all it took to trip the electronic lock, and she darted inside the room. The door was pneumatic, and automatically closed behind her.

A few more moments closer to the titanium container charged her with enough radiation to open the lock that stood between her and the full force of raw Kinemet.

Once it was open, the Kinemetic influence washed over her like a tidal wave. She remembered the ecstatic look on Alex's face when he was in the presence of the rare metal, and for the first time, completely understood it.

The clairvoyant vision started to return to her in stages. At first, she had a disconnected awareness of her surroundings, and then the objects closest to her slowly resolved into discernible forms.

She figured it would take at least an hour for her to be fully irradiated; but less than a minute in, she heard the sound of a footfall in the corridor outside the room.

One of the Cruzados threw open the door. He was momentarily taken aback, glancing at her bare breasts. But then, with a roar of anger, he swung his ion pulse rifle in her direction.

Just as he fired, Justine quantized herself, and the ion stream passed right through her photonic self, doing no harm.

With a look of abject surprise, the Cruzado took a few steps inside the room and let out a curse in Spanish.

Justine floated past him and out the door before it closed. The man charged the door, but before he reached it, Justine used her ability to engage the lock, and then blocked the power to the device.

The Cruzado hurled more muted curses as he tried to physically knock the door down, to no effect. He was fully locked in the room as if it were a maximum security prison cell.

This proved that Justine's plan would work. Unable to overcome the greater force of Cruzados, she would have to take them right out of the situation. The entire observatory complex was run on electronic doors and locks, and Justine was now a master of any electric current she sensed.

As she pushed her essence back down the hall toward the stairs, she hoped she could get back to the lab before it was too late, and before she once again ran out of Kinemetic radiation.

∞

Outside of the workshop's main door, Justine paused and extended her *sight* into the room.

There were several men on the floor, and the remaining five were in a standoff. On one side of the room were Klaus and his uncle, Captain Gruber, who was holding one arm limply to his side, blood soaking his shirt sleeve. They had knocked a metal lab table over and were hiding behind it. They each held a weapon. Gruber had an ion pistol in his good hand. Klaus, holding a pulse rifle, was spitting out curses at the three soldiers who blocked his escape.

Corporal Marks was dead, Justine saw. There was a trail of blood on the tiles from where Gruber had shot him to where he now lay. It looked as if he had not been killed right away, and had been pulled out of the line of fire—in vain, as it turned out.

One of the other soldiers, Private Townsend, was face down on the floor, also dead.

Justine felt a sudden pang of loss and anger. Over the past week she had become fond of all the soldiers in Jeffries' squad.

Lieutenant Jeffries and two men—Privates Vic Genero and Tomas Hodges—were holed up behind a bank of computer servers. Between them, they only had one pulse rifle, obviously taken from one of the dead Cruzados. All three soldiers evidenced wounds and bruises, but nothing looked fatal. The situation was dire, Justine saw when Vic checked the rifle's meter and gave Jeffries a helpless look. The rifle was void of any electrical charge.

Justine tried not to let her emotions get the better of her, but the atrocities committed against her and the people she cared about stacked up.

She couldn't simply seal off the room unless she was able to get Lieutenant Jeffries and his men out first, and the only way she could communicate that plan was to rematerialize.

Scanning the area near the two holdouts, Justine looked for anything electrical that she could use her powers on. If she could cause something to blow up near Klaus, it could possibly disable them or provide enough of a distraction to get Lieutenant Jeffries out. But there was nothing she could see that would do what she wanted.

Justine decided to go for broke and hope Lieutenant Jeffries would figure out what was going on and get himself and his men to safety.

She pushed her quantized self through the small opening in the broken window of the workshop door and into the room.

All eyes turned to her as she floated into the center of the room.

Klaus raised his rifle and fired off a single shot in her direction. The ion stream passed through her harmlessly. As if the result did not completely surprise him, Klaus scuttled toward a computer keypad.

Justine had no idea what his intention was, but Klaus had obviously figured out the ball of light in front of him was her, and by the self-confident sneer on his face he most likely had a theory on how to capture or kill her. Of course, when he started the experiments, he would have thought ahead about how to control any transformed subject.

Lieutenant Jeffries wasn't taking the opportunity, so Justine had no choice.

She transformed back to her human form, and stood in the middle of the room, stark naked.

It had the desired effect on Klaus. He paused in his search for the keypad to look at her.

Justine shouted, "Get out of the room," to Lieutenant Jeffries and, accustomed to following orders, he grabbed both of his men and complied.

When she turned back to Klaus, he had his rifle pointed directly at her, his lips curling up. In his other hand he held the keypad, and his thumb was pressed down on a key.

Justine immediately willed herself to transform into a quantized state, but nothing happened.

"Too late," Klaus said triumphantly. Lifting the keypad up, he winked at her. "Kinemetic damper. The same tech they use in a quantum drive. The whole room has been wired for it, not just the lab. Now, I'm afraid, I'm going to have to terminate your experiment."

Klaus leveled the barrel of the rifle at her head.

There was the distinctive electrical whir sound, and then a frozen moment when Justine's heart stopped.

A puzzled look on his face, Klaus slowly sank to his knees. On his chest, a small circle of blood blossomed, and he fell face down on the floor, releasing the keypad.

Behind him, one of the younger Cruzados, who Justine had thought was dead, lay on his side, a small ion pistol stretched out in front of him.

"*Lo siento,*" he said, and then his arm dropped and he went still.

Justine didn't have time to wonder what had caused one of the Cruzados to turn on Klaus, because Captain Gruber, with a roar of outrage, jumped up from his hiding spot, aimed his own pistol at her, and fired.

But Justine, free from the damper, was able to quantize herself a split second before the first ion stream sliced through her bare skin.

Lieutenant Jeffries and his two men charged back into the room.

His ion pistol spent, Gruber threw it at them in futility. They quickly tackled him and wrestled him to the ground.

Justine, sensing she was nearing the end of her Kinemetic fuel, moved her photonic self to the wall near the door of the lab. Her uniform had been hung on a hook there. She reverted to a physical form and quickly dressed while the lieutenant secured his prisoner.

"What the hell is going on?" Lieutenant Jeffries asked in what Justine thought was a very controlled voice, considering the circumstances. "What was that ball of light? Was that you? I mean, I had a briefing on the Kinemetic effect. Is that what happened to you? That's what Klaus was doing here?"

Nodding, Justine said, "I'll explain everything to you later. Right now, I need to secure the observatory. You find a communications room and get word back to Earth about what happened here."

"Uh, yes, Major."

Justine took a step toward the door, but paused, and knelt down beside the young Cruzado who had saved her life. She felt for a pulse, but the young man was truly dead.

"And, if you could, please find out who this person was. He saved my life."

∞

It took Justine a little less than a quarter of an hour to make a full circuit of the observatory and use her electropathic ability to seal off any Cruzado she found. Taken completely off guard, they didn't stand a chance. By her count, there were at least forty of them held inside the common area, and half a dozen other stragglers she trapped in their individual rooms or work areas.

When she was finished, they returned to the room where the Kinemet was stored. She used her *sight* to look inside. The Cruzado was standing in front of the container, his face painted with anger.

She spoke in Spanish, and pitched her voice for him to hear through the door. "We've taken control of the observatory. Your leaders are dead or captured. We have reinforcements on the way. You don't have any food or water. Put down your rifle now, lay on the floor with your hands folded on your head."

There was a brief moment when she thought he either didn't hear her, or was planning on being defiant. But then he tossed the rifle away from him and got down on the floor.

Justine unlocked the door and stepped inside, quickly grabbing the ion pulse rifle.

"All right, I want you to slowly get up and move into the other room. You'll wait there until we come for you."

Glaring at her, the Cruzado nevertheless complied, and once he was safely locked away in an adjacent room, Justine returned to the Kinemet, sat down beside it ... and basked in its radiance.

∞

Once she felt her energy levels were back to normal, Justine once more tried using her clairvoyant ability. This time, she pushed herself and tried to home in on Alex's weak signal.

It was difficult to get a fix on him because he seemed to be fading in and out.

Having the ability to see at great distances without physically being there was revolutionary. Alex's ability, kept top secret and shared with only a privileged few, had all but dissipated during the years he was not infused with Kinemetic radiation. He had told Justine once that he could only push his senses so far before he became mentally exhausted, even at the height of his power.

It was possible, Justine thought, that Alex had tried to use his power to find her after the hijacking and had exceeded his capacity. If so, he might have exhausted himself and didn't have enough reserves to pull his consciousness back to his body.

Experimenting, Justine confirmed what Alex had told her. At about one hundred and fifty kilometers from the Lucis Observatory, her conscious vision stopped moving forward. It was as if she had hit a barrier, and no matter how much energy she exerted, she could not push past it.

As Justine moved her *sight* back toward the observatory, she took in the deadly beauty of Venus. Unlike Earth, whose surface detail could be seen between patches of cloud, Venus was completely covered by its sulfuric clouds. It was mesmerizing, and Justine wanted to drift out there in space forever, exploring all the celestial wonders of space.

But too many people were relying on her.

Returned to her corporeal self, Justine reflected a moment on the powers she had acquired, and being a trained astronaut, she connected most of the dots.

In order to navigate at luminal speeds, a pilot would need the ability to sense the star beacons as if they were a navigational map. She assumed the clairvoyant *sight* was a reflection of that ability. The electropathy would be twofold. Although she had no empirical data on which to base her theory, it made sense that she would be able to course-correct a quantized ship in flight using the ability. Also, it would be needed once a quantized ship was returned to normal space, in order to dampen the engines and prevent a secondary Kinemetic reaction.

Or, she thought, she might be able to stop the reaction herself without the aid of a damper. There was a lot of experimentation that needed to be done.

She wasn't certain where the enhanced visual memory would come into play. It could just be a side-effect of being a Kinemat.

She remembered that was the word Alex called himself, and had wondered at times if he was still human.

As she processed the thoughts, she continued to bathe in the radiation of raw Kinemet.

∞

When Lieutenant Jeffries found her and gently shook her shoulder, it took everything in her not to ignore him and sink deeper into the influence of the powerful metal.

"We've secured the observatory," he said to her when she opened her eyes. "All of the Cruzados are in the common room, along with Gruber. We can keep them there indefinitely."

"What about the young man who saved my life?" she asked.

"Gruber wouldn't say a word. One of the other Cruzados said the man's name was Terry, but he wasn't really one of the rebels. You'll never believe this: he was the grandson of that Mayan who had the scroll in Honduras. I didn't get the whole story, but apparently Klaus and Jose—the leader of the Cruzados—tricked him into stealing the scroll."

More treachery, Justine thought.

The lieutenant said, "You were right, we did get transferred to another ship, the *Ultio*. It's a space yacht, with some upgrades. It's in dock."

"I assume the *Diana* is lost, then."

The lieutenant nodded, then said, "We did an inventory of the computers in the lab. Most were destroyed in the fight, and if there were any data backups, we can't find them. There's no way to retrieve Klaus's work."

"Did you find the scroll?"

The lieutenant shook his head. "No sign of it. It may have been destroyed once Klaus had what he wanted from it."

"Well," Justine said, "we'll just have to trust that our scientists can reverse engineer ... me."

He looked uncomfortable with reciting the next portion of his report, and it was only after Justine prodded him that he spoke.

"We've removed all the bodies; they're in cold storage."

"Clive?"

"Yeah. Him too. I'm so sorry about that," Lieutenant Jeffries said, gently placing a consoling hand on her shoulder.

"Never mind," Justine said, pushing her feelings deep down. She would think about it another time, when she was more capable of dealing with it. "Did you contact home?"

The lieutenant cocked his head and made an inscrutable face. "It's about a five-minute delay in EPS transmissions, so we don't have the whole story. I've got Private Genero in the communication room. So far, though, it looks like we're going to be on our own."

Justine stood up. "What?"

"Colonel Gagne said it all started with a crackdown in Honduras. Apparently, the Cruzados down there kidnapped the old Mayan and Michael Sanderson, and killed a U.S. national, George Markowitz. Mr. Sanderson managed to escape with the Mayan. The Honduran military moved in and put down the rebels. Apparently, the three of them figured out what was so important about the ancient scroll—probably that the formula for … making someone like you … was in there all along."

"My God," Justine said. "George."

Jeffries took a breath and continued: "But that information was leaked, and now most of the world country corporations know that someone has worked out the solution to Kinemet. Both the People's Republic of China and the Arabic Consortium are howling mad."

"The Arabs?" Justine said.

"I guess since most countries have stopped using oil for fuel, they're scrambling for a way to get back on top. They've issued ultimatums to share the technology under threat of hostilities. The world is in gridlock at the moment. Everyone's borders are closing. There's talk of war."

It took a moment for Justine to process that, but her thoughts returned to George Markowitz. She'd met him a few times. Another senseless death. And there would be many more if matters continued down their current path.

"So," Lieutenant Jeffries said. "What's the plan, boss? We sit here and wait?"

"Did Colonel Gagne give any specific orders?"

"Nothing other than to secure and defend the Kinemet. He's waiting on higher-ups to make a decision."

"In that case, I'd rather not sit around here waiting and doing nothing. Why don't we load this container back on the *Ultio* and head back to CS3?"

The lieutenant looked surprised. "CS3? Why there?"

"You remember that boy we brought on board before the hijacking?"

"Alex, the one you told me to forget about?"

Justine nodded. "Yeah, well, he's in trouble, and I think the only way to save him is with that Kinemet."

"There's only four of us and over forty of the rebels," Lieutenant Jeffries said. "I'm not sure we can handle all of them on a trip back."

"There's enough food and water here on the observatory for at least a few weeks or so; enough time for the U.S. Space Corp. to get up here and take care of them."

Lieutenant Jeffries raised an eyebrow, looking unsure.

Justine stood up and patted the top of the container. She smiled.

"Well, are you heading my way?" she asked. "Wanna lift?"

Canada Station Three :
Lagrange Point 4 :
Earth Orbit :

Although Michael wanted to work through the sixteen-hour flight from Nova Scotia to CS3, he fell into a deep exhausted sleep soon after launch and didn't wake up until the ship began to slow on approach.

While Yaxche had found the skybus trips from Honduras to Toronto and from Toronto to Yarmouth horrifying experiences, he seemed to really take to space travel. After all, there was no turbulence in space.

Michael found him in the forward observation lounge, sitting on a comfortable sofa bench, watching as the two-kilometer-wide space station slowly grew larger and larger as they got closer. There were twenty or so other people in the room, all watching in companionable silence and mesmerized appreciation.

"I could not take my eyes off the Earth as we left," Yaxche said into his translator when Michael sat down beside him. "I have seen videos from my grandson's pocket computer, but it is not the same. I am a simple man from a simple village." He pointed to the massive space station. "This is like something from a dream. It is no wonder the gods reside out here."

"It's addictive, being in space." Michael crossed one leg over the other and leaned back, sharing in the moment. "I've only been a few times. I keep forgetting how beautiful it is."

An attendant entered the room and quickly set his eyes on Michael. He approached and leaned closer. In a soft voice he said, "You have a call from Earth, sir."

"All right, thank you," Michael said, and with a smile to Yaxche, he got up and followed the attendant to a communication booth.

∞

It was Calbert.

"I don't know if you've scanned the newsblogs yet," the CEO of Quantum Resources said, "but the survivors of the *Diana* have contacted Earth."

"Survivors!" Michael said, his voice loud enough that a few other passengers who were taking calls turned their heads at the sound. His face flushed red, not from embarrassment, but from anger and worry.

"Four of the Americans, including Major Justine Turner, managed to overpower a band of Cruzados on the abandoned Venus orbital, Lucis Observatory, and recover the stolen Kinemet."

Michael breathed a sigh of relief that Justine was alive, but a thousand questions flooded his mind. He bit his tongue until Calbert was finished with his story.

"It looks like the Cruzados were led by Klaus Vogelsberg and Trent Gruber. Klaus was killed in the firefight, but they managed to capture Gruber alive."

"Klaus?" Michael hadn't heard that name for years, and had completely dismissed him from his memory.

"Yeah. Apparently, he's been trafficking in information all this time since the *Quanta* hijacking, and over the years managed to set up a network of contacts throughout Earth and the Moon. That fits in with your theory of who was behind all this. He somehow recruited the Cruzados to his cause, as well as quite a few others. They're cleaning house on Luna Station as we speak."

It did explain things, but there was obviously much more to the story. "Are they sending a rescue mission?"

"Not right away," Calbert said. "The prisoners are secured on the observatory, and Major Turner and the American soldiers are on their way to CS3—they're using Klaus' ship, the *Ultio*. We're assuming the *Diana* has been disintegrated by the Sun."

"Did you find out what Klaus was doing there?"

Calbert shook his head. "If the Americans know, they're keeping silent about it so far. Especially since the People's Republic of China has filed an official complaint with the United Earth Corporate Council against USA, Inc."

"The Chinese? On what grounds?" Michael asked.

"Can you believe it? They're citing the Nuclear Ban Treaty of '42."

Michael blinked. "I don't see how that's relevant."

"Well, Kinemet is based on nuclear technology. They demanded that we prove we aren't using it to make weapons."

"That's ludicrous!" Michael said.

With a shrug, Calbert lifted his eyebrows. "There are a lot of country corporations who feel they've been excluded from the technology. With everything that's been happening on Earth, there's renewed interest in new developments. No one wants to get left behind. The Council is convening an emergency session. Talk from SMD is the motion might be ratified. It's a political move."

Michael didn't like the sound of that. He wasn't against sharing technology; if humankind was able to fully develop reliable interstellar travel, he believed everyone on Earth should be a part of it and benefit. However, international corporate politics was renowned for its sluggish pace. Before anyone could move forward with any more research or development, the technology could be tied up for years or decades while the some oversight committee decided whether Kinemet was a danger or not.

"You think they can get it ratified?" he asked tentatively.

"Yes. Who knows, maybe they're trying to develop interstellar travel independently and don't want the competition."

Michael asked, "You think they may have been helping Klaus?"

"I don't know. Our 'big brother' to the south isn't offering up any information to us at this point. Perhaps you can see what you can get out of Major Turner when she arrives. She should be there sometime tomorrow. The Canadian Space Forces have offered protective services for the time being. I know their commander; I'll see about getting you clearance to meet with the Americans."

"Thanks, Calbert," Michael said.

"Oh," Calbert said just before severing the connection. "I also talked to the provost officer on CS3 and got him to release Kenny. Technically, he did break Quantum Resources protocol by not registering his activities—and we'll talk to him about that later—but he swears he was only taking readings. Whatever happened to Alex, it was something completely different."

With a nod, Michael said, "We're going to be docking in an hour or so. I'll call ahead and see if Kenny will meet us at the port. I'd like to get the full story straight from the horse's mouth."

"Sounds good. I'll contact you later tomorrow when we have more information."

"See you later." Michael closed the connection and hurried back to the lounge to watch the final approach with Yaxche.

∞

While he waited for his luggage to be unloaded and brought to him on the conveyor on CS3, Michael listened as Kenny explained what had happened that night in his apartment with Alex.

"...and then he twitched and went into a coma. Only," the physicist added after a moment, "Doctor Amma says it's more of an extreme fugue state than a coma. He responds to stimuli, and appears to be awake. His consciousness, however, is not there."

Yaxche, who was listening to the explanation through his translator, said, "He is on a spirit walk."

Kenny, looking genuinely worried, asked, "Raymond said you might be able to help him; can you?"

"I will try," Yaxche said.

As Michael grabbed the bags when they passed near him, Kenny said, "They have him hooked up to IVs and they've even tried to force-feed him. But he's fading away. The doctor's explanation is that he was in remission the last few weeks, but it was only temporary. Now, whatever deteriorating disease was afflicting him before is back."

He added, "And it's progressing."

∞

It took a lot of fast talking to convince the medical staff in the infirmary to give Yaxche the privacy he needed to see if any of his rituals (Michael called them naturalistic procedures when explaining it to Dr. Amma) would help bring Alex out of his state.

Dr. Amma wasn't buying it, and in the end, Michael had to place another call to Calbert and get him to authorize their attempt.

Michael and Kenny stood in the room, watching as Yaxche pulled a few accoutrements out of the bag he had brought with him from Honduras, including a hand-carved headdress decorated with feathers, and a shawl woven with sea shells and bone. He produced two wooden sticks that rattled when he placed them beside Alex's supine form.

Part of Yaxche's traditional rituals required the use of fire to help lift spirits to the heavens, but he said he would make do with some candles and incense.

Alex looked gaunt and aged. Though his eyes were open, they stared blankly out of darkened sockets. He seemed to breath normally, but made barely discernible moaning noises once in a while. When Michael grasped the boy's hand, it felt cold and listless.

"I must enter the spirit world of dreams," Yaxche told them once he had everything arranged. "Then I will try to commune with the Sky Traveler. It may take a long time. Please make sure we are not disturbed."

Michael regarded the old Mayan levelly for half a minute, waiting for the ritual to begin, when Kenny tapped him on the arm. "I think he means he wants us out of here, too."

Yaxche gave them a toothy grin, and waited patiently for Michael and Kenny to leave the room before turning back around.

Outside, Michael looked indecisive.

"Uh," Kenny said, clearing his throat. "Raymond said they've finished the initial analysis of the Song of the Stars and have transmitted the data to our computers. Do you mind if I go and have a look at it?"

Michael smiled and checked the time on the wall holoslate. "Sure thing. I think I'll go get a bite to eat and wait for the *Ultio* to dock."

But Kenny, ever the scientist, was already halfway down the hall before Michael finished his sentence.

∞

Michael didn't have to wait long. He was in the waiting area of the docking port for less than a half an hour before the overhead monitors flicked on to announce the arrival of the *Ultio*.

It took a few minutes for them to complete docking procedures, and when the gates opened to allow the passengers to disembark, Michael stepped up to greet the survivors.

Before he took two steps, however, a small fireteam of Canadian Space Force soldiers, armed with ion pulse rifles, came marching down the hall.

Before the Luna Station incident with Chow Yin, Canada Station

Three only had a small contingent of five peace officers whose primary role was to keep the seasonal space miners in order when they had come aboard for shore leave. Breaking up a bar fight was the most action many of them had ever seen.

Since then, however, the military had sent up a thirty-six-man platoon of soldiers to bolster internal defense and to provide added security for any international visitors to the station.

Michael didn't recognize any of the soldiers, but they obviously knew who he was. When they got closer, they veered toward him, and the first man lifted his right hand in a salute.

"Sir," he said. "Master Corporal Bixby."

Dully, Michael raised his hand in an attempt to return the salute. "Michael Sanderson."

"Sir," the master corporal said in a clipped military tone, "we've been assigned to escort the American hijack survivors during their stopover on the station. The Minister of SMD informed us you would also be accompanying them."

"Oh?" Michael frowned. "Do you think they are at risk?"

The soldier gave a quick shake of his head and a cursory smile. "Just a precaution, sir."

When the main door to the docking bay opened, Michael glanced over and saw Justine and three men—all looking as if they had been through a warzone—enter and step up to the identiscan one at a time.

Once they were processed and cleared, Justine approached Michael, fighting through a weary grin with a wide smile. She gave him a hug, which he returned with as much emotion as hers.

At first, Michael hadn't noticed, but Justine did not have her optilink or her PERSuit harness on, yet she had spotted him right away and walked toward him unwaveringly.

"Justine?" Although his first instinct was to ask how she was and tell her he was glad she was safe, he found himself blurting out, "Can you *see?*"

She let out a short laugh and smiled at him. "I am still blind … but, yes, I *can* see."

"What—?" He stared into both of her eyes one after another. There was no detectible change in her irises. Her eyes were unfocused, distant.

Justine patted him on the arm. "I'll explain later. Can we go see Alex right now?"

Michael shook his head. "Soon. Yaxche's with him." He detected a sudden pained look in Justine's expression. They needed someplace private to talk; he was acutely aware of over a dozen pairs of eyes watching him.

"Um, is everyone all right?" He looked at each of the American soldiers in turn. One of them looked quite banged up; several bruises were evident on his cheek and forehead. The lieutenant was favoring his arm, and the last soldier had one eye swollen shut.

The master corporal quickly introduced himself to Justine and the others, and said, "We have an area set aside in the infirmary. If you'll all follow me, we'll get you patched up and fed a hot meal. Then you can contact home to make your debriefing. I've been told there are several USA, Inc. directors and NASA officials gathering at the capital to listen in."

"I'm fine," Justine said to him. "I don't need any medical attention. If it's all the same to you, I'd like to confer with Mr. Sanderson while you see to the others." She moved her head towards Lieutenant Jeffries, who nodded his assent.

Master Corporal Bixby called one of his men closer. "Private Ludwig, here, will escort you to our headquarters. We have a conference room set up for the debriefing if you want to use it." He regarded Michael with a calculating look. "But we also have a few smaller offices, if you prefer."

Justine and Michael followed the private while four of the Canadian soldiers took up positions around the entrance to the dock where the *Ultio* was, and the remaining men led the American soldiers to the medical section.

∞

"Are we safe to talk here?" Justine asked once Michael closed the door to a small office. Some thoughtful person had brought in a carafe of coffee and a plate of sandwiches and veggies.

Michael watched as Justine deftly reached for a carrot stick and bit into it with a snap.

"Reasonably," he said in answer. "So, you first. You can see...?"

"What I'm about to say is probably going to be classified as soon as we report back home." Justine sat down and took a deep breath. "Klaus figured out the formula to convert a human into a Kinemat.

464

And," she added with a dramatic pause, "I am proof of it."

"What? Proof? You mean you're——?" A hundred questions all tried to pour out of his mouth at the same time. Michael found a seat and eased himself into it, all the while never taking his eyes off Justine. "Maybe you should start at the beginning."

She did, and relayed everything that had transpired from the moment they had been hijacked to arriving back on CS3, including that they hadn't been able to locate the scroll.

When she finished her story, Justine said, "Colonel Gagne was pissed when he found out we were heading here and not back to Earth. I told him we were running low on fuel. He didn't believe me, but what choice did he have but to arrange for our berthing here?"

"Why did you come here?" Michael asked.

"I knew Alex was in trouble. When I was in a quantized state, I could sense that his consciousness was separated from his physical body."

"Yes." Michael nodded. "And since he's fallen into that fugue state, his body is deteriorating. Yaxche says he's trying to communicate with Alex, to see if he can draw him back. Don't ask me to explain how. I'm not even sure I believe in that kind of mysticism, but I don't have any other ideas. You wouldn't have come here unless you did have a notion. What is it?"

"Before I tell you that, it's your turn," Justine said. "Catch me up. I've been isolated for a week."

"I know the feeling," Michael said cryptically, and then told Justine what had happened in her absence.

Starting with the EPS from Alex when he went through his first fugue, Michael recounted the events up to their capture and escape in Honduras. When he spoke of George's death, his words caught in his throat, and he poured himself another cup of coffee.

"The political situation on Earth has been worsening over the past few days," he said in conclusion. "People aren't dumb. They've figured out there are developments in the area of Kinemet, and are demanding to be brought in. The world economy is in tatters; viable interstellar travel could be a shot in the arm—whether or not there are *others* out there. If the country corporations on Earth knew just how far those developments have gone, it could get worse. Are you going to tell your superiors that you've been transformed?"

After a moment, Justine took a deep breath. "I'm no diplomat, and

I have no desire to be," she said. "I'll make my report and leave policy to them. Meanwhile, we need to help Alex, and time is running out in more than one way. As I said before, once I make my report to the USA, Inc. Board, the cat will be out of the bag. We'll all go into lockdown, and then it might well be too late for Alex."

"What do you mean?" Michael asked. "Do you know something because of ... what's happened to you?"

"I think so." She stood up and paced, gathering her thoughts. "I haven't had a lot of time to explore my new gifts, but, whenever I used any of the extranormal abilities, I could tell that I was using the Kinemetic radiation as a fuel. It worked before, and bringing Alex in proximity of Kinemet might reinvigorate him once more. I know, when I ran out of the radiation, I felt an uncontrollable hunger. I think, if I didn't charge myself with Kinemet, my health would also deteriorate like Alex's."

"So you think bringing him close to some Kinemet will snap his consciousness back?" Michael asked.

Justine shrugged. "Maybe. I think it's worth a shot."

"There's no way we can unload the Kinemet here," he said, thinking out loud. "If any of the station's security sees it, they'll report it to our government. And if we move Alex out of the infirmary, the nurses will sound an alert." Michael chewed on his bottom lip.

"It's a good thing I planned ahead," Justine said. She reached into her pocket and brought out a small control pad. "Klaus gave me the idea. He used a Kinemetic damper on me to stop me from being able to use my abilities. I figured if I was leaking any radiation at the security station, they'd notice, so I rigged up a localized damper to hide myself. And—" She reached into her other pocket and pulled out a small disc of metal attached to a gold chain. "—some Kinemet, disguised as a locket if anyone searched me. This should be enough to irradiate Alex. At least long enough to figure out our next step."

Michael stood up. "Then what are we waiting for?"

∞

On the way back to the medical area, Michael stopped at a communications kiosk and called Kenny at the QR lab. The scientist answered almost right away, but he seemed annoyed at the interruption until he recognized his caller.

"Yes, Mr. Sanderson?"

"Just call me Michael. How are you coming along on the scroll data from Raymond? And I hope you've made redundant backups of everything."

"Of course," Kenny said, pursing his lips in annoyance at the suggestion. "All data is backed up continually."

"Just checking," Michael said, putting up an apologetic hand. "What have you found?"

"We're working on the theory of pitch and frequency. Perhaps Kinemet *is* sensitive to sound vibrations."

"Try converting sound frequencies to light frequencies."

"That's not really a valid physics methodology. There's no direct correlation to—" Kenny's face froze in mid-word as it dawned on him. "It worked, didn't it?" His eyes widening, he said, "Someone solved it, didn't they? It worked on one of the Americans?"

"That's all I can tell you for now," Michael said, suppressing a grin. "We're heading down to the infirmary to see Alex. You can reach me there."

He didn't even have time to say a farewell before Kenny cut the connection, most likely off to run some computer simulations.

∞

They stopped outside the door to Alex's room, and Michael gently knocked before opening it a crack. He didn't want to break Yaxche's concentration, but his caution was not necessary. The old Mayan was sitting on a guest chair in the corner, head drooped from exhaustion. He looked up when Michael entered.

"I had a dream," he said, then noticed Justine. "Hello, Sky Traveler. I saw you in my dream."

"Uh," Michael said. "This is Justine. She was captain of the ship that rescued Alex on Pluto. Justine, this is Yaxche."

She stepped forward and clasped both of her hands around Yaxche's. "I'm so sorry to be the one to tell you this," she started to say.

"My grandson has passed from the world," the old Mayan said, as if he already knew the fact of it. He kept a stoic face, but there was a tightening around his eyes, and he looked away as he lost the fight to hold back a tear.

Justine said, "He died saving my life." Though she did not have the ability to see out of her eyes, they nevertheless conveyed what the sacrifice meant to her.

Yaxche squeezed her hand and nodded. "I would not expect any less. Te'irjiil was a good boy."

"You'll have to tell me about him."

Yaxche nodded. "Yes. We will sit together some time and I will tell you his story."

Justine pressed her lips together and nodded. Then she turned to where Alex lay in the bed and said, "Let's see if this works, shall we?"

She withdrew the amulet of Kinemet and placed it on Alex's chest, tucking his hospital gown up over the metal.

The diagnostic machine beside the bed blipped as Alex's vitals immediately shot up. His pulse quickened, and his vital stats normalized.

Michael quickly leaned over and looked into Alex's eyes, but there was no dilation of his pupils.

"He looks better," Justine said in a soft voice. "It seems to take a few hours for us to fully charge." She shook her head and lifted one side of her mouth in a half-smile. "I say it like we're batteries or something."

But after several more minutes passed, there was no sign that Alex's consciousness had come back to reside in him. The body on the bed was still a hollow shell.

Realizing that Yaxche had not related the details of his dream to them, Michael turned to him. "Is this going to work?"

Ever patient, Yaxche had resumed his position on the chair. The translator did its best to convey the meaning of his words: "The metal of the heavens will heal the body, but not the spirit. The Sky Traveler has always been two parts of a whole. The spirit half is frightened, and has run to the safest hiding place it knows."

Michael asked, "And where is that?"

"In my dream I saw a small station like this one, looking upon three suns."

Michael guessed, "The Centauri System."

Before he could say any more, Dr. Amma raced into the room with a nurse and two attendants. She stopped short when she saw Yaxche in his ceremonial dress.

Michael noticed Justine, who was standing next to Alex, deftly reach her hand down and grab the Kinemet disc.

"What's going on in here?" Dr. Amma demanded. "The monitors went berserk and—" She spotted Alex, looking hale and breathing steadily once more, and rushed to his side. Quickly, she took his vitals manually, and then looked between Michael, Justine and Yaxche.

"I don't understand it. All of his signs seem normal. But he's still in a fugue state. What did you do?"

Shaking his head, Michael said, "Uh, nothing. We were just standing here, talking."

The doctor motioned to the nurse. "I need to run some tests. Can you bring me the sequencer?" Then she shooed the three of them out with a wave of her hand.

∞

In the waiting room, they were on the verge of sitting down when one of the receptionists stepped into view.

"Michael Sanderson?" she asked.

"That's me."

"There's a call for you. I can transfer it to the kiosk over there."

"Thank you," he said, and quickly went over.

The call was from Calbert, and he looked harried.

Michael asked, "What's going on? Is everything all right?"

"No. The United Earth Corporate Council has granted an injunction against all Kinemet experiments until it can determine if it represents a risk to the safety of the world population."

Unable to believe what he was hearing, Michael opened his mouth, but couldn't form any words.

Calbert said, "Yeah. Happened real fast."

"And they have unanimous support?"

"Almost. The only country corporations opposed were USA, Inc., Canada Corp. and the German Federation."

"Germany?"

"The rumor mill is working overtime. Apparently, word got out who was behind the hijacking of the *Diana*, and the Federation denounced Klaus as a disavowed citizen working on his own. They're just covering their bases."

"That's one word for it."

"As soon as we receive the official notice," Calbert continued, "we are obligated to quarantine the QR Labs on CS3."

"What about our Earth-based research sites?" Michael could feel his face flush with outrage.

"They're focusing on CS3 for now. It's a smokescreen. Someone thinks we've unlocked the technology. And they're right—Raymond says Kenny thinks he has a workable theory. We could be less than a few months away from human trials."

"Not if they shut us down," Michael said in a grumble.

Calbert pitched his voice lower. "It gets worse. The Arabic Conglomerates have proposed sending a team of observers from Luna Station to ensure we're following the UECC's edict."

Michael couldn't believe his ears. "What?"

"They're already on their way. Due to arrive in about six hours."

"You have to do something to stop them. What does Ottawa say?"

Calbert tilted his head. "Cooperate. We're under scrutiny from the world court. If we balk at this point, we're admitting we've been hoarding the technology."

Grinding his teeth, Michael said, "If they start snooping around, they'll find out about Alex and everything else…"

He narrowed his eyes. "Calbert, I have to go. I have an idea, and I don't think you're going to like it. If we—"

"No," Calbert said. "Don't tell me. I can see the wheels spinning. Whatever you're going to do, I need to be able to deny knowledge of it."

That made Michael smile for the first time during the conversation. "All right. If you don't hear from me, then it worked."

"Good luck."

Michael cut the connection and quickly strode back to the waiting room where Yaxche and Justine were speaking in quiet tones. They looked up at him as he approached.

He summarized what was happening, and said, "Justine, I can't involve you in this, but I have to get Alex, Kenny and all our Kinemet research away from the Arabian observers."

It did not take her long to figure out his plan, and she put her own spin on it. "Getting us off the station is only half of it. Alex needs more Kinemet, and I know where there is a tidy little stockpile."

Michael noted her use of the word 'us' and he felt a swell of pride.

Justine said, "Turnabout is fair play. How do you feel about commandeering a pirate ship?"

Yaxche gave them that amused grin as he listened to the translation.

Canada Station Three :
Lagrange Point 4 :
Earth Orbit :

Justine knew the assembled Board of Directors for USA, Inc., as well as representatives for NASA and a few generals of the U.S. Armed Forces, would be waiting for her to report to the conference room and link back to Earth with an A/V EPS within the hour. This was only the first of several problems.

She needed to stall for time, but she needed help.

As the three of them neared the infirmary, she said, "We need to take a quick detour."

Michael turned his head to her, though he didn't break stride. "Oh?"

"Lieutenant Jeffries and the others should be in here somewhere. Let's see how they're doing."

About to say something, Michael closed his mouth and gave her a slight nod.

They found the lieutenant in one of the rooms where his men where convalescing. Private Genero had a cast on one arm, and Private Hodges had several stitches on his forehead. Only one of the Canadian soldiers stood post outside, and he saluted as the three of them passed by.

The lieutenant stood up as they entered and gave Justine a bright smile. The other two started to rise, but Justine waved them back down.

"Hello, Major," Lieutenant Jeffries said. "We're just waiting for one of the doctors to clear us, and then we're ready for the debriefing."

"That's what I'd like to talk to you about," she said. "I want you to go to the meeting, but tell them I can't make it."

"Pardon me, ma'am?"

"Just say that there are some health complications from my being held hostage, and the doctors are keeping me here overnight for observation."

The lieutenant could clearly see there was nothing wrong with Justine physically, and his eyes narrowed in suspicion.

"Something more important has come up," Justine said. "I can't tell you what it is, but unless you help me with this, everything we went through on Venus will be for nothing."

He blinked, then made a decision. "Of course I'll help."

"Thank you," she said, and then spoke to the two privates. "How about you? Are you up for the job?"

"Yes, ma'am," said Private Genero, and Private Hodges nodded as well.

"Good," she said, "because I'm going to need one of you to be a dummy."

Private Genero opened his mouth in surprise, but no words came out. Justine smiled at him.

Lieutenant Jeffries laughed. "I think you just volunteered, Vic."

"If you can spare Private Hodges," Michael said, "I might need some help in the QR Labs."

"Wouldn't Calbert or Raymond have already contacted Kenny?" Justine asked.

"Yeah." Michael gave her an odd look. "But I have a crazy notion I need to run by him."

Justine nodded. "All right," she said to them. "Here's the plan…"

∞

Justine waited for Lieutenant Jeffries to step out of the room and speak to the Canadian soldier posted at the door.

She shifted her sight to the hall and watched.

"Private Johnson," the lieutenant said to the young man. "Can you show me the way to the conference room you set up at your headquarters?"

"Uh, just you? Sir?"

"Unfortunately, my men haven't been cleared medically yet, and I can't wait any longer."

"Yes, sir," the private said, and led Lieutenant Jeffries away.

Justine snapped herself back into the room and nodded to Michael and Private Hodges. "You're good to go."

Michael grinned and left the room with the private in tow.

To Yaxche and Private Genero, Justine said, "Let's get set up."

∞

Dr. Amma was the only member of the medical staff in Alex's room when Justine entered. She was silently tapping and swirling her fingers around the haptic control on her holoslate, updating her patient's chart.

"How is he?" Justine asked in a quiet voice.

The doctor glanced up quickly, and then resumed typing. "If I believed in that kind of thing, I would call it a miracle. It's another complete remission. Physiologically, he's in perfect condition. But it's like his mind has shut down. It's unprecedented."

She continued updating her notes, and it seemed to Justine that she was there for the long haul.

Although she needed to be careful when using her Kinemetic talents, in case the station's sensors detected any anomalies, Justine, with a bare flicker of thought, focused her electropathy on the doctor's holoslate.

The screen went dead and Dr. Amma jerked her hand back. She shook the tablet, and when that didn't do anything, she tapped the power node a few times.

"Damn," she cursed. "If you'll pardon me. I need to find another holoslate." With an annoyed set to her face, she hurried out.

Justine watched her disappear down the hall, then signaled in the other direction. Yaxche pushed Private Genero ahead of him in a wheelchair. The private was dressed in a hospital robe and let his head, wrapped with a single bandage that covered half of his face, hang forward, as if he were sleeping.

A duty nurse glanced over as they slowly wheeled their way down the hall, and just as quickly dismissed them.

Once the two were inside Alex's room, Private Genero got out of his robe and pulled the bandage off his head. With his good arm, he helped Justine dress Alex in the costume and put him in the wheelchair. Then the private arranged himself in Alex's bed.

"You have to relax," Justine said as she reached for the diagnostic cables still suctioned to Alex's chest.

After a moment, Private Genero nodded. "All right. I'm good."

In a single deft movement, Justine transferred the sensor from Alex to Private Genero, and the diagnostic monitor blipped only once.

Yaxche once again took up duty as wheelchair navigator, and pushed Alex out into the hall.

"Thank you," Justine said to Private Genero. "And if they try to give you any trouble, just tell them you were under orders and had no idea what was going on."

"It's the truth," Private Genero said with a smile. "Good luck, ma'am."

Justine gave him one more smile, and then followed after Yaxche.

∞

Things had been progressing according to plan, but as she and Yaxche made their way across the station to the port, their luck took a turn for the worse.

Several uniformed men where hurrying about, setting up a perimeter. Justine couldn't see any civilians in the area.

"Sorry, folks," one soldier said, spotting the trio. "We have orders to seal off the area for the rest of the day. If you had a flight, it's been postponed until tomorrow."

"No, we were just going for a walk," Justine said, and smiled benignly. She turned back around and cursed under her breath.

They went back to the main corridor. Yaxche watched her patiently as they walked.

Stepping closer to a communications kiosk, she tried to connect with QR Labs.

A harried looking receptionist answered. "Can I help you?"

"Michael Sanderson, please."

"I'm sorry. He's already left."

Justine pressed her lips together. "By himself?"

The receptionist clearly looked uncomfortable answering the question, but she said, "No, he was with Kenny and a soldier. They were—" Her head moved closer to the camera. "Are you Major Turner?"

"Yes."

"Oh, I'm sorry I didn't recognize you. Mr. Sanderson left a message in case you called. He said..." She glanced to another screen as if to check her notes. "...'Look for me.'"

The receptionist wrinkled her nose. "I don't know what that means."

"Thank you," Justine said, and severed the connection.

Using her *sight* to find one person out of the hundreds on the station would be like looking for the proverbial needle in a haystack, so Michael wouldn't have said that unless he knew she could home in on him somehow.

She took a deep breath and expanded her senses out, and almost right away sensed the signature pattern of an object irradiated from Kinemet.

Focusing on it, she *saw* Michael, Kenny and Private Hodges pushing a large trolley down the cargo hall two floors beneath her. There was something mechanical on the trolley, but it was covered with a black plastic sheet. Whatever it was, it had come into contact with Kinemet at some point.

She quickly scanned the route to the loading area. There were scatterings of workers, but there was no sign of any soldiers.

"Come on," she said in a low voice to Yaxche. "We're going in the back door."

∞

When she reached the main loading bay doors of the port, Michael and the others were already there waiting.

"I hoped you'd figure it out," he said to her, and patted the object on the trolley.

"What is it?"

Kenny answered, "It's a prototype quantum drive. Fully functional. We just need fuel and a few hours to hook it to the ship's main systems."

"Where'd you get a quantum drive?"

Kenny smiled. "Don't forget, Quantum Resources designed the first engine. We were working on an improved version just before you Americans sold your share of Quantum Resources to Canada Corp." He said it as if he had been a part of the process. Obviously, Kenny felt that the actual date of his enrollment in the company was irrelevant to his personal investment in the organization.

Justine turned to Michael. "You're not bringing it aboard just to hide it from the UECC and the Arabs, are you?"

"No," he replied, a wild grin on his face. "We've got a ton of Kinemet, a quantum drive, and a pressing need to bring Alex's body and consciousness back together. You heard Yaxche: Alex's essence is in a world with three suns. What do you say, are you up for it?"

Justine let out a low whistle at the notion. "We have an untested ship, an untested light-speed drive and an untested pilot. Talk about flying blind." She gave a little bob of her head and a quick laugh. "Of course I'm up for it."

∞

They raised a few heads on their way across the deck to where the *Ultio* waited, but they quickly went back to work. Justine was certain they had far too much to do clearing a bay for the unexpected ship to worry about two uniformed soldiers and two scientists wheeling cargo around.

She was sure someone would ask why they had a Mayan in ceremonial garb following them while they pushed someone in a wheelchair, but they were not stopped.

They arrived at the air-locked loading bridge, which was attached to the ship like a long umbilical, traversed its length, and once they reached the end, Justine and Private Hodges turned the latch to raise the bay door. They all helped maneuver the Quantum Engine inside and back to the engine room.

Justine led the private back to the loading bridge.

"Are you up for one more task?"

"Yes, ma'am," he said.

"If we pull this off, pretty much every country corp., news agency, and police force in Sol System will call us traitors or pirates. I want you to do me a favor—and this goes for Lieutenant Jeffries and Private Genero as well."

"Anything."

"Don't defend us."

He looked startled. "Pardon me?"

"If you stick up for us, it will incriminate you. I appreciate everything you guys have done, but the last thing I want is for them to prosecute you. I told Private Genero to say he knows nothing; he was just following orders. Same for you."

"I can't do that," he protested.

"Yes you can. You could even tell them I threatened your life. Maybe you three will get lucky and get through this without a court-martial."

His voice tight with emotion, Private Hodges nodded. "Yes, ma'am. Understood."

She smiled at him. "Good. Now go find the nearest peace officer and report us to him."

∞

Canada Station Three was primarily a launching point for Canada's Space Mining Division. It's secondary function was as a scientific complex with various wings of the station leased out to interested country corporations who might not have the resources to build their own orbital.

Acting as a waypoint for flights between the Earth and the Moon was a distant third in the station's mandate.

There was usually a considerable amount of traffic to and from the station, and it was tightly monitored.

When Justine prepped the ion engines of the *Ultio,* and disengaged the electronic couplings from the loading bridge, it was less than a minute before flight control buzzed in.

"Uh, hello, *Ultio.* This is CS3 Port Control. You have *not* been cleared for disembarkation. Please identify yourself."

Yaxche, sitting in the navigator's chair, looked at Justine to see what she would do.

Instead of answering the call, Justine continued monitoring the ship systems and adjusting power levels.

Michael and Kenny were in the engine room, attempting to install the Quantum Engine. Justine had secured Alex in the captain's quarters, and had placed the disc of Kinemet back on his chest.

The port officer spoke with authority. "Please be advised: If you do not identify yourself, we will have no choice but to report your ship. You will be interdicted at any space port you attempt to reach. This is your last warning."

Yaxche motioned to the speaker. "It is not polite to ignore someone who is talking to you."

Justine made a face. "I'm sorry, Yaxche. I'm just a little too busy at the moment."

"May I?" he asked, and Justine nodded in mild surprise. She pointed to the controls on the holoslate.

Yaxche leaned forward, turned the monitor to face him, and tapped the button to turn on the two-way feed.

The port officer blinked, clearly taken aback by what he saw. Yaxche still had not changed out of his ceremonial garb.

"Ahyah," Yaxche said to the man. "Heloo."

Finding his voice, the port officer said, "Who are you?"

Yaxche gave the man a toothy grin and, remembering to speak into his translator, said, "I am Yaxche. I am on a journey to the heavens."

"Uhm. Sir? Are you the only one on board? Can you turn the ship around?"

Yaxche shrugged his shoulders. "I'm sorry, I am not able to do that. This is only the second time I have been in a space ship."

"Sir, did you press something you weren't supposed to?" the man asked. "If there is anyone else on that ship, please get them to the console. You need to turn the ship around, right now."

Yaxche said, "You look upset. Perhaps if you were to practice meditation, you would be happier. I could show you how."

Frustrated, the man opened his mouth to issue another command, but something off the visual range distracted him, and he leaned away for a moment.

When the port officer turned back, his voice took on a stern tone. "Sir. Mr. Yaxche. I don't know if you are in control of the ship or not, but I've just been informed there is an armed spacecraft on approach. Somehow they are aware of your activities and have issued a warning. Turn around and dock now, or they will pursue and open fire—"

At the last, Justine reached over and severed the communications link with CS3, and quickly ran her fingers over a number of holoslates. When the ship's diagnostics did not provide her with the information she wanted, she stepped back, closed her eyes and concentrated.

She used her *sight* to scan in the general direction of the Moon. Her body shook with the effort of straining against the limits of her power, but the oncoming ship was too far away. It was pure instinct that she changed tactic. Although she could not *see* past the hundred and fifty kilometer range, she could sense any refined Kinemet or any object that was irradiated by Kinemet at a much farther distance. Within a minute, she found what she was looking for.

And cursed.

She opened a communications link to the engine room. "Michael. How are you guys coming with the installation?"

His voice was thin, as if he were speaking at a distance away from the microphone. He would have remote activated the communications console. "Uh, we barely got started."

"I don't think it's an Arabian ship," she said, acid in her voice, "and they're not coming from Luna."

"What?"

"I don't know who they are, but they're coming from Venus."

"Venus? Gruber?" Michael asked in speculation.

"I don't know who it is, but they've got weaponized Kinemet on board. I assume it's been loaded into deep-range missiles."

"What?" Michael repeated, and stepped into the video frame. The side of his face was smeared with grease and soot. He had a laser iron in his hand. *"They're* using Kinemet as a nuclear weapon?"

"Yeah," she said. "They know we're on the run, and they know our trajectory. They're coming straight for us. If they fire their missiles and hit us, the explosion will set off a chain reaction in our Kinemet. We'll be vaporized."

"Why would they want to destroy us? Don't they want the chance to get the secret of the Kinemet from us?"

"Not if they've already figured it out and want to shut us up so they can develop the technology first."

Michael cursed. Then he said, "We're going as fast as we can, but the *Ultio* is using a proprietary operating system. Kenny's rewriting code while I install the engine. You're going to have to give us at least a couple more hours before we can patch it in."

"Hold on to something, then," she said. "I'm going to go to maximum acceleration for two minutes—about three g of thrust. It'll take their ship at least an hour to course-correct. That should buy you another hour and a half before they are within missile range."

"Got it." He broke the link, and Justine's hands were a blur on the controls.

To Yaxche, she spoke while she worked. "You'll have to go back and strap Alex in; yourself, too. It's going to be a rough couple of minutes."

"Turbulence?" he asked, his face paling.

"Yeah. Something like that."

∞

Once Justine had ensured all her passengers were secured, she wiggled her fingers over the haptic console and fired the ion propulsion thrusters.

The *Ultio* was basically a reconditioned space yacht, originally designed for the comfort of its passengers. The military-class vessels used by the U.S. Space Corp used a much more powerful hydrogen engine capable of greater thrust, and Justine guessed that the enemy craft was outfitted with something similar, and could easily overtake them.

After two minutes, the *Ultio's* velocity was less than a tenth of what the *Orcus* ships had been capable of.

They were racing against time, and the worst part was, once Justine disengaged the thrusters, she was completely helpless. There was nothing for her to do but wait and hope Michael and Kenny completed their installation before they were all blasted out of space by their pursuers.

Rather than sit up alone in the cockpit and go stir crazy, she decided to head back and check up on Yaxche and Alex. The captain's cabin had a bridge monitoring station, so she could keep an eye on things.

When she got there, she found Yaxche sitting in a short legged chair he had pulled close to the captain's bed. Alex was safely bundled under a web of canvas straps, and though he was perfectly still, his eyes were wide open and unfocused. It was more than a little eerie.

"How's our patient?" she asked in a quiet tone, as if a loud noise could wake Alex. There was a small nook cut into one bulkhead where a short desk and metal bench chair were installed. She sat down on the seat and leaned forward, resting her elbows on her knees.

Yaxche spoke to her, but his eyes were on Alex.

"The spirit world is a sacred place to us. Our priests meditated all their lives in their quest to learn to walk on the path of dreams and commune with the gods. There is a story I remember my grandfather telling me, about one of our holy men who had mastered the gift of entering the spirit world through dreams. He preferred being there to being in our world, and one day he set foot on the path and never returned, though his body remained until his death."

Justine thought about that. "Are you saying that even if we are able to bring Alex to where his essence is anchored, he may not recover? May not want to come back?"

Yaxche closed his eyes and nodded. "It is my fear. The Song of the Stars is a powerful and mesmerizing thing."

He spoke the truth, Justine thought to herself. When she had been in a quantized state back on Venus, she had heard the hauntingly beautiful sound that emanated from the planets in Sol System. Each voice was distinct in a majestic symphony. In one of Yaxche's interviews, he had called it the Music of the Spheres. She suspected this was one way the Kinemats were able to navigate in space.

For a brief moment back then, when Justine had focused her senses outside the limits of Sol System, she had become aware of the pattern of the star beacons she had sensed in the stellar distance. If she closed her eyes, she could almost hear the much more powerful and eternal composition of the Song of the Stars.

If the stars were the ethereal voices that had been calling Alex home all these years, why would he ever consider returning to normal space? It would be like having an opportunity to be in heaven. What could the mortal world ever offer in comparison?

Justine was just too new at this to come up with any conclusions, let alone viable theories on the cosmic impact of her and Alex's transformations. She was not a philosopher or a priest, nor was she a physicist who might better explain what was happening.

"Yaxche," Justine said after a time. "It occurred to me that we never asked if you wanted to come with us. Worst case scenario, we might all die; best case, if we are able to achieve light speed, it will be over four years before we arrive in Centauri. I apologize for not talking with you before."

It was the better part of a full minute before Yaxche replied. "I know my daughter loves me, but she has built a life with her husband and her two daughters. She does not have time for an old man like me. I had hoped my grandson, Te'irjiil, would follow in my footsteps and become a caretaker for the Song of the Stars, but after his poor Itzel passed, he drifted away from everyone. Now that he is gone, I have no reason to remain in this world."

He looked at Alex. "Except for the Sky Traveler. He needs my guidance, and as long as he needs me, I will go where he goes."

They both fell into an introspective silence then, and without Justine really being aware of it, she started to nod off.

She suddenly sprang awake when the remote monitor sounded an alert.

"Here we go," she said to no one in particular, and hurried out.

∞

According to the Pulse-Doppler radar system, the enemy ship was closing in at five-thousand kilometers distance. If Justine remembered correctly, the outside range any of the U.S. Space Corp. missiles could be fired in space and still be guided with any measure of reliable control was about two-thousand kilometers. At the speed difference between the two ships, the enemy would reach optimal firing range in less than ten minutes.

Justine called down to the engine room.

"Heads up. We've got company. How are you coming along?"

After a long span, Michael answered the communication feed. "Physically, it's installed," he said, his eyes showing how exhausted he was. "We calculated how much Kinemet we would need for the trip out there and loaded it in the quantum drive."

"Perfect," she said.

"Kenny's got the initial computer systems up and working, but we're having trouble calibrating the Kinemetic dampers. There's some kind of interface issue. If we can't get it working properly, we'd have a better chance surviving the missile attack." Unnecessarily, he added, "We'd reach our destination only to blow up thirteen seconds later."

"What's the problem?" Justine asked, and endured the harried look Michael gave her.

He scratched at the stubble growing on his jaw. "There's some kind of delay—about seven seconds—between the generator and the Kinemetic damper. With the five additional seconds it takes for the generator to build up enough power to engage the dampers, that won't give you time enough to rematerialize from a quantized state and start the generator in the first place."

Justine laughed, almost too loud, in relieved surprise.

"What?" Michael said.

"There's no re-materialization on my end," she said. "That's the missing piece of the puzzle. I'm fully conscious and aware during quantization. I can start the generator instantly once we arrive. Alex—and the other test candidates—were never fully transformed into a Kinemat, and had no awareness in the quantized state. Seven seconds may not be ideal, but it is more than enough time."

Michael stood there dumbfounded for a moment, then snapped out of it. "All right, then. I'll get Kenny to map the control functions to your console. He'll have to give you a rundown, since it's a patchwork of commands—"

Justine cut him off.

"Damn," she said. "They're not even going to try to parley."

"What?"

She grimaced. "I can sense a quantity of Kinemet hurtling toward us at high velocity. They've launched a missile."

"Warning shot?" Michael said.

"Can't chance it," she said, her voice tight. "Can we engage the quantum drive now?"

Looking off screen a moment, probably at Kenny, Michael finally shook his head. "At least five minutes to finish mapping the controls."

"We'll be atoms in two."

Michael said something more to her, but Justine didn't hear it. She shut all physical awareness from her mind, and concentrated on pushing her *sight* out toward the oncoming ship.

At the speed the radar estimated the missile was traveling—a little over one-hundred kilometers per second— it would breach the distance between her outer limit of *sight* to the *Ultio* in less than two seconds.

There was a chance she could sense it the moment it came within range of her *sight*, and if her reaction time was quick enough, she might be able to detonate the warhead before the reacting Kinemet got too close and triggered their own cache of the metal.

She waited ... and waited...

Like a lightning strike, the Kinemet burst into her awareness, and for a split-second, she faltered and thought she had missed her chance.

Desperately, she sent her electropathic sense on an intercept course with the missile.

The radar on her holoslate blanked as it was overloaded with feedback.

For a moment, she wondered if she had failed.

Then the *Ultio* bucked like an angry bronco, and Justine was flung hard into the bank of controls. The bulkhead screamed and the diagnostic console lit up as hundreds of sensors reported the sudden change in conditions.

"What the hell just happened?" someone screamed through the comlink.

"How's the Kinemet?" Justine called back, holding her hand to the side of her head and struggling back into the pilot's chair.

"Fine." Michael appeared on the comlink, wide-eyed. "Did you just do what I think you did?"

"Yeah," Justine said, still breathing hard. "One warhead destroyed."

"You all right?" he asked.

She nodded, though her head rang from the movement. "But as soon as they realize their missile didn't blow us to space junk, they'll launch two at a time." She shook her head, wincing. "I can't stop two."

Glancing off screen once more, Michael said, "All right. Kenny just finished the final mapping. Check your console. He's labeled all the commands for you. One to start the generator. Another to engage the damper."

"Sounds simple enough," she said, and then sent her *sight* back out.

After a minute, she *saw* what she had feared.

"They've launched two missiles. They really want us dead." She did a quick mental calculation. There was most likely less than five seconds before the missiles impacted with their ship.

…four…

"Kenny," Michael called out immediately. "Are we clear to engage the Drive?"

…three…

"Yeah," he said, his voice sounding muffled. "I labeled it 'GO.'"

…*two*…

Without further prompting, Justine reached her finger toward the haptic console and tapped the command button and—

…*ONE*…

—the universe shifted.

Partial Entry From Omnipedia :
Subject: Alpha Centauri :

Alpha Centauri is a binary star system averaging 4.37 light years from the Sun. The distance between the two stars varies during their 79.91 year orbit. A third star, Proxima Centauri, lays about .21 light years from the Alpha Centauri stars, and the three companions are sometimes referred to as a triple star system, though it is not determined whether Proxima Centauri is gravitationally bound with Alpha Centauri A and B.

Due to the significant gravitational effects of the system, no gas giant planets have formed. There is evidence that one or more minor planetoids or comets may have found their way into the system at some point, and may be orbiting at the outer rim of the system.

In 2095, the first attempt to travel to Alpha Centauri failed. Though the light speed ship *Quanta* completed the journey, a mishap upon arrival in our neighboring system resulted in the destruction of the vessel. The pilot, Captain Alex Manez, survived in an escape pod and returned to our system in mid-2103.

Tap for more…

Alien Space Port :
Alpha Centauri :
Four Years Later

—**After an eternity** of drifting in the purgatory between the material world and the unreality of the quantized state of being, Alex was abruptly ripped back to his corporeal self.

He screamed. The pain tore through his very essence. It was as if every atom in his body had exploded. He couldn't take the agony—

—and in the nanosecond before he passed out, he welcomed the oncoming blanket of oblivion.

∞

Eons later, or moments for all he knew, reality crashed back in as Alex once more regained consciousness. He could feel a bed under him. There was a musty smell wafting up, and a natural brightness permeated his eyelids. He was in his human state.

Disoriented, he tried to sit up, but gentle hands pushed him back down.

"Easy, now," a voice whispered in his ear.

Alex tried to speak, but he couldn't move the muscles in his jaw to open his mouth. He let out a groan.

"Give yourself some time," someone said. It was a woman, and the voice was familiar. Justine. *What is she doing here?*

"You've been gone for a long time," she said.

He tried to open his eyes, but they were lidded shut. He managed to open his mouth finally, and this time was able to croak out a question. "What happened?"

A second voice, one that Alex recognized right away, spoke.

Yaxche said, "Sky Traveler, you have been on a long journey in the spirit world. We did not know if you would come back to us, so we traveled a great distance to find you. Now, you are whole once more."

Fighting against the sudden nausea that rose up as the blood pressure in his head increased, Alex forced his eyes open. It took him a moment to focus, and a few more moments to identify where he was.

He saw Michael, Justine and Yaxche, but his stomach clenched when he realized they were in a cabin on an unfamiliar space yacht.

"Where am I?"

"The *Ultio*," said Michael. He reached out and touched Alex's shoulder. "How are you, my boy? You had us worried."

"I'm fine, I think." Alex's head was clearing, and he was able to sit up without feeling dizzy. "What happened?" He needed to know.

"Well," Michael said, "it seems you fell into some kind of a fugue state, and your consciousness—Yaxche calls it your dream spirit—was anchored in Centauri System. Kenny's theory is there was an energy link between you and the alien space port. Probably from when you were here last. Naturally, your Kinemetic consciousness gravitated here."

Here? Alex's stomach flip-flopped. "Alpha Centauri?" He stared at Michael. "We're in the space port?"

"Outside of it, actually," he said. "We can't figure out how to get in. You seem very upset, Alex."

Alex gulped. "Uh … it's … I mean, the last thing I remember was being on CS3. Now I'm in another solar system. It's just unexpected."

Michael gave him a comforting look. "Trust me, I felt the same way. I didn't experience anything when we were quantized. It was a blink of the eye for us." He glanced at Justine when he said it.

Justine had a playful smile on her face when she asked Alex, "Are you thirsty?" and reached for a squeeze pack of orange juice beside her without looking.

Alex took it when she offered it to him, and as the liquid hit his tongue he realized he was parched. And starving.

But what had just transpired caused him to look at Justine in surprise. She did not have her optilink on, nor her harness. Yet she had passed him the juice without faltering in the least.

"How did you—?" he asked.

She smiled at him. "Use your *sight.*"

He did. "You're … a full Kinemat?" he asked in wonder.

"Yes." A contented smile on her lips, she nodded. "It was Klaus."

She told him about the hijacking and the experiments.

When she finished her tale, Alex asked her, "You were aware the entire trip here?"

There was a particularly distant look on her face when she nodded.

"Yeah," she said. "It was pretty exciting at first, but after four years and however many months, well…" She fell silent for a moment, and there was a reflection of the pain of loneliness on her face.

"Are you able to sleep?" he asked her, wondering if his insomnia was a typical side-effect.

She shook her head. "No. And that took a while to get used to." Justine smiled. "We are the same in every way, except that I am aware during quantization."

Alex, like Michael and every other person who had not been irradiated by charged Kinemet, had no awareness when he was quantized. Again, that proved to him that he was not fully transformed—he was stuck somewhere between human and Kinemat. But he was overjoyed that humankind had made the next step in its chrysalis. Justine had made that transition, though it had been forced on her by Klaus.

Alex asked, "You all came here just for me?"

"Well," Justine said. "That, and we were kind of chased out of Sol System."

Alex sat up straighter. "What?"

"Are you up to hearing the rest of the story?" she asked. "We can wait until you're feeling better."

Alex shook his head. "Other than needing a sandwich or something else to eat, I'm good. Tell me everything."

They did, Justine and Michael taking turns relating everything that had happened since Alex had shifted out of consciousness, right up until they arrived in Centauri.

"About seven hours ago, we arrived in orbit around the small planetoid you described. The one with this system's star beacon," Michael said. "We scanned the area and found the spaceport you told us about. It only took us about five hours to get here. But now we're just hovering outside the structure. We hoped you knew how to get in."

Alex shook his head.

Michael said, "We've just been doing scans of the port. It looks like the hangar is only half of this structure. There's most likely some kind of working and living area on the other side, but we can't detect any signs of life. We think we found a bay door to the hangar, but can't figure out how to open it."

Sometime during the last part of the story, Kenny had arrived. When he spoke, his voice was measured and controlled.

"I managed to rig one of the spectrographic sensors up to the ship's computers. And I got a reading from the Centauri star beacon."

When everyone looked at him blankly, his jaw rippled in frustration at his inability to get his point across. "You see, when we first arrived in Alpha Centauri, the beacon went dormant right away. You know. Once we had come out of light speed."

There was an inscrutable look on his face, but then Alex connected the dots. His eyes widened.

"You were able to link to it now because it's giving off electromagnetic waves. That means—"

"—Someone's coming," Michael and Justine said in unison.

∞

In a group, the four of them rushed out of the cabin and up to the bridge where Kenny had installed the sensors. The spectrographic readout showed an ever-increasing wave signal.

Alex was a little unsteady on his feet, but the food and the hour of rest had done wonders; physically, he was recovering quickly. His heart, however, beat in his chest like a hammer.

Over the past few years, Alex had had plenty of time on his hands to research every aspect of Kinemetic science, and based on the readings he saw, he quickly calculated that whatever the new arrival to the Centauri system was, it would enter normal space in less than five minutes.

Where it would arrive in relation to Centauri's star beacon and the space dock was unknown. The first time Alex had made the trip here, he'd appeared a little over twenty-thousand kilometers away—a very short distance in astronomical terms. The *Ultio* had also arrived at the same location. The average ion drive could propel a ship that far in a couple of hours, but Alex didn't know if it would take the newcomers that long.

He had to tell the others, but couldn't find his voice. Hope and fear both warred within him.

"Are they coming from Sol System?" Kenny asked. "Did they follow us?"

"Impossible," Michael said in answer, though the crease in his brow showed that he had a kernel of doubt.

Kenny nodded his agreement. "The only two agencies with full access to quantum drive schematics are Quantum Resources and NASA. The security checks I had to go through to get access *after* I had been hired were exhaustive. There've been informational leaks and technological espionage before, but never on this level." He glanced at Michael for agreement.

Justine speculated. "Our pursuers had weaponized Kinemet in their warheads. Maybe they've developed the tech on their own."

Kenny turned back to his monitors. "Any geek in their parents' basement can figure out how to do that. It took Quantum Resources years to develop the first functioning quantum drive. Even if these guys managed to mine their own stash of Kinemet, it would be years before they mastered the technology."

Justine countered. "Klaus was able to make a leap ahead of us, and he was just one guy."

Frowning, Kenny gave a terse shake of his head. "He had access to the scroll. I say it's a ship from *out there.*"

"Aliens?" Michael said in a breathless voice, his eyes filled with wonder.

"Well," Kenny said as the graph on the monitor spiked, and then flat-lined, "we're going to find out very soon."

∞

If the new arrival was, indeed, the mysterious warship that had chased the *Ultio* out of Sol System, and they had somehow paralleled Klaus's experiment and created another Kinemat, then Alex and his friends were in trouble.

But the other possibility was potentially worse.

Alex summoned up the courage and, as the four of them stared at the monitor, he said, "I'm so sorry that I never told you the whole truth."

At first, no one reacted. It was as if they didn't understand a word he had said. But then Michael slowly turned his head toward Alex.

"What truth?"

Taking a deep breath, Alex took a step off to the side and looked at the large holoscreen showing a panographic starfield.

He said, "Outside of you and Justine, I've never told anyone about the space port in this system, except for the oversight committee representative—and I regret telling him that much."

"You could have told me," Kenny said, looking hurt. "I had to find out about this from them."

Alex flushed. "All I told them was that when I came to this hangar on my last trip out, its automated systems attached a portable quantum drive and sent me home. I didn't want that knowledge to get out, because it would only lead to more questions that I couldn't answer."

"Couldn't, or wouldn't?" Kenny said, but there was only a hint of reproach in his words.

But it was Michael who guessed the truth. "You made contact."

Alex nodded. "Yes."

Justine and Kenny turned as one, mouths agape. "You met an alien?" Kenny asked.

"Sort of."

"What do you mean 'sort of'?" Justine asked.

"I mean I don't know who it was for sure. I didn't see anything. When I came out of quantization, I was inside the hangar, and the machines were installing the drive. The only part that I left out of my story was the voice message on my console. Once I listened to it, I had to purge it from the ship's memory."

"Which is why you blew the storage banks," Michael said.

"Yes. I panicked and pushed too hard. But I remember the message word-for-word."

"Your eidetic memory," Kenny said.

"Yes," Alex said. "And the message was in Mayan."

Kenny glanced between Alex and Yaxche. "Mayan?"

Alex nodded, and turned on the ship's translator. He spoke in Mayan, and the others listened to the English version:

∞

I offer my greetings to you, Sky Traveler. I am Ah Tabai, a Sentinel of the Collection. Our people have waited for a thousand years for humankind to walk the path of light, and journey beyond the boundaries of our home system to join with us.

It saddens me that our reunion must be delayed. I am afraid that I bring a message of despair.

Your world is in extreme danger.

Almost one thousand of your Earth years ago, the Grace vanished without a sign of where they went. They were our leaders, our mentors, our elders and caregivers. An ancient race, they were the ones who built the nexus of star beacons and infused them with their essence. The Grace existed in the galaxy eons before any culture Emerged from their systems. There has long been a legend that the Grace hid the sum of their knowledge in an unknown pre-Emerging star system.

The Kulsat, once the favored of the Grace and one-time heirs to their knowledge and wisdom, have turned aggressive and power hungry. When they've become aware of a pre-Emerged system, they've scoured them for signs of the Grace and their legacy. They have not hesitated to destroy everything in their path to find what the Grace have hidden.

I have sent instructions to the space port computer to affix a temporary light-speed engine to your ship, and it will send you back to your system. You must avoid traveling 'outside of light' at all costs, and refrain from returning to this star system, or the Kulsat may sense you.

With luck, your system will remain undetected long enough so that you may learn to fully Emerge. Only then will you be able to defend yourselves against the Kulsat.

Travel swiftly, Cousin. Go with Grace.

∞

Once Alex finished his recitation, he turned to face his friends. They were all stunned.

Kenny was the first one to break the silence. "Why wouldn't you share this with us? I mean, confirmation of alien cultures aside, the fact that one of them might invade and destroy us is information I, for one, would like to have had."

Justine answered before Alex had a chance. "If we did know, the first thing we would have done is work towards improving the quantum drives, and on weaponizing Kinemet. Eventually, someone would notice that much Kinemet being used."

"It's more important for us to 'Emerge'," Alex said. "You heard his last words. Only once we are Emerged will we be able to defend ourselves. I don't know what that entails, but I'm sure if there were any other option, Ah Tabai would have mentioned it."

Michael turned to Yaxche, "He spoke Mayan. The Song of the Stars mentions a time when a great number of your people vanished during a war."

"Ahyah," Yaxche said. "The Great War."

"Then…" Michael started to say, clearly working through the facts.

But before anyone had a chance to add to the conjecture, the ship's console lit up and an alert sounded. On the holoscreen, the faint twinkling of stars turned pitch black as they were blocked out by an enormous object.

It had taken the *Ultio* five hours to travel from the star beacon to the space port. The alien ship made the trip in five minutes.

∞

Everyone's eyes were glued to the holoscreen, watching as the outline of a ship began to coalesce several kilometers away.

"It's huge," Kenny said in a hushed voice. "At this magnification, I would say it's at least fifteen-hundred meters long."

The architecture of the vessel was unlike any craft Alex had ever seen on Earth. It was as if the metal of the hull were made of pure electricity. It glowed and swirled in continuous motion, a dance of solid energy.

The nose of the vessel extended out in a gently tapering cone. The ship's body was shaped roughly like a tube, and ended in a long taper at the back. Overall, the vessel somewhat resembled a narwhal.

As the ship neared, Alex was suddenly awash with the overwhelming sensation of Kinemet. He shivered.

"I can feel it, too," Justine said. "The ship itself is built from Kinemet!"

Once the alien vessel came within half a kilometer, it stopped and floated at that position.

"Is it the Kulsat?" Kenny asked. No one replied. "What are they doing?"

"Maybe they're scanning us. Wondering who we are," Michael said.

At the same time, Justine and Alex nodded.

"Yes," Justine said. "I can…" She gave her head a slight shake. "I don't know how to describe it. When I try to use my *sight*, I'm just overwhelmed by the Kinemet out there. It's like looking directly at the Sun. But, I feel like they are *looking* at us with the *sight*. Like they are *looking* at me—"

Her words were cut off abruptly, and when Alex glanced at her, he saw that she was transforming into quanta before his eyes. There was a look of panic on her face in the moment before she completely turned to light.

Everyone else took a step back as Justine's essence, her collection of photons, floated toward the monitors and through them. They all flickered out as she passed them, and then came back to life when she was through.

Her photons then continued to drift into the hull of the *Ultio* and finally out into space. Unconfined by any material barrier, her essence shot toward the alien ship, almost as if she were being sucked in through a vacuum tube.

"What the hell?" Kenny asked.

"It's not her," Alex said. "It's got to be *them*. They're taking her."

Michael gasped. "Why her?"

"She's the only one of us who is a full Kinemat. I'm incomplete. They probably aren't even aware of my existence."

"What are they going to—?" Kenny started to ask, but the hull of the alien ship brightened to a blinding level, and lance of pale light shot out toward the underside of the *Ultio*.

Kenny screamed, "They're targeting the engines!"

Before anyone could brace themselves, the impact knocked them all to the floor.

Michael let out a cry as he fell, and it looked as if he might have broken an arm.

The electrical systems in the bridge stuttered. One interface console exploded in a shower of sparks, and a panel on the other side of the room popped off, the wires spitting and hissing.

Yaxche, looking frightened out of his wits, had an arm wrapped around the back of the captain's chair.

The lights flickered off and on, and the artificial gravity generator failed. Alex lost contact with the floor, and floated up, smacking his head against a control panel.

There was a secondary explosion, and then the ship listed to port.

Just before the holoscreens went dark, Alex saw the alien spacecraft turn away and leave, as if confident their attack had been a fatal enough blow.

Alex held enough hope that that wasn't the case, right up until the air filters shut down, and the entire electrical system fizzled out.

They were adrift in space. Their ship was disabled, and their life support system was non-functional.

The temperature on the bridge started to drop at an alarming rate.

"Alex," Michael called out. "Can you do anything?"

He could quantize himself, but he had no awareness in that state. In doing so, he might be able to save himself, but there was no way he could navigate the ship or help the others. He pushed his senses out to see if the electrical system was repairable.

"I'm sorry, the generators and batteries are completely melted."

"What about the Kinemet?" Kenny said. "If it fissions, that's all she wrote."

Alex shook his head, then realized no one could see the motion. "It's not there. They must have taken it when they took Justine."

After a few moments, Kenny said, "Is now a good time to panic?"

"Wait a minute," Alex said. He could feel the chill creep in to his bones. The bridge was nearing the freezing point.

The *Ultio* was only a few hundred meters from the space port, and though it was falling away, it was an agonizing thought that they were so close to salvation.

When Alex had been saved before, he was in a quantized state, and had no memory of the events, but if he made one giant assumption…

He concentrated, and pushed his *sight* out toward the space port. He had the sense that it was wrapped in something similar to the Kinemet dampers because when his consciousness reached the outer hull of the complex, he could not push his way in.

There had to be some kind of way to communicate with the space port's computer system, to let it know there was a ship ready to dock. In the case of a disabled ship, they had to have made a provision for some kind of manual override.

He searched the entire surface of the space port, but after the first pass, he had not found any way in.

Willing himself not to panic, he continued his search, and it was only at his second pass over one of the large elliptical bay doors of the hull that he spotted a slight protrusion sticking out a few centimeters. It was a tiny metal rod.

He used his electropathic ability and sent a small shot of energy into it.

Slowly, the bay door started to open, and Alex could feel a magnetic tug coming from within. He returned to his body.

Kenny was wild-eyed. "What's happening? We're drifting the other way now!"

"The space port dock has us. It's pulling us in," Alex said.

Michael cried out with joy. "You did it."

"I'm not sure it was enough," Alex said. "Maybe I only postponed the inevitable. Even if we were to manage to get one of those portable quantum drives attached to the *Ultio,* we'd be dead five minutes after arriving near Pluto."

There was a sharp jarring as the ship came to a stop, and Kenny and Michael scrambled in the dark to manually open the cabin door and lead the way to the main hatch. They opened it to reveal the inside of the alien space port.

The rush of fresh oxygen was pure heaven.

37

Alien Space Port :
Alpha Centauri :

Standing on one of the metal walkways along the pier inside the alien space port, Michael surveyed the damage to the *Ultio*. A full third of the hind section, where the quantum drive and Kinemet had been, was simply missing. The ship was as good as scuttled.

"Maybe destroying our ship was incidental," Michael said, though to no one in particular. "They wanted the Kinemet and Justine, and didn't give us a passing thought."

Kenny glanced up and frowned.

"What now?" Alex asked, sitting down near Yaxche, who had found a spot on the floor to rest.

Michael rubbed the stubble growing on his chin, and winced when he moved his arm. Not broken, but still sore.

The hangar itself was several hundred meters wide in every direction, laced with rows of berths, metal jetties, elevated piers and several walkways floating at various elevations. It looked as if the port wasn't meant for ships much larger than the *Ultio*.

All of the docking bays in the hangar were empty. The jetties were lined with large discs on the end of cylindrical beams. Michael guessed they served as dock bumpers. They gave off a steady electromagnetic hum.

When Michael and Kenny had opened the main loading door from the *Ultio*, they'd been able to manually extend the ramp. Although the electrical systems were dead, and the few small fires had been extinguished, the structure of the *Ultio* was still unsafe. The ship groaned periodically as metal beams collapsed and the contents shifted and fell.

"I'm not sure," Michael said finally. "But we should try to go back in and get food and water. Maybe some blankets or something and make a camp out here."

"What about Justine?" Kenny asked, but the only answer Michael gave was the hard set to his jaw.

The aliens—he assumed they were the Kulsat—had abducted her, and there was nothing Michael could think of to help.

∞

They spent the next fifteen minutes making quick excursions back into the *Ultio* and gathering supplies and enough equipment to make a camp.

Kenny set up a makeshift table using a few storage containers. He brought out several holoslates for testing, and finally found one that wasn't damaged. As he worked on it, tapping, swirling and wiggling his fingers on the haptic console, Michael looked over his shoulder.

"We should conserve the battery," he said by way of suggestion.

Kenny smiled. "No need. There's a wireless electrical current running through the complex. It's powering the computer directly. I'm going to see if the space port has a network I can hook into. Maybe we can download a manual on how to get into the living quarters on the other side."

Alex had already tried to use his electropathy to open the large door at the far end of the hangar, but had reported that there wasn't any kind of switch or lever that he could find.

With Alex's help, Yaxche had used cargo netting to create a hammock between two vertical beams. When Alex went back into the ship to look for a blanket, the old Mayan sank into the netting and closed his eyes.

"Are you all right?" Michael asked, approaching tentatively.

Blinking his eyes open, Yaxche gave him that big grin. He spoke, and his clip-on translator repeated, "Ahyah. Old men get tired. I just need a nap."

Laughing, both in relief, and at the Mayan's equanimity in the face of everything that was happening, Michael said, "Quite a mess we got ourselves in."

"Ahyah," Yaxche said back. "As they say, 'Out of the pot and into the fire'." His grin widened into a full smile.

Before Michael could say anything more, Alex raced out of the wreckage of the *Ultio,* his eyes wide.

"What's wrong?" Michael asked, his heart speeding up.

Alex headed straight for Kenny and the holoslates. "There's something happening. I could feel the electromagnetics activating on one of the other docking bays." He pointed to the holoslate. "Are you able to do any scans on this?"

Kenny shook his head. "No, the external sensor on this unit is damaged."

Just then, one of the magnetic dock bumpers on the next pier over began to extend.

Kenny stood up, his face flush and his eyes bright with trepidation. "Are the Kulsat coming back to finish us off?"

A huge circular section of the hangar wall, the bay door, faded to an almost perfect blackness. The ring of the opening had a vague whitish glow to it. That was the energy barrier Kenny had theorized about earlier. While they were inside the *Ultio* being pulled into the dock, they'd been unable to see what was happening.

Michael could feel his hair tingling with the electricity as a new alien ship appeared in the opening.

It was less than a quarter of the size of the *Ultio.* As with the ship that had attacked them, the hull of the new alien ship looked to be made of Kinemet—the entire surface glowed and swirled, though the colors on this ship were a kaleidoscope of reds and yellows. Its shape was very similar to the bird-like designs of gull-wing planes from Earth. Michael guessed that this ship could serve a dual purpose as a spacecraft and an aircraft. The front of the ship resembled the coned head of a bird, with a beaked nose that came to a point.

Michael's first impression was of a phoenix.

When the vessel had fully entered the bay, the docking bumpers adjusted themselves to uniformly secure it. The hangar wall solidified once more, sealing the area against the void of space.

The four stood there with mouths agape during the entire docking procedure.

Kenny took an involuntary step back when a hatch on the side of the alien ship opened. A broad, rectangular patch of the ship's hull faded to empty space.

A platform held by two large metal arms protruded from the gap and began to descend to the hangar deck.

On the platform stood two aliens.

Both of them were bipedal. One of them was significantly taller than the other, standing almost three meters high, and it was extremely thin. The second alien was a great deal shorter, the top of its head level with the other's elbow.

When the platform stopped several centimeters above the dock, the two aliens stepped off and approached the waiting humans.

The shorter alien wore clothing that was alarmingly close to the ceremonial outfit Yaxche wore. Calf-high boots with beads and tassels were pulled over long beige pants. The alien's torso was wrapped with a tzute style cloth, intricately designed in geometric shapes and earth-tone colors. A scarf hung loosely around the neck, decorated with brightly colored baubles. The alien reached up and removed the feathered headdress, and Michael looked on the face of a being from another world for the first time.

—And it was human. The small man was dark complexioned, with black hair and a long forehead. High cheekbones framed a broad nose and wide brown eyes. He resembled a Mayan.

He gave them an easy smile.

Michael was speechless.

A moment later, the taller alien, dressed also in what Michael guessed was a ceremonial outfit—though it was one he had never seen before, made of some kind of shiny material and arranged in several folds and layers—also removed its mantle, an oblong cap with several long spines protruding from it.

Michael gaped at the tall alien.

She had the same basic features as a human girl, but the lower part of her face was drawn forward to end in a narrow jaw and tiny chin. Her thin lips framed a small mouth set also in a welcoming smile, and her eyes were overlarge and elliptical.

Instead of hair, she had what looked like the down of a bird that, as far as Michael could tell, ran from the top of her head, where it was white, to the back of her neck where it turned a light shade of yellow and extended down behind her clothes. Michael could not see her ears, if she had any, and the skin on her face and the front of her neck was bright yellow and fuzzy.

Together, the pair of aliens approached the four humans and stopped. The shorter alien genuflected.

Michael, the politician of the group, recovered from his astonishment and bowed. He stepped forward.

Kenny reached out instinctively to stop him, but he smiled at the younger man. "It'll be fine. These are not the Kulsat."

The shorter alien spoke in Mayan, and a split-second later, Michael heard English words come from somewhere near the alien's collar.

"I offer my greetings to you. I am Ah Tabai, a Sentinel of the Collection."

The alien extended both arms and clasped Michael's hands in welcome. He glanced at Alex. "It has been a very long time since we first discovered you, Sky Traveler. I am glad you have endured."

Ah Tabai then took a step toward Yaxche, and bowed deeply.

"Grandfather," the alien said. Michael remembered from something Alex had said that it was a general term of respect for one's elders, regardless of the blood relationship. "You have traveled a great distance to be here."

"Ahyah," Yaxche said, a look of surprise on his usually calm face.

Ah Tabai motioned to the other alien, who made a quirky nod.

"My companion is—" He made a high pitched sound, for which his translator found no suitable match in English.

As if realizing this, Ah Tabai said, "You can call her Aliah. She is also a Sentinel. You would know her home star system as 'Gliese'."

With that, the tall birdlike alien woman made a chirping sound and tilted her head almost perpendicular to her shoulders. The translator in her suit said, "Pleased to meet you."

Michael said, "I'm afraid you are not finding us at our best, but on behalf of my friends here and our home world, I am glad to meet you, and extend our friendship to you."

His tone grew somber. "We were attacked by an alien ship—the Kulsat?—and they took our friend."

Ah Tabai's eyes widened. "They did?"

"Her name is Justine," Alex said. "She is the first and only one of us to become a full Kinemat—she has Emerged."

"That is why they took her," Ah Tabai said. "It has happened in the past. They will try to find out as much about your system from her as they can."

"Is there anything you can do?" Michael asked. "Can you rescue her?"

Ah Tabai dropped his eyes. "By now they have taken her back to their home system." He glanced at Aliah. "We hurried from Gliese the moment we detected the beacon in this system was active, but it is obvious we were not quick enough, else we might have been able to save her."

Kenny raised one finger. "Uh, excuse me. From 'Gliese'?" he asked.

Ah Tabai smiled, "Yes. Gliese is the closest member world of the Collection to this system."

"But—" Kenny glanced at Michael. "If you only left there when we arrived *here,* that would mean you traveled, like, twenty light-years in a little over eight hours!"

"Yes," Ah Tabai said, as if this were obvious.

"That's unbelievable," Kenny said. He looked at the alien ship with wide eyes. "You can travel at, what—" He did a rough calculation in his head. "—thirty-*thousand* times the speed of light?"

"You are mistaken in your calculation," Ah Tabai said, as if talking to a child. "It took us that amount of time to get from our planet to the beacon in our system at light speed."

"Then…?" Kenny glanced back and forth between Michael and the alien, but Michael couldn't figure it out either.

Ah Tabai said, "When we use the star beacons, we say that we travel 'outside light'. It is by the Grace that we do this. Only inside a system do we travel by light—though the beacon and the space port in this system are too close for light travel."

"So it's instantaneous between the beacons?" Kenny asked. He glanced at Alex and Michael. "It took us over four years." Stunned, he asked Ah Tabai, "What kind of engine can do that?"

Ah Tabai said patiently, "When we travel outside light, we use the Grace. All star beacons occupy the same space outside light."

Kenny stared. "The Grace. What does that mean?"

Ah Tabai put up his hand to forestall more questions. "I will answer everything as well as I am able. For now, you must listen to me."

He looked at each of them in turn to make sure they were paying attention.

"As much as I longed for the day we would meet, I had hoped you were more advanced than this. If your friend is the only one of you who has Emerged, then your world is in terrible danger.

"Now that the Kulsat are aware of you, they will gather an armada and prepare an invasion of your home system."

Michael blanched. "We thought coming here was our only hope to save Alex."

Ah Tabai nodded. "It was. We do not have much time. We must

board my ship and return you to your world without delay."

His eyes reflected the gravity of his words. "You need to warn your people the Kulsat are coming, and try to defend yourselves against annihilation."

38

Alien Ship :
Alpha Centauri :

Some days I feel my age. I know I am much older than my father was when he passed from the world. My brothers and sisters are all long gone, and my only grandson has died.

When I think about it, I can understand how many people my age start to look forward to the end. It is not that terrible a thing, passing from this world into the next. All things must end, and on the days when my bones ache and I miss my family and friends who have passed, I look to the sunset of my life with a sense of peace and welcome.

Today is not one of those days. Today I feel young and full of excitement, despite the danger to the Earth.

Following the path of the gods, standing on a structure built by the people of the stars, and meeting sky travelers from alien lands, I suddenly long for another lifespan of years.

When Ah Tabai, the traveler who shares our Mayan ancestors, invited us on board his star ship to return us to Earth, the scientist, Kenny, jumped with excitement. If I were not so old and fragile, I would have jumped, too.

As we entered the alien ship, I could feel a tingle of electricity pass through me, and I could not tell if it came from the vessel or from the wonder I feel.

Ah Tabai took us to a passenger room with seats that flow out of the walls. When I sat down, the seat gently formed itself around the shape of my body. It felt like I was floating in the air, and I had the urge to fall asleep, but I fought to stay awake.

Our host told us it will be a short journey to the beacon, and then we will arrive in our home system a moment later. He said he will answer all of our questions when we are in our home system.

As I drift into sleep, I think about the story Ah Tabai told us, and how the gods who created the star beacons have been missing for a thousand years.

And I think to myself:

I believe I know the secret the gods hid on Earth, and I might also know what happened to them.

EMERGENCE

to be continued in *Worlds Away*…

WORLDS AWAY

THE INTERSTELLAR AGE
BOOK 3

VALMORE
DANIELS

1

CHRYSALIS

Quiriguá :
Guatemala :

Long Count: 9.19.19.17.9

It had been seven days since I began my warrior's trial, and I feared I would not succeed in my quest. I would either be captured by the Q'eqchi', the northern tribe, or I would spend the remaining days of my life shamed by my failure. I would not be Subo Ak, the warrior; I would be Subo Ak, the unworthy.

The only way I could return to my people, the Ch'orti', with any dignity was to bring back a trophy.

For the past two days, I had been scouting the forests south of Quiriguá, waiting to catch one of their warriors out alone. I would kill him and take something of his to prove my victory. My hope was to find a warrior who had many kills of his own. He would have tattoos showing his conquests; his skin would be a suitable prize, and might gain me enough status to obtain a wife. I had seen Ysalane smiling at me whenever I passed near...

The Q'eqchi' warriors, however, only went out on patrol in numbers, and they never strayed from their party. They were very disciplined; it was no wonder their tribe had grown so large over the past generation.

They had invaded our lands many times in the past, killed our men or captured them for sacrifice, stolen our women, and burned our crops. My brother, Atal Ak, died from a spear wound during one such raid a year ago. Since then, I have been dreaming of joining the warrior caste and avenging my brother.

We have many story stones that tell of a time when the Q'eqchi' paid tribute to the kings of Copán, when we had been their overlords. That had ended many generations ago when the king of Quiriguá captured our last great king, Uaxaclajuun Ub'aah K'awiil, and took his head. The Q'eqchi' have harassed us for more than a hundred years since then.

Now, Copán is but a shadow of its former glory, and we struggle for our very survival. My village, east of Copán city, has seen our numbers dwindle more every year. We have suffered from poor harvests, sparse hunting, and raids from the Q'eqchi'.

One day, the Ch'orti' will become powerful again, and all tribes in the world will make the pilgrimage to Copán to offer their tribute.

It was my desire.

Before I could help restore power to my people, I had to achieve honor for myself. At this point, I would have attempted an attack on two, or even three of their warriors. I was desperate.

I decided to head east where the forest thickened. Perhaps I needed a better spot to wait for my prey. As I stood to go, I heard the snap of a branch behind me.

Spear in my hand, I turned, ready for combat. Had a warrior crept up behind me? Had I turned from the hunter into the hunted?

A laugh escaped my lips when I saw a dark-feathered turkey a distance away. It was walking through the brush, its head bobbing and jerking while it foraged.

My stomach rumbled. I had not hunted game since I arrived at Quiriguá, and I was down to the last bit of meat in my pack. If I were weakened from hunger, I would never last in a match against a single Q'eqchi' warrior, let alone two or three.

The turkey did not see me. It was my lucky day.

Silently, I lowered my spear to the ground, picked up my atlatl, and placed a long dart in the shaft.

Stepping carefully to avoid any fallen branches that would alert the turkey to my presence, I got as close as I could to the bird. Taking aim, I flung the dart at my prey, and cursed as the tip hit the dirt in front of the turkey.

It immediately took flight. In the confines of the forest, however, it didn't have enough room to get any height. Several times, it was forced to land after swerving to avoid the trunk of a tree.

I gave chase, picking up my spear and my pack as I ran after the bird. If I got close enough, I could try to throw another dart at it.

We were nearing the edge of the wooded area. I knew that once the turkey reached the plain, it could fly faster than I could run. When I saw it hit a tree with a wing, and lose balance, I knew it was my best and last opportunity.

Dropping everything except my atlatl, I quickly loaded another dart and let it fly.

This time my aim was true, and the dart hit the turkey through the upper part of its wing. It would not be able to fly from me now. Though it tried to run, the dart in its wing unbalanced it, and slowed it down.

Drawing my knife from my belt, I ran to the bird and jumped on it. My first strike missed its throat, slicing instead into the meat of its breast. My second cut found its mark, and I held the bird down as it died.

The turkey made a terrible noise in its death throes, however. Several Q'eqchi' warriors, who had been following a path through the woods, heard the sounds and ran to investigate.

I saw them and felt a moment of panic. If I stayed to fight them, they would overwhelm me. They would either kill me or drag me back to Quiriguá for sacrifice.

If I ran, I would only prove that I was a coward, and unfit to be a warrior of the Ch'orti'.

A plan came to me, and I only had a moment in which to act.

Leaving the dead turkey where it was, and the dart still sticking through its wing, I picked up my spear, hurried a distance away, and crouched behind a thick copse of bush.

The warriors would know the turkey had been killed by a hunter; they would most likely be able to identify the dart as one of Ch'orti' design. Their first thought would be that their enemy had decided to flee.

With any luck, they would split up in their search for me. I would then follow one of them. When I saw my chance, I would ambush him.

I waited, daring to raise my head above the top of the bush to see what the warriors were doing.

A few more moments passed, and I still had not heard the sounds of their pursuit. Clutching my spear in both hands, I crept out from behind the bush and searched for them. They were nowhere to be seen.

Puzzled, I returned to the spot where I had killed the turkey, careful to remain as silent as I could. The bird remained undisturbed, and I chanced to move through the woods to the path.

I could not believe my eyes when I finally spotted the four warriors. They were running back to their city. *Cowards!*

Still trying to figure out what had caused them to flee, I turned around, intending to return to the turkey and claim my dinner.

A shadow crept across the path in front of me, and I looked skyward, expecting to see an eagle or some other bird of prey circling as if it had sensed my earlier kill.

It was not a bird, however. I felt cold fear grip my bowels.

One of the story stones at Copán foretold a time when the sun would fall from the sky and burn the world.

For the span of a heartbeat, I believed it was happening right then. Then I realized it was not the sun, but an impossibly bright ball of light streaking across the afternoon sky.

I remembered one of our elders, Yax Kuk, who spoke often of the gods of the sky. On clear nights, sometimes you could see them as they traveled on the backs of firebirds. Once in my lifetime, I witnessed such an event. A thin line of light cut its way across the evening sky, as if one of the stars tried to slice through the blanket of night.

Now, however, the ball of light was much larger than the one I had seen in my youth. Instead of long tendrils of fire and smoke, there was only a faint sparkling, like cooling embers in a campfire.

Unlike the Q'eqchi' warriors, who fled in fear of the strange occurrence, I became emboldened when I realized that the object was not passing through the sky; it was going to land in the mountains to the northwest.

If it were indeed a god in his flying boat, then the first human he encountered would be assured a place of honor. That person would become a prophet.

I had to be that person.

With the blessings of a god, I could lead the Ch'orti', and regain our rightful place as the overlords of all the tribes. I would become king. Subo Ak, savior of all the People.

Thoughts of the turkey and my empty stomach left me as I broke into a run, following the path to the god who had returned to Earth.

2

Alex came out of the photonic state to a scene of chaos. Ah Tabai's Sentinel ship was shaking, and an immense roaring sound filled the passenger compartment.

A klaxon sounded from somewhere, and Alex heard a cry from the other side of the chamber. Michael was on the floor on his side, holding his knee. His face was contorted into a grimace of pain. Kenny and Yaxche were still in their molded seats, hands gripping the sides to keep from being thrown off.

The ship rocked again, and a moment later, the door melted away. Ah Tabai stumbled inside.

"What's happening?" Kenny asked, his voice desperate.

"We ran into something that exploded and breached our hull, perhaps a mine." Ah Tabai motioned his hand, encompassing all of them in the room. "We have to get you to the escape pod."

"Aren't we back in Sol System?" Alex asked as he carefully got out of the molded chair, keeping one hand on the edge for support.

Nodding, Ah Tabai said, "Yes. Someone was expecting your return. The moment we arrived, we entered a minefield of some kind. We hit one, and it disrupted our computers long enough to prevent us from jumping back into Aetherspace."

"Kinemetic?" Michael asked. He was still on the floor, gritting his teeth, but it looked as if the pain from his fall was subsiding. He was in a sitting position.

"I don't think so," Ah Tabai said. "We have defenses against that. The explosion has damaged our hull. Our Aether Engine is offline. There is a ship approaching, and they will be on us in minutes, well before we can make repairs." He turned to Alex. "It's against protocol for us to be here; but to let an un-Emerged society have access to our technology is one of our most serious crimes. We will have to self-destruct. Our escape pod is made with very basic technology; it is your only option. You must hurry."

Kenny got completely up from his seat, went to assist Michael, and got him to his feet. "Did you try to contact the ship? They could be one of ours."

"No," Ah Tabai said. "I ran their signature through your ship's database. It is not in your records."

Alex helped Yaxche up. "It could be the same ship—or same people—who came after us four years ago." It was odd thinking about the span of time. From Alex's perspective, it had only been a day.

"If so, how did they know we'd be back?" Kenny asked.

Michael, on his feet, though favoring his hurt leg as he let himself be led out of the passenger compartment, said, "Probably doesn't matter to them. Whoever it was who attacked us before didn't want our technology; they were already developing their own. I'd guess they've been stationed out here all along with orders to intercept any ship that came out of quantum space."

"Or destroy them. Best way to have a monopoly is to eliminate the competition," Kenny said, his lips pressing together in a sour expression.

Ah Tabai showed them the way to the belly of the ship, and opened a portal to a small, cramped escape pod. It was a circular chamber, with four seats set into the outer wall facing inward.

"You aren't coming with us?" Kenny asked.

"No." Ah Tabai shook his head. "Aliah and I will attempt to return to our system in the command pod—it has a portable Aether engine similar to the one we used for Alex before. We'll try to come back with another ship—and this time, we'll be ready for an attack."

Before heading inside, Alex said, "Won't they fire on our escape pod?"

"We've programmed a trajectory into the pod to take you to the star beacon. The energy field around it should mask you from their sensors. The pod has enough air and liquid nutrients to keep you all alive for several weeks. Alex, you may begin to feel adverse effects by being on Pluto, but you aren't as sensitive as full Aethers. It won't be pleasant, but it's your best chance until we can come back for you.

When our ship self-destructs, the Aether shock should disrupt the attacker's sensors for some time."

"Ah Tabai," Alex said, "thank you."

"No thanks are necessary," he said. "Just keep yourself alive until we can get back to you."

With that, Alex crawled into the escape pod and squished himself between Yaxche and Kenny, opposite Michael. Ah Tabai closed the portal behind him as they strapped themselves in.

The four men shared uneasy glances at each other in the dim light from a monitor display that showed life support levels. There weren't many controls on the pod—obviously, it wasn't designed as a navigable spacecraft.

"Who do you think it is?" Kenny asked. "The attacker, I mean."

Michael, looking as if he were still in pain from his fall, said, "Figuring out who chased us out of Sol System four years ago is less important than the fact that they're still out here, waiting for us."

"How is that more important?" Kenny asked.

"It means things on Earth have changed. Even though NASA funding had been cut back at the time we left, they would have—at the very least—maintained an unmanned alert station out here on Pluto. The star beacon is the most significant discovery we've ever made. It's hard to believe they'd leave it abandoned. If USA, Inc. maintained a presence here, they wouldn't adopt a 'shoot first' policy. The only reason I can think of that they weren't here is that some foreign power has taken control of Plutonian space. Perhaps more than that."

"Foreign power? Wasn't it an Arab Conglomerates signal that came from that ship that chased us?" Kenny said.

"Signals can be disguised. The truth is, we have no idea who it is. All I can say is the situation on Earth must be dire."

All through the evacuation to the escape pod, and the discussion while they waited to be launched, Yaxche had remained silent.

"Are you all right?" Alex asked him.

"Ahyah," the old man said, and offered Alex a reassuring smile. "I am not used to so much excitement."

"We'll be fine." Alex hoped his words would prove true.

A small chime sounded, and they heard Ah Tabai's voice. "We're going to launch the command pod first, to distract the attackers. Once your escape pod is ejected, our ship will begin a one-minute countdown. We'll wait until the pod is near the star beacon before we enter Aetherflight."

"We're all set, here," Alex said.

A sharp rumbling sound came a few moments later, and Alex assumed that was the command pod with Ah Tabai and Aliah.

Ah Tabai confirmed this when his voice came through the escape pod. "We're away. They're firing missiles at us, but they're far too slow. Our countermeasures have disabled them."

The four in the escape pod waited anxiously for what seemed like ages, but was more like ten seconds.

"Prepare for launch," Ah Tabai said, and the entire pod began to shake as the engines propelled them out of the ship.

The pressure suddenly increased, and Alex found himself unable to breath for a few moments until the acceleration leveled out.

"You're on your way," Ah Tabai said over the speaker. "Countdown to self-destruct has started."

As the escape pod's velocity leveled out, they lost gravity, and Alex saw Kenny go pale—many people became disoriented and nauseated in a weightless environment.

"Thirty seconds," Ah Tabai said. "There will most likely be an aftershock. You should grab on to something."

"How are you doing?" Alex asked, and then remembered that he could use his ability to find out for himself. Closing his eyes, he pushed his *sight* out.

The escape pod was hurtling toward Pluto and the *Dis Pater*—Sol System's star beacon. At their current rate, they should arrive in less than five minutes.

In the space around Pluto, the attacking ship was pursuing the command pod. Behind them, Ah Tabai and Aliah's scout ship drifted slowly away from them.

"Twenty seconds," Ah Tabai said, then his voice changed pitch. "They've fired a torpedo at us. It's not Aether-based. Their aim is off the mark. But the concussion wave has caused the main Gliesan ship to change direction."

"What?" Michael asked.

"I'm not sure…" Alex started to say. Then he saw that the attacking ship had changed course.

The Gliesan vessel drifted into another mine.

The explosion sent out enough of a shock wave to crush the command pod's hull.

"Ah Tabai!" Alex called out, but there was no answer.

In the escape pod, Alex didn't feel the aftershock of the blast, since they were already far enough away to escape the effects. When the Gliesan scout ship exploded ten seconds later, however, the concussion wave slammed against them so hard that, even in their restraints, the occupants were knocked around.

The monitor of the escape pod blinked on and off, and Alex had to turn his head as an electric spark shot out of the console.

He could feel the pod tumbling, but the only thing he could do was hold on. There was no way to control its spin.

A low moaning sound filled the chamber, but Alex couldn't tell who it was.

He tried to push his *sight* out again, but before he could focus, the escape pod struck something hard and unyielding. The impact knocked him unconscious.

3

Escape Pod :
Sol System :

Michael was the first to return to consciousness.

It took a long time for him to orient himself. There were no interior lights inside the escape pod, but he could still breathe air. He moved his leg, and pain from his bruised knee coursed up through his body. He tried to bite back a cry, but it came out anyway.

Grimacing until the pain subsided, Michael took a deep breath and reached out beside him. His hand touched Kenny's shoulder, and he gently shook the physicist.

"Kenny, are you all right?"

A low-pitched moan came out of the younger man, and when Kenny spoke, it was with obvious effort. "It's hard to breathe."

"Hold still. Don't move. If you've broken a rib, the last you want is for it to puncture your lung."

He reached out in the other direction and felt Yaxche's hair. Moving his hand down to the older man's neck, he felt for a pulse. It was there, but faint. "Yaxche?" he asked. "Are you hurt?"

Gently, he tapped the side of Yaxche's face, and then repeated his question when he felt the older man flinch.

Yaxche said, "Ahyah. I'm fine, except I think I might be blind."

"The lights are out," Michael said. He was still secured by the restraints and fumbled for the safety latch. "I can't reach Alex. Is he still unconscious?"

Michael couldn't see whether Yaxche nudged Alex or not, but a moment later, the young man groaned.

"What happened?"

Michael said, "I was going to ask you the same question."

"My head hurts. I think I banged it on something."

"Can you use your *sight* to *see* where we are?" Michael asked.

"Yeah," Alex said. "Give me a minute." A moment later, he let out a sound of despair.

"What is it?" Kenny asked.

"I can see the remains of the scout ship, and … I can't tell for sure, but it looks like the command pod is destroyed."

"Ah Tabai." Michael's voice was hoarse. "Aliah."

"I can't feel their Kinemetic signatures. I think they're dead." Alex made a moaning sound. "They risked everything to help us, and they paid with their lives."

Michael felt a deep anger at the news. More lives lost needlessly. Who were these maniacs who had attacked them without warning?

Kenny said, "So that means we're stranded here?"

"We're not that lucky," Alex replied.

"What do you mean by that?"

"We landed on Pluto. The bad news is we didn't land close enough to the star beacon for it to mask us. Our attackers are heading in this direction."

∞

They sat in silence as the long minutes stretched out. Michael knew that even if none of them were claustrophobic by nature, being in the dark in an enclosed space could work on anyone's psyche.

"What are they doing now?" he asked, keeping his voice as calm as he could.

Alex cleared his throat. "I'm not sure. They've established an orbit, but they haven't sent a shuttle or anything. Maybe they're waiting for instructions."

"From where?" Michael asked. "If they're contacting Earth, it could be over eight hours before they get a reply. It seems like a long time to wait."

"Maybe they can't see us," Kenny said, his voice filled with hope.

Alex said, "Our sensors and lights are offline. It's possible that's enough to hide us. They might know the general area where we landed, but can't tell our exact location."

Michael let out a short, hollow laugh. "If that's the case, then maybe we should let them know we're here."

"Are you crazy?" Kenny's voice was strained. "They'll kill us."

"Maybe," Michael said, "but if we don't take that chance, we're dead, anyway."

"What do you mean?"

Instead of answering the question directly, Michael asked Alex, "Is there any way you can be sure that Ah Tabai and Aliah are dead? Maybe they just quantized themselves, like you did."

"I can still sense traces of the Kinemetic radiation around where their command pod exploded. If they quantized themselves, I should be able to detect them the same way. I'm sorry to say it: I don't think they survived."

"Then no one knows we're out here," Michael said. "It looks as if the life-support systems are working fine. We've just lost communications and lights. If we can jump-start the systems, we can send out a distress call."

"Wait a minute," Kenny said. "Don't you think we should vote on this?"

"If you have any better suggestions," Michael said, "now's the time…"

After a moment, Kenny huffed. "Fine. How do we get communications back up?"

"When we were setting up the quantum drive on the *Ultio,* Justine mentioned that she was the spark to engage the damping field and kick-start the main engines. Alex, can you use your electropathic ability to do that here?"

"I can try," Alex said. "Give me a minute. The systems here are completely unfamiliar."

They all waited in silence for a short eternity. Without warning, the cabin lights turned on, and all of them cried out in surprise. Michael, feeling like he'd been blinded, covered his eyes with his hand until he adjusted to the light.

Alex said, "I think I can trace the communications array … ah, yes, here we go."

The display on the wall lit up, showing life support.

"Oh. That was the diagnostics array," Alex said. "Still looking for communications."

While Alex continued to use his abilities to try to repair the communications system, Michael looked over at Kenny. The young physicist wasn't looking very good.

"Are you all right?" he asked.

Kenny, his face drained of color, forced a smile. "It only hurts when I breathe—at least that means I'm still alive, right?"

Alex said, "Got it. We have communications again." He glanced at Michael. "I'm broadcasting on several frequencies."

Nodding at Alex, Michael spoke in a louder voice. "Attention unidentified vessel orbiting Pluto. This is Michael Sanderson, a Canada Corp. citizen. There are three others aboard our pod—Alex Manez and Kenny Harriman, who are also Canadians, and a Honduran translator named Yaxche. We offer our surrender."

The four men looked at one another uneasily until the speaker crackled.

"This is Lieutenant Gao of the Solan Empire. You have arrived in imperial space on a vessel of unfamiliar manufacture. According to our records, the four people you named have all been declared traitors by your respective governments. Furthermore, they have been missing for over four years and presumed dead. We must conclude you are spies for a foreign government, or you are fugitives attempting to disguise yourselves with false identities. In either case, the penalty for espionage is clear."

"We're not fugitives," Michael said. "And we're not spies. We are who we say we are. If our governments have warrants out for us, I'm sure they would appreciate it if you arrested us and turned us over. It's all a big misunderstanding. Please, we have an injured man here. He may have broken some ribs and will require medical attention."

The radio went silent for a moment. With a note of apprehension, Kenny asked, "Why aren't they replying? Does that mean they're just going to fire on us?"

Michael looked at Alex. "Can you *see* what they're doing?"

Alex closed his eyes in concentration. "They're approaching our geosynchronous position. I can't tell if they are arming weapons or not."

"They're going to blast us," Kenny said in misery.

Lieutenant Gao's voice came over the speaker. "Occupants of the escape pod. Stand by. We are sending a shuttle down to investigate. Should you not be who you said you are, you will be destroyed on the spot."

"Thank you, Lieutenant," Michael said.

The lieutenant did not reply, but a moment later, Alex told them a shuttle had been launched from the patrol ship.

Before it arrived, Michael said, "I suggest none of us say anything about Ah Tabai, Aliah, or the Kulsat."

"What do we tell them, then?" Kenny asked. "How do we explain the alien ship, or this escape pod?"

"Play dumb. Tell them we have no knowledge of what happened to us after we left Sol System."

Alex, his voice dry, added, "It worked for me last time."

∞

After latching onto the escape pod with a magnetic clasp, the shuttle lifted off Pluto and headed back to the patrol ship.

Once they were safely in the docking bay, and Alex told them that the soldiers were approaching to surround the pod, Michael said, "See if you can open the hatch."

Alex did so, and a hiss of cool air flowed into their compartment.

A voice from outside called out an order. It sounded like Lieutenant Gao. "Step out of the pod one at a time, slowly, and with your hands on top of your heads."

"Coming out," Michael called back, and got out first, walking gingerly. His knee still throbbed.

Six armed soldiers aimed their pulse rifles at Michael. As if seeing that he was, indeed, human, they all relaxed to a small degree—at least as far as Michael could tell by the expressions on their faces. They still trained their guns on him as they would a dangerous criminal.

Next out was Alex, followed by Yaxche.

Lieutenant Gao stepped forward. Though there was writing on the patch on his chest, it was in Chinese, as was the patch on the epaulet. He was clearly oriental, but he spoke English with no accent. His tone held no humor. "Where is the last one?"

Nodding toward the pod, Michael said, "He'll need help."

"Very well. You three will follow the guards to the detention area. If you do not follow instructions precisely, you will be shot without hesitation." The lieutenant pointed to two of his soldiers. "You two, retrieve the injured prisoner and bring him to the infirmary. Ensure he is fully secured."

"Thank you, Lieutenant Gao," Michael said. "We have been out of the picture for some time. Can you tell me what the Solan Empire is?"

"Be silent," the lieutenant said. "Until we receive further instructions, you will be held incommunicado. You will not speak to your guards, nor will you be given any information."

Michael wanted to watch as the two soldiers reached into the escape pod to help Kenny get out, but one of his guards pressed the barrel of his pulse rifle between his shoulder blades. The three of them headed out of the docking bay, none of them saying anything, as they'd been instructed.

Just before they exited the main doors, Michael swiveled his head around and got a brief look at Kenny. The young physicist hung limply between the two soldiers, and was possibly even unconscious. Michael wanted to race back to help, but he knew anything he did might jeopardize the cooperation of the Solan Empire soldiers—whoever they were.

∞

It was nearly nine hours later before anyone came to their cell. Michael was growing more and more worried that they hadn't heard anything about Kenny, nor had they had any indication from the stoic soldier standing guard as to what their fate would be.

Michael stood up from the long bench set into the wall of the cell when he recognized Lieutenant Gao, who was followed by two other soldiers holding handguns.

"How is he?" Michael asked, glancing nervously at the guns. "Is Kenny all right?"

"That should be the last of your concerns, Mr. Sanderson," the lieutenant said, an ominous tone in his voice.

Alex got up and stood next to Michael while Yaxche remained sitting.

Michael asked, "What do you mean by that?"

"We've received instructions from Central Command. They were explicit." With that, he made a motion with his hand to the two soldiers. Both raised their guns and pointed them at Michael and Alex.

"What are you doing?" Michael cried out. The only response he got from Lieutenant Gao was an amused smile.

The lieutenant nodded at his men.

Alex yelled, "No!"

The soldiers opened fire.

4

Kulsat Ship :
Centauri System :

When Justine had quantized herself in the past, she'd been completely aware of her surroundings.

Not so this time.

Her consciousness only returned to her when she materialized out of the quantized state—through no action of her own. It took her several seconds to remember what had happened to her.

The *Ultio*.

Someone, or something, on the Kulsat ship had scanned her with the *sight* and then, against her will, transformed her into quanta.

… And then what?

Her thoughts were thick; she had trouble concentrating. Where was she?

She opened her eyes to an all-encompassing blanket of darkness. There was no Kinemetic radiation left in her body; she could not use its influence to sense her surroundings.

Panic surged through her, and she fought back a scream. She had to keep her head.

Though she was blind, she had other senses.

She could breathe; therefore, there was oxygen. It smelled musky and a little stale. It reminded her of being in a large industrial complex with climate control.

Straining her ears, she could hear the echo of her breathing; that meant there were walls, and she was in an enclosed space. A prison?

Under her back was a hard floor, cold to the touch. Tapping it with a fingernail produced a high-pitched metallic sound.

Extending her arms around in a fan-like motion, her hands did not come in contact with any walls or other objects in her immediate vicinity. She reached above her and felt no resistance in that direction.

Carefully, she rolled to her stomach, drew her legs under her, and raised herself to her knees. Though her muscles were stiff and sore, she didn't need much effort to push herself up. The gravity level was about half of Earth normal.

She moved her arms around in a circular motion, searching for a wall or ceiling.

"Hello?" she said. Her voice came back to her sounding small and frightened, but there was no reply.

Stretching one hand out in front of her, Justine crawled forward on her knees. She needed to know the limitations of her prison cell, if that were, indeed, where she was.

Her fingers came up against a wall, and she let out a small grunt at the sudden discovery. The surface of the wall was smooth and cool, but unlike the floor, when she tapped her nail against it, the reverberation sounded more like glass than metal.

Rapping on it with her knuckles, she called out. "Hello. Is there anyone there?"

No answer except the echo of her own voice.

She used the glass wall as support and pulled herself to her feet. Reaching up as high as she could, even standing on the tips of her toes, she could not feel a ceiling.

Keeping her hand firmly on the wall, she moved to her left until she came to a corner. The adjoining wall was made of the same glass-like material.

Soon, Justine made a complete circuit of her cell. The room she was in was a cube, each wall at least three meters. She assumed the ceiling was at least a similar height. Although she couldn't reach it, when she was near one corner, she could feel a hiss of oxygen coming from above her.

Was she a prisoner of the Kulsat? Was she on their ship? The hull had been made of Kinemet. She'd sensed that before they abducted her. There had to be some dampening around her, however, because she could not sense any radiation.

Alex, Michael, Kenny, Yaxche! Had they been abducted as well? Killed?

Her military training told her that there was a possibility she would be tortured for information. She remembered the story Alex had told them moments before the alien ship had appeared before them.

The Kulsat wanted to find the legacy left behind by the Grace, which they believed was in a pre-Emerged system. The Sentinel who had left the message for Alex had told them the Kulsat would not hesitate to destroy anything that got in their way.

Justine knew they would question her about her home world: where it was, what level of technology they had, and any other information that would provide them with a tactical advantage. Now that they'd become aware of humanity, it would only be a matter of time before the Kulsat investigated the system.

Earth would not stand a chance against a species who had the level of technology the Kulsat possessed—and for all Justine knew, what she'd seen might only be a small portion of their capabilities.

During her four-year journey to the Centauri system, Justine had been fully conscious in her quantized state. Something during the Kinemetic conversion had altered her body's chemistry in a permanent way.

One of the other major side effects was that she retained information. She could recall the text of every book she'd ever read. Her mind was a storehouse of knowledge that an enemy would be eager to pillage.

Again, she felt her heart rate increase. It wasn't the thought of torture that frightened her; it was the thought that she wouldn't be able to withstand their interrogation techniques. If they broke her, she would essentially be giving up her entire world to the enemy. She didn't know if she could live with that … if she survived.

She couldn't let her imagination get the better of her. Her isolation and the fear of the future were playing with her emotions. Willing herself to be calm, she took a deep breath, and then another. With her back against one of the walls, she sat down and waited.

Although she'd been conscious for only a few minutes, she had no idea how long it had been since she'd been abducted from the *Ultio*. Hours? Days? For all she knew, they could have kept her in the quantized state for years, and there would be no physical evidence to prove otherwise.

She also did not know how long they planned to keep her in the cell. Certainly, it was not set up for long-term confinement. Though she was not looking forward to it, she knew whatever the Kulsat planned to do her, she had to keep all the information stored in her mind from them.

∞

She didn't have to wait very long.

Twelve minutes after she'd regained consciousness, she became aware of another Kinemetic presence nearby.

With her *sight*, she realized that the damping field was not around her cell, which was in a very large room. There was a barrier dividing the room itself from the rest of the ship.

Alex? was her first thought. Had they captured him as well? He was the only other human who had been through the Kinemetic process—though his transformation had not been complete.

When she'd been on Lucis Observatory, she'd been able to recharge herself just by being close to dormant Kinemet. The new presence gave off enough radiation that some of it leaked into her. It wasn't enough for her to quantize herself, but she regained some of her ability to *see,* though in a severely diminished capacity.

It was as if someone had turned on a very dim spotlight. Outside the confines of her cell, at least twenty feet away, a form took shape in her mind's eye.

Just as her hopes started to rise, they plummeted as the presence came closer.

What she *saw* made her stomach clench.

It was not human.

The creature had a large, bulbous head that bore the rough shape of a spade. Two protuberances on either side of its head held large eyes. Instead of a torso, eight long tentacle-like arms, connected at their base by a membranous web, extended out. The alien resembled a cephalopod.

From the top of its head to the end of its arms, it was less than half the height of an average human. She had no way of figuring out what gender the Kulsat was, or even if it had a gender, but in her mind, she thought of it as male.

So this is a Kulsat…

At first, she thought the creature was hovering, or floating somehow. Then his arms expanded and contracted, propelling the alien closer to her prison cell, and she realized he was swimming.

The Kulsat must have a water-based physiology. Was the inside of the alien ship completely filled with water?

That meant that if she were to break the glass of her terrarium, water would pour in and drown her.

In her mind, she'd been preparing for a bipedal alien species, but the realization of how different the Kulsat were from humans came as a shock.

The alien swam closer to Justine's tank, and as he did so, her *sight* grew marginally stronger. While her prison was a perfect cube, the room in which it was situated was far more complicated.

It looked like a complex laboratory, with dozens of open-faced cupboards on the walls. She couldn't identify several large constructs. Tubes extended from them into the ceiling.

There were three long tables. Various objects that could have been tools, containers, or other scientific apparatuses were strewn over their surfaces. Short vertical walls lined the edges, and Justine realized that they were there to prevent anything on the table from falling off—when the alien moved past, his motion created a wake in the water. A number of items shifted position.

When the alien reached Justine's prison, he extended one tentacle to what looked like a control panel attached to the outside wall of the cell.

Though Justine had not absorbed enough Kinemetic radiation to quantize herself, or manipulate any electric current in the area, her *sight* was enough for her to start making out details, rather than seeing rough shapes.

At the end of the Kulsat's tentacle were several wormlike fingers. With these, he touched the control panel in a pattern.

A moment later, a mechanical voice spoke, the sound coming through the glass muted and partially distorted.

"Hello."

Justine flinched, then got hold of herself. She looked at the Kulsat.

"What do you mean, 'hello'?" She slapped her hand against the glass wall, all the anger and fear she'd been suppressing coming out. "Who the hell are you? Why did you kidnap me? What have you done with my friends?" When the alien did not respond, she asked, "What are you going to do to me?"

The alien extended his arm to the control panel again, as if typing.

"What do you mean hello who the hell are you why did you kidnap me what have you done with my friends what are you going to do to me."

Justine took a step back. The alien had mimicked her words.

She asked, "How do you know my language?"

The alien typed. "My do not have language. My have to *do* language."

He motioned to a spot between his eye and one of his arms, and Justine put her hand on her neck near the corresponding area. Her fingers felt a small rectangular piece of metal attached to her collar. A transmitter? The control panel attached to her tank must be a linguistic computer. Everything she'd said must have gone into it and been analyzed. The computer had already interpreted basic grammatical structure based on the few sentences she'd spoken.

While Justine did not want to give the Kulsat any information, she understood the need for communication. Perhaps she would be able to negotiate a treaty between the Kulsat and Earth. Then there would be no need for an invasion.

She started small. With her enhanced memory, she could recall the very first books she'd read as a child. Even without corresponding images to associate with the words or phrases, the alien's computer should be able to build a rudimentary language database.

Taking a deep breath to focus, Justine spoke, beginning with a number of the simpler titles, and moving up to some of her favorite children's books, including *Peter Pan*. By the time was she was on the fifth chapter of that classic, the alien interrupted her.

"You are able."

"Able?" Justine asked. "To do what?"

The Kulsat typed on his console. "You are able to be well."

"Am I hurt?" Justine asked. "No. I am not hurt."

"You are to be not expired? To be continuous?"

Justine struggled to understand the alien's meaning. "Yes, I'll live." She took a breath to illustrate. "Who are you? What is your name?"

"I am being the science leader."

Justine asked, "What do you want from me? What are you going to do to me?"

The alien did not type a reply immediately. It seemed to consider her question. Finally, it reached out to the computer again.

"You are to be cooperating. You are to be giving your knowledge to us. Then you are to be expiring."

5

Sierra de las Minas :
Guatemala :

Long Count: 9.19.19.17.9

With thoughts of glory, both for myself and for my people, I watched as the god completed his journey across the sky and toward the mountains. I fixed the spot where he landed in my mind, and then gathered my packs and my weapons and broke into a slow jog.

I was aware that I was going further into enemy territory the nearer I got to the mountains. To the north, on the other side of the mountains, was Lake Izabal, where many Q'eqchi' villages made their homes. Copán was two days' south through the highlands. If I got into trouble, there would be no help for me.

It would take me the better part of the day to get to the area where the god had come down. I knew, once I had left the relative safety of the forested areas south of Quiriguá, any patrol could spot me easily as I traveled across the river valley toward the mountains.

If anyone else had seen the god, then they might come to investigate. However, they would have to discuss the venture with their leaders before they could organize. For the time being, I had an advantage, if I could get there first.

Halfway there, I stopped beside a stream to drink and to eat the last of my rations, then continued across the valley.

I reached the base of the mountains just as the sun started to dip below the horizon.

I knew I was close. The god had landed about a quarter of the way up from the base of the mountain. It was slower going, picking my way up the face. A few times I stopped to catch my breath and see if any of the Q'eqchi' were following. From where I was, I could see the entire plain to the east. If I strained, I imagined I could see clear to the great ocean.

Night was falling, and if I didn't hurry, I might lose my sense of direction in the dark. Pushing myself, I climbed the rest of the way.

I expected something grand when I arrived. In my imagination, I pictured a tall and imposing god sitting on a glowing throne of jade, wearing a feathered headdress that would put anything I had ever seen to shame. Jaguars would lie at his feet, and a great eagle would perch on one shoulder—or perhaps it would be a firebird, flexing its blazing wings.

Instead, what I saw confused me.

There was no throne, no jaguars, no eagles, and no firebirds.

There was a short boat before me, and it was tilted on its side. A canopy covered the top of it, and it was open. The vessel was made from a material unlike anything I had ever seen. The shell seemed to be in motion, like the running water of a stream. Across the surface, it was as if an artist had created a living painting of bright and glowing colors. I found myself captivated by it.

I heard a faint sound and stepped around the mysterious boat.

A god did not wait there for me. Instead, I saw what looked like a plump young boy. He lay on his side, curled up, arms wrapped around him, with his back to a tree.

Once I got close enough to him, I froze.

His body had no hair, and his pale white skin was leathery, and mottled with blue patches.

His face was unlike any I had ever seen before. The top of his head was shorter than normal, and he had a thick, bony ridge starting where his eyebrows should have been, and wrapped around the sides of his bald head and to the back of his neck. I couldn't see any earlobes, but there was a small bump where his ears should have been. His eyes were large and spaced wide apart over high cheekbones. Although his nose was extremely small, his mouth and jaw were long and beaklike. Overall, he bore a slight resemblance to a turtle without a shell.

"You must help me," the creature said, and he spoke as if he were native to my village.

Overcoming my shock at his strange appearance, I rushed forward to see what was wrong.

He opened his slatted eyes and looked at me. "How are you called?" From this distance, I noticed that the words he mouthed did not match the sounds that came out.

"I am Subo Ak of the Ch'orti'," I said. "Who are you? *What* are you?"

"You may call me Ekahua. The people of the sky call us the Grace, though my people call ourselves Xtôti."

"Are you a god?" I asked.

He shook his head. "I am not. My people once came from a world much like this one."

I saw that he was having trouble breathing, and asked, "Are you injured?"

"I am dying," Ekahua said. "I will not live long on the surface of your planet; it is destroying me. My ship is too damaged to take me back to the sky."

"Will anyone from your tribe come to help you?"

He said, "There are only a few of my people left, and they are very far away. There will be no help from them. No one knows I am here.

"But there are other star tribes who might come. They cannot be allowed to find my sky boat or me. It is too dangerous for them. You must help me."

I glanced at his ship. "How?"

"Inside my boat there is a—" He said something then that sounded like stones grinding together. "It is a box with many square shapes, with many drawings on them."

Leaving Ekahua where he was, I strode back to the vessel. I felt the hairs of my arms stand up when I leaned close to look inside. I didn't want to touch the surface. I feared it would burn me, or that it would suck me into its swirling current.

There was a long, curved seat built into the ship. In front of the seat was a flat box with many smaller boxes outlined within, some larger than others. In the center of the box was a square that contained glowing, moving shapes.

"Touch the shape that has a picture of a circle with a line through the bottom edge."

I looked over the boxes until I saw one that fit the description. Once again, I hesitated. This could be a test or a trap. I didn't know what would happen if I did as Ekahua instructed. He said he was not a god; therefore, I could disobey him without risking any divine wrath. However, he was obviously very powerful; he could sail through the sky in this flying boat.

I remembered my people and how we were being slowly overrun by the Q'eqchi'.

"If I help you, will you help me? Will you help us defeat our enemies, who kill our men and steal our women? My village is near Copán. It was once a great and beautiful city, but our numbers grow smaller every season. We need help, as you do."

He said, "My very presence here is a danger to the future of this world, much greater than the conflict with your neighboring tribes. Having knowledge of me, your entire world is at risk."

I didn't understand what he was talking about, and it seemed he grew sadder.

"I have no weapons to give you," he said. "But I can give you a gift, Subo Ak."

"What gift?"

"I will teach you the Song of the Stars. Perhaps you will pass it on to your children and grandchildren."

"A song?" I asked.

"There is great power to be had in the song."

I was doubtful, but at the very least, I would have something to bring back to my village. A new song would not bring me as much honor as the skin of a Q'eqchi' warrior, but perhaps the song would gain me a level of respect with the elders. It was always good to be in their graces.

I nodded. "I will accept that bargain."

"Press the shape marked with the circle and line," Ekahua said.

I did so, and jumped back when a plate on the back of the boat opened. I stepped over to the opening and looked in. The inside of the boat resembled a mass of roots wrapped around a solid block of dark polished stone.

"There are twelve cords on the top of the—" He said another word I did not understand. I pointed to the top of the block, and when Ekahua nodded, I touched one of the root-like cords.

"It will be difficult, but you must pull them all out, and then put them back in different spots. You will need to work quickly. The ship will—" When I glanced at him, he said, "The ship will become like fire and burn. Within moments, it will turn to light and disappear."

Shocked, I pulled my fingers away from the cords. Suddenly, I became uncertain. The task sounded dangerous, and I did not want to be hurt or killed for a song.

"No harm will come to you, Subo Ak, if you are fast, and so long as the canopy keeps the cords shadowed from the sun. Once you have finished, return to me here where you will be safe."

I considered the device once more. There must be great power inside those roots if they could destroy such a wondrous boat so quickly.

Taking a deep breath, I plucked the first root out of the block. I felt an odd sensation in my hand, as if a small insect were crawling across my palm. A quick look showed me that my hand was empty. I peered into the hole left by the root and saw a small glowing object, no bigger than a grain of sand, resting in the gap.

Mindful that I had to work quickly, I yanked the remainder of the roots out.

"Hurry," Ekahua said, and feeling the urgency in his words, I replaced the roots into the openings in a random order.

"Good, now run back here."

Just as I started to turn, I noticed that one of the glowing grains of sand was resting in a nook partway down the polished block of stone. It must have fallen out when I pulled the roots.

I snatched the pebble up between my finger and thumb, and raced back to Ekahua as quickly as I could.

He was watching the boat, not me, and did not see when I slid the grain of sand inside one of the loose beads on my belt.

I turned to see what was becoming of the boat. At first, there was no change in the vessel.

A high-pitched sound came from it, soft at first, then louder. The swirls on the surface of the boat became frantic, and the vessel began to vibrate. The canopy snapped closed with a loud bark, and the plate on the back dropped back into place.

The ship began to shine bright like the sun.

"Shield your eyes," Ekahua said, and I put my hand over my face, looking at the vessel between the cracks of my fingers.

The sound became louder, and just when I thought I couldn't handle it any longer, the boat burst into thousands of flecks of light. Each of those flecks burnt out within moments.

When I took my hand away from my face, I saw that the boat had completely disappeared. I cautiously approached the spot where it had rested, and could not see any sign that it had ever existed.

"Thank you, Subo Ak," Ekahua said.

I felt a raindrop fall on my cheek and looked up into the evening sky. Clouds had gathered, and we would soon be caught in a downpour.

"We need to find shelter," I said.

"I do not have the strength to rise; you must carry me."

I picked Ekahua up, and he was far lighter than I had expected.

When I had climbed the side of the mountain earlier, I had passed a cliff where I had seen a small crevice. I didn't know how deep the crevice went, but I hoped it would be large enough for us to fit inside.

At the very least, it would keep the rain off Ekahua, and we would be hidden in case the Q'eqchi' warriors sent a scouting party this way.

6

Unknown Station :
Sol System :

To Alex's complete surprise, he woke up.

The last memory he had was of the Solan Empire soldiers firing at them. In retrospect, he realized they'd been shot with tranquilizers rather than bullets or ion pulses.

Opening his eyes, he looked around. He was in an infirmary, along with the other three. They were all hooked up to medical equipment and life support. An oxygen mask pressed against his mouth, and he felt the pinch of an IV needle in his arm feeding him nutrients.

Michael and Yaxche were still unconscious, but Alex saw that Kenny was coming to. A soft moan escaped the physicist's lips, muffled by his own mask, and he moved his head in quick, jerky motions.

Alex recognized the signs of bio stasis. Some people did not come out of it as well as others. NASA had experimented with the technique in the past, inducing a state similar to a medical coma in their astronauts on deep-space missions, but had discontinued the practice after determining the long-term effects were potentially harmful, ranging from muscle atrophy to dementia.

How long has they been in stasis? It was apparent the Solan Empire soldiers had decided it would be easier to put their prisoners to sleep for the trip, rather than deal with them. Depending on how bad Kenny's injuries were, he might have actually benefited from the long sleep, giving his bones time to knit.

Alex had a gnawing feeling deep in his stomach. He hadn't eaten solid food in who knew how long; he was suddenly famished. Quelling the hunger for the time being, he closed his eyes and concentrated.

Where were they?

Pushing his *sight* out, he was shocked to discover that they were no longer on the patrol ship that had attacked them.

He surveyed their immediate surroundings. They were in a large station, the design of which was not familiar to him. In passing, he sensed there were more than a thousand people on the station. It wasn't until he looked beyond the edges of the complex that he realized they were nowhere near Pluto.

From the moment Alex had been exposed to Kinemet on Macklin's Rock, he'd been able to hear the planets—the Music of the Spheres, as Yaxche called it. Every celestial body had a unique combination of forces—radiation, gravity, spin, mineral composition, and chemical makeup. Over the past several years, Alex had been able to identify the planets by their individual frequencies. With an odd feeling, he realized they were in orbit between the inner asteroid belt and Mars.

Based on ion pulse engine technology, it would have taken them four months to traverse the distance. That didn't seem plausible to Alex; he should have suffered far worse aftereffects from the medical stasis in that case. At the very least, he would have had significant weight loss in that time, and though he was acutely hungry, he didn't feel much slimmer than before.

Waking up must have triggered a sensor. He pulled his *sight* back as he heard a door open in the infirmary, and footsteps approaching.

Turning his head, he saw an unfamiliar man in a white lab coat coming toward him. Middle-aged, with a pronounced aquiline nose and a balding pate, the doctor smiled at Alex.

"Ah, I see our patients are starting to wake up."

Alex tried to rise, but couldn't even prop himself up on his elbows. Thick restraints around his arms and ankles held him to the bed.

"Oh, you mustn't try to move around until we can be sure you haven't suffered any muscle damage from your trip." The doctor removed the oxygen mask.

Alex tried to speak. With his dry throat, the words came out as a croak. He moved his tongue around to moisten his mouth, and tried again. "How long have we been in stasis?"

The doctor waited patiently for Alex to finish the question before answering. "Two weeks, my boy."

"Two...?"

The doctor smiled wider as he went to the other three patients and removed their masks as well. "Yes. We've made a few advances since you were last among us."

Kenny had come fully awake, and seemed to have overcome his reaction to the stasis. "Who are you?" the physicist asked.

"Pardon my manners. I am Doctor Naysmith." He went over to the diagnostic computer beside Kenny and looked over the readout. "Ah, good. It looks as if you are making a full recovery. Your ribs will still feel tender for a while, but give it another week or two, and you'll be right as rain."

"I think he meant, who are all of you?" came the question from Michael. "Who are you people? Where are we?"

"As I said," the doctor replied, a cheery note to his voice, "quite a bit has changed in the past four years, and my job is *not* to bring you up to speed. I'm just here to make sure you will be fit for an audience."

"An audience?" Alex asked. "With who?"

"With the Emperor, of course."

"Emperor?" Alex realized he was simply repeating everything as a question, and felt completely in the dark.

"Rest assured," Doctor Naysmith said, "all your questions will be answered in time. For now, if you'll permit me, I will go over your diagnostics and ensure you are all healthy. Do not stress about things which are beyond your control."

As if by unspoken consensus, the four of them pressed the doctor no further, and let him go about his business, reading scans and interpreting the output from the diagnostic computers. When he was finished, the doctor offered a bright smile to all of them, as if he'd accomplished a great feat.

"I will inform His Majesty of your full recovery. Have a pleasant day."

With that, the doctor left the four of them alone in the room. The overhead lights dimmed, leaving them in semi-darkness.

"What the hell is going on?" Kenny asked.

Michael said, "We've obviously stumbled into the middle of something big. We need more information. Alex, do you know where we are?"

Alex nodded, then realized that the others might not be able to see him. "Yes. We're on an asteroid mining and processing station. I'm not sure which station, though—it could be Chinese; I don't know their characters. It's in a solar orbit inside the inner belt."

Michael asked, "In line with Mars' orbit?"

"Yes."

"It's the Qin Station, named after the first Emperor of China, the one who initiated construction of the Great Wall."

Kenny said, "Emperors! Do you think there's been a civil war in China? Did they overthrow the communist party and resurrect the imperial dynasties?"

"It's a possibility," Michael said. "What concerns me is that they've apparently managed to supplant USA, Inc.'s presence on Pluto. I know, when we left, things were dicey back home, but how bad could it have gotten?"

"So what's the plan?"

"For the moment," Michael said, "it looks as if we have to take the doctor's advice. It's out of our hands. Once we've met this Emperor, whoever he is, then we'll know more." He added in a lower voice, "I would suggest that we all continue to be extremely discreet. When we meet this Emperor, let me do the talking."

Alex said, "Fine by me."

"Me, too," Kenny said. He turned his head to the other bed. "Yaxche. You haven't said much. Are you all right?"

"Ahyah," the old man said. "My stomach is upset. I'm a little dizzy."

"That's probably because of the bio stasis," Michael said. "It will most likely pass in a few hours. It looks like we all have to play the waiting game, anyway."

Alex couldn't just lie there and do nothing. He still had enough Kinemetic radiation flowing through him to continue to use his *sight,* so he began to search Qin Station.

For the most part, the station was much like any other mining station, populated with engineers, miners, pilots, administrators, supervisors, and technicians of all the disciplines required to keep the operation going. Expecting a mostly Chinese population, Alex was a little surprised to find an even representation from all Earth cultures.

The question remained: whoever this Emperor was, would he be in a position to defend Sol against the Kulsat? However much power he'd accumulated, it wouldn't matter if the Kulsat wiped them all out.

While he searched, Alex became aware of an area of the station where his senses could not penetrate. The moment he got close, it was as if he hit a wall.

A Kinemetic damper surrounded the large area, which could have been rooms, offices, or labs, for all Alex knew.

After all his effort, Alex didn't have much more information than when he started. It looked as if they would have to follow the doctor's advice after all, and wait.

∞

It was nearly twelve hours later when a squad of armed soldiers entered the infirmary, accompanying the doctor.

"Good news," Doctor Naysmith said, "the Emperor will see you now. First, however, we need to get you all cleaned up. Once I remove the stasis equipment, you'll have one hour to acclimate yourselves. We've kept gravity at two-thirds on the station, so it should be easier for you to get your feet. No doubt, you all are feeling hunger pains. It's been a while since you've had solid food, so we'll provide you with a nutrient paste for today. Your stomachs should be back to normal by tomorrow. Now, I hope you will all give me your complete cooperation."

Alex frowned. Having spent two weeks lying on a bed, he wasn't sure he could offer any resistance if he wanted to. Though the bio stasis kept muscle tone up with electrotherapy, all four of them would have the physical responsiveness of newborns for at least a while.

Without waiting for a reply, the doctor began to shut down the remaining bio machines. He unhooked Yaxche from his IV first, and unlatched his restraints. With the help of one of the soldiers, he assisted him into a sitting position.

"How are you feeling?" the doctor asked.

Yaxche nodded. "Like an old man."

With a short, polite laugh, Doctor Naysmith said, "Private Lund will help you to do some stretching exercises."

The doctor signaled one of the other soldiers to assist him with Kenny, following the same procedures. He got Michael up next, and Alex last.

When all four of them could walk around unassisted, the doctor motioned toward a door on the other side of the infirmary. They followed him into the next room.

"There are showers here," the doctor said, "as well as toiletries and clothing. I will return in half an hour to check on your progress. If you require assistance, any of the guards will be more than happy to help."

The soldiers entered the room behind them. It looked like they weren't going to have any privacy.

Turning on his heel, the doctor hurried out of the infirmary, and left the four prisoners to put themselves together.

In silence, Alex and the others cleaned up, showering, shaving and getting dressed. The clothes were simple jumpsuits with black leather boots. The epaulets had the sigil of the Solan Empire on them.

When the doctor finally returned, he gave them all a conciliatory nod of approval.

"Gentlemen, my purpose has been served. Thank you for your time. Please follow these soldiers; they will take you to your audience. Have a nice day."

Alex automatically said, "Thank you." Kenny looked at him and lifted an eyebrow as if asking why he was being polite to their captor.

They all exited the infirmary. The doctor went down the hall in one direction, and the rest of them headed in the other.

As they went, several of the station's residents looked at them curiously, but no one spoke.

Reaching the end of the hall, they stopped at an elevator, and got in once the doors opened. One soldier tapped a button for the top floor, and Alex remembered that the area surrounded by the Kinemetic damper was there.

He felt the growing anticipation as they approached the barrier his senses could not penetrate.

The moment the elevator went past the damping field, Alex's senses were overwhelmed by the sheer quantity of Kinemet stored on that level. There was enough to power hundreds of quantum ships. It was more Kinemet than USA, Inc. and Canada Corp. had mined in ten years.

The overwhelming radiation made him reel. He was so distracted by the sensation that he hadn't thought to use his senses to see if there were any people there.

It was only when the elevator doors opened that he realized there was a large welcoming party waiting for them.

He hung his mouth open in shock when the Emperor of Sol System, surrounded by a dozen armed soldiers, spoke to him.

"It's been a long time, Alex."

7

PRC Penal Station :
Earth-Sun Lagrange Three :

During the latter third of the last century, several observational stations had been put into orbit in the Lagrange Three point, on the opposite side of the Sun from the Earth. These stations were designed to forecast sunspots, flares and coronal ejections, giving advance warning of solar disturbances.

At one time, quite a few of the stations had been populated, but as it turned out, it was such an unpopular assignment—there was a psychological effect of never being in a direct line of communication with Earth, since the Sun interfered with most radio signals—that the world's governments had abandoned their efforts there, and only maintained the unmanned stations. All except one.

That orbital, built by the People's Republic of China, had been converted to a penal station for those criminals the government decided could not be rehabilitated: serial killers, traitors, drug lords, terrorists, human traffickers, and war criminals. Since the Chinese government had abolished capital punishment, they decided this was the next-best thing.

There were no guards, and the inmates themselves were charged with the maintenance and operation of the station as part of their sentence. Should the convicts fail to organize, it would be their own undoing.

The only contact the penal station had with Earth was the monthly transport—a military PRC warship—which brought supplies, equipment, and new prisoners. Sensors all over the outside of the station would broadcast an EPS alert to the government of China via relay satellites should any unauthorized vessel approach the station.

This station was where Chow Yin, convicted of nearly every capital crime in the Chinese justice system, was sentenced to spend the rest of his days.

Chow Yin wasted no time, and began to plot his escape from the moment he embarked on the military transport to the penal colony. On Luna Station, he'd built a criminal empire in a very simple, but effective manner, and now applied the technique in his current situation.

The first day on the military transport, he sized up the four other prisoners. There was Tza, a heavily muscled opium smuggler; Huan, convicted of espionage; Sang, who—if the newsvids could be believed—was a serial killer who had murdered more than forty women over the past twelve years; and Sian, a frail young man who had somehow managed to hack into China's largest bank, where he'd worked, and embezzle close to a half-billion yuans.

The cargo bay of the transport was magnetically sealed, and that's where the five of them would spend the fourteen-day journey to the penal station. There was no need for guards, since there was no possible way any of the prisoners could breach the hold's security system.

Four long tables made from metal were set up along one wall of the bay, on the opposite side from the six sleeping cots, which were little more than sheets of canvas wrapped around a plastic frame. Those were the only furnishings in the area, except for the one lavatory set into the farthest corner of the hold.

At mealtimes, a dumbwaiter opened in one wall to reveal trays of food on paper plates. They were not provided with utensils, so the prisoners were only able to use their fingers to feed themselves.

Even in the low gravity, Chow Yin's legs were all but useless. Having spent months on Earth during the trial, his condition had worsened until the point when he required the constant use of a molded plastic wheelchair.

He expected to become the first and obvious target of one of the other prisoners, but to his surprise, Sian was the focus of Tza's first attempt at extortion.

At the first meal, Chow Yin held back and observed. Sian got up before anyone else and headed over to the dumbwaiter. Without hesitation, he grabbed a plate and made his way to the tables.

Tza, instead of going to the dumbwaiter to get his meal, approached

Sian.

"You're the runt of the litter," he said. "You don't need as much as the rest of us."

With that, he backhanded Sian, knocking the smaller man to the ground, and picked up the plate.

"You can have my scraps, if there are any left," he said in a snarl, heading to the dumbwaiter and grabbing another plate.

The big drug lord paused a moment, glancing at Chow Yin. "You got something to say, cripple?"

Shaking his head slowly, Chow Yin remained where he was, still waiting. Moments later, Sang and Huan decided to split Chow Yin's plate before he even approached to get it. Both smirked at him as they divided their spoils.

Only after Tza, Sang, and Huan had eaten did Chow Yin approach Sian.

Shaking and looking miserable, the young computer hacker glanced up at Chow Yin. His eye was already swelling up. "He would have killed me if I fought back."

"Of course he would have," Chow Yin said.

"Next time I'll be smart like you, and let them go first."

Shaking his head, Chow Yin said, "No, next time you will go first again, except you will get a plate for me as well."

With a look of horror at the thought, Sian said, "That's suicide."

"Trust me," Chow Yin said, and wheeled himself away to the farthest table, positioning himself at it as if waiting to be served.

It was several hours later, when the dumbwaiter once again sounded that a meal was being delivered, that Sian glanced at Chow Yin, who nodded confidently.

Tza, seeing Sian get up and approach the panel first, laughed and said to the others, "Do you believe this? Some people never learn."

Chow Yin, still at the farthest table, waited for Sian to bring him his meal.

Sian, sweating and shaking in fear, grabbed two plates the moment the door panel opened, and hurried over to Chow Yin's table.

Tza guffawed at the action, and slowly stood up. He put his fist in his hand and cracked his knuckles.

"Watch this," he said, and lumbered over to Chow Yin and Sian. He stood over the two, as if deciding which of them to punish first.

Chow Yin pushed his plate a centimeter toward Tza. "We were

foolish to try to take what is rightfully yours," he said, his words obviously surprising both Sian and Tza. "Please accept our apologies."

"Damn right, it's mine," Tza said, and reached down to grab the plate.

Tza's eyes bulged when Chow Yin casually flicked his hand out and stabbed the smuggler in the neck with a short shiv, slicing into the carotid artery.

Both the body and the wheels of Chow Yin's wheelchair were made of plastic. For the past few hours, Chow Yin had loosened one plastic axle a few centimeters, and snapped it off. He had spent the rest of the time rubbing the shiv against the bottom of the metal table, sharpening the point.

It was obvious Tza could not figure out what had happened. As the opium smuggler fell to the deck, clutching at his neck and trying to stem the flow of blood, Chow Yin casually took his plate back and began to eat.

A biosensor detected Tza's condition, and an alarm sounded. By the time the soldiers entered the hold to assess the situation, Tza was dead.

Though the guards did not seem to express any outrage at the death of a known criminal, they had to follow protocol, and the remaining prisoners were secured to their cots for the remainder of the trip. From that point on, they were only released one at a time for meals and biological needs.

The restrictions did not matter to Chow Yin; he'd already achieved his goal. By the time the military transport arrived at the penal station, the remaining prisoners had sworn complete allegiance to him.

∞

For the next twelve years, Chow Yin did not simply rule the cadre of criminals in the penal station. He enforced a strict regimen of education on them. Doing what the justice system could not, he turned these criminals into productive soldiers in his burgeoning empire. He found out what each inmate's unique talents were, and schooled them on how to use those abilities more effectively. Whenever a transport came, he would sort through the newly arriving prisoners and indoctrinate them to his cause.

No matter how much control he had, however, he could not tip his hand to the outside world. Whenever the military inspectors arrived, they found what they'd always come to expect: a typical prison environment, the station maintained to its minimum standards, and the occasional dead body—if the soldiers reported back that everything was perfect, that would arouse suspicion.

Though there were grumblings from his subordinates that their escape was taking too long, Chow Yin knew that any premature action would result in their recapture. Freeing himself of the penal colony was a secondary consideration; before he could make any move, he had to be certain that his escape was permanent. His ultimate goal was not simply freedom; the only way he could ensure his future was a complete reversal of the game he played on Luna Station. He would not skulk in the shadows. It was time for him to seize control of his future, and nothing less than the complete domination of Sol System would do.

All electronic communications were monitored by the government satellites throughout the Lagrange Point, so Chow Yin had no way to communicate with the rest of the solar system. Before he left Earth, he'd managed to send out a short message to a trusted subordinate through one of his lawyers, but he had no way of knowing if it was received, or if the man would be successful.

Finally, his patience was rewarded.

When the monthly military transport arrived, the entire population of the station gathered in front of the docking bay doors, as they always did.

This time was different. When the ship opened its cargo doors, instead of prisoners disembarking, seven soldiers marched out onto the dock and formed a line in front of the gate.

To the inmates' complete surprise, the pilot of the ship, a grizzled officer, opened the gate and took a step forward. He stood at attention in front of Chow Yin and, with a salute, said, "We are at your service, Emperor Yin."

"It took you long enough, Mr. Leong." Chow Yin's words were only half-reproachful.

It would have taken Captain Leong years to get himself assigned to the penal station duty, and to get the military transport staffed with those who were loyal to the movement.

During the months of his trial, Chow Yin had spent a considerable amount of time listening to the news. He realized that there were people from all areas of China who had become disillusioned with the policies that had turned the PRC from one of the most powerful nations in the world to its current state as nothing more than a puppet for the Earth Council. The military, becoming less of a necessity as China slowly moved away from communism and toward democracy, had particularly suffered in the interim. Many officers and enlisted, who had dedicated their lives to the defense of the country they loved, believed it was time to restore the old system of divine leadership. The Emperors of China had always relied heavily on their military to enforce their rule.

Before he'd been captured on Luna Station, one of Chow Yin's hobbies had been genealogy. He had been able to trace his lineage back to the Qing, the last imperial dynasty of China two centuries before. With a legitimate claim through bloodlines, all he had to do was to get a message to imperialist sympathizers of his incarceration.

Before his exile from Earth, Chow Yin had managed to convince the imperialists, through Leong—who had never managed to make a rank higher than captain in the PRC Space Force—that they should set their sights higher than simply retaking China. With Chow Yin as a figurehead, it was only a matter of time before the disillusioned officers managed to organize and put their plan into effect.

Captain Leong said, "My apologies for the delay, Sire."

"You are here now," Chow Yin said, then added, *"General* Leong."

Though the newly promoted general's expression did not change, Chow Yin saw that he stood a little straighter.

Chow Yin gestured to the inmates of the penal station. "I'd like to introduce you to our newest recruits."

General Leong took a step forward and surveyed the growing crowd of convicts.

He spoke in a booming voice for all to hear. "We don't have much time before the false Chinese government realizes we've commandeered their ship, so I'll be brief. We need to ensure no one suspects that we have liberated you from the station. Your cooperation is mandatory." He made a gesture, and four of his men came out of the ship, carrying two heavy crates between them. They set the crates down beside the general and pulled the lid off.

General Leong continued his speech. "I need everyone to grab an incendiary canister and bring it to your quarters. Place it in the center of your cell. They're connected with a remote, which we will activate once we have left dock."

One of the inmates, the serial killer named Sang, spoke up. "What about our stuff?"

"You must leave all your personal possessions behind. Inspectors will come. If you've packed all your things, they will know the escape was planned. We want them to investigate all possibilities; this will delay their efforts."

Chow Yin cleared his throat and gave the general a furtive look.

General Leong opened his holoslate and said, "Would the following prisoners please step forward." He read off a list of eleven names, including Sian, the hacker.

As the eleven men separated themselves from the main group, four more soldiers jogged out of the transport ship, pulse rifles in their hands, and circled them.

Sang said, "What's this all about?"

Holding up a hand, General Leong gave the man a conciliatory nod. "Not to worry. There are some who do not deserve to be part of the new Empire. We will ensure the purity of our cause."

Giving the eleven another assessment, Sang nodded. "I see what you mean." The separated men shared common traits: they were all considered the weakest of the inmates. Over the past few years, Chow Yin had had to intervene several times to spare them a beating from one of the other more violent inmates. "Besides, you probably want to leave a few bodies behind to throw off the scent." A number of the other prisoners chuckled.

Sian gave Chow Yin a look of panic. Chow Yin did not even glance in his direction.

General Leong spoke in an authoritative voice. "Gentlemen, we are embarking on a new chapter in the history of Sol System. Today marks the first day in the rule of the First Empire of Sol. Please do as I instructed."

With alacrity, the seventy-one remaining inmates rushed to the crates and picked up an incendiary canister. As they filed out of the docking area and back to the main compound, Chow Yin looked up at General Leong.

"Tell me she is safe."

Nodding, the general said, "It wasn't easy, Sire, but we've secured her for you. You were correct; she was integral in developing the weaponized Kinemet."

"Good."

After a moment's hesitation, General Leong said, "I have other news, Emperor. Klaus has been located. He has made himself a hidden base on Venus. We believe he has made a breakthrough in the process—"

Chow Yin waved an impertinent hand at him. "That will be our first destination, then. I trust we have enough resources to accomplish our objective."

"Yes, Sire. More than enough. General Zhang has given us his full support, and he controls over a hundred-thousand troops. We also have four colonels, six members of the state council, and several private sector CEOs who have chafed under PRC rule. We have people in every level of government. As you suspected, all seven nations we reached out to have informally offered support and a willingness to sign fealty to an imperial charter—it seems the USA, Inc. stranglehold on future technologies is a sore point with them; they'd like nothing more than to see the giant fall."

"Excellent," Chow Yin said.

Once the last inmate to grab an incendiary left the bay, General Leong signaled his men surrounding the eleven who had been held back. The soldiers all raised their pulse rifles.

"Quickly now," the general said to the eleven in a low voice, "board the ship. Not a word."

Confused, the men stared at him.

"Would you rather be shot?" the general asked. "Move it!"

The men, glancing at the soldiers nervously, did as they were told, and hurried aboard the ship. Sian tried to catch Chow Yin's eye, but the self-styled Emperor was wheeling his chair to a control center at the main bay doors of the prison.

As he tapped out a few commands, one of the prisoners, Sang, was returning to the dock area from his task. The bay doors began to close.

"Hey!" he called out, and broke into a run. A soldier who had been standing watch over his Emperor raised his pulse rifle, leveled it at Sang, and fired. The electric whir of the rifle was followed by a meaty thud as Sang's dead body fell to the cement floor. A few other prisoners noticed the closing doors and the body, and within a few moments, they stampeded for the docking bay.

The soldier only had to fire two more shots to put down the lead prisoners before the door closed, locking electromagnetically.

Shouldering the rifle strap, the soldier quickly raced behind Chow Yin's wheelchair, grasped the handles, and wheeled his Emperor onto the ship, which immediately lifted off.

Once Chow Yin was on the bridge, General Leong issued a command to one of the other officers. "Detonate the incendiaries."

Chow Yin could not observe the dozens of small explosions within the prison compound, but he knew the fire would quickly spread throughout the station and gut the colony.

If there was one thing that serial killer Sang was right about, there would be plenty of bodies for the Chinese investigators to find.

∞

Sitting in his wheelchair on the bridge of the ship six weeks after breaking out of the penal station, Chow Yin forced himself to keep his temper in check.

General Leong carefully watched the monitors at his station and did not turn around to face his Emperor. If he knew how angry Chow Yin was, he didn't give any indication.

First, they'd arrived at Lucis Observatory too late: Klaus was already dead; his research destroyed. After questioning Klaus's uncle, Gruber, they'd learned two things before the man had succumbed to the wounds sustained during questioning. The first was the general process Klaus had used to develop the Kinemetic conversion—the Kinemet had to be 'primed' somehow. Secondly, Gruber told them that Major Justine Turner had been converted to a Kinemat and was on the way to Canada Station Three, where Alex Manez was kept under military protection.

Chow Yin glanced at Sian, who sat at the main computer terminal. The programmer had been able to monitor the communications between the Earth Council and Canada Station Three, and learned about the injunction against Kinemetic research. He'd also picked up a message that the Arab Conglomerates were sending a team of observers to CS3—Chow Yin, knowing Alex and Justine's history, made a guess that they wouldn't just sit idly by and wait to be put under a microscope. "We need to be ready to intercept them," he told his crew, and General Leong put in a course for CS3.

His hunch had proved correct: Alex and Justine were trying to get away from CS3 before the observers arrived, and Chow Yin ordered

General Leong to pursue them.

"How many of the Kinemetic torpedoes do you have on board?" he asked.

"Three," the general responded. "If we use them, we'll destroy their ship."

"That's the idea," Chow Yin said. "According to Captain Gruber, no one knows Klaus's process; the secret died with him. The last thing we need is for someone to leak the information; we cannot have competition. In order for us to control space, we need to have a monopoly on the technology; anyone who is undertaking research must be eliminated."

"Understood, Sire," General Leong said, but their efforts to destroy the *Ultio* and its passengers fell short when, to everyone's surprise, their first Kinemetic torpedo detonated before it impacted. When the general ordered the launch of the remaining two torpedoes, the *Ultio* quantized and disappeared from normal space.

The silence on the bridge stretched out for several minutes before Chow Yin finally spoke.

"Well, there is no help for it." He turned to General Leong. "We must return to our original plan."

The general nodded, and gave the order to his pilot. "Lay in a course to Qin Station."

Chow Yin swore under his breath, "It's time I took back what is rightfully mine."

∞

Over the following four years, Chow Yin wrested control of all space operations in Sol System through a combination of force and misdirection.

His greatest asset was to use the paranoia of Earth's nations against them. Before he launched his first strike against Luna Station, he arranged for the detonation of a Nepali nuclear warhead on Bhutan soil. Key members of the PRC Parliament, as directed by Chow Yin, called for immediate sanctions against Nepal.

India, a long-time ally of Nepal, called for sanctions against China, who then declared war on India. Within months, nearly every nation on Earth was taking sides, and military conflict was at an all-time high.

Once the superpowers withdrew the bulk of their military forces back to Earth, Luna Station was Chow Yin's for the taking. The most tenuous moment in his plans for empire came when the United States Space Force launched a major offensive to retake their four mining stations near the asteroid belt—which was important to the war effort, since asteroid mining was the only way to replenish their stocks of metals. Earth had been depleted the majority of their resources long ago.

Instead of protecting those mining stations, Chow Yin ordered their complete destruction—which served as a warning to any other nation that attempted a similar action.

In a public relations move, he relocated all the personnel on those stations to the Qin Station. He made it a point to have the news feeds report that there had not been any loss of life in the action. The reality was that Chow Yin valued those engineers and scientists more than the stations they worked on.

At the same time, Chow Yin informed every news agency about the catastrophic losses of Chinese military in the conflict, most of whom had died at the hands of American soldiers. With world sentiment rising against the USA, Inc., Chow Yin instructed the members of the PRC state council who were loyal to him to declare war on USA, Inc.

The declaration went through, and China launched its first strike— Chinese troops managed to get a foothold on the pacific coast before finally being repelled from American soil.

The conflict proved an effective distraction, and kept the news focused on the terrestrial conflict, and away from events in space, which was what Chow Yin wanted in the first place.

Any vessel—whether military or civilian—launched from Earth was intercepted, the crew given the choice to swear fealty to the new Emperor of Sol System, or be ejected into space.

His military strategy, however, was considerably more successful than his scientific ones. After four years, his team of scientists was no closer to figuring out the key to Kinemetic conversion. Not that they hadn't tried. Chow Yin had no problem coming up with hundreds of 'volunteers' for the experiments, none of whom survived.

The furthest they'd been able to push his technology agenda was to convert Kinemet to a super fuel, giving their ships the ability to fly at ten times the velocity of ion pulse engines. The first Orca mission to Pluto had taken nearly six months; Chow Yin's engineers had developed engines that would propel their ships from Luna to Pluto in two-and-a-half weeks.

It was not nearly fast enough for Chow Yin. When he received the communication from the patrol ship he had placed in Plutonian orbit that an alien vessel had materialized in Sol System space, he longed for near-light-speed travel.

The captain of the patrol ship reported that the alien vessel had been destroyed by the minefield they'd placed there.

Grimacing as he listened to the message, knowing the events described had already occurred four hours previous, Chow Yin breathed a sigh only when he heard the last sentence:

"…and we have recovered four passengers who used an escape pod—all humans. We have identified them, and have them in custody. Alex Manez, Michael Sanderson, Kenny Harriman, and the Mayan historian, Yaxche.

"Sire, your instructions were to destroy anything that entered Sol's space, but we wanted to confirm those instructions, considering the identities of the prisoners."

This was one time Chow Yin was happy his subordinates did not completely obey his instructions. With the difficulties he had in replicating Klaus's research, having access to those four might give his team of researchers a catalyst to perfecting the Kinemetic process. The only person who would have been more beneficial to him was Major Turner. He wondered what had become of her.

Chow Yin encoded a return message to the patrol ship. "Excellent work, Lieutenant Gao. You are to return to Qin Station immediately with the prisoners. We'll send a relief patrol ship to replace you."

Once he sent the message, he contacted the lab facility and informed them to prepare for the impending arrival of their 'guests'.

8

Qin Station :
Sol System :

"Chow Yin?" Michael blurted out.

The criminal who had once secretly controlled Luna Station from the shadows stood in front of them, beaming as if pleased that he had suitably surprised his guests.

When he'd been arrested on Luna, Chow Yin had barely been able to get around the station with the aid of a cane. During his trial in China, the stress of the planet's gravity had done considerable damage to his already weakened legs, Michael recalled. At the time of his incarceration, Chow Yin had been confined to a wheelchair.

Now, Michael saw, he'd been fitted with a full set of biomechatronic legs, similar to the braces Alex had used on Canada Station Three. The prosthetics were bulky, making him look disproportionate, but it gave him the ability to walk around under his own power.

Chow Yin did so, stepping forward amid the mechanical hum of the electronic pistons, and nodded to Michael. "Mr. Sanderson, welcome back to Sol System. I see you've noticed my new legs. My engineers just fitted me with them. Tell me, do they make me look too tall?"

Michael ignored the question. "Why have you kidnapped us?"

The Emperor only widened his smile. He turned to the others. "Kenneth Harriman, Yaxche, pleased to have you join us."

A thousand thoughts raced through Michael's mind. The last he'd heard, Chow Yin had been sent to a penal station on the L3 point on the opposite side of the Sun. In the span of four years, Chow Yin went from prisoner to Emperor. Michael wondered at the events that had led to this development.

Alex took a step back. "I won't do it."

"Now, now," said Chow Yin. "I had hoped we could be civil."

At first, Michael didn't know what they were talking about, but a moment later, it came to him. Assuming it was Chow Yin's engineers who had advanced Kinemet technology to the point where they could fly a ship from Pluto to the asteroid belt in two weeks, they still hadn't mastered the element's superluminal aspect. As powerful as Chow Yin had become, carving out his own empire, it was obvious he still had not been able to develop a Kinemat.

That's why he'd captured them, instead of killing them. Alex was the only living Kinemat in Sol System, though he was not fully converted. They would need him for study. Kenneth had been working with Alex, and was one of the brightest quantum physicists in the community. Though Quantum Resources had made recordings of Yaxche's recitation of the Song of the Stars in Mayan, it was more than likely they had not allowed those to get into Chow Yin's hands. Without the musical recipe, they could spend a century trying to get the frequencies correct to prime Kinemet for a transformation.

The Emperor needed Alex, Kenny, and Yaxche.

He did not need Michael, and proved it a moment later when he nodded to one of the soldiers near him. The man raised his rifle, aiming directly at Michael's head.

Chow Yin said, "I had a banquet planned, where we could have something to eat while we negotiated our partnership. It's disappointing that you've brought us to the ultimatum stage so quickly. You're taking all the fun out of it, Alex." With a look of forced patience, he spoke slowly. "You will help us, or your friend will die. There. Is that simple enough for you?"

Michael gritted his teeth. "Don't do it, Alex. Don't give this madman anything."

"Ah, I see you think I am bluffing. I assure you. I am not." The Emperor's expression turned grave. "A demonstration is in order." To the soldier, he said, "Kill Mr. Sanderson, if you would be so kind."

"No!" Alex shouted, and instinctively tried to push Michael out of the line of fire.

Kenny was a second faster, and hit Michael with his body. The ion pulse that was meant for the older man seared through Kenny's chest, instantly killing the physicist.

Alex changed direction, reaching out to catch Kenny's falling body. A cry of outrage and despair escaped him.

"You murdered him!" he yelled, though the words came out incoherently.

Michael, who had recovered his balance, slowly stood up straight. He couldn't believe Kenny was dead. A primal savagery began to grow inside him. Thought did not control his actions. On pure instinct, he launched himself at Chow Yin with only the image of his hands wrapped around the self-styled Emperor's neck to fuel him. He had no care that he would most likely be shot dead by a soldier before he got more than half way to their leader. Kenny had never hurt anyone. He didn't deserve to be cut down like an animal.

Instead of shooting Michael, the soldier who had killed Kenny reversed his rifle and hit him with the butt square in the head. Michael fell to the floor in a heap. His head exploded with pain, but the blow hadn't knocked him unconscious.

"I see you continue to test my resolve," Chow Yin said. "Perhaps we need to repeat the lesson."

Michael slowly looked up; any action sent waves of agony through him, and a sickening nausea gripped his guts.

"Leave him alone," Alex said. "I'll cooperate." A moment later, he added, "On one condition."

"Yes?" Chow Yin asked.

"Send them all home." Alex, who had knelt beside Michael to check on his friend, stood up. "Send them back to Earth. I'll give you what you want."

It took Michael a moment to understand the words. "No," he said in protest, his voice weak. "Don't give the bastard the satisfaction. I'd rather die than give him that kind of power."

"What you fail to realize, my dear Mr. Sanderson, is that the power has always been mine. Alex's decision was inevitable." Chow Yin turned around on his biomechatronic legs and walked away.

∞

Michael was brought back to the infirmary, two soldiers on either side of him grasping him by the arms. The blow to the head had been hard enough that he didn't have any fight left in him now, even if he'd wanted to do anything.

The soldiers led Alex and Yaxche in a different direction, while several other guards brought in a gurney on which they loaded Kenny's body.

The suddenness of the young man's death was almost too much for Michael to process. He'd only known Kenny for a short time, but the two of them had worked very well together. The younger man was extremely intelligent, and as far as Michael was concerned, he would have had a brilliant career ahead of him.

Grief and regret edged into Michael's consciousness as he realized he didn't even know whether Kenny had any family. He should have taken the time to get to know the other man better.

Chow Yin. Michael couldn't wrap his mind around it. How had he escaped the penal station? How had he enlisted so many to his mad cause? How had he managed to wrest control of space from the nations of Earth? There were a hundred other questions he had. Ignorance was as big an enemy to Michael as Chow Yin. Without more information, Michael was at a complete disadvantage; he was at their mercy.

After strapping Michael onto the infirmary bed by the forearms and ankles, the soldiers stood guard until Doctor Naysmith returned.

"Back so soon?" the doctor asked, with that same innocent smile on his face. "Oh, it looks as if you've had an accident."

"How can you work for these animals?" Michael asked. "They murdered Kenny right in front of me."

"Sad to hear it." The doctor pulled out a tray from one of the rolling cabinets and extracted a few sheets of medical absorbent cloths. He stood over Michael and examined the head wound.

His voice low in a growl, Michael said, "Chow Yin is a madman who wants more than to rule the world; he wants to rule the entire universe. If you work for him, you're just another traitor."

While he gently placed the cloth on the injured spot to soak up the excess blood, Doctor Naysmith leaned in and said, "My life is medicine. It's all that matters." He continued to work on Michael, maintaining his smile. "I took an oath: 'I will not permit considerations of religion, nationality, race, gender, politics, socioeconomic standing, or sexual orientation to intervene between my duty and my patient.' Everyone has a right to medical treatment, Mr. Sanderson, even madmen."

Doctor Naysmith reached into the tray again and retrieved a laser suture gun. He pointed it at the gash on Michael's head and pressed the trigger.

There was an uncomfortable pulling sensation that grew more painful as the skin on his forehead mended. Just when Michael thought he couldn't handle it anymore, the doctor finished the procedure.

"There," Doctor Naysmith said, giving Michael a pat on the shoulder, "good as new."

∞

It was a few hours later when the soldiers came for him. With ruthless efficiency, they unstrapped him from the gurney. Michael hadn't seen Doctor Naysmith since he'd tended his head wound, and there was no sign of him now.

The soldiers didn't give him time to get his balance. When his pace proved too slow for them, two of them grabbed his arms and dragged him out of the infirmary.

"You're ripping my arms out of their sockets," Michael said, not expecting his words to have any effect.

"We're almost there," the squad leader said, as if to reassure him that the discomfort was temporary.

They led him through the halls and back to the elevator, though this time they descended to the lower levels. When the doors opened, Michael saw that they were in the main docking bay area.

Yaxche was there, standing beside a metal casket. The moment Michael's guards let his arms go, he hurried over to the old man. The soldiers fanned out, rifles at the ready, but they didn't stop him.

"Are you all right?" he asked, and felt a surge of relief when Yaxche nodded.

"Ahyah. They only wanted me to tell them my story."

Lowering his voice, Michael asked, "The Song of the Stars?"

Nodding, Yaxche said, "Alex said to go ahead and do so; that it would make no difference."

That puzzled Michael, and he gave Yaxche a quizzical look. The Mayan shrugged one shoulder. "Alex could have sung it from memory, but I think he wanted a chance to say goodbye to me."

Michael put his hand on the casket. "I feel bad for Kenny."

"He makes the final journey. I do not worry; his is a wise spirit."

The sound of boot steps got Michael's attention, and he looked around to see Lieutenant Gao approach.

"Mr. Sanderson, I've been assigned to transport the three of you to Luna Station, where you will then be put on a rapid transit capsule, which we will send to the Nova Scotia Space Port. I trust you will not resist, or cause any trouble during the flight. I would rather not put you into bio stasis again."

Michael took a deep breath, then nodded. "You have my word." He glanced at Yaxche, who gave the lieutenant a toothy smile.

"Good," Lieutenant Gao said. He took one measured step back, and gestured toward where his ship was docked. "If you will follow me, we'll get you situated in secure quarters. The flight will last approximately three days, and the capsule trip should take less than twelve hours."

They trailed behind Lieutenant Gao as he led them to his ship, while the Solan soldiers followed, watchful for any transgression.

In the ship, one of the officer's quarters had been converted to a temporary detention area. It was cramped for two people, but at least they had some privacy.

Michael wanted to share his theories on what had happened in Sol System, but Yaxche didn't seem very interested in conversation or company.

At one point, Michael asked if there was anything wrong with him, to which Yaxche shook his head. "I have not had much time for meditation," he told him. "I am a simple man; I am not used to all this excitement. I only wish to go home."

Once they reached orbit around the Moon, they were given an hour to stretch their legs before they were taken to the capsule area of the ship.

Lieutenant Gao was there to see them off. "I can't promise you it will be a smooth ride," he said. "It will only get rougher when you hit the atmosphere. If you make it through that without any serious damage, you should be fine. We're aiming for a splashdown off the coast of Nova Scotia. I've been authorized to notify your government of your return; they should be waiting for you."

Michael's diplomatic side compelled him to say something. "Unlike certain others, you've treated us decently, Lieutenant."

"Of course," the lieutenant said with a slight nod.

"It's not too late to change your ship's course. Come with us. Turn yourself in. I will speak on your behalf."

"I'm sorry. I'm afraid my loyalty is unwavering."

Michael said, "I understand."

With that, he and Yaxche got into the rapid transit capsule and waited as two soldiers strapped them in securely. A moment later, they sealed the hatch, and darkness surrounded the two passengers.

The power of the sudden thrust as they were launched into space toward Earth was surprising to Michael, even though he was expecting the terrific forces pounding his body.

It was nothing compared to the shock he got twelve hours later, after landing in the Atlantic Ocean. When his rescuers opened the hatch of the capsule and pulled him and Yaxche out, a military police officer slapped handcuffs on the two of them.

"Michael Sanderson," the officer said, "you are under arrest for the crime of treason against Canada Corp."

9

Kulsat Ship :
Centauri System :

Justine couldn't think straight. A cold chill ran through her entire body.

You are to be expiring.

They were going to extract information from her and then kill her.

"No," she said. "I'm not going to cooperate."

The alien typed. "Where is your kind to be living? How many are they being? How many are Risen? Describe your discovery of the Gift."

Instead of answering, Justine shook her head, though she wasn't certain the Kulsat could interpret the gesture.

"We have biology information. Your kind does not see. Why do you motion respond?"

He thought all humans were blind, based on Justine's condition. She wasn't about to correct his wrong assumption.

The alien typed. "Why does your kind have eyes, if you do not see? Are you unit-defective?"

The Kulsat were obviously an intelligent species, and Justine assumed this one would eventually figure it out, but she wasn't about to speed up the process.

"Biology information," the machine voice said. "Your kind is to be communicating with sound. We require testing."

A low humming sound filled Justine's tank, growing louder and louder until she felt the vibrations go through her body. The intensity increased. Her muscles began to ache, as if she'd just run a marathon. Unsteady on her feet, she had to lie down.

The sound waves pounded through her, and she started feeling nauseated. Her heart beat erratically, as if trying to match the pulse of the vibrations.

She let out a groan, and held her stomach as every nerve in her body ignited in pain.

The low hum changed, rising in pitch. The sound waves no longer affected her body, but her hearing. She clapped her hands over her ears. It felt as if her eardrums were going to burst. If the torture continued, she would lose her hearing, and she would be deaf and blind.

The agony grew, and as much as she tried to hold it in, she couldn't bear it anymore.

"Stop!" she screamed. "Enough!"

The sound abruptly stopped, but there was a persistent ringing in Justine's ears. She rubbed around her lobes and moved her jaw to increase blood and air flow.

"Sound communication able to be causing discomfort," the machine voice said. "You are to be cooperating, or there is to be additional discomfort."

The alien was going to torture her with sound waves. Justine didn't know how much of that she could take before he broke her, or before he went too far and ruptured either her eardrums or another internal organ. Sonics could be used as a very powerful weapon.

The science leader had just proven to Justine that he had no compassion or concern for her well-being outside of what information she could provide him. If he were representative of his kind, then a species like that would not hesitate to bring destruction to any world that got in their way. The story Alex had told them was proving true.

Justine had a choice.

She could cooperate and avoid torture; but the alien had already told her he would kill her once he was done with her. The Kulsat would then, most likely, plan their invasion of Earth.

Alternatively, she could defy him. That would mean torture until he decided she was of no use to him. Then he would 'expire' her, and still plan the invasion ... but her resistance might delay those plans. Space was big; without more information, the Kulsat could conceivably spend years trying to find Sol System.

If Alex and the others had managed to escape the Kulsat attack, they might be able to return to Earth and warn them about the invasion. Justine had no idea how they would accomplish that, since

Alex was not a fully transformed Kinemat; but any chance she could afford them, she would take.

She got to her feet. Though she was still unsteady from the sonic attack, she stepped closer to the glass wall and put both hands on it.

"Do your worst," she said, and braced for another blast.

The alien twitched, and his entire body rippled. Justine had no basis on which to interpret Kulsat body language, but she thought she'd managed to annoy the creature.

It typed something on the computer, and the machine voice spoke. "Comprehension difficulty. Risen being is superior to others. You chose discomfort to protect unGifted and Deficients. You are unit-defective in your eyes. Are you unit-defective in comprehension?"

"I'm not crazy," Justine said. "I value the lives of all of my kind, even if they aren't 'Risen'."

The alien typed. "Units not Risen do not contain true value. Demonstration."

Turning fluidly, the Kulsat made a rippling gesture with one of his arms. At the other end of the room, another Kulsat, smaller than the first, swam into the area of Justine's *sight*. The newcomer, she sensed, was irradiated with Kinemet.

The scientist made several motions with his arms, and after a few moments, Justine realized he was using a form of sign language to communicate with the other Kulsat. That made sense. If they were physiologically comparable to cephalopods, then they had limited hearing capabilities, and most likely had not developed vocal cords.

When the leader finished signing, the smaller alien swam over to a table and retrieved a long, thin object. On one end, there was a loop, which the alien wrapped a tentacle around to carry it. The other end of the device came to a point, like a needle.

The smaller alien gave the tool to the science leader, who typed for quite some time on his computer.

He waited while the mechanical voice spoke to Justine.

"This unit was offered the Gift, but failed to become Risen. He is of limited use. This Deficient serves me, but should he expire, there are millions of Deficients to replace him."

Then, to Justine's horror, the science leader plunged the spike directly into the other alien's head.

"No!" Justine cried, but it was too late. The smaller Kulsat's body twitched, his arms flailing about for several seconds. Then he went still, floating away with the spike lodged in his head.

The science leader made another motion toward the entranceway, and three other small aliens swam in quickly. They grabbed the dead Kulsat and dragged him away.

"Without the Gift of Light, that unit would be expired soon. Deficients are having little value. There is no loss."

Justine couldn't believe what she was seeing and hearing. The Kulsat had been the favored of the Grace? From what she'd taken from Alex's story, the Grace was a benevolent race. Either someone had been sorely mistaken about the Kulsat, or the cephalopod race had undergone a radical societal change in the past thousand years.

Justine knew she couldn't impose her own system of values on another culture, but she couldn't condone murder under any circumstance.

The Kulsat typed. "If you are unit-defective, then you are to be expiring. There are several more of your kind in this system. They are not Risen, but they are possible to be not unit-defective. We will retrieve them now and increase knowledge of your kind."

"No," Justine said.

She was aware the Kulsat had given her vital information. Alex, Kenny, Michael and Yaxche had not been captured. Some of them, if not all, were still alive.

She had to give them as much time to escape as she could. If she didn't cooperate, the Kulsat would simply kill her and go after the others.

While the Kulsat possessed advanced technology, she suspected that they might not be a superior race. Perhaps she could distract them.

She said, "I am not unit-defective. I will cooperate. But I need something from you."

"What are requirements of cooperation?"

Justine noted that the linguistic computer had improved its capability for translation. She would have to choose her words carefully in the future.

"I need time to recover from your sonic attack, and I need to eat." She took a breath before adding, "I also require more Kinemet—the Gift of Light. With it, I am able to see."

"Ability to see is not required for cooperation," the alien typed back. "You will be allowed sustenance and rest. Cooperation will resume after a delay of time."

With that, the alien swam to one wall and tapped a sequence on another control panel.

Above Justine, near where the oxygen flowed, there was a scraping sound, and when she looked up, she saw a cylindrical container, the size of a kitchen pail, descending from the ceiling on a cord. A few drops of water, smelling like brine, fell from it and splashed on her cheek.

Once the container reached the floor, the cord separated from it, and retracted into the ceiling again. Justine put her hands on the cylinder. The sides of it felt as if it were made from the shells of clams or mussels. Instead of a solid lid, there was a membranous skin covering the top. When she put her fingers against it and applied pressure, the skin broke away.

Inside the container, there were two compartments. One half held a clear liquid. When Justine dipped a finger in and brought it to her lips, she was relieved that it was fresh water.

In the bottom of the other half of the container was some kind of gelatinous substance.

Justine tentatively stuck her finger in. It was slimy, cold, and thick. When she pulled her finger out, the gelatin stuck to her skin, and she used her thumb to scrape most of it off. Her stomach rolled at the thought of eating whatever it was they'd served her, but she was mindful that the Kulsat was observing her. If she did not eat, as she'd requested, it might arouse suspicion.

Steeling herself, she lifted her finger to her mouth. Before tasting the food, she sniffed. It smelled fishy, but not overpowering.

It took every bit of her willpower to stick her tongue out to taste the viscous gelatin on her finger. To her relief, it had a rather bland flavor. The problem was that it had the consistency of nasal mucus.

Trying not to think about what she was eating, Justine scooped up a small amount with her fingers and stuffed it in her mouth. She gagged, but stopped herself from vomiting it out. With an act of sheer stubbornness, she forced herself to swallow it.

It felt disgusting going down, and tears sprung to Justine's eyes. She had a task to undertake, and an act to play out. She lifted the container and angled the water half toward her, careful not to let any of the gelatin pour out on her. Tilting the container to her lips, she drank to wash the gelatin down, and that helped.

To take her mind off the food, she thought back to what her captor had said when he killed the other alien, that the smaller Kulsat had failed to become Risen, and that there were many others who had undergone the process unsuccessfully.

On Earth, there had been several volunteers during the early days of the quanta experiments. Even when Klaus had discovered the formula hidden in the Song of the Stars, he still had more failures than successes. The thought that made her blood run cold at that moment was that there might not be a single, guaranteed process. Even if Klaus had gotten every factor right, there was a chance that Justine might not have survived the experiment.

It was an important piece of information, one she needed to bring back with her—if she managed to convince the Kulsat that she was more valuable alive than dead.

Just as she finished the last of the slop, Justine noticed another small Kulsat enter the room. He approached the leader and signed for more than half a minute. The leader made a few signs in reply, and the smaller one swam away quickly.

Approaching the control panel, the leader typed. "Time delay is increased. You will rest now. Cooperation will resume after one sleep cycle."

He turned around to one of the machines behind him, tapped something on the pad on the front of the machine. Then he swam away toward the exit.

Justine heard a whirring sound from above her, where the oxygen was pumping into her tank. She smelled something gaseous a moment before she realized she was being tranquilized.

She reached her hands out to break her fall, but before she hit the floor, she was already deep into a dreamless sleep.

10

Sierra de las Minas :
Guatemala :

Long Count: 9.19.19.17.9

The opening in the crevice was barely wide enough for me to crawl through, but I was able to pull Ekahua inside after me. As I went deeper, the gap became much wider, and the cave floor was big enough that we could both lie down, if we had to spend the night there.

There was a small crack in the ceiling that allowed a thin stream of moonlight into the cave. It was barely enough light to let me make out the shape of my own hand when I held it up in front of my face.

"Are you hungry?" I asked Ekahua. "I could go hunt something for us, though I don't think we should risk making a fire."

Ekahua said, "No, thank you. By the time you returned, I would be gone."

I shifted, uncomfortable at how casually he spoke about his own death. It did not seem like a glorious death to me. Fading away in a cave was not how I wanted to die. If I were to meet my end in battle or on a hunt, then my tribe would sing of my heroism.

"I didn't see any wounds," I said to Ekahua. "What is killing you?"

He seemed to think about how to explain himself to me. "It has been eons since our world, Xtôtix, was destroyed. I, like all of my people, have spent my life among the stars; I am one of the last of my kind.

"It is because of the Grace—which gives us power to travel the stars—that we cannot survive on a planet. We become like fish on dry land."

"Then why did you not stay in the sky?" I asked, trying to understand what he was telling me.

"I have been visiting your system for quite some time, watching your world from the sky. You have grasped the nature of the universe much quicker in your evolution than other races. It is very interesting to follow your progress.

"This time, there was a flare in your sun that hit my sky boat. By the time I got control, it was too late." He made a sound, which I decided was a laugh.

Not understanding half of what he said, I asked, "You said there are only a few of you left. Did they also come to the world and die?"

"No." He closed his eyes. "The Grace—what we call the power of light—that lets us travel the stars also gives us very long lives, Subo Ak. I have lived for thousands and thousands of your years. But everything has a cost. You see, there was an accident on our world. Only a few of us survived, and we were changed. Unfortunately, though we have great power, we are not able to have children. Once, there were many Xtôti; now, there are only a few. It has been a long time since I have seen another of my kind. For all I know, I may even be the last."

I felt him reach out to me and rest his trembling hand on mine. It must have been a terrible effort on his part; it was a moment before he spoke again.

"That is why it was important to destroy my ship, and why none of the other tribes can find me. If they learned how to use the full power, as we did, their people would also begin to die out. We cannot allow that to happen."

There was a pleading look in his eyes. "You must promise me that when I die, you will build a fire. Make it as hot as you can, and burn my body so that not even ashes remain. Make sure you get very far away, so that you will not be harmed. Will you do this for me, Subo Ak?"

I was so stunned by his story and request, I didn't realize I had been holding my breath. I let it out and said, "You will not have any path to the Underworld. Let me bury you. This cave is a sure way to the spirit world. I will bring you many gifts for your journey."

"No," Ekahua said. "I know it is not your tradition to do as I ask, but you must promise to do so."

For a time, I thought about his story. The power he talked about was mighty, and I dreamed about what I could do if I lived for thousands of years. Then I felt a moment of doubt. It would be an offense against the gods if we never had children. The Ch'orti' were already dying out because of our wars with the northern tribes. We needed to increase our numbers, not lose them.

I thought I understood what Ekahua was trying to tell me, and I nodded. "Yes, I will do as you ask."

"Thank you, Subo Ak." He closed his eyes. "There are many cultures in your world, but I believe yours is the most promising. Already you look to the stars to guide your lives." Ekahua smiled.

"Of course," I said. "We all await our rebirth among the heavens."

"It is for that reason I have left a message for your people, once you begin to explore beyond the shores of your world."

"What message?"

"It is more of a marker to point the way." He opened his eyes and gave me an odd look. "Though I am not certain I have managed to write it correctly; your symbols and glyphs don't always bear the same meaning as your spoken words."

I waved a hand. "We leave the writing to the priests and elders. I prefer *hearing* the stories."

"And so, now you must listen carefully to my story. I will teach you the Song of the Stars. It is very important to learn it exactly, and pass it along to your children. The knowledge will give your people power in the generations to come."

Ekahua sang a song to me in a language that I could not understand. Respectfully, I did not interrupt him, but listened as carefully as I could.

"I do not know what those words mean," I said to him when he'd finished.

"The words are not important." He turned his head toward me. "The meaning is in the song itself. You must be able to sing the melody as I have. I will sing it again, and then you can try."

"What is this song?" I asked. "How will it give my children power?"

Some time passed before Ekahua said, "It is the song that we hear when we become one with the Grace. One day, that Song will allow your people to travel across the stars."

We practiced throughout the evening, until Ekahua finally told me that I had learned the song correctly. When I sang the song, I could feel something powerful in the music. It was as if it were a reminder of an event in my life I had never experienced.

Ekahua said, "Come closer, Subo Ak, and I will give you a final gift. You have heard the song from me; now you will hear the song from the stars themselves."

When I moved over to him, he raised one hand and placed it on my forehead. My first reaction when his body began to glow and light up the cave was to pull away, but though he was weak, his grip was strong, and he held me there.

It was as if he became light itself. A quick thought came to me that maybe Ekahua was a god, and had only led me to believe otherwise. What person could become light?

A soft ringing in my ears caught my attention. That sound grew louder in my head until it fully consumed my thoughts. I detected the faint melody of the song, and once I did so, it was all I could hear.

The Song enveloped me, took me away from my mortal self. It was stronger than any dream I'd ever had, more powerful than any spirit vision I'd ever heard of. Soon, my entire being became that Song, and there was nothing else in the universe.

∞

When I woke up, it was morning, and faint light streamed through the crevice into the cave.

I reached out to shake Ekahua, but pulled my hand back when there was no resistance. He made no sound. I held my fingers at his mouth and felt no breath.

Ekahua was dead. The effort of that last gift to me must have been too much for him.

Though I had only known him for a short time, I felt a heavy sadness in my heart and a great loss. I wanted nothing more than to hear that Song again and for the rest of my life. Now, I only had the memory.

Slowly, I made my way out of the cave. Squeezing through the small opening in the cliff face, I blinked at the sudden brightness of the morning sun.

Ekahua's last request was for me to make an offering of his body through fire. I thought, perhaps it was so that the smoke would carry his spirit back to the sky to join his people. It was important to honor the dead, and I intended to do as I was asked.

Before I gathered dried wood to build the fire, though, I went in search of food, taking my atlatl and two darts. I had gone too long without eating, and I needed to keep my strength up if I were to make the long journey home and tell my strange tale to the other villagers.

I was in luck, and found a bird's nest with three eggs. My hunger got the better of me, and I quickly cracked the shells open and sucked the eggs down.

After finishing the third one, I heard a sound from a distance behind me. Dropping down to a knee, I searched through the woods. Soon, I saw the forms of three Q'eqchi' warriors. They were walking in the direction of the crevice where Ekahua's body rested.

I could not let them find him. They would be certain to take his remains back to Quiriguá. I would not be able to honor Ekahua's final wishes, and would risk angering his dead spirit.

Desperate to lead them away, I stood and loaded a dart in my atlatl. Immediately, I threw it toward the three warriors. I had no thought to hit any of them. My plan was simply to get their attention. My dart struck home, however, running right through the neck of one of the warriors. He made a gurgling scream as he fell to the ground.

As one, the other two warriors spun on their heels, crouching defensively until they could spot their attacker.

Turning, I broke into a run. In the back of my mind, I congratulated myself. I had accomplished my original mission to either capture or kill an enemy, though I didn't know whether I would be able to take a trophy of my victory.

The two warriors spotted me. One of them threw his spear at me, but it went wide. The other warrior broke into a run, chasing after me through the forest.

I had to lead them as far away from the crevice as I could, but I could not let them catch me. If they did not kill me, they would bring me to Quiriguá to become a slave, or a sacrifice.

I scrambled as fast I could down the mountain. If I could reach the valley floor, I might be able to outrun them.

My foot caught on a root sticking out of the ground, and I lost my balance. I fell hard on my stomach, and pain lanced through my body as the breath rushed out of me.

Cursing, I fought to suck air back in and get to my feet.

The lead warrior was almost upon me, and he drew back his spear and aimed at me. I grabbed a handful of dirt and flung it in his face.

He yelled as he turned his head away and threw his hand up to protect himself.

Taking the opportunity, I picked up my atlatl, which had fallen from my grip, and swung it like a club at the warrior's head. The end connected with his temple, and he fell to the ground in a heap.

The second warrior was only a few paces behind his companion, and caught up during the fight. Still at a run, he jumped at me, swinging a long knife at my throat.

I batted at the knife with my atlatl and knocked it out of his hand. At the same time, I tried to duck under the warrior's flying body, but he hit me with his entire weight. Both of us crashed backward into a tree trunk. I felt a snap, a surge of pain, and knew that one of my ribs was broken.

The agony made my head swim. My breath came in painful gasps.

Having bounced off me and landed a few steps away, the enemy warrior jumped back to his feet. He let out an animal roar and rushed at me.

I threw myself to my back and, in one motion, reached out to grab the first warrior's spear and bring the point up.

The second warrior tried to turn away at the last moment, but he was running at me too quickly. The spear caught him in the chest and went straight through him.

He gave me a puzzled look, and then the life went out of his eyes as he toppled over onto his side.

I could not believe it. I'd defeated three of the Q'eqchi' warriors by myself.

The pride I felt was short-lived. I could barely breathe, and I knew if I did not find help, I would not survive. With my rib broken, I would not be able to hunt for food. If more warriors came, I would not be able to outrun them.

With great effort, I drew myself to my feet. Picking up my atlatl, I slowly picked my way back to the crevice where I had left my pack.

Even if I managed to build a fire to burn Ekahua's body and send his spirit to the sky, I did not have the strength to pull his body out of the cave. As it was, I didn't know if I had the strength to make it back to my village outside Copán, which was a two-day march away.

As I hefted my pack, grimacing at the pain and holding one arm close to protect my broken rib, I vowed to return. If I had to, I would bring more warriors with me to complete the ritual and honor the sky traveler.

11

Qin Station :
Sol System :

Alex was taken deeper into the laboratory section of the station without being given the opportunity to say goodbye to his friends. His thoughts were clouded with outrage over Kenny's murder, and he was barely aware of his surroundings when they arrived at the destination.

The lab was similar to the one Klaus had set up on the station orbiting Venus—Alex recognized it from the description Michael and Justine had given him. There were two sections: the main lab area, and the room where the subjects underwent Kinemetic process trials.

He took a hard look around, and it was only then that he saw there was another person in the lab besides his guards and himself.

An oriental woman, who looked to be in her mid-thirties, her long jet-black hair tied back in a ponytail, and wearing a white lab coat, glared at him as he entered.

Three of the guards, having completed their escort mission, stepped back out of the lab without a word and sealed the door behind him. One guard remained inside the lab, standing in a relaxed but attentive position, with his rifle cradled in his arms across his chest.

Alex, feeling decidedly uncomfortable, cleared his throat. "My name is—"

"I know who you are," the woman said. "And I don't need you here. I told him that. I can do this myself."

"Do what?" Alex asked. "And who are you?"

She gave him an inscrutable look. "Do you know nothing? This is a waste of my time." Storming to a communications console in the wall, she tapped something on the control, and a voice came through.

"Yes, Your Highness?"

"I told you, Dr. Yin will suffice. Get my father."

Dr. Yin! Alex reeled from shock. This young woman was Chow Yin's daughter?

He glanced at the guard in the room, as if he could give Alex some kind of confirmation. The guard did not so much as react.

The monitor lit up, and Chow Yin appeared on-screen. "What is the problem, Alice?"

"I told you I didn't need this boy to help me. I am perfectly capable of discovering the process on my own."

"You've had four years to do so," the Emperor said.

Alice Yin's face flushed visibly. She protested, "Now that we have the Mayan's story recorded, it's only a matter of time."

"Time is a luxury we can no longer afford. After all, the Americans had the story for over a decade, and they never solved the problem. There is obviously a missing element. Alex Manez knows the secret; he has been in close contact with the involved parties all along. He has agreed to cooperate."

"I can figure it out myself," Alice said, though her words were not as vehement as before.

"Of course you could," Emperor Yin said, giving her a patient smile. "I have every confidence in your abilities. We are on a timetable, however, and so I ask you to set aside your pride and work with the Westerner. Make me proud." He cut the communications link before his daughter could say anything more.

Alice Yin stared at the blank monitor for several seconds before turning around. Alex got the impression she was trying to compose herself.

Her efforts, apparently, were not enough. She gave Alex a hateful glare and stormed out of the lab through a door on the opposite wall.

When Alex glanced at the solitary guard, the only reaction the man made was a very slight relaxing of his shoulders. It seemed high drama ran in the Yin family.

∞

Much had happened in so short a time, and Alex felt more than a little disoriented. Kenny's death hadn't fully hit home yet; his initial outrage at the killing had settled into a strange, disconnected numbness. When he'd first met the young physicist, he and Kenny had done nothing but butt heads. Their friction had turned to friendship. Alex didn't want to think about it, didn't want to process the finality of the other's death.

Alone with the uncommunicative guard, Alex felt helpless. As a distraction, he took it upon himself to take a tour of the lab.

On a hunch, he tried to initialize one of the computers, and it prompted him for a password. He tried a few others but could not get access. The lab had a Kinemetic damper, so Alex could not use his electropathy to circumvent the computer's security protocols.

From his quick investigation, he concluded that they had all the necessary equipment to perform the Kinemetic process. All they were missing was Kinemet and a subject.

He gravitated toward the experimentation room, and his thoughts drifted back to Klaus, who had killed several American soldiers in his attempt to refine the process before succeeding with Justine.

The last time Alex had seen Klaus was at his uncle's base several hundred kilometers from Luna Station. He'd spent a few years in the company of the young man. Though they'd never indulged in conversation, and had been barely polite to each other during Alex's stay, he always felt Klaus could have matured past his abusive childhood.

Initially angry and bitter, Klaus had become quiet and introspective over the first few years, and had spent his time focusing his studies on physics and chemistry, rather than on computer technology. At one point, Alex thought he might take Klaus into his confidence, and see if either of them could understand Alex's condition.

That was never to be. Word reached Klaus through his uncle that his estranged father had died from liver failure, a legacy from his alcoholism. His mother, who had left them years before, refused to acknowledge Klaus and rebuffed all attempts at communication. Klaus became increasingly agitated and violent. He went on several raids with his uncle, and Alex came to understand the young man had taken someone's life unnecessarily.

It was then that Alex realized he could no longer depend on Klaus or his uncle to harbor him. With his deteriorating health, Alex knew the clock on his life was ticking, and made the plan to hijack the *Quanta*. Though he'd tricked Captain Gruber into helping him, Alex had not thought about what his deception would have done to Klaus. It was only years later that the repercussions became evident, when Klaus enlisted the Cruzados to aid him in his experiments.

Now, Klaus was dead, but his mad pursuit had been picked up by Emperor Yin and his daughter.

Alex was, once again, right in the thick of it. He had promised his cooperation to save his friends, and couldn't think of any way to back out. Even if they told him Michael and the others had been returned to safety, there was no way for Alex to know whether it was the truth or a lie.

If he refused to cooperate now, it would only be a matter of time before they rediscovered the formula for the Kinemetic process. Alex had to do his best to delay their progress by any means necessary.

The Kulsat were on the hunt for Sol System. They would eventually find it. Humanity needed Kinemats to defend themselves against the threat; but someone like Emperor Yin would never use the technology to save Sol System. He would use the knowledge for his own gain, and sacrifice the masses.

Alex started and let out a gasp when he realized someone had come back into the lab. Alice Yin studied him with cold, dark eyes.

"I didn't see you there," Alex said, struggling to even out his breathing.

"It seems we must work together," Alice said. Her voice was even, but Alex could sense the hostile undertones. She was struggling to keep her anger in check.

"That was the arrangement." If she was going to play it cold, so would Alex.

"Then tell me the big secret. Tell me what I've been missing all this time."

Alex shook his head. "Not until I am satisfied my friends have arrived on Earth alive."

"You doubt my father's word? He is the Emperor of Sol System. Argh," she said, throwing up her hands in frustration. "Do you not understand? Once your 'friends' are in the custody of your government, they will tell them the secret. We must succeed before they do."

"That would be too bad," Alex said, unable to keep the sarcasm from his voice.

She pointed a finger at him. "You gave your word you would cooperate. If you do not, then we have no reason to ensure their safety. So long as you are helping me, your friends will safely continue their journey to Earth. Once we have developed the Kinemetic process, it won't matter that they also know it," she said. "We have amassed more Kinemet than they have. We can create hundreds of Kinemats before they have their first one."

"You're mad," Alex said, the accusation coming out before he could stop himself.

Alice's face turned a bright shade of red, and for a moment, Alex thought she would attack him.

He couldn't help himself. He asked, "Don't you care that you're killing innocent people in your experiments? If you do succeed, you surely know the Emperor will use the power to kill thousands—perhaps millions—of others. How can you be a part of that?"

"Why should I care?" Alice said in a hiss. "Humanity turned its back on me a long time ago. Anyone who opposes us will get what they deserve."

She glanced at the guard, and then back at Alex.

"You will cooperate now, or I will give the guard the order to shoot you on the spot."

12

Department of Defense HQ :
Ottawa, Canada :

Michael had never felt so despondent in his life.

After three days in a holding cell in the military detention center, he thought he would never see a friendly face again. They had not even let him contact his family to let them know he was still alive. Until they could assess the national security risk he posed, he was kept incommunicado.

They gave him access to a computer for the purposes of filing a statement, but he'd been supervised for the duration. Though he'd submitted the report a day ago, no one had come back to let him know what his status was, or whether they would simply leave him in his cell indefinitely.

From the moment Michael and the others had re-entered Sol System, he'd been imprisoned in one form or another, and he'd had his fill of the experience. All he wanted was to speak to someone in authority and plead his case. Even if they decided to lock him away forever, he wanted someone to take his warning of the Kulsat threat seriously, at the very least.

When one of the two guards outside his cell unlocked the door, Michael first thought it was to bring him a meal, but the man who entered the cell was not a soldier.

"Calbert!" Michael said. "You have no idea how happy I am to see you." He stood up and took a step forward, but Calbert Loche put up a hand, motioning for Michael to sit down on his cot again.

"You may not be so happy once you hear what I have to say," he said.

"Oh?"

Calbert glanced around the holding cell quickly. There was a small, plain desk with a chair on one wall. He pulled the chair out by the backrest and turned it around. Slowly, he eased himself down on it.

"I'll cut to the chase: they're not going to drop the charges against you," he said, "…yet."

"Yet?" Michael asked. "Then there's a possibility."

"Maybe. Your report made a lot of people unhappy." Calbert took a deep breath. "Billions of dollars were spent on Quantum Resources and Alex Manez. Now, from your statement, we find out he was lying to us from the moment he returned from Centauri—some even doubt he made the initial trip.

"Half the senators on the oversight committee think you were operating in collusion with Chow Yin—after all, how did he manage to figure out how to weaponize Kinemet?"

"That's ridiculous," Michael said. "Why would he ship us back here if we were working with him?"

"I don't know." Calbert shrugged. "Maybe he needs more information, and thinks you can get it for him."

Grimacing, Michael said, "Ludicrous."

Calbert continued. "The rest believe you're not a traitor, but simply guilty of gross incompetence."

"What?" He couldn't keep the shock from his face.

"From the beginning, Quantum Resources faced failure after failure; it was only after your retirement that the company turned itself around. Once you were brought back into the fold, things went sour in a hurry."

"They want a scapegoat? Pin everything that went wrong on me?"

"It wouldn't be the first time something like this happened."

"So either I'm a traitor or an idiot," Michael said.

"Don't forget 'a liar'," Calbert said. "All of them think your report of some super alien species massing an invasion is pure fiction, a legerdemain designed to distract us from your other activities."

"Are you serious? I wouldn't make something like that up." Michael felt the figurative noose tightening around his neck. He looked Calbert in the eye. "What does Alliras think?"

"Alliras is no longer the Minister of Energy, Mines and Resources. He recommended me for the minister's ballot before he left the position. I've been in the seat for a year now."

"You got political?" Michael gaped. "What about Quantum

Resources?"

"Dissolved. Since Chow Yin has put an embargo on space operations for all earthbound nations, we lost our mandate. Space Mining Division has been gutted. The country has more important needs, such as fighting the war."

"The war?" He gasped, feeling completely out of touch.

"I have to say, it was a brilliant move on Chow Yin's part. He corrupted a good portion of the PRC government, got them to start trouble in Asia. Within months, everyone was picking sides, and I mean everyone. The rub of it is that World War III is nothing more than a distraction. While we're all busy fighting each other, Chow Yin's been taking advantage and securing control of the rest of Sol System."

"Murderous bastard," Michael said, grinding his teeth.

"Yes, I'm sorry about Kenny Harriman." Calbert bowed his head a moment before continuing. "A month ago, the PRC government regained control of China. They're in the process of rooting out the imperialist sympathizers, and they've initiated a ceasefire. Everyone is in a holding pattern at the moment."

"That's good news," Michael said. "We can turn our attention back to Chow Yin and the Kulsat."

Calbert clicked his tongue. "That might take a bit of time, and might be more problematic than realistic. There were a lot of shots fired by both sides. It'll take years to smooth out ruffled feathers. Worldwide resources are already taxed. We need those space-based production stations controlled by Chow Yin. There's been talk that it would be easier to negotiate a deal rather than commit resources to another fight, especially when the Solan Empire has the high ground."

"I can't believe my ears." Michael's eyes were wide. "They're going to give in?"

Lifting his shoulders in a sign of helplessness, Calbert said, "The economy was tenuous when you left; now, it's reaching a critical point. The war exhausted everyone's reserves. People are tired of fighting."

"Well," Michael said, his voice upset, "people better get un-tired. The Kulsat are going to find us, and when they do, we'll be wiped out."

With a half-smile, Calbert said, "It would be easier to convince the government to swallow the Moon, than to swallow that story."

"And you?" He looked at Calbert through the corner of his eye. "What do you believe?"

Taking a long time to answer, he finally said, "I believe that if your story is true, then we're all in very serious trouble."

"That wasn't what I was asking." Michael held his breath.

Finally, Calbert nodded, "We are all in very serious trouble."

Though Michael felt a surge of relief when he heard that—at least someone in the entire world didn't think he was either a complete moron or a traitor—he knew his situation was far from optimistic.

"To break it down," he said, pulling at his lip, "we've got two problems: Emperor Chow Yin, and the Kulsat Consortium. I hate to say it, but Yin is the lesser of the two evils. He wants to rule Sol System; the Kulsat want to decimate it."

"What do you suggest?"

Michael scratched an eyebrow. "Do we have the technology to weaponize Kinemet?"

"Before Quantum Resources was shut down, we bandied a few theories about. The first problem is, we don't have any Kinemet stockpile to test the theories. Second, even if we did, those theories can't be tested planet-side. Unfortunately, Chow Yin has all the marbles, and he's not sharing."

"It sounds like you're trying to convince me that making a deal with Chow Yin is the sensible option." He gave Calbert a sharp look.

"The devil you know…"

Shaking his head, Michael sighed. "I can't believe that option is on the table."

Then he noticed Calbert looking at him oddly.

"What?"

A smile crept into Calbert's lips. "You realize that, not once in this conversation did you ask about what's going to happen to you?"

Tilting his head, Michael let out a hollow laugh. "I thought it was a foregone conclusion. I figure I'm the administration's worst nightmare. If they reveal I'm back, the newsvids will investigate. The moment they find out about an alien invasion, there'd be mass panic. If they prosecute me, they'll have to disclose certain facts to the public, and hide others. Anything they hide will come back to bite them later; a cover-up is a sensational scandal."

With a bittersweet smile, he said, "If I were them, I'd keep pushing the paperwork from office to office indefinitely, or just bury it. Put me in a hole somewhere and forget where they hid the key."

Calbert gave him a hard look. "You're not wrong about that. It's taken a lot of fast-talking to keep knowledge of your return limited to the oversight committee. At this point, there are only about twenty people in the world who know you're still alive."

"Well," Michael said, trying to keep the defeat out of his voice, "no matter what happens, I appreciate you taking the time to come down here in person."

"I wanted to come down here," he said, "but not just because I consider you a friend."

"Oh?"

"I wanted to ask you about Yaxche."

"He's a good man." Michael leaned forward. "I hope you realize that he had nothing to do with anything. He just came along to help save Alex."

Calbert put up his hands. "There are no worries on that part. We've actually contacted the Honduran Departmental and arranged for his return to his village."

Letting out a sigh of relief, Michael said, "That's good."

Slowly, Calbert said, "I'm glad you vouched for him."

Michael narrowed his eyes. "I never knew you for someone to beat around the bush."

Calbert laughed. "Normally, I'm not. I guess this last year of glad-handing politicians and captains of industry has made me more circumspect."

"Just you and I here," Michael said. "Spit it out."

"All right." The minister took a moment, as if to sort out what he was going to say. "I spoke with Yaxche in private yesterday. He remembers me from when we met at Quantum Resources—just a few weeks ago from his perspective, but over four years ago for me." He held Michael's eye. "At first, he didn't want to talk to me, but when I reassured him I only wanted the best for you, and I believed your story about what happened in Centauri, he relented and said something I wasn't sure how to take.

"He said the Kulsat were once the favored of the Grace, and that they're trying to find the legacy of the Grace."

Nodding, Michael said, "That's what the Gliesans told Alex. I have no idea what it really means. We didn't really have a lot of time to talk about it before the Kulsat blew up our ship."

"Right." Calbert scratched his jaw. "Yaxche said he believes the Grace could be the gods in the Mayan pantheon."

Michael frowned. "He never mentioned that to anyone."

"And he said he might know how to find the old gods' legacy."

"How to find——?" Michael gaped. "You mean it might actually be here, on Earth?"

Calbert made an uncertain face. "He says it might be somewhere near his village."

"No wonder he didn't want to say anything. Chow Yin's agents could have been listening the whole time." He stood up. "You need to send someone with Yaxche. If you can find this legacy, it might just be the thing we need to deal with the Kulsat."

"It might be a long shot—no, it's definitely a long shot—but I agree it's worth exploring," Calbert said. "But, since we don't want to leak anything to the public about this, we need to send someone with Yaxche who we can trust, and who can get the job done."

Michael searched his memory for someone who would fit the bill. Then he noticed Calbert looking at him oddly again, but this time with a playful smile on his face.

"What?"

"How'd you like to go back to Honduras?"

Stunned, Michael opened and closed his mouth without saying anything. When he finally recovered his senses, he asked, "Me? How?"

"First of all," Calbert said, pulling a folded letter out from inside the breast of his jacket, "I need you to sign this affidavit stating that you have been operating undercover as an agent of the Canadian government for the past four years under direct authority of the Prime Minister."

Signing that would immediately exonerate Michael of any charges the Department of Defense had on him.

"As long as you agree to a full retraction of your earlier statement, we've prepared a replacement statement detailing how you've spent the last four years infiltrating Chow Yin's empire."

Michael couldn't believe it. "How did you get Prime Minister Dolbeau to agree to that?"

Calbert's smile widened. "I didn't. I got Prime Minister Rainier to agree to it."

"Alliras? But I thought you said——?"

"I just said he was no longer the Minister of Energy, Mines and Resources."

Michael pointed a finger at him. "You damned trickster."

Laughing out loud, Calbert said, "Just sign the affidavit so we can get you on a skybus to Honduras."

13

Kulsat Ship :
Centauri System :

A pounding headache woke Justine. After she regained consciousness, she decided it was most likely an aftereffect of the sleep agent the Kulsat had introduced into her tank.

She pushed herself up on one arm, but the motion made her stomach heave, and she let herself lie back down until the queasiness faded.

Darkness filled her awareness. The minute amount of Kinemetic radiation she'd absorbed from the presence of the Kulsat science leader was gone and her *sight* with it.

Two conflicting emotions warred inside her: if the Kulsat returned, she would absorb enough of the radiation to *see* again; but that meant the interrogation would resume. Justine was running out of tricks to delay the science leader.

Her situation was looking more and more hopeless.

"Is it true?"

Justine jerked at the sound of the mechanical voice. She couldn't *see* anyone—or anything—but someone had obviously used the linguistic computer to communicate with her.

She made a guess. "You're not the science leader."

"He is undertaking other tasks, and will not return for some time."

"Who are you?" Justine asked.

There was a long pause, and for a moment, she thought the newcomer might have gone away.

The mechanical voice said, "I am being the cleaner of floors and walls."

"What is your name?" Justine asked, but only a long silence

answered her. "Do you have a name?"

"I have an identifier. There is no corresponding sound."

Perhaps the computer needed a frame of reference. "My name is Justine."

A moment later, the mechanical voice replied, "The computer does not have a corresponding motion for that word."

"It means 'just' or 'fair'. What does your name mean?" she asked the newcomer.

"I have a circle-shaped red spot above my left eye."

"Is that how you identify each other," Justine asked, "by distinguishing marks?"

"Yes, you have knowledge now."

"May I call you 'Red Spot' for short?"

"The computer is using the correct motion for my name, Justine. What is your station?"

"I'm..." For a moment, Justine was going to say she was a retired major, but she didn't know whether the language computer could interpret rank. "I am the pilot of our ship."

"You are the transportation leader?"

"I guess you could call it that." A moment later, she asked, "Does your science leader have a name?"

"He has a pattern of three dark crescents on the webbing of one limb."

"Three Crescents?" Justine said.

"Yes. He is one of the oldest Risen in the Consortium."

Justine felt a kernel of hope growing inside her. The newcomer seemed curious, and was much more communicative than the science leader. Then a thought hit her: maybe the Kulsat were employing a psychological trick. The science leader was the bad cop; Red Spot was the good cop.

"Are you a Risen?" Justine asked, testing to see if the alien would lie. "Or a Deficient?"

"I have not been offered the Gift," Red Spot said. "I am not of suitable station yet to attempt to Rise."

"Are you not supposed to be here?"

The mechanical voice spoke. "The science laboratory is for the science leader and his servants. This room is restricted from Potentials. It is an offense to disobey rules. You will report my offense?"

"I won't say anything." Justine shook her head. "If it is against the rules, why did you take the risk to talk to me?"

The mechanical voice spoke. "I need to know if it is true."

"If what is true?"

"We were told you are a scout for a barbarian army that wishes the expiration of our kind."

"That's not true," Justine said. "For the most part, our people are explorers."

"Then you practice deception?"

Shocked at the accusation, Justine asked, "What makes you say that?"

"You related a history of your conduct. There is violence. There is atrocity. There is abduction. You are no different than the other races."

Gasping, Justine realized that the Kulsat must have analyzed the story she'd recited for the translation computer, *Peter Pan,* and thought she was talking about something that had happened in her past. Without a cultural reference, the story must have sounded terrible to an alien species.

"That was a fantasy," she said. "For entertainment."

"You do not practice atrocity? You do not cut off the limbs of your enemies and feed them to animals?"

Justine let out a huff. "Not as a rule, no." Then she thought that if she told Red Spot a truth, she might engender trust. "It is true that there are some individuals from our world who break our laws, but we have a system in place to punish the offenders and to protect the innocent, and to protect those who do not have power."

"Your system protects those with no value?"

"Red Spot," she said, "our kind believes all beings have value."

There was a long silence, and for a moment, Justine thought Red Spot might have left, but then the mechanical voice came through.

"Green Stripe Over One Eye shared time with me. He was assisting me to increase my station so that one day I may attempt to Rise. He provided companionship. He had value … to me. Now he is expired."

At first, Justine didn't know what Red Spot was trying to tell her, but then she understood. Green Stripe must have been the Deficient who the science leader had killed. She guessed the two of them had some kind of intimate relationship—though Justine really didn't have a basis to understand what that would entail. In her mind, she began to think of Red Spot as female.

"I must go," Red Spot said via the mechanical voice. "I will be discovered."

"No, wait!" Justine cried out, but then she smelled the familiar scent of the tranquilizer agent, and before she had a chance to protest, she fell back to the floor, unconscious.

∞

The headache was worse the next time she woke. At least some of her *sight* had been restored. Of course, that meant one thing: Three Crescents was back.

Justine struggled to a sitting position and used her *sight* to look around. The science leader was not alone. There was another Kulsat in the room, floating a few meters away from Three Crescents. The Kinemetic radiation in him was much stronger than that in the science leader.

Three Crescents typed. "You have completed your sleep cycle. Cooperation will resume now."

"Good morning," Justine said, and watched as the two Kulsat signed to each other.

Three Crescents turned back to the computer. "Irrelevant information. We require specifications of your home system. Population. Location. Technology level. Describe your understanding of the Gift. Do you possess the final component?"

When Justine didn't reply right away, the Kulsat typed again. "Cooperation was assured."

"You didn't even introduce me to your new friend." She got to her feet and gave the other Kulsat a nod. "My name is Justine," she said.

All eight of Three Crescents' tentacles twitched. "Your name is a deception."

"It's just a name," she said. "Something to call each other. Certainly, no harm will come from sharing our names."

Three Crescents turned to the other Kulsat. Whatever it was they were discussing, it seemed to be a heated debate. By the end of the conversation, Three Crescents was quivering. Justine guessed it was in frustration.

He moved away from the control panel, and the other Kulsat approached.

"I am Ship Leader Long Fingers On Two Of His Limbs. We have analyzed your confession. You are the shadow form. You are to be using stealth techniques to capture our spawn. We are familiar with this purpose. You wish to examine our biology, and develop a means to destroy us."

"You've got it all wrong," Justine said, wishing she'd never picked *Peter Pan* to recite. "I had no intention of kidnapping anyone. It was you who abducted me, remember?"

"All aliens that encroach on our territory wish to destroy us. Your confession has confirmed this fact. We are validated to collect you."

"It wasn't a confession." Justine had to restrain herself from slapping the glass; that would only demonstrate that she was capable of violence, and it was imperative that she be as diplomatic and politic as she could. "It was a story. If you'll let me explain, I'm sure we can come to an understanding—"

Long Fingers typed. "It is apparent your kind practice deception. Any information you provide may be false. You attempt to conceal the final component of the Gift. We will attempt to search for other specimens of your kind, should they exist in this system, and extract biological information."

The ship leader turned from the computer and signed something to Three Crescents. Justine didn't need a translation program to interpret its meaning.

As Long Fingers swam out of the room, and Three Crescents turned to one of his other computers, Justine's frustration boiled over.

"I said I would cooperate. I'm not lying. I'll talk to you, if you'll just listen to me. This is all a big misunderstanding."

When the science leader continued working on his machine, ignoring Justine, she slapped the glass to get his attention, not caring how it looked to them.

"Three Crescents," she said. "I'm talking to you."

He turned around, and a ripple went through his body as he stared at Justine with those large eyes of his. Finally, he propelled himself to the translation control panel and typed.

"I have never offered my identifier. How did you acquire this knowledge?"

Cursing herself for the slip, Justine said, "It was a guess. I see the three dark crescents on the web between your tentacles. You name yourself after distinguishing marks, don't you?"

Three Crescents seemed to consider her answer. "You are practicing additional deception." He went to another computer station and typed on the control panel. For the first time, Justine could see one of their displays, but the information on it was meaningless to her. It looked like a series of squiggles and dashes—obviously their written language—but there was no way she could interpret them.

Turning back to the translation computer, Three Crescents typed to her. "There has been unauthorized access to this laboratory. We have a traitor. Did you promise information of final component to gain assistance from the defector? Reveal the conspirator, and there will be no discomfort in your expiry. Refuse cooperation and I will apply continuous discomfort."

Backing away from the glass, Justine felt the terror growing in her. She had no idea how much torture she could endure, and didn't know if the sonic attack was the limit of what they could do to her.

She wasn't about to give up Red Spot to them. Even though she was a Kulsat, she'd demonstrated that not all of their kind had the same disregard for life as Three Crescents or Long Fingers. Red Spot had grieved for the death of Green Stripe, even though their society had labeled him a Deficient. She had also put her trust in Justine not to betray her.

Three Crescents typed something. "Discomfort will begin now."

The familiar hum of the sonic attack filled the tank, and before Justine could yell out a curse at Three Crescents, she doubled over in pain.

The torture went on for some time...

∞

At one point, Justine began to wish her tormentor would just finish her off and put an end to the agony. She was certain the sonic blasts had caused some internal damage. The low-wave attacks made her vomit, and the high-pitched sonics left her dizzy and disoriented.

When she felt a trickle of blood leak out from one ear, she yelled at Three Crescents in frustration. "How can I hear your questions if I'm deaf?"

The sonic blasts ceased, but the ringing in her ears continued. Even through that, she heard Three Crescents' next question.

"You are prepared to cooperate? Please identify the traitor."

She shrugged. "I can't tell. You all look the same to me."

"Describe distinguishing marks."

Justine found it difficult to concentrate, and felt nauseated, but she had to keep delaying Three Crescents. Every minute she stalled him was another minute for Alex and the others to get farther away.

She said, "I don't know. He had a green stripe running down one arm."

"Deception. That Deficient has expired." Three Crescents typed for a few moments. "You have provided verification that your kind are an imminent threat to the Kulsat and must be eliminated. Once you are all removed from existence, we will investigate your world for the final component."

"No, you can't do that," Justine said. "Why won't you listen to reason?"

"Identify the traitor."

Justine shook her head. "There is no traitor."

"You have displayed the willingness to endure discomfort to protect conspirators, though they are not your species. Should conspirators no longer exist, you will have no reason to withhold cooperation."

He turned around and signed to one of the other Kulsat floating just outside the laboratory's entranceway. That Kulsat swam away in a rush.

Within a minute, he returned with what looked like an army of Kulsat. They all tried to fit inside the laboratory, but it soon became too crowded. Three Crescents signed something to them, and the majority of the aliens swam back outside, but remained in waiting.

Justine counted twenty Kulsat still in the laboratory, not including Three Crescents. Of those, three had Kinemetic radiation in them—Deficients—and the rest were normal Kulsat. With her senses, she detected seven other 'Deficients' among those waiting outside the laboratory. Justine had no idea if Red Spot was among the twenty.

Three Crescents typed on the computer.

"All Kulsat who have been in this section since your arrival are displayed here. One of them is the traitor. To be assured, all twenty will be expired. The others will learn the result of betrayal."

Three Crescents swam a short distance to one of the worktables and picked up a device that looked like a soldering iron. It had a long cord that was attached to the nearest wall. With two of his tentacles, he pointed the sharp end of the tool at one of the Kulsat in the line.

A thin stream of something jetted out from the device, detectable only because of the rippling of the water between Three Crescents and his target. Justine heard a deep thrumming sound and felt the vibrations of what must have been some kind of sonic agitator. The Kulsat at the receiving end of the wave began to pulsate, and his arms started to contract and expand in sharp movements. His entire body seemed to go into a rapid series of spasms, and then the water around him turned murky as his flesh burst into a cloud of black and red.

On the wall behind the victim, a large circular opening appeared and, as if it were a giant pump, began to draw water into it. The dead alien's body drifted back to the opening and was sucked out of the room.

The nineteen remaining Kulsat did not make any sign of protest, or attempt to flee.

Justine, unable to fathom the horror she was witnessing, struggled to her feet and pounded on the glass separating her from the others.

"You monster!" she screamed. "Stop killing them. They're innocent!"

Three Crescents gave no indication that he was aware of her protest. He raised the device up at the next Kulsat in line, a small one with orange mottling on his arms, and fired again.

Again, the Kulsat spasmed, the water around him clouded over with his bodily fluids.

"Stop it!" Justine screamed. She punched and kicked the glass as hard as she could but the only damage done was to her fist.

"Name the traitor. The others will be spared."

How could she betray one Kulsat to save the rest of them? How could she watch more sentient beings die horribly to keep her word to an alien being who she barely knew? No matter what she did, Red Spot was going to die.

"All right," Justine said, choking back the tears. "I'll tell you. Just stop killing them."

"Name the traitor."

Pointing to the second murdered Kulsat, Justine said, "That was the one. You got him already."

"Deception has been employed." Three Crescents typed. "These twenty have never been in this section before. It is apparent that your kind cannot be trusted. Your species are an imminent threat, and will contaminate all Kulsat you contact. We will now expire all Deficients and Potentials in this section of the ship. We will report to our superiors and recommend the expiry of all your kind."

The overwhelming futility of it consumed Justine. No matter what she'd done, Three Crescents had been single-minded in his purpose and his conviction that she, and all humankind, was a threat. The story Alex had conveyed was now confirmed in her mind. Paranoia drove the Kulsat to destroy any new alien species they encountered.

Not knowing if any of the other Kulsat could see the translation monitor, Justine nevertheless called out to them. "Save yourselves. Fight him. He's only one. You outnumber him."

Three Crescents made a rippling motion with his arms, similar to when Justine had caused him frustration earlier, and he touched something on the computer. The soft hum on the transmitter on her collar—a sound she hadn't noticed up until that point—disappeared. The Kulsat had shut off the translator.

The alien then raised the energy emitter device in his tentacles and began to fire into the remaining Kulsat in the room.

Justine couldn't understand why the Kulsat simply waited for their death. Had the elite class—those like Three Crescents—so completely conditioned the others to believe they had no value unless they were Risen?

Even knowing in her heart it would make no difference, that none of the Kulsat could understand her, Justine slapped her hands against the glass. "Fight him, damn you. Defend yourselves."

It was as if one of them had heard her. From the entranceway, a small Kulsat flicked all eight of her tentacles and dashed toward Three Crescents. Red Spot? Justine spied the distinctive mark above her eye.

Intent on murdering the non-Risen Kulsat in the lab, Three Crescents didn't see her until she was right next to him.

He twisted around to aim the rod at Red Spot, but her plan wasn't to attack him. Instead, she darted to the wall where the cord of the energy rod was attached. She wrapped three tentacles around it and yanked. It came free before Three Crescents could fire at her.

With a huge ripple of frustration going through his arms, Three Crescents quantized her. In the place where the small Kulsat had been, now there was only a collection of light particles.

The pump in the opposite wall was working overtime, sucking in the remnants of the other dead Kulsat. It was also creating a current in the water, and the quantized bits of the small alien were slowly being drawn across the lab.

Three Crescents, having dealt with the situation, swam over to the wall and went about repairing the connection to the energy rod.

He was going to resume his killing spree.

When Justine had been fully irradiated with Kinemet, she'd been able to quantize herself at will. It had never occurred to her to try to quantize another being. She believed a quantum engine was required to begin the quantization process. It was only after the quantized state existed that Justine had been able to reverse the change of state and return the ship and its passengers to their tangible selves.

With her senses, she could not detect any Kinemet in this section of the ship, whether charged or dormant. How had Three Crescents done that to Red Spot? When she'd been quantized and removed from the *Ultio,* her suspicion had been that the Kulsat had developed some kind of technology they'd used to target her. Now, she wondered if it was another stage in the development of a Kinemat.

Even though Justine barely had any radiation in her system, she had enough to see ... and maybe, if she concentrated, she might have enough to reverse the quantization on Red Spot before the ship's pumps sucked her out of the room and to destinations unknown.

Willing herself to focus, she reached out with every trace of the Kinemetic radiation in her. The strain was incredible, and her entire body shook with the effort.

The effort completely drained her, and panic streaked through her when she suddenly lost her ability to *see.*

14

Long Count: 9.19.19.17.11

I had no sense of time. It seemed as if I had been walking for tens of days. The pain in my chest was worse since I started on my way back to my village, and with every step I took, it felt as if I were being struck in the ribs with a heavy club.

I paused to drink whenever there was a stream of water, and eat whenever I came across a bush ripe with berries.

I could not recall when I stopped to sleep, though I must have, because I found myself lying on the ground in the morning, looking up into a cloudless sky.

The thin wisps of a dream floated away as full consciousness returned. The pain surrounded me like a blanket, and I wondered if I would ever rise again.

Somehow, I managed to get back on my feet, gather my pack, and complete the journey to my village.

Papan, one of the hunters who had taught me how to track prey, was the first to spot me, and he let out a cry to others to come and help me.

Knowing that I was among family and friends, I let myself succumb to my weariness, and passed out as several strong men picked me up to bring me to my hut.

∞

I don't know how long I slept, but when I woke, my chest was wrapped with a bandage, and I was covered with several woven blankets.

There were three others in my hut. My father, Tohil Ak, stood over me, his face beaming with pride. Beside him, my mother, Xmucane, clasped her hands together and gave me a look that was a mix of relief and worry.

The third person in the tent was Balam Ix, our priest, who was the oldest person in our village.

"Subo," my father said, "it is good to see you awake. Your mother feared the worst."

I tried to sit up, but it felt as if a boulder pressed down on my chest.

"Don't try to move," the priest said. He put a wrinkled hand on my shoulder. "It will be many days before you are healed."

I relaxed my muscles and lay back. "I have succeeded, father." Smiling up at him, I spoke with pride. "Three Q'eqchi' came upon me. I did not take their skin, but I defeated them."

"That is good, my son." He nodded. "The warriors will welcome you to their ranks once you are able."

Balam said, "There is much more to your story, young Subo, is there not?"

I looked back and forth between the holy man and my father, who said, "You spoke of it in your fever sleep. Is it a dream, or a vision?"

"You must tell me," Balam said, "now, before we bring the story to the council. You had a holy vision. Did a god grant you audience, young one?"

Though it was difficult to do so, I took a deep breath. "He said he was not a god, but he was a sky traveler. I saw his boat flying through the sky while I was waiting for a Q'eqchi' warrior to fight."

I told them Ekahua's story from beginning to end. When I was finished, I could feel myself tiring from the effort.

"Do you remember the Song of the Stars he taught you?" Balam asked. His voice was pitched low, full of wonder. I saw in the way he looked at me that he did not doubt my story.

"Yes," I said, and closed my eyes as I sang the song in Ekahua's strange language.

When I sang the last line of the song, I looked again at our holy man. He nodded.

"It is a powerful Song. It is a great gift he has given you, Subo Ak.

It will take you your entire life to understand its meaning. Perhaps you will never understand. We will study the song together."

"Together...?" I asked, wondering at Balam's words.

"Yes." He stood, then. "I have been to Copán and spoken with King Ukit Took about your fever dream. This Ekahua is a spirit who visited you in a vision. It is a sign from the gods. Only a prophet may receive such portents from the Underworld."

My father spoke the words before I could. "Subo is to be a warrior. He has achieved a great victory over our enemies."

Balam smiled and nodded. "Only with the power of a great spirit was he able to defeat three Q'eqchi' warriors. It has been decided, Tohil. Subo will become my apprentice, and one day he will take my place as the high priest of the village. It is prophesied."

He turned to me. "In seven days, you will begin your training." With that, Balam took his leave of us.

I was completely stunned by the news, and I felt a rising anger at the king's decision.

Me, a holy man? I had never thought about being anything other than a warrior like my father, and to honor the memory of my slain brother.

I could see the disappointment in my father's eyes. From the time I was a child, he'd schooled me in the ways of battle. Now, all that effort was for nothing.

Clenching his jaw, my father turned on his heel and strode from my hut. Only my mother remained, and she would not meet my eyes.

Ysalane! She could not marry me. Holy men did not take wives, and would never have children.

It did not matter to me that the priest was one of the most revered members of our people, that the elders took counsel with him, and that he commanded the respect of all in the village. Right then, I felt I'd been cheated out of my reward, and I cursed the day I had seen Ekahua's flying boat.

∞

Over the next few days, I healed, and soon I could get up from my bed and walk on my own. I tired quickly, and could only make short trips at first. Soon, however, I could wander around for long periods of time.

Our village had twenty houses spaced out over a sizeable area. The largest building was in the center of the village, near the common circle, and was used by the elders to hold their meetings. One house was reserved for the priest. The others were for the families of the elders, weavers, toolmakers, traders, and the warrior-hunters.

There were several temporary huts for those of us who were unmarried, but who no longer lived with our families. It was where we stayed until we completed our manhood rituals, and until our parents and elders arranged a marriage for us.

Most of the villagers lived on their own compounds outside of the village, where they tended their fields.

Everywhere I went, the other villagers would watch and stare as I passed. No one would approach or talk to me other than my mother and father. Word had spread that I was going to be apprenticed to our village's priest.

Returning to my hut, I lay on my bed and thought about how miserable my life had become. I would have to learn numbers, stars and the calendar; I would need to learn to write glyphs to record our stories; I would need to learn to help heal the sick with potions and rituals; I would have to advise new families on what to name their children. There would be hundreds of other tasks I had never wanted.

At that moment, I decided I would sneak away from the village once I was healed enough to do so. I would return to Quiriguá and kill as many of our enemies as I could before they captured and sacrificed me. Then, at least, there would be songs sung of my heroic deeds.

The Song. Over the past few days, I had been trying to avoid remembering it, but once I let it enter my thoughts, I couldn't put it out of my mind.

Without being consciously aware that I was doing it, I began to hum the song. Soon, the humming turned into singing, and a sense of peace crept into my troubled heart.

I was angry at my fate, but I could take comfort in the great gift Ekahua had given me.

When I finished singing, I started it again from the beginning.

I was so consumed by the song, I wasn't immediately aware that the ground was shaking underneath me. It only lasted a few seconds, but I knew from experience that small earth tremors often led to larger earthquakes.

Rolling off my bed, I bit my tongue as a sharp pain went through my chest at the sudden movement. It took me a moment before I could get to my feet and step outside my hut.

Several of the women were running across the village common, calling out for their children to come to them and find a safe spot to hide.

A second tremor hit, sending me off-balance. I had to grasp the supports on my hut to keep it from collapsing.

One of the huts on the other side of the village toppled over. The story stone in the center of our common vibrated, sending rock dust down in plumes.

My father, who had been preparing a skin by the fire outside his hut, hurried over to see if anyone was in danger and needed help.

A small child, who had been knocked over by the tremor, screamed in fear, not understanding, even as he threw his arms out for his mother. She raced over and scooped him up in her arms.

My father and I shared a quick glance, but it seemed as if a collapsed hut and a frightened child was the extent of the damage.

"Tohil," Bil'al, a young warrior-in-training who had stayed back from the hunt because of a broken ankle, said to my father, "is everyone all right?"

Nodding, my father surveyed the village, taking a head count of everyone who should be there.

"Everyone seems to be unharmed," he said, but then he changed his expression.

A moment later, I realized there was one person who had not come out of their house at the commotion: the priest, Balam Ix.

As quickly as I could, I headed for the priest's home. It was a larger dwelling than my hut, but not as big as the family houses. My father got there well before I did, and looked inside. Instead of going in, he paused at the doorway, and I could see his shoulders slump.

He backed out just as I arrived.

"What?" I asked, searching his face before I ducked inside the priest's hut to see for myself.

Balam Ix had been the oldest person in our village, and had lived for many more years than most would. Everyone suspected he would not live for much more, but witnessing him lying on his bed without moving, his eyes open but not seeing, lips slightly parted but not breathing, I felt a momentary twinge of disbelief. Balam had been a part of everyday life in our village all my life, and now he was gone.

My father spoke in a muted tone. "The Underworld has called for him."

"It is an omen," I said, though I kept my voice too low for anyone to hear.

My father put his hand on my shoulder. He said, "When the others return from the hunt and patrol tonight, we will prepare him for burial."

One other result I had not immediately considered became alarmingly clear when Bil'al, who had come up behind us, asked, "Is Subo the priest of the village, now?" Widening his eyes, he added, "I hope you can remember all the words to the prayers."

∞

I spent the rest of the day sweating, and not because of the heat. Only a short while ago, I was on the path of the warrior, moving toward the future I desired. Now, the villagers were expecting me, who had not yet seen eighteen summers, and who had not spent a single day in religious study, to be their spiritual leader—at least for the time being.

In cases where the high priest of a village died without an apprentice, the elders would send a request to the High Priest of Copán to provide them with a temporary holy man. The elders had, indeed, charged one of the warriors to travel to the city to deliver the news, and he'd returned at dusk. Because of the earthquake, the Holy Order was too busy aiding the citizens of Copán, where the damage had been more severe than in our village. It could be several days before they sent anyone, perhaps longer.

It was up to me to lead the ritual.

We'd had several burials in the past few years, and I had to admit that I had not given them my full attention. To my relief, my father and the other warriors took charge of preparing the priest's house for the burial. After gathering the priest's story stones and calendars, they tore the building down. All the construction materials were removed from the site except for the floor, which they raised high enough so that several others could dig a grave for the priest.

The three elders, Yax Kuk, Ohtli Ti, and Nentil Mo'Nab, brought me to their house, where they instructed me on how to wear the priest's headdress and costume. It did not fit me very well; I was much taller than the priest had been, and rounder of the shoulder. I endured and followed the elders back to the priest's house.

Balam's body lay on the ground in front of the remains of his home. Ensuring that I assisted throughout the entire process, the elders prepared the priest's body. First, they wrapped him in a cotton shroud and then they filled his mouth with maize. Without thinking about what I was doing, I began the ritual.

"Accept this food to sustain you through your journey through Xibalba."

At the elders' prompting, I placed a jade bead in the priest's mouth on top of the maize.

"The road to rebirth may be long; the jade will give you breath in the Underworld."

The elders wrapped his head with the shroud.

"We wrap you to protect you from the cold of the Underworld."

The slaves picked up the priest's body and carried him to the grave they had dug under where his house once stood. Gently, they placed him in it.

I lifted a ceramic pot full of water and slowly poured it over the priest, starting at his head and moving down to his torso.

"The Underworld is a world of water. You must enter the water to begin your journey."

One of the elders lit sticks of incense and placed them in the ground outside the grave as the others arranged the priest's possessions around his body.

"Accept these gifts. May they help you on your path to rebirth."

I stepped back as other members of the village came forward to make offerings of their own and to speak prayers for the man who had been their priest all their lives.

Catching my father looking at me thoughtfully, I realized that I had spoken the ritual word-for-word. I did not make a single mistake. It was as if I had performed the rites of burial a hundred times before. The thought came to me that, had I never met Ekahua and learned his Song, I would never have been able to remember the words of prayer today. Somehow, when he'd touched me with light, he'd changed me.

The men filled in the grave, and then lowered the platform floor over it.

We would begin building my home on top of the priest's grave tomorrow. His spirit would watch over and guard the new dwelling, and perhaps visit me in my dreams.

15

Qin Station :
Sol System :

Alex knew he couldn't use any more delaying tactics right then, at least, not under direct threat of being shot.

"As long as you can promise to give me periodic updates on my friends' progress home, I will cooperate. I gave Chow Yin my word."

"His Highness," Alice corrected, but it sounded more like an automatic response. "So," she said, "what's the big secret?"

"The big secret is that I don't know what Klaus discovered."

Seeing Alice's eyes widen in outrage, Alex held his hands up. "However, I know the road he took to get there."

"The Song of the Stars. Is the formula hidden in it?"

"Yes, though it's not precisely what you think."

Alice folded her arms across her chest. "I'm waiting."

"The words in the story are unimportant. It's the melody itself. There are certain notes that translate to sound frequencies. These sound frequencies have a corresponding light-wave frequency. Those light-wave frequencies are used to bombard Kinemet before initiating a reaction—in essence, priming it—to achieve the desired effect on a person. The result, of course, is irradiating that person, and attuning them to the radiation signature of Kinemet."

"What notes?"

"I'm not certain. I believe Klaus wrote a computer program that disseminated the most likely possibilities. Unfortunately, that program was destroyed along with the station on Venus."

Alice chewed her lip. "We have many computer programmers with us. I'm sure we can reproduce that algorithm. I assume you have some idea which notes are important and which ones aren't?"

Nodding, Alex said, "I listened to Yaxche recite the song several times. I have some ideas."

"Good." Alice went to her computer and typed something. "Sian is my father's best programmer. We'll get him here to write the code." A moment later, a message came back on-screen, and Alice smiled. "Good. He's currently finishing an assignment, but should be here in a few hours."

She logged off the computer and faced Alex. "I will have some food delivered here for you. If you require rest, there is a cot set up in the storage room over there." She pointed to a door on the other side of the lab.

"Thank you," Alex said. There was no point in being impolite. After all, the more cooperative he seemed, the easier it would be to delay their progress.

"A guard will be posted in this room at all times. He has my permission to shoot you if you do anything to arouse suspicion."

"Understood," Alex said amicably.

Narrowing her eyes at him once more, she strode out of the lab.

∞

Alex presumed Alice was off either to report to her father, complain about the working arrangement, or have something to eat. No matter which it was, Alex wouldn't have much time.

Confidently, he walked over to the computer Alice had used to contact the programmer. Just as he started toward it, the guard turned his rifle on him.

As casually as he could, Alex took a seat in front of the console and typed in Alice's password—she had not been careful enough to hide it from him. Perhaps she thought he could not see what she typed from across the room, or that he couldn't use a keyboard with Chinese characters on it. Though there was a Kinemetic damper in the room, that only prevented Alex's electropathy and his *sight*. His eidetic memory was intact, and though he didn't know how to interpret the characters on the keyboard, he remembered precisely which keys Alice pressed and in what sequence.

"What are you doing?" The guard took a few steps forward, and pointed his rifle directly at Alex.

Forcing a calmness into his voice that he didn't feel, Alex said,

"Cooperating. What did you think I was doing?"

The guard didn't reply, but neither did he lower his weapon.

Affecting a sigh of irritation, Alex turned in the seat to face the suspicious guard. "If you must know, I'm going to access the recording of the Song the Stars and begin logging the sound waves of each note. It could take some time."

Without waiting to see if his explanation satisfied the guard, Alex turned back to the computer and tapped a key to see what it would do. A navigation screen appeared. "After all," he said, "that's what they brought me here to do, isn't it?"

He tapped another key, and then another and another, memorizing each of their functions. Once he had a baseline, deciphering the remaining characters only took a few minutes. By the time he had a working knowledge of the computer's operation, he noticed the guard had retreated to his post, and had adopted his previous watchful position.

What Alex needed was more information, both on how much they knew about Klaus's progress, and about their empire.

The first database Alex accessed prompted him for a password. He entered Alice's and smiled; she was one of those people who used the same password for everything. It occurred to him that he had no idea what that password was, and opened a translator and frowned when it spat out the English letters: qinguangwangfoursevensevenzero.

At first, he thought it might be a random string of characters, but then he had an idea, and did a general search. Qin Guang Wang was the Chinese ruler of the first court of Feng-du, the equivalent of the Western version of hell. He judged the dead and decided whether their souls went to paradise or were sent into hell for punishment.

Using her password, Alex accessed Alice's personnel file and confirmed the date of her birth. 4770 was the Chinese equivalent to 2073 in the Gregorian calendar.

Alice used the Chinese god of retribution and her birthday as her password.

What events had occurred to make Alice Yin the person she was? There was such anger in her.

Quickly, Alex skimmed the rest of her file. It gave some basic details, but not enough to paint a complete picture. Alex didn't know how much access he had, but he did a comprehensive search throughout the entire station's databases for any document that would give him a hint to Alice Yin's background.

With his enhanced memory, he only needed to glance at each document once to retain everything on it. By the time his lunch arrived, Alex had read all the information in the database concerning the Emperor's daughter. Whatever wasn't there, he could fill in himself.

∞

When Chow Yin had started to build his criminal organization in the depths of Luna Station, he'd done so despite his disability. For the kind of man he was, he believed the only women who would be attracted to him were those seeking his money, power, and security. To let himself become romantically involved with someone was a weakness, a vulnerability he could not afford. He was still a man, however, with a man's needs. Those needs were met by those women who provided such services.

To prevent any possibility of such a woman becoming familiar with him or his operation, he never contracted the same person twice, and always ensured they were on Luna temporarily.

Chow Yin took as many precautions as he could, but no safeguard was infallible, as he found out when one of the women contacted him and attempted to extort money: their union had produced a baby girl. Alice.

In an attempt to plug the breach in security, Chow Yin sent a man to eliminate the two. Some paternal weakness in him made him change his orders at the last moment: let the baby live.

Since the woman had no living relatives, Alice ended up in China's orphanage system. Though Chow Yin had no desire to meet or publicly acknowledge his daughter, he nevertheless checked in on her from time to time.

When he received a report that Alice had an affinity for the sciences, he arranged a scholarship to Peking University in their Astrophysics department, and ensured various professors and university officials monitored and encouraged her progress.

After Chow Yin was arrested on Luna Station, the media dug into every aspect of his life.

A reporter from Beijing broke the story, linking Chow Yin to Alice.

It became a media circus for her: daughter of the most infamous criminal of the century. Her scholarship funds were seized by the government. Trying to dispel any suspicion of bribery, the university administration immediately expelled her from their program. She lost her apartment and all her friends.

No legitimate company would hire Alice after that, and—homeless, destitute, and desperate—she ended up working for an arms dealer who was developing biological weapons.

Three years after her father was prosecuted and sent to the penal colony on the other side of the Sun, the organization Alice worked for was raided. Alice was convicted and sentenced to life in Chongqing Prison.

A follow-up piece several years later illustrated how prison life was unkind to Alice. The prison had a reputation for torture by the male guards, severe deprivation, and brutality among the inmates.

The last article Alex read was about an unexplained fire in a poorly maintained section of the prison that killed more than a dozen inmates and guards, including Alice Yin, a month before Chow Yin's own escape from the remote penal station.

Alex guessed Chow Yin had arranged for her escape and brought her to Qin Station to work for him.

She'd been working on the Kinemetic process since then. The only means of testing any Kinemetic theory was to use human subjects; and there had not been any successes in all that time.

With horror, Alex wondered how many people had died in her experiments.

At thirty-six, Alice Yin was as brilliant and insane as her father.

16

Tegucigalpa, Honduras :
Central American Conglomeration :

As much as the radical events that had occurred in the four years he'd been away had alarmed Michael, the overwhelming sameness of the Honduran capital was a sharp contrast. The country had always had a struggling economy, and the war that had ravaged the world since Michael had left hadn't improved the standard of living for the people of Honduras.

The last time Michael had been here was with George, and they'd been on a fact-finding mission. This time, the only difference was that he was accompanied by Yaxche. For the duration of the flight, through the landing at the Toncontin International Airport, and the sluggish wading through the country's customs procedures, neither of them spoke of anything of importance. They kept their conversation light, and off-topic from their mission, just in case any other curious passenger or official overheard them.

Yaxche, as a returning national, had an easier time passing the customs interview, but when Michael offered up his identification, he was flagged. He had to spend an hour in a small room while the officers contacted Canadian officials. Michael's name had been plastered all over the local newsvids after his involvement in the events at the Ruiz plantation four years before, then again after his disappearance from Canada Station Three. Whoever the Honduran officers contacted back home, they managed to convince them that Michael was not only *not* under suspicion for any wrongdoing—any outstanding charges had been rescinded—but he was a fully authorized government agent, whose current mission was to escort Yaxche to his home.

Michael's first task was to check in to the consulate, and then head to the bus terminal to catch the daily shuttle to Santa Rosa de Copán. Customs had taken so long, they only had half an hour to get to the Tegucigalpa bus terminal, which was almost across the city.

It proved harder to find an autotaxi than to get through customs. When Michael, with Yaxche quietly trailing behind, went to the kiosk to get one assigned, there was an attendant there, a young kid who couldn't have been more than fifteen.

Though his Spanish had improved over the past while, Michael was glad he'd remembered to bring his translator with him.

"Sorry, sir," the attendant said. "All the computers are down this morning. The autotaxis are grounded."

"For how long?" Michael asked.

"They're doing some kind of upgrade—it's been needed for a long time. They were supposed to be finished overnight, but it's taking forever."

Michael made a grunt of displeasure and looked around.

"A city bus should arrive in twenty minutes, if you want to wait."

There was no way they would make the terminal in time.

"How far away is a car rental office from here?" Michael asked.

The attendant said, "Oh, the del Angel Vehicle Hire is right over there, near the north end of the terminal. You could walk there in five minutes."

"Thank you." He gave the attendant a tip, and then hefted his luggage. He glanced at Yaxche. "I don't think we're going to make the daily shuttle in time. If we can rent a car, we could drive to Santa Rosa ourselves after we check in with the consulate." Yaxche gave Michael a nod that he agreed with the plan. He had a backpack full of souvenirs he'd bought at the Pearson gift shop, and he slung it over his shoulder before following.

When they entered the rental agency, the harried clerk behind the counter shook his head. "If you're looking to rent, all our cars and trucks are gone. With the autotaxis down, we sold out almost an hour ago."

If they hadn't been so delayed by customs…

Not only would they miss the shuttle out of the capital, but they also seemed to be stranded at the airport.

Michael grimaced, and looked at Yaxche. The older man was looking pale; after spending so long in air-conditioned space craft, and in the cool Canadian climate, it would take a bit of time for them both the acclimatize to the heat of Honduras.

"Maybe I'll call the consulate, and see if they can send a car."

They stepped back out of the rental agency, and Michael scanned up and down the terminal for a comm kiosk. He strode over to it, logged in, and placed the call. A young-sounding female voice answered.

"Thank you for calling the Canadian Consulate of Honduras. Beth speaking. How may I direct your call?"

"This is Michael Sanderson. I'm a special emissary escorting a Honduran national. I believe Allan Perkins was informed of my arrival. It seems we're stuck at the airport without transport, and we've missed the daily shuttle to Santa Rosa de Copán." A moment later, he remembered to give her his official access code to verify his identity.

The secretary said, "I'm sorry, Mr. Sanderson. Consul Perkins had an all-day conference today. Unfortunately, because of budget cuts, we no longer have any vehicles for official use. We contract with a chauffeur service, but they don't travel outside the capital. I could send one to bring you here. There's a hotel near here where you can stay until tomorrow."

Trying not to sound ungrateful for the offer, Michael said, "We were hoping to make Santa Rosa de Copán today."

"I'm sorry, Mr. Sanderson," the secretary said.

It seemed they didn't have any other choice. "Thank you, Beth. We'll be waiting at the north parking lot."

After disconnecting, Michael said to Yaxche. "We might as well find a shady spot and sit down."

There was an outdoor food vendor, where Michael bought two iced teas. They sat at one of the round patio tables and took refuge in the shadow of its umbrella.

"How does it feel to finally be back home?" Michael asked.

Looking around the busy streets, Yaxche said, "This is not home."

"Well, with luck, we should be in your village tomorrow evening at the latest."

"It has been a long time since I slept in my own bed." He gave Michael a toothy smile. "Your beds are all too soft."

Since his release from the detention center in Ottawa, Michael hadn't pressed Yaxche on specifics, taking the older man at his word that he might know the whereabouts of the alien race Ah Tabai called the Grace. Thinking about it, the information the Mayan had given them was fairly thin—that he *might* know where they'd gone—but then again, everyone had discounted that the ancient Song of the Stars document contained the key to unlocking the photonic properties of Kinemet. Michael was prepared to go on a little faith, but his curiosity got the better of him.

Casually, he asked, "So, what is it we're looking for?" When Yaxche glanced at him questioningly, Michael added, "I mean, is there another ancient scroll or something?"

"I don't know."

"What do you mean, you don't know?"

"It's possible, but I do not think so."

Michael looked at Yaxche pointedly. "If it's not a scroll, then what is it?"

"It is a story."

"What story?"

"I cannot tell you. It is not my story." After a moment, he said, "I already told you *my* story."

Michael cleared his throat. "Now you're just being cryptic."

Yaxche, as if enjoying teasing Michael, smiled wide. Letting out a small laugh, he said, "We need to speak to an old friend of mine. Perhaps, if he likes you, he will tell you his story."

"The story of the Grace?"

Keeping his smile firmly in place, Yaxche shrugged helplessly. "It is best to hear the story from the storyteller."

Michael recalled that the key to the Song of the Stars wasn't the story itself, it was in the telling, and he resigned himself to be patient.

Yaxche patted him on the arm. "Do not worry. I think my friend will like you."

By the time they finished their iced teas, they spotted a long black car pulling into the parking lot. The decal on the door read 'Tegucigalpa Chauffeur Service'. Michael stood and hefted his luggage as the car pulled up.

The driver spoke in English with a heavy Spanish accent. "Mr. Sanderson for the Canadian Consulate?" The man, who was short but quite stocky, wore an odd-fitting black suit. The tie around his neck was loosened, and the top button of the collar was undone. As if realizing the fact, he quickly did the button up and tightened the tie.

"Yes, that's us," Michael said.

Reaching into his vehicle, the driver pressed the trunk release, then hurried over to help Michael and Yaxche with their luggage.

Once Michael and Yaxche climbed into the back seat, the driver engaged the navigation computer and typed in their destination.

They drove along the Bulevard Fuerzas Armadas, weaving in and out of traffic, and Michael looked out of the window at the city. When he glanced over to Yaxche, he saw that the older man seemed not to take any interest in the city.

When they reached the Boulevard Centromerica, instead of turning north toward the Canadian Embassy, they kept going east.

"I think you missed the turnoff," Michael called out to the driver.

"Construction," the driver said. "We'll take a side street around. It'll be faster."

Sitting back uneasily, Michael searched his memory. It had been a few months—his time—since he'd been in Tegucigalpa, and though he didn't have as keen a memory as Alex or Justine, he'd taken the time to look at a street map of the capital more than once. There were no side streets from the turnoff until they crossed the Anillo Periférico. Even in a roundabout way, that would more than double their travel time.

"City's going through a lot of problems this morning," Michael said.

"*Sí.*"

The man didn't seem to be acting suspiciously. Perhaps Michael was just being paranoid. He decided to wait and see what happened.

When they reached the turnoff to Anillo Periférico, and continued heading east, Michael sat forward.

"Where are you taking us?"

"Please relax, *señor.*" The driver drew a pistol from inside his suit jacket and held it up a moment for Michael to see before putting it back. "It's for your own good."

17

Kulsat Ship :
Centauri System :

Blind both physically and Kinemetically, and trapped inside a small tank surrounded by water on a hostile alien ship was enough to make Justine feel overwhelmed. Knowing there could either be a mass slaughter or a revolution just outside her reach, the outcome of which would directly decide her own fate, Justine fought to keep herself from succumbing to the emotional overload.

Sounds didn't travel very well into her terrarium, but what she could hear, she couldn't interpret. Had her efforts returned Red Spot to physical form? Had Three Crescents repaired his energy rod and blasted her? Was he finishing his insane task of killing every non-Risen on the ship?

The Kinemetic radiation coming from the alien Risen started to seep back into Justine's system, and her *sight* returned to her slowly.

In the span of a few seconds, she saw what had transpired during her blackout. Three Crescents had reconnected his energy rod and was blasting it at the other aliens, but he was doing it out of desperation. As if Red Spot's courage had bolstered them, the other Kulsat charged Three Crescents. They grabbed loose tools and canisters to use as weapons. So far, none of them had gotten close enough to strike Three Crescents, but he'd killed more than half a dozen of them and wounded several others.

Red Spot was still alive, Justine saw, but she was injured. One of her tentacles hung limply from her torso—perhaps a graze from the energy weapon.

Helplessly, Justine watched the army of cephalopods throw themselves at Three Crescents, but he seemed an expert in his aim and kept fending them off.

The sheer numbers were on the rebels' side, though. As if sensing that he couldn't keep up his defense forever, Three Crescents quantized himself. In control of himself in that state, he raced out of the laboratory, leaving the survivors and Justine behind. He was no doubt going to report to Long Fingers.

Justine didn't know how many Risen were on board the alien ship, but one was all that was needed if they decided to quantize the entire vessel. Once everyone was neutralized in a photonic state, the pilot could navigate back to their home system, where the numbers would undoubtedly favor the elite Kulsat rather than the rebels.

Red Spot swam to the terrarium and turned on the translation computer with a flick of one long tentacle. The familiar hum of the link on her collar gave Justine a sense of comfort she hadn't expected.

"Red Spot," Justine said. "Are you all right?"

The little alien typed. "Your concern is unexpected. I will continue. I am not certain our actions were wise, however. We have no power against Long Fingers."

Behind her, dozens of Kulsat waited, as if unsure what to do now that they had succeeded in scaring Three Crescents away.

Justine said, "Is there a shuttle on this ship?"

"Yes, we have six such vessels. They are used to mine the Gift of the Grace on asteroids. The shuttles do not have the engines to use the Grace."

The Grace. According to Alex's story, that was what Ah Tabai had called the race who created the system of star beacons. Maybe, for the Kulsat and the other Emerged races, the name was homonymous for the power of Kinemet, the photonic state of being, and for the race that had first mastered the technology.

"Do you have any of the Gift on board?" Justine asked. "If we can get some of it to my friends and our ship, we might have a chance."

Red Spot turned to the aliens behind her and signed to the group. Several of them signed in return, and the back and forth went on for what seemed like forever—at least, to Justine.

She waited, barely containing her impatience, as Red Spot spun back to the computer and took a very long time to type the results of the conversation.

"There are several stores of the Gift on board. We can collect a quantity of it and load it on the mining shuttle. The problem we have is how to bring you to the shuttle. Your observation platform is affixed to the hull. Even if we could move it, the loading door to the shuttle is too small for it to fit. There is no provision for one of your kind on the shuttle. Our alien biologist informs us that you are an air-based species and cannot process oxygen under water. It will only be a short duration before Three Crescents and Long Fingers return to destroy us."

A few times, Justine tried to interrupt the message that came in, but since it had been pre-typed, there was no way to stop the translation. She bit her lip until the machine voice finished speaking.

"Bring some of the Gift here, to me. Once I'm recharged, I can turn to light and follow you to the ship. We won't have any way of communicating while I'm in that state, but if we can find my ship and my friends, they will be able to help us."

Red Spot made a unique set of signs to her, which Justine took as acknowledgement. The little alien then turned around and handed out instructions to the small band of revolutionaries. The individual Kulsat swam off to complete their assigned tasks. Only Red Spot remained in the lab.

"Is everyone with us?" Justine asked.

"We are conditioned to obey those in authority. The Kulsat on board regard me as their new sub-commander. I told them Three Crescents is unit-defective and wanted your alien technology for himself. That is the reason they attacked him. They are all still loyal to the Consortium. If they encounter Long Fingers, however, he will be able to counter my instructions."

Justine felt herself grow frustrated with the Kulsat's culture. They were alien to her in every sense of the word.

"Are you still loyal to the Consortium?"

Red Spot replied. "Yes." She continued to type. "Our kind has been persecuted throughout history. When the Grace disappeared from the universe, the other races became jealous of our knowledge and warred against us. They invaded our home world. Only because of our superiority were we able to survive. Now, we are the dominant race in the galaxy, but we are not secure. The other races continue to plot against us. Only with the final component will we assure our continued survival."

If what Red Spot said was true, then the Kulsat had reason to be paranoid of other worlds. Justine asked, "Why did you save me?"

"The Consortium believes all non-Kulsat races are an imminent threat and must be expired to ensure our continuance. The Consortium believes non-Kulsat have no value. The Consortium believes Deficients have no value." She held Justine's eyes as her next statement filtered through the translator. "You believe all beings have value. There is validity in that. Perhaps there is an opportunity to reevaluate some of the polices of the Consortium."

Justine was overwhelmed by what she was hearing. How many other Kulsat felt their culture was overzealous in its xenophobia? Although it was difficult to avoid imposing one's own values on other cultures, Justine didn't know how a society could progress when it completely discarded those who failed to achieve the Kinemetic change.

She would save her philosophizing for later. Right now, time was working against her.

From what she gathered, Three Crescents and Long Fingers were completely ensconced in their status as elites. They believed the rest of the Kulsat were thoroughly subjugated; the ship didn't have much in the way of internal security. That slight advantage would disappear the moment Long Fingers felt the situation was out of his control.

Even if they all managed to get on the shuttle and flee the ship, the moment the two Risen became aware of the exodus, they could easily pull her back, as they did when she was on the *Ultio*. Then they could blast the shuttle to bits at their leisure.

Justine had to increase her chances of escape, somehow, and ensure the other Kulsat weren't killed in the process.

"Red Spot," she said, "are there any other Risen on the ship besides Three Crescents and Long Fingers?"

"No. We are not military. We are a mining vessel. There is only one science leader and one ship leader on board."

"Can you describe the layout to me? Where is the main cabin, engineering, crew quarters, loading dock, everything?"

"Yes. I can explain that." Red Spot typed for a long while.

∞

By the time Justine absorbed all the information Red Spot gave her, she had a very solid idea of the ship's geography.

She sensed one of the non-Risen Kulsat returning to the lab. He was carrying a small quantity of Kinemet—the Gift of the Grace—in a spherical container. The radiation level was minimal, and Justine assumed the enclosure was made of some kind of damping material, like the titanium they had used in Sol System to keep the Kinemet from playing havoc with nearby electronics.

As the alien got closer to Justine's tank, she felt a surge ripple through her. Although she'd been able to absorb second-hand radiation from Three Crescents, that had been little more than a drop of water on the tongue; nowhere near enough to quench her thirst. Even sealed by the damping container, Justine could feel every fiber of her being reaching out for the nourishment of Kinemet.

When Klaus had conducted his experiment on her, he'd used a milligram of the kinetic metal. Justine sensed the Kulsat had brought her at least a full gram. If she never quantized herself, that much would most likely be enough Kinemet to sustain her for the rest of her life. It was being in the photonic state that consumed Kinemet at a rapid rate.

Hungrily, she waited for the Kulsat to get to her tank. With Red Spot's assistance, the two swam up to the top of her glass cage and placed the container in the cylinder that had been used to feed her previously. They placed the cylinder in the delivery mechanism and triggered the winch.

As the Kinemet was lowered within her reach, Justine heard Red Spot's message come through the translator.

"Only a Risen is capable of opening the container."

For a moment, Justine's impatience got the better of her, and she felt a rush of heat to her cheeks.

Whatever substance the container was made of must be impenetrable by physical means. Since a Risen had the ability to quantize others at will—as they had done to her—then it followed that they had the ability to quantize objects as well. Once the sphere was converted to photons, the Risen had full access to the Grace inside.

The problem was that, even if she were fully irradiated, Justine didn't have any idea how to quantize anything except herself. Radiation still leaked out of the container, but at a rate so slow it would take her an hour or longer to become charged enough to make the change—and even then, she would use up that charge very quickly.

They didn't have that kind of time. It was hard to tell how long it had been since Three Crescents had fled the lab, and she expected him and Long Fingers to show up any moment and take control of the situation. When the Kulsat had quantized her to bring her aboard their ship, Justine had not been conscious in that state, much the same as none of the other passengers on the *Ultio*—Alex included—had been aware during the journey.

Justine didn't know nearly enough about the 'Gift' of light, although she'd spent over four years in that state. Given the chance, she was determined to learn as much as possible.

She held the sphere close to her chest, and sat on the floor of the tank, letting the Kinemetic radiation flow into her. She would hold on as long as she could.

Soon, another alien entered the lab and signed to Red Spot, who conveyed the information to Justine. "We have loaded the shuttle with the Gift. Squiggles Over A Small Circle spotted Long Fingers on the bridge, but did not interact with the ship leader. Perhaps Three Crescents has not reported us to him yet."

That was good news, Justine thought to herself. That would give them more time. It also hinted that Three Crescents may have exceeded his authority, if he was afraid of letting the ship leader know what was happening.

Red Spot typed. "The rest of the crew are on the shuttle waiting for instructions."

Justine said, "I need a little more time with the Grace before I am charged enough to quantize myself. You three get to the shuttle and get off the ship—"

The mechanized voice interrupted her. "The others are helping only to get you away from Three Crescents. If we leave you here, they will see no reason to leave the ship."

"I promise," Justine said, "I will get to the shuttle as soon as I am capable." She didn't know if Red Spot could interpret the sincerity in her words, so she looked through the glass at the cephalopod so that the alien could see it in her eyes.

"You have not employed deception to me in the past. I do not believe you will employ deception in the future. We will be waiting for you on the shuttle. Utilize haste, Justine."

With that, Red Spot and the two others flicked their tentacles and darted out of the lab.

It had only been a few minutes with the Kinemet, but Justine was already feeling the effects of its influence. She wished she knew how the Kulsat Risen were able to quantize others. After decades of experiments, the only method NASA and Quantum Resources' scientists had discovered for quantizing a ship was to use a quantum drive.

Justine had read many of the theoretical papers about the process, and while she sat there waiting to be fully charged, she reviewed all the texts stored in her memory. The crash-course took her several minutes to complete, but by the end, there was nothing in the experiments to suggest the possibility of external quantization. Of course, no one had imagined that it was possible to quantize anything without a quantum drive—which, basically, was a high-powered hydrogen bombardment device.

Something tickled the back of her mind.

What would happen if she was in a quantized state, and bombarded an atom of Kinemet with a photon of her own? Would that, in turn, begin the quantum change in an external object? And if so, could she somehow target that energy?

Justine didn't get the chance to test her theory. With her *sight,* she sensed the arrival of a Kinemetic presence outside the lab.

She stood up, clutching the sphere to her as Three Crescents entered the room, holding what looked like a portable energy rod.

The moment he spotted Justine, he aimed the rod at her tank and fired.

The glass shattered and thousands of liters of water slammed into her.

18

Sierra de las Minas :
Guatemala :

Long Count: 9.19.19.17.18

I spent the following days in my hut, waiting for my new home to be finished. I felt terrible that I was not able to help. Although I seemed to be recovering faster than expected, I still had difficulty with simple tasks. I could walk around, but I couldn't lift a bucket of water without pain shooting through my chest.

Though I hated my new chosen role in the village, I owed it to my people to become the best priest I could. As a warrior, I'd had some lessons in reading glyphs. It was important to understand decrees or orders from the king's guard. Until a priest arrived from Copán to begin my lessons, I decided to try to teach myself.

The scrolls the priest had left behind were far beyond my understanding. At first, when I tried to read them, I quickly became frustrated. Without a teacher to guide me, I might as well have tried to learn the language of birds. Even still, I kept trying. After all, I had nothing else to do, and lying down for hours on end was maddening.

After most of a day trying to figure out the meaning of a certain glyph that was repeated many times in the scrolls, I decided to bring my question to Ohtli Ti, the oldest of our elders.

It was bad form to approach an elder without first requesting an audience, and even worse to ask an elder to lower themselves to the role of teacher. Without another priest to guide me, however, I had no other choice.

I picked Ohtli only because, when I was a child, he'd taken supper with my father and our family several times.

My ribs ached from the effort, and I stood outside the doorway of his house in silence, as much out of respect for his position as to catch my breath.

I was certain he had noticed me right away, but he went about his own tasks for several minutes before lifting one hand for me to enter his house.

Bowing and keeping my head lowered, I said, "Forgive me for being familiar, Elder Ti. I mean no disrespect."

"The king has decreed you are to become the priest of our village, Subo. It is only right that the elders listen to the counsel of our holy men."

I felt a heat rise to my cheeks. "I would not dare to offer my opinions to those who are more learned than I."

"But you will." He nodded to me. "You must become accustomed to your new rank."

"Thank you, Elder Ti. I will do my best."

I looked up, and he smiled at me.

"I'm sure you will," he said. "Now, do we have business today?"

"Please excuse my ignorance, Elder. I am trying to learn to read Balam Ix's scrolls, but I am having difficulty."

"Show me."

I held the scroll out to him and pointed to the glyph that kept appearing.

He glanced at it and then looked up at me in surprise. "Do you not remember your first lesson? I thought warriors were taught the difference between sound symbols and word symbols."

As he said it, I recalled that there were often two ways to write the same word: it could be written out with a symbol for each sound, or a single symbol that represented the word. Most of Balam's scroll was written with sound symbols, but the one I was not familiar with was a word symbol I had never seen before.

I flushed. "My apologies, Elder. I should have known. If you could, please tell me what that symbol represents."

"Flower," he said. "Or the essence from that flower."

"Thank you, Elder Ti," I said, and bowed as I backed out of his house.

Hoping none of the other villagers had witnessed my

embarrassment, I headed back to my hut and worked my way through the first scroll. By the time the sun set, I had a basic understanding of the scroll's meaning: it was a recipe for a paste that would soothe light burns.

I was excited that I had made so much progress. Over the next two days, I went through as many of Balam's writings as I could. By the time my new home was completed, I was able to figure out the meaning behind each of the scrolls I had inherited.

I didn't let the other villagers know how far I had come. If I told them that I had learned in three days what it would take most others three months to understand, they would regard me with suspicion, and might think I had been replaced by a demon.

One other thing happened that was more difficult to hide. My ribs were healing faster than they should. I knew, from others who had broken bones, that it could be as many as two *winals*—forty-days—to recover. At the rate I was healing, I would be fully recovered in a few more days.

I became nervous that the other villagers would realize that I was different. Though I hated to deceive them, I pretended to be worse than I actually was. If someone questioned me about how I was healing so fast, I would tell them that perhaps I hadn't been as injured as we had first thought.

My only explanation was that when Ekahua had put his hand on me and taught me the Song of the Stars, he had somehow changed me. Whether it was a gift or curse, I couldn't say. I knew that my being different from the others would only draw their fear. At the same time, I couldn't help but feel grateful for my ability to learn as fast as I had been, and to heal quickly.

On the fourth morning after we had buried Balam, I woke up and decided to confess everything to my father. He'd heard the story about Ekahua already, and I hoped he would understand that I had not been changed into a demon; that my new abilities were a gift from the sky traveler.

Before I could reveal myself to him, however, a small squad of warriors from Copán arrived. To my disappointment and confusion, they were not accompanied by a priest.

Several villagers came out to greet the newcomers. Our smiles of welcome turned to frowns of concern when we realized it was a war party.

The leader of the squad—a man I had not met before—quickly identified my father, and spoke directly to him. His words were spoken loud enough for the rest of us to hear.

"Tohil Ak, I hope I find you well."

My father greeted him with a hand gesture. "Chaan Xiu, I am well. May we offer you shelter and food?"

"No," Chaan said. "I bring orders from Copán. King Ukit Took has been in discussion with the holy order and the council of elders. They have all agreed that the earthquake four days ago was a sign from the gods. The time for us to attack Quiriguá is now. It has been long overdue, do you not agree, Tohil?"

"I do." My father glanced around the villagers and spotted me. He pointed to me. "My son has recently come back from his warrior's trial, where he defeated three Q'eqchi' fighters. Our enemies have grown weak and lazy."

Chaan nodded to me. "I have heard of this conquest by young Subo, who is blessed of the gods." Turning back to my father, the war leader said, "We are calling all able men to gather in the ceremony field south of Copán tomorrow morning. We will march to Quiriguá and attack at dawn two days from now. Our victory will be sung to our great-grandchildren's grandchildren."

With that, my father and Chaan clasped hands, and the war leader ordered his men on to the next village to spread the call to arms.

Immediately, my father gathered the eight hunter-warriors in our village and gave them orders to prepare weapons and supplies, and to visit each of the farms in the area to call all men of fighting age to the village. Although they were not dedicated warriors, the farmers had all been trained in basic combat in case of invasion from the Q'eqchi'.

Once his men were set to the task, my father approached me. My expression of hope turned to disappointment when he put his hand on my shoulder and said, "I am saddened that you must remain here in the village. I promise you I will bring home many Q'eqchi' slaves for sacrifice. It will be our honor for you to perform the rituals."

My father must have mistaken the look on my face for one of uncertainty, because he squeezed my arm. "I have seen you with Balam's scrolls. You are already able to read them. One of them will describe the ritual of sacrifice, and you will have time before we return to learn what to do. The only thing that would make me more proud than to have you join us in victory is to have you bless our victory with the holy rites."

"I will do my best," I said to my father, trying to hide my personal disappointment as he left me behind and went off to prepare for war.

∞

I woke up the next morning well before the sun rose, and watched from my hut as all the men of the village gathered in the common area, waiting for my father's order to begin their march to Copán. Their wives and children hovered outside the common area with the few older men who were no longer capable of fighting.

Before the troop left the village, my father spotted me and waved me over. I approached him, and when I stood next to him, he spoke to the crowd of fighters.

"Good warriors," he said, "before we march to battle, I ask that we all pray for a swift and glorious victory. My son, Subo Ak, will lead us in that prayer."

For a moment, I froze under the sudden attention from more than a hundred people.

Somehow, my mind called up the prayer Balam Ix had recited to me before I began my warrior's trial. Using that as a starting point, I spoke.

"Nacon, god of war, give our warriors a great revelation of the spiritual and the natural realms. Let them see the strategies of our enemies, give them the might to drive our enemies from their camp, and grant them the strength to withstand any attack.

"Go with all speed, and return with honor."

The warriors raised their arms and cheered. Out of the corner of my eye, I saw my father smile and nod to me, and his approval filled my heart.

Many of the warriors reached out to touch me for additional blessings as they marched out of the village.

∞

I spent the rest of that day elevated in spirit. I'd performed a service to the village, and offered courage and blessing to the warriors. Perhaps becoming the village priest wasn't the worst thing that could have ever happened to me.

My mother also benefited. With her husband being the village's war chief, and her son soon to be the village's holy leader, her status was greatly raised. Only the elders' wives received more respect.

Several of the women in the village brought me food. One of the weavers, Tepin Cen, offered to make me a new set of priest's clothes. Balam's were ill fitting.

I did not have the skill to make my own costume, and so I said, "Yes, please."

Since I was still not fully healed, and she did not want me to stand while she took measurements, she asked me for some of my other clothes to use for comparison.

I gave her the pack I had used on my warrior's trial, and she picked it up and left my home, promising that she would have something for me to try on the next day.

Having nothing more to do, I spent the rest of the afternoon trying to read Balam's scrolls, proud that I could understand most of what he wrote.

It was less than an hour later when I heard a scream from the other side of the village. My ribs were still tender, and I could not run, but I walked as fast as I could to where a group of people had gathered around Tepin's house. The women were all speaking at once, pointing and asking each other what had happened.

When I arrived, they parted for me. Though I had no skill in healing, I was still their priest. A few of the women looked at me expectantly.

In front of the weaver's house, Tepin was lying on the ground. The skin on her hands and face was blistering and turning black, as if she were being burned by fire. She looked up at me, and made a horrible sound, pleading for help.

Beside her was my pack. Several of the items in it were strewn about on the ground, as if the pack had been upturned.

Neither her body nor my pack was what drew my attention. She had taken the items out of my pack. Near my belt, there was a tiny ball of glowing light on the ground in front of Tepin. Slowly, it grew brighter and brighter.

I remembered the grain of what I had thought was sand, which I had taken from Ekahua's sky boat, and I recalled his warning not to let the sun shine on the stone block, which held those grains.

One of the younger girls, Mizquixaual, who was standing very close to Tepin, cried out and fell over. Her skin began to blister and bubble.

I grabbed her and pulled her away from the growing star grain, but the effort of it sent a sharp pain through my chest, and I suddenly felt like throwing up.

Elder Nentil Mo'Nab, who arrived moments after I had, pointed at the glowing ball and said, "It is a tear from Kinich Ahau, the sun god! It is a weapon sent by the Q'eqchi'."

I saw my mother push her way through the gathering crowd. She had a stick in her hand. Before I could yell at her to stop, she swung it at the glowing grain. I was certain her only intention was to send the burning object as far away as possible. I watched with growing dread as the stick connected with the star grain, sending it arcing through the air straight for the fire pit in the common area.

"Run!" I yelled to everyone, and despite the sharp pain in my chest, I grabbed Mizquixaual by her arms and dragged her behind the weaver's house.

The burst of light that washed over the village was brighter than the sun at noon, and hotter than the biggest fire we'd ever built in the common area. The power of it knocked me off my feet, and the breath rushed out of me when I hit the ground.

It seemed like hours before I could focus and look around the village. Most everyone was still lying on the ground. Some were curled up, either moaning in pain, or crying in fear. Others, closer to the common area, were not moving at all, and I feared they might be dead. Everyone I saw had burns on their skin.

Elder Mo'Nab was on the ground beside me. His eyes were open, but unseeing. I saw a trickle of blood coming from under his hairline, and his head lay on a jagged rock. He was dead.

On the other side of me, Mizquixaual was alive, but the burns she'd gotten earlier had begun to peel and bleed.

Groaning with the effort, I pushed myself to my hands and knees.

Where the fire pit had once been, there was now a huge crater. The entire common area was blackened and scorched.

Several of the houses closer to the common area, including mine and the elders', were ablaze. Wincing with every step, I hurried over, but long before I got there, I knew there were no survivors.

Several women, who had been far enough away to have escaped the blast, ran to the stream outside the village, buckets in hand. I knew I would not be capable of helping fight the fire, but I had another job to do. I was the village priest, and it was up to me to help heal the wounded.

My mother was on her feet. Though she'd also suffered burns, the look of shock on her face was not because of her injuries. She was staring in the direction of the common area, as if trying to understand what had happened.

"Mother," I said to her. When she didn't react, I grabbed her arms and gave her a gentle shake. "Mother."

She looked at me, and her mouth opened, but no words came out.

"You must help me," I said. "My house is destroyed, and all the priest's scrolls and medicines are gone. We need to make a salve to ease the burns. I need you to find pots and utensils. I will gather the flowers I need to make the medicine."

When my words sank in, my mother nodded and said, "Yes, of course. I have everything in our house. I will get them ready for you."

I called out to the more able women who were helping the others, and instructed them to bring everyone to my mother's house, where I would try to heal them.

As I made my way out into the fields, searching for the plants and flowers called for in Balam's recipe scroll, there was one thing I realized. Though everyone else who was near me had suffered burns when the fire pit exploded, I'd remained completely untouched and unharmed.

19

Qin Station :
Sol System :

"What do you think you are doing?" Alice asked in a shrill voice when she came into the lab and saw Alex at her computer station.

Forcing a disarming smile, Alex looked up at her. "Like I told the guard, I'm beginning to outline the notes for the Song of the Stars, and convert the sound frequencies to their light-wave counterparts."

"How did you get onto my computer?" Alice demanded, striding forward and looking at the screen. Indeed, Alex had begun to build a comprehensive analysis of the song.

Shrugging, Alex said, "I used your password. I thought I'd take the initiative and get started. After all, the faster we finish this, the sooner you'll let me go, right?"

There was a clouded look on Alice's face that told him not to get his hopes up, no matter whether they promised to release him.

He noticed another person in the room following closely behind Alice. Alex glanced up at him and said, "Hello."

Alice introduced the newcomer. "This is Sian. He's our computer genius."

"Ah," Alex said, and got up from the chair. He gestured to the seat. "I got it started for you."

Sian, giving Alex an inquisitive look, sat down and went over the work. Letting out a grunt of approval, Sian said, "Good start. If you can finish this analysis, I can begin writing an algorithm to determine the most likely possible combinations for the primer."

Alice, seeming a little out of her depth in this area, gestured to another computer terminal. She said to Alex, "You can use that one." To Sian, she asked, "How long will it take to write the program?"

Sian bobbed his head back and forth, calculating in his mind. "Alex seems to know his way around a computer. With his help, we should have something ready in a week or two."

"A week or two!" Alice looked positively outraged.

Sian seemed to shrink into himself. "If I had a team of programmers—"

"No!" Alice glared at him. "No one else. Can't you do it any faster?"

"Maybe if we had Klaus's notes..."

Alice shook her head. "They were destroyed in the attack."

"I'm sorry, Your Highness," Sian said. "It's a complex algorithm. I'm sure Klaus worked on it for months before getting the raw data. At least we have that advantage."

As if sensing that any further browbeating would not speed up the process any more, Alice said, "I'll hold you to your estimate. I'll prepare samples and ready our subjects. The moment you receive the first possible combination for the bombardment formula, you will inform me, and we'll begin the trials."

∞

For the following two days, Alex worked alongside Sian.

The first afternoon, he finished converting frequencies for the song. After that, he assisted the programmer in coming up with identifiers on which frequencies were most likely part of the priming sequence.

They didn't engage in any conversations of a personal nature; the guard standing in the room was an effective deterrent. When they did talk, they kept it professional, limiting their exchanges to technical aspects of the program and the desired results.

When Sian was done for the day, the only words he spoke to Alex were, "Until tomorrow."

A new guard came in to relieve the other one, and turned off all the computers, giving Alex a look of warning.

With nothing else to do, Alex spent the night thinking about how to delay, or even stop, Alice and Chow Yin. Deep into the night, when his thoughts started to turn to his parents, Kenny Harriman, George Markowitz, Ah Tabai, Aliah, and even Klaus, Alex despaired at the enormous loss of life that had happened from the moment of discovering Kinemet.

To keep despair at bay, Alex distracted himself by offering to play a game of cards with the guard.

"It is not permitted."

"What about solitaire?" Alex asked. "What harm could it do?"

The guard spoke into his communicator, and within five minutes, another solider arrived with a deck of cards for him. Since Alex could not sleep, and he soon tired of the more familiar games, he made up his own versions. It was mind numbing, but it was better than staring at the wall.

∞

The second day unfolded much the same as the first, but at the end of the third day, Alex knew Sian was stalling. From what he saw of the programming, the coder should have been able to complete that portion of the application in one day. Alex was far from an experienced programmer, and he hadn't spent much time pursuing it since he was a teenager. He saw, however, where Sian included several unnecessary redundancies in the code, as well as dozens of extraneous pages of instructions.

When Alex followed a logic thread and found himself in an infinite loop, he was certain something was up.

He didn't give anything away, and carried on assisting as if everything were progressing as it should have.

To test his theory, Alex, added a small code to the program. When Sian ran that segment, his computer's clock would begin to run in reverse. It was a question, and soon after Sian ran the segment, Alex saw that his code had been deleted, and a new code was in its place.

He didn't need to run it: he recognized it as an 'oxbow code'—a fragment that was once needed, but no longer.

Alex knew that once his efforts were successful, his usefulness would be at an end, and with it, his life. Sian was obviously aware of this, and most likely thought he was in the same situation. He was playing for time, trying to help the both of them.

In response, Alex sent back a code that would produce a false positive, intending to let Sian know how he should proceed.

They did not share any more messages through code after that, or else they might risk alerting anyone monitoring them that they were in collusion.

∞

On the fourth day, Alex had nothing more to contribute to the effort until the algorithm was completed. When Alice came to check on their progress, she ordered him to follow her out of the lab and leave Sian to his work.

She brought him to an adjacent room with a plain table and two chairs. It was obviously someone's office, perhaps even Alice's. Now, it served as an interrogation room. There was one window, but it was covered with a blind.

Gesturing for Alex to take a seat, Alice sat opposite him.

"We held up our end of the bargain," she said, her words hard. "You have not held up your end."

"Michael and Yaxche...?"

"They have been delivered as promised. You, however, have withheld vital information."

"I'm not sure what—"

"Please," Alice said. "Don't insult our intelligence. We were aware you were keeping secrets, but we didn't want to press you until we had proof."

Alex felt his skin grow hot. "Didn't want to press? You killed my friend, held a gun to our heads. I'm surprised we weren't tortured."

Leveling her eyes on him, Alice said, "Don't worry. Unless I get the answers I'm looking for today, I have been authorized to engage in more aggressive interrogation techniques."

Pushing thoughts of torture to the back of his mind, Alex spoke in a calm voice. "What information do you imagine I'm withholding?"

Letting a small smile escape her lips, Alice said, "First of all, we are all aware that a quantum drive can only fly just under the speed of light. Your first adventure to the Centauri System took a little over eight-and-a-half years, round trip. Now, you're back in half that time."

"We were—"

She held up a hand to stop him. "If you're going to come up with some excuse that you turned around halfway there, or that you were hiding just out of range all this time, spare me.

"No," she said, "we are quite confident you traveled to the Centauri System. It would have taken you the four years or so to get there, but the return trip must have been near instantaneous."

Alex pursed his lips.

"That led us to speculate on the means. Up until a few hours ago, we had no evidence, but now we do."

She stood up from the table and drew the blinds from the window.

Alex looked out into the large room beside him. There, being dismantled by a crew of engineers, was the Gliesan escape pod. A sinking feeling in the pit of his stomach, Alex realized there was no way for him to deny it. He'd hoped it would take months, if ever, for someone to return to Pluto and recover the pod near the *Dis Pater*.

"The moment we received word they'd found you, we launched a nearby salvage ship. It arrived here this morning. Oh," Alice said, a smug smile playing over her face, "at first we thought it was just an unfamiliar design ... until we got to the communications computer."

Drawing the blinds once more, Alice sat down and folded her hands in front of her on the table. "Now, please leave out no details. Who are the alien species? What is your relationship with them? What is their level of technology? What are their intentions here?"

A dozen thoughts raced through Alex's mind, then. Every one of them ended with the same conclusion: he couldn't hide the truth from Alice and Chow Yin any longer. If he did so, they would see through it.

Also, he knew the clock was ticking. Sol System was running out of time, and though he had hoped to play for that time, and give the nations of Earth a chance to gain the upper hand on Chow Yin, he knew he was gambling with the lives of billions of people.

After all, sometimes it was better to side with the devil you knew.

"There are tens of thousands of species out there, but the ones you need to worry about are called the Kulsat. They are like the Huns of the galaxy, but they don't care about conquest; their purpose is the annihilation of any race who stands in their way. They've had millennia to build their armada of warships, and have destroyed thousands of alien cultures."

Alice's eyes slowly grew wider as Alex spoke, but her mouth opened in a silent gasp when he concluded:

"And they're actively hunting for Sol System. For all I know, they could arrive any minute. If they do, we're all dead."

20

Tegucigalpa, Honduras :
Central American Conglomeration :

It wasn't until they were several miles outside Tegucigalpa that the driver pulled off the highway and down a dirt road to a small industrial development.

For the duration of the trip, the driver did not speak to them, not even to respond to Michael's questions. At no time did they slow down enough to let anyone jump out. Even if Michael had attempted such a foolish escape, Yaxche would never be able to follow him. Most likely, neither of them would survive the fall.

It occurred to him at one point that he was an old man in a young man's game. The problem was, there didn't seem to be anyone else to play his role.

At the end of the country road, they turned into a long driveway leading to what looked like a storage facility. There weren't any signs on the property or the building, but Michael spotted several guards wandering around, all armed with hunting rifles.

Shutting off the engine after he parked in front of a bay door, the driver turned in his seat. "Say nothing and follow me."

He got out, and stepped back to open the passenger door for his two captives. They slid out of the car and looked around. The heat of the morning hit Michael like a wave. Of course, the last time he'd been in Honduras, it had been later in the year. High summer was nearly unbearable.

Holding a finger to his lips to make sure the two kept their silence, the driver headed toward a door off to the side. Without knocking, he stood in front of it and waited. Michael assumed there was some kind of camera or recognition system in play, for a moment later, there was a short beeping sound, and the door swung in.

The driver motioned for them to go in first.

Reluctantly, and with a sidelong glance at the driver as he passed, Michael went in, his imagination running wild. Was he simply a lamb going meekly to his own slaughter?

It was completely dark beyond the door, and Michael hesitated. The driver waved him in again. It seemed there was no other option.

Michael stepped in, Yaxche following, and the door closed behind them, trapping them in darkness and silence.

Holding his breath, waiting for the sharp crack of a rifle shot, or something worse, Michael was startled when he heard the hum of electricity surrounding him. It lasted a few seconds, and then someone turned on a light. He winced against it, but his eyes quickly adjusted.

In sharp contrast to the ragged, worn building outside, the chamber they'd stepped into was high-tech. Michael recognized what it was: a security gate similar to the one at the airport terminal. Providing state-of-the art metal detection, x-ray, and electromagnetic scanning, they didn't come cheap.

The gate was completing its cycle. When it finished, a stocky, olive-skinned man with a thick mustache appeared at the other end of the gate. His short-cropped hair showed streaks of gray at the temples, a change from the last time Michael had seen him.

Mind racing to figure out what was going on, he blurted, "Humberto?"

"*Sí.*" He had a wide smile on his face. "It is good to see you again." He nodded and focused his eyes behind Michael. "Yaxche, my old friend. You look well."

"As well as can be."

Facing Michael once more, Humberto said, "I must apologize if I alarmed you. We needed to take precautions."

"Against what?"

Pointing to the security gate, Humberto said, "We found several listening devices planted on you. They have been disabled. Unfortunately, your luggage has a GPS tracker in it. We put an EM damper in the trunk of the car to kill the signal. Our driver, Migel, will drive to another location and dump the baggage to throw them off. Don't worry; we'll get you fresh clothes."

"What is going on?" Michael asked.

Humberto motioned for them to step out of the security gate, and he led them down a long hall to an office.

Inside was a sofa against one wall. The back of the office had a boarded-up window, and in front of it was a plain desk and chair. There were a few folders and papers on the surface of the desk, as well as a palm-sized portable holoslate. Humberto sat on the edge of the desk and picked up the slate. He tapped a few commands into it as Michael and Yaxche sat on the sofa, and then handed the slate to him.

Michael looked at the readout. It was written in Spanish. He glanced up at Humberto.

"It's a list of encrypted messages sent from a private commlink of a guard at La Granja Prison."

"A guard?"

Nodding, Humberto said, "The first message, sent an hour after you left Canada, is to a customs agent at the Toncontin airport, telling him of your arrival this morning, and to delay you as long as possible. The second message is to Servicio Informático Rápido—the computer company subcontracted to the autotaxi service—instructing them to shut down the taxis. A third message was sent to a driver who works for Tegucigalpa Chauffeur Service, with instructions to take you to the Canadian Embassy."

"That doesn't make a lot of sense."

"There are several other messages—twenty, in fact—to various organizations and companies across Honduras. All of them are instructions to follow you and find out what you are doing here. Everything is set up to ensure their people are near you at all times. It's easier to keep track of you if one of their operatives is accompanying you."

"Operatives?" Michael asked. "Whose operatives? Not the Honduran Conglomerate?"

"No." Humberto took the holoslate back and laid it down on the desk. "Though it could easily look that way. We managed to get Migel, who works as a mechanic for the chauffeur service, to pick you up first."

"You?" Michael couldn't believe what he was hearing. "You set this all up?"

"No. Our man in the prison is a double agent. Do you remember Oscar Ruiz?"

Michael blanched. "Yes. I never followed up on what happened here after I left. George and I thought he might have been coerced by the Cruzados."

"As it turned out in the investigation, he was one of their main sympathizers. Though he never condoned the violent aspect of the organization, he did not speak out against it either."

Then Michael made the connection. "Let me guess; he's in La Granja?"

"Yes. He still has a lot of power, and controls quite a few large companies in Honduras, though not in name."

"What does he want with me?" Michael asked. "Revenge?"

Shaking his head, Humberto said, "I don't think so. No, I believe he is like every other powerful man; he simply wants more power. He suspects you are back in Honduras for a reason other than to escort Yaxche home. Whatever information he can get from you, he could then turn around and sell it to the highest bidder. I understand the Emperor of Sol System is generous in such matters."

Chow Yin! If that madman found out what Michael was doing, he would use every resource available to get that information and keep it for himself. Once again, Michael realized he'd been naïve to think that the Emperor's reach wouldn't extend so far.

He looked up at Humberto. "Where do you come into this?"

"We are what we should have been: the Cruzados. When last we spoke, I told you I believed in their cause. Now, we work to restore ourselves to our rightful place." He smiled widely. "Our mission is to protect the heritage of the Mayan Civilization. For the most part, we lobby for advocacy groups in Honduras, Guatemala, and Mexico. There are many corporations and countries that wish to exploit our culture. We do everything in our power to prevent that."

"Including kidnapping me?"

Humberto shrugged. "I prefer to think we liberated you from covert surveillance."

"Then you are not holding me hostage?"

"Not at all. You are free to go any time you like. We will even take you back to your embassy, if you want—though I must insist that Yaxche remains under our protection. He's one of our own. Without our assistance, he will be vulnerable to Oscar Ruiz and those who are like him."

Michael glanced over at Yaxche, who was listening, but didn't seem very affected by the discussion.

"What do you want with Yaxche?" he asked carefully.

"We'll bring him home, make sure he's safe. Two of our men will remain in his village for protection."

Michael sat back on the sofa. "And that's all you want to do, protect him?"

Humberto nodded, then said, "Unless there is something more to your interest here? Perhaps we can help?"

"You saved my life," Michael said. "For that I owe you, but as you've illustrated, a lot has happened in the past four years."

"I see you do not trust me, *mi amigo,* and you are wise to be cautious." He spread his hands. "However, I do not see how you have any other choice? Your government has little power here. Our government is not suited for subtle operations, and there is corruption everywhere. You need help from someone, or your purpose will have failed before it even started."

Michael still wasn't completely convinced of Humberto's intentions, but he wasn't about to turn tail and go back to Canada with nothing to show for his efforts. Even Calbert would think him either incompetent, or that the entire mission had been a sham all along.

"Let's say I do trust you—" he began.

"That would be nice." Humberto gestured to Yaxche. "But it does not matter that you trust me. Only that *abuelo* trusts me, no?"

Michael gave Yaxche a sharp look, but the older man regarded Humberto with consideration. "Ahyah," he said finally. "I think my friend will like you, too."

21

Kulsat Ship :
Centauri System :

The water was freezing, and the shock of it caused her to gasp. She swallowed a mouthful of the salty liquid and tried to choke it back up.

Panic set in as she realized she was going to drown. In desperation, she tried to quantize herself, but she hadn't charged herself nearly enough to make the transformation. If she didn't do something, she was going to die.

Three Crescents, whether he'd been pulled in by the current or had come closer of his own volition, was almost on top of her. He pointed his energy rod at her, but he seemed to be hesitating before finishing her off. Perhaps he was curious to see an air-breather drown. Whatever the reasons for his delaying the death blow, his proximity had the effect of pumping more radiation into Justine.

It still wasn't enough to let her convert her entire self to protons, but maybe, if she concentrated, she could convert a portion of herself. Knowing she had only seconds before she would pass out from oxygen deprivation, she tried to focus on her hand, wrapped around the sphere containing Kinemet.

All she needed—she hoped—was a single proton to penetrate the outer shell of the container. The quantum drives they had developed at NASA had used hundreds of thousands of free protons to initiate the reaction in charged Kinemet. She had no idea what to expect, if her experiment worked.

A ripple went through Three Crescents' tentacles. He must have seen her clutching the sphere of Kinemet, Justine guessed. Bringing the energy rod up, he fired.

Without consciously thinking about it, Justine willed her hand to convert from the physical to the photonic state. In a microsecond, the change occurred, and her hand passed through the sphere and to the grain of Kinemet within.

Whatever the container was made of dampened the Kinemetic radiation, but wasn't resistant to Justine's photons.

The boost of radiation was enough for her to quantize herself a split-second before the beam of energy would have sliced through her body, and before the water in her lungs would have drowned her.

In the quantized state, she could no longer effectively hold the container, and the sphere fell to the floor of the lab.

Justine instinctively stretched out her essence, one point reaching for the pebble of Kinemet, the other point extending toward Three Crescents. The moment she felt her photonic self come into contact with the Kinemetic atom, she willed a single proton to hit that atom with as much force as she could generate.

A wave of energy coursed through her, coming up from that one point and traveling out of the other point, which had reached Three Crescents.

As the Kulsat had done to her when she was on the *Ultio,* Justine converted Three Crescents into particles of light. She hoped, because he'd been quantized by her, rather than having done it himself, he would not be aware while he was in that condition, as Justine had not been conscious when they'd done it to her.

She waited for a few moments, carefully watching the collection of photons—Three Crescents—to see if the Kulsat would once again flee. The quantized essence continued to float where it was, and Justine's theory was confirmed. The science leader was neutralized.

Though she could manipulate electricity in her quantized state, she had no ability to move solid objects. She couldn't convert back to her human self, or she would drown, and she wasn't about to leave the Kinemet where it was. It was precious.

She had an idea.

Pushing her *sight* out, she saw that the non-Risen Kulsat were all aboard the shuttle, and it had already launched. They were several hundred meters away from the Kulsat mining ship. Changing direction, Justine searched the Kulsat ship. Her exploration confirmed that Long Fingers was the only other Risen on board. He was on the bridge, all eight tentacles working at a rapid pace on a bank of computer consoles.

Justine felt a gravitational shift as the Kulsat ship slowed and banked, obviously coming around to pursue the shuttle. Deep down, she knew Long Fingers would destroy the other aliens.

Extending herself back to the Kinemet on the floor, Justine attempted to quantize the Kulsat ship.

She didn't have nearly enough power. The attempt was like trying to open a magnetically sealed door by ramming it with her body. The ship remained unaffected, and Justine nearly knocked herself unconscious with the effort. If she lost awareness, she would be at Long Finger's mercy.

The Kulsat ship had completed its turn, and it rumbled as the engines went into overdrive. Whatever distance the shuttle had managed to gain would soon be cut short.

There had to be another way to distract Long Fingers.

She formed a plan, but before she tried it, she reached out to the Kinemet and absorbed all of its radiation as quickly as she could, becoming fully charged in a matter of seconds.

With the layout of the ship clear in her mind, Justine raced toward the engine room, which housed both the Kulsat's quantum drive and their normal space engines. She didn't know what kind of propulsion the Kulsat used, but she did know they would use some form of electric power to run the computers. Risen or Kinemats—whatever they were called—could manipulate electrical current. She would shred every conduit and computer in that room.

When she got to the engine room, she headed for the normal space engine first. It was unlike any other engine she'd seen before, but she detected trace elements of plasma. She guessed their engine used a form of ion propulsion, similar to what was equipped on the majority of ships in Sol System.

Justine had to stop the Kulsat ship from accelerating. Reaching out with her senses, she traced the various conductors and capacitors, and forced as much electrical current through them as she could.

Many of the systems were waterproofed, but as the first circuits overloaded and blew, the explosions ruptured the firewalls, and salty water poured into the computer banks. The few brief sparks were extinguished quickly, but the water itself did more damage than Justine. The entire array of computers beside the normal space engine fizzled and died.

The plasma engine cooled, and then ceased to function.

Next up was the quantum drive. Justine intended to cripple the

Kulsat ship.

Before she could turn her attention to the computers on the other side of the room, the quantum drive turned on. Long Fingers must have realized his ship was being sabotaged. If the ship were quantized, it would effectively stop any further destruction. Long Fingers could travel at light speed to the beacon, and simply return to his home system. Once there, he could marshal the military, warn them of the threat humanity posed, and return in force.

Also, Justine had no idea what would happen to her if she were on a ship that quantized while she was already in the quantized state. Would she be trapped on the ship? Would she retain her consciousness? She didn't want to find out.

By force of will, she pushed her essence through the water environment toward the quantum engine control computers. Before she got there, however, she ran into something. That fact alone shocked her. She was made of photonic particles; what substance out there was dense enough to stop her?

She realized there was some kind of damping shield around the quantum engines. Perhaps, she speculated, it was there to contain or focus the quantization procedure. The scientists back at Quantum Resources and NASA would kill to study the Kulsat technology. Whatever the reason for the damping field, it prevented her from sabotaging the engines. She could sense they would fire in a matter of seconds.

Directing her energy toward the hull of the ship, she streaked to it, through it, and out into space mere moments before the Kulsat vessel quantized. It raced away at the speed of light.

With her *sight*, she tracked it for the two seconds it took to reach the star beacon, over six-hundred-thousand kilometers away. One instant, the ship existed, and the next, it disappeared from the Centauri System.

∞

Using her ability to visualize the space around her, Justine scanned for the Kulsat shuttle, and soon spied it flying toward a large asteroid in the distance. The shuttle had traveled over a hundred kilometers away in the few minutes since it had left the Kulsat ship. Justine propelled herself toward the small vessel. With her *sight*, she saw that she was closing the gap, though slowly. Although she was made of photonic particles, she did not seem to have the ability to push her essence even a fraction of the speed of light—obviously, another reason for a quantum engine.

Even though she'd been fully irradiated, Justine knew from the experimentation on the Lucis Observatory that she would not be able to maintain her quantized form for more than a few hours without additional exposure to Kinemet. The shuttle, however, carried enough of the metal to fuel her for the rest of her life. With it, she would be able to scan the entire sector of the Centauri System in search of Alex and the others. She just needed to reach the shuttle before her radiation levels dropped to the point where she turned corporeal again.

A nagging thought crept up from the back of her mind as she raced forward. When she'd been on Venus, she'd been able to sense Alex on Canada Station Three, even though his essence had been very faint to her. Now, she did not sense him at all. Although the Kulsat ship had traveled quite a distance away from the space port, it wasn't even a fraction of the distance from Venus to Canada Station Three. Three Crescents had given her no indication that they had killed her friends, and the science leader had said that if she weren't going to cooperate, they would gather the others for questioning.

It made no sense to her, unless something had happened in the last few hours.

After what seemed like an eternity, Justine halved the distance between her and the Kulsat shuttle. She estimated she would reach it before it arrived at the asteroid.

Her *sight* still extended, she sensed the star beacon pulse. A moment later, a ship appeared in the Centauri System. Had the Kulsat returned already?

Justine knew they would be able to sense her, and would head straight toward her. Even if she changed her course, they would eventually find their wayward shuttle and recover the cargo. She also knew there was a good chance they would kill all the Kulsat on board.

With renewed determination, Justine pushed the limits of her powers. Though she had no idea what she was going to do when she got there, she knew she had to get to the shuttle before the Kulsat ship did.

The newly arrived ship quantized, and the streak of light crossed the distance between the beacon and her in a blink.

It rematerialized a few hundred meters away from her. Unlike the Kulsat ship, whose shape resembled a gigantic narwhal, this ship had the contours of an enormous bird. The hull, also made of Kinemet, swirled with reds and golds. *Was this a Kulsat warship?* Justine wondered.

The ship seemed to sense the shuttle beyond them, and changed course, powering toward the helpless vessel. Even going as fast as she could, Justine knew she would never reach the shuttle in time. In a desperate gamble, Justine put herself on an intercept course with the new ship. She would do the same to it as she had to the first Kulsat ship; with the last bits of her Kinemetic power, she would tear it apart from within.

When her essence raced through the hull, and into the belly of the ship, she felt a momentary disorientation. It took her a moment to realize she wasn't floating in water. The inside of the new ship was filled with air. Instead of the dull gray sheen of metal that covered the walls and floors of the mining ship, the inner surfaces of this ship were painted in a mosaic of bright patterns.

This isn't a Kulsat ship, she realized.

Detecting two Kinemetic presences on board, Justine flew in their direction instead of trying to find the engine room.

At the bridge, she froze in momentary shock when she saw two tall, bird-like bipeds sitting at the controls. In front of them was an electronic display showing the Kulsat shuttle. Though Justine could not understand any of the words on the readout, she was very familiar with what a targeting system looked like.

The new aliens were preparing to blast the shuttle, along with Red Spot and all the other Kulsat passengers, out of space.

22

Sierra de las Minas :
Guatemala :

Long Count: 10.0.0.0.0

For the next two days, I treated the burns and did as much as I could to help the survivors recover from the tragedy.

My mother and some of the other women had set blankets around the outside of her house to serve as beds. While they all had burned skin, soon they began to complain of upset stomachs. Some became so weak, they could not even lift themselves up off the blankets. Some soiled themselves where they lay.

Those who were still able helped to bury those who had died, while I tended the sick as best I could.

The three elders were dead, leaving me the only remaining adult male; and I was still not completely healed from my broken ribs.

When one of the women from a nearby farm came to the village, I bade her travel to Copán and ask them to send help. By the time she gathered supplies for the journey there, she'd fallen ill and didn't have the strength to pick up her pack, let alone hike the distance.

Of the fifty-two women and children in our community, seventeen had been in the village itself when the star grain exploded. Four women and one child had been killed in the blast, and two children and an older woman had died from their burns the first night. By all accounts, there should have only been nine wounded left for me to tend, but as I surveyed my patients, I counted fifteen women and four children who needed my aid. Some of the women who had been on their farms were showing the same symptoms.

My mother became ill as well, and had fallen into unconsciousness a number of times.

She died that night, along with the rest of the women and children who had been in the village during the blast.

By morning, every surviving member of our community made their way to me, begging me to help them.

I had no idea how to do that. I had only read a few of Balam's healing scrolls, and those had only told me how to heal physical wounds. Nothing I had read had given me the knowledge to treat inner sickness.

Ysalane, who lived on the farm farthest from the village, was one of the few women left who could still walk around on their own. When she'd come to us with her two younger brothers yesterday, she had not shown any signs that she was burned, but by mid-morning, blisters were appearing on her arms and legs, and both of her brothers had started vomiting.

By that afternoon, she became too weak to stand.

I was completely overwhelmed by the death and pain surrounding me. There was nothing I could do to save them, and I couldn't stand listening to the dozens of pleading voices begging me to ease their suffering.

I ran into the woods east of our village, trying to escape the desperation I felt. When I reached the stream where we got our water, I fell to my knees along the bank and looked at my rippling reflection.

For the first time since I was a child, tears rolled down my cheeks.

Why had I not been affected by the illness and burns? Did it have something to do with Ekahua sharing his gift with me? Had that, somehow, made me immune to the effects of the star grain?

I was so consumed by my own misery, I did not immediately notice that the sky was growing brighter. When I finally looked up, my breath caught in my chest, and I rose to my feet.

It was another sky boat.

Unlike Ekahua's vessel, which had streaked across the sky and crashed into the mountain range, this one was coming to land on the ground near our village in a very slow and controlled manner. It was large, and resembled a massive phoenix. The hull of the ship looked to be made of the same kind of material as Ekahua's.

My first thought was to run for the ship, and call whoever was in there to come out and help save the women and children of our village. Then I remembered Ekahua's warning, that others might come looking for him. I didn't know why he didn't want to be found, but by the way he'd said it, I assumed their intentions might not have been pure.

Were these Ekahua's enemies, then? Or his rivals?

I stopped myself from rushing forward, and hid behind a tree until I could figure out what these newcomers wanted from us.

The ship landed on eight long, thick legs. Some of the women in the village were shouting in alarm, but none of them was strong enough to get up and flee. I felt guilty for not running to their rescue, but I knew I had no power to defend my villagers against the newcomers.

A rectangular opening in the side of the ship appeared, and a platform slid out from inside the vessel. Two impossibly tall people stepped onto it.

I could not believe what I was seeing. They had arms and legs just like any other person, but they wore costumes unlike anything I had seen. Their outfits were made of a shiny material, almost like polished stone, and covered every part of their bodies except their heads. Instead of hair, they had what looked like a headdress of white and yellow feathers. The lower parts of their faces were drawn forward, ending in small mouths and chins. Like Ekahua, they had no ears that I could see.

From where I was, I couldn't make out the words they spoke, but it sounded like the chirping and squawking of a bird.

They carried something in their hands, but it did not look like a weapon to me—it was shaped more like a small box. They pointed it around the village, and there were portions of the box that seemed to light up. It reminded me of the picture boxes in Ekahua's sky boat. The creatures made more chirping sounds, this time quite excited.

My heart skipped a beat as the platform lowered to the ground, and the sky travelers stepped off. Some of the women yelled curses at them; others cried out in fear. They were too weak to get up and fight the invaders.

I felt terrible for not doing anything, but though I was not as weak as the others were, I knew I was powerless to stop the sky travelers.

When they approached Ysalane, however, I stood from my hiding place and had every intention of charging them. I had no idea what I could do to stop them, but I had to do something. When I saw that they were not trying to grab her, I stopped, and moved back behind the tree once again.

They spoke to Ysalane, and though their words came out in chirps and squawks, a moment later, a secondary voice spoke in our language.

"I am a Sentinel of the Collection; I am a protector," the sky traveler said to Ysalane. "You have been touched by star fire. If you come with us into the sky, we will complete the change in you and your people. Your lives will continue. If you remain here, this world will consume you and you will die."

"You can save us?" she asked, looking at her brother, who was lying on the ground beside her, curled into a ball. "You can save him?"

"Yes, but you will never be able to return here."

Ysalane looked at some of the others, who nodded to her. She said, "We will go with you. Just save my brother."

The leader motioned to the other sky traveler, and they assisted all the villagers off the ground and to the platform. In groups of four, they lifted the women and children up and into their sky ship.

Once all the survivors of the blast were inside, the leader approached one of the dead women—I couldn't see whom. He swept the box over her body. He made a squawking sound, and then gestured to the other. They picked up the woman's body and carried her back to the platform. The sky travelers repeated the process for all the dead.

When all the villagers, both living and dead, were in their ship, the leader took something out of one of the pouches on his costume. It looked like a large ball, similar in size to the ones used at the ball court in Copán. This one, however, was not made of rubber. The surface of the ball was similar to the stone block from Ekahua's sky boat.

The sky traveler stepped over to the blackened crater where the common fire pit once stood, and placed the ball in the center. He returned to his ship, and went inside.

Stepping on the platform, which lifted him up and into the ship, the sky traveler made a gesture with the box in his hand moments before the rectangular opening in his ship closed.

The ball on the ground began to glow and vibrate.

When I realized what the ball was for, I knew I had to flee.

The sky ship rumbled and lifted off the ground.

I turned away from the village and, trying to ignore the pain in my chest, ran as hard as I could.

By the time I reached the closest farm, a blast of light, many times brighter than the one that had ripped through our village before, covered our entire village.

I turned my head before it blinded me, and dove inside the house on the farm just as an ocean of heat, more intense than I could ever have imagined, washed over me. It burned the very air around me, and I could not breathe.

Certain that I would die, I prayed to the gods. Perhaps they heard me. Just when I thought I could hold my breath no longer, the heat and light faded, and air filled my lungs when I opened my mouth and inhaled.

When I felt strong enough to rise, I made my way back to the village, but it was no longer there. No buildings, no common area, no trees, and no grass; there was nothing but a huge circle of bare earth. It was as if a thousand farmers had come and tilled the soil.

For a very long time, I could only stand there and wonder at what had happened. I knew everything that had occurred over the past week was greater than anything written in any of the story stones at Copán.

The affairs of the gods were beyond me, and though I had been thrown into the center of these events, I could not divine their purpose.

I don't know how long it was before I returned to the farmhouse, but the sun had begun its slow descent from the sky, and the moon had come out from hiding.

Sleep was not something that I thought about, but exhaustion got the better of me, and by the time I woke up, it was morning again. It had been five days since the men of the village had gone to war.

I searched through the house for some basic supplies—a pack, some tools, a knife, and food—and then I set out on the trail for Quiriguá.

∞

By the time I arrived near the area where the Ch'orti' army was encamped, I'd had plenty of time to think about what had happened. Unfortunately, I was just as confused as I had ever been.

The sky travelers had said they would heal the women and children of the village, but the same time, they would never be able to return. Did that make them good or evil? Were they taking them away to become slaves? There was no way I could know.

Ekahua had asked me to burn his body, rather than bury it. I didn't know if he didn't have the desire to journey through the Underworld and be reborn in Heaven. In my mind, I had not felt any remorse that I had left him buried in the cave, and not burned his body as he'd requested. Now, however, I was having doubts.

He'd told me that other sky tribes would arrive and look for him, and I could not let his body be found by them. Without knowing the birdlike sky travelers' intentions, I had to believe that Ekahua had been right all along. After all, he'd given me a gift that had protected me from the star fire.

Instead of continuing on to the warrior camp, I went wide around them, being as stealthy as I could. I decided to find the cave where I had left Ekahua, and burn his body as he'd instructed me to do.

It was several hours before I reached the mountain, and I realized that my chest no longer hurt. My ribs had healed, and my breathing was once again strong and sure.

With a little searching, I finally found the cliff where the crevice was, but to my dismay, the entire area was covered in rocks, boulders, and gravel. The earthquake must have caused the cliff wall to crumble.

Even with a team of twenty men, it would take a hundred days to dig through to the cave, and there was every chance the cave itself had collapsed in on itself. For a single man, it could take years.

The cave-in had hidden Ekahua's body from the bird-like sky travelers. They would never find him. After all, who would think this enormous pile of rubble was a grave for a sky traveler?

I had one duty left: to find my father and the other Ch'orti' warriors and tell them what had become of our village. It was a task I did not want to undertake, and I sat down among the ruins of the cliff and thought long and hard about how I was going to tell them their wives and children were either dead, or taken by invaders from the sky tribes.

They would never understand about the star fire, or about sky ships. The elders of my village, and the King of Copán, believed Ekahua was a god, no matter what I'd said. If I told my people exactly what had happened, they would doubt my words. I had to tell them the story in a way they would understand.

A thought came to me, then. The Song of the Stars. The words Ekahua had used for the song were gibberish to me, and he'd said the words didn't matter—it was the melody that was important for our descendants.

I would use the Song of the Stars, replace Ekahua's words with my own, and tell the story of our downfall. I had to make certain the story was powerful. I might have been protected from the star fire at the village, but I knew I would pass on to the Underworld one day. Combining the story of my village with the song was the best way to ensure that both would survive me.

Over the next few hours, I created the story, and composed the words to match the melody of the Song of the Stars.

The bird-like sky traveler who had spoken to Ysalane was Kinich Ahua, the firebird god and messenger of Hanab Ku, creator of the People. The other sky traveler was Kukulcan, the feathered serpent.

Kinich Ahua must have been angry with us because of the war with the northern tribes, and this was his punishment.

I did not sleep that night. Instead, I worked on the story, and completed it as the sun rose in the morning.

I headed down the mountain and across the valley to look for my father and the other warriors, and found them before the sun set that night.

Though more tired than I had ever been in my life, I told them the story, and I felt their grief as they listened.

After hearing the tale, my father spoke to the King of Copán. The war council agreed that the gods did not approve of the war with the Q'eqchi', and we would return home.

My father and the other men of our village decided to erect a monument to the memory of our lost ones where we were, to remind any Ch'orti who came north not to engage in war with the northern tribes.

In the following months, I carved the story into the stone of four mighty columns, and vowed to return every year to recite the story and honor my people.

23

Qin Station :
Sol System :

Alice stood straight up, her face reddening with anger. "You idiot!" she screamed at Alex.

Taken aback by her reaction, he sat there as still as he could.

"This is exactly the reason the nations of Earth have driven themselves to the brink of destruction," Alice said through gritted teeth. "They didn't need any alien enemy; they're doing a good enough job all on their own. They've been on a downward spiral for a century. Corruption and apathy in the government, greed and avarice in the economy, cruelty and malice in the people."

She swung an accusatory finger toward Alex. "And you kept this information from the one person in the system who has the resources and the strength of will to save it. My father was right; you are a petty, selfish little child."

The words stung, and Alex felt they were unfair. He had a brief urge to refute her claim. After all, Alex had sacrificed everything from the moment his parents had died on Macklin's Rock.

He shot back at her. "All those words you used—corruption, apathy, greed, avarice, cruelty, malice—those are all good words to describe your father. He may have fooled you, as he fooled so many others; as he tried to fool me. He plays on your weaknesses, preys on your feelings of abandonment. When he sees someone who he can use for his own purposes, he befriends them, tells them they are important and powerful. But once he has what he wants from you, he chews you up and spits you out."

Alice shook her head. "You lie!"

"Why do you think he ended up in prison? Because of me?" Alex let out a hollow laugh. "It was Klaus, if you must know. Your father underestimated him. When I was kidnapped, your father thought he no longer needed him. Klaus figured out where he stood pretty quick, and took steps to take down your father first." He swung a hand around as if to encompass everyone on the station. "Look around. Why do you think your father surrounds himself with people who have run afoul of the law, or are repressed, or who've been ostracized by society? Not out of the goodness of his heart, I can tell you. It's because they let their anger and desperation rule them, and because of that, they're easy to fool."

Alice looked ready to burst. "I'm not a fool," she said, but her voice was low.

"You've been deeply hurt. Betrayed and shamed by society for something that wasn't your fault—I'm sorry; I know about your history: your mother, the newspapers in Beijing. It wasn't fair, but your life was still ruined. Now, you want to make someone pay." He shook his head at her. "But just because they did this to you, it doesn't give you the right to conquer them or kill them."

Looking suddenly like a little girl, Alice lowered her head.

Alex said, "I know you're angry, but you don't want to watch the world burn. If you did, you would simply do nothing and let the Kulsat do your dirty work for you. No, you got angry at me because, deep down, you care."

There were tears streaking down her cheeks. "I don't care."

"Yes, you do," Alex said, his voice taking on a soothing tone. "And so do I. The Kulsat will destroy us. It will be quick. Emperor Yin is going to take his time about it, but he'll end up doing the same thing. I won't trade one doomsday scenario for another. But you—"

Alice looked up. "What about me?"

"You have the power to make a difference. There is a chance to stop the Kulsat. I've been told there is a way, but in order to get to that point, we need to work together."

Narrowing her eyes, Alice said, "Against my father...?"

Alex nodded. "Yes." Seeing her teetering on the brink of a decision, he added, "He was directly responsible for the murder of my friend, Kenny, and he's given the order for many others all in the name of power. You've watched the newsvids; surely not everyone is telling the exact same lie about him."

Alice wiped the tears from her cheeks. "Say I believe you," she said.

"Say I want to help you. What do we do?"

Alex lifted one shoulder in a half-shrug. "We continue our work."

Looking up sharply, Alice spoke in a breathy rush. "What?"

"The goal is the same. We need Kinemats. Only then can we learn how to defend ourselves. I told the truth: I have no idea how long it will take the Kulsat to find us. It could be minutes; it could be a millennium. When they do find us, we need to be prepared. Other systems have been able to defend themselves. It's possible."

"Then you will tell Sian to stop delaying and complete his algorithm?" Alice asked, and gave him a sly smile. "I told you: I'm not a fool. Don't worry, my father is occupied with other matters; I need not concern him with every little detail."

"Thank you," Alex said.

"If we do solve the formula for priming the Kinemet, we're going to have to test it."

Alex shook his head. "We're not going to sacrifice any more innocent lives."

"Then how will we know if it works?"

"I have a thought about that," Alex said. "As someone who is attuned to Kinemet and its radiation, I may be able to tell if the formula is correct or not."

Alice stood up. "What are we waiting for?"

24

Copán Departmental :
Honduras :

Yaxche insisted that they return to his village, and would not give anyone a hint of his friend's location until they agreed. Five of them piled into a hydrogen-powered crew cab. Yaxche sat up front with Migel, who continued his role as the driver. Michael sat in the back with another Cruzado named Diego, and Humberto, who squeezed between them. After the five-hour drive, Michael was thankful to get out and stretch his legs.

Little had changed in Pueblo de Santa Brio since Michael had been there last. Even the older woman selling handcrafted trinkets sat on the same wooden chair in the same spot as before. She smiled at him, as if recognizing him. He nodded to her, returning the smile, though he didn't stop to peruse her wares.

There was a young tourist couple in town, recording their journey on a digital recorder. Humberto gave them no more than a cursory glance before dismissing their presence.

The house that was once Yaxche's now belonged to another family. Four years was too long to remain vacant, and without news, the village would have assumed he wasn't alive.

Yaxche headed straight for a different house, and before he reached it, a middle-aged woman ran out, tears streaking down her face and a cry on her lips. Michael recognized her as Yaxche's daughter.

The two embraced, and it was a long time before the woman stopped crying.

Michael, not wanting to intrude on the reunion, turned to Humberto. "We might be here a while."

"Oh?"

"I feel like an ass," Michael said. "I was so wrapped up in everything else that's happened in the past while, it completely slipped my mind. Four years ago, Yaxche's grandson, Terry, was killed on Venus." The sharp memory of Kenny's recent murder cut through his mind. He intended to contact the young physicist's family and extend his condolences, and vowed to do so the first chance he got.

"Ah." Humberto nodded. "Te'irjiil. Another victim of Jose's madness. I regret my part in involving him in that mess."

When Michael looked up, he noticed Yaxche waving him over. Humberto followed a few steps behind.

Yaxche said, "My daughter wants to thank you for bringing me back to her. She wishes us to spend the evening to hear the story of my grandson's sacrifice. There is plenty of room on the floor, and she has spare blankets for the night. In the morning, we will go."

"Of course," Michael said.

Humberto turned to his two men and instructed them to park the truck on the outskirts of the village. "The three of us will set up rotating patrols."

Michael followed Yaxche and his daughter into the house, where they waited for her husband to return from work before they ate supper. Yaxche's two granddaughters, Rosalia and Maria, clung to their grandfather and would not let him do anything for himself.

Michael's translator had been disabled by Humberto, in case it had a tracker, and he fervently wished he'd had time to pick up another one. He had some difficulty following the conversation among the Hernandez family, and had to rely on Humberto to translate.

They spent the evening listening to stories of Terry's youth, and his love for Itzel. When it came time for Michael to share what he knew of Terry's fate, he told his mother that he was sorry that he'd never had the chance to meet the young man.

To his surprise, Humberto told of his experiences with Terry, and didn't gloss over his role in inducting the youth into the Cruzados.

"He had the heart of a crusader," Humberto said in conclusion. "And it is because of his true spirit, and those like him, that we continue our fight."

Michael expected Yaxche's daughter to be outraged at Humberto, but instead, she held her husband's hand and said, *"Te'irjiil le habría perdonado, estoy segura. No podemos hacer menos."*

"Gracias," Humberto said, his voice solemn.

The next morning, the five of them piled back in the truck and headed out. Yaxche would not tell them their destination. He merely indicated which turns to take.

As they headed west toward Copán Ruinas, Migel gave Humberto a concerned look.

Humberto, checking his holoslate, leaned forward and spoke to Yaxche. "It looks as if you are taking us to the border crossing of Guatemala. If that's our destination, we need to stop. We can't get past the border patrol."

Having read up on the region, Michael knew that under ordinary circumstances, crossing into Guatemala wouldn't be a problem. The custom's office was more of a prolonged toll operation and casual check stop. If Michael gave them his passport, however, it would register on the national-security grid, flagging him to Ruiz and his operation.

"Head north at the ruins," Yaxche said to Migel, and Humberto let out a sigh of relief.

"We've only got a few more hours' hydrogen in the tank," Migel said. "How far north is your friend?"

"We will be fine," Yaxche said.

Sensing everyone else's discomfort, Michael asked, "Can you show us on a map?"

Turning in his seat, Yaxche said, "I have not seen my friend since I was a young man, but I will remember how to get there."

Realizing that, for a great number of cultures, landmark navigation was the primary means of travel, Michael sat back in the seat and looked out the window, watching the farms and forests fly past.

After a little over an hour, turning one direction and then another on dirt roads, they arrived at a small plantation. Michael glanced at Humberto's holoslate.

"We're here," he said, pointing to a spot on the small map on the holoslate display. "Right near the border."

There weren't any signs telling them what plantation it was, and Michael fervently hoped they had nothing to do with Oscar Ruiz.

A horse and rider plodding along the edge of the main entranceway spotted them, and turned toward them.

Migel spoke to the man in Spanish, and Michael wished he had a translator with him. He didn't want to ask Humberto what was being said every time.

The rider looked across the seat to Yaxche, who spoke rapidly. A moment later, the rider replied, and pointed farther north along the road.

"Gracias," Migel said, putting the truck into gear.

Yaxche, sounding excited, said, "My friend has retired from the plantation, and has a villa down the road."

The road, little better than a goat trail, cut left and right several times before leading to a small clearing. A modest house stood there. A dozen chickens walked freely around the property. There was a small barn with a pen holding a few pigs.

As Migel pulled up, a man who could only be described as ancient stepped out from the doorway, a wide grin on his face as he waved to his visitors.

Stepping out of the truck, Yaxche hurried over to his friend, shook his hand and gave him a heartfelt slap on the arm.

They spoke in Spanish, and Michael didn't need Humberto to figure out they were re-acquainting themselves with one another.

If they hadn't seen each other in over half a century, there would be a lot of catching up to do.

Michael noticed that Migel and Diego automatically migrated to either end of the property, trying to look casual as they set up watch posts. The paranoia might not be necessary, this far away from any major population, but then again, if something happened, help was a long way off. He decided to be thankful the men were on guard.

Humberto patiently waited until the two older men finished saying hello to each other.

Yaxche turned and said, "Michael, Humberto, I am pleased to introduce my oldest friend to you. This is Patli, who is also the grandnephew to my grandfather's brother. He does not speak English, but he has agreed to talk to you for a time. Perhaps he will share his story with you. Come, sit."

They followed Yaxche and Patli to a small area on the side of the house opposite the pen, where several wooden chairs were set out around a barrel.

"Patli does not often get visitors, but he always has a few spare chairs just in case."

The four of them arranged themselves around the barrel, and Patli spoke, looking at Michael with a kindly smile.

"He says he wonders if this is the first time you have stepped out into the sun." Yaxche grinned. "He's never seen a person so pale before."

With a nod, Michael said, "I come from a land far to the north, where it snows half of the year. The sun is much colder there than here."

Yaxche translated, and then said, "He has never seen snow, but he heard a story about a man made of snow once, and thought someone was pulling a trick on him."

Michael laughed. "It's true. I've made a few myself, when I was younger."

They spoke casually like that for an hour, allowing Patli to get to know them.

Just as the noon sun peaked, Patli spoke at length to Yaxche.

Humberto narrowed his eyes at what he heard, and Michael's anticipation grew.

Turning to Michael, Yaxche spoke. "I have told my friend that you and George were the first ones, besides my grandson, who understood the Song of the Stars, and that you needed to hear the rest of the story. Patli says he has not told the story in many years—no one is interested in the ramblings of us old men—but he is happy that you have shown patience today. If you have a little more patience, he will tell you the story that was passed down from his grandfather's grandfather many generations back.

"It is the story of the dying god, and of the young hunter who discovered him, and who was the first to hear the divine Song of the Stars. He was my and Patli's ancestor, who wrote the Song of the Stars as told to him by the dying god. His name was Subo Ak."

25

Gliesan Ship :
Centauri System :

"Stop," Justine said the moment after she returned to her corporeal self on the bridge of the alien ship. "Don't kill them."

To her surprise, the two bird-like bipeds stopped their attack. A power indicator on the display of the control array leveled down.

Both aliens, sitting on chairs that floated a meter off the floor, turned to face her. Their faces were vaguely human in shape, except that the lower halves were drawn forward and came to a point, like a soft beak. Neither had hair; instead, their heads were covered with a feather-like down. One of them had predominately blue and green coloring, while the other was yellow and orange.

Both regarded her with cocked heads.

It was only under their scrutiny that Justine realized she was completely naked. When she'd quantized herself, she had not converted her clothing, since she'd only just developed the theory on how to quantize other beings or objects. Her attention had been focused on Three Crescents' attack, and defending herself by changing him into photons. She realized that, from this point on, she should be able to quantize her clothing and spare herself further embarrassment when she returned to her physical form.

Self-consciously, she threw one arm over her breasts and used her other hand to cover her lower regions. As hard as she could, she willed herself not to let her face flush red with embarrassment.

Justine's discomfort was forgotten when the blue-and-green-colored alien spoke, and she heard the translation a split-second later. The voice was male and soft-spoken; a complete contrast to the impersonal machine voice of the Kulsat translator computer.

"Apologies. You must be Major Justine Turner. We sensed your Aetherform." He pointed to the ship on his display console. "We believed you were trying to destroy the Kulsat shuttle, and we were attempting to assist."

Justine, stunned that they knew her name, said, "The Kulsat on the shuttle helped me escape the mining ship where I was taken prisoner by two of their 'Risen'."

Although she'd been one of the first to discover the evidence that the universe was home to thousands of different species of sentient beings, and had just spent the last few days interacting with a race of cephalopods, it still took her some time to adjust to meeting a new life form. She wished the circumstances were less dramatic and proper introductions could be made.

"It is amusing," the alien said, and Justine wasn't immediately certain the translator was working correctly. "We came to the Centauri System to attempt to rescue you from the Kulsat. Now, you are rescuing the Kulsat from us."

"Rescue me?" Justine asked. "Who are you? How do you know who I am?"

The pilot got up from the floating chair. A moment later, the chair slowly sank down and seemed to melt into the floor, as if being absorbed into the superstructure.

Standing well over three meters in height, the alien made a bowing motion and fluttered two wing-like hands.

"Forgive our impoliteness. Our names are not completely pronounceable in your language, but a reasonable representation of mine is 'Naila'. I am the Primary Sentinel of the *Fainne*, our ship. This is 'Fairamai'. She is the navigator and copilot. We are from the system you call Gliese."

The other alien stood up and made a bowing gesture of her own. Her translation voice was feminine with dulcet tones. "Pleased to meet you, Solan being."

"I'm Justine," she said. The two Gliesans made a funny little cock of their heads, and Justine flushed when she remembered that they already knew who she was. "Uhm. Is it possible to borrow some clothing?"

The two aliens conferred, and Fairamai nodded to Justine. "We have some nesting fabric that may be long enough for you to use as an outer wrap, if that is suitable."

"Thank you," Justine said, and offered a grateful smile as the tall alien exited the bridge, presumably to retrieve the clothing.

Naila resumed his story. "We received a report from one of our patrol vessels detailing your arrival in this system, followed by the Kulsat attack and your abduction. They requested we come to this system to investigate and should you still be here, retrieve you."

"Patrol?" Justine asked. "Did they find my friends, our ship?"

"According to our readings, the remains of your vessel are on a disused port several hundred-thousand kilometers from here. Your ship is no longer serviceable. It was severed with a mining energy beam. Your friends are no longer in this system."

His last sentence had a reproachful tone to it.

"Where are they?" She looked up as Fairamai returned with a long, multicolored sheet of thin fabric. It was very soft and bore a faint floral scent. Justine wrapped it around herself in a makeshift toga, and immediately felt less vulnerable.

Naila made a clucking sound. "Our colleagues have escorted your friends to your home system after transmitting their report to us."

"That's a relief," Justine said. "Can you take me to my system as well?"

The alien made a vibrating motion with his head, which Justine interpreted as a negative. "I'm afraid travel to your system is forbidden to us by law. Aliah and Ah Tabai have broken protocol. When they return, they will certainly face criminal charges for their transgression."

Justine felt herself grow more frustrated. New obstacles seemed to develop at every step.

"Why is it forbidden?"

"Yours is not an Emerged system. The ancient law of the Grace forbids interference with non-Emerged cultures. I will be happy to explain this all to you, but for now, it is vital we leave Centauri and return to Gliese System."

"Will the Kulsat return?" Justine guessed.

Naila nodded. "Centauri is barren of a native population. The Kulsat frequent this system, looking for Aetherock to mine—I believe you refer to it as 'Kinemet'. They obviously detected your presence."

"What will they do now?" Justine asked.

Naila said, "They will report your presence here, and the Kulsat will return in force. We must leave this system."

Justine's mind was awhirl with all the information. Her immediate concern was the safety of her friends and Earth. "Won't the Kulsat be able to follow us to Gliese?"

"No. Emerged systems have some defense against attack. Our star beacons are masked. Only when a star beacon is active can an Aetherbeing detect it."

"So the Kulsat won't be able to follow the other patrol ship to my home system, either?"

Naila shook his head. "Only if they were close enough to the star beacon to sense the activation. If that were the case, they would be in your solar system now. We do not have any indication that is the case."

"Why wouldn't they just go to the nearest solar system in this area of space?" she asked, aware that Centauri and Sol were close neighbors.

Naila crooked his head in what Justine assumed was a sign of amusement. "There are billions of systems in the galaxy, and spacial proximity is not a factor when traveling by the star beacons. You could have arrived here from anywhere. The star beacon in your system is unknown to the Kulsat or the galactic network. The Gliesans are the only ones who know its location, and we have guarded the secret for a very long time."

"How will they find us, then?"

Naila said, "The Kulsat will most likely set up a permanent post in Centauri at first. Should anyone from Sol System travel here again, the Kulsat will be able to track them."

It took a moment for Justine to absorb it all. The next ship to use the star beacon to travel to Centauri would be flying into a trap. She felt overwhelmed. "So what can I do?"

"Return to our home system with us. You will be safe until our Council can make a determination."

"Determination?"

"On whether yours is to be considered an Emerged system or not."

"And what will that accomplish?"

"If you are invited to join the Collection of Worlds, we may offer your system the technology to defend yourselves." Naila paused before he added, "If you are not granted status as an Emerged system, we cannot interfere, even if the Kulsat invade you."

Justine took that all in. She knew she was a guest aboard the Gliesan patrol ship. Though she didn't want to seem ungrateful, she couldn't accept or understand their policy.

"If you can't interfere, then why are you helping me?"

"Simply put," Naila said, "there is an ambiguity in the galactic law. You, individually, are physically outside your pre-Emerged system. We may assist you, personally, without actually interfering in the pre-Emerged progress of your world. Though we can offer you amnesty and protection, we are not permitted to offer you technological advances. You will be remanded to a holding station at the outer edge of our system until a decision can be made, and you will not have access to any restricted information or material."

"What happens if you break the law and interfere?" Justine asked.

"The other member systems of the Collection would turn against our world. This is the reason we are at war with the Kulsat; they broke the law of the Grace."

"And you've been at war for how long?" Justine asked.

"The equivalent of over one-thousand Solan years." Naila seemed to be growing impatient with all the questions. "Though there are more than twenty-thousand member systems in the Collection, the Kulsat outnumber us. They have colonized thousands of non-populated systems."

"Twenty-thousand?" Justine remembered the writing on the *Dis Pater*, the monument housing the star beacon on Pluto. "I thought there were over thirty-thousand races out there?"

Naila dropped his head. "At one time," he said, "there were. Many systems were destroyed in the early days of the war, before we developed technology to restrict how many Aetherbeings can enter our system at the same time." He made a gesture to the display showing the Kulsat shuttle. "We cannot delay anymore. Once we are in Gliesan space, I will grant you limited access to our history files, though I must warn you, many of our records will be off-limits."

"I understand," Justine said. "Thank you for taking the time to explain what you have. I look forward to meeting with your government."

Naila nodded to Fairamai, who used her feathery fingers to tap instructions into their control computer. The targeting system went back online, and the power level indicator rose.

"What are you doing?" Justine barked out.

"We must destroy the shuttle," Naila said. "If they report our presence here to their masters, the Kulsat will focus their aggression on Gliese. Even with our technology, they may eventually be able to swarm us."

Justine took a few steps forward. "You can't kill them. They're innocent. Red Spot risked her life to save me."

"Red Spot?"

"She's a Potential." Justine hoped the Gliesans were familiar with the Kulsat social structure, and understood what she was trying to tell them. "The science leader on the ship, Three Crescents, killed her friend, Green Stripe, just to scare me into talking. Then he went on a rampage, and was going to kill all the crew. Red Spot saved the other Kulsat from destruction, and she saved me."

Naila continued to regard Justine as if her words weren't translating properly.

Exasperated, Justine said, "Not all Kulsat have a complete disregard for life."

The two Gliesans exchanged glances with one another, but made no comment.

Justine took a deep breath. "From what I've experienced, it seems the Risen are the aggressive caste in Kulsat society. The others are subservient, almost like peasants."

"Kulsat hierarchy is familiar to us," Naila said. "Though the non-Risen on the shuttle pose little direct threat, they would reveal knowledge of our system should they ever escape and return to the Consortium. Bringing them with us to Gliese is a security risk, as is leaving them here."

"Red Spot said there are other non-Risen who don't agree with the Consortium's policies," she added. "She could prove to be a valuable ally."

"The Solan may be right," Fairamai said to Naila. "Perhaps the Potential will give us tactical information on their fleet movements."

That wasn't what Justine had in mind. She didn't think Red Spot would betray the Consortium, but as long as the Gliesans didn't destroy the shuttle, she would go along with them.

Naila nodded. "Very well. I will leave the decision to our commander." He turned back to his console. A blob of Kinemetic material rose out of the floor and formed into a seat that floated up behind the Gliesan. Automatically, he sat and began to flick his feathery fingers over the computer controls. "We will take them with us as prisoners of war." He glanced back at Justine.

Justine nodded. However the Gliesans chose to consider the Kulsat on that shuttle, she thought of them as political refugees, not soldiers.

26

Qin Station :
Sol System :

After his conversation with Alice, Alex gave her a brief rundown of the events that occurred from the moment he first entered the Centauri system over more than fourteen years ago, to the point when they were captured by Chow Yin's patrol.

He left out a few choice tidbits, such as the fact that Ah Tabai was human, and that Justine had been captured by the Kulsat. Instead, he told her that his friend had died when the alien ship was destroyed by the mines around Pluto.

When he'd finished his story, the two of them returned to the larger lab and approached Sian. The programmer gave him an inquisitive look.

"How is it coming along?" Alex asked. He kept his voice even.

Sian blinked. "Slow going. There are a lot of variables."

"Is there anything I can do to help?" Alex asked. "We need to speed up the timetable."

Glancing at Alice, Sian took on a look of concern.

Alice turned to the guard. "Leave us." At first, the soldier didn't budge, but under her continued glare, he finally nodded.

"Your Highness," he said, and stepped outside.

Alice closed the door behind him and faced Sian. "I am aware that you and Alex have been dragging your feet on this project." She held up a hand. "Not to worry. I will report that you were merely being meticulous in your calculations. There are new developments that require the utmost efficiency."

Sian said, "There's a lot of work to do, in that case."

Stepping over to the other computer, Alex opened the program code. "Just tell me what you need. It's been a while, but I catch on quickly."

∞

Over the next two days, Sian and Alex worked through the program to create the algorithm to disseminate the frequencies hidden in the Song of the Stars. While they wrote code, Alex wondered at how Klaus had managed to create his program so accurately: according to Justine's report, he ended up with six possible combinations of the code.

At one point, Alex couldn't follow Sian's work anymore, and he was just getting in the way.

Every few hours, Alice came in to check on their progress. Whenever she was there, she ordered the guard to leave them alone.

One such time, as the code was nearing completion, she motioned for Alex to join her on the other side of the lab.

"Yes?"

She turned on a holoslate and called up several astrophysics charts.

"I don't know how much you learned from your alien friends, or how much you've theorized on your own, but I have a few thoughts I'd like to run past you."

"Of course."

"It has to do with the nature of the star beacons. When you traveled to the Centauri System, you did so just under the speed of light—though you were not conscious for the duration. However, once the Gliesans returned you here, the trip was near instantaneous."

"Yes," Alex said. "They said the star beacons exist at the same point in space."

Alice's face clouded over. "That would imply some kind of quantum entanglement, but that's not what you said earlier. You said, 'outside light, the star beacons all occupy the same space.'"

"Right."

She shook her head. "That's not the same thing."

"I don't understand."

"For centuries, physicists have been toying with the concepts of faster-than-light travel. For example, Einstein-Rosen bridges, or wormholes. They've toyed with the concepts of quantum tunneling based on the Casimir effect. There's the slipstream theory, which you might know as hyperspace. Now, one might assume 'outside light' is a reference to this. After all, how can light exist if you are traveling faster than it? But something doesn't add up. I don't think that's the answer."

"Then what?"

"Well, how can two or more objects occupy the same space? It's a physical impossibility."

"What about decoherence?" Alex asked. "Some kind of a quantum immortality and quantum suicide relationship?"

Alice nodded. "That's what I was thinking. But I think there's something more to it."

"Go on."

"Well, that's where I run into a wall. I can't help but think that many of these concepts have roots in ancient religions. It's almost as if our ancestors from thousands of years ago had a better grasp of the metaphysical aspects of the universe, and weren't encumbered by our need to quantify it in scientific terms."

"You think this all might have something to do with religion?"

"Well," Alice said, "a great deal of your Mayan mysticism is based on your ancestors' contact with these 'luminous' beings. The Grace, as you called them. Is it such a stretch that other religions and cultures may have had some kind of contact, and developed their own explanations for it?"

Not certain where the conversation was going, Alex asked, "So you think the ancient religions had a better understanding of the universe than we do?"

"Maybe not in a scientific way, but their lack of hard astrophysical knowledge didn't hinder them from coming up with theories." Alice raised a finger. "Now, if we examine your alien friend's use of the phrase, 'outside light' again, we must admit the possibility of dimensional transference."

"You think the star beacons can send a ship to another dimension—"

"Where there might exist a corresponding star beacon at a fixed point in their space."

"—and then send the ship back into our dimension in a different point in space."

"That would explain it, wouldn't it?"

Alex nodded. "I guess it would."

For the first time since meeting Alice, Alex saw that her expression was one of pure wonder. Gone was the angry and bitter young woman.

Astrophysics was her calling, and he could tell it was what made her the happiest. Deep inside, he wished the events that had led her here had never happened, and that they'd met in other circumstances.

Alex was aware that, though he was over thirty-years old chronologically—only a few years younger than Alice—because of the time he'd spent in photonic travel, he was biologically an eighteen-year-old. There were too many differences between the two of them besides age.

A sharp pang of regret ran through him over how the course of his life had affected him. Suddenly, Alex felt more alone than he ever had.

"Done!" Sian said, shocking him out of his reverie.

Practically jumping out of her seat, Alice hurried over to look at the completed code. Alex followed at a slower pace.

"It's compiling," the programmer said. "Give it a minute, and then we can run the algorithm."

Together, the three of them watched, as if that very act could speed up the process.

When the program was ready, Sian looked up at them. "Shall I run it?"

Alice nodded, her face revealing that she was too excited to say it aloud.

Sian ran the program. Within seconds, it spat out two possible combinations for the priming sequence.

"Two?" Alice said, frowning.

The programmer gave a slight shake of his head. "I'm not sure how Klaus managed to get the sequence correct the first time." He turned in his seat. "The only thing I can think of is that he must have used Yaxche's grandson's recitation, whereas we used Yaxche's—and yes, we have two recordings of it." Taking a breath, he said, "It's possible the old man's voice has become weaker over the years. He was off on one note."

"At least we don't have to worry about variables," Alex said. "Klaus didn't have access to me, or to Quantum Resources' trials, so he had to test for environment conditions, gravity, atmosphere, Kinemet volume and so forth. From the records of our trials, and from what Major Turner told me, I can recreate the necessary conditions."

Alice took a deep breath. "But it still means we only have a fifty-fifty chance of getting it right. Which means—"

Another voice cut through their discussion. "Which means there will have to be a necessary sacrifice."

Alex hadn't noticed the main door to the lab had opened. In the frame, standing up with the aid of his biomechatronic legs, Chow Yin put his hands on his hips and surveyed the occupants of the lab.

He gave them a disapproving glance. "Did you think I would leave you to your own devices without monitoring you every step of the way?"

"Sire!" Sian said in a gasp.

"I expected betrayal from Mr. Manez, but you, Sian? I rescued you from life imprisonment. I'm very disappointed."

Then he wagged an accusatory finger at Alice, his face pulled into an expression of disapproval. "And you, my daughter." Then his lips spread into a wide smile. "You were correct. All you needed to do was to play the damsel in distress who needed rescuing, and look, your knight in shining armor gave up all his secrets for you."

Alex's stomach did a lazy flip-flop. He'd been duped, and easily at that.

A crooked, satisfied smile on her face, Alice separated herself from the other two and made her way over to stand beside her father.

Shaking his head, Chow Yin motioned for the guards who had accompanied him to enter the lab and seize the prisoners.

Sian took a step back, and tried to resist when one of the guards grabbed his arm. "What are you going to do?"

Chow Yin, Emperor of Sol System, said, "It's quite simple. We have two possible formulas to create a Kinemat, and now we have a volunteer."

27

Cerro Azul :
Guatemala :

When Patli finished his story, Michael noticed Humberto's eyes boring not into the storyteller, but into him, as if trying to measure his reaction. It was an incredible story, and if Michael had not encountered Ah Tabai, Aliah, and the Kulsat, he would have immediately discounted the tale as nothing more than a fable. Now, however, he was inclined to believe the story had merit. From the description of the Grace's ship and its destruction to the radiation sickness caused by the piece of active Kinemet brought back to the camp, and ending with the villagers' rescue from the tall, bird-like aliens—it all made sense with what Michael had already learned.

It was obvious that he had not hidden his belief as he listened to the story; Humberto's expression as he considered Michael was proof of that.

For one fleeting moment, the thought of denying the story went through Michael's mind. After all, the fewer people who knew the truth of the galaxy's history at this point, the less chance of the information getting back to Chow Yin, who would use it to his advantage.

Humberto's track record of assistance and reliability prompted Michael to trust in the Cruzado.

As if sensing Michael had come to his decision, Humberto asked, "Do you think this is all true?"

"For the most part, yes." Michael rubbed at the stubble growing on his chin. "I'm not supposed to go into the details. It's a matter of international security, and I've been sworn to secrecy by my government. I trust you won't reveal what you learn here to anyone?"

Nodding, Humberto said, "So long as I have your word that our people won't be exploited anymore. It sounds like there is a connection between our ancestors and whatever it is out there." He pointed skyward.

"Let me put it to you this way," Michael said. "There's a very real and imminent threat in the galaxy, known only to a handful of people. The 'god' described in Patli's story is most likely a member of a powerful race of aliens who, at one time, could restrain the other systems in the galaxy. In the past millennium, they've disappeared, and the threat grew."

"I take it you are talking about something more dangerous than Emperor Chow Yin?"

Michael said, "We encountered this menace. They ripped our ship apart with a single strike, and from what we learned, the only reason they didn't destroy us is that they didn't consider us to be worth the effort."

Nodding toward Patli, Humberto said, "And you believe the only defense might be found within a thousand-year-old tale?"

Michael shrugged. "The formula for Kinemetic conversion was in this storyteller's tale, the Song of the Stars. Apparently, it was passed along to this Subo Ak by the dying alien. Perhaps Subo Ak left more clues that might help us."

Humberto spoke rapidly in Spanish to Patli, who then nodded and replied. The Cruzado said, "He says the shrine is in a mostly forgotten area of the Cerro Azul—the Blue Hills. It is where the warriors of the lost village first learned of the fate of their loved ones. It is in the shrine where Subo Ak etched the story on stone columns. Patli has not made the journey there in more than twenty years, but he remembers the way."

The two spoke in Spanish some more, and Humberto said, "The shrine is just over the Guatemalan border. He says there is a horse trail that might be wide enough for our truck. There are no border guards out here."

"And he's willing to show us the way?"

Humberto nodded. "He seems more than happy to do so. Few people have shown this much interest in his story." He said something to Patli who, despite his age, sprang from his chair and hurried into his house. When he returned, he was wearing hiking boots and had a large sack full of food. He was ready to go.

Together, they went to the truck, and Yaxche and Patli squished themselves into the front beside Migel, while the other three piled into the back.

"We've probably got enough fuel to get there," Migel said as he pulled out onto the dirt road and headed north under Patli's directions, "but I doubt we'll have enough to get back to Copán Ruinas."

"No problem," Humberto said. "Los Amates is only twenty or thirty kilometers north of the border. We should be able to make it there to refuel. If not, I have some friends there who can bring us some hydro."

To Diego, Humberto said, "If this horse trail is passable, it will let us go back and forth to Guatemala discreetly."

As it turned out, the trail was passable, but only on foot or hoof. The truck was too wide, and the ground too soft for the tires to get traction. They all had to get out and walk. While the three Cruzados wore military boots, and Patli had hiking gear, both Yaxche and Michael had street shoes on. According to the old man, they were only a few kilometers away from the shrine. By the time they got there, Michael's feet were completely caked with mud, and his ankles burned with the strain of the hike. He was so miserable, he barely registered it when they finally reached their destination.

The area, as Humberto had told them while they hiked, was part of a national park. While there was a healthy tourist industry there, he didn't think many people would venture that deep into the hills. Even if they did, very few people could interpret the Mayan writing on the shrine.

"It doesn't look like anyone has been here in a very long while," Humberto said, pointing to the tall grass in the clearing, and the overgrown vegetation.

Near the tree line, there was a series of four stone columns, no more than two meters high. Mayan glyphs covered their entire surface.

Patli, barely winded from the hike, went to the columns and ran the palms of his hands over them. He gave Michael and the others a wide grin and started speaking in Mayan.

Yaxche, who didn't look like he'd managed much better on the journey than Michael, said, "He's telling us what each glyph means."

"The story he told us back at his place seemed much longer," Michael said, surveying the four columns.

Humberto nodded. "The glyph-style of storytelling is more like point-form. The priest telling the story would fill in the narrative when he recited it. There's a lot of room for interpretation."

"Tell me about it," Michael said. "When our linguists tried to decipher the Song of the Stars, we had a dozen different versions, and every translator insisted theirs was the correct one."

Humberto held up a finger, and a crease appeared in his forehead as he questioned Patli. When the older man replied, the cruzado spoke to Michael. "He says the only thing written on the columns that talks about where the alien might have been buried is that it took Subo Ak from sunrise to sunset to walk the distance across the valley from the Sierra de las Minas."

"Twelve hours." Michael looked behind him. "How far did we come from where we left the truck?"

"About ten kilometers. It took us a little under four hours."

"And we're not all exactly young and fit." In his head, Michael calculated. "If he could make better time than us, we're looking at a maximum range of, say, thirty kilometers from this spot." A moment later, Michael added, "Of course, that's based on our interpretation of the glyphs."

Humberto took out his holoslate and called up a terrain map. "In a generally northern direction, I would say we should be looking in this section, along the southern edge of the mountain range."

Michael blanched. "That's over ten-thousand hectares, easily. It could take us weeks to cover that much ground."

Humberto brought up another screen. "There's a mining operation supplier in Guatemala City. The Guatemalan Minister of Culture is one of our supporters." He glanced up at Michael. "I can trust him. I'll ask that he send satellite survey maps to us—we should be able to narrow down any caves in the area. We should get some equipment as well: laser scanners, that kind of thing."

"Get a radiation detector," Michael said. "The half-life of Kinemet is in the hundreds of thousands of years. That might help."

"Good." Humberto typed a message. "According to the topographical map, there's a tributary to the Motagua River a few kilometers from here, and a small village a few more kilometers downstream. I'll tell my friends in Los Amates to come get us there."

Michael's excitement was quickly dampened. "The fewer people who know who we are and what we're doing, the better."

"Not to worry," Humberto said, "I trust these men with my—"

He was cut off when the crack of a rifle shot split the air. Diego, who had been standing at the southern edge of the clearing, flew backwards as a bullet ripped through his shoulder, and he disappeared into the long grass.

Migel swung around and shot into the forest, but the bullet that struck was the one that hit him in the leg, spinning him around before he fell with a loud cry.

Before anyone had a chance to react, a loud voice yelled out in Spanish. *"¡No se mueva!"*

28

Gliesan Ship :
Centauri System :

Justine watched as the Gliesans maneuvered their patrol ship close to the shuttle. At the last moment, the shuttle veered to port and accelerated away.

"They think we're attacking them," Justine said. "Is there any way we can communicate with Red Spot? I could explain what we're doing."

Naila reached out a feathery finger to an open space on the wall beside him, and touched the flowing surface. A shimmering console molded itself out of the wall. The alien pressed a series of small squares on the device.

"It is rare that a Kulsat ship will respond to a hail, but you may make the attempt. Direct your message into this receptacle. Our communications program will translate to the Kulsat computers."

He ran his finger along a section of the console, and a thin protuberance formed out of the wall that Justine assumed was a microphone.

Justine stepped up to it and said, "Red Spot, this is Justine. If you can hear me, please respond. We are not trying to destroy you or your ship. The Gliesans have agreed to help us."

Just when Justine thought there would be no reply, a monotone voice spoke. "There will be no help. They will torture us. Death is preferable."

"I promise that is not true," Justine said. "They have given me their word."

Several moments passed before Red Spot replied. "You cannot guarantee our continuance. Our enemies practice deception on you,

Justine."

Trying to bridge these two very different worlds was frustrating. Justine gave Naila an exasperated look. "Is there anything you can do to prove to them they won't be tortured?"

Naila and Fairamai shared a look. The pilot looked back at Justine. "You show uncommon compassion for a violent species that shows no compassion for others."

Shaking her head, Justine said, "You can't judge an entire culture based on the policies of those in power. Red Spot proved that not all Kulsat are like the Risen. She protected her people from Three Crescents' murderous rampage, and she helped me—an alien—escape him."

Cocking his head in a manner that Justine interpreted as bewilderment, Naila bent toward the microphone.

"This is Naila of the *Fainne*. Do you have the ability to broadcast my words to your entire ship?"

"All Kulsat on board can hear you," came the monotone reply.

Formally, Naila said, "On behalf of the Collection of Worlds and the Parliament of Gliese, I am willing to offer you and the other members of your crew the right of asylum in return for your parole that you will renounce all hostilities against the Collection now and in the future. You will live, but you never be permitted to leave Gliesan space for the rest of your lives. Do you agree to these terms?"

A few long moments later, Red Spot replied, "All are in agreement. We accept your conditions."

"Cut your engines. We will latch your shuttle to our ship and enter Aetherflight."

"Thank you, Naila," Justine said.

Naila made a low throaty noise. "Do not thank me yet. Their shuttle is much larger than our patrol ship, and our scans indicated there are over one hundred of them. If the shuttle is secured to our ship, and we push our quantum drive to its capacity, we should be able to convert them to Aethersleep, but I cannot guarantee they will all survive the Aetherflight."

Justine opened her mouth to ask him to elaborate, but Fairamai got up from her seat and gestured to the corridor leading toward the back of the *Fainne*.

"If you will follow me down the passageway, Justine, I will take you to the passenger compartment. It is for your safety."

As Naila began the docking procedure, Justine followed Fairamai and asked her a question. "What kind of danger was Naila talking about?"

"I'm sure you are aware there can be disorientation when coming out of Aetherflight."

"Actually," Justine said as she trailed the Gliesan, "I've only been on a quantum ship once, and I was the pilot at the time. I had no idea what I was doing—though I learned quickly—but I seemed to be able to manage the transition all right."

"For our flight," Fairamai said, "only the pilot will be in Aetherform and remain aware. It is the way of it. All passengers and crew of our ships, regardless whether they are Aethers or not, are placed in Aethersleep before Aetherflight. It is for their safety. You will not be conscious during the flight, and neither will I. Unfortunately, Naila will not be able to put all the Kulsat into Aethersleep. He will only be able to maintain a link with a dozen or so." A moment later, she spoke in a low voice. "The Kulsat Risen apparently do not bother to induce Aethersleep in their crew, and let their quantum engines perform the conversion. The Kulsat may have more advanced technology, but that doesn't mean they are more enlightened."

Justine guessed that Aethersleep must be the term for quantizing another being, whether by a Kinemat, or by a quantum drive. Sensing the deep emotion behind Fairamai's last statement, Justine was curious about the difference. "Why don't you use the quantum drive to start the photonic change in passengers?"

The alien shook her head. "There is a significant risk of passengers not returning to the physical state if the Aetherdrive initiates Aethersleep."

"Uh…"

"Were you not aware of this problem?" Fairamai asked. "Did you experience a noticeable delay when your ship came out of Aetherspace?"

Gulping at the thought that there had been a chance that all of them aboard the *Ultio* could have been stuck in the quantum state, Justine said, "Yes. That was one of our greatest hurdles when we began experimenting with quantum drives." The more she learned, the more she realized how much more there was to learn. "Many of our test pilots died…"

Fairamai had reached the passenger compartment, and gestured for

Justine to enter first.

"I am sorry to hear that," the alien said. "We undergo years of training to master Aetherform and inducing Aethersleep before we are allowed to take a ship into Aetherspace."

"Since we both have the ability to become photonic," Justine asked, "why are we going into Aethersleep?"

"Only one consciousness can pilot a ship in Aetherstate. If there are two consciousnesses, there will be conflict and instability. The chance of returning to normal space is severely diminished."

Justine felt her stomach sink at the thought. It would have been another fatal lesson for NASA and Quantum Resources to learn. At the back of her mind, she was aware that, in the four years since she'd been in Sol System, any number of disasters could have taken place if Earth continued quantum experiments.

Fairamai said, "The report we received from the other patrol ship indicated that your journey to Centauri was entirely in Aetherspace. The risks of mishap would have been greatly increased if you had gone outside light. You are lucky to be alive."

Fairamai touched a spot on the wall, and a hammock-like seat formed out of the fluidic metal.

"You will be secure here."

Justine didn't move to the seat, however. Her mouth hung open in shock.

"Is there a problem?" Fairamai asked.

"What do you mean by 'outside light'?"

With a slight jerking motion of her head, Fairamai made a chirping sound. She sounded surprised when she said, "You were not aware of this, either?"

Justine shook her head. "I thought there was a problem with the translation computer when you said the other patrol ship had sent a report to you before traveling to my solar system. I thought maybe you meant they'd left a report here for you, in Centauri; but they actually *went* to Gliese, and then to Sol System, didn't they?"

"Yes." Fairamai nodded. "It is by the Grace that we travel outside light. Inside a system, we travel in Aetherspace—inside the speed of light—but once we reach the star beacons, we are able to arrive in another system instantaneously."

Justine couldn't wrap her head around it. "How?"

"Outside light, the star beacons all occupy the same space."

"Are you talking about quantum entanglement?"

"It is one theory. However, our experiments in that area have proven inconclusive."

Chewing her lip, Justine asked, "Could 'outside light' be another dimension?"

"That is not known. When we are outside light, none of us has consciousness. It is only by the Grace that we are able to return to Aetherspace in another system."

Stunned, Justine made her way to the seat and laid back into it. "I spent four years in a quantized state," she said in a hoarse voice. "And I could have made the same journey in the blink of an eye."

"It is unlikely," Fairamai said. "You do not have the training, and your ships do not have the proper technology. All of that will come in time."

Springing up to a sitting position, Justine said, "Then you must train me and show us how to use the star beacons correctly."

"We cannot." The alien shrugged her delicate shoulders. "We are forbidden to interfere in your technological evolution. It is a knowledge you need to discover for yourselves. Already, I am in ambiguous territory by warning you of the dangers."

"I really don't understand that policy," Justine said.

"It is because of the Kulsat that the Grace made non-interference a law."

"The Kulsat?"

Fairamai made a tapping gesture to the wall beside her, a console appeared showing writing that Justine couldn't read.

The alien said, "We still have some time before Naila is finished attaching the shuttle. I will tell you the history while we wait—it is not restricted material." She flicked her fingers across the panel, and it disappeared back into the wall.

Another reclining seat, similar to Justine's, formed underneath Fairamai, and she sank into it.

"The Grace, who called themselves Xtôti, discovered Aetherspace nearly a million years ago. They explored our galaxy, and erected a star beacon in every system with a life-supporting planet, or cache of the Aetherock, so that they would not have to spend years or centuries to return to those systems.

"The Kulsat were the second species in the galaxy to achieve space flight—we believe this occurred approximately eight-thousand-years ago. From your own history, you understand that societal evolution can take a very long time. The Grace were perhaps too impatient. They brought knowledge of Aetherspace to the Kulsat as a gift. The Kulsat had not matured as a society, and quickly splintered into a caste system of those who could achieve Aetherform, and those who were unable to make the change."

Justine interrupted. "The Deficients." She thought about Alex. "They weren't able to transform fully."

"Yes. It is rare for it to happen in the other races, but there is some kind of physiological issue with the Kulsat species. Less than one in ten thousand is able to transform into a 'Risen'."

"That is why the Risen have cultivated their elite status."

"That," Fairamai said, "and because of the lifespan differential."

"Lifespan?"

"A normal Kulsat has a life expectancy of approximately two to three years." The translator calculated the time equivalent for Justine's reference. "Those who fail the conversion process have their normal life expectancy reduced to an average of one quarter—it is the same rate with any other species when this happens."

Justine swallowed hard. "One of my friends from the *Ultio,* Alex, wasn't able to complete the transformation. Do you mean to say his life expectancy will be cut short as well?"

"Yes. I am afraid that is the case."

The average human lived to a hundred-and-twenty. Alex had been exposed to Kinemet when he was ten. That meant that he most likely only had twenty or thirty years from the time on Macklin's Rock left to live.

Fairamai said, "We make every effort to ensure those unconverted are comfortable. Though they can never exist within the gravity well of a planet or moon, we have many stations in our system where they work and live out their lives."

"There's no cure?" Justine asked, to which Fairamai shook her head.

She said, "The Kulsat call them Deficients, and do not treat them very well. Often, since they rarely have more than a year of life left in them, they are sent out to mine Aetherock, or they are used as front-line troops in combat missions against the Collection."

Justine was aghast. "And the Xtôti didn't do anything to stop the Kulsat?"

"The Kulsat did not begin their war with the Collection until after the Grace disappeared from the galaxy. Before that point, the Grace were able to keep the Kulsat reined in. No one knows how this was accomplished; otherwise, we would have used the knowledge long ago to stop them."

After a moment, Fairamai continued, "The Grace realized that interference could have unforeseen consequences. They decreed that all species would retain autonomy over their own affairs in all matters, especially when it came to technological advances. Only once a system Emerged could they petition to become a member of the Collection of Worlds and share technology."

Justine said, "That answers some of my questions about the Kulsat's internal culture, but why are they so aggressively paranoid about other species? Surely, there has to be a way to stop the war between them and the rest of the galaxy. You said it's been going on for a very long time." Justine shook her head in astonishment at the thought of a thousand years of war. "Does it have something to do with this 'final component' they kept asking me about?"

Fairamai gave a shrug of uncertainty. "At this point, there can only be speculation. Over the centuries, many of our records have been lost, and those that remain are in dispute. We believe the Xtôti—the Grace—possessed a higher level of technology concerning the Aetherock than any we have been able to develop. There are two aspects to this advancement that we have debated endlessly.

"While those who fail the Aether conversion have their life expectancies shortened, those who convert successfully often more than double their life span. There is a theory that, individually, each of the Grace had lived for a million years."

Justine blanched, unable to imagine living so long. Doubling life expectancy was a more familiar concept; humankind had been exploring that for all history. Primitive peoples often only lived twenty or thirty years. Currently, it was becoming more common for people to celebrate their hundredth birthday, and still be quite active and lucid.

For the Kulsat, the difference between five or six years as a Risen and the immortality of the Grace was a goal that would be hard to ignore.

"You said there were two aspects."

"The second thought is more speculative in nature," Fairamai said. "We hypothesize that the advanced technology gives the Grace the ability to remain conscious outside light. That is the only explanation we can think of for how they were able to create the star beacons. Of course, the last Xtôti disappeared from the galaxy nearly a thousand years ago, and when they were among us, they did not share their secrets. Many in the Collection of Worlds have tried to discover this technology, but so far, we have not advanced our knowledge very much since the time of the Grace. The war with the Kulsat has taken its toll on our societies and resources. If the Kulsat gain the technology, they will control the star beacons, and thus, control us."

Justine said, "In the message Ah Tabai left for my friend Alex, he indicated the Kulsat believe this technology was hidden on an un-Emerged world. Is there any validity to that?"

"Since the Collection of Worlds adheres to the Grace's galactic laws, we have not explored this surmise. So far, the few worlds that have Emerged before the Kulsat destroyed them have not yielded the lost secret."

Bringing the conversation back around, Justine asked, "If the Collection of Worlds grants Emerged status to Sol System, that means you will offer us protection from the Kulsat?"

"We cannot guarantee the safety of any system," Fairamai said. "Indeed, in the last century alone, we have seen the cultures of more than a hundred Emerged systems destroyed by the Kulsat armada. However, we will all offer what assistance we are able to, in order to shore up your defenses. There are ways to limit travel through your star beacon. It is a difficult process, and requires the combined effort of many Aetherbeings to accomplish this."

A chime sounded from somewhere in the wall, and Fairamai said, "Naila has secured the Kulsat shuttle. He will put us into Aethersleep soon. When we awaken, we will be in Gliesan space."

"One more question," Justine said. "Just because we've achieved what you call Aetherflight, that doesn't mean the Collection will consider us Emerged, does it?"

"For Gliese, it was years from the first discovery of Aetherock before we were able to travel outside light."

Justine cursed to herself. The Kulsat were probably already looking for Sol System. Earth didn't have years to play catch-up.

Before she could form any other thoughts, she felt herself transforming into the photonic state as Naila induced Aethersleep in her.

29

Cerro Azul :
Guatemala :

Michael immediately rushed over to Yaxche and Patli, intending to push them out of the line of fire. Humberto pulled out his pistol, dropping to a crouch as he did so, and scanned the wooded area for their assailants.

"I said, don't move!" the gunman yelled out in English.

Michael froze and looked in the direction the voice had come from. He couldn't see anything. Glancing at Humberto, Michael said, "They have us surrounded."

"Put your weapons on the ground, step back, and put your hands on your heads." A moment later, the assailant added, "I don't want to have to kill any of you, but I will."

With a low growl, Humberto complied. Only once the four of them put their hands on their heads did two people, a man and a woman, step out from behind the bushes. With a measure of alarm, Michael recognized the tourist couple from the day before. They'd followed them all this way. Who were they?

He hadn't paid them much attention at the village, but now he got a good look at them. They were both of Spanish heritage, and both were tall and thin. The man's black hair was cut short, while the woman had her long hair tied back in a ponytail. Neither of them wore smiles, and their eyes radiated anger. There was something familiar about the man.

Both held high-powered rifles. The man aimed at Humberto, while the woman slowly slung her weapon at the rest of them one at a time.

"Who are you?" Humberto asked. When the two didn't reply, he continued, "Can I check on my friends?"

The man gave a slight shake of his head and spoke English with a heavy Spanish accent. "I am an excellent marksman. I did not shoot them in any vital areas. Shoulder and leg. Both will live. If you do not do precisely as I say, however, then I will ensure they do *not* survive."

Careful not to let his aim waver in the slightest from his target, the man walked toward Humberto. Only when he was right in front of the Cruzado did he stop. Without glancing behind him to make sure his partner had him covered, the man slung his rifle over his shoulder. Standing tall, keeping his eyes fixed on Humberto, he reached out and grabbed the holoslate, which the Cruzado had slipped into a belt pouch.

He flicked it on with a swipe of his finger and looked at the readout. "It is fortunate for you that you did not have time to send your message; otherwise, we might have had to take more extreme measures."

"Who are you?" Humberto asked again.

Continuing to examine the holoslate, flipping through the screens to read the history, the man said, "What is this map of? Why is that area so important to you? Why do you wish to excavate there?"

A wave of relief went through Michael. If these were Ruiz's people, then his organization had no idea what he was doing in Honduras and Guatemala. The attempt to kidnap him and Yaxche was nothing more than a fishing expedition. Under no circumstances could he let them know his true mission.

"It's a jade deposit," Michael said.

The woman narrowed her eyes. "Jade?" She let out a laugh of disbelief.

"I used to work for a Canadian resources company," Michael said. "A mineral satellite that ran over the area several years ago indicated there might be a deposit there. It was too small for my company—it wouldn't have been worth it for a big company like that to lease the rights. It might be valuable for a smaller operation, though. If I can find it, I can sell the information for a ten-percent finder's fee. At my age, I have to think about my retirement."

The man and woman didn't look convinced, and Michael added, "I asked my friends to help me find the deposit."

"If we've mistaken you for someone else, I'm afraid we're going to have to kill you all." The man smiled conspiratorially. "After all, we do not need witnesses." He raised his rifle to Humberto again.

"No, wait!" Michael said, holding out his hand.

"Why?" the man asked, lifting one eyebrow. "Do you have a different story to tell me, Mr. Sanderson?"

Michael gaped. How did he know his name?

The man nodded, and his smile widened. "Yes, we know all about you. Your government's attempt at misinformation might fool the newsvids, but not us."

"What do you want?"

"Do you remember Señor Oscar Ruiz? He offered you his hospitality and protection, and in return, you led the police to his plantation, ruined his name, and stole the knowledge possessed by Señor Yaxche for your own purposes."

Michael glanced at Humberto, and then back. "You work for him?"

"Work for him?" the man said, looking offended by the suggestion.

Humberto narrowed his eyes. "He is your father. You must be Alondo and Nadia. I see the resemblance now."

"And so," Alondo said, finally, "now that we all know who everyone is, let us try this again."

"What do you want with us?" Michael asked.

Nadia spoke. "Once, you came to Honduras and stole from our nation. You took knowledge from us, and you and your country prospered. Now, you are back, and I think you are here to steal more. This time, you will steal it for us. We will carve out our own legacy."

"I'm not here to steal anything."

With a sneer, Nadia said, "You are looking for information, as you did before. Do you deny this?"

Michael couldn't, not without giving away the lie—he was too physically exhausted from the march and too emotionally wrought from the violence to be a convincing actor.

Alondo said, "You will explain what you are doing, illegally crossing the border to Honduras, and what is really buried in this mountain range. I promise you, I have more bullets than you have friends."

Expecting that Alondo and Nadia would think he was still lying and kill him anyway, Michael said in a flat voice, "Based on a folk tale, we believe an alien creature was buried somewhere in those mountains over a thousand years ago."

"An alien, you say?" Alondo grinned. "That is quite the story. Let's investigate this fairy tale, shall we? I will make the arrangements."

∞

Alondo permitted Humberto and Michael to tend to Diego and Migel, and they did their best to bind the men's wounds. The two carried the injured men closer to the stones one at a time, where there was more shade. After asking if it was all right with Alondo and Nadia, they left the two men with a few canteens of water.

"I will send someone back to fetch them," Alondo said, and instructed his remaining prisoners to march north overland to the small village Humberto had spotted on his map earlier.

As it turned out, Alondo Ruiz and his sister were not without resources. Along the way, once he received a decent satellite signal, Alondo made several calls on his commlink. He didn't attempt to hide his conversations from his prisoners.

He contacted a mining operation they partly owned, and ordered them to start the paperwork to excavate the area.

Sensing Michael's confusion, Alondo laughed. "What, did you think you were just going to walk into a national park with a few shovels and start digging? The police would be on you before you broke a sweat. No, for appearances' sake, it will all be legal. The CEO knows how to grease certain Guatemalan officials to get the permits quickly. Fear not, we will begin surveying by this time tomorrow. Once you've found the location for us, we will excavate."

After three more grueling hours of marching, they arrived at the village and were greeted by two armed men driving a two-ton cargo truck. The captives were herded into the canopied bed. Michael sat on the floor, welcoming the relief from his blistered and burning feet. Both Patli and Yaxche looked worse for wear. Humberto was more angry than exhausted, but he kept his head down.

The siblings rode up front with the driver, and the other armed man sat in the back with the prisoners, his rifle at the ready.

They drove north for half an hour, and stopped when they reached an isolated farmhouse.

Michael and the others got out of the truck. Alondo led them to a barn and motioned for them to go inside. There were several stalls with straw on the ground. The doors were chained and bolted, and the one window in the loft was sealed shut. There weren't any animals in the barn, but there were a few barrels filled with what Michael hoped was drinkable water.

Alondo looked outside and waved his hand. Another man entered, holding a large cooking pot. Placing it on the floor, he removed the cover to reveal a corn, bean, and rice mix. It didn't look particularly appetizing, but it had been a long time since they had eaten last, and Michael was ravenous. There didn't seem to be any cutlery, as if Alondo expected them to eat with their hands.

He said, "My father believed in treating his guests with courtesy." He glared at Michael. "You, however, are not guests. I trust you will *not* have a comfortable stay."

30

Gliese Outpost :
Gliesan System :

Justine came out of the photonic state—Aethersleep—immediately.
There was no delay between the intangible and physical states of being
that she'd experienced on her last journey. While some people
experienced momentary disorientation when waking up from normal
sleep, Justine had always been one of those people who were instantly
alert. This process was no different.

She opened her eyes and looked around the passenger
compartment. Fairamai took a few moments to open her eyes. The
Gliesan made a quick ruffling movement with her head, as if to shake
off the effects of the Aethersleep, and then she looked at Justine.

"We are here," she said. "Home."

Pushing her *sight* out, Justine quickly sensed that she was in a new
solar system, one with a red dwarf star at its center. There were several
small planets orbiting close to the star, and four larger bodies outside
those. A number of tiny planets that would most likely be considered
dwarf planets orbited the outer edge of the system. From what she
could sense, there weren't any gas giants in Gliese.

"I would love to be able to visit your home world," Justine said to
her, wondering which one of the four planets in the habitable zone was
their prime.

"Even if it were permitted, you would not be able to survive for
more than a few days."

"Oh?" Justine asked. "How come?"

Fairamai got up from her hammock, and it melted back into the
wall. "Our physiology has been altered by the Aether process. The
gravity of a planet, or even a moon, puts an incredible pressure on our

cells. It interferes with the Aether, and dampens its ability to sustain us. Our internal systems begin to shut down."

"Alex, the first of us to be changed by the Kinemet, lived several years on our moon before his health deteriorated," Justine said.

"As you said before, he is not fully transformed. He might even be able to survive several months on the surface of a planet. We are beings of light, Justine. We are no longer true members of our own species."

There was one question that Justine hadn't asked yet, and she realized it was because it was something she wasn't certain she wanted to know. Kinemet was a miracle element, and would give any world the ability to venture beyond the borders of its solar system. For those who successfully underwent the Kinemetic change, and were forever altered, there were numerous benefits: the ability to pilot ships between the stars, electropathic control, and enhanced memory. It was a dream-come-true on many levels.

The change came with some serious disadvantages. There were many dangers involved with utilizing the Kinemetic power itself, but it was the secondary effects that would give potential candidates pause. Never being able to set foot on her home planet again without risking death was a significant downside. If Justine had had a choice in her conversion, and had known about this drawback, she would've had a very tough decision to make. It was a big enough issue that it would deter many from going down the path to becoming an interstellar pilot.

The Kinemetic change altered a person at the cellular level. What other side effects would this change produce?

Hesitant to ask the question, Justine nevertheless spoke it. "Whatever you want to call us—Risen, Kinemats, Aetherbeings—we can't have children, can we?"

"Not once we are altered," Fairamai said, as if that were a well-known fact.

The confirmation was like a punch in the stomach to Justine. Though she'd made the decision not to have a child of her own long ago, the option had always been there if she ever changed her mind. Now, there was no hope. Klaus had taken away a great deal more than anyone thought when he'd forced Justine into the change.

The anger surged in her, but she had no place to direct it. Klaus hadn't survived Lucis Observatory, but if he had, she would track him down and make him wish he hadn't.

Fairamai led her back to the bridge, and by the time they arrived,

Justine had managed to regain control of her emotions.

The display on the main console panel showed dozens of Gliesan patrol ships in the vicinity around the star beacon. A distance away, there were a number of larger ships that looked like they were military cruisers of some kind—she could sense a variation of weaponized Kinemet on board them. Considering the ongoing war with the Kulsat, Justine assumed that if an enemy ship were to travel to their system, they would quickly be engaged in battle.

Naila said, "I have transmitted our report to Commander Analock. We will be escorted to Skanse Aerie—our outmost station." Glancing over his shoulder at Justine, he added, "The Commander is not pleased that we brought the Kulsat shuttle with us … or that I offered them asylum."

Setting her jaw, Justine asked, "What did he have to say about me?"

"With Ah Tabai and Aliah breaking protocol—and galactic law—and with my decision to spare the enemy, his response to your presence was … not repeatable. He has, however, dispatched a courier ship to Gliese Prime for further instruction."

Justine felt acutely guilty at the mention of the 'enemy', remembering Fairamai's warning about how unstable the conversion to and from Aetherspace was for normal beings. "The Kulsat," she said. "Did they all make it?"

"There is one less life form registering on our monitors," Naila said.

Gritting her teeth at the news, Justine was silently thankful that her ignorance had not cost any of her passengers on the *Ultio* their lives.

As Naila plugged in the course to the station, Fairamai stroked her long, taloned finger on the control panel on her side of the bridge. A workstation of sorts emerged from the wall on one side of the bridge and a contoured chair rose up and floated above the floor. The Gliesan motioned for Justine to take a seat.

"Skanse Aerie is approximately two-hundred-thousand kilometers away—too short a distance for quantum travel. We'll have to use normal space engines. It will be at least forty minutes before we arrive. Perhaps you would like to access some background material on our history before you meet a representative from the Collection of Worlds and present your case. It would be best if you were as informed as possible."

"Thank you, Fairamai," Justine said, and settled herself into the floating chair. When she'd been standing up, the display screen had looked like a two-dimensional representation; once she sat down, the image before her expanded into a volumetric holograph. Haptic technology had just started to become popular on Earth, and Justine extended her hand to manipulate the image in front of her.

"No," Fairamai said, "the educational database has a synaptic interface."

"How do you operate it?"

"Simply focus your concentration on any rendered object or word." She pointed to a small antenna above the display. "It will receive your neuropulses. To manipulate the display, form one of the basic commands in your mind. I've entered translations of 'Go', 'Back', 'Follow', and 'Return'. You can customize other commands with the interface at the bottom. Subvocalize searches to begin. I would suggest that you start with the Xtôti entries before moving on to Kulsat history."

Silently amazed at the remarkable technology, Justine looked at the display. There was a single phrase hanging in three-dimensional suspension: *Please supply search parameters.*

"Xtôti history," Justine said under her breath, and the display launched the first page in the database, comprising text as well as a dimensional image of what looked like a humanoid turtle without a shell. For a moment, Justine gaped. In her mind, she hadn't really formed an image of the Grace, but this was not what she had expected.

Before reading the text, however, she wanted to be sure she had a handle on the interface. She focused on an arrow on the bottom of the display and thought, *next.* Immediately, the page transitioned to a topic list. *Back,* she thought, glancing at the right side of the page. The first page returned. The top line of the text read, 'Introduction', and Justine focused on that and thought, *go.* A generic definition of 'introduction' appeared on the display.

She played with the controls for a few more seconds until she was confident she could navigate the database.

The synaptic interface was as close to a telepathic link as technology could get. On Earth, thought-link implant surgery allowed for a very rudimentary Meshstream to be uploaded through the optic nerves, with commands still based on vocalization. A true synaptic interface had never been developed.

Turning to Fairamai, Justine asked, "Can you use this for communication?"

Shaking her head, Fairamai said, "Far too many conservatives in the Parliament. They've banned synaptic technology for anything other than databases and medical emergencies." She made a short screeching sound that Justine took for amusement. "One of the first demonstrations proved embarrassing to a certain member of Parliament…"

Justine turned back to the display and immersed herself thoroughly in the history of the galaxy.

∞

The amount of information she absorbed was incredible, but she knew she had only uncovered the tip of the iceberg. Even with her accelerated learning ability, it could take her years to learn everything available in the database.

A few key points stood out from the research.

Although there wasn't a direct match in the species catalogs between the evolved worlds throughout the galaxy, there were significant similarities among them. With a few rare exceptions, the animal kingdoms of the diverse worlds could be categorized along the same basic families. As humans evolved from the primate family and became the dominant species in Sol System, the Gliesans—whose home world's geography was dominated by mountainous regions and forests—evolved from a species of flightless birds that was something of a cross between an ostrich and an owl.

The anthropology of the *Aves,* as they called their species, was fascinating, and Justine had to stop herself from spending the entire session learning about them. There was time for that later. She needed to learn about the Kulsat.

Ninety-two percent of the Kulsat home world's surface was water. The cephalopods on that planet were the first to use tools for survival. They had created underwater cities and developed agriculture around the same time as humans were still living in caves. The Kulsat had discovered electricity thousands of years before the first human hut had been erected in Mesopotamia.

One statistic that surprised her was, among the thirty-thousand species that had developed space flight—or were on the cusp—less than twelve percent had evolved from land-based mammals. By far, the majority of dominant species evolved from oceanic environments.

It only followed, Justine thought; after all, mammals were latecomers on the evolutionary scale of Earth.

As Fairamai had mentioned earlier, the Kulsat had been the second species to expand beyond their planet's surface and into the space of their solar system. A million years ago, the reptilian Xtôti had already mastered light-speed travel, and had discovered a way to circumvent normal space. Justine had difficulty imagining spending that amount of time alone in the galaxy, knowing that there were tens of thousands of other sentient species with the potential of becoming galactic neighbors.

If the Xtôti had not provided technological advancement, the Kulsat might not have developed light-speed travel for many more millennia—their system was barren of Kinemet. The nearest solar system was eighty-seven light-years away. With the short lifespan of the Kulsat species, they would've had to develop generation ships to explore the systems in their sector.

Without Xtôti interference, the Kulsat would most likely have Emerged around the same timeframe as the majority of the other members of the Collection of Worlds. According to the database, there was a mass confluence of advancement throughout the galaxy. The majority of worlds had emerged between two and four-thousand years ago—it was practically simultaneous, in the context of galactic time.

Sol System was a straggler. A question arose in Justine's mind, and she did a quick search. While interference in un-Emerged systems was against the law, observation was not. The Xtôti had been notoriously close-lipped about the existence of other systems, having learned their lesson with the Kulsat.

A question occurred to Justine, and a few thought-strokes later, she found her answer. Galactic scientists estimated there were over two thousand more un-Emerged systems in the galaxy. When Justine read this, she wondered how they'd arrived at that number. With her mind, she focused on that fact and thought, *follow*.

The monuments housing the star beacons, she read, all contained the same catalog of language samples. Apparently, the Xtôti kept a close watch on developing systems. At some point in the evolution of that culture, the Xtôti would sample local languages and leave a message on the monument housing the star beacon as a way to welcome them to the galactic fold. There were 2,341 unidentified writing samples.

Justine wondered at the translation they'd found on the *Dis Pater*. She knew the Mayan language had dozens of dialects, and even modern-day linguists argued over the meaning of many of the symbols and icons.

'Behold the Mighty Door of Kinich Ahua; Eternity is Now Before You; Beware the Power of Kukulcan.'

It sounded ominous, and she wondered what the message really meant.

She turned to Fairamai. "I have a question about the writing on the star beacon monuments. Actually, I have two, but the first one is, 'What do those messages really mean?'"

"I am not certain the translation program will give you the correct context of our message," Fairamai said. "The line was written in one of the earliest languages from our southern continent. No one has spoken it in thousands of years, but according to our linguists, it reads, *'Observe the gate of creation and the endless sky of your future. Great and terrible is the power of Aether.'*"

Justine deduced that, in a rudimentary form, the messages were similar, and could be written in any number of ways. *Here's the star beacon. With it, you can travel to other solar systems. Use the technology with care.*

"The database says all the monuments have the same writing samples," Justine said. "So yours, out here, has our Mayan message on it. Did the Xtôti write on all the beacons?"

Shaking her head, Fairamai said, "You still do not comprehend. The star beacons all share the same space outside light. Some of our scientists believe there may only be one star beacon, and what we see in normal space is a metaphysical representation. Our technology cannot accurately measure the star beacon. We can only hypothesize. The monuments are connected to the star beacons on a level we do not understand."

"So, if the Xtôti wrote on one, the writing would appear on all of them?"

"That is our theory," Fairamai replied.

"So," Justine asked, drawing her words out, "if one of them were destroyed…?"

Giving that amused screech of laughter, Fairamai said, "They cannot be destroyed. Believe me, it's been attempted many times by many different systems."

31

Sierra de las Minas :
Guatemala :

In the morning, Nadia came for Michael.

"Your friends will remain here to ensure your cooperation," she said, casting a suspicious glance at the others. Her rifle was crooked in her arm, and it was as if she wanted someone to try to escape.

"You said you would send someone back for Diego and Migel," Michael said.

"Yes. We brought them here last night. They're in the main house." She glanced at Humberto. "They will both live as long as you all continue to cooperate."

Michael didn't want to give her any excuse to follow through with the threat. Sharing a concerned look with Humberto, he got up and followed the young woman out of the barn. Before he left, he looked back. "It will all work out," he said. Yaxche gave him a nod.

Outside, there were several more people than the day before. A second cargo truck was there, and it was filled with both electronic and digging equipment. Tucked deep inside the cargo area was a compact excavator.

Alondo was standing near the rear of the truck, going over an inventory list. He looked up as his sister and Michael approached.

"I think we have everything we will need," he said to his sister, "provided it is not too deep a cave."

"So long as we are not chasing a fairy tale," Nadia said, raising an eyebrow at her brother.

"I can't guarantee what's there," Michael said, and felt a shudder go down his spine at the malevolent scowl he got from the siblings.

Nadia practically spat out her words. "For you and your friends' sake, let us hope we find something worth our while."

In a businesslike manner, Alondo said, "We have four laser radiation detectors. Once we reach the mountains, you will program the frequency into them, and instruct the teams what to look for. Your map showed an area of ten-thousand hectares. We have used a recent satellite scan to eliminate more than eighty-percent of the area that does not show any subterranean gaps. I've marked the remaining possible locations on these maps. With four teams, we should be able to survey all possibilities in one or two days. We've paid the local authorities to look the other way for that amount of time. If we haven't found what we are looking for by then…" He gave Michael a hard look.

They all turned around at the sound of a third truck rumbling up the dirt road. It pulled a long trailer, on the back of which were four military-style all-terrain vehicles.

"A loan from a colonel in the Guatemalan army," Alondo said.

A knot formed in the pit of Michael's stomach. Once again, he was being swept along with the tide of events. At one time, he was the CEO of one of the most important corporations in the world, and was at the forefront of future exploration. Now, in less than two decades, he was nothing more than a pawn in an international and interplanetary power struggle.

How was he possibly going to be able to save Sol System from the Kulsat when he hadn't been able to save Kenny or Alex from Chow Yin? Even Humberto's intervention had only delayed his being abducted and used by Oscar Ruiz's children.

Now, if he didn't cooperate, more innocents would die. There was every possibility they would all die anyway.

Michael couldn't remember ever feeling so low.

∞

The troop set up a base camp fifty meters outside the tree line at the base of the mountain range and waited while Michael calibrated the radiation detectors.

While raw Kinemet gave off ultra-high electromagnetic radiation— more so than gamma rays—and could disrupt any electronics in the nearby area, the radiation of a Kinemat, such as Alex, was non-ionizing electromagnetic in the extremely low-frequency range. If a Kinemat was not utilizing the radiation, the only means to detect it was with highly sensitive detectors.

When Michael was finished, Alondo split up the men into four teams and handed out coordinates of the most likely locations. Nadia stayed at the camp with the trucks and the excavator. Her task was to coordinate the search with the teams, and provide a communications hub for them.

Alondo took Michael with him. After taking his place in the back seat of one of the terrain vehicles, Michael sat back and kept quiet. Until they found the cave that entombed the alien—if it did, indeed, exist—he didn't have much to do other than go along for the ride.

The forest of the range was sparse, and the trees were spaced far enough apart for them to ride between the trunks. There was also an intricate pathway system the park officials had maintained for years. From the story Patli had told, it was doubtful the cave would be too far up any of the mountains. Michael doubted they would have to walk any great distance from the vehicles.

While he concentrated on keeping his teeth from clattering together, and his bones from rattling from the jarring ride, Michael considered the younger man beside him. It was alarming how much groundwork Alondo had done in such a short span of time. His attention to detail was meticulous, and he commanded the men with an ease that seemed to be an inherent trait. If he'd put his skills to legitimate trade, Alondo could easily have led a company to prosperity. It was too bad he had baser motivations. Internally, Michael sighed. It seemed the universe ran on greed, jealousy, and revenge.

When they arrived at the first prospect—a small area of rock surrounding an outcrop—Alondo got off the vehicle and motioned Michael to grab the radiation detector from the storage compartment on the back.

As they approached the outcrop on foot, Alondo called his sister to let her know where they were. Once he'd finished checking in, he turned to Michael.

"All right, let's see if there's anything there."

Michael set the laser radiation detector on a tripod in front of the rocks, turned it on, and aimed at the center of the pile of rubble. It was a similar device to the ones surveyors used on asteroids. Idly, Michael wondered if the Kinemet would react to the laser and produce an effect similar to the one that had quantized Macklin's Rock.

After the initial discovery of Kinemet, every mining company on Earth went on the hunt for the element in the hopes of improving their fortunes. After years of surveys, however, no sign of Kinemet was found.

Now, here they were searching again, but this time it wasn't for the element itself, but the residue of the element. They were working off a lot of assumptions, but the one thing Michael clung to was that if there had, indeed, been a Kinemetic being buried here, he would give off the same electromagnetic signature as Alex. It was a well-documented frequency.

It took several seconds before the readout spat out the results of the scan. Every spec of matter on the Earth gave out its own form of radiation, and the computer listed every frequency it found: oxygen, silicon, iron, calcium, magnesium, and many other innocuous elements.

Michael adjusted the laser a few degrees and waited for a second readout, which ended up being similar to the first except for a trace of jade—a quantity much too small to warrant the effort of excavation. He continued to play the laser around the area, and only stopped after half an hour of searching.

All the while, he could feel Alondo's hawk eyes watching him.

"Sorry," Michael said finally, "there's nothing in there. From a geological standpoint, it's probably nothing more than a crevice caused by a natural shift."

He expected an outburst, but was surprised when Alondo spoke into his radio to touch base with his sister and inform her that the first coordinate was not a hit.

Alondo crossed the spot off his map. To Michael, he said, "One down, fourteen more to go."

∞

By late afternoon, they'd surveyed five locations. Some of the areas were buried by rock slides, some from sunken earth, and one had been a wide-open tunnel whose opening was half a meter in diameter. Both Alondo and Michael had started when a lowland paca darted out. The rodent had obviously adopted the cave as a home, and was more frightened by the encroaching humans than they were of it.

After their pulses returned to normal, Alondo said, "We'll do two more today, then complete the rest of them tomorrow. You look dehydrated. Have some water, and I'll check in and see how the other teams are doing."

Michael had just enough time to find the canteen on the seat of the vehicle and take a sip before Alondo hollered at him.

"Team Three thinks they may have found something." He hurried toward Michael, trying to read his map while he moved. When he got to the vehicle, he put the map on the seat and found the location of the other team. "There. We can get there in ten minutes."

Despite himself, Michael found his heart thrumming with excitement. Was their long shot really going to pay off?

He climbed onto the back seat, and held on while Alondo drove to the site.

∞

By the time they got there, the other two teams had arrived, and within minutes, Michael could hear the engine of the compact excavator as it slowly picked its way through the forest to them. Nadia stood on a riser outside the cab, one hand holding her close to the vehicle. She had her rifle in the other hand.

A dozen meters out, she jumped from the excavator and trotted up to meet her brother.

Alondo smiled at her, and then turned to Michael. "All right, let's verify the findings."

They scaled a short rise to an area where there had been a massive landslide. From the looks of the overgrowth, it could have been decades or centuries since anyone had been there. There was only one way to tell whether this was the spot.

Michael approached the laser operator, but his eyes were on the readout. "What did it find?" he asked.

"Kinemet," the man said, and Michael gave him a sharp, questioning look.

"Surely, you mean you detected the ELF radiation?"

Shaking his head, the man pointed to the readout. "See for yourself."

Michael refreshed the screen and read the results. It was positive for the high-frequency radiation of Kinemet. The laser indicated there was a very tiny amount of the element, but left no doubt that it was there.

Perhaps the story had been wrong, and there wasn't an alien buried beneath the mountain. There were dozens of other possibilities to explain the presence of Kinemet, the least of which was an alien visitor.

Seeing Michael's expression, Alondo asked, "What does this mean?"

"It's possible there's a natural deposit of Kinemet here. Perhaps a meteorite heavy with the element fell to the Earth a long time ago." He shook his head. "For all we know, someone could've stolen some and buried it here sometime in the past twenty years."

Alondo and his sister shared a greedy look. "A gram of Kinemet is worth a million on the black market, what with the Emperor's embargo. Perhaps, if we continue to search, we will find more than that."

Nadia turned and signaled for the excavator operator to move closer.

Slapping Michael on the shoulder in congratulations, Alondo said, "It seems we may have found the pot of gold at the end of your rainbow." He laughed. "An alien grave site. What a story! I knew you were trying to—how do you say it?—pull a fast one."

∞

It took the excavator operator nearly half an hour to remove enough of the rubble to reveal a narrow crevice in the face of the mountain. A blast of fetid air rolled out, and Michael had to hold his nose together with his fingers.

From a case on his belt, Alondo produced a handheld spectrometer and leaned over to make himself small enough to fit in the crevice. In his free hand, he aimed a high-powered flashlight into the darkness within.

Nadia, with her rifle, motioned for Michael to go next, and she followed right behind him.

The cave was dark, and the flashlight cast eerie dancing shadows on the walls. They didn't have far to go before the spectrometer lit up, indicating they were right on top of the source of the Kinemet.

To everyone's surprise, there wasn't a deposit, or a vein from a meteorite, or even a buried cache of the kinetic element.

What they found was a perfectly preserved body, covered in a thick layer of dust.

The figure was short, like a boy, but the head was reptilian in shape, with a curved eye ridge that traced around the sides of its bald head. It had large, wide-spaced eyes and a beak for a mouth. Its skin was leathery; pale white and mottled with blue patches.

Michael was the first to recover from the shock, and he knelt beside the creature, feeling at its neck and wrist for a pulse.

It had to be the alien from Patli's story. The Grace? If so, he'd died over a millennium ago.

32

Skanse Aerie :
Gliesan System :

"We've arrived," Naila said, breaking Justine's concentration.

When she looked up at the front display, Justine saw that the *Fainne* was approaching the deep space orbital the Gliesans called Skanse Aerie.

While Earth stations were largely built using basic architectural forms as their foundations—a collection of tubes, like Canada Station Three, or wheel-shaped with spokes, like Lucis Observatory—the Gliesan station looked like a starburst, with hundreds of spires extending from the central hub. It was an immense, brightly lit construction, set against the backdrop of the stars.

"How many people are there?" Justine asked in wonder.

"About one-hundred-thousand." On the display, Fairamai pointed to a spot halfway up one of the long spires, which must have been nearly a kilometer in length. "I live there with my mate, Havena. He's one of the gravimetric technicians."

"This is your permanent home?" Justine asked.

"Yes." Fairamai clicked her taloned finger on an icon at the bottom of the display. A series of images in a small sub-window showed several portions of the station: markets, offices, workshops, hallways, and hundreds of elaborate gardens. One of the last sets of images showed dozens of hangars with several spacecraft. "The aerie is primarily a military outpost, and also serves as the first stop for visiting emissaries from other worlds—the population is mainly transitory. Several spires are set aside for Aethers, since we cannot live on our home world."

As they approached the central area of the aerie, Justine spotted a landing bay. A tug emerged from it and latched on to the Kulsat shuttle. It towed the shuttle off to another section of the station.

"Where are they taking them?" Justine asked.

"We have … facilities to house them," Fairamai said. Before Justine could ask, she added, "They are not the first Kulsat we've had here, but they will be treated according to our highest diplomatic conventions. Rest assured, they will not be harmed."

Relaxing at the Gliesan's assurance, Justine watched as the *Fainne* completed its docking procedures. As they pulled into their assigned bay, Naila spoke through his communicator. The translation machine didn't interpret for Justine, and she wondered if they were talking about her.

When he'd finished his conversation, Naila said, "We will disembark now. An ambassador from Gliese has been assigned to escort you from this point on—he will meet you at the main gate. They've set aside quarters for you on the station while the Collection's assessment council deliberates on your situation. I'm sure they will contact you for debriefing at some point, though I can't say for certain; I am simply a pilot, not a politician."

Justine smiled. "How long do you think they'll take to decide?"

"I have no idea," Naila said. He motioned to the communication console. "I've been given some instructions. Before we can let you off this vessel, I must formally inform you of the following:

"On behalf of the Collection of Worlds, the Gliesan Parliament extends you, Major Justine Turner, political asylum and shelter from enemy attack. In return, you will not undertake to acquire our Aether technology, and you will give your oath that you will uphold all Gliesan and Galactic Laws. You will be restricted from traveling to or contacting any being in Sol System until said system is granted Emerged status and membership to the Collection of Worlds. Do you agree to these terms?"

At first, Justine balked at the official words. What if the Collection decided Sol System wasn't Emerged? She would be stuck out here, alone and away from home, for the rest of her life. What other choice did she have, though? She would just have to do everything in her power to convince the politicians to come to a favorable decision.

"I accept," she said.

Fairamai put a feathered hand on Justine's shoulder and made a soft whistling sound. "Welcome to Gliesan System."

∞

From the moment Justine had re-materialized in physical form aboard the *Fainne,* there had been a nagging thought in the back of her mind. She'd been so caught up in the excitement and wonder of making contact with an alien culture that it took her until now to realize something. Naila and Fairamai had been completely composed when she—an alien life form to them—had appeared on their ship.

Was it so commonplace to meet a new species that there wasn't any exhilaration left in the occurrence of first contact? Ah Tabai and Aliah had briefly jumped into Gliese System to give their report before heading to Sol System, but from what Justine gathered, they would not have remained in the system, since what they planned on doing was breaking galactic law. Certainly, they would have transmitted images of the 'Solan beings'; but even at that, why would Naila and Fairamai have been so casual at Justine's arrival on their ship?

When Justine disembarked from the scout ship, and followed the walkway to the main gate, she quickly learned why her appearance had not elicited any surprise in the Gliesan pilots: They had seen humankind before.

Justine stepped through the doorway into the gate room, and a human male stepped forward, a huge grin on his face as he extended his arm toward her to shake her hand.

Though there was the distinct possibility that humaniform beings had evolved from primates on another world, Justine knew this was not the case in this instance. The man could have been a brother or cousin to Alex Manez or Yaxche. He was most definitely Mayan in origin.

"Good Morning, Major Justine Turner. I am Yoatl Cen, the Gliesan ambassador to Sol. I must apologize if my etiquette is not correct. I've never had the pleasure of visiting Sol System, and I have only been able to reference the data we received from Alex Manez's ship."

Justine's mind spun. There was so much conflicting information, she couldn't process it. The Gliesans had spent a great deal of time telling her that Sol System was off-limits, and that interference was strictly prohibited. Yet, here before her, was evidence to the contrary.

Numbly, she reached out to shake his hand.

Yoatl, shorter than Justine by a few centimeters, nodded to her, a wide smile on his lips. "You must have many questions. I have even prepared a speech to explain it all to you. We have set aside quarters for your stay; you may wish to tend to personal needs or perhaps meditate for a few hours. When you are ready, I will give you a tour of the aerie, and bring you up to velocity before your briefing with the Collection representative."

"Thank you," Justine said absently, and gathered her makeshift toga around her as she followed the—*her*—ambassador through the processing area and into the corridors of the station.

One of the first things she noticed was the aesthetics of the station. The organic décor of the interior was a sharp contrast to the futuristic architecture of the outside of the station. Many of Earth's space stations were designed for efficiency, and while there were attempts to make it seem a little more homey for the long-term residents, no one who visited any of the stations made of the mistake of forgetting they were in space.

The corridors of Skanse Aerie station were anything but straight. The path wound left and right, sometimes gradually, sometimes sharply. Sculpted to resemble the walls of a canyon, the surface had rocky areas with outcroppings housing plants and flowers. Justine was surprised when a small bird she thought was a decoration flapped its wings and flew off ahead of them. The floor rose and fell unevenly, and the base narrowed and widened randomly. Above them, a wide-open green-blue sky housed several cloud formations and the image of a small, red sun. The ceiling obviously used some kind of projection technology. Although the expense must have been enormous, the Gliesans must have believed it was worth it to create a natural-looking environment for those who were stationed on the outer rim of the system either temporarily or permanently. To Justine, it felt as if she were taking a stroll through a national park on Earth.

"On the other side of the wall to our right is a transport conveyor for those carrying supplies, or for those who do not wish to walk the distance from the central hub to their destination. You can access them here."

He pointed to what looked like a sawed-off branch coming out of the wall. With a quick motion, he waved his hand over it, and a section of the wall vanished, revealing a short passageway to the transport tunnel. There were two pathways there; one leading up to the far side of the tunnel, the other descending a shorter distance to the lower level, where the floor itself moved slowly up the length of the spire.

Though she couldn't see the floor on the upper side, she assumed it held a similar moving floor heading the opposite direction.

"The upper pathway," she said. "How is it suspended?" There wasn't any scaffolding propping it up, and she couldn't see any wires leading from it to the ceiling of the tunnel.

"There's an electromagnetic field, though I can't pretend to understand the specific technology; it's not my area of expertise."

Stepping back into the main corridor, Yoatl gestured to another cutoff branch sticking out of the other side of the wall, though he didn't wave his hand over it.

"On the left side of the wall are the compartments for living quarters, working environments, industrial complexes, life support gardens, or storage facilities."

Justine said, "I'd love to see those gardens."

"Once we've completed the briefing, you'll be assigned a security level coded to your biosignature. I assume you'll be granted access to all the common areas—which includes the gardens—in addition to your quarters. You may visit any unrestricted areas at your leisure. Until then, you'll need me to escort you around the station."

"Understandable."

He nodded and then gestured to the branch marker on the wall. "Temporary visitor quarters are inside here. They are fully equipped with every amenity you should require, though I'm sure once we've established your diplomatic status, you'll be assigned a more appropriate dwelling." Waving his hand over the branch, he took a step back when a portion of the wall vanished, and motioned for her to enter first.

Inside, there was another corridor, though this one did not look quite as natural as the main pathway through the spire. The walls and floor were smooth and straight, but the ceiling still benefited from the projection of the sky. It was a very comforting illusion.

There were several apartments along the corridor, and when they reached the last one, Yoatl opened the door for Justine and politely waited at the entrance for her to enter.

"My wife, Ekthin, did not have much time to synthesize clothing for you; I hope the garment style she selected is to your liking. There is nutritional refreshment in the cold storage unit, a sonic shower, and a reclining platform if you wish to rest or meditate. I have reserved a private space in one of our most popular eateries where you can sample some Gliesan cuisine, and we can talk. I will return for you in two hours."

Justine shook her head. "But I have so many questions."

"I am sure everything you've experienced must be overwhelming, even for an Aetherbeing. You will benefit from some time to gather your thoughts and—how do you say it?—'catch your breath'. Besides," he said, giving her a conspiratorial wink, "I must report my first impressions of you to the Solan Society. Your arrival has created quite a stir among us, and I fear there might be an uprising if their curiosity is not satisfied."

She wanted to protest again, but Justine realized that he was right; too much had happened in too short a time. She needed a few hours to clean herself up and get her head straight.

Whatever the Kinemet had done to alter her on a cellular level, one of the side effects was that her suprachiasmatic nuclei stopped inducing the sleep aspect of her circadian rhythm. While she'd only spent a small portion of her time since the Kinemetic change in physical form, she realized that quieting her mind was still a necessity. Even Alex had spent several hours a day in a meditative state. Since arriving in the Centauri System, the only time Justine had not been conscious was when the Kulsat had quantized her, and that had been more like a state of suspension than affording her any real rest.

When she entered the small apartment, and Yoatl closed the door behind her, Justine's first impulse was to review everything that had happened over the past few days; but when she saw the reclining platform set into a small alcove at the back of the room, she changed her mind. Instead of a flat mattress, there was a hammock-like bed that looked irresistible.

One thing she had to do first, however, was clean up. She'd spent several days in the Kulsat terrarium. Yoatl had been polite not to mention how badly she smelled. There was another recess on the other side of the room, and Justine stepped out of her makeshift toga and entered the sonic shower. It was simple to figure out. A single lever turned the device on and off. She didn't know if there was a time allotment, but she figured she must have spent a good half an hour letting the sound waves wash over her. Never in her life had she been so thoroughly scrubbed and cleaned.

While she showered, she thought about sonic technology. Scientists on Earth had long thought that sound was one of the most powerful forces in nature. At the right frequency, sound waves could melt metal, shatter glass and rock, and—as she had witnessed—explode organic cells. For over a century, engineers had used sonic welding in electronics to bond metals. The nature of the star beacons suggested that the Grace had somehow tapped into the sound frequencies of all stellar objects, using that technology to help those attuned to it to navigate between the beacons. It was no wonder the Kulsat had developed sonic weapons and tools.

If Justine listened hard with her newfound ability, she could hear more than the Song of the Stars, or the Music of the Spheres—she could hear something beyond. When she had time, she would have to discuss it with other Aetherbeings.

Her skin tingled from spending so much time in the sonic shower. She turned off the device and stepped out.

Naked, she went back to the reclining platform, crawled in and was surprised when the foam wrapped itself around her in a form-fitting cocoon. It felt as if she were floating, and she was able to put herself in a relaxed state very quickly.

It was the very thing she needed, and she remained there right up until a soft chime sounded. She assumed Yoatl had come to retrieve her.

"Just a moment," she said, wondering if he could hear her. She took a one quick glance at the makeshift toga lying in the heap on the floor. No matter what the fashion in the Gliesan System was, she was sure it didn't include long swaths of fabric tied haphazardly around her torso.

A few moments searching was all it took before she found a small closet with half a dozen clothing selections. She picked the one that looked most appealing to her—she was always drawn to darker colors; perhaps a carryover from wearing her military uniform for so many years.

After slipping on a long one-piece outfit with baggy leggings that seemed to produce the dual effect of looking like a jumpsuit and an ankle-length dress at the same time, she went to the door and opened it.

Yoatl bent his head in admiration and smiled. "Perfect selection."

"Thank you," Justine said, and followed him back out to the main corridor.

∞

The hub of the aerie was bustling with activity. If the station had over a hundred-thousand people, the majority of them had congregated in the central area.

When they exited the spire, they were several dozen meters above ground level, and at a perpendicular angle. They had to use a floating platform to descend, and Justine was completely unaware of any gravitational shift as the platform altered pitch to match the common area's perspective; the Gliesan technology was seamless.

The architecture of the hub followed the nature theme of the corridor. Like a multi-layer landscape, replete with canyons, grottos, forests, cliffs and waterfalls, it was enough to put any of Earth's theme resorts to shame.

"This is primarily a military outpost?" Justine asked.

"The well-being of our citizens is of utmost importance. We have a number of permanent residents. They can be proud to call this home. Besides, we need to set a good impression for ambassadors from other worlds."

Although she'd read about the proliferation of alien species, Justine was still taken aback seeing the variety for herself. While the majority of the population was Gliesan, she spotted a number of people who had evolved from other species. A being with four short legs, a squat body, and a round head on a long neck sauntered past them. He had no arms, but he had a long prehensile tail with a half-dozen 'fingers' on the end of it. He turned his head and bowed to them, while waving his tail-hand.

Yoatl nodded back. "Ambassador Etrevius," he said to Justine. "From Beta Monocerotis. And yes, he's a dinosaur—mammals never evolved on his planet at all."

"So many people…" Justine could spend a lifetime learning about all the denizens of the galaxy, but she would have to wait for another time. They had arrived at the restaurant.

Quickly, Yoatl ushered her in and they found their cubby. It wasn't a typical chair and table setup, however, and it took Justine a moment to figure out that the space was a representation of a bird's nest. Following Yoatl's example, she climbed in and sat on the floor of the nest, resting her back against the curved wall, which was lined with a foam-like material and was quite comfortable.

Yoatl settled himself in, crossing his legs. "I've taken the liberty of ordering for us. The main entrée should arrive soon. In the meantime, if you want water or another beverage, simply use the control panel there to indicate your preference." He demonstrated by tapping one of the icons on the panel, and a section of the wall folded out. The platform held a bowl-shaped container of liquid. "A form of wine, quite sweet, like nectar. Did you want one?" he asked, and Justine nodded. He closed the panel and tapped the icon again to produce another drink for Justine.

She sipped it, and found it extremely pleasant-tasting.

"Thank you," she said, and then waved one hand to encompass the station. "All of this is fantastic, and the explorer in me wants nothing more than to spend the rest of my life experiencing all these wonderful new worlds. But..."

Smiling, Yoatl said, "But we have more pressing matters, and I promised you a story."

"Yes. And start with how there are humans here, in the stars."

"Very well." He took one more sip of his nectar wine. "I hope this answers most of your questions."

Taking a moment to gather his thoughts first, he began:

"According to the report Naila filed, you have accessed some basic history of the galaxy, correct?"

Justine nodded.

"Let me give you a bit of background on the Grace, the Xtôti. A million years before the Mass Emergence—which is what we call the era when the majority of systems began to discover light-speed travel—the Xtôti home system was destroyed when their star went supernova. They were unable to evacuate their system, and the tragedy decimated their population. The survivors were those who were at the edge of their system, or in other solar systems: namely, Aetherbeings. Some speculate that the supernova may have been caused by experiments. We only have scattered accounts of what happened at that time. You must remember, this was a million years before most of our species began to evolve into sentience.

"There is a theory that those Xtôti who were in the system at the time of the supernova became the Grace. Slowly, over time, as each Xtôti who was outside the system—and who had not ascended to the Grace—reached the end of their life cycle, their numbers dwindled, leaving only the Grace to remain."

Yoatl paused as a chime in the back wall sounded, and he touched another icon on the control panel. A length of the wall folded down out formed a long, narrow table. Several dishes of food slid out from inside the wall, and the smells wafted up to Justine's nose. Her stomach growled with hunger.

She couldn't identify the type of food Yoatl had ordered for them, and gave him a questioning look.

"It's called *biantha*. A vegetarian mash baked in a crusted bread container, which is also edible. Try it."

Justine did so, and the flavor exploded in her mouth. "Delicious," she said. "Tastes like a pot pie."

Yoatl took a bite before continuing his story around mouthfuls of food. "The Gliesans discovered Sol System by accident twelve-hundred-and-seventy-nine years ago."

Justine gaped. "You know that exactly?"

"Yes." Yoatl nodded. "The Galactic Law of non-interference had been in place since before the Gliesans Emerged. One of the ways that was enforced is through the star beacons themselves. Somehow, the Xtôti were able to 'lock' those beacons orbiting developing worlds. They are completely masked; our computers can't even detect them in the galactic grid. Any radio signals you send out are dampened at the outer limits of your system. You are, for all purposes, invisible to us until you Emerge.

"One Gliesan scouting ship, however, had been monitoring a lone Xtôti—even back then, they were rare. I do not blame the pilots for being curious. The Grace were so much more than celebrities; they were—are—like gods to us. So, when the Xtôti traveled to your system, temporarily activating your star beacon, the Gliesans recorded the location of your beacon. I'm certain they had no intention of breaking Galactic Law, but were rather 'star struck', as it were, and did the unthinkable: they followed the Xtôti to Sol System."

"They remained near your beacon while the Xtôti went to your planet. No one knows what his purpose was. However, there was a noticeable Aether event on your world several days into the visit, and the Gliesans raced to investigate. If the Xtôti were in trouble, they would try to help.

"Even though Aetherbeings cannot survive on a planetary body for long, the Gliesans took the risk and landed at the location where they'd detected the explosion. There was no sign of the Xtôti, but a small village had been irradiated by Aether. If left unaided, they would all die. The Gliesans are a very compassionate people, and though they knew their actions could be subject to penalties, they offered to take the afflicted villagers away to save their lives.

"Those humans," Yoatl said in conclusion, "were members of a Mayan tribe near Copán, Honduras."

"The 'Song'," Justine interrupted. "One of my friends who came with us to Centauri, Yaxche, was the keeper of an ancient story called The Song of the Stars. It contained the key to unlocking the power of Kinemet, but the story in it told of a time when the 'gods' abducted their people."

Smiling, Yoatl said, "I'm certain it would have seemed so to them."

Finishing the vegetable mash, Yoatl picked up the bread plate and took a bite out of it. "Many of the villagers had been exposed to lethal levels of Aether radiation. In such cases, transforming a person into an Aetherbeing is the cure. Once they cured the villagers, the Gliesans brought them here, to Skanse Aerie, where they lived out the remainder of their lives in comfort.

"There were several pairs of humans who had only been partially affected, and they were otherwise physically normal. They chose not to become Aetherbeings, and made their homes on Gliesan Prime. They were welcomed into their society, married and had children. Over time, our numbers grew to over six-thousand. Though our citizenship is officially Gliesan, many of us remember our Solan roots, though we may never visit the planet of our origin."

Justine had finished her bread plate as well, and a moment later, a second dish slid out from the recess in the wall. It was in a cup that looked like the same kind of bread as the entrée.

Yoatl made a happy sound. "Ah, desert. It's a kind of whipped desert made from the sap of one of their tropical plants. You can eat the utensil as well as the cup."

Justine tasted it and smiled. It had the consistency of rice pudding with a slight hint of syrup.

"About a century ago, several of us sought to reconnect with our roots. We formed the Solan Society. We petitioned the Parliament for permission to set up a spaceport in the nearest system to you, Centauri, for when you Emerged. Historically, most systems who discover Aetherflight naturally attempt to visit their closest neighbors.

"It was a little over ten years ago that our sensors detected the first traveler from Sol System, Alex Manez. Ah Tabai, one of the Solan Aetherbeings who had volunteered to become a Sentinel, had the privilege of making first contact. It was from his ship's computer that we were able to find out about your history. We have all been waiting for a second meeting with excitement."

"Ah Tabai is human?" Justine remarked. She'd originally been under the impression that he was a Gliesan.

Yoatl lowered his voice. "Yes. He is young and impetuous. I do not know how he convinced Aliah to accompany him; but should they return to Gliese, I fear they will be arrested."

"They were only trying to help us," Justine said.

"The Law is the Law." Yoatl raised both of his open hands in front of him. Then he offered Justine a conciliatory smile. "I will do what I can for them."

"Thank you."

Having finished dessert, Yoatl tapped on the console one more time, and the recess produced two small glasses of liquid, which seemed to change color from red to yellow.

"It's called *ljúka,*" he said as he passed one of the glasses to Justine. "The final course." With that, he picked up his own glass and drank it down in one motion.

Following suit, Justine was surprised at the taste. She'd been expecting something fruity and sweet, but the drink was slightly spicy. As it hit her stomach, she felt a tingle go through her. Whatever the drink was, it had the effect of reinvigorating her. Yoatl placed his empty glass back in the recess, and Justine did the same.

"That was very nice," she said, and Yoatl smiled. "Thank you for the meal."

"No thanks are necessary. It was my pleasure."

"So," Justine said, "what happens now?"

Considering his words, Yoatl rubbed a knuckle on his chin. "Now comes the hard part."

"Oh?"

"While you were resting, I received a message from the Collection's ambassador. One of the requirements before a system can be granted Emerged status is that you are able to travel outside light, utilizing the Grace. Since you did not, they have decided that Sol System has not yet Emerged."

Justine stared at him, wide-eyed, as she heard the news. The Collection had not even debriefed her. "Then they won't help us?"

"I'm afraid they will not. Not yet, anyway." He had a pained look on his face.

"And they won't let me go home, either," Justine said.

Yoatl nodded, his eyes cast down. "I'm sorry. You have been exposed to too much of our technology."

Feeling the frustration and anger grow in her, Justine willed herself to remain calm. From the moment she'd escaped from Lucis Observatory, everything that had happened had been out of her control. She'd done the best that she could to survive, but her personal survival wasn't enough, especially if the Kulsat invaded and destroyed Sol System.

Yoatl said, "Every effort will be made to ensure your comfort. They've assigned you permanent quarters on the station. Should you choose to, you may request work duties, though it is not mandatory. I would be honored if you would consider taking a position in the Solan Society."

"I don't want a job here," Justine said, then she gave him a hard look. "You're human; how can you just sit there when you know the Kulsat are going to wipe us all out?"

"I don't want that to happen any more than you, but I believe in the Law. Ah Tabai's scout ship accessed your database. The Collection is aware of your history. There are many conflicts in your world; it was one such that caused you to flee. If we were to extend the knowledge of Aether technology now, who can say if humans won't become the next Kulsat?"

She didn't want to hear those words, and though her first impulse was to deny the possibility, in her heart she knew humanity still had some maturing to do.

However, she believed they needed the time and opportunity to find their way in the galaxy. The Kulsat would destroy their future.

There had to be a way for Justine to stop them…

33

Sierra de las Minas :
Guatemala :

Alondo swept the spectrometer over the alien, and nodded to Michael. "It is made of Kinemet."

"How can that be?" Michael gasped. Kinemats, such as Alex, were altered at the molecular level by Kinemetic radiation. It seemed as if this creature—the Grace?—had a quantity of the element as part of its physiology.

What did that mean?

Michael's mind raced. Did the Grace have Kinemet as part of their natural biological makeup? Or had they figured out a way to infuse themselves with the element, and alter themselves on a genetic level? Was it because of this that they were able to create the network of star beacons? Or had the star beacons been there all along, despite the legends, and the Grace had somehow changed from a million years of exposure? If the Grace were made of Kinemet, then perhaps they would not decompose like a normal biological being; it was possible the Kinemet in them would sustain the body's cells until the element decayed slowly over hundreds of thousands of years, though the creature's brain would cease to function.

Another question entered his mind: if the Grace decayed rather than decomposed, then there should be millions of alien bodies strewn throughout the galaxy. There were not; what had happened to them? He recalled the story, how the alien had asked Subo Ak to cremate him. Is that how the Grace slowly disappeared? They came to a planet and arranged for their own death? Go out in a blaze of fire? Michael initially balked at the thought, but then he realized that he didn't truly understand their motivations.

He needed more information on the Grace, the Kulsat, and the origins of Kinemet. Everything he knew, he'd surmised from what little Ah Tabai had divulged before his death.

He wished fervently that George and Kenny were still alive. Both loved to speculate on such things. Often, throwing around ideas led them down paths none of them would think of on their own. Both were friends as well as colleagues.

As if assuming Michael had all the answers ready for the asking, Alondo waved his hand over the alien's body. "What does this mean?"

"It means there is no deposit of Kinemet for you to mine."

The other man frowned, and Michael could almost read the thoughts going through his mind. How would they be able to monetize this discovery? Selling Kinemet would be a straight black market trade, with a definitive value per quantity. Who wanted the alien body, and how much would they pay for it? It was a more complex proposition for Alondo, and he looked at Michael as if to ask for a hint on what the next step should be.

"There are only two governments that have the experience and resources to explore this discovery," Michael said. "USA, Inc. and Canada Corp. Do you want me to contact my superiors and set up a meet?"

Alondo scoffed at him. "Nice try, Mr. Sanderson. But I think we will make our own plans." He pointed at the alien. "How do you suggest we handle the body?"

"I would recommend we leave it as is for now. We have no idea what will happen if we alter the environmental conditions. Kinemet can be a volatile element. Exposure to sunlight can have a detrimental effect. We need to be extremely careful."

Together, the three of them filed out of the cave through the narrow crevice, Nadia taking the lead, followed by her brother, with Michael last.

When he reached the opening, Michael was blocked by Alondo's legs, and he suffered a moment of claustrophobia, wondering if the young criminal had decided to cut him out of the equation and leave him there.

Someone from outside the cave barked out an order in Spanish, *"¡Alejese!"* A moment later, Alondo stepped out of Michael's way.

Holding his breath, Michael pushed himself outside. His stomach knotted when he stood up and looked around. The entire area was surrounded by Guatemalan soldiers, all pointing their rifles at them.

The captain of the soldiers and Alondo exchanged several heated words in their native language, speaking too fast for Michael to understand. Even still, he got the impression that both men were familiar with each other.

After they finished their exchange, the soldiers put down their weapons. Alondo turned to Michael, his face red and his eyes narrow. "It seems our plans have been made for us."

Alondo shared a sour look with his sister. "All right. Let's get packed up."

∞

The captain left one squad of armed soldiers to secure the area while he directed the rest of his men to escort the Ruiz's and the others back to the base camp. Several more military trucks were in the area. A squadron of Guatemalan soldiers had taken over the operation.

Michael and the Ruiz siblings rode in one truck with the captain and four of his guards. Together, they headed away from the camp. Once they reached Los Amates, they turned east. A little over an hour later, they arrived at their destination, a beachfront estate on the Caribbean Sea.

During the trip, none of the soldiers spoke to them, and though both Alondo and Nadia whispered to one another, they ignored Michael.

Once they got out of the truck, the three of them were greeted by a small squad of Guatemalan soldiers, who escorted them to the main building.

Inside, dressed in the uniform of a general, a dark-haired, middle-aged man with a thin, black mustache, which drooped at the corners of his smiling mouth, stepped out from a side room and gave Michael a conciliatory nod of his head.

"Once again, I must apologize for your treatment. Welcome to my home."

Michael couldn't believe his eyes, and though he opened his mouth, no words came out.

Nadia, her voice cracking with shock, said, *"¿Papá?"*

"What are you doing here?" Alondo asked, more outraged than surprised. "I thought you were still in prison?"

Obviously enjoying himself, Oscar Ruiz made a dramatic bow and said, "I haven't been there for years, my son. It suited me to let the world believe I was still incarcerated. It gave me freedom to accomplish a great many things."

"Why didn't you tell us?" Nadia asked, then she frowned. "Is this why you would not permit us to visit you in La Granja?"

"I assure you, it was necessary. My apologies, my children. Of course, you will forgive me."

Both the siblings looked hesitant.

Then Oscar waved his hand at them. "Come, we have much to discuss, and my other guests are waiting."

Numbly, Michael let himself be led into the adjacent room. He guessed who was in the room before he got all the way inside.

Yaxche, Patli, and Humberto were sitting beside one another on a long couch, looking refreshed.

"Are you all right?" Michael asked Yaxche, his eyes encompassing all three of them.

"Ahyah," the old Mayan said with a grin. "We've been here since noon."

Humberto glared at Señor Ruiz. "Where are the others?"

"Do not worry yourself. I 'liberated' everyone from my children's custody and brought them here. Your injured friends are in another part of the complex being treated as we speak. You see, I am not an uncivilized man."

Oscar Ruiz gestured to a table with trays of meats, fruits and pastries. "Please, eat something. I must apologize if the coffee is not quite as good as what we grew on my plantation."

Alondo and Nadia made no move toward the refreshments, but Michael's stomach growled. He wasn't certain what Oscar's intentions were, but from his last encounter, he decided the man's sense of hospitality would prevent him from having his guests harmed out of hand.

Michael picked up a small dish and filled it with a few choice selections from the table. He found a chair and sat down.

Around the food in his mouth, Michael said, "You arranged to have me abducted at the airport."

"I prefer to say that I tried to extend an invitation to you, Mr. Sanderson, without the knowledge of the Honduran or Canadian authorities. I've been paying a great deal of money to ensure everyone thinks I am still incarcerated in La Granja Prison. If my 'old friend' Humberto had not interceded, we all could have saved a great deal of time."

He glanced at his children. "I am sorry if you have suffered in the past few years, but it was necessary to maintain the fiction. I know you are angry with me, but now that you are here, we will combine our efforts, and once again become prosperous."

"In Guatemala?" Alondo asked.

"Honduras is aligned too closely with the northern countries. The Cruzados are now nothing more than a group of nostalgic farmers and peasants—I'm sorry if that insults you, but it is the truth," he said to Humberto. "However, the CEO of Guatemala Departmental understands where the future is, and together, we are working to ensure our place in the Empire."

Michael had a sinking sensation in his gut. "The Solan Empire?"

He couldn't believe it. Somehow, Chow Yin had aligned himself with the government of Guatemala. Had this been his plan all along? Was this why he had really let Michael go, rather than simply to appease Alex? If so, how had Yin known what Michael's purpose was? Even Michael hadn't known what he was looking for until he got here. Or had Chow Yin merely been playing the long odds?

Oscar smiled. "I will answer all of your questions, Mr. Sanderson," he said, "and I will ensure your friends are returned to their homes in Honduras unharmed."

"I sense a condition," he said.

Nodding, Oscar said, "And I'm certain you can guess that condition."

During the long ride in the truck, Michael had plenty of time to think through the various possibilities. It all came down to one, however: possession of the alien body. Michael had hoped that no one knew the true purpose of his journey. Now that Oscar revealed that he was working for the Solan Empire, he knew a message would have already been dispatched to Chow Yin, informing him of the discovery.

He suddenly lost his appetite. "You want me to work for you."

"His Highness has sent word to provide you with the most state-of-the-art laboratory facilities and equipment available, and to extend every convenience to you. Your stay with me here will be comfortable, I assure you. Once you have completed your work, we will make arrangements to send your friends home."

Michael felt like he'd been kicked in the gut.

Alondo, the look of anger having changed to one of anticipation during the course of the conversation, said, "What of us, Father?"

"Ah," Oscar said. "I would like you to return to the dig site and take over once again. I am certain Mr. Sanderson will instruct you on the precautions you need to follow in order to transport the alien body here safely." He winked at his son. "It is time for me to take you under my wing, and mold you to become my heir in the new empire."

To Nadia, he said, "My daughter, I have a very important mission for you. With all our new guests, I require someone to run the household—" At her sour look, Oscar held up a hand to forestall any protest. "—and to liaise with the Guatemalan CEO's office as an official ambassador of the Solan Empire. Do you think you are up to the task?"

For the first time, Michael saw the young woman's eyes light up. It would be a prestigious position.

"Now," Oscar said to Michael, "you have to excuse me while I report the good news to His Highness."

Michael dropped the plate of food on the table, its contents uneaten, and shared a miserable look with Humberto. He'd been a pawn in Chow Yin's game all along.

34

Justine accompanied Yoatl to his apartment on another spire, where she met his wife, Ekthin. She was a dainty woman, who spoke with a very soft voice.

"Welcome to our home," she said by way of greeting. "I hope the outfits I chose are to your satisfaction."

"They're perfect." Justine grabbed the fabric of her top and stretched it out. "What's it made of?"

"There's a small species of animal on Gliese, similar to the opossums of Earth, that produces this for their nests. We've managed to synthesize the material. It's very durable and warm. We call it *swa.*"

Yoatl gestured to a living room area. "Come, make yourself comfortable. I hope you don't mind, but before I take you to your quarters, there are several of the Solan Society's members I would like you to meet. I hope that will be all right."

"After I retired from NASA, I got a job as a public relations hostess for diplomats and ambassadors." Justine laughed. "I am more than comfortable with crowds."

Smiling widely, Yoatl said, "Excellent. I will let them know you are ready to meet them."

∞

Justine spent the better part of the evening chatting with the dozen guests Yoatl invited. For the most part, they were more interested in her personal history than world events. They wanted to hear stories of her time in NASA as a pilot. Her history with Alex and Michael was a hot topic, but when she spoke about Yaxche, everyone grew excited.

"From what we've learned, we share common ancestry with him; his forefathers and ours were from the same region on Earth," one of the older men said. "I would have enjoyed meeting him."

"I didn't spend a lot of time with him," Justine said. "But he is very wise. I'm sure he'd love to meet you someday."

The evening went on for longer than Justine had expected, and when Yoatl finally announced that it was time for their guest of honor to retire, she was more than grateful.

Saying goodbye to the visitors took another hour, and by the time the last one was gone, Justine was exhausted.

He escorted her to another apartment at the end of the spire. "There was some debate on where to house you," he said. "The commander of the station thought you might be more comfortable with the other Aethers, but we convinced him you would adjust to life here faster if you were surrounded by Solans."

Justine didn't want to tell him that it didn't matter to her where they put her; she had no intention of adjusting to life on Skanse Aerie, as wondrous as it was. Instead, she smiled at him and shook his hand as they stopped outside the apartment door of her new quarters.

"Thank you," she said to him.

"I will come by tomorrow morning, and we can begin your orientation."

"That would be perfectly fine." Justine waved her hand over the protrusion on the wall—as she'd seen Yoatl do at his apartment—and her door slid open. They both said their good-nights, and Justine went inside.

She was too tired to take a full tour of the apartment, and only looked around long enough to spot the reclining platform. A few hours' meditation there was just what she needed.

∞

After resting, she explored her new quarters. There were four rooms. Besides the lavatory and reclining platform, there was a kitchen with a nest-shaped area for eating. Justine climbed on and played around with the console until the panel in the wall folded out. Pressing a few other buttons on the console produced a breakfast dish—at least, she hoped it was breakfast. A shallow container appeared in the recess, filled with something that looked to be of the same consistency as the vegetable mash from last night. She tasted it, and decided it was palatable. She remembered how to order water, though she would have preferred coffee—she had no idea if Gliese had anything like caffeine.

Once she'd eaten, she went to the large, central room that she decided was the main living area. There was some odd-looking furniture placed around the room. Instead of chairs, there were soft pedestals. She assumed the Gliesans were more comfortable perching on these than sitting. Yoatl's apartment had more earth-style furnishings, all designed for humans. She'd have to ask him about getting some for herself.

Along one wall, she recognized a computer area, set up similar to the one aboard the *Fainne*. Immediately, she sat down on the curved chair, and the holographic monitor flickered on.

It didn't look as if the computer had a synaptic interface, but she was just as comfortable tapping the controls with her fingers.

Previously, she'd researched the ancient history of the Kulsat. She needed more current information, and she spent the next hour scouring the Gliesan database for anything that would help her understand them, and provide her with a means of stopping them from destroying Sol System.

The Kulsat home world was largely a mystery to the rest of the galaxy. They were a highly paranoid society, and they had a contingent of several hundred warships guarding their star beacon at all times. The Collection sent Sentinel scout ships on reconnaissance to the Kulsat System on an unsystematic cycle. The ships would materialize in Kulsat space, take as many readings as they could, and fly back seconds before the Kulsat Risen could close access to the star beacon, and before the warships could fire on them.

Over the past several hundred years, major offensives had been launched. At one time, before the Aetherbeings worked out how to limit access to the star beacon, more than a dozen systems had sent thousands of Collection ships to attack Kulsat in a concerted effort.

They'd managed to get past the first line of defenses, but before they could meet the bulk of the Kulsat armada, every Kulsat ship that had been in other systems returned home. The Collection ships were trapped between the two forces, and had been decimated. It was the last time anyone had attempted to bring the fight to the enemy.

The Kulsat, with their numbers and technology, had attacked and destroyed over ten-thousand cultures since the war had started a millennium ago.

So far, the only effective defense against them was to remain as unnoticeable as possible, and not to pose an immediate threat. As in Gliese, all star systems maintained a permanent patrol around their star beacon. Should it activate from any Kulsat-occupied system, the Aetherbeings would all work together to suppress access through the star beacon. Although the technique was effective against an armada, it would not stop a small number of ships from passing through. There was always a military presence on hand to deal with such situations.

In order for Sol System to defend itself, it would require enough Kinemats to do the same thing to their star beacon, and they would need a fleet of warships to interdict any Kulsat who managed to get through the restricted opening. Also, they would need to understand the technology the other systems had developed to read and control the star beacons. For all Justine knew, that could take years...

Growing despondent in the knowledge of what seemed like insurmountable odds, Justine called up some non-military information, wondering if there was some other way to defeat the undefeatable force.

As a society, the Kulsat evolution was driven by necessity. Their home world, mostly oceanic, was a harsh environment, filled with dozens of underwater predators. In their history, the Kulsat were easy prey, and had needed to develop the ability to use tools and weapons to ensure their survival.

Their progress had been geared toward industrial endeavors, and their social structure was based on technological merit; the more advanced they were, the higher their chance to protect their species against their enemies—and they considered any non-Kulsat an enemy. It was almost as if they had a genetic predisposition toward paranoia.

One social theorist in the Collection posited that meeting the Grace would have been one of the most frightening experiences in Kulsat history: a force so far advanced that they were completely at their mercy. As with many militaristic cultures, the Kulsat, realizing they were powerless, had become subservient to the Xtôti, biding their time until their own technology advanced to the point where they no longer felt threatened.

Once the Xtôti died off, the Kulsat had begun a thousand-year campaign of expansion and domination that terrorized the galaxy.

Justine lifted her head when she heard the chime at her door, and quickly stepped over to answer it. Yoatl was waiting for her.

"I trust you had a restful night?" he asked.

Nodding, Justine said, "Yes. I have to say, that hammock is one of the most comfortable beds I've ever been in. I just wish I could experience sleep; then I could take full advantage of it."

"It's an extension of the nests the prehistoric Aves made. Warm, supportive, and protective." Yoatl crooked his head. "Have you thought about my offer to join the Solan Society? We're much more than just a casual affiliation of humans; many Aves are also members. We are strong advocates for future ties between Gliese and Sol, when they eventually become members of the Collection."

"That does sound promising," Justine said. Although Yoatl had already shown that he was a man who believed in the Galactic Law, and would not go against it, there might be others who were more sympathetic, and could provide Justine with other means to accomplish her goal: stopping the Kulsat.

"Before we do anything else, is there any way I can see Red Spot, and see if she's all right?"

"Of course," Yoatl said with a kind smile. "Though they have not been afforded nearly as much privilege as you, the Kulsat have been granted official refugee status from the Parliament. We can head there right away, if you like."

"Yes, please."

Stepping back to give Justine enough room to exit her apartment and join him in the long hall, he said, "On an interesting side note, Gliese has been, historically, very welcoming to species from other worlds. I believe nearly eight percent of the Gliesan citizenship are xenomorphic in origin. Should Red Spot and the others desire to work toward citizenship, they would be the first Kulsat in the history of Gliese to do so." A moment later, he added, "I'm sure, if you should decide to apply for citizenship, we could push for a quick approval. There are only five Solan Aetherbeings—including Ah Tabai—I'm certain you could become a role model, and perhaps convince others to attempt the conversion."

"Only five?" Justine asked.

"The Solans on Gliese are highly family-oriented, and we have kept many of our ancestral traditions, including a great reverence for nature. The sacrifice of being away from home and hearth for the rest of one's life is a difficult decision to make. I believe the Solan Society would gain political status with the Parliament if we could contribute more to space industries."

They'd reached the central hub of the station, and Yoatl directed Justine to another platform that floated above the large area and ended near the entrance of a guarded spire.

Two Gliesans looked up as they approached, and one of them faced Yoatl. "Ambassador," he said, shooting a glance at Justine. "We weren't expecting you."

Yoatl gave the guard a polite nod. "Last-minute decision to see to our other new guests."

"One moment, please."

The other guard tapped something on a podium in front of him. Justine assumed it was a computer or a communications console, because a few moments later, the guard nodded to his colleague. "The commander has cleared them for visitation."

The first guard stepped aside for them. "I trust you know the way, Ambassador?"

Yoatl said, "Thank you, yes. I promise, next time, I'll get my office to clear it first."

"Pleasant day to you," the guard said, and then took up his position in front of the entrance once again.

The spire itself was far more utilitarian than the others, designed more for efficiency than for esthetics. It was unmistakably a military area. The long canyon-like hallway with the ceiling projection of the other spires was not in evidence. Yoatl led Justine to the automatic transport platform and both stepped on, patiently waiting as the conveyor took them all the way to the top of the spire. Instead of narrow corridors connecting the transport platform to the main body of the spire, there were wide hangar-like bay doors. Many of them were open to allow quick access for the hundreds of Gliesan soldiers, mechanics, engineers, clerks and supervisors as they went about their duties.

"Kulsat gravity is slightly higher than Gliese," Yoatl explained. "We have the last segment of the spire sectioned off and converted to a self-contained water environment as closely matched to their home world as we could. There's plenty of space for all of them, though quite of few of the Kulsat have had to double-up until we can install more individual domiciles."

When they reached the last section, they were stopped again by two more guards who took biosignature readings before allowing Yoatl and Justine in.

A small hallway led to a glass viewing area.

"There's a visual monitor on the inside and a computer interface for the Kulsat to use. Their interpersonal communication is based entirely on a complex sign language. Their written language is technical in nature, and was developed mostly to forward their industrial advances. Even with our communication computers, things sometimes get lost in translation."

Though the glass covered the wall in the room, it didn't show the entire water environment on the other side. There was a rocky wall that obscured the view. Even the Kulsat deserved a little privacy.

As a small Kulsat swam by, oblivious to the two humans standing on the dry side of the glass, Yoatl, raising his voice a notch, spoke in the direction of a receiver jutting out of the floor in front of the glass.

"Hello, my name is Yoatl. I am the Gliesan Ambassador to Sol. I would like to speak to Red Spot, if she is available."

The small Kulsat turned to them, approached the computer on his side, and tapped on the console.

"I will inform her of your presence. You will wait here."

He swam off, and Justine shared a look with Yoatl. He said, "They are a very old society. Even though they are in our space, and confined in our facility, Kulsat sensibility still considers all non-Kulsat beings as inferior. Diplomacy is not one of their priorities."

Soon, a familiar Kulsat approached. Justine recognized her from her unique marking right away, but she saw that one of Red Spot's tentacles was hanging limp under her as she swam closer.

"Are you injured?" Justine asked, casting a glance at Yoatl to see if he was aware of this development. He looked as concerned and surprised as she was.

Red Spot typed. "We have had a minor conflict between us. Several of the other Potentials were outraged that we surrendered. They launched an attack. There were casualties. Two Deficients and one Potential were killed in the fighting."

"In the fighting?" Justine said. "When did this happen?"

"We resolved the situation," Red Spot responded.

At that, Yoatl said in a tight voice, "I'll alert the guards. There should be safeguards in place to prevent this. I'll be right back." With that, he strode out of the room.

Turning back to Red Spot, Justine said, "I'm sorry this happened to your people."

"It is fortuitous it occurred," Red Spot typed. "I have established command as senior Potential. The other Kulsat will not rebel again. The Deficients have sworn fealty to me as well. We will continue."

"I don't know what to say." Justine took a step toward the glass and put her hand on the surface. She had no idea if Red Spot could sense her sincerity. "You saved my life; I don't want to see you—or any of the others—hurt."

"Gratitude, Justine. The Gliesans have provided the necessities. There is no cause for further concern."

Just then, Yoatl came back into the viewing room. "It looks like the fight took place out of sight of the security monitors. The guards are sending in medical staff to see what they can do to help, and to retrieve the bodies. Unfortunately, there was nothing they could do to prevent the fight."

Red Spot typed. "It is an internal matter, Ambassador. Interference is not required."

"Of course," Yoatl said.

To Justine, it seemed as if Red Spot had not extended her trust to anyone besides her. She asked, "Is it possible for Red Spot and me to speak in private? Do the translators record our conversation?"

Yoatl gave her a considering look. "As refugees, and not prisoners, the Kulsat do have more rights under Gliesan law. Privacy is one of those rights." He seemed on the verge of asking a question, but then smiled and gave Justine a bow of his head instead. "I'll wait outside for you."

"Thank you, Yoatl."

When he'd gone, Justine spoke to Red Spot. "I don't want to ask you to do anything to betray your people, but I need to protect my world. I need to warn them that your military will attack them."

"It is understandable. While I do not agree with our policy to attack un-Emerged systems, I do not know how I may assist you, Justine."

Taking a deep breath, she said, "I have given the Gliesans my word that I would not seek to learn about their Aether technology, and I don't believe in breaking my word. Their Galactic Law forbids sharing, but since the Kulsat do not subscribe to that Law…"

"Of course, Justine," Red Spot typed, catching on to the loophole.

"I will be glad to teach you everything I know about the Gift and the path to becoming a Risen being."

"Thank you," Justine said, but she was interrupted. Red Spot continued typing.

"However, warning your system of our attack will be futile. Our warships are far too powerful. They outnumber you. They will crush anything your technology can send against them. If you wish to save your home system, there is only one way."

"What do I have to do?"

"You must stop the Kulsat Risen."

Justine laughed. "That's the number-one question on everyone's mind: how to accomplish that."

"The answer is obvious, Justine," Red Spot typed. "Obtain the final component."

35

Caribbean Coast :
Guatemala :

Over the next few weeks, Michael worked in an underground laboratory on the coastal property.

True to his word, Señor Ruiz provided him with the most up-to-date diagnostic equipment with which to study the alien. Michael's expertise was more in the fields of planetary geology and astrophysics.

Two lab assistants arrived to assist. When they saw the alien body for the first time, they both stood and stared for several minutes, their mouths open in shock. After recovering, they started to babble uncontrollably, as excited as children in a theme park.

One of the assistants was a biochemist from the Universidad de San Carlos de Guatemala. His name was Felipé, an older man who spent a great deal of his time talking about his fishing boat, and where he was going to sail once he retired with the money he was making from this job.

The other was Tristán, a young biologist from La Aurora Zoo who had spent a few years in oceanographic exploration. He was the one who quickly categorized the alien, surmising it had evolved from a creature much like the *protostegidae* family."

"A sea turtle?" Felipé asked. "But it has no shell."

Tristan smiled. "Look at this x-ray." He pointed. "Obviously, over time, it no longer needed the shell for protection, and it gradually shrank. There's still the remnant of a carapace running along the spine of the creature. It's sub-dermal, but it's most definitely a shell under its skin. Very similar to the *dermochelys coriacea*—the leatherback turtle."

The two debated and speculated on the origins of the species. What kind of environment did it come from? What level of intelligence had it achieved? What cultural dynamic had it developed? How had it managed to be buried on Earth? The one thing they agreed on was that it had evolved on a different planet, in another solar system.

While Michael listened to their conversations, and sometimes joined in the discussion, he was far more interested in a completely different aspect of the alien's physiology. Namely, that every cell in its body contained a single molecule of altered Kinemet.

Very quickly, they determined that the element would have to have been introduced some time after physical birth; the Kinemet, while providing a constant source of energy to the cells, also had the effect of halting the aging process.

It took Michael well over a week of inputting and collating data from the thousands of diagnostics they performed to conclude that the infusing of raw Kinemet into these creatures would increase their normal lifespan by a factor of thousands.

Was that the legacy the Kulsat sought? Virtual immortality? If that conclusion was accurate, then where had the Grace gone? Certainly, not all of them had strayed too close to the gravitational well of a planet, where the forces that played on the cells would be too strong for any physical being to endure. That, they decided, had been the cause of death in this case. Kinemet was such a heavy element that the proximity to Earth, and the strain of its geomagnetic force, had caused the cells to overload.

No, there had to be another explanation for the fate of this race, the ancient beings that had explored space and created tens of thousands of star beacons to connect the galaxy.

Michael wrestled with these questions during the day, and they even pervaded his thoughts in the evenings, when he ate dinner with Yaxche and Patli. Michael wasn't permitted to speak to anyone else. All information about the outside world was restricted from them.

Humberto was secured in another building with his two Cruzado friends—they were all still considered a threat. Humberto had effected Michael's escape once before. Señor Ruiz would not make that same mistake again.

Every morning, Michael had to give a progress report to Oscar Ruiz, who would then presumably pass it along to Chow Yin.

Michael dreaded the day he made the final connection. His initial exultation at the realization of the relationship between the Xtôti and Kinemet was quickly marred by the fact that he knew he could not keep the information from his captors for long.

He suspected the Kulsat did not want the secret of the Grace merely to extend their lives. They wanted it for something far more powerful. Something that could, and would, change the entire order of the galaxy.

The discovery happened quite unintentionally.

Since Michael did not have access to any Kinemet for experimentation, he extracted a few of the alien's skin cells—using a high-density laser set a frequency he knew would not cause a reaction with Kinemet.

The problem arose when he tried to separate the Kinemet from the biological cells. The element was bound to the cell at a subatomic level.

For two days, Michael struggled with the problem, but nothing he did could extract the Kinemet. It was as if it had become an integral part of the alien's physiology.

One of the known reactors to Kinemet was hydrogen photons. Michael decided to see what would happen to the Kinemet-infused cell when bombarded with hydrogen photons.

He set up his experiment on the other side of the lab, away from the alien's corpse, in a vacuum-sealed container.

Before he initiated the emitter to produce the photons, there was an explosion from outside the lab. For a split-second, Michael thought his experiment might have caused it, but there was no possible way for that to happen.

His alarm turned to fear when he heard the distinct sound of machine-gun fire. The complex was under attack.

He ran to the window and lifted one of the blinds to look outside. It looked like a battlefield in the compound. Dozens of guerrilla soldiers were storming the property. Cruzados? How had they tracked the captives here?

A stray bullet splintered the wall beside Michael, and he jumped back with a start.

Something bright caught his eye, and he realized the bullet had hit the hydrogen emitter. Sparks flew from the unit, and it caught on fire, which spread quickly.

When the fire burned through the container, the Kinemet in the skin cells he'd extracted grew bright.

Instinctively, Michael backed away, remembering Patli's story. Even though there were only a few molecules of Kinemet on the table, the reaction could be highly energetic.

Then Michael felt a sudden heat from behind him, from the alien body. It was glowing.

He checked the computer display monitoring the cells. Somehow, the Kinemet in the skin cells Michael had removed were entangled with the Kinemet still in the alien's body. What happened to one cell, happened to all the cells.

That was his last thought before a wave of Kinemetic radiation rapidly filled the room, completely encompassing Michael. He did not even have time to scream before he was entirely consumed.

∞

When Michael woke up, he felt like the weight of the world was pressing down on him. He was being crushed, but when he opened his eyes, he saw that there was nothing on top of him.

A sensation went through him then, and for the first time, he felt a tiny fraction of what Alex felt, of what those soldiers Klaus had experimented on felt, and what the ancient Mayan villagers had felt.

Michael was irradiated. He didn't have any of the powers of a Kinemat, because he wasn't converted.

There was a tickle at the edge of his consciousness. But, like a half-formed thought, whatever was there eluded him. He could not fully identify what the connection was.

There came a sober realization, though, when Michael struggled to breathe.

He was going to die.

A stream of light cut through the room, and a shadowy figure entered. Hastily, it approached him.

"Michael?" Humberto asked. "You are alive. The Cruzados have found us. They are liberating us. We will be home soon."

"How?"

Smiling, Humberto said, "At Alondo's ranch, Diego and Migel managed to get word to my men in Honduras, who contacted some of our friends in the government here. There's a revolution going on in the Guatemalan capital—it seems not everyone was on board with the CEO's policies, nor his involvement in the kidnapping of Honduran and Canadian citizens. Both our governments are sending troops to police the transition. The Guatemalan army got new orders this morning to liberate this complex. They've already arrested Oscar. Both

Alondo and Nadia have been killed."

Then he gave Michael a concerned look. "Are you all right?"

Michael was barely able to whisper. "Something's wrong. I can't move."

"Are you paralyzed?"

"No," Michael said. "I can feel everything, but it feels like I weigh a hundred kilotons."

Humberto looked down at him with a helpless expression.

"The alien," Michael said. "Is it still there?"

Standing up, Humberto glanced at the metal table that once held the alien body. "No. Where did it go?"

"It reacted when the emitter caught on fire. Now, I'm irradiated with Kinemet. I won't survive this."

"I will get one of the other scientists—"

"No. Listen to me," Michael said. "Come closer."

He was finding it more difficult to breathe with every passing moment.

"What is it?" Humberto asked.

"You need to get a message to Alex Manez. I don't know how. He's being held on a mining station in the asteroid belt by Emperor Yin."

"What do you want me to tell him?"

"Tell him what happened here, that the alien's DNA was infused with Kinemet." His lungs felt thick, as if he were drowning. "It's some kind of entanglement. That's the secret."

Humberto grasped Michael's arm. "What's happening to you?"

"Promise me," he said to Humberto. "Only for Alex's ears. No one else must know."

"I promise," Humberto said, but Michael could not hear him.

36

Qin Station :
Sol System :

Over the next two weeks, the guards shadowed Alex's every move. He was confined to the lab, and Sian was locked in the experiment room with guards of his own. Apparently, Emperor Yin didn't want the young programmer to do anything foolish, such as harm himself. Sian was no longer trusted to work on the project independently, so the final setup was left to Alex.

Checking Alex's progress every step of the way, Alice never failed to flash him a condescending smile. The entire time he was setting up the first trial, Alex couldn't stop remonstrating with himself. If the situation hadn't been so dire, he could have blamed it on his screwed-up physiology causing him to think with his emotions rather than his logic. A part of him recognized that he might have wanted to believe in Alice's change of heart despite her history.

The game hadn't changed, just the players. The Kulsat were still on their way at any moment in the future, and Alex could not hold out hope that anyone on Earth would be able to crack the code and develop an army of Kinemats to stop both Chow Yin and the impending alien invasion. For all he knew, Justine was dead, and no one on the Gliesan home world had any idea what had happened.

At the back of his mind, he still nurtured the possibility that he would be able to find a way out of his predicament. He couldn't give over to despair.

While he prepared for the first experiment, he kept coming back to the conversation he'd had with Alice. Her theory that the star beacons were inter-dimensional devices had some merit, but there was a nagging thought that it wasn't exactly the correct answer.

Back on Canada Station Three, when he and Kenny performed their unauthorized experiments, Alex had been lost in some otherness that he couldn't explain. Yaxche had called it a spirit walk, a dream state—though Alex had not been able to sleep or dream since the moment he'd been exposed to Kinemet on Macklin's Rock.

There were so many ancient myths and legends about the nature of the universe that it was difficult to sift through all of them. One aspect penetrated them all, however: that there was a level beyond the physical plane, something to which all humanity could and should endeavor to attain.

The problem Alex had with that idea was how the star beacons played into it. Were they some kind of bridge to an alternate level of existence? He found it hard to believe that something so tangible and prevalent was the answer.

Though he only had Ah Tabai's very brief account of the history of the galaxy, it seemed the Grace were a terrestrial species. They were not gods; they'd merely attained a significant level of scientific advancement.

If they had created the star beacons, then there had to be another explanation for how they worked. The words 'outside light' kept playing over and over in his head.

He knew there was some kind of physical explanation for the star beacon's mechanism; there was no need to get into the metaphysical or mystical to find the answer.

Once Alex had completed all the calculations for the first Kinemetic conversion trial, he informed one of the guards, who immediately spoke into a communications chip on his wrist.

Within a few minutes, Alice arrived.

Behind her, several workers carted in a large container made of a transparent thermoplastic. Big enough to fit a person, it was hooked up with several electronic wires and circuits. A small tube inserted in the back of the container led to an oxygen tank. The only opening was the door, which was electromagnetically sealed.

Alex instinctively knew what the container was. "A Kinemetic damper?"

Nodding, Alice said, "Well, we want you on hand to observe the experiment, but the moment we lift the damping field in the lab, you would have the ability to thwart the experiment."

Sourly, Alex spoke in a low voice. "We can't have that, can we?"

Pretending not to hear him, Alice said, "Unfortunately, my father is attending other business, so we'll postpone the trial until later this evening."

From the small room, Sian watched on through the window. Alex could feel his despair.

Another person entered the lab. Doctor Naysmith, his perpetually good-humored smile on his face, gave Alex a nod as he passed by and headed for Sian.

"What's going on?" Alex asked.

Alice said, "We need to be sure there's nothing physically wrong with him. There can be nothing that will skew the results of the test."

While the doctor performed a thorough examination of Sian, Alice ordered the guards to set up the lab for the experiment, placing chairs facing the experiment room window, and setting up monitors so everyone watching could follow the progress of the trial. Alex wondered how many people were going to be there.

Since no one seemed to be paying attention to him, Alex took a step toward the lab door, but a sharp-eyed guard spotted him and snapped his weapon up, the barrel of his rifle pointed at his head.

Alice snickered. "Perhaps you would be more comfortable waiting on the other side of the lab. Lie down on your cot and get some rest. You don't want to miss the show."

Feeling as helpless as he'd ever been, Alex retreated to the cot and sat down, but there was no way he was going to get any rest. Inside, he was far too frustrated and angry.

He willed himself to think about something else, and came back to that nagging sensation that had been haunting him since CS3.

How could something be 'outside light'?

Light was simply electromagnetic radiation. Human senses could only detect a relatively small band of its wavelength.

Was Ah Tabai talking about the absence of light? If so, then how did that relate to being in a photonic state? Did the star beacons negate the effects of the quantum drive?

Alex shook his head. That didn't explain anything. The travel between the star beacons was, as far as he knew, instantaneous.

What about the opposite end of light? Gamma rays were at the top of the spectrum. The galaxy was flooded with their bursts, whether from black holes or hypernovae. Many of the corresponding frequencies in the Song of the Stars were charted among the gamma wavelengths. It was these frequencies they were going to use on the sample of Kinemet and change its physical properties to the point where, once bombarded with hydrogen photons, it could properly irradiate a person, in turn altering their physiology where they became sensitive to light and all things in the electromagnetic spectrum.

Was there something beyond gamma rays? Some high-energy wave that had previously been undetected, which was somehow used to create the star beacons, much as a Kinemat was created? When Macklin's Rock had traveled through Sol System at near light speeds, the readings Justine's crew had taken of the star beacon they'd dubbed *Dis Pater* was off the charts.

What could possibly produce that much energy?

The thought vanished from his mind when he realized someone was standing over him, a personable smile on his face.

"Doctor Naysmith?" Alex said.

"And how are you today, young man?"

Frowning, Alex glanced over at Sian. "How can you pretend to care, when you know he could die from this experiment?"

The perpetual smile on the doctor's face wavered for a fraction of a second. He cocked his head. "From my understanding, he could live."

Looking up sharply, Alex stared into the doctor's eyes.

Doctor Naysmith said, "Everyone has the right to medical treatment. Now, your checkup has been overdue. If you will permit me, I would like to scan you."

His first impulse was to continue haranguing the doctor, but then Alex realized he would only be wasting his breath.

The doctor pressed a sensor against the side of Alex's neck and looked at the readout on his holoslate.

"Hmm," Doctor Naysmith said, for the first time looking concerned.

"What is it?" Alex asked, wondering if the time away from the influence of Kinemet was starting to drain him.

"Your blood pressure is a bit high."

Laughing involuntarily, Alex shook his head. "Is that it?"

"Well," the doctor said, reaching into a pocket of his lab coat and withdrawing a hypodermic gun. "According to my records, your diet is well within guidelines. It could just be the stress of the day, but there's always the possibility of hypertension. I'd like to inject you with a micro-monitor. It will record your blood pressure over the next twenty-four hours and send the results to my lab."

Without waiting for consent, the doctor pressed the tip of the gun against the inside of Alex's wrist and pressed the trigger. Alex let out a short cry and rubbed the spot until the pain dissipated.

Putting the hypodermic gun back in his pocket, the doctor said, "If the area becomes irritated, let me know."

Alex looked up as Alice approached. She glanced back and forth between him and the doctor. "Everything all right?" she asked.

The doctor gave her a warm smile. "Right as rain."

"Good," she said, and looked at Alex as she pointed to the glass cage. "My father will be here soon. It's time to start."

∞

When Alex realized he was pacing like a caged animal in the glass encasement, he willed himself to stand still. He watched as Alice and several technicians set up for the first trial on Sian.

Though the young programmer was in the experiment room on the other side of the laboratory, Alex could see the worry on his face. He didn't blame him. There was an even chance that Sian would suffer an agonizing death by being subjected to the Kinemetic radiation. Going through all of his calculations in his head once more, Alex could not think of any way to eliminate one or the other of the two sequences. The trial was the only way.

When Alex had been exposed to the Kinemetic radiation on Macklin's Rock, he'd been partially shielded by the electromagnetic barriers in the TAHU, which was specifically designed to protect against the numerous radioactive waves floating through Sol System. If not for that shielding, Alex knew he would have died as his parents had, since the Kinemet had not been primed before activation. It was a cruel truth.

Absently, he scratched at the spot on his wrist where Doctor Naysmith had injected the micro-monitor. When he looked down, he saw the skin had turned a faint shade of red. It was probably caused by the rubbing and scratching.

Alice stood in front of the communication panel on one wall, her hands balled into fists and resting on her hips. She exchanged a few heated words with whomever was on the other end, but Alex couldn't make out what she was saying through the glass.

Finally, she turned to look at Alex, and then a moment later strode over to him. There was an intercom system set up on the encasement, and she pressed the button to turn on the microphone. Her voice came through the speaker set high up on the glass wall.

"Well, it looks as if we're going to have to start without His Highness." She did not attempt to hide her bitterness. "We're to record the trial for playback later. I can't imagine what is more important right now."

"Why not postpone?" Alex said.

She gave him an irritated glare. "No. We'll do this now. It will only take a few more minutes to set up the recorders. I'll have a monitor brought up here so you can follow the progress of the trial. If there is any anomaly, you will let us know right away."

"Of course," Alex said with a terse nod.

Alice narrowed her eyes. "Do I need to remind you that any trickery will earn you swift punishment?"

Though Alex did not want any harm to come to Sian, the logical side of him knew this trial was necessary. Once the procedure for creating a Kinemat was ascertained, they could begin creating a defensive force against the Kulsat.

"I know what's at stake," Alex said. "You don't have to threaten me."

A look of annoyance crossed Alice's face, showing Alex that she didn't completely believe him. Someone who had gone through what Alice had would most likely never lose that level of paranoia.

As the Emperor's daughter walked off to oversee the last-minute details, Alex found himself scratching at his wrist again. The skin was turning bright red. He wondered if he should get the doctor back into the lab to have a look. Instead, he made a conscious effort to thrust his hands in his pockets and not scratch.

After fifteen more minutes of prep, Alice and a technician wheeled a monitoring station over to the glass cage and positioned the screen so that Alex could see the readout. The display showed a score of diagnostics, including Sian's vital signs, the ambient temperature in the experiment room, the luminosity, gravity, air pressure and content levels. From his first summary glance, Alex couldn't see anything out of the ordinary.

"All right," Alice said through the intercom after one of the technicians gave her thumbs-up sign. "Alex, we're going to bring in the Kinemet sample now, so we'll be turning on the damper in your encasement. The shielding will cut off all electromagnetic waves, including the speaker system. If you feel the experiment needs to be aborted before the priming, knock on the glass three times. Once I engage the priming sequence, there's no turning back."

Alex nodded that he understood her. She took a few steps away and sat down at a nearby workstation.

A minute later, he heard a slight hum of the electromagnetic shielding indicating the Kinemetic damper was engaged. He saw Alice press another command on her console, presumably to disengage the lab's damper.

A technician wheeled a trolley, with a sealed container resting on top, through the main door. It must be the Kinemet. Though it was very close, Alex could not sense the radiation from the metal. Just knowing it was there sent a sensation of longing through him. It'd been days since he'd been in the presence of the Kinemetic radiation. Like a junkie, his entire body ached for it.

Pushing the trolley into the experiment room, the technician donned a radiation suit before transferring the container to the priming station. Sian, strapped onto the operating table in the middle of the room, tried to turn his head to see what was happening, but he couldn't find the right angle. Alex could imagine the man's fear, and he swallowed the sudden surge of guilt that coursed through him.

Exiting the room, the technician closed the door behind him. Alice hit another command key, and the window blackened. The only images those in the lab could see were on their monitors, which would blank the moment the reaction took place.

Alice programmed in the first formula sequence, and Alex watched on his monitor as the milligram of Kinemet—magnified several hundred times by the camera—was bombarded with a series of electromagnetic waves. The display indicated the Kinemet was transforming its elemental signature on a microscopic scale.

Everything was going as Alex expected, except that his wrist felt like it was on fire.

He pulled his hands out of his pockets and grew alarmed when he saw the red blotch on his skin had tripled in size. There was a large lump forming, as if he'd developed some kind of sebaceous cyst.

Was the minute amount of Kinemetic radiation in his system

reacting with the micro-monitor?

Unable to help the impulse, Alex scratched at the spot, which was turning white at the top. Pressing down, he detected something hard under his skin. It felt like a metal sphere. There was a sudden flare of heat, and the capsule popped open.

The sensation that went through Alex was completely unexpected.

It was raw Kinemet inside the capsule, at least a half a gram. The doctor had not injected him with a monitor. He'd given him a strong dose of the kinetic metal—enough to power him for several months. The doctor? Alex wondered. Was he a saboteur? An agent? Whatever his motivation, had he not known that the greatest weapon against the Emperor was a fully irradiated Kinemat?

Starved from the lack of radiation, Alex could almost feel every fiber of his being soak in the effects.

The electromagnetic shielding around the cage was set to the lowest level in an effort to minimize any effect it might have on the trial. That level was more than enough to contain the trace radiation Alex previously had in his system. Now, however, with raw Kinemet surging through his system, the damper field was like a thin sheet of paper against a hammer.

Instinctively, Alex pushed against the shielding, and the damping coils burst above the glass encasement.

Alice and the other technicians jumped at the sound and spun around to see what was happening.

The door of the cage was no longer electromagnetically sealed, and Alex slammed his shoulder into it. Bursting open, the door hit a technician who had rushed over to stop Alex.

The impact sent the technician reeling backward toward Alice and her command console.

She shrieked as the man flailed about to get his balance, and threw up her arms protectively.

In the chaos, the tech must have hit the door lock command to the experiment room, and it unsealed and rolled back with an electric hum.

Out of the corner of his eye, Alex saw on his monitor that the priming sequence was complete.

"No!" Alice screamed, trying to reach for the failsafe button on her console to stop the Kinemetic trigger.

Without the Kinemetic damper in the experiment room to shield them from the reaction, they would all be exposed to the Kinemetic process.

The entire lab was bathed in a blinding light as that section of Qin Station, and everyone in the area, quantized.

37

Skanse Aerie :
Gliese System :

Over the next few weeks, Justine acclimated to life on the station. During the days, she worked with the Solan Society in a diplomatic capacity, meeting with ambassadors of hundreds of other worlds to strengthen future ties between Sol and the other systems when the day finally came that Sol System gained membership in the Collection of Worlds.

At first, encountering so many new life forms had been overwhelming, and she was certain she'd committed dozens of social *faux pas*, but with her increased capacity for learning, she quickly overcame her anxiety and awkwardness.

Within a short time, Yoatl was able to get the Collection to recognize Justine as the Envoy of Sol System. While this did not give her any significant power in the Collection, it did give her a voice, and increased her status in the Solan Society.

When she wasn't establishing relationships with other worlds, Justine spent time with the Gliesan-humans, talking to them about Solan culture, history, science and politics. As Yoatl had hoped, her stories of their home system inspired several of their younger members to enlist in the Gliesan Space Force and undertake Aether training. It would be years before they were ready to become pilots, but it was a step in the right direction.

Justine also spent some time with the other human Aetherbeings in the system, and though they were restricted from discussing Gliesan Aether technology, they were allowed to help Justine learn more about her altered physiology—aspects common to all beings who had undergone the quantization process.

While in physical form, Aetherbeings were unable to sleep in the classic sense of the term, but they still required rest and time for their minds to process all the information of the day. They showed her meditation techniques that proved quite effective in giving her both requirements. During her four-year flight from Sol to Centauri, Justine had been fully conscious; there had been times she thought she was going to go mad from boredom and loneliness. When they'd learned of her extended time in Aetherspace, the others had been alarmed, and wondered that she hadn't gone insane. Aethers rarely spent more than twelve hours at a time in the Aetherstate.

"Books," Justine told them. "I was able to recall every book I ever read. They kept me company."

One of the human Aetherbeings, Na Huama, told her that word had come through the ranks that the Kulsat had posted a single warship to patrol the Centauri System. It was likely the ship would remain there for months, perhaps even years. The Sentinels, Fairamai and Naila, decided to go on reconnaissance trips to Centauri once every few days to check on their enemy's status.

In her off-hours, Justine visited Red Spot and went over the plan to get back to Sol System. She also undertook the training she needed to accomplish that goal.

One of her first questions was what the final component was.

"We do not know, specifically," Red Spot told her. "It was a tool of subjugation. With it, the Xtôti were able to nullify the Gift."

"Like a damper?"

"A damper will only suppress the power. We have devices that will quell the Gift from an enemy or their vessel, but it is a temporary effect. Whatever technology the Xtôti had, if they used it on a ship, it would render the Gift permanently inert—whether it was in a quantum engine, or in a Risen. If a ship were too far from a station or planet, it would never return. Any Risen exposed to this technology would perish."

If the Kulsat had that technology, they would be able to eliminate any other system's ability to travel between stars. With that kind of threat, no world would dare to resist the Kulsat.

The alien didn't have any more information other than that, and Justine was left with only speculation on how she could identify the final component.

"What if it's not on my home world?" Justine asked.

"Then you will have to continue searching other worlds until you find it. Our people have the advantage in that we are the only race looking for the final component."

She listened as the alien went into minute detail over the Kulsat training exercises for Potentials. Though Red Spot only knew the theories, she was able to convey to Justine many techniques of control while in Risen form.

Justine practiced quantizing herself. Red Spot, along with several other Kulsat, volunteered to let her practice on them as well. Soon, Justine could quantize twelve of the aliens at a time, maintaining a photonic link with them for over an hour without becoming depleted.

She learned several other techniques besides quantizing objects and beings. The first was how to hide her quantum signature while in a photonic state.

When she'd escaped from the Kulsat mining ship, luck was on her side in more than one way.

If the ship leader had extended his *sight*, he would have detected her moving about the ship. He would have initiated a section-by-section damping field to trap her and return her to her physical self. In that event, she would have drowned.

Red Spot remarked that the hull of their ships had an external damper—a basic defense against alien Aethers boarding their vessels. To conserve energy, the shields were not normally charged unless there was cause. She was lucky to have passed through the hull without being converted to her physical self out in the cold of space.

Another ability, which many Risen were unable to master, was to learn how to resist being quantized by another being. Three Crescents had not yet perfected the technique, since Justine had been able to quantize him.

Justine could not practice hiding her signature or resisting being quantized by another. There was no one to practice on, or against.

She'd promised the Gliesan Parliament that she would not try to learn their—or the Collection's—technology, but there was no rule that said she couldn't learn how the Kulsat did it. If the Collection of Worlds or the Parliament of Gliese found out she was learning the techniques, however, they might decide she was going against her oath by using that loophole, and restrict her from visiting Red Spot.

The most important ability she needed to learn was how to travel outside light. Red Spot informed her that the technique was universal, no matter how the quantum engines had been constructed.

Once again, however, Justine could only learn the theory; there were no Kulsat quantum engines for her to practice on. She hoped the theory would be enough when the time came.

The skill was a compound of all the attributes of becoming a Kinemat.

The navigational principle was similar to when Justine had flown the *Ultio* from Sol's star beacon to Centauri's. Her *sight* was able to mark the spacial locations of the two beacons, and her enhanced memory kept the two points in her thoughts when she engaged the star beacon.

In order to travel outside light, the pilot would have to use the electropathic ability to link herself to the star beacon much the same way she linked herself to the quantized passengers on her ship. In this regard, it was akin to quantum entanglement. For a brief time, she, her ship, her passengers, and the star beacon would be a single entity. The star beacon would 'know' her navigational intentions.

Once she reached the star beacon, instead of sling-shotting past as she'd done before, the star beacon would take over, and absorb the photonic energy of the ship and its passengers.

That's when the mystery began.

Everyone she spoke to gave her an identical explanation: outside light, the star beacons shared the same space. That made no sense to Justine.

If it were a form of dimensional travel, then the star beacon would simply transfer the photonic signature from one beacon in this plane of existence to its counterpart in another dimension, then back to another beacon in a different region of space. There was no way Justine could conceive of this without there being a delay. Travel between two star beacons was instantaneous; therefore, it wasn't dimensional transference.

It couldn't be true entanglement, which would mean the star beacons were, in effect, the same beacon existing in different places at the same time. If that were the case, anytime someone activated a star beacon, they would all activate.

No one knew the secret, or how the Xtôti had built the star beacons. The only thing they agreed on was that they had developed the technology nearly a million years ago.

Justine wished she had Alex and Michael to talk to about it; perhaps they would have some theory to explain it.

Each day, she went over the lessons with Red Spot, but without a practical application, she wouldn't know if she had mastered the abilities. Under no circumstances would she share the fact of her knowledge with anyone outside of Red Spot and the other Kulsat.

Learning the techniques without being able to practice them was a significant obstacle, but a bigger hurdle was managing to get on board a vessel heading for Sol System.

No ship from the Collection of Worlds would break protocol and travel there. Speaking with Na Huama, Justine had learned that Ah Tabai had always been something of a rebel. As much as the human Aetherbeings wanted to help, they would not follow down their colleague's path.

Justine had given her word that she would not break Gliesan Law, and she was not one to go back on her word. She'd worked hard over the past few weeks to establish relations with nearly one-hundred systems; if she broke the Law, she would also break the trust she'd engendered with those races. Of course, if Sol System were ravaged by the Kulsat, those diplomatic relations would be meaningless. Justine was torn.

When she related her concerns to Red Spot, the alien's reply hit her like a bombshell. She couldn't believe what she heard. For a brief moment, she thought that, despite all the time they had spent together building trust, Red Spot had been secretly plotting against her all along.

It was only after the initial shock began to wear off that Justine realized it was the only way for her to uphold the Laws of Gliese and the Collection, and to get home and try to find the final component.

Red Spot told her, "If no Collection ships will travel to Sol System, and you will not commandeer a ship, then you must be on board a ship that is already heading there ... you must find a way to board a Kulsat ship."

38

Qin Station :
Sol System :

For the first time in months, Chow Yin took no pleasure in walking around the station with the aid of his biomechatronic legs. The sense of freedom that came with the technological prosthetic paled in comparison to another, more unfamiliar feeling.

Loss.

From the time he was a child, he'd never formed a close attachment to another person like the one that had developed between him and his daughter. They'd only been reunited for the last few years; their time together had been painfully short.

He'd imagined grooming her as an heir to the Solan Empire once he moved on to conquer the galaxy. Now, there was no one left to pass his legacy on to.

It was all because of Alex Manez and Doctor Naysmith.

Chow Yin had reviewed the recording of the last hours of his daughter's life a hundred times while his technicians and engineers repaired the damage that had nearly destroyed Qin Station.

Though Chow Yin had done his share of betrayal over the years, and uncovered more than a few traitors in his ranks, the doctor had been singularly successful when he'd slipped Alex a small quantity of Kinemet.

It had restored the boy to his full powers, which he'd exercised at the most unfortunate time: simultaneous with the activation of the Kinemetic process on Sian.

The photonic explosion quantized the lab and the top few levels of the space station. Unlike the accident on Macklin's Rock years earlier, there was not nearly enough Kinemet to launch the affected section toward the star beacon at near-light speeds. Less than a day after the event, Chow Yin's sensors picked up fragments of the station hull several thousand kilometers away.

The salvage mission recovered the bodies of all those affected by the photonic conversion, including the technicians in the lab, several other workers in the nearby levels, as well as Sian and Alice. Medical staff quickly determined that all of them had been partially converted to Kinemats, as had those who were subjected to Klaus's first trials. Of the two priming sequences, their first attempt was the wrong one. Even if the cold vacuum of space had not killed his daughter and the others within moments of returning to normal space, the unsuccessful conversion would have killed them soon enough.

The only body they had not recovered was that of Alex Manez. Chow Yin could only surmise that his previous conversion somehow kept him alive. Perhaps, as his records indicated, Alex managed to remain quantized. There was no way to tell how long he could maintain himself in a photonic state. According to those reports, Alex had no awareness in that form. Depending on how much Kinemet the doctor had injected him with, Alex could remain out of Chow Yin's reach for months or even years.

At least Chow Yin had been able to arrest the doctor before he escaped the station. Though Chow Yin did not believe in torture, he believed in poetic justice, and he'd had the doctor launched out into space to suffer the same fate as his daughter.

There was a silver lining to the entire tragedy, and Chow Yin clung to it. Now, they knew the priming sequence for converting a person into a Kinemat. Once they finished rebuilding the Kinemetic conversion chamber, Chow Yin could create as many squadrons of quantum pilots as he needed to subjugate Sol System, and later, the galaxy.

Chow Yin had never been a superstitious man, and did not hold with the power of chance, but he thanked his lucky stars that he'd received word about the liberation of Michael Sanderson in Guatemala. That had prompted him to speed up work on the quantum ship his engineers were building in the dry dock station several kilometers away from Qin Station. Chow Yin had decided to oversee the final stages of the operation.

It was a grand warship. With a crew of only twelve, it had enough firepower to take on any of the USA, Inc.'s space destroyers and win.

Chow Yin's engineers had long ago learned to weaponize Kinemet into torpedoes, and the warship carried thirty-six of those, as well as an additional twenty-four conventional and nuclear missiles. A believer in stacking the odds in his favor, Chow Yin also had a dozen twenty-pound gun turrets installed, each with a five-kilometer range, just in case of those rare times the ships came within proximity to one another.

Chow Yin visualized its maiden flight, once he'd successfully undergone the Kinemetic conversion to become a quantum pilot. His first target would be Canada Station Three, in revenge against Alex and his country. Even though his Solan forces had already taken over that station, he would destroy it as a symbol of his power and will. The United Earth Corporate would know the temerity of his purpose. If they did not immediately surrender the corporate nations of the world to him, he would launch Kinemetic warheads at their capital cities until they capitulated. Once he had bent Sol System to his will, then he would focus on these Kulsat Alex had told Alice about.

Though the information he had on them was thin, he'd already developed a plan of attack: if they were so interested in some artifact on Earth, he would offer them free access to the planet to search for it. Why not feign cooperation, make them drop their guard? Once they'd found whatever it was they were looking for—presumably some kind of weapon they feared—then Chow Yin would swoop in and take it from them, and use it against whatever armada they sent against him. With that weapon in his arsenal, the galaxy was his for the taking.

"Your Highness," someone behind him said. "There you are."

Chow Yin stopped walking and turned to see General Leong hurrying to catch up.

"General." He gave a slight bow of his head. "I was on my way to inspecting the progress on the lab repairs."

The general said, "They should be complete by the end of today."

Resuming his pace, with full expectation that the general would follow, Chow Yin said, "And the warship?"

"We're going through final diagnostics. The quantum drive has passed all tests. The ship will be ready for its maiden voyage by this time tomorrow."

"Ensure there is ample Kinemet on board. I fully expect to test the quantum drive at that time."

"Are you certain it is wise to undergo the conversion yourself?" the general asked, raising a concerned eyebrow. "Perhaps it would be more prudent to test the formula on someone else first."

Chow Yin turned his head and growled, "And sully the memory of my daughter? She gave her life to prove which sequence is valid. No, I shall make the conversion tonight."

"Of course, Your Highness."

∞

It was the first time since he was a child that Chow Yin felt apprehension. He knew, in his mind, that the priming sequence was the correct one, but there was a small nagging thought that there could be another factor which might cause the trial to fail.

For a fraction of a second, he wanted to heed the general's advice and have someone else undertake the first trial, but then his pride drowned the notion. How could he face his men if he showed even the smallest hint of fear?

Purposefully, he strode into the lab, taking pleasure in the heavy thumping sound of his biomechatronic legs as they stomped against the ceramic floor. It was a grand way to make an entrance; no one could mistake who had arrived.

The general was there, as well as several of his top officers, watching on as the technicians made the final preparations.

Without any sign of hesitation, Emperor Yin continued through to the Kinemetic conversion chamber. Inside, instead of an operating table with straps, there was a chair. Chow Yin would not be able to wear his biomechatronic legs during the event. The electromagnetic signature could interfere with the Kinemetic priming sequence.

With the assistance of two technicians, Chow Yin unlocked the legs and, leaning heavily on the men, allowed himself to be maneuvered into the chair.

Beside the chair, the Kinemet was already placed inside the priming device. Chow Yin imagined he could feel the radiation penetrate through him.

He looked out through the viewing window at the general and the other officers, taking on a look of supreme confidence, as the technicians hooked up sensors to him.

When all was ready, one of the technicians nodded. "We can begin whenever you are ready, Your Highness."

Chow Yin waited until everyone had exited the chamber and sealed the door behind them.

Once everyone in the lab focused their attention on him, Chow Yin said, "Gentlemen, today marks the beginning of the greatest era in our history. From this day forward, the course of human existence will be shaped by us. Burn the memories into your minds; you will be able to tell your grandchildren that you were among the honored witnesses to the birth of the first galactic empire."

Having finished his speech, Chow Yin slowly raised one hand, lifting one finger and, after a dramatic pause, pointed to the technician to begin the priming sequence.

The chamber became eerily silent as the Kinemetic damper engaged, and the room sealed electromagnetically. Beside him, the milligram of Kinemet in the conversion device, which was so small when dormant that Chow Yin had to squint to see it, began to glow as it was primed with the sequence of light waves. Once the procedure was complete, and the Kinemet was too bright to look at directly, the bombardment device opened a thin tunnel from which a beam of hydrogen photons penetrated the kinetic metal.

The reaction was all-consuming.

∞

Chow Yin had never been much of a patron of the arts, and held little interest in music. The sound that filled his mind and body when he became a photonic being transcended everything he'd experienced before in his life, and the music penetrating his soul was beyond description. It was the end-all of all things. Forevermore, the elegant symphony of the heavenly bodies throughout the universe would be an integral part of him. He was the song, and the song was him.

He could sense the subtle signature of the Kinemetic damper around the chamber, and with a mere thought-impulse, he penetrated through it and turned off the electromagnetic seal.

A collection of photons, Emperor Yin pushed himself out of the chamber and into the lab, reveling in the looks of awe on his men as they watched a being of light appear before them.

Chow Yin knew he truly was a god.

Just as the thought came to him, he became aware of something else in the vicinity, another presence, and he instinctively knew it was of a magnitude more powerful than he was.

For the first time in his life, Chow Yin felt fear.

39

Unknown :
Unknown :

Nothing.
Then something.
The smallest whisper.
A crescendo of sound.
Everything inside him was outside.
The infinite universe filled his essence.
Answers just out of reach.
Music of the Spheres?
Song of Stars?
Cosmic Opus?
Key.
A rift.
Absence of light.
The inexistence of time.
A dichotomy of spacial matter.
Convergence of light, space and time.
Everything outside him was inside.
Simultaneous divergence of matter.
Invariance and covariance.
Quantum absence.
Everything.

40

Low Earth Orbit :
Sol System :

His first thought was that he had died and gone over to the other side.

A feeling of completeness came over Michael as he regained consciousness. The soft, cradling warmth that flowed through his body was unlike anything he'd experienced before.

The ever-present ache he felt in his knees and hips as he grew older came back, and that was when he realized he wasn't dead. Every cell in his body was on fire, and he knew this was because he'd been irradiated by the reaction to the Kinemet in the alien. It had not been enough radiation to kill him immediately, however. Then why had he felt like he was going to die?

He opened his eyes and looked around. To his confusion, he realized he was in officer's quarters on a ship. There was a desk with an old-fashioned DMR casement. The screen held orders for the captain of the ship, and the name was all too familiar.

Michael struggled to understand how he'd ended up back on Lieutenant Gao's ship.

In space?

His disorientation and confusion sent his heart racing. What was going on? How did he get here?

Fighting against the feeling of weakness running through him, he got up, and a wave of pain coursed through his torso.

He had a broken rib. Something must have fallen on him during the explosion. That was why he'd felt heavy. Shock had tricked him into thinking he was going to die.

With one hand, he felt the bandage around his ribs. It still hurt to breathe, and it took him a bit of time to approach the computer console. There, he read the status report on the screen.

The ship was in orbit at the L3 point on the opposite side of the Moon from the Earth. That region was long-held as a launching point for missions to the outer planets. It had been one of Chow Yin's first targets.

The status report indicated that there were dozens of ships sharing the same orbit, and the majority of them were models used by USA, Inc., Canada Corp., UK PLC, and Deutschland, AG. More than half the ships, however, were of Chinese manufacture. Was Chow Yin massing an armada to invade Earth? Had he captured all these ships? Had he captured Michael?

His confusion heightened when Lieutenant Gao entered the quarters and smiled at him.

"I see you are awake and well, Mr. Sanderson."

Dropping all pretext of civility, Michael demanded, "What the hell is going on? How did I get here?"

Putting up a hand to calm his guest down, Lieutenant Gao said, "You are safe, I assure you. If you feel up to it, I can explain."

Though he knew the radiation in his body, combined with the broken ribs, was sapping his strength, he felt more than up to an explanation.

"Please do," he said, bringing himself to a sitting position on the edge of the bunk.

Lieutenant Gao pulled a chair out from a small desk set into an alcove on the wall, and eased himself down. "We only have a few minutes, so pardon me if I give you the highlights."

"Go on."

"I am, and always have been, an agent for the PRC, planted among the Solan Empire to undermine Chow Yin's rule. When you arrived in Sol System, we sent an alert to avoid the mines, but the alien vessel did not receive the warning in time. When I saw it fly toward another mine, I sent a warning missile to get it to change course. I had no idea the vessel would explode. I am so sorry about your friends."

A mix of emotions went through Michael at the admission, but soon enough, he nodded to Lieutenant Gao to continue.

The lieutenant said, "Over the past few months, we have been secretly amassing a fleet out here, launching during solar flares to mask our movements. In one hour, we will begin to take back Sol System, and we require your help."

"Me? What do you think I can do?"

"You were captured by rebels in Honduras, who were working for Chow Yin, is that correct?"

"Yes," Michael said. "The last thing I remember, the complex was under attack. Humberto, a friend of mine, said the Guatemalan army was liberating us." He gave the lieutenant a hard look. "How did I get from there to here?"

"When the authorities found you, the Cruzado informed them that you had sustained injuries and would only speak to Alex Manez. Of course, that was impossible at the time, but he finally agreed to speak to Minister Calbert Loche, one of your top officials."

"What did he tell him?"

"You had sustained a few broken ribs, and that you had been exposed to Kinemetic radiation. Word was sent through diplomatic channels from your government to the Americans, then to my government who has been working in cooperation with them. My ship was in low-Earth orbit on a routine patrol when I received instructions to break my cover and take you aboard. The Guatemalans launched a small vessel to rendezvous with our ship. You've been here for several days, drifting in and out of consciousness. Now, our ship's doctor has verified that you are well on the road to recovery from your physical injuries."

Michael, his mind racing with all the information he'd just received, reached the most vital conclusion. "You broke cover. That means—"

"Chow Yin is aware of my duplicity. We already have information that he is gathering his forces at Qin Station—he is obviously protecting something very important. Our fleet will launch within the hour, but General Gates, the commander of the flotilla, needs to debrief you before we finalize our mission specs."

"Debrief me?"

"You may be the only person who can contact Alex."

"Alex?"

The lieutenant nodded. "I was able to send off Humberto's encoded message to an agent at Qin Station; Doctor Naysmith. We have no way to verify whether Mr. Manez received it, and we've lost contact with the doctor."

It took a moment for Michael to wrap his head around all the new developments. He asked, "What about the others, Humberto and his men, and Yaxche and Patli?"

"As far as I know, they have been escorted back to Honduras, and are under the protection of their military. They are fine."

A chime sounded, and the lieutenant stood. "Ah, it's ready."

"What is?"

"We have prepared a shuttle to take you to the general's flagship."

∞

The *Liberty* was the largest battle cruiser in the US Space Force. It had eight torpedo tubes with both nuclear and conventional warheads, twelve short-range missile launchers, and two dozen heavy gun batteries. There were six portals on either side of the ship for small fighter shuttles to dock. The ship utilized the latest high-tech countermeasures, and was equipped with state-of-the-art computer technology.

What got Michael's attention was not the weaponry or the firepower. As his shuttle neared the warship, he saw on the monitors that someone had installed a quantum drive. From what he could tell, it was the same configuration as the prototype he had installed on the *Ultio*.

This was the first he'd heard of a light-speed capable military ship—of course, all they were missing was a Kinemat who could pilot it.

By the time he docked, disembarked from his shuttle, and was led to the bridge to meet General Gates, Michael was bursting with questions.

Before he could say anything, however, the general pulled him into a small conference room away from the other officers.

"Mr. Sanderson, welcome to the *Liberty*. Thank you for assisting us."

"How can I help?"

"We plan to attack Qin Station, which is Emperor Yin's base of operations. We have reports coming in that Emperor Yin has four times the number of our ships, but most of them are scattered around this area of space. If we stand any chance, we must arrive in force before he has a chance to gather his fleet. Our attack must be unexpected. No doubt, you are aware that our ion engines have improved over the past few years. It should only take us two or three days to arrive there once we launch."

"What is it you want from me, then?" Michael asked.

"It is our belief that Emperor Yin is building a quantum ship of his own. Should he successfully create a Kinemat, he will have an advantage over us. We know he has coerced Alex Manez into assisting him; we must retrieve him alive if we are to have any chance of creating our own force of Kinemats."

"Alex had no choice…" Michael said.

"We know. That's not important. What's important is that he may not know whom to trust. That's where you come in."

"Of course. I will do anything to help."

"Good." The general nodded, and then took a moment to form his words. "We don't believe we've been able to contain news of the Guatemalan revolt, which is why we believe Emperor Yin has moved up his timetable. Once he has what he wants from Alex—"

"He'll kill him," Michael finished.

41

Qin Station :
Sol System :

There was no sense of time or space. It was a complete metaphysical metamorphosis. Alex was unaware that he'd ever been a corporeal being. His consciousness was filled with the entire scope of the universe's existence. At the same time, he was suspended in a moment of a pure energy.

He could have existed in that state for all time, and not known the difference—or cared, for that matter. It was the end and the beginning of all things for him.

In an instant, he became aware of his unawareness, and he willed himself to become conscious.

There was another sentience near him, and the edges of his perception told him it was a presence similar to him.

The overwhelming bliss called him back, and he was very near to dismissing the anomalous sense that there was someone or something near him. All he wanted was to exist in that glorious fragment of time and space for all eternity, the suspension of all reality.

Still, there was something in his psyche that would not let him remain in his current form. What was it? If he had the perception of consciousness, did he not have an obligation to embrace it? Otherwise, the infinite inexistence was a lie.

He concentrated, and became cognizant that there was a material universe surrounding him.

Galaxies, solar systems and planets. Elements, particles, molecules, and quanta.

Time slowed down and returned to him, and his memories were restored.

From one moment to the next, he realized a great many things.

He was different from before. For nearly twenty years, he'd been affected by the radiation of Kinemet. Now, the Kinemet was a part of him. Every cell in his body, his very DNA, was altered. Kinemet was part of his fundamental physiology now. He was no longer a failed conversion, no longer a half-human, half-Kinemat—he was different enough that he'd become another species, even though he knew his physical appearance would not show the changes.

The Grace! Was this what the Grace were? Alex sent his consciousness out. Though he could always sense every planetary body in Sol System, he could not send his awareness more than a hundred-and-fifty kilometers away from his photonic self. Beyond that limitation, the details were completely obscured. Now, if he concentrated, he could push his awareness out to every point in Sol System.

Like a lighthouse beaming directly into his soul, the star beacon on Pluto shone brightly. No longer was it a distant pin of luminescence in the farthest reaches of his *sight*.

And ... Alex could see beyond it. Not in the physical sense. It wasn't as if he could see past it on a spacial basis. Though he could still detect other star beacons throughout the galaxy, his new perception of Sol System's beacon was beyond anything he'd imagined before.

An ethereal symphony emanated from it, something much more majestic than the Music of the Spheres, or the Song of the Stars. It was all-encompassing perfection, and it called to him. The message had been there since Macklin's Rock, but now it was much more powerful than ever before.

Alex, come home.

How had he changed? The doctor! How had Doctor Naysmith known that injecting Alex with Kinemet before the conversion process would have this effect? Or had it been an accident?

That was the final key, Alex knew. Priming the Kinemet to match the Song of the Stars was only half the equation. Exposure to its radiation would convert a physical being to a Kinemat, but a Kinemat was merely the halfway point. Infusing the converted Kinemet during the conversion process changed Alex into a full quantum being.

Was this the secret the Kulsat had been searching for over the past thousand years? In theory, it sounded right, but there was a seed of doubt in Alex's mind. He would need to think about it more.

Another realization came to him, this one more immediate. There was something important about the secondary presence he'd sensed.

There was a physical distance between him and the other photonic being. Several thousand kilometers. Before he could think about the question, he had the answer. Alex, in his quantum state, had drifted outward from the Sun. A quick calculation of his position among the planets told him he'd been in the alternate awareness for several days.

Using his *sight,* he focused on the presence, and realized it was very near Qin Station.

It was another Kinemat, and Alex focused his perception to identify it.

When he realized it was Chow Yin, Alex pushed his photonic self forward.

At one point, he'd thought the only option for saving Sol System was to help the self-styled Emperor of Sol System. Now that he'd discovered how to create Kinemats, Chow Yin would not stop in his mad quest. The last thing they needed was a maniac running around with that power.

Chow Yin had to be stopped.

Though his perception traveled at near-light speeds, Alex still had limitations, and could only push his photonic self at a fraction of that speed.

As he neared Qin Station, Alex felt the presence of a significant quantity of raw Kinemet, the entirety of which was loaded on a large warship. He could sense Emperor Yin's Kinemetic presence on that warship, and he detected there was a quantum drive installed in the vessel.

By the time Alex's essence had reached Qin Station, the warship had moved a few kilometers away and was coming about.

Chow Yin's ship launched a Kinemetic torpedo at the station.

As Justine had caused the torpedoes to explode years before when they were being chased from Canada Station Three, Alex pushed his senses out at the weapon and detonated the Kinemetic torpedo before it hit the station.

Immediately, the Emperor's ship launched a conventional missile, and Alex could do nothing but watch in horror as Qin Station was obliterated.

How many innocent people had been on that station?

No! Alex raged. He had a crazy thought: as he'd detonated the weaponized Kinemet on the torpedoes, perhaps there was a way he could detonate the Kinemet on the Emperor's warship.

Before he could push his senses out, Chow Yin activated his quantum drive, and the warship disappeared in a streak of light.

It was then that Alex sensed another quantity of Kinemet. A fleet of ships were coming his way. His first thought was they were the Emperor's reinforcements, since many of the ships carried markings of the People's Republic of China.

When he looked closer, he realized the ships did not carry weaponized Kinemet warheads. One of the ships bore a USA, Inc. signature and had a quantum drive installed, and several hundred kilograms of Kinemet on board—more than enough to power the ship for years.

At the same time, another group of ships converged on the newcomers from another direction; they must have been the remainder of Chow Yin's forces.

As the two fleets met, they began to fire on one another. Alex was helpless in the fight.

If this had been a vid, or a rendition of Nova Pirates—the game Alex had loved to play as a youth—he would have enjoyed the epic space battle that ensued. He would have reveled in the conflict, cheering his side on.

Now, Alex could only watch in horror as dozens of ships, and hundreds of soldiers on either side, were destroyed in the fight.

After what seemed like hours, but was in truth less than five minutes, the battle was over.

Chow Yin's forces, without the Emperor at their head, quickly broke ranks, the ships turning away from the fight and fleeing from certain death.

The Earth forces had won the battle.

But what of the war?

Certainly, Alex knew, there were pockets of imperialists throughout Sol System, but without their Emperor, the odds favored Earth.

Alex had been distracted by the fighting, but now that the conflict was over, he scoured the main Earth ship. Were they truly from his side?

When he focused his perception on the bridge, he felt a surge of relief.

Michael!

Pushing himself forward, Alex passed through the hull of the ship and onto the bridge.

Michael, as if expecting him to arrive all along, said, "It's so good to see you, Alex."

His warm smile was in complete contrast to the look of shock on the officers' faces when Alex materialized into physical form.

∞

In the captain's cabin, Alex sipped a cup of hot chicken broth while Michael and the commander of the fleet, General Alan Gates, brought him up to date.

"And so," Michael said, "Chow Yin must have initially prepared to repel us—"

"But then he sensed me," Alex said, and shook his head.

Michael said, "With you on one side, and us on the other, he would have realized he was outgunned without the bulk of his fleet. Like any coward, he fled."

General Gates growled. "Not until he was sure to destroy Qin Station behind him, whether to distract us, or to hide his research."

Giving Alex a level look, Michael asked, "Where do you think he went?"

"He went to look for more allies."

"Where?" the general asked. "The Jupiter moons?"

"No," Alex said, and took a deep breath. "Centauri. He knows about the Kulsat. He thinks they will join forces with him, if he gives them what they're looking for."

General Gates frowned, and looked at Michael. "None of this was in your report. The Kulsat?"

"It's time you heard the truth," Michael said. "I briefed my government, but my report was discounted as a fabrication."

Together, Michael and Alex told the general everything they knew about the Kulsat threat.

When they were finished, the general didn't question the truth of their story. He asked, "What about these Gliesans you mentioned, the ones that saved Alex on his first trip, and the rest of you this last time?"

Michael said, "I'm not sure if they have the resources to stand against the Kulsat. I got the impression they're severely outgunned. Their Kinemats have helped us, but I believe they have done so of their own accord. Their actions might be unofficial, and they might have been breaking their own laws to assist us." He shook his head. "There's no way to guess what stance their government has adopted concerning us."

Alex said, "Up until now, the Kulsat haven't had any idea where in the galaxy Sol System is. The star beacons have a kind of interstellar cloaking mechanism, hiding our location from anyone who doesn't know our coordinates."

"And hiding them from us," Michael added. "This is why none of our long-range sensors have recorded anything outside our system."

General Gates stood up and paced in the small room. "And you say this was set up by these ancient aliens, the Grace?"

"As far as we know," Michael said. "We weren't able to debrief the Gliesans in full before Chow Yin's mines struck. And the only other information we have is the stories from Yaxche and his friend, Patli. It's possible some parts of the story could have been altered or lost over the past thousand years."

Drawing himself up to his full height, the general nodded to himself. "I will send a report to HQ."

"We don't have time to wait for them to debate this," Alex said. "If we don't follow Chow Yin and stop him, he'll lead the Kulsat right to us."

"I don't have the authority to do that," the general said, and then glanced at Michael. "Besides, if your government has discounted your story, my government might do the same. I can't just run off to another solar system based on conjecture."

"What if I could prove it?" Alex stood up.

Raising one eyebrow, the general asked, "Prove the Kulsat threat?"

"Yes."

"How?"

"You have a quantum drive on board."

Slowly, the general nodded. "Yes, but I understand neither of you are fully capable of piloting the drive."

"Things have changed," Alex assured him. "Don't worry; it will be a short trip."

"A short trip?" The general frowned. "To where?"

Alex smiled. "Back to Pluto."

∞

When the general went to send in his report, insisting he needed someone higher up the food chain to sign off on the proposal, he left Alex and Michael alone in the cabin.

"You've been irradiated by Kinemet," Alex said.

"I have, but I don't seem to have any of the powers of a Kinemat. I just feel the bad side effects. If they hadn't got me off Earth, I'm sure I would've died. Now, I can handle it—at least for the time being. Judging from past cases, I might not have more than a few days or weeks before the radiation starts to kill me."

"Tell me what happened?"

Michael quickly outlined everything that had happened since they'd parted ways after Kenny's death. "I realized that the alien had Kinemet infused in his DNA. Of course, that revelation came seconds before the lab blew up."

"It wasn't natural Kinemet," Alex said. "It was already altered, as if it had undergone the priming sequence."

"Yes." Michael frowned. "I got Humberto to send the message to you letting you know that was the final key. I assumed…"

Shaking his head, Alex said, "Doctor Naysmith must have snuck Kinemet into my bloodstream just before the first trial. The sample they used on Sian was incomplete—everyone else in the lab died. I was insulated against that; I assume because I've been previously irradiated. I quantized myself moments before the explosion. Somehow, while being quantized, I managed to process the Kinemet in my system. The conversion must have altered it. If you were to take a genetic sample of me now, you'd most likely find that I share the same Kinemetic DNA markers as the Xtôti you examined."

"So you…"

Alex nodded. "Technically, I'm no longer a human. I'm one of the Grace." He laughed. "Unfortunately, I have no idea what that entails. Other than being aware in the photonic state, the only other ability I seem to have is to be able to extend my awareness throughout the solar system."

"So that was the legacy the Kulsat were looking for? The infusion of Kinemet? It was the alien's body that gave us the clue."

Alex frowned. "I think the infusion may only be a part of the legacy, an important step. There's a piece missing in this equation, and for the life of me, I don't know what it is."

"We need a lab, and a lot of time," Michael said. "We have neither."

A moment later, he added, "I don't know how much time I have, either."

"I'm sure you'll have all the time in the world," Alex said.

Michael squinted at him. "What do you mean?"

"You told me Patli's story, about how other aliens abducted the irradiated villagers a millennium ago."

"Yes."

"I believe the rescuers were Gliesans, and the villagers were Ah Tabai's ancestors."

Nodding, Michael looked at the floor, thinking it through. "That makes sense."

"So, all we need to do is get Ah Tabai and Aliah to fix you, as the Gliesans fixed the villagers."

Michael jerked his head up. "What?"

"What better way to prove our story than to get it straight from the horse's mouth?"

"Ah Tabai? Aliah? They survived?"

Alex nodded. "Yes. The same way I did when I first went to the Centauri System. They're waiting out there, in the photonic state. Why else would I want to go to Pluto?"

∞

At first, the general wanted to get authorization, but Alex pointed out that a message sent to Earth from their position would have taken nearly fifteen minutes each way, and adding in the time it would take for someone in command to make a decision, Chow Yin would most likely be an hour or two ahead of them, traveling at very near the speed of light.

"Also, if he is fully converted to a Kinemat, he can utilize the star beacons. The moment he travels to the Centauri System, he could signal the Kulsat."

"My original mandate was the capture of Chow Yin," General Gates said after considering Alex's words. "Technically, nothing has changed." With that, he gave the order to get the quantum drive online.

It only took the engineers a few minutes to prepare everything, and when the general was notified that all systems were ready, he nodded to Alex. "You're sure you can do this?"

"Yes," Alex said, finding his way to the console area built

specifically for a quantum pilot. "Now more than ever."

"Very well, I'm transferring navigation to your station. Let us know when you're going to engage the drive."

Taking a deep breath, and familiarizing himself with the controls, Alex was suddenly reminded of the first time he'd piloted a luminous vessel, when he'd hijacked the *Quanta*.

He closed his eyes, and could feel a connection to the Kinemet already loaded aboard the quantum engine. At the same time, he became acutely aware of Michael and the other three officers on the bridge, as well as the six engineers on board the ship. It was almost as if he could reach out with a thin tendril of his own essence and touch each of them.

Alex hesitated as something revolutionary occurred to him.

"What is it, Alex?" the general asked.

"Something's not right."

Michael got out of his seat and stepped over, looking over Alex's shoulder at the console. "It looks fine to me."

"No," Alex said, "not with the drive; with the procedure." He glanced up at Michael. "Do you remember one of the primary reasons I took the place of the first pilot of the *Quanta?*"

"You thought a pilot who had not undergone the Kinemetic conversion process would not be able to dampen the secondary Kinemetic reaction."

"And I was right." Alex looked back down at the quantum drive controls. "Since that time, I've always thought there was something fundamentally wrong with our theory, that the secondary reaction should never have been an issue."

General Gates approached, a harried look on his face. "What's the delay? Weren't you the one who convinced me time was of the essence?"

"All this time we've been using the theory a quantum pilot is for navigation and to control the ship's return to physical space." He smiled. "But there's much more to it."

"What do you mean?" Michael asked.

Alex waved the two men back to their seats. "Not to worry. I think I know what I have to do."

"You think?" the general asked, his eyes wide and disbelieving.

"Instinctually," Alex said and gave him a firm nod. "Trust me."

Slowly, the two men returned to their seats, and Alex faced forward.

Closing his eyes, Alex reached out with his photonic essence and connected with the crew. Then he formed a bridge between them and the quantum drive.

Michael said, "We're ready—"

As Alex had been able to quantize himself in the past, he knew, deep down, he could convert the crew to photons by willing it to happen. He did so, and a moment later, he quantized himself. He was fully aware in that state, and with his electropathic senses, he engaged the quantum drive…

…A little over four hours later, he disengaged the drive, then returned himself to physical form moments before rematerializing the crew.

It had been the smoothest flight Alex could ever have hoped for.

"—when you are," Michael finished, then paused with his mouth open when he saw the main casement on the bridge showing him that the ship was in orbit around Pluto.

"We're here?" General Gates said in a breathless rush. With a slight shake of his head, he added, "It felt instantaneous."

"It's just a matter of perception," Alex said. "To me, the flight took four hours, eight minutes, and twenty-seven seconds."

"Pluto." General Gates stared at the image on the casement screen. "I never truly thought I would see it."

"If you think that's remarkable," Alex said, "prepare to be amazed."

"What—?" the general began to ask.

Two photonic essences came out of the bulkhead and floated down in front of the officers on the bridge. Slowly, both of them coalesced into bipedal forms.

"I'd like you to meet Ah Tabai," Alex said, standing up and approaching the two. He shook hands with the shorter of the two beings, who looked Mayan in appearance. "And Aliah, of the Gliese System." He bowed to the tall, bird-like alien who gave him an excited chirp of greeting.

"Alex," Ah Tabai said. "I didn't know if you would realize we were here, waiting. Thank you for rescuing us."

Smiling, Alex clapped a hand on his shoulder. "It was my turn to save you."

Aliah spoke in her whistle-like language, and the words came out from the translator at her collar. "You are more than an Aetherbeing, Alex. I can sense it." She and Ah Tabai glanced at each other.

Ah Tabai nodded. "Yes, I can feel it, too. You are—" Then his eyes widened. "—you are in a state of Grace! How—?"

Aware that all eyes were on him, and not certain if he should be telling anyone the secret, Alex realized that it was only a matter of time before the truth came out.

"Michael discovered the body of one of the Grace on Earth, and saw that he'd infused Kinemet with his DNA. I was injected and exposed to a conversion." He shook his head. "I'm surprised no one else has ever stumbled on that."

"No," Ah Tabai said. "That has been attempted before. It never resulted in ascension to the Grace." With a concerned look at Aliah, he added, "The results of that experiment have always been fatal."

Michael asked, "Then how did Alex survive it, and become—how did you say it—ascended?"

"That is the question," Ah Tabai said.

Aliah spoke. "We sensed another activation of the star beacon a little while ago. It was on course for the Centauri System."

"Yes," Michael said. "That was Chow Yin." For Ah Tabai's and Aliah's benefit, he added, "He's a criminal who is trying to contact the Kulsat."

His expression turning alarmed, Ah Tabai said, "You must not allow that. The Kulsat will not make allies with him. They will destroy him, and then come here. We must stop him."

"My sentiments, exactly," the general said. Up until that point, he had not spoken. Instead, he'd been staring at the alien on his ship. "Perhaps we can all formally debrief later. Right now, can we get to Centauri and stop Chow Yin in time?"

Alex took a deep breath. "We had better." He turned to Ah Tabai. "I've never used a star beacon correctly before. I don't think we have time for a lesson. Would you do the honors?" he asked, glancing at the general for approval.

Once General Gates nodded, Ah Tabai said, "Of course."

…And then Alex became aware that he, the crew, and the entire ship, now existed in deep orbit around the Centauri star beacon.

To his perception, the trip had been instantaneous.

The next moment, they were under heavy fire.

42

Aerie Skanse :
Gliese System :

Deep down, Justine had hoped the day would never come, but when she received the message from Naila, she held her breath as she listened.

"We have picked up a signal from the Centauri star beacon. It is activating, indicating a new arrival. It could be a Kulsat ship coming to relieve the other one, but from what our sensors could detect, the warship in the system has raised Aethershields and primed its weapons systems. We presume the new arrival is not expected. If you are coming, you had better hurry. We're flying into Centauri in fifteen minutes to investigate."

Justine, who had been at dinner in Yoatl's apartment, looked to the Ambassador. "It's time. Are you still willing to help me? I know you've had your doubts."

Yoatl wiped the corner of his mouth with a napkin as his wife started to clear the table. "It is a terrible risk. If the Parliament finds out, you'll have sacrificed your position here for nothing. It's not too late to back out."

Standing, Justine forced a smile. "This might be my only opportunity. I'm willing to take the chance."

"Just remember," Yoatl said as he went to the computer console on the other side of the room. "If it is one of your ships, and they have arrived using the Grace, you still may not share any Aether technology with them until the Collection verifies their method of travel. Warn them to return to Sol, and then come back here immediately." He began typing a series of commands into the computer, granting her permission to accompany the *Fainne* on their reconnaissance mission.

"If the Parliament finds out I did this, they'll revoke my ambassadorship."

"Don't worry, Yoatl. I won't break Galactic Law. It's the same loophole Naila and Fairamai used to save me."

Yoatl faced her, taking a deep breath. "Be careful. The Kulsat will be quick to attack." He gave her a long look. "I would hate myself if anything happened."

"You've been a wonderful friend, Yoatl. I will do everything I can to return to Gliese safely."

∞

By the time Justine got to the area in the space port where the *Fainne* was docked, Naila and Fairamai had the ship prepped and were ready to fly. The spaceport controller noticed her striding purposefully toward the ship. He was a tall Gliesan with red plumes on the top of his head.

With his long legs, he quickly caught up to her. "Envoy Turner, you aren't supposed to be here," he said. "You don't have clearance."

"Actually," she said to him, "I do. There is a possibility the new arrival is from Sol System. As envoy, it's my responsibility to be there to warn them of the Kulsat danger."

The controller cocked his head in doubt.

Justine shrugged. "Call Ambassador Yoatl, if you like. He'll verify the orders. But you're delaying the *Fainne*. We only have a small window of opportunity."

As if imagining the effort of going through official channels to get verification of Justine's statement, the controller nodded. "All right. Go ahead."

"Thank you," Justine said, and hurried to the ship. The portal closed behind her, and the vessel launched a moment later.

Fairamai was in the bay, and motioned for Justine to follow her to the passenger compartment where she helped secure her in the molded seat.

"You remember what we talked about?" the bird-like alien asked, and continued to spell it out before waiting for a reply. "Once the *Fainne* arrives in Centauri, Naila will scan the area for ship signatures. If it is Kulsat, he will return us to Gliese immediately. Should the new arrival come from Sol System, you will have less than twenty seconds to send them a warning; that is the amount of time a Kulsat ship needs to lock on to our ship, charge weapons, and fire."

"Yes," Justine said. "I know. I'll be ready."

Frowning, Fairamai said, "We are more than capable of sending the transmission. You do not need to come on this mission. Remain here, be safe. We will return with news."

"No." Justine shook her head. She could feel the vibrations of the *Fainne* as it banked around the Skanse Station, lining up for the run at the Gliese star beacon. "It's my responsibility."

A communication speaker in the room hummed, and a moment later, Naila said, "Engaging Aethersleep in 5 ... 4 ... 3 ... 2 ... 1—

∞

Justine had conditioned herself to react the moment she came out of the photonic state. She did not wait to find out the origin of the arriving ship, because it didn't make a difference to her plan.

A split-second after returning to normal space in Centauri, Justine quantized herself and pushed her particles outside the hull of the *Fainne*. Utilizing the technique Red Spot had taught her, she shielded her photons—essentially making her invisible to detection—and used her *sight* to scan for the other ships in the area. She figured there would be an even chance between one of two possibilities.

If the new ship was Kulsat, Justine's intention was to stow away on board. So long as the Kulsat didn't suspect their unseen passenger, Justine would be able to feed off the Kinemetic radiation of the ship and exist in her photonic state indefinitely. At such time as the Kulsat discovered Sol System, Justine would hitch a ride and return to her home world, and there do the best she could to aid in the defense of her people—by finding the final component, if it existed on Earth.

If the ship were from Sol, Justine would go on board and do everything she could to evade the Kulsat warship, and return to Sol, even if she had to commandeer the ship and pilot it herself.

She felt guilty for deceiving Yoatl about her intentions, but her promise held: she would not share technical knowledge of Kinemet. It was possible she wouldn't have to. It had been a while since Alex, Kenny, Michael, and Yaxche had returned to Sol System. They would do their best to prepare for a Kulsat invasion, and to advance their own Kinemetic technology as far as they could.

No matter what they did, though, she knew the one thing that could save her system was to do what Red Spot had suggested: possess the only technology more advanced than the Kulsat's, and make them surrender.

The first ship she sensed was the Kulsat warship, a behemoth compared with the mining ship that had abducted her when she first arrived in Centauri. She could feel the overwhelming quantity of Kinemet on board—they were stocked, enough to supply a fleet for years. To her surprise, they were already firing their weapons, not at the *Fainne,* but at the Solan ship that had just arrived.

She became aware of several things at the same time:

The Solan ship had traveled from Sol to Centauri outside light. For the first time since she'd left her home system, Justine could momentarily sense the star beacon from Sol, attached to the *Dis Pater* monument. It was faint, and the signal dissipated quickly, but it was there nonetheless. The technology that had hidden it and Sol System from the awareness of the rest of the galaxy had been tripped by the very act of using the star beacon. In the back of her mind, she knew it would only be a matter of time before the Gliesans became aware of this and, with Justine already having laid the diplomatic groundwork, ratified Sol System into the Collection of Worlds.

Those thoughts came and went in a blink. What captured Justine's attention was when she realized the Solan ship had the same markings as the ship that had chased her and the *Ultio* out of Sol System.

The flashback of narrowly avoiding destruction from a Kinemetic torpedo gave Justine pause. For a very brief moment, she didn't know which ship she would rather see blown apart.

Only a few thousand meters apart, the Kulsat and the Solan ship were firing on each other, the Kulsat with their sonic energy beams, the Solans with the Kinemet-modified nuclear warheads.

To Justine's surprise, the Solan ship was holding its own. Many of Earth's industrial ships, especially the long-haul vessels which traveled between planets, were still heavily reliant on electroceramics—a highly durable material which provided insulation against solar radiation and other forms of energy, including sound—to bolster the titanium hulls. The *Ultio,* being a private yacht designed for short excursions, did not have the electroceramics shell over its titanium hull. The mining ship, with its sound energy beams designed to rip through asteroidal metals, had torn the *Ultio* right apart.

Even still, the sonic blast was enough to cripple the Solan ship. Panels of the hull shattered and flew off. The vessel listed, as if its internal stabilizers had malfunctioned.

As she pushed her photonic particles forward toward the battle, she could sense the Kulsat ship changing the aim of one of its energy beams. She had not noticed, but the *Fainne* was coming about and attacking the Kulsat warship. Their weapons were no match by themselves, but in concert with the Solan ship, they helped to even the odds.

The distraction gave the Solan ship enough of an opportunity to shift itself a few degrees below and to the starboard of their enemy.

The Solans fired a conventional torpedo at the belly of the alien ship where, by Justine's estimation, their quantum engine was.

Unlike the Kinemetic ordnance, the conventional torpedo caused damage. It didn't disable the warship, but it shredded a section of the Kulsat's hull, and Justine could sense a level of protective radiation diminish. If the Solans followed up with another torpedo in the same spot, or if the *Fainne* fired its weapons, they might be able to inflict heavy damage.

Apparently, the Kulsat were aware that if they suffered another hit they would be dead in space; instead of returning fire, the ship changed course, pointing toward the star beacon, and engaged its quantum drive. It vanished from Centauri space.

Justine watched as the *Fainne* moved off from the Solan ship. There was no way for Naila or Fairamai to know where Justine was, or if she was still in Centauri space. They also had no way of knowing if this Solan ship were friend or foe. Their only two options were to go back to Gliese for further instructions, or stand by and see what happened. They chose to wait.

Not wanting to contact Naila, since he would most likely charge her to return to Gliese, Justine approached the Solan ship, and experienced a moment of trepidation.

This group was the same that had tried to destroy her four years before. She knew they had not followed her right away—the reappearance of the Sol System star beacon in her photonic consciousness proved that whoever piloted the ship had not only developed the ability to create Kinemats, but had also discovered how to travel outside light.

She could only come to one conclusion: one of Earth's more

aggressive nations had mastered the ability to travel faster than light. The fate of her friends suddenly became uncertain to her.

Under her current circumstances, however, she did not have another option. Now that the Sol System star beacon had activated on the interstellar grid while the Kulsat monitored it, the armada would head there as soon as they marshaled their forces.

Mentally steeling herself, Justine pushed her photons through space toward the Solan ship. It took her quite a while to get there. At first, she had the impression the ship was flying away from the star beacon, but as she got nearer, she realized it was drifting. It had not come out of the fight unscathed. Perhaps the ion engines had been damaged in the fight, she wondered.

She could also sense that many of the electrical systems on board were blown out. Once she pushed herself through the hull and into the ship, she heard the cries of the crew who were badly hurt; some of them were dead.

As she floated near one section with several bodies on the ground, she examined them. The first thing she noticed was that they were multiracial. Pausing near one man, she looked closer. The style of uniform and the insignia on the sleeve were unfamiliar to her, but the words written on the epaulet sent a wave of dread through her: her Chinese was rusty, but she swore it translated as 'Solan Empire Space Force'.

The hallways were strewn with metallic rubble, overhead lights sparked, and smoke filled the air. Still in her photonic state, Justine was able to navigate through the ship to the bridge.

It was there that her suspicion was confirmed. The captain of the ship was, indeed, a Kinemat. Justine could sense the radiation emanate from him. When she saw who it was, she couldn't believe her senses.

Standing with the assistance of a bulky set of biomechatronic legs in front of a bank of computer consoles, Chow Yin shouted orders to the half a dozen men to get the ship's controls back on line. Justine was glad she'd learned how to mask her photonic form from other Kinemats and Kinemetic sensors. She was free to eavesdrop until she had enough information before she decided what course of action to adopt.

An older uniformed man, with general's stars on his collar, stood at a console beside Chow Yin. He looked up and said, "Emperor Yin, we have reports that the fires in the ion engine room have been put out, but it will take several hours to repair the damage."

"What about the quantum drive?"

"Intact, Sire."

"What about torpedoes."

The general called up a readout. "Two conventional, four Kinemetic, Sire."

Chow Yin pointed to him. "Ensure they are all armed. That other ship could decide to fire on us at any time. Meanwhile, put as many men as you can on repairs." He let out a throaty growl. "And keep your eyeballs on that star beacon readout."

"Yes, Sire. That other ship is maintaining its distance. It doesn't look like it's attacking."

"If it changes position, let me know. Otherwise, ignore it. We don't know if they are the Kulsat or another race."

Everything was happening far too fast for Justine to figure out what was going on. She needed more information. Coalition? Solan Empire Space Force? Emperor Yin? What had happened in the years since she left Sol System?

She watched for the next several minutes as the crew desperately tried to repair their vessel.

In a panicked voice, one of the helmsmen called out. "Sire, the sensor indicates the star beacon is activating. We have no way of knowing if it is the aggressor returning, or the Coalition."

Waving his hand dismissively, Chow Yin said, "It doesn't matter who it is. Prep the torpedoes. Fire both a conventional and a Kinemetic warhead the instant any ship rematerializes."

Justine felt a moment of panic. She didn't know who the Coalition was, but if they were opposing Yin, then they had to be the good guys. She highly doubted the Kulsat would return to Centauri; now that the Sol System beacon was revealed to them, they would be able to head there from any point in the galaxy.

The general said, "They should be arriving in five seconds. Three … two—"

With a thought, Justine shifted to normal space.

"Stop!" she yelled.

She expected Chow Yin and the officers would be surprised at her unexpected appearance, at the very least. The moment she became a physical being, however, the general pivoted toward her. He had a phase pistol in his hand, and fired without hesitation.

The only thing that saved Justine was that she was close enough to Chow Yin that the general aim was off to avoid hitting his Emperor.

Outraged, Justine quantized him.

Chow Yin's reaction was a fraction slower than his officer's, but much more effective. He tapped a control on the console on the arm of his computer and activated a Kinemetic damper.

The entire bridge became a null zone for the Kinemetic energy.

When Klaus had used the damping technology on Justine on Venus, she'd been in physical form. The effect was that she'd been unable to shift into light, or use the energy.

The general, already in a photonic state, suffered a much different effect.

Without Justine's Kinemetic link to guide the reversal, the photons became physical, but they did not realign with the general's original form.

A mass of flesh appeared in midair, hung there for a moment, and then fell to the deck in a bloody pile. Justine gagged and looked away before she threw up.

Ignoring the dead general, Chow Yin barked an order to the nearest other crew member on the bridge. "You, put a gun on Major Turner. If she moves, kill her."

The man drew a gun and pointed it at Justine. She put her hands up.

Chow Yin pointed to another officer and yelled, "You! Get over there and fire those damned torpedoes."

Justine looked up at the holo casement on the front wall. Another ship had entered Centauri space, and its architecture was familiar. It looked like one of the U.S. Space Corps' warships.

Just as the crewman raced to the general's station and launched the torpedoes, the U.S. warship opened fire, spraying Chow Yin's vessel with thousands of projectiles that ripped through the already damaged hull and breached the inner compartments. On the screens, the two torpedoes exploded halfway between the two ships.

The blowback rocked Chow Yin's warship. Alarm klaxons sounded. The ship was venting atmosphere.

The helmsman called out, "Sire, we must abandon ship."

"The hell you say! We can send repair crews to patch those holes. Launch more torpedoes. Their countermeasures can't possibly stop all of them. Blow them out of space. Damn it!" he yelled, and pressed a control on his console. "I'll do it myself."

The U.S. warship launched a torpedo of its own; it wasn't weaponized Kinemet, but it carried enough of a conventional blast that the force knocked everyone on the bridge back. Chow Yin started to tip over, and the self-styled Emperor fought to keep his balance.

Some of the electrical systems were going offline because of the widespread damage. To Justine's amazement, one of those systems had been powering the Kinematic damper. Her power came back to her in an abrupt rush, and she didn't waste a moment.

She quantized everyone on the bridge.

∞

The U.S. ship was launching another volley of projectiles. In a panic, Justine raced for the communications console and looked for the radio controls. From her days at NASA, she remembered which emergency channels the military used during conflicts, and hoped they had not changed protocol.

"U.S. vessel, this is Major Justine Turner aboard the enemy ship. I have secured the bridge. Cease fire. Cease fire. I repeat: I have secured the enemy bridge." She tried two more channels before she received a reply.

"Major Turner, this is General Gates. Verify your identity."

"Recall code: seven-alpha-seven-five-five-alpha."

"Verified."

Justine breathed a sigh of relief. "Welcome to Centauri, General."

"It was quite the welcome," the general said wryly. "What is your status, Major?"

"Chow Yin and the bridge officers are quantized. The ship itself is badly damaged; it may not be salvageable. There are at least a dozen wounded, several dead."

The general said, "If you have access to the internal communications, inform the crew to surrender and prepare to be boarded."

"Understood, General." Before Justine complied with the orders, she asked, "Do you mind if I ask, who is the Kinemat on your ship?"

"I'll let you talk to them yourself," the general said.

"Them?"

A moment later, a very familiar voice came over the speaker.

"Justine," Alex said, "I have so much to tell you."

"You're all right," Justine said, feeling the weight of worry lift from her heart. Then she asked, "Wait a minute. You're a full Kinemat?"

"Sort of," Alex said. "It's a long story."

Justine shook her head in wonder, even though no one could see her. "You're going to have to give me the condensed version. We have another problem. Moments before you arrived, Chow Yin was engaged in battle with a Kulsat warship, and he managed to wound it enough that it retreated."

The general came back on the radio. "Are we expecting it to return with reinforcements?"

"No, General, it's much worse: The Kulsat armada has at least a hundred-thousand warships. They are now aware of Sol System, and their standard response will be to send an invasion fleet there and destroy everything and everyone they consider a threat. I'm afraid they are not open to negotiation. How many Kinemats do we have?"

"Counting Alex and you," the general said, "Four."

Four? Justine wondered.

She could hear the apprehension in his voice when the general asked, "Do we have any allies who will intervene?"

"The situation is dire," Justine said. "The Kulsat are the dominating force in the galaxy. The Collection of Worlds cannot stand up to them. And even if they could, they hold to an ancient law which prevents them from interfering. I'm afraid we're on our own, General."

"We're almost to you, Justine. We'll secure the enemy ship and transfer the prisoners."

"Don't forget the Kinemet," she said. "There are several kilotons here."

"Right. Then we can go into a thorough debriefing."

∞

Alex and Michael were waiting in a large conference room just off the bridge, and Justine could barely contain her emotions. It had been less than two months since she'd seen them, but it felt like a lifetime.

Standing up and throwing his arms around Justine, Alex said, "You gave us all a scare. We thought the worst."

"I'm alive," she said, and gave him a wide smile. "I'm so glad all of you are all right."

"Thanks to Ah Tabai and Aliah," Alex said, and then formally introduced everyone to each other. Aliah excused herself to contact Naila aboard the *Fainne* and give them an update.

Justine shook hands with the Gliesan of Mayan descent. "I've been spending quite a bit of time with Yoatl."

Ah Tabai raised his brows and formed a guilty smile. "I'm sure he'll have a few choice words for me when I get back."

Justine narrowed her eyes at Alex. She could sense the change in him. "You have to tell me how you managed to complete the Kinemetic conversion. It's not something anyone else in the Collection has been able to do."

"You won't believe it," Alex said, smiling.

"Try me." Then Justine said, "Better yet, start from the beginning."

They all sat down at the conference table.

Alex told his story, beginning from the moment Justine had been abducted by the Kulsat mining ship. He updated her on the political upheaval in Sol System, Chow Yin's Emperorship, and the research into rediscovering Klaus's process.

Michael took over the story then, explaining about the ancient tale of Yaxche's friend, Patli. When she heard this, Justine quickly filled them in on what she knew about it, confirming that it had happened as it was told to them.

"It was touch and go," Michael said after describing his research on the alien body they found, and how the Grace's DNA was infused with molecules of altered Kinemet.

"While they brought me into space quickly enough to stop me from dying, we got word to a double-agent in Chow Yin's organization—he managed to inject Alex with Kinemet before a conversion trial. Of course," he said, glancing at Ah Tabai, "apparently that wasn't the actual reason Alex entered the state of Grace."

Justine put her hand on Alex. "However it happened, I'm glad you are altered. According to what I learned, those who fail the conversion process have a shorter life expectancy. You don't have to worry about that, now. Quite the opposite, in fact."

Alex said, "I have many questions for you. Like how you survived the Kulsat ship."

Justine let out a humorless laugh, and she told them what had happened to her, about the Kulsat and how Red Spot saved her from Three Crescents. Then she described her rescue by Naila and Fairamai, the journey to Gliese, and the events leading up to her residency and political appointment as Envoy of Sol System.

Partway through her story, General Gates entered the room. He'd been busy overseeing the transfer of prisoners from Chow Yin's ship, and directing his crew to effect repairs. He sat at the conference table and listened in.

"Political envoy, huh?" the general said when Justine finished. "It's too bad you can't use your influence to rouse the Collection."

"I got the process started, but it could take a while before they give Sol System 'Emerged' status."

"So what do we do, just sit here while our solar system is destroyed?" he asked, his tone more exasperated than accusatory.

"Maybe not." All through Alex's story, Justine had a nagging thought in the back of her mind. To Alex, she said, "Red Spot's advice might still stand. She said we could make the Kulsat surrender to us if we found the final component first."

"How?" Alex asked.

Justine gave him a quizzical look. "Are you up for an experiment?"

"Sure. What are you thinking?"

"Back when we were chased out of Sol System—by Chow Yin, apparently—he launched a torpedo with weaponized Kinemet. I was able to ignite it before it reached us."

Alex nodded. "I did that earlier, when Chow Yin tried to destroy Qin Station." His face grew dark. "I couldn't stop his second attack, however."

"I wonder if you, having the full powers of the Grace, have something more than that, concerning the Kinemet."

"You want me to blow up every Kulsat ship with Kinemet on it?" Alex asked, his face pale. "Even if I could, I don't think I would."

"No," Justine said, shaking her head. "But there's something about the way Red Spot talked about the Grace that led me to believe they had an ability that inspired even more awe."

"More than setting off a Kinemetic explosion a thousand-times more powerful than any atomic bomb?" Michael asked.

Justine turned to the general. "Do you have a small quantity of Kinemet we could use?"

He nodded and spoke into his communicator.

While they waited, Justine described the techniques she had learned from Red Spot: how to hide her photonic essence while in a state of light, and how to resist being quantized. To test it out, Alex quantized himself, and a moment later, Justine was unable to sense his presence. A few moments later, he reappeared in physical form. She tried to quantize him, and couldn't.

"Very interesting," Alex said. "I can see how these techniques came in handy, letting you get close to Chow Yin."

"I think there might be an extension of these techniques that only someone who is fused with Kinemet can perform."

"How do you mean?" Alex asked, and looked up as a lieutenant entered the room with a container holding a milligram of Kinemet.

"If someone threatens you with force, a natural reaction is to either defend yourself or go on the offensive. However, if you know someone has the power to take your power away, render you useless, you can neither defend yourself, nor fight. Perhaps this is what the Kulsat fear the most, being at the complete mercy of every other race in the galaxy."

"What do you want me to do?"

"Alex," Justine said, "I'm not sure how you would go about it, but can you try to nullify the radiation from that sample?"

"Nullify?"

The general cleared his throat. "That gram of Kinemet represents a considerable amount of money."

"It'll be worth it," Justine said, then turned to Alex. "If you can make Kinemet inert, you might be able to disable any Kulsat ship."

"I'll try," Alex said, and focused his concentration on the Kinemet. Justine kept her attention on it as well, and cried out in delight when she sensed the radiation in the sample dissipate completely.

Ah Tabai, who had remained quiet through the reunion, gasped. "You did it. You are, indeed, one of the Grace. The first in a millennium."

"So we can disable their ships?" the general asked, giving Ah Tabai an uncertain glance out of the corner of his eye.

"Yes." When she noticed the general frowning, Justine asked, "What's wrong? This is good news."

"We have one ship going up against how many, a hundred thousand?" the general said. "Even with this ability, Alex can only do so much. The Kulsat will swarm him. We don't have the time to convert enough Kinemats to give the Kulsat pause, at least not before they obliterate us."

"I might have an idea," Alex said. He turned to Justine. "You mentioned earlier that the Collection had tried to take the fight to the Kulsat home world once before."

Ah Tabai answered. "Yes. We all know the story. Their entire armada returned within a short time and destroyed the invading force."

Justine squinted at Alex. "If we were able to lure them all back to their home system, you really think you'll be able to nullify their ships as they enter Kulsat space?"

"Like the Battle of Thermopylae?" Michael asked, and turned to Alex. "As the general said, there's only one of you, and a hundred-thousand of them. No matter how fast you can nullify the Kinemet on their ships, all it takes is one conventional missile, and they've won."

"And the general is right," Alex said. "A hundred-thousand ships is a lot. There's no way I can nullify all of them."

"I don't think you have to," Justine said. "Once word reaches their leaders that one of the Grace is disabling their armada, they will surrender in order to preserve what they have. Why do you think they were subservient to the Grace for so long?"

"Now, wait a minute." The general gave them all a hard stare. "I can't authorize this kind of action. We need to return and transmit an update to my superiors—we only had a mandate to follow Chow Yin and apprehend him. And we've done that.

"Any further action needs to be sanctioned. We don't have the right to make unilateral decisions concerning the fate of Sol System, let alone the galaxy. I can't just let you 'invade' another solar system. Not to mention that we have to bring Chow Yin back to Earth for trial—everyone there needs to know he is in custody."

"General," Justine said, "there is every possibility that Sol System could be under siege at this very moment. I hate to sound cliché, but these are desperate times. Correct me if I'm wrong, but the ranking officer in any theater of operations has the authority to determine their individual force's plan of action should he not have the opportunity to receive orders from their superiors. The Kulsat invasion is impending, if not already underway. We need to take those desperate measures to give Sol System a fighting chance."

"Well..." the general said finally, "it *will* draw them away from attacking Sol, temporarily at least. That might give someone time to get back to Sol with this information to create more advanced Kinemats like Alex." He cocked his head. "You realize that it's a suicide mission."

"If you can get Chow Yin's ship patched up," Alex said, obviously making an effort to keep his voice steady, "I'll do it."

Justine said, "I'll go with him."

The general shook his head. "No. First of all, Chow Yin's ship would require nine months in dry dock. Secondly, we can't afford to sacrifice both of you. Besides, you're already established in the Collection of Worlds' political sphere. If we get through this, we're going to need you in that capacity."

"With all due respect, General," Justine said, "I don't think the entire Kulsat armada will return to their home world because of one broken-down Earth ship with a single Kinemat on board."

"And you think they will feel more threatened with two?"

"No, they won't," Ah Tabai said. Everyone in the room turned to stare at him when he added, "But they might take notice if their home world is being invaded by twenty-thousand ships."

"Twenty-thousand?" Michael asked.

"Yes. That is approximately how many Sentinels there are in the galaxy." He glanced at Aliah, who nodded her agreement. "Our ships are small, but we have experience out-flying the Kulsat battle-cruisers. I will send word out to everyone."

Justine gave him a long look. "What about the ancient law? The Collection would never condone this action."

Ah Tabai smiled. "We are not going to interfere in the evolution of Sol System. Our purpose is to protect the galaxy from the Kulsat." He looked at Alex. "And to follow the rule of the Grace."

Taking a deep breath, Justine looked at the general. "Do you have a better plan?"

Slowly shaking his head, the general said, "No."

"All right, then." Justine stood up. "What are we waiting for? Let's get this war party started."

43

USSF Warship *Liberty* :
Centauri System :

Assuring them the repairs required before they could be underway to Gliese would be quick, General Gates left Alex, Michael, Justine, Ah Tabai and Aliah in the conference room with a final admonition.

"You realize that I'm giving you a lot of leeway here. I fully expect a thorough briefing at some point."

Michael nodded to him. "You have my word. Once this crisis is behind us, we'll ensure you have all the information you need, General."

Once the officer was gone, Alex turned to Ah Tabai, and gestured to Michael. "I'm not sure what's happening to him. He was exposed to a Kinemetic blast."

Michael quickly explained what had happened with the alien body on Earth. When prompted, he outlined the story Patli had told him.

"We are all under great stress when we are within the gravity well of a planet," Ah Tabai explained. "The Xtôti—the species of being whom, until now, were the only race to ascend to the Grace—were much more sensitive. They had technology far beyond anything we've been able to achieve. They could manipulate the Aetherock a hundred ways, making it a thousand times more powerful than anything we have. One of the side effects of this was the altered Aetherock's extreme sensitivity to sunlight and fire. The radiation from the altered Aetherock is what affected those villagers so many hundreds of years ago, and what is affecting you now, Michael."

"So how do we heal him?" Alex asked.

"We don't." When everyone gave him a puzzled look, he said, "We merely complete the process. He must undertake the conversion. If it is successful, then he will become an Aetherbeing, like the rest of us."

Alex asked, "Could that have been a solution for me all along?"

Ah Tabai shrugged. "Yesterday, I would have said yes. Now, however, I am not certain. You are Grace, after all. There is an unknown factor remaining in your case. Perhaps your initial exposure on the asteroid when you were a child was unique, in some way. Once we are past this crisis, we can explore your condition in greater depth."

Michael cleared his throat. "The Grace thought it better not to share the technology." He gave Alex a stern look. "Maybe you should think long and hard before going down that path."

Ah Tabai immediately bowed. "Of course, the decision will be entirely up to the Grace. As Galactic Law prohibits us from sharing technology until a system has Emerged, I expect the Grace will follow the same philosophy, and withhold knowledge until we have met a greater standard."

Alex, looking uncomfortable with the notion of all that responsibility, gestured to Michael. "So, all we have to do is prime some Kinemet and expose him to it after it activates?"

Michael cocked his head. "I hope you have a conversion chamber nearby … Chow Yin blew up our only one."

"We have a facility at our aerie in Gliese," Ah Tabai said, "but that won't be necessary this time."

"It won't?" Michael asked, glancing back and forth between Ah Tabai and Aliah, who made an odd ruffling motion with her neck feathers.

Pointing to Alex, Ah Tabai said, "In addition to all the techniques shared by Aetherbeings, the Grace has always had the ability to initiate the Aether process themselves."

"What?" Alex asked. "How?"

"Do you know how to quantize people?" Ah Tabai asked.

Nodding, Alex said, "It was something that just kind of occurred to me. I did that to get everyone to Pluto."

"Unlike other Aetherbeings, you have altered Aetherock in your molecules. You do not require a conversion chamber. Perhaps, if you think about it, the Aether process will come naturally to you."

Michael stood up and faced Alex. "If you think you can help me…"

Getting to his feet, Alex squared off in front of Michael and seemed to be considering him for a very long time. Then, just when Michael thought the answer would elude his young friend, Alex's face lit up.

"Of course!" he said, and quantized Michael.

Unlike the previous times Michael had been rendered into a photonic state, this time he retained complete awareness of his surroundings. He was a floating cloud of light. The sensation was beyond anything he'd ever experienced or imagined before in his life.

Like a child who just discovered how fun it was to splash in a puddle of mud, Michael pushed his essence around the conference room. He reached out with his senses and saw the three stars in the Centauri System. Though there were no planetary bodies, there were millions of large asteroids scattered throughout the system. He, somehow, was able to sense their exact location in relation to where he was.

Like a powerful lighthouse, the star beacon glowed bright beside him; and, to a lesser degree, he could detect thousands of other beacons scattered throughout the galaxy.

The ship itself was a living thing to him, thrumming with electricity, and Michael could feel the electrons pulsing like veins and arteries. Instinctively, he knew he could reach out with his senses and manipulate that electricity, if he chose.

So, he thought, *this is what it feels like? I never want to stop!*

But, there was much more to do.

With a thought, he returned himself to physical form.

Justine glanced at Ah Tabai. "Do you think this will be enough proof that we are Emerged? We need to practice some of our techniques."

The Sentinel nodded. "As far as I am concerned, Sol is an Emerged system. Certainly, it will be ratified. It is a minor breach of protocol, but the techniques may be necessary to prevent you from harming yourselves or others."

Over the next few minutes, Ah Tabai gave Alex and Michael a crash course in being a Kinemat—or, Aetherbeing, as they called it. The Kulsat called them Risen. Michael wondered if every species in the galaxy had different names for the same thing.

Michael learned how to quantize inanimate objects without Kinemet; how to hide his photonic signature; how to resist being quantized, and the theory behind using the star beacons.

Just as they were finishing the lessons, General Gates entered.

"All systems are operational—it's not pretty, but it will do." He looked at each of them in turn, his gaze lingering a little longer on Aliah. "Have we all caught each other up to speed so far?"

"We're ready," Justine said, and then addressed all of them in the room. "There are quite a few people I can't wait for you to meet."

44

Skanse Aerie :
Gliese System :

Any alien ship that appeared unexpectedly in Gliesan space had a matter of seconds before the patrol ships guarding the star beacon would attack them.

Naila and Fairamai would have already reported the details of the battle between the Kulsat and Chow Yin's forces, and that Alex and the other Solans were on their way, but Ah Tabai said it was better to follow protocol. The moment the *Liberty* entered Gliese space, Ah Tabai transmitted his identity through the communications system, as well as who he'd brought with him.

Moments later, the return message came through from Commander Analock. The translator on the ship was not yet programmed with the Gliesan language, so Ah Tabai let them know what the reply was.

"We acknowledge our Solan neighbors. Welcome to Gliese System. Please remain at your current position and refrain from additional broadcast until we update central command."

To Ah Tabai, General Gates asked, "What can we expect?"

"The majority of Gliesan government responses are dictated by a rigorous set of laws and protocols," Ah Tabai said. "As with many Emerged systems, we consider ourselves under a constant state of siege. Though no Kulsat ship has invaded our system in over a hundred years, no one knows what might prompt them to take notice and launch a surprise attack; it's happened before. Our protocols are in place to give our system advance warning in that event. Once central command is made aware that we are not hostiles, we'll be formally invited to visit to Skanse Aerie, which is our main diplomatic hub."

"It's an incredible station," Justine said. "You'll no doubt be astounded by the representatives of the different star systems." She smiled at Michael. "If you thought international politics were difficult to navigate, interstellar politics not only deal with different languages and cultures, but different biology. The ambassador from Mebsuta System is physiologically similar to a sea anemone; his mouth is also his anus, and they do not consider public defecation to be socially unacceptable. It can sometimes be unsettling for other cultures, like ours, to interact with his species."

"I imagine so," Michael said, his eyes wide.

The general interrupted. "How long will it take their commander to respond?"

"Very soon," Ah Tabai said. "But it will take us a little time to fly there. Once we are cleared, I will contact the Committee of Sentinels and begin to organize them."

Looking back and forth between Michael and Justine, the general said, "If they're anything like our military, this mobilization could take a bit of time. What if the Kulsat attacks Sol before we organize?"

Justine nodded at the question. "From my experience, the Kulsat are a highly structured hierarchal society. Their report will have to go up their chain of command. Once their leaders make their decision, then they will begin preparations and invade our system *en masse.*"

Impatiently, the general asked, "And how long do you think that will take?"

Ah Tabai answered, "Historically, anywhere from one of your days to a month, depending on how much resistance they expect from the target system. Considering your criminal, Chow Yin, was able to defeat their patrol ship, they will consider Sol a high threat. They will mobilize as quickly as they can, but they will also utilize the bulk of their armada. The Kulsat believe in overkill."

Michael asked, "What if the Committee of Sentinels doesn't approve of our plan? Also," he added, "what if the governments of the Collection decide to forbid the action?"

With a reassuring smile, Ah Tabai replied, "The governments only have authority over their own systems. They can set policy for Sentinel protocol while in their systems, but the Galactic Law set by the Grace supersedes local governments. When we are in a neighboring jurisdiction, we must obey local laws. When we are in an unregulated region of space, such as the Centauri System, we need only to follow Galactic Law. I am confident, once the Committee learns of the return of the Grace—Alex—they will be enthusiastic. For the past millennium, we have strived for a way to eliminate the Kulsat menace."

Their conversation was interrupted when Commander Analock opened a communication channel with them. Ah Tabai translated:

"On behalf of the Collection of Worlds, the Gliesan Parliament extends you, General Gates, official welcome to our system. During your stay, you will not undertake to acquire our Aether technology, and you will give your oath that you will uphold all Gliesan and Galactic Laws. As your system is not recognized as Emerged, you will be granted limited access to our station and restricted from venturing outside the station-star beacon corridor. As commander of your ship, you must accept responsibility for the actions of your crew and passengers while in our system. Do you agree to these terms?"

Nodding to Ah Tabai to translate, the general said, "I do so agree."

∞

The *Liberty* wasn't nearly as fast as the *Fainne,* and the trip to Skanse Aerie took almost three hours.

In the meantime, Justine spoke to Alex and Michael at length about everything she'd read on the Kulsat, their history, and their solar system.

By the time they reached the station, Ah Tabai informed them that he'd sent word to the Committee of Sentinels, and that they'd approved the plan. With one of the Grace on their side, everyone believed history had come to a turning point.

Though most systems in the Collection had numerous Kinemats, few of them chose to join the Sentinels. Many systems did not have any representative Sentinels; uncommonly, Gliese system had four. With their membership spread out among the twenty-thousand or so Emerged systems in the galaxy, it would take some time to get the message to everyone.

The plan was to have all the Sentinels converge in Gliese, where the Grace was, and then jump to Kulsat in small waves—the only way to get into an Emerged system guarded by Aetherbeings.

The attack would take place in twelve hours.

∞

On Aerie Station, Ambassador Yoatl was at the dock to greet the new arrivals from Sol System.

"Envoy Justine," he said. "You should not have given me such a scare." His words were tinged with remonstration, but he smiled through them. "I'm glad you are unharmed."

General Gates said, "We have a number of prisoners on board. Is it possible that we can transfer custody of them to the station while we make repairs and prepare for the incursion to Kulsat?"

"Of course," Yoatl said. "I will make arrangements. I'm sure you'll find our holding facilities more than adequate." He spoke into his collar communicator in a series of whistles and chirps. When he finished, he glanced at Justine. "Speaking of which, Red Spot has been asking after you. Once she learned that you were back in Gliese with one of the Grace, she requested a meeting with both of you."

Justine nodded. "I was hoping to see her, anyway." She turned to Alex. "Unless you need some rest, did you want to go now?"

"Absolutely."

Michael said, "If it's all the same, I was wondering if I could have some time with Ambassador Yoatl." When Justine raised an eyebrow at him, he added, "Whether we're successful in stopping the Kulsat or not, we will need to join the galactic community. I'm sure there will be a lot of protocols and procedures to becoming a member of the Collection of Worlds."

"That is a fact," Yoatl said. "It is a long, complicated process. There is much to learn." He nodded approvingly at Michael. "I will bring you to the offices of the Gliesan Councilor. That will be the best place to start."

"I know the way to the holding facility," Justine said.

General Gates looked up as a tall, imposing Gliesan approached. Military men seemed to recognize other soldiers automatically, and the general saluted.

"I'm Commander Analock," the Gliesan said, the translation coming out from his collar translator a fraction of a second later. "I am at your disposal, General." The two officers headed off to organize repairs and the transfer of Chow Yin and the other prisoners.

Yoatl pointed to the opposite end of the docking bay, at an awaiting shuttle. "It will be quicker to fly to the Councilor's offices from here. He has a private dock where we can land."

"We'll catch up soon," Justine said to Michael and Yoatl, and motioning for Alex to follow, she led him out of the docking bay and to the holding area where Red Spot waited. All the while, she gave him a running commentary of the workings of the station.

∞

Though she'd described the Kulsat in detail to Alex, she still saw his look of amazement when Red Spot swam up to the computer console to greet them.

"Justine," she said. "You are continuous."

With a smile, Justine replied, "Yes, thank you. How are you?"

"I continue as well." A moment later, she said, "The Gliesans informed us of the return of the Grace." It was difficult to tell if Red Spot was looking at her or at Alex.

Justine gestured to her young friend. "This is Alex Manez. He is the first of the Solans to attempt the Rising, and he has become one of the Grace."

Red Spot waved three of her tentacles in a rippling motion. "It is my honor to be in your presence, Your Grace."

"Please, call me Alex."

"It is not permitted to be so familiar, Your Grace."

Justine caught Alex's puzzled expression. She said to the Kulsat, "Now that the Grace have returned, we hope your Consortium will end their conflict with the rest of the galaxy. We have made plans to journey to your system and make your people aware of the Grace."

"That will never happen," Red Spot said, and Justine paled, not sure if there was trouble with the translation.

"What do you mean? You said they would surrender if we found the final component."

Red Spot said, "No, Justine. I said the only way to stop them is to find the final component. The Risen will not surrender. It does not matter if the Grace has returned. We are all well-schooled in our history and our people's enslavement by the Grace."

"Enslavement?"

"How else could it be described? We had to obey the Grace, or they would take away our ability to travel beyond our solar system."

"But," Justine said slowly, "how, then, do we stop the Kulsat?"

"I will explain." Red Spot typed on the console for a few more moments. "Until we attempt to receive the Gift, we Kulsat are slaves.

To us, it will make little difference who are our masters; the Grace, or the Risen. The Risen, however, will never relinquish their status. They will die first. Finding the final component, and bringing about the return of the Grace *is* the only way to stop the Risen. Alex Manez must destroy all Kulsat Risen. Only then will the non-Risen once again swear fealty to the Grace, and begin to rebuild our society."

The pallor that came over Alex's face at the statement spoke volumes. Justine was aghast at the notion. It was tantamount to genocide. Even if he agreed to such a horrible undertaking, the obstacles just became insurmountable. Disabling hundreds or thousands of ships was one thing. Seeking out and killing hundreds of thousands—perhaps even millions—of Risen was an impossible task. Discounting the moral implications of such an action, doing so would take a lifetime.

"No," Alex said. "I won't do it. There has to be another way."

"Over the past millennium, the Risen have become completely consumed by their power. They will never stop."

Alex turned to Justine. His face reddened with rage and horror. "We need to stop the invasion. Even if I were insane enough to go through with this, there's no way I can do it by myself. Maybe if there were hundreds of us with the power of the Grace—" He shook his head. "No, it's unthinkable. If I had the knowledge to convert someone to the Grace, I wouldn't if I knew they were going to do this."

Taking a deep breath, Justine nodded. "Neither would I. It's monstrous."

While the two were talking, Red Spot continued typing. Her words came out. "There is only one way to stop the Kulsat without destroying the Risen. It is an enormous risk to us, but it is possible."

Both Alex and Justine said, "How?" at the same time.

"I will only tell you once we are in Kulsat System." When neither of the humans responded immediately, she typed again. "You must return me and my comrades to our home. This is not negotiable."

"Red Spot," Justine said, her mind racing to figure out if the Kulsat had planned this from the beginning, or whether she was playing them now, "how can we know if you are … practicing deception?"

"I will not betray my world," Red Spot said through the translator. "Neither will I betray the Grace, nor the galaxy. The only way to stop the threat of the Risen is to save Kulsat from them. Only the Grace can achieve this. For the sake of the trillions of my people who are at the mercy of the few million Risen, you must help us."

"Save Kulsat?" Justine asked. "How?"

"I will only give my knowledge to the Grace, and only once we are in Kulsat System."

Red Spot typed again. "Your Grace, will you save us?"

45

Skanse Aerie :
Gliese System :

"There's no way," General Gates said when Alex and Justine approached him and explained what Red Spot had told them.

The two found the general in the Gliesan councilor's suite. Michael and Yoatl were also there.

The general's face grew a deep shade of crimson as he spoke. "Not only are we already so far beyond my mandate that I'm probably going to be court-martialed when we get back home—if I'm lucky—but even if I had any inclination to follow through on this mission now—which would be sure sign I've had some kind of psychotic breakdown—I can't imagine the Council of Sentinels would go on what's tantamount to a suicide mission." He took a deep breath when he finished his rant, his eyes flicking back and forth between the two.

"It's not a suicide mission," Justine said, but her next words were cut off when the general raised a forestalling hand.

"First you tell me that, no matter what we do, the Kulsat won't surrender. Then you say there is some kind of secret method to stop the Kulsat—by saving them!" He shook his head in disbelief. "But the only one who knows how is one of the Kulsat prisoners, who won't tell us how unless we bring her with us." Giving Justine an exasperated look, he asked, "And you don't find anything suspicious about that?"

After the general gave Councilor Ijallanna a pleading look, the tall Gliesan ruffled his dark-gray neck feathers and said, "Officially, our government has no say in whether you undertake this action—Sentinel business is not in our purview. However, if the Sentinels are on board with this, I'm certain I can convince our security council to hand custody of our Kulsat guests to you, General Gates. After all, we have taken precautions against giving them access to any vital information on our system."

At the general's incredulous look, the councilor said, "Perhaps we should invite the Sentinels into this discussion." He strode to his computer console and spoke a few commands into it.

Within moments, the monitor flared to life. Ah Tabai stood in the frame, with Aliah, Naila, and Fairamai in the background.

"Councilor Ijallanna," Ah Tabai said. "I was just about to let you and the others know. Word has come back from the Sentinel Council. Every available Sentinel will be ready to go to Kulsat System within six hours."

"There seems to be a significant hitch in the plan, Sentinel Ah Tabai. I will let the Grace explain."

Alex took a step closer to the monitor and said, "We have information that the incursion may not convince the Kulsat Risen to surrender. Red Spot indicates that they are so power-mad, they will most likely fight to the death. There's an alternative, but we don't have all the facts. Instead of an offensive, we require the Sentinels to provide a distraction. We need to bait all Risen in the galaxy to return to Kulsat, at which point Red Spot will reveal how to stop them permanently. She won't tell us how until we are in the system, however."

Ah Tabai frowned. "Do you believe she's telling the truth?"

Alex, shooting a quick look at Justine, who nodded, said, "It might be our only option."

Taking a moment to confer with the three other Sentinels, Ah Tabai returned to the screen. "We'll need to get confirmation from the Council, but we all follow the law of the Grace. I see no reason not to follow you, Your Grace."

The general let out a deep sigh. Justine and Alex looked at him.

He gave a terse shake of his head. "I must be as crazy as the rest of you." Addressing the Councilor, he asked, "Is there any way your people can assist us in building a grapple to secure the Kulsat's shuttle to our ship?"

∞

Five hours later, Alex stood on the bridge of the *Liberty*, along with the general and his staff as they went through a final systems check. They, and the twenty-thousand sentinel ships, were in formation around the Gliesan star beacon.

Red Spot and the ninety other Kulsat were already aboard their shuttle, which was firmly secured to the *Liberty* with an electromagnetic grapple. A direct communications line was set up between the shuttle and Alex's station on the bridge. When he'd reminded Red Spot about a quantum pilot's limitation of how many beings they could quantize, the Kulsat leader had assured Alex that they were all more than willing to take that chance.

While Michael stayed on Aerie Skanse—he did not have any practical experience either as a Kinemat or as a pilot—Justine had insisted on doing her part.

"I've been training for this all my life," she'd said. "I've studied the Sentinel ships. I can fly one. You need every able body." When the general and the Council of Sentinels approved her participation, Justine hadn't been able to hide the elation from her face. Alex knew, from previous conversations, she'd never believed she would ever pilot a spacecraft again, and—he kept the dark thought to himself—this might be the last time she ever did.

Though they'd gone over the plan several times, the general reiterated it for both Alex's and Red Spot's benefit. "We'll go through the star beacon into Kulsat space last. Once we arrive, we won't directly engage the Kulsat. We'll get out of the thick of the battle, and hang back until we're certain the bulk of the Kulsat Risen ships have returned to the system.

"Alex, you will nullify the quantum drive of any enemy ship that comes close to us, and we'll retreat out of their line of fire. Once the bulk of the Kulsat armada is in the system, and Red Spot lets you know whatever it is you're supposed to do to save the Kulsat, you do it. Then we'll get the hell out of there." He shook his head in bewilderment as if he couldn't believe he was going along with the plan.

A moment later, he continued, his voice taking on a hard edge. "Red Spot, I expect you to hold up your end of the bargain."

A mechanical voice came through the bridge speakers. "I do not practice deception," Red Spot said. "Expect several waves of Kulsat. The Sentinels will meet their initial defense patrol, but they will not provide much resistance—they will alert our home planet, and then they will exit the system to call for reinforcements.

"The largest force will come from within the system. The Sentinels must hold them off for as long as possible to allow those who are outside the system to return." According to consensus, that would take anywhere up to a quarter of an hour.

The problem would come when the off-system Kulsat ships returned. The Sentinels would be trapped between two armadas.

The general asked, "And how long will it take Alex to … do whatever it is you want him to do?"

"It will not take long," Red Spot's translated voice said through the speakers. "Before Alex saves us, you must ensure you have released our shuttle, and all non-Kulsat have exited the system. Only then will I share the knowledge with you."

Alex could hear a very low growl come from the general, and though he could sympathize with the sentiment, he trusted in Justine's judgment. Red Spot had risked everything to save her—an alien—and had given no indication that she would betray them.

"How long until the operation begins, General?" Alex asked, more to distract the officer than anything else.

The general was in constant contact with the Sentinel squadron commanders through his upgraded communications console. There were five-hundred squadrons in total. From the instant the first wave of Sentinel ships went through to the last wave, it would take nearly a quarter of an hour. The *Liberty*, with Alex as the quantum pilot, would launch a minute later. The entire time, the Sentinels would be under heavy fire. Alex didn't want to think about the potential casualties.

"If I read these monitors correctly," the general said, scanning the screens, "the first wave will quantize in thirty minutes."

"Which squadron is Justine in?"

"The last," the general said. "She told me she plans on joining the Sentinels once this is all over. For some reason, flying billions of kilometers through the vast blankness of space is more appealing to her than a cushy political assignment."

A moment later, he said, "I'm getting an alert on the screens."

"What is it?"

The general raised his head and gave Alex a hard look. "The Sentinels have a tracking sensor aimed at Sol System's star beacon. They say it's activating. The Kulsat are invading us right now."

A cold bead of sweat rolled down Alex's spine. "How many of them?"

"No idea. Could be hundreds, for all I know. The Sentinel commander is giving the word to launch against Kulsat now. He hopes the Kulsat patrol will send out the alert to their armada to return before they get too far into our system to turn back in time."

The general asked, "Are you ready for this? The first wave is engaging ... now. We're up in about fifteen minutes."

"That's too long," Alex said.

"What?"

"We need to get to Sol System right now." Alex wasn't about to stand around and wait while an armada of genocidal Kulsat Risen were on their way to Earth. He knew, even if their leaders sent a messenger to recall them, they would be too far into the system to turn around. Earth was wide open to their attack.

Before the general could say another word of protest, Alex quantized all the passengers on the *Liberty*, and all the Kulsat on the mining shuttle.

A moment later, he quantized the ship itself, and headed for the Gliesan star beacon, setting a course for *Dis Pater*.

The instant before he reached the star beacon, he was still in photonic space—an elemental being within the physical universe.

The next instant...

46

Unknown :

Welcome home, Alex.

It was the haunting voice that had been calling to him for nearly two decades, and he struggled to understand it.

Though he'd been in a photonic state a number of times, before the tragic experiment on Qin Station that had completed his transformation, he'd never been 'aware' while quantized.

Since Qin Station, he'd initiated the change in himself several times—and marveled in the awareness he had while in that state of being.

He'd never traveled using the star beacons as the quantum pilot, however. Both times, from Sol to Centauri, and then from Centauri to Gliese, Ah Tabai had been in control. When another Kinemat quantized someone, it was the only time that being would not retain awareness in the photonic state.

Alex wasn't sure what he had expected. Indeed, his thoughts had been so preoccupied with getting to Sol System that he hadn't fully anticipated what would happen. After all, everything the other Kinemats had told him was that, once they reached the star beacon, there was no consciousness during transit to the destination until after they arrived in the new system.

As far as anyone knew, the journey between beacons was instantaneous.

Now, Alex knew different.

For him, the journey was simultaneously immediate, and of an infinite duration.

Though the physical universe contained vast stretches of emptiness, there was always a faint signature of electromagnetic radiation in all parts of space, however immeasurable it was to technological sensors.

The star beacons were not portals to another dimension, as Alice Yin had theorized.

Alex recalled the description Ah Tabai had given him before: "Outside light, the star beacons occupy the same space." Without proper perspective, that was the only rational explanation for how the star beacons existed.

His mind struggled to understand the reality, and it seemed to take eons for him to realize the truth.

The star beacons did not occupy the same space, because the place it touched did not have light, or space, or time.

The monumental artifact they called *Dis Pater* was nothing more than a physical construct, built with altered Kinemet, surrounding the star beacon.

The star beacon was an anomaly—something of a fracture in the fabric of the universe. It was the absence of the universe.

Somehow, Alex guessed, the Xtôti had not been content to travel throughout the galaxy at the speed of light. After all, it would take over fifty-thousand years to get from one edge of the Milky Way to the other. The physicists at Quantum Resources had theorized that there were countless ways to prime Kinemet, and create powerful results from the alteration.

The Grace had experimented with this a million years ago. Instinctively, he realized that one of these experiments had caused their sun to supernova. Dimly, he wondered if that reaction had caused their metamorphosis from Kinemats to the Grace…

Was it possible the Xtôti, like Alex, had no idea how they'd evolved past Kinemats and become the Grace? If they had, they would have created more Grace and not have died out. They would have continued expanding throughout the Milky Way and, possibly, ventured to neighboring galaxies.

Was Alex, truly, the last of the Grace?

If so, it was up to him to rediscover the process and repopulate the galaxy with more Grace. But how? Was there some kind of similarity between that and what had happened to Alex on Macklin's Rock?

He recalled that the first readout from the security receptacle had indicated something was coming at them at light speeds. Could that cosmic event have, indeed, happened at the same time his parents had drilled into the asteroid and exposed the deposit of raw Kinemet?

Whatever had happened, it must have had something to do with the Sun itself, Alex guessed. Perhaps it had been the same kind of unexpected solar event during an experiment that had inadvertently caused the supernova of Xtôti's sun.

If the Grace had never figured it out, then how was Alex going to?

The thought came to him then: even if he could figure out how to raise someone to the state of Grace, should he? Perhaps the galaxy wasn't ready for that. Maybe there were some secrets that should be kept a mystery.

But he would have to think about it another time. After all, according to what Justine had told him, he might have an abundance of that commodity to meditate on the topic.

Right now, he needed to understand the nature of that null-space between star beacons.

The story Justine had related to him on the history of the Grace indicated that it was after the Xtôti sun's supernova that they'd begun their outward expansion through the galaxy, creating the system of star beacons to connect individual solar systems.

As Grace, they'd figured out how to tear holes in the universe, and 'sew' the tears back together with 'threads' of altered Kinemet—which were metaphysically connected to each other, as if in a state of quantum superposition.

Traveling through the star beacons was, in actuality, traveling through rips in the universe.

The monuments themselves were incredible feats of advanced technology designed to monitor and house the 'threads'. They also had the power to shield the location of the star beacons for populated solar systems.

Kinemet was a quantum element. Using it and entering the photonic state, Alex was aware of others who were also in that state, and could sense the Kinemet in quantum drives.

He imagined, if he tried, he could also sense raw deposits of Kinemet. In a way, all Kinemet throughout the universe was connected, entangled on a metaphysical level. And the hub of those connections was in that tear in the universe; it was the center of everything.

At the same time, that existence between star beacons was the purest state of Kinemet. Alex, and all those who had achieved the state of Grace, was a creature of that element. It was fundamental to their

DNA. It was such a powerful concentration of pure Kinemet, it was the closest thing to 'home' there could be for someone like Alex.

Aside from those who'd died by mishap, this is where the majority of the Grace had gone. A million years of life was more than enough time for any sentient being to exist. Alex couldn't imagine it. One-by-one, they must have made a decision to take that final voyage to the null-space outside the universe, and remain there.

Instinctively, Alex knew he could stay in that place between star beacons for eternity, and be perfectly content for the rest of his metaphysical existence. It *was* home.

But … there was something more important for him to do than remaining there, and his conscience would not let him stay.

Sol System was in danger.

He was the only one who could save it.

47

USSF Warship *Liberty*:
Sol System:

...he was back in a physical state, on the *Liberty*.

"What the hell do you think you're doing, young man?" General Gates asked in a growl, though he was quickly distracted when the connection to the Sentinel fleet was lost. His communications array went silent. His second-in-command tapped a few haptic symbols on his own console, and the main casement on the bridge lit up with their current coordinates: they were in orbit around Pluto.

Ignoring the general's question, Alex quantized himself, though not to avoid reprimand from the officers. Instead, he used his photonic senses to cast out through the solar system, looking for signatures of the Kulsat Risen.

When he found them, a wave of trepidation coursed through him.

During the planning phase of their military action, the Sentinels speculated that the Kulsat would send anywhere between a dozen and a few hundred of their warships to Sol System.

Alex detected well over ten-thousand Risen, all in a photonic state racing at near-light speeds toward Neptune.

A moment later, his astonishment at the sheer number of them passed when he wondered why they would be heading to Sol System's outermost major planet. There wasn't an occupied outpost there, only a few monitoring stations orbiting the ice giant.

Then he realized the Kulsat wouldn't know which of the planets were populated with Solans, and which were barren of life. They would have to fly from planet to planet until they found Earth, where they would begin to look for the final component, wreaking destruction on any humans who got in their way.

Elated, Alex returned to his physical form on the bridge of the *Liberty*, and informed the general that there were over ten-thousand Kulsat ships heading for Neptune.

"Its orbit is very close to Pluto's right now," he said matter-of-factly. "It's only about two-hundred million kilometers away. The quantum drive can get us there in about twelve minutes."

"What?" the general asked. "The ten-thousand Kulsat are heading for Neptune?" He seemed to realize he was just repeating Alex. "What does that mean?"

"They don't know Earth is our primary world. They need to drop out of photonic space to check each planet on their way in. I would imagine they'd take a bit of time to scan each one before heading for the next. We need to follow after them."

"And just what do you imagine we can do if we get there before they leave? One ship against ten thousand?" He spoke the number in a hoarse voice.

"We're going to send them a warning."

"A warning?" the general asked, obviously not understanding Alex's intent.

"Not from us," he said, "from Red Spot. We'll get her to alert them that the Sentinels have taken advantage of the situation and are attacking their home world."

"Ah," the general said with a light nod.

Alex opened a communications line with Red Spot and outlined his plan. The Kulsat agreed to help.

She added, "Once we have delivered the message, we must leave before they scan your ship and decide that we practice a deception."

"Understood," Alex said. "The moment we arrive in Neptunian space, you must be ready to broadcast the warning."

Red Spot replied. "Understood, Your Grace."

Alex gave General Gates a questioning look, and when he got a nod of assent, he immediately quantized the crew and ship, and flew toward the Kulsat armada.

48

Patrol Ship :
Gliese System :

Justine couldn't believe what had happened. No one expected Alex to take off to Sol System like that. The entire communications network of Sentinels was swarmed with everyone trying to figure out what was going on and what to do.

Without Alex, there was no point going to Kulsat System. They would be outnumbered five to one, and each of the Kulsat warships was heavily armed, whereas the majority of the Sentinel ships were two-person scout ships. It would be a slaughter.

Justine sat in the pilot's chair of the small vessel the Gliesan Councilor had loaned her. Though it was not designed to Sentinel standards, it had enough Kinemetic armor to absorb one or two mining laser shots. She knew her role in the invasion wasn't so much for direct combat, but to monitor Alex on the *Liberty*.

She had failed that mission even before she started.

A communications alert came through her console, and she recognized the caller's identification. It was Councilor Ijallanna. When she opened the channel, she saw Yoatl and Michael in the casement frame.

"Envoy Turner," the councilor said. "What happened?"

"I'm sorry, Councilor. When Alex heard that the Kulsat had invaded Sol System, he went after them."

"By himself? What does he hope to accomplish?"

"I'm not certain, Sir." Justine addressed Michael. "Do you think he'll try to take them all on himself? That would be suicide."

In the background, Michael looked gravely concerned. "There's only one way to find out. Someone has to go there and see what's happening."

Yoatl said, "Sol System has not been ratified as Emerged. No one is officially permitted to travel there."

Ah Tabai and Aliah had gone against protocol to take Michael, Alex, Kenny and Yaxche back there. They had only done so because they did not believe they would be detected by the Solans. Justine had learned that the Committee of Sentinels were going to launch an investigation into their actions, and they could possible expel the two from the organization for what they'd done.

Now, with practically every Sentinel in the galaxy gathered in one place, none of them would break protocol without explicit orders from their leaders. That kind of political decision would not be made unilaterally.

It was up to Justine. She wasn't a Sentinel, and the only thing stopping her was her parole to the Gliesan government.

"Councilor Ijallanna..." she said.

"Of course," he replied. "You are released from your bond. Go. Find out what's happening and return here immediately. We need to know."

Before the councilor had finished speaking, Justine quantized herself and her vessel, focusing her consciousness on the star beacon, and initiating a connection directly to Sol System.

∞

The journey from Gliese to Sol System was instantaneous, and when Justine materialized in her home system after months of being away, she felt a kind of elation in returning.

Just as quickly, the feeling left her. The space around Pluto was barren of any ships, conventional or quantum. In physical form, she could only push her *sight* out a hundred-and-fifty kilometers, but in a photonic state, she could extend her senses to detect other Kinemetic signatures throughout the solar system, provided they weren't hiding themselves.

When she quantized herself and sent her senses out, she gasped when she detected a mass of Kinemetic beings—the Kulsat!—heading directly for her.

They were coming from the direction of Neptune.

Swallowing her panic, she realized that Alex must have managed to get their attention somehow. Focusing, she saw that there was one signature ahead of the pack by a narrow margin. It had to be Alex.

They were only half a minute of travel time from the star beacon. Justine's initial impulse was to launch herself through first and return to Gliese with the news, but she willed herself to wait.

Sure enough, she detected the star beacon activating, and with the ship's sensors, saw that it was connecting with the Kulsat System. As she guessed, Alex was leading them back there.

There was one big problem with that, she knew, and felt the iron grip of panic. If Alex led them to Kulsat, he would be there by himself, caught between the thousands of pursuers and the tens of thousands of warships in the system. He would be on his own, and would not last long without help from the Sentinels.

With the star beacon activated, Justine was helpless to do anything until Alex and the Kulsat had passed through to the other solar system.

The moment they were gone, Justine activated the star beacon once more, and went through it back to Gliese.

∞

Moments after arriving, she blasted the news out for everyone to hear.

"Alex managed to lead the Kulsat back to their home system. He's there alone. We need to mobilize immediately."

Hundreds of voices flooded the communications system until the Sentinel commander sent out a squelch, silencing the chatter.

Once he had everyone's attention, he sent out the order. "Prepare to launch for the Kulsat system. First arrivals, once you are there, find Alex's signature and move in to protect him. Everyone else, be prepared for heavy fire. Ready? Launch."

Justine, barely able to get her breath, intended to go in with the first wave—damn the protocol—but the moment she quantized with the first few hundred Sentinels and oriented to the star beacon, she realized there was something wrong.

The star beacon would not activate for the Kulsat System.

After repeated attempts, all she could do was return to physical space.

Through her communications console, she heard the commander issue a statement. "Sentinels, somehow the Kulsat have completely blocked their star beacon. We are not able to penetrate it."

Justine's senses swam with the implications.

Alex was trapped in the Kulsat System with no hope of rescue.

49

USSF Warship *Liberty*:
Kulsat System:

Everything seemed to happen at once.

Upon entering the Kulsat System, Alex and the *Liberty* returned to physical space.

The patrol ships guarding the star beacon detected their presence and began to lock their weapons on the intruder.

Alex knew that he only had seconds before the Solan ship was blasted out of existence, and he was on the verge of quantizing the ship again with the intention of traveling deeper into enemy territory, but his communications console streamed a message from Red Spot.

General Gates, obviously realizing where they were, was shouting at him, but his words were lost on Alex.

The message. The secret that Red Spot knew, which no one else seemed to know. There it was on his readout, but for the life of him, Alex could not understand its meaning.

"The Kulsat did not fear the Grace only because of their ability to nullify the Gift. The Kulsat feared the Grace because they could dismantle the star beacons."

In the span of a moment, Alex's mind made several connections.

The transformation into a Kinemat extended the natural lifespan of the affected being by a factor of two or three.

The Kulsat's natural life expectancy was about two or three years, and a Risen's average lifespan was five to six years.

The Kulsat System was on the farthest tip of one of the spiral arms of the Milky Way, eighty-seven light-years from the nearest system.

Without a star beacon, it would take a Kulsat ship generations to travel from their home system to their nearest neighbor.

The Kulsat System had no natural deposits of Kinemet. The Risen would hoard whatever Kinemet they had.

The Kulsat Risen had become self-serving, egomaniacal beings since the disappearance of the Grace. Perhaps in the future, they might evolve and be willing to make that kind of sacrifice to reconnect with the galaxy, but it was unlikely to happen for centuries.

If Alex nullified the Kulsat star beacon, he would cut them off from the rest of the galaxy, and end their threat.

At the same time, that would insulate the Kulsat from the other species of the galaxy, protecting them from any possible retribution—at least for the next century or so.

He would save the galaxy from the Kulsat, and save the Kulsat from the rest of the galaxy.

Given their nature, it was unlikely the Risen would squander any Kinemet to create more Risen. Logic and foresight rarely entered into the reasoning of power-mad beings.

"Release my ship, as you promised," came the follow-up message from Red Spot.

With how strong a personality Red Spot had, and with her exposure to other cultures, it was possible that she might become a force for revolution in the Kulsat System. If she were able to get her story out, perhaps more of the native Kulsat would rebel against the Risen. For the first time in a millennium, their culture would have a new purpose. Perhaps in a few hundred—or thousand—years, the Kulsat might mature enough as a society to be ready to rejoin the galaxy.

All these thoughts occurred to Alex in the span of a few seconds.

He didn't release Red Spot right then, however. In the midst of the Kulsat patrols, she would be in danger. Also, he needed to be certain the armada had returned to Kulsat space.

"The lead ship is firing—" General Gates began to say, but Alex quantized the ship, and pushed the *Liberty*'s quantum engines to fly at light speed for the duration of one second.

They were over three-hundred-thousand kilometers away from the star beacon when Alex returned the ship to physical space. He reached out to his console and disconnected Red Spot's shuttle from the *Liberty*.

General Gates was red-faced. It was obvious he was not used to being at the mercy of someone else's decisions, especially one who still looked like a teenager. "You will tell me, this instant, what is going on," he ordered.

Alex, making certain Red Spot's shuttle was on its way safe and sound, said, "I'm really sorry to do this to you and your crew, General, but I have no other choice."

For the last time, Alex quantized the *Liberty*. Very soon, he sensed the arrival of the Kulsat armada. Aside from any possible stragglers—mining ships in unpopulated solar systems—the vast majority of Kulsat Risen were here.

Alex focused on the star beacon.

This time, he did not do it with the intention of flying the quantum ship through it to another system.

This time, he pulled at the Kinemetic 'thread' connecting the Kulsat star beacon with the galactic network. He knew, instinctively, he could not have done that outside of the Kulsat System.

Without that 'thread', the tear in the fabric of the universe repaired itself.

The Kulsat star beacon did not exist anymore.

Alex, along with the *Liberty*, was trapped within the Kulsat system.

50

Pueblo de Santa Brio :
Copán, Honduras :

January 2197

My name is Rosalia Chiquita Hernandez, and I am the first of my village to celebrate my one-hundredth birthday. It is a milestone, by the standards of any human culture. Of course, the Kinemats of Sol will live two- or three-hundred years, they tell me. In the same breath, they also tell me that those who have become Star Travelers are something beyond human, and something less than gods.

My birthday is bittersweet, to me. It is also the anniversary of my grandfather's death. Yaxche, who never liked his Spanish name, passed away when I turned twenty. Though it has been so long since then, I remember him and his legacy every day. He passed the care of the Song of the Stars to me, and bade me guard the ancient scroll. I have grandchildren and great-grandchildren. Juan, the gentlest of them, wishes to carry on the tradition when I pass on to Mitnal. That will be soon, I suspect. But not yet.

I have had a very full life, and often I reflect back on my one-hundred years.

After the Emperor's defeat on Qin Station, the coalition of nations retook the solar system within a matter of days. While the alliance that had formed for that task might have dissolved over time, the return of Major Justine Turner and Ambassador Michael Sanderson caused an interplanetary stir; they brought alien emissaries from Gliese to Sol System.

While stories of the Kulsat threat—and the destruction they could have brought—both thrilled and frightened people everywhere, it was the offer to become a member of the Galactic Collection that prompted Sol System to revolutionize its political system, since the Collection would only recognize a single centralized government from each member system.

The United Earth Corporate was disbanded, and the Solan Synergy was created. Country corporations and planetary subsidiaries were replaced with democratic cooperatives, which recognized the authority of the Synergy.

Kinemetic technology was advanced with cooperation from the Collection. With cheap space travel and access to the solar system's resources, there was a population explosion on the other planets and moons of Sol System. Even the poorer regions of Earth prospered, not just economically, but in matters of health and wellness.

It was the beginning of the Fifth World, an era of prosperity and human progress.

Every year, on my birthday, thousands of people from all over the solar system—and even a few from other species in the galaxy—make the pilgrimage to my village. Kinemats and Sentinels, who cannot bear the gravity of the planet, are present in holoform, servo-assistants projecting their images and recording the sights and sounds to send back to them in orbit around Earth.

We host a daylong celebration in honor of my grandfather and his friends, Sentinel Justine Turner and Ambassador Michael Sanderson, who have both attended every year. We honor the fallen heroes, George Markowitz, Kenny Harriman, and all the soldiers who fought and died in the years up until the Emergence.

In the afternoon, I tell the tale of Subo Ak and the Dying God, taught to me by the wise Patli, who had no heirs.

At sunset, I recite the Song of the Stars, which was taught to me by my grandfather, in honor of the Lost Grace, Alex Manez, and the brave crew of the *Liberty*, who sacrificed themselves by leading the Kulsat armada away from Sol, and thereby saving our solar system.

This year, however, before I am able to begin the Song of the Stars, Ambassador Michael Sanderson asks to speak to the crowd before the final ceremony begins.

He stands before them, and there is much emotion in his wizened face.

"Friends, citizens of the Solan Synergy, Kinemats and Sentinels. A few minutes ago, I received word that the star beacon in Heraiea, the closest system to Kulsat, had activated, the signal originating from Kulsat System."

When he says this, there is a collective gasp from those gathered together. For decades, we were told how unlikely it was for the Kulsat Risen to attempt to cross such a vast distance. Stories of the Kulsat had endured, however, and they were considered to be the bogeymen of the galaxy.

Ambassador Sanderson holds up both of his hands to quell the crowd. "It was not the Kulsat who arrived, however. It was a century-old warship." He paused for dramatic effect. "The *Liberty* and its entire crew have returned to us, alive and healthy after eighty-seven years."

His last words were drowned out by the resounding cheer from the crowd. It was only once he had their attention again that the ambassador spoke.

"His Grace, Alex Manez, is among them.

"He is coming home."

METAMORPHOSIS

…the end of The Interstellar Age

About the Author :

Valmore Daniels has lived on the coasts of the Atlantic, Pacific, and Arctic Oceans, and dozens of points in between.

An insatiable thirst for new experiences has led him to work in several fields, including legal research, elderly care, oil & gas administration, web design, government service, human resources, and retail business management.

His enthusiasm for travel is only surpassed by his passion for telling tall tales.

Visit ValmoreDaniels.com